BUNTER'S RICH RELATION

by Frank Richards

The volume contains the first eight issues of the much admired Carter series.

Billy Bunter must earn the approval and esteem of his rich Uncle Joe Carter. But Bunter's cousin, new boy, Arthur Carter, has other ideas . . . Who will inherit the wealthy relative's riches?

BUNTER'S RICH RELATION

The titles of individual stories
contained in this volume include:
Billy Bunter's Rich Relation
Bunter the Bragger
Rivals for Riches
Bunter's Big Bluff
Getting His Own Back
The Schemer of the Remove
A Ventriloquist's Vengeance
Billy Bunter's Dead Cert

Magnet issues. Nos. 1561 to 1568

BUNTER'S RICH RELATION

by

Frank Richards

HOWARD BAKER

LONDON

Bunter's Rich Relation

Frank Richards: (The Magnet, 1938)

ISBN: 0 7030 0135 3

Greyfriars Press Books are published by
Howard Baker Press Ltd.,
27a Arterberry Road, London, S.W.20, England
Printed in Great Britain by
Per Fas Printers Ltd., of Croydon, Surrey

Frank Richards

The writing phenomenon known to the world as Frank Richards (real name Charles Hamilton) died at his home in Kingsgate in Kent on Christmas Eve 1961 at the age of eighty-six.

By then it is estimated that he had written the equivalent of one thousand full-length novels.

His work appeared continuously for over thirty years in those famous Fleetway House magazines *The Magnet and The Gem*. Most famous of all was his immortal creation Billy Bunter, the Fat Owl of the Greyfriars Remove, whose exploits together with those of the other boyhood heroes Harry Wharton and Co., delighted generations of readers from 1908 to 1940.

The war unhappily saw the end of *The Magnet* but though the post-war years brought the return of Greyfriars stories in other formats nothing ever quite recaptured the evergreen magic of the original much-loved boys' paper. It was for this reason that, some years ago, W. Howard Baker presented the first of his now world-renowned faithful facsimilies.

The brilliant character studies of boys and masters created by Frank Richards ensured his own immortality. Apart from the boys of Greyfriars, not forgetting Horace Coker, the duffer of the Fifth, there was the unforgettable Mr. Quelch, the Remove form-master ('a beast, but a just beast'), the Rev. Dr. Locke, venerable Headmaster of the School, William Gosling, the crusty, elbow-bending school porter who firmly believed that 'all boys should be drownded at birth', Paul Pontifex-Prout, the pompous form-master of the Fifth, the excitable but kind-hearted 'Mossoo' (M'sieu Charpentier, French master), the odious Cecil Ponsonby, involved in murky goings-on at The Three Fishers, and peppery Sir Hilton Popper, irascible School Governor. All these characters and many, many more are to be found in the pages of these volumes.

Each of the Howard Baker editions contains a series of stories from *The Magnet's* great golden age. And each is a fitting memorial to the glowing imagination, the humour, the humanity and the well-nigh incredible industry of its brilliant author.

Frank Richards loved writing for the young, and affirmed that no writer could do any better work in life than this. Certainly none did it better than Frank Richards himself.

The Magnet

2D

Billy Bunter's Own Paper

NOTHING DOING!

Join Up for Another Peep Behind the Scenes with—

The GREYFRIARS GUIDE

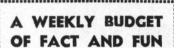

A TOUR OF THE SCHOOL. The Music-Room.

(1)

Hark, there comes a sound like
 thunder,
Study walls are rent asunder,
Faces wear a look of wonder
 Not unmixed with gloom!
Not an earthquake or volcano,
Not an air raid just began, no—
It is merely the piano
 In the Music-Room!

(2)

Every Lower School old stager
Knows the row, and he will wager
It's the Study in D Major
 Brilliantly portrayed
By its addlebrained composer,
Hoskins of the Shell, who throws a
Famous man like Bax or Brosa
 Wholly in the shade!

(3)

Hoskins' row is simply fearful,
Patrick Gwynne is far more cheerful,
He can give a pleasant earful
 With his hearty boom!
Then the fags at music practice
Give us headaches, and the fact is
That the one place always packed is
 NOT the Music-Room.

AFTER SCHOOL HOURS
The Midnight Feast!

(1)

Oft in the stilly night,
 E'er slumber's chain has bound us,
We sit in candle-light,
 With tons of grub around us!
Old Mauly stands the spread
 (Though he himself is sleeping!)
The rest are out of bed,
 And careful watch we're keeping!

(2)

For if it meets the eye
 Of any prowling master,
Such feasts are followed by
 Unmerciful disaster!
The grub for which we've yearned
 Is quickly confiscated,
And all the chaps concerned
 Are walloped, lined, or gated.

(3)

But one of us, at least,
 Has no spare time to worry,
When Bunter's at a feast,
 He's always in a hurry!
His jaw works up and down
 In strong and steady rhythm,
Those pies and pastries brown—
 He's playing havoc with 'em!

(4)

Then whispered healths are drunk,
 And candle-flames cease gleaming,
And soon, in slumber sunk,
 The guests have started dreaming.
A groan sounds here and there,
 There isn't any question
The groans aren't in despair—
 No fear! They're indigestion!

THE GREYFRIARS ALPHABET

CEDRIC HILTON,
the Dandy of the Fifth Form.

H is for HILTON, and I suppose
He's not so bad, though no one knows
What causes him to chum with Price,
Who's full of dirty tricks and vice.
With lots of money, tons of sense,
Good-natured, too, and never dense,
He might have found a worthier chum—
But he is under Price's thumb.
The blackguard of the Fifth, in fact,
Might easily get Hilton sacked;
For if there was a row about,
You bet that Price would wriggle out
And leave his chum to stand alone,
And face the music on his own.
Well, Hilton knows—so, after all,
It's really his own funeral!

ANSWER TO PUZZLE

Three minutes. If both trains took
the same time to pass a fixed point,
they'd take the same time to pass each
other.

GREYFRIARS GRINS

Kipps, the Remove conjurer, recently
made a half-crown vanish from his
hand into the pocket of Fisher T. Fish.
He hasn't succeeded in making it re-
appear again yet!

There is a rumour that Dabney of
the Fourth may be leaving the school.
In order not to miss his chum, Temple
is going to buy a parrot, and teach it
to say, "Oh, rather!"

Coker of the Fifth has broken the
world's impot record by bagging
150,000 lines. When Prout, at a lan-
tern lecture on the Rockies, showed a
slide of a grizzly bear's carcass, with
himself standing proudly beside it,
Coker asked which was the bear.

Dicky Nugent, of the Second, seen
looking glum, said that he had been in
hot water. Don't be alarmed—he
meant trouble, not a bath!

Frank Nugent has been chosen to play
the beauteous Ophelia in the forthcoming production of "Hamlet." The
claims of Bolsover major were not
treated seriously, because he must have
imagined the play to be Tarzan of the
Apes.

Peter Todd, tall and thin, has been
practising the long jump, and claims to
have covered 47 ft. with one leap. He
covers nearly that much with one suit!

Skinner has been caught smoking,
and is afraid Quelchy will "raise
Cain." Personally, I'd be more afraid
he would bring it down!

BILLY BUNTER'S RICH RELATION!

By FRANK RICHARDS

Carter stared as Billy Bunter approached, then he turned on his heel and walked away, leaving the fat junior blinking in astonishment!

THE FIRST CHAPTER.

Not According to Programme!

"LIKE this!" said Bob Cherry.

"Better not play the goat, old man!" advised Johnny Bull.

"I could do it on my head!"

"More likely to do it on your head, than not, if you ask me."

"Well, as a matter of fact, I didn't ask you, old bean!" said Bob, cheerily. "Just watch!"

Bob put on speed and shot ahead on his bike.

Harry Wharton and Frank Nugent, Johnny Bull and Hurree Singh, rode after him in a bunch, and watched—rather uneasily.

It was a half-holiday at Greyfriars, and the Famous Five were on their jiggers, on the Lantham road, enjoying a spin in the clear, frosty air.

Getting near Lantham, they slowed down, for the last mile into the town was uphill. But it was just then, when four members of the Co. were disposed to take it easy, that Bob Cherry proposed to do stunts.

Bob could do anything—or almost anything—on a bike. He liked riding with his hands in his pockets, turning corners merely by a gentle swerve of the body.

Plenty of fellows could ride downhill with their hands in their pockets—if they chose to take the risk of a tumble. Plenty could ride on the level, in the same reckless manner. But riding uphill in that way was an altogether difficult and dangerous performance. Even with a hefty pair of legs—and Bob's legs were hefty enough

—it was not easy to keep up the necessary speed.

However, Bob could do it, he had said that he was going to do it, and he proceeded with the doing.

He shot ahead of his comrades, and, having gained the necessary momentum, released the handle-bars, and shoved his hands into his trousers pockets.

Sitting thus in the saddle, grinding hard at the pedals, and with the wheels revolving like lightning, Bob sailed cheerily onward and upward.

"Fathead!" remarked Johnny Bull.

◆━◆━◆━◆━◆━◆━◆━◆━◆━◆

Tip-Top Story of Schoolboy Adventure, featuring HARRY WHARTON & CO., the Cheery Chums of GREYFRIARS.

◆━◆━◆━◆━◆━◆━◆━◆━◆━◆

Johnny was a practical youth, with no use for stunts.

"The fatfulness of the esteemed Bob's head is terrific!" agreed Hurree Jamset Ram Singh.

"Watch for the bump!" remarked Frank Nugent.

"Chuck it, Bob!" called out Harry Wharton.

Bob Cherry did not chuck it.

So long as he was able to keep up the speed, he was safe. He was going —if he could—to arrive at Lantham with his hands in his pockets, just to demonstrate that it could be done:

and that he, Robert Cherry, of the Greyfriars Remove, could do it.

But he did not allow for the chapter of accidents! Bob was not an ass, and had a car appeared on the road, he would have grasped his handle-bars fast enough. But no car came in sight —the road was perfectly clear—until a rabbit suddenly shot across it, from the wood on one side, to the wood on the other.

It was not uncommon for a rabbit to shoot across that country road. If one met a passing car, it never reached the other side. This particular rabbit met Bob's bike.

It whisked by under his front wheel, so suddenly and swiftly, that Bob hardly saw it, if he saw it at all. But it made the bike wobble.

That wobble did it!

The rabbit escaped, hardly touched. It whisked away into the wood, and vanished. The rabbit got off all right —the cyclist was not so lucky! As the bike wobbled, Bob's hands shot from his pockets and grabbed at the handle-bars, a second too late.

The bike curled up.

The next item on the programme was a terrific bump! It was immediately followed by a fearful yell.

The bike crashed and clanged. Bob Cherry sprawled beside it, hardly aware, for the moment, what had happened.

"Ow!" he roared. "Wow! Oh! Ah! Oooooogh! Ow!"

"Oh my hat!" gasped Harry Wharton.

"Come on!" exclaimed Nugent.

The four juniors rode quickly to the

THE MAGNET LIBRARY.—No. 1,561.

spot. They jumped off their bikes, ready to render first-aid.

Bob sat up, dizzily.

"Ow!" he repeated. "Wow! Oh crikey! Wow!"

"Hurt, old chap?" asked Harry, anxiously.

"Oh, no! Enjoying it!" gasped Bob. "If there's one thing I like better than another—ow—it's a bang, on a hard road—wow! Silly ass! Yow-ow!"

Bob's usually sunny temper seemed to have suffered a little!

He tottered to his feet and wriggled. He rubbed half a dozen places where there were aches and pains.

"Well, you're lucky!" remarked Johnny Bull. "You might have broken something, playing the goat like that!"

"Ow!" Bob rubbed aching bones. "Wow! It was a rabbit, or something —some beastly thing ran under the front wheel—ow! My napper! Yow-ow!"

"I told you you were more likely to do it on your head than not!" remarked Johnny Bull.

"Fathead! Ow! Ass! Wow! Idiot! Yow-ow!"

"Well, it's nonsense to call a fellow names, because he told you so!" said Johnny, staring at him. "I did tell you so, didn't I?"

"Chump! Ow! Blithering idiot! Wow!"

"If you're going to slang a fellow, simply because he told you you couldn't do a thing that you jolly well couldn't do——" said Johnny, in a tone of patient argument.

"My esteemed Johnny," murmured Hurree Jamset Ram Singh. "Speechfulness is silvery, but silence is the cracked pitcher that saves a bird in hand from going to the well!"

"I'll jolly well show you whether I couldn't do it, you fathead!" roared Bob Cherry, in great wrath. "I tell you it was a rabbit bunged into the bike! I'm going to do it, see?"

"Bob, old man——" urged Harry Wharton, as Bob limped to his fallen jigger, to pick it up and re-start, after the interval.

"Don't jaw!" said Bob crossly. "I tell you I'm going to do it, if only to show that silly ass Bull what a silly ass he is."

"Well, I did tell you so——" said Johnny, stolidly.

"Shut up!" roared Bob. "Now watch!"

He picked up the jigger. His comrades looked on in dismay. Bob's back was up: and he was going to do it now, whether he could or not. But even if he could have done it before, it was quite improbable that he could do it now, in his present bumped and limping state.

But the anxiety of the Co. was soon relieved. The bike, when it was lifted, revealed at once that it was not a going concern. That crash on the Lantham road had damaged the cycle as well as the cyclist.

A pedal was bent, a mudguard was broken, and a wheel was twisted. So far from riding that bike uphill with his hands in his pockets, Bob could not have ridden it downhill in the ordinary way! He could not ride it at all! It was likely to be a difficult task to wheel it!

"Oh crumbs!" said Bob blankly. "The dashed thing's crocked. Oh crikey! I shall have to wheel it into Lantham and leave it for repairs! Oh scissors!"

"All the better, old chap, if you could only see it!" said Johnny Bull.

THE MAGNET LIBRARY.—No. 1,561.

"It will save you from another tumble."

Bob Cherry gave him a look. Johnny Bull had more solid common sense than most fellows in the Remove. On the other hand, he had less tact than a good many. His present remarks were much more sensible than tactful.

"Idiot!" said Bob, briefly. A dozen bumps and bruises distributed over him, and a crocked jigger on his hands, had not improved Bob's temper. He had, at the moment, absolutely no use for solid common sense.

"Abuse is no argument," Johnny pointed out. "I think——"

"You don't!" interrupted Bob. "You can't! You've got nothing to do it with. If you could only think, you wouldn't talk such rot!"

"Look here——"

"Let's push the jiggers on to Lantham!" interrupted Harry Wharton, hastily. "You'll have to walk it now, Bob, and we'll walk it, too——"

"No need for you to walk, that I can see!" growled Bob. "You were going round by Redclyffe, and back. Get on with it, while I push that dashed jigger into Lantham. I shall have to come back by train, anyhow."

"But——"

"Oh, blow your butting! Think I want four silly owls to trail after me, and Bull talking rot all the time? Rats!"

And Bob heaved his disabled jigger into motion and shoved it away up the hill into Lantham—leaving his comrades standing by their machines.

"The absurd Bob is terrifically infuriated!" remarked Hurree Jamset Ram Singh.

Harry Wharton laughed.

"The old bean will get over it by the time we see him again at the school," he said. "After all, we may as well finish the spin. Come on!"

And the four remounted, taking the first turning off the Lantham road, to ride home by Redclyffe. Bob Cherry, not in his customary exuberant spirits, wheeled his clinking, clanking jigger up the hill into Lantham, to leave it at the cycle shop for repairs, which, to judge by the bike's musical effects, were likely to be extensive.

THE SECOND CHAPTER.

Getting Tidy in Study No. 7!

BILLY BUNTER blinked round Study No. 7 in the Remove through his big spectacles, with a peevish and disparaging blink.

He grunted several times—the grunts, like the blinks, expressive of disparagement.

Peter Todd, who had the pleasure, or otherwise, of sharing that study with the fat Owl of the Remove, glanced at him. Bunter did not seem satisfied with the study. He seemed, indeed, to be turning up his fat little nose at it. What was the matter with him, Peter could not guess. There was, so far as Toddy could see, nothing wrong with the study, except that it had Bunter in it.

"This won't do, Toddy," said Bunter, at last turning his spectacles on Peter with an irritated blink.

"What and which?" inquired Toddy.

"The room's untidy—in fact, slovenly," said Bunter. "Look at it."

Peter did not look at it; he looked at Bunter. He looked at him in astonishment.

This was the very first time in history that William George Bunter, of

the Greyfriars Remove, had objected to slovenly surroundings. As Billy Bunter was the most slovenly fellow in the Remove, this was quite surprising.

Bunter was the only fellow in the Remove whom Mr. Quelch had ever sent out of the Form-room to wash, or to put on a cleaner collar. In his study he never put anything away, and he left traces of jam in numerous spots.

Now, all of a sudden, Bunter seemed to have become particular on the subject. Naturally it made Toddy stare.

"Look at that marmalade on the table," said Bunter contemptuously.

"You smeared it there," remarked Peter.

"Well, you might have wiped it off. Look at those papers lying about the floor."

"You dropped them on the floor."

"Well, I don't see why you couldn't have picked them up, if I did. Look at that lock on the cupboard—busted!"

"Why, you fat villain, you busted it with the poker to get at a cake I'd locked in the cupboard."

"You can jaw as much as you like, Toddy, but this won't do. We can't have the study slovenly like this. That rotten old armchair is all chipped and torn; the stuffing coming out. I suppose you gave about ten bob for that rotten old armchair!" said Bunter scornfully.

"Fifteen," said Peter. "Nobody's stopping you from buying a more expensive one, old fat bean."

"Look at the seat of it—all squashed out!"

"That's through a porpoise squatting in it."

"You've got your football boots on the shelf. You might shove your rotten old boots out of sight. Don't you ever think anything about keeping up appearances?" demanded Bunter. "Look at all those inkstains on the table!"

"Where you spilt the ink!"

"You might have cleaned the table, I think. What would a fellow, coming from another school—a very expensive and swanky school—think of this study?" snapped Bunter. "Look here, Peter, I expect you to buck up, and get it a bit cleaner and tidier—see?"

Peter could only gaze at him. It was true that Study No. 7 was the untidiest study in the Remove. It was equally true that Billy Bunter was the fellow who made it so. Really, it was not for Bunter to find these faults. Neither had he ever shown any particularity on the subject.

"Are you trying to pull my leg, or what?" asked Peter, mystified.

"I think a fellow's study ought to be a bit decent!" snapped Bunter. "Pick up those old papers, Toddy. Get out the duster, and give the table a rub, and put those books and things away, and——"

"I'll watch you do it," suggested Peter.

"I wish you'd talk sense. There's another thing I'd better mention, too," went on the Owl of the Remove. "I'd like you to change out of the study, Toddy."

"What?"

"I mean we're three here—you, me and Dutton," explained Bunter. "Some of the studies have only two, you know—like Wharton and Nugent in Study No. 1. Well, with three in the study, Quelch isn't likely to put a new fellow in here, is he?"

"I hope not," said Peter. "What

are you driving at, you fat chump? Is there a new kid coming this term?"

"Yes, there jolly well is, and I want him in this study. I'm going to ask Quelch to put him in here."

"I'll scalp you if you do!" roared Peter. "Wharton and Nugent can have him in Study No. 1. There's only two of them."

"There'll only be two here if you change out," said Bunter. "I want you to make room for him, Toddy. And it's not only that. The fact is, if you don't mind my mentioning it, you're hardly the class of fellow I want to show off to my relation—see?"

tin—if any—and he's not coming into my study."

"It won't be your study if you change out," explained Bunter "I really want you to, Peter. It's bad enough having that deaf ass Dutton here; but, after all, he's not a freak like you, is he, old chap?"

"Not!" gasped Peter.

"Well, no; and he's got some decent people, too," said Bunter. "I'm no snob, of course. You can't say that I haven't always treated you decently, Toddy, though your father's a measly solicitor in Bloomsbury. I don't care much about such things Fellows of

Study No. 3, with Ogilvy and Russell. The fact is," said Bunter, in a burst of generosity, "I don't care where you go, so long as you clear out of here, Peter."

"Oh!" gasped Toddy. "Is that the lot?"

"Yes, that's about all," said Bunter, with a nod. "Arthur won't be here before six. Lots of time to get the place spruced up a bit, if you put your beef into it, you know. You might as well begin at once."

"I will," said Peter.

He stepped across to the shelf, and picked up a cricket stump.

" If you think I'm going to sweep up grates——" began Bunter. Whop! " I mean, all right ! Keep off, you beast ! "
With Peter Todd standing over him with the cricket stump, the fat Removite set to work tidying up the fireplace and fender !

"You fat, foozling, frabjous freak!" gasped Toddy. "Mean to say you've got a relation coming into the Remove this term?"

"Yes; one of my wealthy connections," explained Bunter. "His people are awfully rich——"

"So you want him in this study?"

"I'm going to take him up and look after him a bit at his new school, Toddy. That's only friendly, as he's a relation," said Bunter. "He's rolling in money. His uncle's got thousands—I mean millions."

"Not billions?" asked Peter. "Or trillions? Sure it doesn't run into quadrillions or quintillions?"

"Oh, really, Toddy! He's fearfully rich, anyhow," said Bunter. "He's been to St. Olaf's. That's a fearfully swanky school."

"Never heard of it."

"Well, you wouldn't, in your humble sphere," said Bunter cheerily. "I can tell you St. Olaf's is a cut above Greyfriars. Awfully rich people send their sons there—just juicy with oof. I can't make out why Arthur is leaving to come here. But I'm jolly glad, of course."

"You would be, if he's got any tin," assented Peter. "But I don't want his

really good family don't, you know. Still, I don't want Arthur to find you here. There's a limit"

Peter Todd stood gazing at Bunter. He seemed to find some difficulty in breathing.

This was the first he had heard of a relative of Billy Bunter coming to Greyfriars. New fellows generally turned up on the first day of the term; and the term was now a week old. It was not, in Peter's opinion, a case of better late than never. He did not want any more Bunters. He had as much of the Bunter tribe as he wanted, and a little over.

"So if you'll change out, old chap, all right," said Bunter breezily. "Mind, I don't mean that I'm going to drop you. I wouldn't do that to an old pal. I may tea with you sometimes. I shan't forget you, Peter."

"Not at tea-time."

"Oh, really, Toddy! Only look here, as my relation is coming to-day, I want the study a bit decent," said Bunter. "Set to and get it tidy, Peter. Clean it up all round—see? Then you can shift your things into another study. I dare say Wharton would take you into Study No. 1. Or you might shift into

Billy Bunter gave him an impatient blink.

"No good collecting your things till you know where you're going to take them, Toddy," he said. "Where——"

"I'm going to use this here," explained Peter. "I'm not changing out of the study, old fat bean! Not quite! If any relative of yours butts in here, I shall slaughter him stone dead—but I'll leave that till he does."

"Look here, you beast——"

"But there's one point on which I agree entirely," continued Peter, "and that's about making the study tidy. I think you're right there."

"Well, I'm glad of that, at least!" yapped Bunter.

"Glad you're glad!" said Peter. "Get down to it!"

"Eh?"

"Don't I speak plain? Get down to it!" said Peter cheerfully. "You made the study untidy, old fat man, and you can put it to rights! I'm going to stump you till you do."

"You—you—you silly ass!" gasped Bunter. "I—I—I think perhaps the study will do, after all——"

"I don't!" grinned Peter. "If a

fellow from a swanky school, a cut above Greyfriars, is going to poke his nose in here he's going to see this study tidy! Pick up those papers."

"I—I—I've got to go and meet his train——"

Billy Bunter made a strategic movement towards the door.

Peter Todd's long legs whisked across the study.

Whop!

"Yoo-hoop!" roared Bunter, as the cricket stump landed on his tight trousers. "Ow! Beast! I say——"

"Picking up those papers?"

"No!" yelled Bunter. "I——"

Whop!

"Yaroooh! Leave off, you beast!" howled Bunter. "Keep that cricket stump away, you rotter! I'm picking up the papers, ain't I?"

Bunter picked them up and crammed them into the wastepaper-basket. He gave Peter Todd a glare that almost cracked his spectacles.

By that time, probably, Bunter regretted that he had raised the subject! He had not expected this outcome—though really he might have!

"Now that marmalade on the table!" grinned Peter.

"I can't——"

Whop!

"Yoo-hoop! I mean, I'm just going to!" shrieked Bunter.

Bunter cleared the smear of marmalade off the table.

"Now put all your books tidily on the shelf——"

"Look here——"

Whop!

"Yaroooooooh!"

For the first time since Billy Bunter had had school books they were all put away neatly!

"There's a smear of jam on the armchair," said Toddy.

"I—I—I can't see it, Peter."

"Take my word for it! If it's still there in half a minute you get a whop!"

The smear of jam was cleaned off the armchair under the half-minute.

"Now put those football boots away in the cupboard!"

"They're your boots!" shrieked

Bunter. "Think I'm going to put your boots away for you, Peter Todd?"

"I think I'm going to whop you till you do! We're going to have this study tidy or bust something. Now then!"

"I jolly well won't——" yelled Bunter.

Whop!

"Yaroooh! I—I mean, I jolly well will!" howled the fat Owl.

"That's better!" said Peter, with a nod of approval. "The study's looking much tidier already! I'll keep you up to this, Bunter, now you've suggested it! No more slovenliness in this study! The grate looks a bit untidy! There's a brush in the locker! Get to it!"

"If you think I'm going to sweep up grates——"

Whop!

"I mean, all right! Keep off, you beast!"

With Peter standing over him with the cricket stump Bunter set to work, and the fireplace and fender were soon newly swept and garnished. Peter looked round the study. There was no doubt that its appearance was considerably improved already. But Peter was not satisfied yet.

"Bit dusty," he remarked. "Take the duster and go over the whole room, Bunter! We can't have a dusty study."

"I—I—I don't mind a spot of dust, Peter!" groaned Bunter.

"I do!" said Peter.

"Look here, you rotten beast——"

Whop!

"Ow! Wow! Where's that duster?"

Billy Bunter's fat face was crimson with rage as he dusted Study No. 7. A very cursory dusting would have satisfied Bunter. But it did not satisfy Peter. Peter was getting very particular about the tidiness of that study. Several whops from the cricket stump spurred Bunter on. There was hardly a speck left in Study No. 7 when he had finished.

"Good!" said Peter approvingly. "Now, there's only one thing more you can do to improve the look of this study!"

"What's that?" hissed Bunter.

"Get outside it!"

"Look here——"

Whop!

Bunter got outside the study quite quickly.

THE THIRD CHAPTER.
A Highcliffe Rag!

"GREYFRIARS cad!"

Bob Cheery's blue eyes glinted.

That pleasant observation was not addressed to him. But it was spoken for him to hear, and he heard it.

Bob was walking up and down the platform at Lantham Station. He was feeling neither merry nor bright.

He had a considerable number of aches and pains lingering from that bang on the hard high road. He had had a lot of trouble getting the disabled jigger up the hill into Lantham. He had left it at the cycle shop for repair—it was not going to be sent home for several days, and quite a little bill was going to be sent home with it! Added to which he had arrived at the station just after a train had gone out, and he had to wait half an hour for the next.

It was cold and windy on the platform. There was hardly anybody about, and he had the windy platform to himself to tramp on—till four Highcliffe fellows came on.

Ponsonby & Co. of the Highcliffe Fourth walked warily at the sight of Bob Cherry. As the Famous Five generally "went about" together on a half-holiday they supposed that Bob's friends were probably in the offing. If all the Co. had been there the Highcliffe knuts would have avoided them very carefully indeed, regardless of old quarrels.

But after a time they realised that Bob was alone. Having made that discovery, Ponsonby saw no reason for not making himself unpleasant.

Ponsonby and Gadsby, Monson and Vavasour, walked past Bob, and as they passed Pon drawled "Greyfriars cad!" for Bob to hear.

Bob's eyes glinted round at him. After the chapter of accidents that afternoon he was in no mood to stand cheek from Pon of Highcliffe.

However, he restrained his irritation and walked in the other direction. Bob was generally full of beans, but that bang on the Lantham road had knocked a lot of the beans out of him. He had a big bruise on his knee, which made him limp a little, and another on his right elbow, which would have taken a lot of the vim out of his usual punch. He was, in fact, in no state for a scrap—and the enemy were four to one, and so it was evidently judicious to avoid trouble if he could.

Pon winked at his friends.

Bob was so hard a hitter that, even four to one, the Highcliffians were not fearfully keen on a row. But if Bob was avoiding one, no more than that was needed to encourage Pon.

The quartet wheeled round and walked after Bob again.

"Greyfriars cad, I think!" said Pon cheerily. "Look how dirty he is!"

Bob's ears burned at that cheery remark behind him. It was true that his roll on the Lantham road had made him a little muddy.

"They never wash at Greyfriars, y'know!" remarked Gadsby.

"Never, I believe!" agreed Monson.

"Absolutely!" chirruped Vavasour.

Bob paused a moment—breathing hard. He was powerfully inclined to turn round and charge the four—and had he been in his usually exuberant state he would certainly have done so.

But a pang in his knee and a twinge in his elbow reminded him that he was in no state for a battle against heavy odds.

It was fairly clear, however, that he could not keep clear if he remained on the platform with the Highcliffians, so he went into the waiting-room.

No one else was there; Bob and the Highcliffians were the only waiting passengers on that side of the line at present.

There was a chuckle from Cecil Ponsonby.

"Dodgin' us, old beans!" he murmured. "Not his usual style—he's generally rather like a bull at a gate! Come on!"

Pon led his flock into the waiting-room after Bob. The good Pon was quite determined on trouble now.

Bob's eyes gleamed at the four as they came in. He was getting very near the end of his patience.

"Oh, here's that Greyfriars cad!" drawled Ponsonby. "Barge him out! Can't have the fellow in here with us."

"I'd like to see you barge me out, you Highcliffe nincompoop!" roared Bob.

"Now, isn't that lucky?" said Pon blandly. "Because that's just what we're goin' to do. Barge him!"

The four barged together.

Bob Cherry forgot his game knee and his crocked elbow. He hit out with right and left.

Gadsby gave a roar and rolled over. Vavasour yelled and stumbled over him.

Then there was a heavy bump as Bob went down, with Pon and Monson grasping him.

"Back up!" yelled Pon, as Bob struggled, and Gaddy and Vavasour scrambled up to join in again.

Bob was not easy to hold. His left came jolting up, landing under Pon's chin with a crack like that of a hammer, and the dandy of Highcliffe gave a yell of anguish. He felt, for the moment, as if his chin had been knocked through the top of his head.

But it was Bob's last punch. The four Highcliffians piled on him together, and he was spread out helplessly on the floor of the waiting-room, pinned down by the four.

"Got the cad!" grinned Monson. "Chuck him out—what?"

Pon, with his knee on Bob's chest, rubbed his chin.

"No; we're not done with him yet!" he snapped.

"I say, the train's due in five minutes," said Gadsby.

"Lots of time to catch it, but that Greyfriars cad isn't goin' to catch it," said Ponsonby coolly. "We'll leave him fixed up here to wait for the next—or the next after it."

"But how——"

"Tie up his fins!" said Pon.

"I say," began Gadsby, "I——"

"Don't jaw, Gaddy; just do as I say. Take his hanky and tie his fins!"

Bob struggled savagely as his handkerchief was taken, twisted, and tied round his wrists. He had waited nearly half an hour for his train, and the idea of being left in the waiting-room while it went on to Courtfield without him was intensely exasperating.

But his struggles did not avail. His wrists were tied together. He was in the hands of the Philistines, and there was no help for it.

"Now his hoofs!" said Ponsonby.

"I say——" began Gadsby.

"You talk too much, old bean! Tie up his hoofs. His necktie will do—and your hanky. Gaddy."

"You rotter!" roared Bob.

His ankles were tied together. Then the Highcliffians released him, and grinned down at him as he lay helpless on the floor, wriggling.

Ponsonby rubbed his chin, with a vicious gleam in his eyes. That punch was going to be paid for.

"I rather think he won't catch that train now,' he remarked.

"He will yell for a porter, fathead!" said Gadsby. "There'll be a porter about as soon as the train's signalled."

"He won't," said Pon coolly. "Give me your hanky, Vav."

"Oh, you cad!" gasped Bob. "You—grooooogh!"

With his hands tied he could not resist as Ponsonby forced his mouth open. The handkerchief, twisted, was stuffed in, and Pon tied it there with a length of string.

Bob could not even gurgle.

"Think he'll call to a porter now?" grinned Pon.

"I say, it's too thick!" muttered Gadsby.

"Shut up, you ass! Now stick him on one of those chairs and tie him to it. Can't be too careful!" chuckled Ponsonby.

Bob was swung up from the floor and plumped into a chair. Pon had a whipcord in his pocket. He cut it into lengths, and Bob's arms were tied to the back of the chair, and his ankles to its legs. He sat in the chair unable to stir a limb or to utter a sound. And his enraged glare had no effect whatever on the grinning Highcliffians.

"Now stick him behind the door," said Pon. "Somebody might wander in here, and we don't want him to be spotted."

Pon was evidently full of bright ideas that afternoon.

"I say——" began Gadsby uneasily.

"Shut up, Gaddy! Don't be soft!"

"Well, look here——"

"Shut up, you noodle! Now, then, all hands!" said Ponsonby.

The chair was shoved behind the door. That door stood wide open, back against the wall. Pon pulled it out sufficiently to allow the chair to be placed behind it. It was a cold and chilly spot, the stove in the waiting-room being at the other end.

"Right as rain!" grinned Pon. "I rather fancy he won't catch this train—or the next, I rather think. Shouldn't wonder if he sticks there for a couple of hours."

"I say——"

"Do shut up, Gaddy! Anythin' more we can do for you, Cherry?" asked Pon.

Bob gave him a petrifying glare in reply.

"Come on, you men!" drawled Pon. "Only a minute to the train now. Good-bye, Cherry, old bean! Have a good time!"

"Ha, ha, ha!"

Pon & Co. walked out of the waiting-room.

A minute or two later Bob heard the train come in, and heard it roll out again, carrying away the Highcliffians. Bob had no chance of catching that train, and he wondered, dismally and furiously, whether he was going to catch the next—or any train at all that day.

THE FOURTH CHAPTER.
The New Boy!

"COME in here!"

"The train——"

"It is ten minutes yet."

"Oh, all right!"

Those two voices were only a few feet from Bob Cherry, but they might as well have been two miles for all the chance he had of making his predicament known.

For about twenty minutes Bob Cherry had sat exactly as Pon & Co. had left him, for the good reason that he could do nothing else.

He could not shift a limb. He could not utter the faintest sound. Pon had done his work well—perhaps a little too well! Bob could do nothing to attract attention, even if anyone came into the waiting-room. Unless somebody looked behind the door he could not be seen. And it was improbable, to say the least, that anyone would look behind the door.

Two passengers, waiting for the next train, appeared in the doorway. Through the aperture between door and jamb, Bob had a glimpse of them.

One of them was a man, dressed in black, with elastic-sided boots that squeaked as he moved. He had a hard, cold face, with fishy-looking eyes.

The other was a boy of about Bob's own age, whose resemblance to the man showed that they were relatives.

On their looks, Bob would have liked neither of them, but he would have been extremely glad to attract their attention at that moment.

He hoped that they might come along to the end of the waiting-room, and chance to glimpse him behind the door. But it was unlikely, as the stove was at the other end, and it did not happen.

The rusty-looking man walked at once towards the stove, and stood warming his hands in front of it. The boy followed him.

Both disappeared from Bob's sight; but he heard the scratch of a match and smelt tobacco, and supposed that the man was smoking. That, however, was an error, as he learned the next moment as he heard the man's voice, which had a squeaky sound like his boots.

"You had better stop that, Arthur."

"Last chance before I get in at the school, Cousin Gideon," came the voice of the smoker.

"You young fool! Do you want to ask for the same trouble at Greyfriars that you had at your last school?"

"Oh rats!"

Bob was not in the least interested in the conversation of strangers, and would have preferred not to hear it had it been avoidable; but he was a little interested as he heard that.

This fellow, it seemed, was going to Greyfriars, joining up a few days late after the beginning of the term. The man he called Cousin Gideon, it appeared, was taking him to the school.

"I am speaking for your own good, Arthur!" said the squeaky voice.

"Well, you needn't!"

"Look here, you young rascal——"

"Oh, chuck it!" said the cheery Arthur. "You're not my father-confessor, that I know of. You're my legal adviser!" Bob heard him chuckle. "Or perhaps I'd better say, illegal adviser! What?"

"If you will not take my advice——"

"I will when it suits me."

"If you were anything but a self-willed, selfish, bad-mannered, disgraceful young blackguard, you would listen to good advice, Arthur."

"Especially as I'm getting it free of charge—what? You don't often advise your clients free of charge, do you, Gideon? Or are you going to send in a bill, Mr. Gooch?"

And he chuckled again.

"Listen to me, Arthur! I am your cousin, and have no responsibility for you, and no interest in you except——"

"Except a share in the loot! What?"

"You young fool!" The squeaky voice came like a rasp. "You have already been kicked out of one school for bad conduct. Do you want to be kicked out of another, with so much at stake?"

"I'll watch it!" said the cheery Arthur. "They won't nail me at Greyfriars. Besides, they don't sack a man for smoking!"

"You had better give it up, as well as all the other foolish and vicious things you did at your last school."

"Oh, don't be an ass, Gideon! I don't want sermons from you—a dashed hole-and-corner solicitor on the make!"

Bob would not have been surprised if the next sound had been a smack on a head. But there was no such sound. Gideon Gooch seemed amazingly patient with that remarkable new boy for Greyfriars!

"You are a fool, Arthur!" came the rasping voice. "It was not easy for your uncle to manage to get you into Greyfriars, after you were turned out of your last school. If you are turned out again——"

"I'll watch it, old bean! Not much chance of playing the goat there, as I shall be hard up all the time. Half-a-crown a week pocket-money—unless my Cousin Gideon squeezes out a quid occasionally. The old hunks! The old ass! The dashed old curmudgeon!"

"You have only yourself to blame, Arthur! You have lost a fortune by your folly—you know that your uncle altered his will after you were expelled from school—fifty thousand pounds. Have you forgotten that?"

"Am I likely to?" snarled Arthur.

"You had better bear it in mind. What would have come to you, now left to a more distant relative. I have absolutely certain information on that point. Your uncle will do nothing for you now, except pay your bare school fees! Last term you had all the money you wanted, at an expensive school—what have you this term, at your new school?"

"No need to rub it in!" growled Arthur savagely.

"I am trying to make you see sense. You are going to the same school as your relative, who now stands in your place as heir. You have one chance and one chance only, of getting back into the old man's good graces. That relative may disappoint the old man as you have done——"

"He will, if I get a chance!" snarled Arthur.

"And if, at the same time, your own conduct is good——"

"Oh, don't jaw! I'm going to play up! I'm going to be a dashed model! growled Arthur. "I'm going to be Good Little Georgie, who loved his kind teachers! I'm going to keep a diary of all my good deeds! I shan't smoke—if I can help it; and if a fellow talks about backing a horse, or a hundred up, I shan't even know what he means! I'm going through with it—if I can stand it!"

"You had better contrive to stand it, Arthur, if you have sense enough to know what is good for you! You have two tasks ahead of you at Greyfriars—to prove that you have completely reformed, and to prove that the relative who has cut you out is no better than you were at your last school. Both of these are equally necessary."

Bob Cherry almost wondered whether he was dreaming, as he heard this.

"Leave it to me!" snarled Arthur.

"I'll fix that cad who's cut me out, somehow, if I have a dog's chance!"

"Your own conduct is equally important——"

"Oh, give us a rest!"

"Well, I can do no more than advise you, and leave it to your common sense, if you have any!" snapped Gideon. "Don't light another cigarette."

"Oh, rats!"

A match scratched again.

"You will have to see your headmaster and your Form-master when we reach Greyfriars! If they detect tobacco-smoke about you——"

"They won't! I've got some cachous to scoff in the train."

"You are an incorrigible young rascal, Arthur."

"Same to you, with knobs on—except for the 'young.' Do shut up and give a chap a rest!"

"I have a great mind to box your ears, Arthur!"

"Do—and I'll jolly well hack your shins, Gideon!"

"There is the train!"

Footsteps passed the door again. For the umpteenth time, Bob Cherry made wild efforts to make himself heard. But it was in vain; and Mr. Gideon Gooch and "Arthur" walked out of the waiting-room, without the faintest idea that anyone was there.

And a few minutes later, Bob heard the train roll away with them to Courtfield—and wondered, with inexpressible feelings, whether somebody would come in and find him before the next!

THE FIFTH CHAPTER.
Glorious Prospects for Bunter!

"ONE of my rich relations!" said Billy Bunter impressively.

Whereat there was a chuckle in Study No. 1 in the Remove.

Harry Wharton & Co., as well as the rest of the Lower Fourth Form at Greyfriars, had heard all about Billy Bunter's rich relations.

But their knowledge was limited to hearsay from Bunter. They had never seen any of those rich relations of the fat Owl's. They rather doubted whether Bunter had!

"Is the richfulness terrific?" asked Hurree Jamset Ram Singh.

"Oh, pots of money!" said Bunter airily. "Pots and pots!"

"And he's coming here?" asked Frank Nugent.

"Yes! I don't know why he isn't going back to St. Olaf's. He's coming to Greyfriars—getting here this afternoon. His name's up in the Form list already. It was all fixed in the hols, I suppose. I say, you fellows, he's simply rolling in money! You'll be glad to meet him."

At which Study No. 1 chuckled again.

Four members of the famous Co. were in that study. They had rather expected Bob Cherry back by that time, but he had not yet come in. As they had ridden round a good distance before riding back to school, Bob had had time to get in by train.

But he had not turned up, and the four were getting a handsome tea ready for him when he did; which would help the clouds to roll by, if there was still a spot of bad temper about.

When Billy Bunter rolled in, they had no doubt that he had spotted supplies being brought in from the school shop. But Bunter, for once, did not seem to be thinking of food. He handed out the surprising information that a relation of his was coming to Greyfriars.

"It's too jolly thick!" grunted Johnny Bull.

"Eh? What is?" asked Bunter.

"We've got too many Bunters here already!"

"Oh, really, Bull——"

"You in the Remove, and your brother Sammy in the Second! Is it going to rain Bunters?"

"His name isn't Bunter, fathead! If you'd looked at the Form list, you'd have seen him there—A. Carter."

"A carter!" exclaimed Nugent.

"Yes!"

"Well, a carter's a jolly useful sort of man—more useful than a millionaire, really—but I never heard of carters being rich!"

"Ha, ha, ha!"

"You silly ass!" roared Bunter. "I don't mean that he's a carter—I mean that he's A. Carter!"

"That's lucid, anyhow!" remarked Harry Wharton. "Sure you don't mean that he's a chauffeur?"

"Ha, ha, ha!"

"A. Carter! roared Bunter. "Arthur Carter, you fathead! The Carters are fearfully rich. Old Carter—that's his uncle—just rolls in oof. He's our rich relation—I mean, one of our rich relations. Blessed if I see anything to cackle at! My pater says he gets richer every time he goes bankrupt."

"Oh crikey!"

"Pots and pots of money!" said Bunter. "Young Carter is his nephew, and he will get it all some day, or most of it. I saw old Carter when I was a kid—bit of a beaky old merchant, and he rather liked me——"

"No accounting for tastes, is there?"

"Well, I mean to say, a good-looking and well-mannered Public school chap does make a good impression on these City people, you know——"

"Oh crumbs!"

"Young Carter didn't like me much. I fancy he thought I might be after the old bean's money. Me, you know! You know I'm not the sort of fellow to want anybody's money but my own! I say, you fellows, I want you to lend me a pound——"

"Ha, ha, ha!"

"What are you cackling at now?" demanded Bunter. "The fact is, I've been disappointed about a postal order, and I want to stand young Carter something rather decent when he blows in. See? I'm going to be very friendly with him. He had an enormous allowance when he was at St. Olaf's."

"That's why, is it?"

"Well, I'm fond of him, you know. I've seen him once——"

"Ha, ha, ha!" roared the chums of the Remove.

If Billy Bunter had seen that relative once, they hardly supposed that a deep affection was founded on that single encounter! It really began to look as if A. Carter really had pots of money!

"Smithy, here, swanks about his money," went on Bunter. "Bet you Arthur will put him in the shade! Just juicy with oof, you know. I'm going to get him in my study, if I can, only that beast Toddy won't clear off! I've asked him to change out, you know, because he's hardly up to the mark to associate with my rich relation, and he seemed to take offence about something, and cut up rusty——"

"Now, I wonder why!" gasped Nugent.

"The whyfulness is terrific!"

"You see, I want to be pally with the chap, of course, and see him through at his new school, and all that!" said Bunter. "I'm going to be his very best friend here! Me and my Cousin Arthur,

Marjorie Hazeldene gave a gasp at the sight of Bob Cherry, gagged and tied up like a turkey. "Why—what—who——"
Bob gazed at the three Cliff House girls, his face crimson. Never before had he felt such an utter ass, as at that moment.

you know, like Raymond and Porteous——"

"Do you mean Damon and Pythias?"

"Well, you know what I mean, loyal pals, and all that——"

"Cousin, is he?" asked Johnny Bull.

"Well, actually, he's a sort of second cousin twice removed, or something," said Bunter. "But I shall call him Cousin Arthur, because——"

"Because he's got pots of money?"

"Yes—I mean, no! Naturally, I care nothing for his money. I may get him to cash my postal order, perhaps. We shall feed pretty well in Study No. 7, if I can get that beast Toddy to change out and let him in. You'd hardly think that Toddy has refused to change out, would you, though I explained to him that he wasn't socially up to my Cousin Arthur——"

"Didn't Toddy boot you?" gasped Wharton.

"He pitched into me with a cricket stump, for some reason. The fact is, there is never any relying on Toddy's temper. He breaks out any minute, you know, in the middle of a friendly talk! But I say, you fellows, what about that pound?"

"Ask again next Christmas!"

"I hope you fellows are not going to be mean. I'm stony, owing to my postal order not having come. I can't borrow of Arthur the minute he sets foot in the place, you know. Now, could you, Wharton?"

Harry Wharton laughed.

"No; but I don't see why you couldn't, old fat man! You may as well begin soon, as late! Bring him up in the way he should go, in fact."

"Well, look here," said Bunter, "you've got a pretty good spread here. Anything special on?"

"Only waiting for Bob to come in."

"Never mind him! Look here, suppose we keep it for my Cousin Arthur?"

suggested Bunter. "It doesn't matter about Cherry——"

"Doesn't it?"

"No; and you fellows can tea in Hall. It's not too late! You've got enough here for Arthur and me. I'll do the same for you when my postal order comes. What about it?" asked Bunter.

"Ha, ha, ha!" roared the four. That bright suggestion of Bunter's seemed to strike them as a joke!

"I say, you fellows, I think you might back a fellow up, for once!" urged Bunter. "I don't have a rich relation come to the school every day, you know. It's a sheer stroke of luck for me, Arthur leaving St. Olaf's, and coming here. A lot depends on first impressions, you know. I don't want to borrow off the chap, first shot! He might think me a needy sort of chap, always borrowing money——"

"He might!" gasped Wharton.

"The mightfulness is preposterous!" chuckled Hurree Jamset Ram Singh.

Herbert Vernon-Smith came up the passage and glanced into the open doorway of Study No. 1.

"You fellows heard anything about a new kid?" he asked.

"Just heard." answered Harry, looking round. "Has he blown in?"

"There's a kid just come in a taxi from Courtfield, with a rat-faced blighter, who looks like a legal johnny. He's gone in to Quelch. Some new kid for the Remove, I suppose."

"Oh! He's come!" gasped Bunter. He rolled to the door. "Good!"

The Bounder stared at him.

"You know him, Bunter?" he asked.

"Yes, rather! One of my rich relations!" grinned Bunter. "I say, does he look fearfully wealthy, Smithy?"

"Not that I noticed."

"Oh, he's frightfully rich," said Bunter. "His Uncle Carter allowed him no end of money at St. Olaf's. You

can chuck up swanking about your money now, Smithy. I can jolly well tell you that Carter's going to put your nose out of joint."

Study No. 1 chortled. The expression on Vernon-Smith's face, at that happy remark, was quite alarming—if the fat Owl of the Remove had not been too short-sighted to observe it.

"But I must go down!" added Bunter. "Can't waste time talking to you chaps, now Arthur's come!"

Bunter rolled through the doorway. The Bounder's foot shot out as he rolled, and Bunter went into the passage quite suddenly. He roared as he went.

"Yoo-hoop! Why, what—— You beast! Wharrer you kicking me for, you cad?" howled the indignant fat Owl.

But Bunter did not wait for an answer to that question. The Bounder's foot was rising again. The fat Owl shot away to the stairs, equally anxious to meet his rich relation and to get out of the reach of Smithy's boot.

THE SIXTH CHAPTER.
Not Nice!

BOB CHERRY wriggled.

He was quite tired of wriggling. He ached all over. But he wriggled, and wriggled, in the hope of getting loose.

It was in vain!

The man in black and the cheery Arthur had gone, without knowing that he was there! After the train had gone out a porter came in, warmed his hands at the stove, and went out again, without a suspicion that a hapless schoolboy was tied to a chair behind the door.

Bob began to wonder whether he was booked to remain there till the station was closed for the night. Really, it looked like it.

Pon, of course, had not meant it to be so bad as that! He had meant to make Bob lose his train, and perhaps the next after it. But Pon was quite reckless of what he did when he was on mischief bent. Really, Pon did not care a straw if Bob remained there for hours, and was late back at school for call-over. In case of official inquiry into the matter, Pon was cheerfully prepared to deny his own actions—hard lying being the good Pon's usual way of dodging consequences.

In a boiling state, so far as his temper was concerned, and in a chilly and almost frozen state otherwise, Bob wriggled, and wriggled.

He hoped that other passengers would come along for the next train, and that somebody would somehow spot him there. Several times he heard footsteps and voices on the platform outside.

But it was getting towards time for the next train before footsteps came in at the doorway of the waiting-room. He heard a voice—which was familiar to his ears. A fat squeak, very like Billy Bunter's!

"It's cold out there, Miss Bullivant."

It was the voice of Bessie Bunter, of Cliff House School.

"Nonsense!" came the decisive tones of Miss Bullivant, the games-mistress of Cliff House. "You can keep warm by walking, Bessie."

"I'm tired."

"Nonsense!"

"It is really rather windy, Miss Bullivant!" came another voice, and Bob recognised it as Marjorie Hazeldene's.

He ceased to wriggle. Bob was glad, at all times, to see Marjorie; but he did not want Marjorie to see him tied up in this ridiculous way. Much as he desired to be released, he did not want to meet the eyes of a party of schoolgirls just at this moment!

"Frightfully parky, you know!" came another voice—that of Clara Trevlyn, of the Fourth Form at Cliff House.

"Don't be so slangy, Clara!"

"I say, you girls, come in—there's a stove here!" said Bessie.

Miss Bullivant gave a grunt. She was a hardy lady, and the cold wind on the platform did not worry her. However, she allowed the three girls to enter the waiting-room and seek the warmth of the stove. She remained in the doorway herself, looking out, the tip of her nose glowing an attractive crimson in the frosty air.

She was hardly three feet from Bob, only the door was between. A wriggle might have attracted her attention. But Bob did not wriggle now. He did not want the Bull's surprised stare to fix on him; he did not want to hear Bessie Bunter's fat giggle, or to see Clara's smile. He did not even want Marjorie to discover him thus. Anything was better than looking such an ass. So he remained quite still.

"Won't you come to the fire, Miss Bullivant?" asked Marjorie.

"Thank you, no," said Miss Bullivant. "I will walk on the platform. It is much healthier to keep warm by exercise."

Her heavy tread woke the echoes, and died away up the platform.

"Cat!" remarked Bessie Bunter.

"Little beast!" said Clara.

"What are you calling me names for, I'd like to know?" demanded Miss Elizabeth Bunter.

"The Bull's just taken us to a matinee!" said Clara. "She's stood the

tickets—and stood you, which nobody else at Cliff House can do! And you call her a cat! You're a little beast, like your brother Billy, Bessie!"

"Yah!" said Bessie. "So she is a cat! You're a cat too, Clara! I say, shut that door, will you? There's a beastly draught!"

"No; it's stuffy enough in here already!"

"Cat! Shut the door, will you, Marjorie?"

"Well, if you really want it shut, Bessie——"

"Don't I keep saying so? You sit there, taking no notice, while I perish of cold! You shut that door!"

"Can't you shut it yourself, if you want it shut?" demanded Clara.

"I'm sitting down!" said Miss Bunter, with dignity.

"Don't you get up, Marjorie! If you go and shut that door, I'll knock your hat off!"

"Oh, Clara——"

"Mind, I mean it! I'll knock it off, and tread on it, if you shut the door for that fat lazybones!"

"Cat!" said Bessie.

And she rolled along to shut the door herself.

Bob Cherry sat dismayed! He would rather have sat there another hour, or another two or three, than have been discovered by a party of schoolgirls. But there was no help for it now. Once the door was pulled out from the wall he would be revealed.

Bessie Bunter grabbed the door, and pulled! The next moment, she caught sight of the figure behind it, and gave a shriek!

Marjorie and Clara looked round, startled.

"What——" exclaimed Marjorie.

"Little idiot!" said Clara.

Shriek, shriek, shriek!

Bessie was startled, which was only natural. Being startled, she felt entitled to shriek—and she did!

"Bessie, what is it?" exclaimed Marjorie, and she ran along the room, followed more slowly by Clara.

"Oh! Oh dear! There's somebody behind the door!" shrieked Bessie.

"Rubbish!" said Clara.

"I saw him! Oh dear! I—I—I think it's a boy!" gasped Bessie.

"Well, boys don't bite, even if it is a boy!" said Clara. "Besides, how could a boy be there, fathead?"

Shriek!

Marjorie caught hold of the door-handle and pulled the door away! Then she gave a gasp of astonishment.

"Bob!"

"Bob Cherry!" exclaimed Clara, in amazement.

"Oh!" gasped Bessie. "Is it Bob Cherry? Playing silly tricks—hiding behind a door! I'll tell Miss Bullivant, and she will smack his head!"

Bob gazed at the three. His face was a beautiful crimson. Seldom, or never, had Bob felt such an utter ass, as at that moment.

"He's tied up!" said Clara, in wonder. "What sort of a game is this? He's got something in his mouth! What——"

Marjorie stepped quickly to Bob. Amazing as it was to see the Greyfriars junior in such a position, bound and gagged, she very quickly realised that what was wanted was prompt assistance. In a few moments she had got the gag away, and Bob could speak.

"I—I say——" he gasped.

"What is it—a rag?" asked Clara. "Who tied you up like a turkey, Bob?"

Marjorie, asking no questions, sorted

a penknife out of her bag, and began to cut the cords.

"Sorry to startle you!" gasped Bob. "I couldn't help it—I was tied up by a gang of Highcliffe cads—I've been here nearly an hour——"

"Playing silly tricks!" yapped Bessie. "Hiding behind a door——"

"I wasn't!" gasped Bob. "Can't you see that I was tied, and couldn't move or speak, you silly?"

"Well, you shouldn't be!" said Bessie. "Why did you let them tie you up?"

"I couldn't help it!"

"You should have helped it!" said Bessie.

"Shut up, old dear!" said Clara.

"Cat!"

Bob was very quickly released. He gladly rose from the chair, and stretched his stiffened limbs.

There was a smile on Clara's face—as he had fully expected. Marjorie was not smiling, which was a comfort. Bessie was giggling.

"He, he, he! I say, you looked awfully funny tied up there—like a turkey! He, he, he!"

"Be quiet, Bessie dear!" said Marjorie.

"Shan't!" said Bessie. "He looked funny, and you know he did! Never seen anybody look so silly—even a boy!"

Bob Cherry breathed hard. Had Miss Bunter been Master Bunter, Bob would probably have put in some nose-punching next. But he could not punch Miss Bunter's fat little nose.

"I say, you girls, fancy Bob letting them tie him up like a turkey!" giggled Bessie. "Were you afraid of them, Bob?"

"There were four of the cads!" hissed Bob. "They were too many for me."

"He, he, he! They must be laughing!" said Bessie. "I expect they're fearfully amused! Don't you?"

"I'm so glad we found you, Bob!" said Marjorie. "Don't mind Bessie—she can't help being silly——"

"Cat!"

"Thank you for letting me loose, anyhow!" stammered poor Bob, "I dare say I looked a bit of a fool, sitting there —but what could one chap do, against four of them——"

"He, he, he!"

"Do be quiet, Bessie!"

"Shan't! He, he, he!"

"The train!" came Miss Bullivant's powerful voice from the platform; and Bessie rolled out, followed by the smiling Clara.

Marjorie hesitated a moment.

"Your train, Bob?" she asked.

"Oh—no—I—I'm taking the next!" gasped Bob.

"Good-bye, then!"

Marjorie ran out after the others.

Bob would have been glad to take that train; but he had had enough of Clara's smiles and Bessie's giggles. He had a faint suspicion that even Marjorie was suppressing a smile.

He stayed in the waiting-room till the train was gone, with Miss Bullivant and the Cliff House girls. Then he tramped out on to the platform, glad to restore his circulation with a little vigorous exercise.

He had half an hour to wait for the next train. But he was, at all events, free to take it now, when it came in. And at long last, it came—and he rolled homeward; his thoughts dwelling chiefly on Pon, and ways and means of getting into touch with that playful youth—and there was some consolation in reflecting on the alteration in Pon's features that would follow!

THE SEVENTH CHAPTER.
Surprising !

HARRY WHARTON & CO. were waiting at the school gates when Bob Cherry came trailing wearily homeward.

They had waited long for Bob; but as he had not turned up, they had had their tea. Still he did not turn up; and at last they came down to the gates to look out for him, as the time for calling-over drew nigh.

"Here he is!" exclaimed Harry, as Bob came in sight at last.

A taxi was turning out of the gates as Bob arrived. He glanced at the fishy-eyed man in black who was seated in it. It was the man who had talked to the cheery Arthur in the waiting-room at Lantham.

Evidently he had landed Arthur at Greyfriars, and got through his business there, and was now returning to the railway station.

He did not glance at Bob; never having seen him before, and quite unaware how near he had been to him at Lantham.

But Bob glanced after him very curi-

(*Continued on next page.*)

LEARN TO PLAY FOOTBALL!
OUR INTERNATIONAL COACH
BY

HALF-BACK PLAY

I THINK this week we had better get our game going again, after the long pause in which you have heard, and I hope learnt, some very important things. I guess most of you have forgotten where we were when we left the game to talk about tackling. I haven't. Our side had scored a goal, the ball was kicked off by the centre-forward of the other side, and our inside-right got a special pat on the back when he went in to tackle the opposing inside-left. We decided that the only thing wrong with the tackle was that the ball rolled wide, instead of coming out at the feet of our inside-right.

So the game is on again. Already, I can see developing a position which will show you, in practice, the value of a player who can draw an opponent—the important subject we discussed last week. Our right-half, seeing the ball run loose, dashes up, gets it under control, and starts to dribble it forward.

The left-half of the other side has no one to mark at the moment, because our inside-right is on the ground some yards away, so he comes up to tackle our right-half. But our player is a lad who has been practising his ball-control, and who has been watching first-class players. He manages, by a clever trick, to avoid the tackle, and the opposing half-back is left on the ground, while our right-half goes on his way with the ball at his feet.

He mustn't worry about the fact that for the moment he has wandered away from his position. Half-backs must take the ball through occasionally—put that down in your note-book, wing-halves—and another player will fall back in case of emergency.

"WELL PLAYED, GOALIE !"

NOW have a look at that diagram, with the twenty-two players, I suggested you should make for yourselves last week. You see what has happened. Our inside-right, and the inside-left of the other side, are out of the way for the moment. The opposing left-half, too, has been beaten, and our right-half has the ball at his feet. Someone must come to tackle him, or he will be away with a clear run to goal.

The opposing centre-half decides that he must leave his post to tackle the player with the ball. And that means

> This week's "lesson" by our special contributor deals with corner-kicks—and tells how they can be turned into goals. Follow his advice very carefully, chums.

what? Our centre-forward is left on his own in the middle of the field. Our right-half passes the ball to him—oh, this half-back is a good player; that pass was delivered with the inside of the boot, and the ball never left the ground. It is easy for the centre-forward to bring the ball under control. He does so, runs on a bit, and then shoots. A good shot—perhaps a bit too high—but the goalkeeper gets his fingers to it, and the ball goes round the post. Nearly another goal for us, and all because our right-half seized his chance, drew two opponents out of position, and then gave a fine pass to his centre-forward.

We have had a "lesson" on goal-kicks, haven't we? After the ball has gone out of play over the goal-line, one of the defenders has to kick it off from inside the goal-area. This time, the ball has gone behind the goal-line in the same way, but the circumstances are rather different. The last player to touch the ball before it went out was the goalkeeper—one of the defending side. So the game must be restarted by a corner-kick.

You see, if one of the attacking side sends the ball over the goal-line, there is a goal-kick, which is like a free-kick for the defending side. But if one of the defenders sends it off, there is a free-kick for the attackers—a corner-kick.

A corner-kick has been described as being worth half a goal. You might think it ought to be, too. Unfortunately it is a fact that, even in first-class football, somebody has worked out that a goal is scored from only one corner-kick in every eighteen.

TRICKS OF THE TRADE

LET me tell you how a corner-kick is taken, and then you will see why it should be easy to score a goal from one. On your map of a football field you will see, marked in the four corners, little quarter-circles,

like arcs in geometry. For a corner-kick, the ball must be placed inside one of these arcs. On whichever side of the goal the ball goes out of play, the kick is taken from that side. Corner-kicks are usually taken by the wingers. Not long ago West Bromwich Albion had a plan whereby Billy Richardson, their centre-forward, took all the corner-kicks. And at one time Jacky Bestall, of Grimsby Town, took all Grimsby's corners, although he was an inside-forward. There is no reason why you shouldn't let somebody other than the wingers take the kicks; but they are the usual fellows for the job.

The idea is that the player taking the corner-kick kicks the ball into the middle. He should try to send the ball just high enough to go over the heads of the first players and about three or four yards out from the goal, so that the goalkeeper cannot jump up above all the other players and punch the ball away.

Watch a player like Eric Brook, the Manchester City and England winger, take a corner-kick. He places the ball just right. And also notice that he, as well as most other first-class players, takes corner-kicks with what he would call his wrong foot. That means that an outside-left takes the corners with his right foot, and an outside-right takes them with his left foot.

This is done in order to get the proper swerve on the ball. If, in taking a corner from the right wing, the ball is kicked with the right foot, it will tend to swerve away from the goal. If the kick is taken with the left foot, the ball will swerve "inwards," which is much more useful. Try it and see.

Probably the wing men in our game will not be able to kick sufficiently strongly with their "wrong" feet to get the ball into the middle from the corner-flag. What shall we do? That's easy: we'll let the right-winger take the corners from the left, and vice versa. There is no harm in doing this. I remember a time when Mark Hooper, Sheffield Wednesday's outside-right, used to take the corners on both sides of the field.

I am afraid it is time for your "luncheon interval" now. But I can tell you many more stories about the tricks which first-class players get up to to score goals from corner-kicks. I'll let you into some of their secrets next week.

THE MAGNET LIBRARY.—No. 1,561.

ously as the taxi drove away towards Courtfield.

In his painful position in the waiting-room at Lantham, wriggling to get loose, he had almost forgotten that strange talk that had come to his ears there. The sight of the man in rusty black recalled it. "Arthur"—whoever Arthur was—was evidently at the school now—and Bob hoped that he was not in the Remove.

"You've turned up, old chap!" said Nugent amicably. "You've been a jolly long time getting in!"

"Try riding that bike again?" asked Johnny Bull.

"Oh, don't be an ass!" grunted Bob gruffly. "I've had a rotten time, you fellows—lost train after train! Did you notice that sportsman in black who's just gone? Has he left a new kid here?"

"Yes—chap named Carter——" said Harry.

"Arthur Carter?"

"Eh? Yes! How did you know?" asked Harry, in astonishment.

"I didn't know the Carter part—only the Arthur part!" grunted Bob. "Precious sort of a rotter to let into Greyfriars!"

His chums regarded him in amazement.

They had never heard of Bunter's relative before that afternoon, so it was astonishing to hear this from Bob.

"You don't know the chap, surely?" asked Harry.

"No; and don't want to!"

"You seem to know his name."

"Yes, I know his name. I hope he's not coming into the Remove," growled Bob, as he tramped across the quad with his friends.

"As it happens, he is—I suppose it was fixed in the hols, though he didn't get here first day of term."

"Rotten!" grunted Bob. "We don't want a cad like that in the Form."

"Well, it may be rotten," said Harry, more and more astonished. "But as you've never seen the chap, I don't quite see how you know."

"I saw him at Lantham Station," grunted Bob. "Heard him, too."

"Oh! You haven't rowed with him, I suppose?"

"No, ass; he never saw me."

"You saw him without his seeing you?"

"Oh, I suppose I'd better tell you," grunted Bob. "A gang of Highcliffe cads got me there—nobody else about—and they tied me up in the waiting-room. I was stuck there over an hour. I should be there still, I expect, only some Cliff House girls came in—they'd been to a matinee with the Bull, and they found me——"

"Oh, my hat!"

"The cads left me stuck behind the door—tied on a chair, with a hanky stuffed in my mouth!" snorted Bob. "I might have stayed there till midnight, for all I know, only Bessie Bunter wanted the door shut—frowsty, like all the Bunters—and she saw me, and yelped."

"Lucky she did, if you were fixed like that——"

"Oh, frightfully lucky!" said Bob sarcastically. "It was so nice to be found tied up like a turkey by a party of schoolgirls, and giggled at! I enjoyed it immensely, I can tell you."

"Is that why you've come back in a bad temper?" asked Johnny Bull.

Bob looked at him.

"Who's in a bad temper?" he inquired, with dangerous calm.

"Aren't you?" asked Johnny. "You look it."

"Well, cackle from a silly fathead is enough to make a fellow a bit bad-tempered," said Bob. "Can't you go and talk rot to somebody else?"

"Hem!" said Nugent loudly.

"My esteemed Johnny——" murmured Hurree Jamset Ram Singh.

"But how did you see the chap if you were parked behind a door?" asked Harry, rather to change the topic than from a desire for information.

"Between the door and the post, as I'm not blind, as he came in, with that rotten rascal who's just gone."

"That what?"

"Rotten rascal!"

"You're not in a bad temper," said Johnny Bull, "but you call a man you don't know a rotten rascal, and a chap you don't know a cad. If that's good temper——"

"I call him a rotten rascal because he is one; and I call the fellow a cad because he's a cad!" answered Bob. "And if you think it out for a year or two—or perhaps a century or two—it may occur to you that I heard them talking, while I was stuck behind that door, and so I know what a pair of rotters they are!"

The Co. made no reply to that. Whether Bob's remarks were justified or not, it was clear that he was not in his usual good temper.

"So the fellow's name is Carter, is it?" said Bob. "I don't know of any Carters here! But he's got a relation here—I wonder who?"

"Bunter," said Harry.

"Oh, don't be an ass!"

"Thanks!"

"Well, what do you mean?" snapped Bob. "The cad's got a relation here. I heard that when they were gabbling in the waiting-room at Lantham. It can't be Bunter."

"Why can't it?"

"Well, it's rot! I couldn't make much sense of what they were saying, except that they were a pair of worms —but it didn't sound as if they were speaking of a fool like Bunter. How do you know this chap Carter is a relation of Bunter?"

"He told us so."

"Oh!" said Bob. "Not making a silly mistake?"

"Not at all!" said Harry dryly. "But perhaps you are, old bean!"

Grunt from Bob.

"He's one of Bunter's rich relations!" grinned Nugent. "Nephew and heir of a jolly old bean who's juicy with oof, according to Bunter."

"A rich relation, is he?" grunted Bob. "Bunter will find out a mistake there, I fancy. Of course, he might have another relation here, as well as Bunter —if Bunter's really related to him. Blessed if I make it all out."

"We've kept some stuff for you, hot, in the fender!" said Nugent, as they went into the House. "I suppose you're hungry."

"Hungry as a hunter—or a Bunter!" said Bob, with a spot of his usual good-humour. "By gum, I could eat a mule's hind leg!"

"Come up to the study, then!"

The Famous Five tramped up to the Remove.

A bright fire was burning in Study No. 1; the kettle was singing, and the study looked very bright and cosy and hospitable.

Bob Cherry's clouded brow cleared a little as he came in. He was cold and tired, and had several aches and pains, and altogether disgruntled by the hapless happenings that afternoon—added to which, he was fearfully hungry. But

a cheery grin came over his face as Frank Nugent lifted a plate of sosses and chips from the fender, Johnny Bull handed up a stack of toast, and Harry Wharton made the tea.

"By gum! This is better than that beastly waiting-room at Lantham!" said Bob, as he sat down and started.

"The betterfulness is probably terrific!" agreed Hurree Jamset Ram Singh. "Next half-holiday we will go and look for the execrable Highcliffians and slay them slaughterfully."

"Tuck in, old chap!" said Harry. "It won't be long to call-over now."

Bob Cherry tucked in.

There was no doubt that a rest in the warm and cosy study and a square meal made him feel ever so much better.

He had finished that late tea, and was washing down a final chunk of cake with a third cup of tea, when there was a tap at the study door.

"Totter in, old thing!" called out Nugent.

The door opened, and Mr. Quelch, the master of the Remove, was revealed.

The juniors jumped at once, Nugent crimsoning. He had not guessed that it was his Form-master there when he bade the "old thing" totter in!

The Remove master glanced round at a junior who had followed him up the Remove passage.

"Come in, Carter! This is your study."

"Yes, sir!"

The new junior came in, and Bob, with a deep breath, fixed his eyes on the fellow who had smoked and talked with the man in black at Lantham Station.

THE EIGHTH CHAPTER.

Bunter's Relation!

ARTHUR CARTER glanced at the fellows in the study with a keen, cool eye.

New boy as he was, there was nothing of the new boy in his looks; not a spot of sheepishness or nervousness about him.

That, of course, was accounted for by the fact that he came from another school; life in a big school was nothing new to him.

At the same time, his cool self-assurance was not exactly pleasing to the other fellows.

As Bunter's relation—rich or not—he was of some interest to the juniors, especially to Bob, after what he had heard at Lantham.

He was absolutely nothing like Bunter to look at.

So far from being fat, like the fat Owl, he was slim, and looked fairly active and sturdy. He was not bad-looking—and his eyes were uncommonly keen. They seemed to take in the whole study and everybody in it in one flash.

"Wharton!" said Mr. Quelch. "This is Carter, the new boy in the Form. Carter, this is Wharton, the head boy of the Remove."

The two gave one another a nod and a grin.

"I have decided to place Carter in your study, Wharton——"

"Oh!"

"As there are only two in this study, since Bullivant left last term," said Mr. Quelch.

"Oh, quite!" said Harry. "But——"

"But what, Wharton?" asked Mr. Quelch, rather sharply.

It was not for a Remove fellow to explain to his Form-master that he did not want new boys landed in his study. Wharton and Nugent were accustomed to having Study No. 1 to themselves,

In a very secluded spot, almost hidden by ivy and the old stone pillars, Billy Bunter spotted his man. Cousin Arthur was leaning against a pillar, smoking a cigarette! The searching Owl grinned as he spotted him!

though the whole Co. generally tea'd there. A stranger in the land, so to speak, was likely to be disturbing to the accustomed harmony.

But that was not all. It was clear already that Bob Cherry was not going to be friendly with the new junior, and that was likely to make matters awkward, if he were assigned to Study No. 1.

On the fellow's looks, Wharton neither liked nor disliked him; but he did not want him there, if he were going to row with Bob.

All that, however, certainly could not be explained to the master of the Remove. Wharton thought of another tack.

"I think Carter has a relation in the Form, sir," he said. "He might like to be put in his relation's study."

Mr. Quelch raised his eyebrows. It seemed that this was news to him.

"Indeed," he said. He turned to Carter. "Have you a relative here, in my Form, Carter?"

"Not that I know of, sir!" answered Carter.

"It appears that you are mistaken, Wharton!" said Mr. Quelch, with a touch of asperity. Perhaps the Remove master did not need telling that old-established occupants of a study did not exactly like new boys bunged in on them!

Bob Cherry looked hard at the new junior.

That the fellow had a relative in the school was a certainty, for he had heard it, in so many words, at Lantham.

That relative's Form, however, had not been mentioned, or his name; and, so far as Bob knew, it might have been any man at Greyfriars from the Second to the Sixth. And certainly he had no likeness whatever to Billy Bunter.

"I—I thought——" stammered Harry, quite taken aback.

"I fail to see why you should have

thought so, Wharton, as you have never seen Carter before, I imagine!"

"No, sir; but——"

"Have you any relatives at Greyfriars at all, Carter?" asked Mr. Quelch.

"I don't know of any, sir."

Bob set his lips.

That, at all events, was a falsehood! A fellow might easily be ignorant of a distant relative, and not know whether he was in the school or not. But the fellow's own words at Lantham proved that he knew.

"Really, Wharton——" snapped Mr. Quelch, "I repeat that I quite fail to see why you should have thought anything of the kind."

Harry's face was red. He was not going to leave it at that.

"I was told so by a Remove fellow who said that Carter was his relation," he said. "I supposed it was so, as he said so."

Carter gave him a quick look.

"Indeed," said Mr. Quelch, less sharply, "Carter may have a relative here whom he does not know. In that case, no doubt, he would be glad to meet him. Who was the Remove boy to whom you refer?"

"Bunter, sir!"

"Bunter!" repeated Mr. Quelch. "Carter, there is a boy in my Form named Bunter! Is he a relative of yours?"

"I hardly think so, sir," said Carter. "I believe we have some very distant relations of that name, but I don't know anything about them."

"Bunter said he had met you once at your uncle's!" said Harry.

"Did he?" said Carter, indifferently. "I don't remember!"

"If Bunter is such a very distant relative that Carter has forgotten his existence, I see no special reason for placing him in Bunter's study, Wharton," said Mr. Quelch. "There are three

already in Bunter's study, and only two here."

"Very well, sir!" said Harry.

He made a mental resolve to kick Bunter. Evidently—as it appeared, at least—the fat Owl knew his "rich" relation, or pretended that he did, better than the rich relation knew Bunter! After Bunter's talk, Wharton had naturally expected the name of Bunter to be familiar to the new fellow. It seemed, however, that he had hardly heard it.

"Carter will share this study with you and Nugent," said Mr. Quelch. "You will make the new boy welcome here, Wharton."

"Oh, certainly, sir."

"I will leave Carter here now," said Mr. Quelch. "You will come down to call-over with Wharton when the bell rings, Carter."

"Yes, sir."

Mr. Quelch left the study. Carter was left with the Famous Five, quite easy and assured in his manner, with that little crowd of strangers.

"You don't seem fearfully keen on having me in this study!" he said, with a laugh. "Sorry to barge in!"

"Oh, not at all!" said Harry, with a touch of compunction. "You see——"

"I see perfectly! I've been through it at my last school—I had an absolute blighter landed on me once," said Carter. "I'll try not to be a blighter, if you'll give me a chance."

Four members of the Co. laughed.

Bob Cherry stood grimly silent. His friends were rather taken with the new boy's way of speaking.

"That's all right!" said Harry. "I've no doubt we shall get on all right. This chap is Nugent, your other studymate."

"Pleased to see you, Nugent—more than you are to see me, probably," said Carter. "By the way, who's that fellow Bunter you were speaking of? Does he

(Continued on page 16.)

THE FORM-MASTER'S SECRET!

A Spanking Fine Yarn of Jack Jolly & Co. of St. Sam's

By DICKY NUGENT

GREYFRIA...

No. 275.   EDITED BY HAR...

"Dusty!" gasped Mr. Lickham.

The master of the Fourth sounded serprized and horrified.

At St. Sam's, Mr. Lickham was usually looked on as a bit of an old donkey. But now he sounded a little horse.

He stood in the doorway of his study and stared with bulging eyes at the unkempt figger that occupied his armchair.

The unkempt figger wore a grin. He also wore rags and tatters—not to menshun a week's growth of beard. And yet, in spite of this, he bore an uncanny likeness to Mr. Lickham.

This likeness seemed even stronger when he spoke, for his voice, though less refined, was almost eyedentical with that of the master of the Fourth.

"Yuss, Izaak!" he cried. "It's me—your long-lost cuzzin, Dusty Lickham! 'Ow are yer, me old covey?"

Mr. Lickham shuddered. He hurriedly closed the door.

"What are you doing here?" he demanded feercely. "Do you think I want people to know that I have a cuzzin who is nothing more than a common tramp—a work-shy and a down-and-out? Let me tell you, Dusty, there is not a single Lickham who will acknollidge you to-day. You are the black sheep of the fambly!"

"Keep your wool hon, old covey!" grinned Mr. Lickham's visitor. "I may be the black sheep, but if you ram it down my throat I won't eggsactly take it like a lamb!"

"Don't act the goat!" snapped Mr. Lickham. "I want to know why you have turned up here like a bad penny, Dusty. What is it? Munny?"

Dusty Lickham rubbed his griny palm against the corner of his cuzzin's desk and grinned a grin of antissipation.

"Yuss, that's it, Cuzzin Izaak!" he said. "I hain't eaten a square meal or 'ad a nite's lodgin' for a week. It's your munny as I want."

"And it's munny I want myself!" retorted Mr. Lickham. "The fakt is, I need it more than you do yourself, if only you knew it!"

"Wot, an' you a master in a posh skool like this 'ere?" cried Dusty Lickham "Himpossibul!"

But, impossibul as it seemed to Mr. Lickham's frowzy cuzzin, it was only too true!

The new term had begun badly for the master of the Fourth. During the Christmas hollerdays he had forgotten to keep paying the instalments due on a new cap and gown he had bought during the previous term. The result was that the first thing he had found on returning to St. Sam's was a blue envelope containing a court summons.

Ten shillings would have staved off the trubble that threttened. Unforchunitly, during the hollerdays, Mr. Lickham had spent munny not wisely, but too well, and he was unable to raise ten pence, let alone ten shillings. So now he was in the unhappy position of eggspecting the hand of the law to descend on him at any moment.

Small wonder, then, that Mr. Lickham sighed weerily as he gazed at his grimy relative.

"Impossibul or not, there it is!" he said. "I am stony broke—or, to put it vulgarly, I am suffering from acute financial embarrassment! And now, to add to my trubbles, you turn up!"

Plonk! Plonk! Plonk!

It was the sound of footprints echoing along the passidge outside the study.

Mr. Lickham's jaw dropped.

"Ye gods! You must

hide!" he breethed. "If this is Doctor Birchemall and he finds you here, there'll be the very dickens to pay! Quick!"

The master of the Fourth seezed his cuzzin by the scruff of the neck and farely rushed him into a curtained-off recess in a corner of the study.

The next moment the door opened.

Mr. Lickham looked round. Then a groan burst from his lips.

Standing in the doorway a grim figger in blue.

"The perlice!" groaned Mr. Lickham.

"Izaak Jolliwell Lickham, I arrest you in the name of the law!"

JOHNNY BULL IS STARTING A BAND!

Shrieks CLAUDE HOSKINS

The cheek of it! The nerve of it!

How a Remove kid like Bull can have the face to set up seriously as a band conductor simply beats me!

For years and years I have been the acknowledged authority on musical matters at Greyfriars. The very least I should have expected from anybody who thought of starting a band was that he should come to me for help and advice.

Do you think Bull came to me for help and advice? Not a bit of it! I went to him, instead!

The reason I went to him was that my musical feelings simply could not stand the thought of the ghastly mess Bull would make of things if left to his own resources. I could picture him placing his reed and string players in the wrong positions, for instance. I could imagine him descending to vulgar dance music, instead of sticking to the masterpieces of the great composers like Wagner and myself. (Pardon the personal note!) All sorts of possible horrors might happen, I thought, unie ss I went along and sto pped them from the start.

So I went along to the Rag to help.

I was greeted by the most appalling din imaginable. It sounded almost as bad as the average dance band! And the instruments! There were mouth-organs and even worse than that! Two fellows were playing, if you ever heard of such a thing, on combs and paper!

In a state of frenzy, I rushed into the room. My hands were over my ears and a look of agony was on my face.

"Stop! Stop!" I cried. "Vandals! Barbarians! Stop it at once, I tell you!"

You might have thought they would have been grateful for advice from a recognised musician. Nothing of the kind! None of them looked at all pleased—least of all Bull, who put down his conductor's baton and simply glared at me.

"What's wrong with it?" he growled.

"Ask me what's right with it, and save time!" I replied kindly. "My dear kid, everything's wrong with it! There's only one thing to do. Sit

down and let me see if I can make a band of it!"

There was generosity, if you like! A magnificent offer, if ever there was one! I fully expected that on hearing it, Bull would fall on my neck and weep with joy. I quite anticipated that the rest of the band would crowd round me, wringing my hand and thumping me on the back.

But how different was the reality! Instead of Bull falling on my neck and weeping with joy, he fell on my neck and whacked my jaw—while the rest of the band

crowded round me, trying to wring my neck instead of my hand!

I retired in disorder, and left Bull and his band to carry on without me. But if they think I've given it up, they're soon going to find out their mistake! Watch out next week—and if I don't have a very different story to tell, my name's not Claude Hoskins!

HARRY WHARTON

Have you broken all your New Year resolutions yet, chums? Most of them, I'll wager!

I don't mind admitting that all mine have gone west—with one exception. Fortunately that exception happens to be the most important of the lot.

The resolution is to make the "Greyfriars Herald" even brighter and better than it has ever been before!

How to do it is a problem that has been occupying my mind since before the Christmas hols. I think I've solved it now. The keynote is "More rarity!" I am going all out to obtain news and views from a host of new contributors.

Please don't think that this means your old favourites will be forgotten. Nothing of the kind, I assure you! Bob Cherry, the Bounder, Dick Rake, Peter Todd, and all the other star turns of the past will continue to write for the "Herald." But I intend to spread my net a little wider and see if I can land a few more contributors who have something original to say and can say it in a way that is likely to appeal

to ...
Hera...
Jus...
start...
au ...
Quele...
reaso...
sider...
Form...
I hop...
bers ...
mast...
own ...
for th...
up the...
The ...
make ...
all li...
selve...
now ...
frank...
us fr...
ters ...
Grey...
eager...
sibly ...
of ap...
Dic...
gerin...
Sam'...
prince...
our fa...
and, ...
unare...
less t...
recen...
you r...
obligo...
all h...
"sup...
No ...
this i...
for ...
talk ...
week...
Cl...
HA...

This ...
perlice ...
harsh ...
as he ...
study ...
of the ...
Lickha...
the lip...
"W...
manni...
"O...
keepin...
ments...
bough...
Baggs...
of Mu...
the co...
glance...
in his ...
tip an...
Lickha...
He ...
ment ...
projoc...
gave ...
Fourth...

s HERALD

STOP PRESS NEWS

HARTON.   January 15th, 1938.

MY FORM IS THE BEST AT GREYFRIARS!

Says H. S. QUELCH, M.A.

I hope there will be no raising of eyebrows amongst my friends at the idea of my contributing to the "Greyfriars Herald." It is quite true that Wharton's paper is one which I can hardly view with unqualified approval. The lack of respect for authority which characterises its articles and features, for instance, is something on which I frown most severely—while Nugent minor's orthography is truly shocking! But, for all that, I consider that the "Greyfriars Herald" is, on the whole, a commendable enterprise, and I am quite pleased to accede to Wharton's request to write in it my reasons for thinking that the Remove is the best Form at Greyfriars.

I am certainly very firmly of that opinion. Do not, however, for the moment, think that I look on them as paragons of virtue. The reverse is the case, I assure you! They are as mischievous and troublesome a collection of youngsters as were ever assembled in one Form-room.

But the high spirits shown in their fun have a valuable side which it would be unfair to ignore. The zest which they display in "rags" and "japes" becomes a great asset in sport—and surely nobody can deny that they throw themselves heart and soul into sport! Furthermore, though this may surprise some of my readers, many of them apply themselves to their studies with equal vigour. Wharton, Linley, Todd and Penfold, to name four at random, are quite brilliant scholars and most of the Form, in their school work, reach a gratifying standard of excellence.

What is still more important, the majority of them are extremely likeable boys, possessed of courage and common sense and a sturdy independence of character. There are black sheep among them, as in every fold, but even these are often all the better for the wholesome influence of the others.

Undoubtedly, my Form is the best at Greyfriars!

(Next week Mr. Prout will tell you why he considers the Fifth is the best Form in the school. Don't miss it!)

Fisher T. Fish says that when he played in a Rugger match in New York, he converted no fewer than twenty "tries." We wish somebody would convert Fish from his habit of telling tall stories!

...LING!

...friars ...ders.

...way of a ...e secured ... by Mr. ...ring the ...y he con- ...the best ...reyfriars. ...ture num- ...et other ...wish their ...to qualify ...ur to put ...uments. ...les should ...t hit. We ...see our- ...ers see us ...gain, and ...ons about ...own mas- ...e read by ...ellows with ...and pos- ...in amount ...ision! ...ent's stag- ...ies of St. ...still be the ...eature in ...little paper ...quantity is ...a little ...has been ...am sure ...cky will ...eeing that ...ns are of ...cality!

for more Look out ...r topical ...me next

...chums! ...HARTON

...what the ...said, in a ...rcuss voice, ...d into the ...t the sound ...words, Mr. ...t white to

...for?" he ...gasp. ...unt of not ...your instal- ...p and gown ...Messrs. ...ks, tailors, ...!" replied ...e, after a ...dockument ..."Take my ...e quietly,

...the docku- ...s belt and, ...truncheon, ...ster of the ...rt tap on

the head that nocked him spinning. Before he could get up again Mr. Lickham had been securely handcuffed.

"Isn't it possibul, officer, for me to leave the skool without being seen?" he groaned, as the perliceman yanked him to his feet and began to bundle him out of the study. "The disgrace of being marched off like this will be simply garstly!"

The perliceman pawsed. Underneath his stern exterior he was a kindly man, and he did not want to do anything that would hurt Mr. Lickham's feelings.

"Got a sack?" he asked, after pondering deeply for some seconds. Mr. Lickham looked mistified.

"I've got several sacks if you want them; but what——"

"Give me one and I'll carry you off the premises if you like," said the constable, with a kindly smile.

"Thanks, awfully!" said Mr. Lickham, gratefully.

He went to his desk and drew out a sack from one of the drawers. And the kind-hearted perliceman, after giving him another crack on the nut with his truncheon, put him in the sack and carried him off to the station.

The door slammed behind him. His footprints died away.

And then a grinning and grimy face peered out from the curtained-off recess in the corner.

"My heye! Pore old Izaak!" muttered Dusty Lickham.

He ambled out into the middle of the room and rubbed his unshaven chin reflecktively. And as he did so, a sudden gleem came into his eyes.

"My 'at! Wot a chance this is for me to git free board an' lodgin' for a week or two!" he muttered. "Nobody in this 'ere skool knows Izaak 'as gorn. An' I'm 'is livin' image. If I can only tog up in 'is duds, nobody won't know as I hain't my skoolmaster cuzzin! Haw, haw, haw!"

He crossed to the door and turned the key in the lock. Then he set to work.

Within five minutes he had acheeved wonders.

First he had shaved himself with a razor he found in one of his cuzzin's cupboards. Then he had divested himself of his ragged clothes and donned Mr. Lickham's Sunday worst instead. And finally, he had put on the unlucky cap and gown which had led to Mr. Lickham's present predicament.

Dusty Lickham had quite a shock when he stood in front of the mirror and looked at himself. He looked so much like his cuzzin Izaak that for a moment he thought he had returned! But Dusty Lickham had no time to reflect over his reflection before there was a clatter of feet in the passidge, followed by a nock on the door.

Dusty Lickham made a dive for the door and unlocked it.

A moment later, a bearded figger entered, followed by four grinning juniors.

"Ah! Here we are again, Lickham!" chirped the bearded

figger, who was, of corse, none other than Doctor Alfred Birchemall, the revered and majestick headmaster of St. Sam's. "Sorry we're a day late for the new term."

"How do you do, sir?" corussed Jack Jolly & Co.

The next moment, the newcomers had the shock of their lives when the man they thought to be Mr. I. Jolliwell Lickham, replied to their greeting.

"Wotcher, me old sparrow! 'Ow do, young coveys!" he chortled.

"Bless my sole! Is there something wrong with my ears, Lickham, or did you really call me 'old sparrow'?" asked the Head, quite faintly.

Forchunitly, before the bogus Form-master had time to reply to that question, the dinner-bell started ringing, and the Head and Jack Jolly & Co. turned on their heels and galloped away.

For the time being the mistery of Mr. Lickham was forgotten. But not for long. There were breakers ahead for Dusty Lickham of St. Sam's!

(The bogus Form-master makes things hum in next week's instalment. Don't miss it!)

LET ME MAKE YOU STRONG!

Says BOLSOVER MAJOR

If you're a puny, undersized rabbit, with knock knees, pin toes, watery eyes and a sloping chin, come to me! In one term, I'll turn you into a raging lion, with bandy legs, splayed feet, blazing orbs and the square jaw of a real he-man!

And there's nothing to be nervous about, either. "Moderation in all things" is my motto, and you need not fear that I shall overdo it in any way. If you want anyone to confirm this, ask Snoop!

I took Snoop in hand last term. He was as nervous as a kitten. He thought I was going to knock his hea ? off.

Of course, I did nothing of the sort. True to my idea of moderation, I merely blacked both his eyes and knocked out two of his teeth.

I put him through a gentle course of physical culture all the term. We just took it steadily.

We didn't get up in the morning at six o'clock. Not likely! Five minutes past six was quite early enough for us.

We didn't do a three-mile run and exhaust ourselves. About two miles and three-quarters was our moderate average.

We didn't plunge into a freezing bath at the finish. No fear! I preferred to strike a happy medium—about one degree above freezing point!

So you see, there's nothing to fear if you put yourself in my hands. I get my result by gentle, persuasive means—not by rushing at the thing like a bull at a gate.

If you don't believe me, ask Snoop, as soon as he recovers from his present unfortunate breakdown in health. He'll tell you I'm speaking the truth—or, if he doesn't, I'll break every bone in his body!

Let me make you strong, then, lads, and let me do it this term in my sensible, moderate way!

Apply early and avoid the rush!

BILLY BUNTER'S RICH RELATION!

By FRANK RICHARDS

(Continued from page 13.)

really make out that he's related to
me?"

"A distant relationship—second cousin
twice removed, I think he said,"
answered Harry, laughing. "I suppose
you must be the chap he was speaking
of—there can't be two Arthur Carters."

"Hardly!"

"Bunter's Carter was at a school
called St. Olaf's. Was that your
school?"

"That was it! My uncle has a fancy
that the sea air may be good for me, so
he's hooked me out of St. Olaf's and
planted me here!" said Carter. "St.
Olaf's is right in the Midlands, as I
dare say you know."

"I'm afraid I'd never heard of it
before," said Harry. "Not till Bunter
mentioned it."

Bob Cherry stepped a little nearer to
the door. He was beginning to feel that
he could not breathe the same air as
this fellow.

Unless he had been dreaming, in the
waiting-room at Lantham, he had heard
Carter and Gooch mention, quite
plainly, that the fellow had been turned
out of his last school for bad conduct.

Certainly the fellow could not be expected to mention that, at his new
school. But there was no need to roll
out lies.

Bob, certainly, had no intention of repeating what he had heard by accident,
and thus causing the new fellow trouble
in his new school. But he was feeling
that he could not stand him personally.

"I think I'll cut, you fellows!" said
Bob abruptly, and he left Study No. 1
before anyone could answer.

Carter's quick eyes flashed after him.
"Who's that chap?" he asked.

"Bob Cherry!" answered Harry.

"Friend of yours?"

"Yes, rather!"

"He doesn't seem to like me a lot—
I've never seen him before, that I know
of," said Carter, puzzled. "If he's a
friend of fellows in my study, I don't
want to be unfriendly with him. What
the dickens has he got his back up
about?"

The Co. were rather uncomfortably
silent. At the same time, they could
not help being struck by the new fellow's
swiftness of observation. In those few
minutes, and without Bob speaking a
word, he had sensed his dislike.

"Sorry if he doesn't like me," added
Carter. "I like him, on his looks.
Looks a fearfully healthy sort of chap."

"One of the very best," said Harry.
"Best chap in the Remove, really—
you'll like him all right! Like the
study?"

"Topping!" said Carter. "Better
than my study at my last school! Greyfriars seems a jolly sort of place, from
the little I've seen of it so far."

"The jollifulness is terrific!" declared
Hurree Jamset Ram Singh.

Carter jumped.

"Eh, what? Would you mind saying
that again?" he ejaculated.

"I remarked that the jollifulness of
THE MAGNET LIBRARY.—No. 1,561.

this esteemed school is terrific, and
indeed preposterous, my esteemed
Carter."

"Is that a joke?" asked Carter,
mystified.

Harry Wharton chuckled.

"That's Inky's English," he said. "He
learned it under the wisest moonshee at
Bhanipur, and since then he's used no
other."

"I say, the chap's name ain't really
Inky, is it?" asked Carter.

"Inky for short—full name, Hurree
Bang Wallop Jampot."

"Oh, my hat——"

"My esteemed and absurd Wharton!"

"You haven't seen Bunter yet?" asked
Nugent.

"Bunter? No! I wonder if he's
really a relation!" said Carter. "I
know we've got some distant connections
of that name—I may even have seen
the chap, of course, and forgotten him.
The fact is, I believe they're a rather
hard-up branch of the family, and my
uncle sort of barged them off! Funny
thing to find a relation in a school
without knowing it."

"Well, he hasn't forgotten you, if
you've forgotten him," said Harry.
"You'll see him all right! Hallo,
there's the bell. Come down to Hall."

The juniors left the study together.

Bob Cherry was in the passage, and
he made a movement to join up, as the
little crowd of fellows poured out of
Study No. 1. But as he saw Carter with
the Co. he checked himself.

"Come on, Bob!" called out Harry.

"In a minute—don't wait!" called
back Bob.

Five juniors went down the Remove
staircase, quite cheerfully, together.
Bob Cherry followed more slowly.

THE NINTH CHAPTER.
A Blow for Bunter!

"I SAY, you fellows! Seen my
Cousin Arthur?" asked Billy
Bunter anxiously.

Harry Wharton & Co. grinned.
As Carter, the new fellow, was with
them, Billy Bunter really seemed under
no necessity to inquire after his
"Cousin" Arthur.

Apparently the fat Owl did not know
the rich relation, of whom he had talked
so much, by sight.

Whether Carter knew Bunter by sight
or not was not apparent in his face. If
he had met the fat junior only once, a
considerable time ago, it was probable
that he might have forgotten the meeting. On the other hand, Bunter was a
fellow who, once seen, was not easily
forgotten. His circumference, at least,
was likely to be remembered.

"I've been looking for the chap
everywhere," went on Bunter. "First
he was with Quelch, and then I heard
he was with the Head; and after that I
went along to the House-dame's room,
but Mrs. Kebble told me he had gone.
He's not with Quelch now; Quelch is
jawing in Hall with Prout. I say, I
wonder where he is?"

"I wonder!" grinned Johnny Bull.

"The wonderfulness is terrific!"

"Well, I want to find him!" said
Bunter, evidently quite unconscious that
"Cousin Arthur" was quite near at
hand. "Haven't you seen him?"

In a school of some hundreds of
fellows, there were, of course, plenty
whom other fellows hardly knew.
Bunter, who plainly did not know
Arthur Carter by sight, did not notice
him specially coming down the stairs
after the Co. It did not seem to occur
to him that this fellow was a new fellow,
and therefore probably Carter.

Carter stopped on the stairs and
leaned on the banister, carelessly glancing down at the fat Owl. If he was, as
Bunter had said, a sort of second cousin
twice removed, the relationship was
hardly near enough for a fellow to feel
very enthusiastic about it. At all events,
it did not seem that Carter was keen
to be claimed as a relation by Billy
Bunter.

He took no notice of the fat junior,
and Bunter, blinking anxiously at the
Co., did not notice the fellow on the
staircase.

"You see, I don't want him to feel
that I'm neglecting him," explained
Bunter. "He will be jolly anxious to
see me, you know."

"The knowfulness is not preposterous!" grinned Hurree Jamset Ram
Singh.

"Oh, really Inky—I mean to say,
we're awfully attached to one another,
you know!" said Bunter. "Fearfully
pally, and all that! Queer that I
haven't spotted him yet."

"You'd know him at once?" asked
Nugent.

"Oh, yes, rather!"

"Ha, ha, ha!"

"Blessed if I see anything to cackle
at! I say——"

"What's he like?" asked Harry
Wharton.

"Oh, not a bad-looking chap, I
believe!" said Bunter. "Not handsome,
you know. The good looks are all on
our side of the family——"

"Oh crikey!"

"But skinny," said Bunter—"I mean,
he hasn't a figure like me, you know.
As skinny as you, Wharton! About as
good-looking, too—I mean to say, good
looks ain't his long suit!"

"Oh, thanks!"

"To tell you the truth, I believe he
was a bit jealous of my good looks,"
said Bunter. "Plain fellows are, you
know. But I don't mind that! I'm
used to it, you know."

"Ha, ha, ha!" yelled the juniors.

"I wish you fellows wouldn't cackle
whenever a fellow opens his mouth! I
say, have you seen the chap or not?"
demanded Bunter.

"Yes, we've seen him," said Harry,
laughing. "Quelch brought him to my
study, fathead! He hasn't a figure like
yours, old fat bean, that's a cert. He
didn't have to squeeze in at the
doorway!"

"Yah! Well, where is he now?"
asked Bunter. "I want to take him in
to call-over. Is he in the study?"

"Sure you'd know him if you saw
him?" grinned Johnny Bull.

"Eh? Oh, yes! I—I think so. Is he
coming down?"

"He's come, fathead! There he is!"

Harry Wharton made a gesture
towards the new junior leaning on the
banisters.

"Oh!" ejaculated Bunter. He turned
his eyes and his spectacles on the new
fellow. "I—I say, are you my Cousin
Arthur?"

"Not that I know of!" answered
Carter coolly.

"Eh—what? Look here, are you
Carter?"

"Yes, I'm Carter."

"Then you're my Cousin Arthur!"
declared Bunter.

"Mistake somewhere!" said Carter,
shaking his head. "I have only one
cousin in the wide world, and you're not
the man!"

"Well, not exactly a cousin," said
Bunter. "Second cousin twice removed,
or third cousin once removed, or—or
something of the kind. I suppose you
know me?"

"Not in the least!"

"Look here——"

"If your name's Bunter, you may be some distant connection of mine," said Carter coolly. "As the relationship's so distant, would you mind keeping as distant as the relationship?"

"Oh, really, Arthur——"

"If you call me 'Arthur' again, I shall boot you!" said Carter.

"Why, you cheeky beast——"

"If you're a relation of mine—which I don't believe—you don't look one to be proud of!" said Carter. "Blow away, you bloated bluebottle!"

Billy Bunter stood blinking at him. He seemed as utterly taken aback as a full-rigged ship, under full sail, caught in a sudden head wind. He could only blink.

"Let's get into Hall!" said Harry Wharton hastily.

"Come on!" said Nugent.

The juniors moved on, followed by Carter, leaving the hapless fat Owl rooted to the floor, still blinking.

In the study, the four had rather liked Carter; but they did not like the way he had spoken to Bunter.

Bunter, it was true, was "on the make"; it was plain enough that he wanted to hook on to Carter because Carter was a rich relation. The chap was entitled to keep him at armslength if so disposed. Still, there were ways of doing these things, and Carter's way did not seem very pleasant. They could not help thinking that he might have let the fat and fatuous Owl down a little more lightly.

"Oh!" gasped Bunter at last, blinking after them as they went. "Oh! Swanky cad! Beast!"

Bob Cherry, coming down after his friends, had been a witness of that little scene. He stopped to tap Bunter on a fat shoulder.

That Carter had some relation at Greyfriars he knew, though the fellow had lied about it. From what he had been told, it seemed that that relation was Billy Bunter. That, however, now seemed rather doubtful.

"Look here, Bunter," said Bob gruffly. "Is that chap really a relation of yours or not?"

"Yes, he jolly well is!" yapped Bunter. "Not a near relation, of course, but he's a relation. He jolly well knows it, too."

"You never knew him by sight?"

"Well, I've only seen him once, and it was a long time ago. But he jolly well knew me," said Bunter. "I'm a bit more distinguished, you know! People don't forget me like they do commonplace chaps!"

Bob grinned.

"He didn't seem to know you," he said.

"Swank!" said Bunter. "They're frightfully swanky at St. Olaf's. Why, I wrote to him there once, and told him I'd come and see him if he liked, and he never even answered the letter!"

"Has he any other relations here?"

"Of course he hasn't, except my brother Sammy. If he had, they'd be my relations, too."

"I suppose they would, if you're really related to him," said Bob.

"Well, I jolly well am! I say, this is pretty thick, ain't it?" said Bunter. "Fancy Wharton bagging my rich relation like that!"

"Wha-at?"

"After his money, of course!" said Bunter.

Bob stared at him.

"You silly owl!" he snapped; and he walked on.

"Beast!"

Billy Bunter rolled away to Hall, with a frowning fat brow. Carter was

already there, in the ranks of the Remove. Bunter gave him a blink, utterly unnoticed by the new fellow. Arthur Carter seemed oblivious of his fat existence, and, after calling-over, he left Hall with Wharton and Nugent, still blankly oblivious of Bunter.

THE TENTH CHAPTER.
A Very Distant Relation !

THE Famous Five grinned.

So did a dozen other fellows. It was in break, the following morning.

Arthur Carter, the new member of the Remove, was in the quad when Billy Bunter came out, blinking to and fro through his big spectacles.

Having spotted Carter, the fat junior rolled across to him, with a grin of affectionate friendship on his fat face.

Carter gave him a stare as he approached, turned on his heel, and walked away.

Bunter was left blinking.

He blinked after Carter's back as he went, then blinked round at a score or so of grinning faces.

"Cheeky cad!" gasped Bunter.

Billy Bunter was not a sensitive fellow. He had a fairly thick skin, and, considering his manners and customs, he needed it. Still, even Bunter was not impervious to this sort of treatment.

His relation—if Carter was his relation—had turned his back on him in open quad, before a crowd of fellows. If Bunter had a use for a rich relation, it was clear that Arthur Carter had no use for a poor relation!

"I say, you fellows, did you see that?" gasped Bunter.

"Sort of !" grinned Johnny Bull.

"Think he was cutting me?" asked Bunter.

"The thinkfulness is terrific, my esteemed fat Bunter."

"Swanky cad!" said Bunter. "I've a jolly good mind not to take him up at this school at all!"

"Doesn't look an easy thing to do, does it?" grinned Vernon-Smith.

"Yah!"

Bunter rolled away, disconsolate.

The fat Owl's pursuit of the new junior was causing a great deal of entertainment in the Remove.

In the dormitory, the previous night, he had spoken to Carter two or three times, without receiving an answer once. At the breakfast table he had given him a friendly grin, which Carter had completely ignored. In early school, he had whispered to him in class, and Carter had turned his head away. Now, in break, Carter had turned his back on him in quad. Bunter was a sticker; but even Bunter was expected to "chuck" it after that.

That he was related to Carter was probable; but it was clear that the relationship was a distant one, which Carter did not choose to acknowledge.

That the Carters and the Bunters were not in touch, was, in fact, plain enough, as Bunter had not even known the new junior was coming to Greyfriars until the day he came.

Billy Bunter was not, perhaps, a relation whom any fellow might have been proud and pleased to find in his new school. Some fellows might even have been annoyed thereby. Carter, at any rate, was making it very clear that if Bunter was his distant relative, he preferred the distance to the relationship.

"Fat ass!" remarked Johnny Bull,

as the Owl of the Remove rolled away. "Why can't he let the fellow rip? Carter's not a soft ass like Mauly, to let a fellow stick on him because he's rich."

"Is he rich?" grunted Bob Cherry.

"Well, he looks pretty well off, and Bunter thinks so, at any rate. He wouldn't care two hoots about him if he wasn't."

Back into Bob's mind came those words, which he wished he had never heard, in the waiting-room at Lantham.

Arthur Carter had been rich, but his riches had taken unto themselves wings and flown away. Bunter still regarded him as a rich relation; but Bob Cherry knew that he was nothing of the kind.

He had many expensive things, which a good many fellows had already noticed, which bore out Bunter's belief. Obviously, they were left over from the time when he had been a rich uncle's heir, with a large allowance.

It was no business of Bob's, and he was very far from being a fellow to concern himself about what was not his business. He would gladly have dismissed that talk at Lantham entirely from his mind.

But he could not help knowing what he knew; and he knew that Carter had been turned out of his last school as a bad hat; and that he had told falsehoods in Study No. 1. He felt an instinctive dislike for the fellow.

But that was not what bothered Bob chiefly. He could not help thinking of what he had heard—with regard to Carter's intentions towards his relation at Greyfriars.

How was he going to "fix the cad who had cut him out," as he had viciously expressed it?

He came to Greyfriars as the enemy of his relation there! Was that relation Bunter, or had he some other connection, unknown, in one of the other Forms?

Bob did not like thinking about it; but there was a hint of treacherous scheming in the matter that made it difficult for him to get it out of his thoughts.

Anyhow, he could not stand the fellow; and he was not going to have anything to do with him; which was rather awkward, as he was now a member of Study No. 1. It was all the more so because he felt that he could not repeat what he had heard accidentally about another fellow's private affairs. He realised that he had said rather too much already, as a matter of fact.

When the bell rang for third school, the Famous Five were going in together, when Carter joined up. That was natural enough, as he belonged to Wharton's study, and Wharton and Nugent were on more or less friendly terms with him.

But Bob's face clouded at once, and he quickened his pace, and joined Vernon-Smith and Redwing, who were a little ahead.

Carter walked with the other four, who hoped, rather uncomfortably, that he did not notice that Bob was avoiding him.

If he noticed it, the new junior made no remark on it. In the Form-room corridor Bunter rolled up. Apparently he had recovered from that "facer" in the quad, for he hooked on to Carter's arm.

"I say, Arthur, old chap——" he began.

Carter pitched the fat hand off. Then he took out his handkerchief, and THE MAGNET LIBRARY.—No. 1,561.

deliberately wiped his sleeve where the fat paw had clutched.

Billy Bunter crimsoned with wrath. It was true that his fat paws were generally sticky; but, really, a fellow did not need to wipe his sleeve after Bunter had touched him.

"Look here, Carter——" he gasped.

"Keep away, you fat fool!" said Carter.

"Why, you cheeky beast—— I mean, look here, old chap——"

"Oh, shut up!"

Carter walked on, and again Billy Bunter was left standing—gasping with indignation. Really, it began to look, even to Billy Bunter, that he was not going to benefit hugely by the arrival at Greyfriars of his "rich relation."

THE ELEVENTH CHAPTER.
Bunter Sees It All!

"PRETTY sickening, isn't it?" said Billy Bunter bitterly.

It was in the Rag, after class.

Bunter was addressing the room generally.

Class was over early enough that day for a spot of football practice to follow. The Famous Five, and some other fellows, were taking advantage of the fact—Carter with them.

After what he had heard at Lantham, Bob Cherry had not expected to see the new fellow keen on Soccer; and when Carter joined up for practice at the first opportunity he rose some slight degree in Bob's estimation.

Billy Bunter had no use for Soccer; he preferred the fire in the Rag. A dozen other fellows were there, and they all grinned when Bunter rolled in. His desperate attempts to hook on to his rich relation, and Carter's determination to stall him off, had become a sort of standing joke in the Remove already.

"Putrid, I call it!" continued Bunter, blinking round through his big spectacles. "Not what I should have expected of Wharton. I see it all now, of course."

"What's Wharton done?" asked Skinner, with a grin. "Taken that new man off to the footer? They won't be long, old fat man! In fact, I don't think Carter could keep away long—he's so fond of his relations."

"Ha, ha, ha!"

"Sucking up to a chap for his money!" said Bunter bitterly. "Mean, I call it—absolutely outside! Not the sort of thing I could do!"

"Eh?"

"What?"

"Bagging a chap's relation, you know—bagging him for his study and sticking to him like glue!" said Bunter. "If there's one thing I really despise, it's greasing up to a chap for his money."

"You do?" yelled Skinner.

"Ha, ha, ha!"

"You can cackle!" said Bunter. "But I call it sickening! Wharton puts on a lot of airs and graces—now look at him! Sticking on to my cousin because he's got pots of money!"

"Oh, my hat!" gasped Skinner.

"The whole gang of them!" said Bunter. "Sticking round my cousin Arthur like flies round a jam-pot! I was a bit of an ass to tell them that he was rich! I see that now!"

"Ha, ha, ha!" shrieked all the Rag.

"Oh crikey! I'd like his High Magnificence to hear that!" gasped Skinner. "Wharton would like this!"

Lord Mauleverer sat up in his arm-chair.

"Bunter, you silly ass, shut up!" he said.

"Shan't!" retorted Bunter. "When I despise a fellow, I'm not afraid to say so. I'd tell Wharton so to his face, if he were here. I'm not saying it now because he's gone down to the footer."

"Ha, ha, ha!"

"I was going to get him into my study," went on Bunter. "Not because he is rich, you know. You fellows know that I never think about a fellow's money. I was going to take him up and be kind to him, and all that, as a new fellow here. And Wharton goes and bags him for his study before I'd even seen him! I dare say he's borrowing money off him already."

"You silly ass!" said Bolsover major.

"Oh, run on, Bunter!" exclaimed Skinner. "You don't know how jolly entertaining you are, old fat thing."

"Coming between me and my relations, you know!" said Bunter. "Practically kidnapping the chap——"

"Ha, ha, ha!"

"It's my confiding nature, you know," said Bunter. "I tell them that my rich relation is coming here, and they go and bag him first shot, without even giving a fellow a look-in. Pretty sickening, ain't it? Unscrupulous!"

And Billy Bunter, having thus relieved his mind of a weight of indignation, rolled out, leaving the Rag in a roar.

It was not a laughing matter to the fat Owl. He rolled away to the Remove passage with a morose brow. It had seemed to Bunter real pie to have a rich relation coming to the school. He had revelled, in happy anticipation, in the crumbs that fell from the rich man's table. But no crumbs had come Bunter's way so far.

Had Toddy only been a bit more reasonable, and had Bunter bagged the new fellow for his own study, Study No. 7 might have been like unto a land flowing with milk and honey.

Instead of which, an unscrupulous gang of fellows had bagged the wealthy one, leaving Bunter out in the cold. That, at least, was how Bunter looked at it, and it roused his indignant wrath.

The fat junior was on the Remove landing when Harry Wharton came up. The other fellows were still in the changing-room, after football; but the captain of the Remove had got out first to do some shopping for tea. He came up with a package in his hand.

Bunter blinked at it—and at him—with a disdainful blink. Wharton went into the study and unwrapped the package on the table, disclosing several good things, among them a cake. The fat Owl blinked in at the door.

"Asking me to tea?" he inquired with withering sarcasm.

Harry looked round.

"Sorry, old fat bean, but Carter doesn't seem able to stand you," he said. "It's his study now, you know, as well as mine."

"And he's my relation, not yours!" sneered Bunter. "I must say I despise this sort of thing, Wharton."

"Eh?"

"Did you borrow the money off him to get that?" asked Bunter.

The captain of the Remove stared at him.

"No, you howling ass! Do you think I'm the fellow to borrow a chap's money?" he hooted.

"What are you sticking on to him for, then?" sneered Bunter. "I've

been telling the fellows in the Rag that I think it pretty sickening! Bagging a fellow's relation away from him because he's rich——"

"You fat Owl!" roared Wharton.

"Yah! I suppose that's a sprat to catch a whale—what?" asked Bunter, pointing a fat and grubby forefinger at the goods on the table. "You'll get something pretty good out of him after that—what?"

Harry Wharton stared blankly at the fat Owl of the Remove. Really it was rather hard for him to realise that Bunter judged him by his own measure, and had no doubt that he was "sucking up" to a rich fellow for his money.

"You—you—you——" gasped Wharton.

"Well, I call it mean!" declared Bunter. "Not the sort of thing I would do. The very least you can do, Wharton, is to whack it out."

"Whack it out!" gasped Harry.

"Yes! I really think that!" said Bunter firmly. "You've got hold of my rich relation, and sponging on him. Well, he's my relation, not yours. After all, he's got pots and pots of money. I dare say he won't miss what you get off him——"

"You—you——" stuttered Wharton.

"But where do I come in?" argued Bunter. "Whacks all round is fair as he's my rich relation, not yours. I call it absolutely mean to keep it all to yourself! I must say that. In fact, it's unscrupulous!"

Harry Wharton, with a richly red complexion, made a stride to the door. His expression rather alarmed Bunter. Bunter revolved on his axis and shot up the passage.

But he did not shoot fast enough to escape a pursuing boot.

Thud!

Bump!

"Wow!" roared Bunter as he went over on his fat hands and knees. "Ow! Oh crikey! Beast! Wow!"

Harry Wharton walked away to the stairs to go down for his friends, leaving the fat Owl waking the echoes.

Bunter tottered to his feet. He cast an infuriated blink after the captain of the Remove. Why Wharton had cut up rusty Bunter did not know. So far as Bunter could see, "whacks all round" in the plunder of the rich relation was a fair and reasonable proposition.

"Beast!" gasped Bunter. "Mean beast! Rotter! Wow! Beast! Ow!"

It was clear—to Bunter—that the captain of the Remove wanted to keep that rich prize all to himself.

The fat Owl shook a fat fist after Wharton as he disappeared down the stairs, then he rolled into Study No. 1.

The fellows were not likely to be long in coming up—but Bunter did not need much time for what he had to do in that study.

He grabbed the cake with one hand, and a bag of doughnuts in the other; then he rolled out of the study again—and, like the River Iser, he rolled rapidly. Whether that mean and unscrupulous beast liked it or not, Bunter was going to have his whack; and he had it, and beat a prompt retreat with it.

THE TWELFTH CHAPTER.
Tea in Study No. 1!

BOB CHERRY paused at the door of Study No. 1 and looked in. Seeing four juniors there, he stepped inside. The four were his friends, and as the new fellow was

" Didn't I say tea at five, Tubb ? " growled Loder, swishing his cane. With neither cash nor credit, the bully of the Sixth expected tea all the same. " Yes, Loder," faltered Tubb ; " but——" " I'll give you another ten minutes ! " said Loder.

not present Bob concluded that he was teaing down in Hall, or that some fellow had asked him into another study to tea.

Which was a relief to Bob; for he was extremely unwilling that the usual happy circle should be broken up if it could be helped—and he was not going to sit down to tea with Arthur Carter.

"Hallo, hallo, hallo!" said Bob in his cheery voice as he tramped in. "Footer gives you an appetite in this weather ! Anybody ready for tea ?"

"Yes; we're only waiting for Carter," answered Harry. "No need to wait, though; he will blow along in a few minutes."

Bob came to a sudden halt.

"Carter's coming up ?" he asked.

"Yes. He only stopped to speak to Smithy," said Harry. "He seems to be getting rather friendly with Smithy."

"He would !" said Bob curtly.

Wharton gave him a quick look. He had rather forgotten Bob's apparently unaccountable dislike of the new junior—and he was not pleased to re-member it now.

It was utterly unlike Bob to take un-reasonable dislikes to anyone. In fact, he seemed incapable of hard or bitter feelings; he could hardly have disliked an enemy very much if he had had one. So this repugnance for a new fellow, who had, so far as his friends knew, given no offence, was puzzling, and not a little irritating. Bob was the last fellow at Greyfriars who might have been expected to make unnecessary trouble.

"What do you mean by ' He would,' exactly ?" asked Harry quietly. " I don't quite follow. Why shouldn't he get friendly with Smithy ?"

"Birds of a feather, I mean," said Bob. " I suppose he's spotted already

that Smithy's the bad hat of the Form. He's pretty keen, I've noticed."

"I don't think that a very fair thing to say, Bob. The chap's only been here a day, and he's done no harm so far that I know of; he seems to me decent enough."

Bob opened his lips—and closed them again. He knew what he had seen and heard, but telling what he had seen and heard was another matter.

"What the dickens have you got against the chap, Bob ?" asked Frank Nugent. "You said something yester-day about hearing something or other, and——"

"I heard it by accident, and that means that I can't tell it out all over the school," grunted Bob. "The fellow's affairs are no bizney of mine. I don't want to say anything against him."

"You've done so," said Johnny Bull calmly. "Yesterday you told us he was a cad, and that the man who brought him here was a rotten rascal. Don't you call that saying something against him ?"

Bob flushed.

"Well, I spoke without thinking," he said. " I wish I'd said nothing—con-sidering how I knew. It was through that cur Ponsonby. I should never have known anything about him but for that rotten trick. It can't be helped now. I don't like the fellow."

"Well, why not ?"

"I don't !" said Bob stubbornly. "I'm not going to run him down. Leave it that I'm an unreasonable ass if you like. I don't want to row with him, and I suppose I can be civil if I come across him, but I'd rather keep out of his way. If he's teaing here——"

"I suppose a fellow can tea in his own study !" said Harry rather tartly. "Of course he can. I'm going to tea

in mine," said Bob, turning round to the doorway.

"Now, look here, Bob, don't be an ass !" exclaimed the captain of the Re-move. "We always tea together here. We had a new kid landed on us last term and it made no difference. Why should Carter make any difference ?"

"I can't sit down and feed with a chap I can't stand !" grunted Bob.

"Are you going to cut tiffin in the Hall, then ?" asked Johnny Bull, sar-castically.

"Oh, don't be a silly ass, if you can help it !"

"But look here, Bob," exclaimed Nugent. "We can't turn the chap out of his own study. Quelch landed him here, and that's that ! If you've really got something against him—something serious—you can tell us what it is, and we'll turn him down fast enough, along with you."

"Yes, that's so !" assented Johnny Bull. " If the chap isn't good enough for us, we can cut this study, and tea in mine, or Bob's. But I jolly well know that I'm not going to cut a chap, and insult him, for nothing."

"Give it a name, Bob !" said Harry.

"I can't !" said Bob. " I heard what I did without being supposed to, and how can I repeat it all over the shop ? Besides, it was as much the way they spoke, as what they said. They——" He paused. " If I'm mistaken about the chap, as you seem to think, all right—leave it at that ! If I'm not, you'll find him out soon enough, without my help. He can't keep up this game all the term."

"What game ?" demanded Wharton.

"Oh, nothing—I'm talking too much again, as usual. Look here, I shall row with that chap if I see much of him, so the less I see of him, the better."

"Certainly, if that's the case—we

THE MAGNET LIBRARY.—No. 1,561.

don't want a row for nothing. But you can't expect us to understand——"

"I fancy you'll understand soon enough—wait till he shows the cloven hoof!" grunted Bob; and he walked out of the study, and went up the passage.

The four looked at one another, worried and rather exasperated.

"The esteemed Bob has his back terrifically up!" remarked Hurree Jamset Ram Singh. "It is an idiotic mystery."

"What the dickens can he have heard Carter and that man Gooch saying, to put his back up like this?" asked Nugent. "Might have been plotting a gunpowder plot, at this rate."

"Well, if Bob chooses to play the goat, we can't be uncivil to a new chap, who's done nothing!" said Harry. "Here he comes!"

The four were uncomfortably silent as Arthur Carter came into the study. The sight of him was not, as a matter of fact, very welcome. His presence was causing a rift in the lute.

But to blame him for that, when the blame seemed all due to Bob, was too unjust. Except that he seemed to them rather unnecessarily disagreeable to Bunter, the juniors had no fault to find with him, so far.

"Not keeping you waiting?" asked Carter, cheerily, as he came in. "By gum, I'm ready for tea—you get a terrific appetite in this wind. Can I lend a hand? Where do you fill the kettle?"

"Tap along the passage," answered Harry. "Sort out those things, you fellows—why, hallo—where's the cake?"

"Was there a cake?"

"There jolly well was—and a bag of doughnuts, too!"

"Bunter been about?" asked Nugent, laughing.

"Oh!" Wharton remembered. "Yes—that fat ass saw me bring the things in! By gum, I'll boot him up the passage and back again."

Carter, who was going to the door, kettle in hand, glanced back.

"What's Bunter done?" he asked.

"Snaffled our tea," answered Harry. "He's bagged the cake and the doughnuts."

"Do you mean that he's pinched them?"

Wharton looked at him. He did not like the word, and he did not like Carter's way of using it.

"No, I don't!" he said, and his voice was sharp. "You don't know Bunter, yet, Carter—though he seems to be a relation of yours. He bags tuck the same as he breathes. He hasn't the sense to know that he shouldn't."

"You'll get used to Bunter," said Nugent, laughing. "You see, whenever he sees a cake, he thinks he ought to have it."

Carter shrugged his shoulders.

"Mean to say you let him raid your grub, and nothing said?" he asked.

"Well, he gets booted a great deal! We rather make allowances for Bunter," said Nugent. "You see, he's such a howling ass."

"I don't quite see it," said Carter, dryly. "I suppose the beaks wouldn't take the same view, if they knew?"

"They don't know!" said Harry, curtly.

"I should call it pilfering, and I should think that Quelch would!" said Carter.

"I dare say Quelch might, being a schoolmaster, but Nugent's just told you that we make allowances for Bunter!" said Harry. At that moment he shared Bob's dislike for the new

junior. "He can't help being a silly fathead."

"Well, pinching is pinching!" said Carter. "Do you mean that he would take other things, as well as food?"

Harry compressed his lips.

"I mean nothing of the kind," he said. "Bunter's as honest as any fellow at Greyfriars—but, he can't resist tuck. You can leave that expensive wrist-watch of yours lying about the study, quite safely."

An unpleasant tone crept into Wharton's voice; he could not help it. Carter flushed faintly.

"Oh, all right!" he said. "If you fellows don't mind! But I can't say that I should feel the same. If anybody pilfers from me, he will land into trouble."

He left the study, with the kettle. Harry Wharton breathed rather hard.

"After all, he doesn't know our prize porpoise, yet," said Nugent, with a grin, "and really and truly, you know, it is pilfering, though that fat idiot can't get it into his fat head. Quelch would jump on him, if he knew."

"That's so!" said Harry. "But——"

"Perhaps the esteemed Bob is not quite so unreasonable as we absurdly supposed!" murmured Hurree Jamset Ram Singh.

"I was just thinking so!" said Harry. "If that fellow's going to make the worst of everything, and call everything by the nastiest possible name——"

"Oh, he'll get used to Bunter," said Nugent, "and really, you know, he wants some getting used to."

Harry Wharton nodded, and the subject was dropped. Carter came back with the kettle; and there was tea in Study No. 1.

Perhaps the new fellow realised that he had made a bad impression. He said no more about Bunter; but he turned the talk to the subject of Soccer. That was a subject in which all the fellows were keenly interested; and as Carter was keen on the winter game, too, the atmosphere very soon cleared.

Cheery talk ran round the table; and when Bob Cherry, a little later, passed the door, he heard a buzz of voices from within the study—and his face was glum as he went on to the stairs. He had left a vacant place in the circle —but his friends seemed to have filled it, very soon, and very easily.

THE THIRTEENTH CHAPTER.

Catching Carter !

"CARTER coming?"

Bob Cherry asked that question, rather abruptly.

It was Saturday afternoon. Being the first half-holiday after the Lantham affair, it was the first opportunity Bob had of looking for Ponsonby of Highcliffe. He was not letting the grass grow under his feet.

His comrades were going with him —on the hunt!

All of them agreed that Pon had to be made to answer for his sins; all the more, because his wretched trick on Bob at Lantham had been the cause of Bob's trouble with the new fellow, Carter.

Pon, of course, had no idea of that unexpected outcome of his action; still, it was certain that if he had not left Bob tied up in that waiting-room, Bob would never have heard whatever it was that Carter and Gooch had said to one another, which had made him dislike the new fellow so much.

Pon had, in fact, exceeded the limit, as he often did in a rag; and all the Famous Five were keen to bring him to book.

"Carter?" repeated Harry, as Bob rapped, rather than asked the question.

"No—Carter's not coming, that I know of. We shouldn't be likely to ask him to, when you can't see the chap without wanting to bite his head off."

"Why the dickens should Carter be coming?" grunted Johnny Bull. "He's got no row on with Highcliffe, in fact, I've heard him say that he knows some of the fellows there—knew them when he was at his last school. He's met Pon in the holidays, I think."

"Sort of fellow he would take to, I dare say!" grunted Bob. He checked himself at once. He had made up his mind to say nothing against the new fellow; but it was not always easy to keep to his own resolutions. "Well, if Carter's not coming, all right! I fancied that perhaps you couldn't part with him."

"Don't be an ass, old chap!" advised Johnny Bull.

Grunt from Bob. He was looking his old sunny self, as he went out of gates with his comrades.

His dislike of Carter, instead of wearing off, as his friends had hoped it would, seemed to have intensified. He carefully avoided the new fellow—which in effect meant that he was with his chums a great deal less than of old.

"I say, you fellows!" Billy Bunter was adorning the gateway with his fat person as the Famous Five went out.

"I say, where are you off to?"

"Walking Highcliffe way, old fat man," said Bob. "Like a walk?"

"Well, what about taking the bus?" asked Bunter "I'll come, with pleasure, old chap, if you're going over to tea with Courtenay and the Caterpillar. They stand you a jolly good tea, those chaps! But let's take the bus! I'll pay the fares, if you like. I'm expecting a postal order——"

"Think the bus conductor would let you have the tickets for the postal order you're expecting?" inquired Bob.

"Oh, really, Cherry! What I mean is, you fellows can lend me some money, and I'll settle out of my postal order!"

"We're not going to tea at Highcliffe," said Harry, laughing. "We're going to see Ponsonby, if we can."

"Eh? You're not pally with Ponsonby?"

"That's why we're going to see him!"

"Come on, Bunter," said Johnny Bull. "We may meet a crowd of them, and we shall be glad of a fighting-man like you to back us up."

"You—you—you silly ass!" hooted Bunter "Think that I'm going to walk miles to look for a scrap? You fatheads! If it ain't tea, I ain't coming! Jolly glad you're going, though," added Bunter. "A chap may have a chance to speak to his own relation without a lot of sponging blighters hanging round him."

"Kick him!" said Johnny Bull.

Bunter hastily scuttled into the quad, without waiting for the kick for which he had asked.

Harry Wharton & Co. disappeared—leaving Bunter glad to see the last of them. Whether it was because the Co. had "bagged" Bunter's rich relative or not, it was certain that Bunter had not yet had a chance of sampling the crumbs that fell from the rich man's table.

Arthur Carter not only kept him at arm's length, but at foot's length—having booted him two or three times for displaying the natural affection he felt for a rich relation. It was very discouraging to Bunter.

But hope springs eternal in the human breast.

That his relation had any secret and hidden reason for disliking him, naturally never occurred to Bunter. He had known next to nothing of Carter before the fellow came to Greyfriars, and supposed that Carter knew next to nothing of him.

Knowing what a real nice and attractive fellow he was, Bunter felt that his relative really ought to have taken to him at sight. It was clear that he hadn't; and it was a satisfactory explanation, to Bunter's fat mind, that a lot of unscrupulous fellows had bagged his rich relative, with an eye to the loaves and fishes!

Now that that unscrupulous crew were safely off the scene, for the afternoon, Bunter hoped for better things!

He proceeded at once to look for Carter.

Carter, however, did not seem easy to find.

Billy Bunter inquired up and down and round and about, for his "Cousin Arthur," eliciting many grins and chuckles from the fellows of whom he inquired.

It was Skinner who put him on the track at last.

"Look in the Cloisters!" suggested Skinner.

The cheery Skinner suggested the old, wind-swept Cloisters, as the least likely place in which any fellow was likely to be found. It was his amiable intention to pull Bunter's fat leg, and give him a search for nothing.

Happily unaware of that, the fat Owl rolled away to the Cloisters in search of his rich relation.

As it happened, Skinner's suggestion was better-founded than Skinner supposed! He had sent Bunter rolling off to the Cloisters, because he did not suppose for a moment that Carter was there. But, as a matter of fact, he was there!

In a very secluded spot, almost hidden by ivy and the old stone pillars, the searching Owl spotted his man.

He grinned as he spotted him.

Carter was leaning against a pillar, smoking a cigarette! That, as Bunter easily guessed, was why he had sought that retired and solitary spot. A fellow who smoked had to be rather careful about it, as it meant "six" from an ashplant if he was spotted by a prefect.

"Oh crikey!" murmured the fat Owl, as he saw him.

He had not suspected "Cousin Arthur" of this sort of thing. There were fellows in the Remove who smoked, like the Bounder and Skinner: but Carter had not seemed, hitherto, to be of the same kidney. It was quite a surprise to Bunter.

Carter gave a start, as he saw the fat Owl, and flung his cigarette into the ivy. His face reddened with rage. Clearly, he was intensely annoyed at being caught.

"You fat fool, what do you want?"

he exclaimed furiously, and he advanced on Bunter, with a threatening stare.

"All right, old chap, don't get shirty!" exclaimed Bunter, in great haste. "I ain't going to tell Wingate or Loder! He, he, he! It's all right—I put on a smoke myself sometimes. I say, I'll have one, if you like."

"You spying worm!" exclaimed the new junior, savagely.

"He, he, he! I'll bet they don't know in Study No. 1 that you've got smokes about you!" chuckled Bunter.

"I say—— Yarooooooop!"

He jumped back just in time, as Carter smote.

"I say—look here, you beast—oh crumbs!" gasped Bunter, and he fairly turned and ran, as the new junior came at him.

Cousin Arthur had been far from pleasant to Bunter all the while he had been at Greyfriars. But he had never been so unpleasant as now! He followed Bunter up, landing out with one foot and then another, fairly dribbling the fat Owl out of the Cloisters.

Bunter roared and flew.

He had been very anxious to find his rich relation! Now he was still more anxious to lose him again!

How many kicks he collected, before he got out of the Cloisters, Bunter did not know! It seemed to him like hundreds. He bolted across the quad, spluttering, and did not halt till he crashed into Peter Todd.

Toddy grabbed him by a fat ear to steady him.

"Steady the Buffs!" said Peter. "What the thump are you charging about for like a mad elephant, you potty Owl?"

"Ow! That beast is after me——"

"Loder?" asked Toddy.

"Ow! No! That cad Carter——"

"Your jolly old rich relation?" chortled Peter. "Have you been trying to get him to cash your postal order?"

"Wow! No! He pitched into me because I saw him smoking!" gasped Bunter.

"Rot!" said Peter.

"I saw him——"

"Rats!"

"I tell you——"

"Bosh!"

"Look here, Peter Todd, you beast—-"

"Bow wow!" said Peter, and he sat Bunter down in the quad, and walked on.

THE FOURTEENTH CHAPTER.

Up to Tubb!

GERALD LODER, of the Sixth Form, picked up the ashplant from his table, and swished it in the air in a thoughtful sort of way.

George Tubb, of the Third Form, eyed him uneasily.

Tubb of the Third had the pleasure —or otherwise—of being Loder's fag. Sometimes it was not so bad. Sometimes it was horrid. The present time was one of the horrid times.

When Loder was in funds he could be generous. Often and often had Tubb been allowed to carry off liberal remnants of ham, half a dozen eggs, or half a cake, for a feast with his pals in the Third. That sort of thing made Loder more or less tolerable as a fagmaster.

But when Loder was hard up it was quite a different matter. Then the bully of the Sixth made Tubb feel that a fag's life was hardly worth living.

Loder was hard up now.

He had brought back quite a lot of pocket money after the Christmas holidays. He had set out to double the amount by backing a horse strongly recommended by Bill Lodgey at the Three Fishers. That horse had unfortunately come in eleventh.

Loder was stony now—and not only stony, but he owed money, he had exhausted his credit at the school shop, where he owed a long bill: and he had to sponge on his friends, Walker and Carne, for cigarettes.

Now Loder wanted tea in his study.

In flush times the matter was simple. Tubb took an order to the tuckshop, either to be chalked up to Loder's account, or with cash in hand to pay for the goods. Now there was neither cash nor credit—but Loder, like the bully he was, expected his tea all the same.

Tubb had been through this before. He had developed amazing gifts as an amateur brigand, in supplying his fagmaster's requirements on such occasions.

If Loder found tea on the table, without having provided cash for the same, he never asked questions. Whether Tubb had to beg, borrow, or steal was Tubb's own happy business. All Loder cared about was having his wants supplied.

"Didn't I say tea at five, Tubby?" asked Loder, as he gently swished the cane in the air.

"Yes, Loder," faltered Tubb. "But——"

"I've got a fellow coming to tea," said Loder. "I can hardly keep him waiting, Tubb! This won't do."

"Yes, Loder, but——"

"I haven't whopped you yet this term, have I?" asked Loder, pleasantly. "My mistake—I suppose fags have to be whopped!"

"I—I say——" groaned the unhappy Tubb.

"Well, I'll give you ten minutes," said Loder, laying down the ashplant. "I'm going along to speak to Walker.

(Continued on next page.)

Have tea ready when I come back, Tubb."

"Yes, Loder," moaned Tubb.

Gerald Loder strolled out of the study. Having waited till he was gone, Tubb of the Third shook a fist after him.

Then he, too, left the study—on the prowl. Prowling for provisions for Loder was no new experience for Tubb. Had he been in funds it would have been an easy matter. Loder would have paid up next time he had money. But Tubb's financial resources at the moment were limited to threepence !

Loder had to have his tea, or else there was a whopping for Tubb! Tubb had to prowl for provender till he found the same. Both his cash and his credit were as low as Loder's.

His friends in the Third, when he sought them, were sympathetic, but not helpful. Paget advised him to tell Loder to go and eat coke. Easy advice to give, but not to take! Bolsover minor offered to lend him all he had, but as he had only three-halfpence that was no present help. Paget, however, had heard that Hobson of the Shell was standing a spread in his study, and George Tubb prowled away to the Shell, in his character of a bold bad brigand !

He found that the news was correct— Hobby was standing a spread in his study. But as Hobson and Stewart and Hoskins, and three or four more of the Shell were in the act of disposing of that spread, there was no chance for Tubb. Hobby threw a tomato-tin at him when he looked into the study, which was all Tubb got by prowling in the Shell.

His next visit was paid to the Fourth. Cecil Reginald Temple, of that Form, was well known to splash money about, and often had something very decent in his study cupboard.

But Tubb's luck was out. He found the study empty, and looked into the cupboard; but before he had even time to ascertain whether there was anything decent there or not, Temple came in.

Temple of the Fourth promptly kicked him out of the study, and Dabney and Fry, in the passage, gave him a few more as he fled.

In a desperate state, Tubb wandered into the quad. His face brightened at the sight of Coker of the Fifth coming out of the school shop with a package of considerable size swinging by a string in his hand. Potter and Greene were with him, with such chummy expressions on their faces that it was clear that Coker was going to stand a spread.

"I say, shall I carry that for you, Coker?" piped Tubb.

The burly Coker glanced down at him. "Eh? Yes, if you like," he said. "Stick it in my study."

Tubb could hardly believe in his good luck as Coker handed that parcel over. Coker, of course, would kick up a row later, if he found that that parcel had been taken to the wrong study, and was not to be heard of again. Still, Loder was a prefect, and would stand by his fag—he would have to. Anyhow, it was a case of any port in a storm. The chance of a thrashing from Coker was not so bad as the absolute certainty of one from Loder.

Tubb, indeed, as he grabbed the parcel, felt that it was almost too good to be true. As a matter of fact, it was !

"Hold on !" said Potter of the Fifth. "Here, give me that parcel. I'll carry it, young Tubb."

Tubb panted.

"Coker gave it to me to carry !" he objected.

"Leave him alone, Potter !" said THE MAGNET LIBRARY.—No. 1,561.

Coker. "Why shouldn't he fag for me? Lot of rot—fags for the Sixth, and not for the Fifth !"

"I fancy he may be fagging for the Sixth, not for the Fifth, at this very minute !" grinned Potter. "I'd keep an eye on him, anyhow."

"Oh !" said Coker. "Tubb, carry that parcel in. I'll follow you up to the study. Come on, you men !"

Tubb could have groaned. He had to carry the parcel now, but it was quite clear that he could not bolt into the Sixth with it, with Coker walking at his very heels. Coker was not a suspicious fellow, but Potter did not fancy Tubb had offered his services simply because it was a privilege and pleasure to fag for the great Horace.

With Horace Coker, George Potter and William Greene walking just behind him, Tubb carried that parcel up to Coker's study—and left it there. He went away afterwards with feelings that could hardly have been expressed in words. He was having absolutely no luck in the brigandage line.

More than the stipulated ten minutes had elapsed now. If Loder was waiting for his tea, his temper would not improve while he waited. Tubb cut back to the school shop, with a wild hope of inducing Mrs. Mimble to let him have the required goods on "tick."

"And a dozen jam tarts," a junior was saying, as he came in.

Tubb glanced at him.

It was Carter, the new fellow in the Remove. He seemed to be giving a shipping order, to judge by the stack growing up in front of him.

Tubb eyed that stack hungrily.

He had heard of Carter. Some fellow had told him that he was a relation of that fat ass Bunter in the Remove, and that he was rolling in oof. The orders he was giving looked as if he had plenty of money.

"And a tin of peaches," said Carter, "and a bag of meringues."

"By gum !" breathed Tubb.

"And a pound of cheese biscuits, and half a dozen cheese cakes, and two pots of jam," said Carter.

Tubb's mouth watered.

That new man Carter seemed to be laying in supplies for a tremendous feed. If there was the remotest chance——

The brigand of the Third lingered by the door, while Carter's magnificent supply was wrapped up for him. It cost Carter over a pound. He came out swinging a large parcel.

Tubb did not offer to carry it for him. That was all very well for a fathead like Coker of the Fifth, but one glance at Carter showed that he was no fool. Tubb elaborately took no notice of the Remove fellow as he passed, but when he was gone followed on his track into the House.

It was not tea-time in the Remove yet, and Tubb considered that there was a sporting chance, at least, that that gorgeous supply was not to be immediately consumed. If Carter of the Remove took his eyes off it for sixty seconds, Tubb knew what he was going to do.

Breathless with eagerness, he trailed Carter up to the Remove passage. That bundle in Carter's hand was Tubb's last hope.

THE FIFTEENTH CHAPTER.
Not for Bunter !

BILLY BUNTER knitted a fat brow.

Loafing on the Remove landing, he blinked at his "Cousin Arthur," as that youth came up with a big parcel.

Bunter's eyes and spectacles dwelt hungrily on that parcel for a moment or two. Considering that he was the chap's relation—and prepared to be a very affectionate relation—the brute might have asked him to share the good things in that big bundle.

But the fat Owl had realised at long last that there was nothing doing. That booting in the Cloisters had made it clear, even to Bunter, that Cousin Arthur had no use for him. It was not, after all, a case of a lot of unscrupulous rotters bagging his rich relation; that relation was absolutely insensible to the claims of relationship. He barred Bunter, and, in such circumstances, all that Bunter could do was to bar him back, as it were.

So the fat Owl knitted a fat brow, frowned, and fixed a contemptuous stare on his rich relation.

He turned up his little fat nose—an easy task, as Nature had rather started it on the way. He curled a fat lip, with an expression of scorn that was, in Bunter's opinion, almost blood-curdling.

With that aspect of scornful disdain he stared at Carter as he came across the landing. Deeply did he regret that he was no fighting-man. He would have liked to punch Carter, and then to kick him along the Remove passage. But as that was not practical politics he had to content himself with scorching, searing scorn.

Carter, however, did not look scorched or seared by Bunter's scorn. He did not seem to notice it. Indeed, he did not seem to see Bunter at all. At all events, he did not look at him.

Passing the fat junior, he dropped the parcel.

It burst open at one end, and a bag of meringues rolled out, and several loose doughnuts, and a pot of jam.

Bunter ceased to frown scornfully, and eyed the good things with a hungry eye. This really was cruelty to animals. Bunter was hungry. Bunter was always ready for a meal before a meal was ready for Bunter.

And his was a hard case that afternoon. His postal order, for some inexplicable reason, had not yet arrived. Peter Todd and Dutton were teaing out, and there was nothing for Bunter in Study No. 7. Harry Wharton & Co. had gone out for the afternoon, and looked like missing tea, though Bunter was waiting hopefully for them to come in.

A blink into Study No. 4 had been rewarded by a football boot, hurled by the Bounder, who thus vigorously made it clear that he did not want guests to tea. Lord Mauleverer—always Bunter's last hope—was not to be found.

"Doorsteps and dish-water " in Hall loomed dismally before Bunter, and at such a moment that beast Carter displayed these enticing things right under his eyes and his spectacles !

Heedless of Bunter's longing blink, Arthur Carter stooped to collect the fallen goods, and as he did so, several more things rolled out of the parcel— another pot of jam, a tin of peaches, and a bag of biscuits !

It was too much for Bunter ! Scorn and contempt were all very well— barring the cheeky beast who barred him was all very well ! But grub was grub ! He made a step towards Carter.

"I say, let me help you pick those things up, Arthur !" he said eagerly.

"Get out !"

"Oh, really, Carter——"

"Clear off, you fat Owl !" snapped Carter.

"Beast !" hissed Bunter.

Carter gathered up the scattered goods, crammed them into the parcel, and

" Cannot you understand that it is dishonest to take anything that belongs to another person ? " said Mr. Quelch, sternly.
" But I never——" yelled Bunter. " Bend over that chair at once ! " " Oh crikey ! " Tap ! The study door opened
and Lord Mauleverer presented himself. Mr. Quelch turned a freezing eye on the interrupter.

walked on to his study. Bunter's yearning eyes followed as he went into Study
No. 1 and disappeared.

"Rotten beast !" groaned Bunter.
Why Carter had laid in that immense
supply of tuck, the mere sight of which
made Bunter's mouth water, he did not
know—unless he was standing a spread
when his studymates came in. He could
hardly intend to demolish such a stack
on his own—no fellow in the Remove,
except Bunter, could have dealt with so
much at one sitting !

Whatever he intended, he obviously
did not intend to ask his relation,
William George Bunter, to the festive
board.

Billy Bunter leaned on the landing
balustrade and blinked down in the hope
of seeing the Famous Five coming.

But there was no sign of them. The
only fellow Bunter saw was a fag of the
Third—young Tubb !

Tubb was lounging on the stairs, as if
watching or waiting for something or
somebody ; but he had no interest for
Bunter, who gave him only one careless
blink.

The fat Owl blinked up the Remove
passage. Carter was coming out of his
study.

Bunter's little round eyes gleamed
behind his big round spectacles.

Carter had left that consignment of
tuck in Study No. 1 ! Now he was
going ! Possibly, as a new fellow in the
Remove, he was not aware of Billy
Bunter's little ways in the matter of
tuck ! Bunter hoped so, at any rate !
For if Carter left that stack of tuck un-
guarded Bunter knew what was going to
happen !

Carter did !

He came along the passage, passed
Bunter on the landing, and went down
the stairs, taking no notice of the fat
Owl.

Bunter fairly gasped.

This was tremendous luck ! It was
almost unbelievable luck ! He waited
only till Carter's head was below the
landing. Then he cut up the passage
with unaccustomed speed.

Carter had left the study door wide
open. Bunter blinked in—at an enticing
and dazzling array on the study table !
Really, it looked as if Carter, for some
mysterious reason of his own, was
actually bent on tempting the fat grub-
raider of the Remove !

The bundle had been unpacked ! The
good things were in view on the table—
doughnuts, meringues, cheese cakes and
biscuits, peaches, jam, jelly ! Billy
Bunter gazed blissfully.

"Oh crikey !" said Bunter.

He gave a blink up the passage ; no
one was in sight ! He blinked down the
passage—and frowned, at the sight of
Lord Mauleverer coming up from the
stairs !

Ten minutes ago he had been anxious
to see Mauly ! Now the sight of Mauly
was awkward and irritating. Even
Bunter could not raid a study under
witnessing eyes !

He waited for Mauly to pass and go
into his own study, farther up the
passage. Mauly, generally, was glad to
get past Bunter without stopping. That
annoyed Bunter as a rule, but now he
was glad of it. All he wanted was to
see the last of his lordship, and see it
quick. Then he was going to whip
swiftly into Carter's study and annex
the good things before some other
annoying beast came barging along.

Contrary to expectation, Mauly
stopped. He stopped—with a grin on
his face. Mauly was not a fearfully
observant fellow, but he did not need
telling why the fat Owl was lingering
at the doorway of a study when there
was a stack of foodstuffs on the table
within.

Bunter blinked at him in intense
annoyance. At any other time he would
have been glad for Mauly to stop and
speak. Now he was not glad.

"Jolly old Peri at the gate of
paradise—what ?" said Mauly, grinning.

"Eh ? What ? You going in to tea,
Mauly ?"

"Yaas."

"Well, hadn't you better cut on ?"

"Hadn't you better, old fat man ?"
suggested Mauly. "Didn't you get booted
last time you raided that study ?"

"Oh, really, Mauly ! If you think I'd
touch that tuck——"

Lord Mauleverer chuckled.

"Look here, you cheeky beast, you
clear off !" said Bunter warmly. "I'm
not going into that study ! I—I'm just
standing here to see Carter's stuff safe—
see ? There are chaps in the Remove
who would bag it if they saw it lying
about like that !"

"One chap, at least !" agreed
Mauleverer.

"Beast ! I mean, is Vivian getting
tea in your study, Mauly ?"

"Yaas !"

"I shouldn't keep him waiting, old
chap !"

"You fat villain !" said Lord Mauleverer, with another chuckle. "Leave
that tuck alone ! Look here, come along
to tea with me !"

"Oh !" said Bunter.

Tea with Mauly was always good, and
at any other time Bunter would have
jumped at it. But his eyes lingered
lovingly on the stack in Study No. 1.
Even Mauly's tea-table was not likely to
be stacked like that.

"Come on !" said Mauleverer.

"Another time, old chap !" said
Bunter. "I'll tea with you to-morrow,
Mauly ! I—I've got something else on
to-day."

THE MAGNET LIBRARY.—No. 1,561.

"Oh, quite!" said Lord Mauleverer. He grabbed a fat ear between finger and thumb. "Comin' to tea in Study No. 12?"

"Yow-ow-ow-ow! Leggo!" howled Bunter.

"Better come!" advised Mauleverer. "I'm takin' your ear, old fat man—hadn't you better hike along with it?"

"No—yes—— Ow! I'll come—— Leggo! Wow! All right! Beast! I mean, all right, old chap!" gasped Bunter.

Lord Mauleverer led that fat ear along the passage. Bunter really had to accompany it! Mauly was not going to part with that ear—neither, of course, was Bunter! So he went!

Jimmy Vivian, in Study No. 12, stared as Mauly led Bunter into that study. He did not seem fearfully pleased to see Bunter.

"What's that fat image here for, Mauly?" he asked.

"Tea!" said Mauly. "Sit down, Bunter!" He released the fat ear. "Sosses and chips, old fat man——"

"Oh!" Bunter's fat face brightened. He liked sosses and chips, and he spotted a large cake on the table. "Well, if you really want me, Mauly, I'll——"

"Not at all!"

"Look here, you silly ass——"

"Tuck in and shut up!" said Mauly. "You're not goin' to raid Wharton's study, you fat bandit! Go it!"

Bunter went it! His fat thoughts lingered on that lavish supply of tuck in Study No. 1! But it was quite a good spread in Study No. 12, and, on the whole, Bunter was satisfied.

He was happily unaware that that stack of tuck in Study No. 1 was no longer available. Tubb of the Third had not missed his opportunity. Having watched Mauleverer and Bunter out of sight, and seen that the coast was clear, Loder's fag lost no time. While Bunter was teaing in Mauly's study there was another lavish spread going on in Loder's study in the Sixth!

How Tubby had provided it Gerald Loder neither knew nor cared. It was provided, and that was all that Loder cared about. He had his friend Walker to tea, and there was more than enough for both!

———

THE SIXTEENTH CHAPTER.

A Bad Look-out for Bunter!

HARRY WHARTON & CO. came in at the gates—a little tired, rather late for tea, and extremely hungry. They had had quite a long walk round that cold, frosty afternoon, with wary eyes open for Pon & Co. of Highcliffe. But they had seen nothing of Pon, and punishment had to be postponed.

Carter was waiting for them at the gate. He had been waiting some little time. He gave them a grin as they arrived.

"Any luck?" he asked.

"No!" answered Harry. "We've seen nothing of Pon."

"Ready for tea?"

"What do you think?" said Johnny Bull.

"Come on, then! I've got the stuff in the study—my treat!" said Carter. "No objection to me standing a spread—what?"

"None at all, if you like!" said Harry, laughing. Then he glanced at Bob, whose face was expressionless. That ruddy face had been quite cheerful after a long walk and several hours in

the fresh air. But the sight of Carter seemed to have dashed its cheerfulness.

"You'll come, Cherry, won't you?" asked Carter, as the bunch of juniors walked to the House.

"Thanks, no!" said Bob. "I'm teaing in my own study, with Linley and Wun Lung."

"Oh, all right!" said Carter carelessly.

They went up to the Remove passage together. Passing Study No. 1, Bob's friends all gave him rather expressive looks.

He did not seem to see them, however. He went on up the passage to Study No. 13—his own study.

The other four went into Study No. 1 with Carter.

"By gum! I'm ready for tea!" remarked Johnny Bull. "Jolly thoughtful of you to lay in the prog, Carter! Trot it out!"

Carter was standing and staring at the study table. On that table he had left almost a mountain of good things. Nothing was on the table now, but an inkstand.

"In the cupboard?" asked Nugent.

"No," said Carter quietly. "I left the stuff on the table, here, about half an hour ago. What's become of it?"

"Oh crumbs!"

Carter's face set hard. The other fellows exchanged glances. There was an uncomfortable silence for a moment.

"Much of it?" asked Harry, at last.

"Twenty-four shillings' worth!" said Carter. "I thought you fellows would come in hungry, after tramping about all the afternoon, and I thought we'd have a bit of a feed."

"Oh, my hat!"

"It's gone!" said Carter, in the same quiet tone. "I'm not standing this!"

"Bunter about when you left it here?" asked Nugent, with a faint grin.

"Bunter? Yes; he was watching me all the time, I think. Yes; I remember he offered to pick up some things I dropped on the landing, and I told him to get out."

"The fat brute!" growled Johnny Bull. "Look here, you fellows, I'm getting fed up with this! Bunter's worse this term than he was last! Bagging a bag of bullseyes is one thing—but snaffling more than a pound's worth of tuck is too jolly thick. It's time Bunter had a lesson."

"The thickfulness is terrific!" said Hurree Jamset Ram Singh. "The bootfulness is the proper caper."

"If Bunter had it——" said Carter.

"Well, there's not much doubt about that, if you left it here under his eyes," said Harry Wharton. "You might have been a bit more careful, Carter, after what happened the other day."

Carter looked at him.

"What do you mean?" he asked. "I'm new here, of course; but at St. Olaf's we never had to lock up our things. Is a fellow supposed to lock things up at this school?"

Wharton's eyes glinted.

"No. Don't talk rot, Carter! But we told you about Bunter; and you know he bagged a cake here the other day. You might have shoved the things in the cupboard, and turned the key."

"I suppose I might have," said Carter. "But if I'd thought of it I shouldn't have. I'm not going to lock my things up against pilfering. You fellows can, if you like; but I don't choose to. If there's a fellow in the Remove who can't be trusted not to steal, he ought to be booted out of the school."

"I told you about that fat ass. He would no more steal than you would!" snapped the captain of the

Remove. "He bags tuck, like a silly kid bagging plums out of a Christmas pudding. We'll jolly well boot him for this, but it's no good making a fuss about it."

"You booted him last time, didn't you?"

"You know we did."

"Has it stopped him?"

"Looks as if it hasn't."

"Well, then, you can boot him, if you like, when he pinches your things. I'm going to stop him from pinching mine!" said Carter. "Once is enough for me, and it's not going to happen again."

"You can't scrap with Bunter, if that's what you mean," said Harry. "A fat ass in specs can't scrap; and you won't be allowed to lay hands on him, Carter, if you want it plain. He jolly well deserves to be booted up and down the passage—but you're not going to thrash a duffer who can't put up his hands."

"I'm not thinking of thrashing him. It's not for me to judge in matters of pilfering. If I'd lost anything at St. Olaf's I should have gone to my Form-master about it. That's what I'm going to do here."

"You're not going to Quelch?" exclaimed Nugent.

"I jolly well am!"

"My esteemed Carter——" murmured Hurree Jamset Ram Singh.

"Cut it out, Carter!" grunted Johnny Bull. "I'm fed up with him, as I've said; but we can't sneak in the Remove."

"I don't think it should be called sneaking. If Bunter had taken your watch, or your notecase, would you let him keep it?"

"Don't talk rot!" growled Johnny. "Bunter wouldn't do anything of the kind. You know that!"

"I don't know it. He's taken more than a pound's worth of stuff here. If I'd left a pound note on the table——"

"Bunter wouldn't have touched that!" said Harry sharply.

"What's the difference?"

The four juniors looked at Carter.

Strictly speaking, there was no difference. Pilfering was pilfering. But the Remove fellows were not accustomed to taking strict views of Billy Bunter's little foibles.

"Now, look here, Carter," said Harry Wharton, after a long pause. "This won't do. I don't know what things were like at your last school, as I'd never heard of St. Olaf's. But here, and at most schools, there's a certain amount of give and take. If a fellow can't find his own shirt in the changing-room, he's quite likely to bag the next man's shirt. The Head's down on it, and the beaks are down on it—so are the prefects. All the same, I've seen Gwynne bag a shirt of Wingate's, and seen Loder with Walker's boots on. I've got a pair of Bob Cherry's socks on at this very minute, but if Bob spots them he won't accuse me of pilfering them. I dare say he's got my necktie on! Well, that fat ass, Bunter, carries the same idea into matters of tuck—see?"

Carter shrugged his shoulders.

"I know he's a fool—a born idiot—an unscrupulous young rascal," said Harry. "But he's not a thief, and you're not going to call him one."

"I'm not going to call him anything!" said Carter "I've been robbed, and I'm going to put it up to my Form-master, as I think right."

"If you choose to call it that——"

"I don't know what else to call it."

"Well, it's no good arguing the point," said Harry "I can see that you're down on Bunter. I suppose because he claims you as a relation, and you don't like it——"

"He's not my relation," said Carter savagely, "or, if he is, it's so distant that it doesn't count. I don't care a boiled bean about him—but I'm not going to have my things pilfered. My watch may go next."

"That's rot, and you know it!"

"It's not rot, and I don't know it!"

"You're not going to Quelch about this?"

"I am!"

Harry Wharton drew a deep breath. "You'll get Bunter a flogging! It might be the sack. You never know how the beaks may look at a thing."

"That's his look out. I never asked him to pilfer, did I?"

"Well, it comes to this," said Harry. "You've lost something worth twenty-four shillings. We'll make it up to you."

"Yes, settle it that way, for goodness' sake," said Nugent. "You're right, in a way, Carter, but you're jolly well wrong in another. If you don't lose anything on it you're all right. We can find the cash."

Carter looked round from face to face. "You're willing to clear yourselves out of pocket-money to protect a pilferer?" he said, with a sneer.

"We don't look at it like that," said Harry. He did not disguise the contempt in his look and tone. "We're willing to pay up to prevent you from landing that silly young idiot in a fearful row."

"We'll find the money all right!" said Johnny Bull.

"You can keep your money!" retorted Carter. "That won't set it right, and you know it. I don't care a bean about the value of the things. But I do care about not being able to leave anything about my own study. If you fellows don't agree with me, I'm sorry—but I'm going to do what I think right."

And with that, Arthur Carter walked out of the study and went along to the stairs.

"Come back, you fool!" roared Johnny Bull.

Carter did not come back.

The four juniors looked at one another rather blankly.

"Has he really gone to Quelch?" gasped Nugent.

"Looks like it." Harry Wharton set his lips. "He loathes that fat ass, of course—he hates being claimed as a relation by Bunter! That's natural enough. But—but—— You fellows, I don't know what Bob's got against that chap, but old Bob's right! He's a worm!"

"The wormfulness appears to be terrific!"

"We can't stop him!" said Nugent. "No!"

Harry Wharton stepped to the doorway and looked out. Carter was gone. He was, in fact, tapping at Mr. Quelch's study door at that moment.

THE SEVENTEENTH CHAPTER.
Bunter Knows Nothing!

BILLY BUNTER stopped at the door of Study No. 1 and grinned into that apartment. Lord Mauleverer and Jimmy Vivian, who had walked down the passage with him, went on to the stairs.

Bunter blinked round over a fat shoulder as they went.

"I say, Mauly——" he squeaked.

"Yaas!"

"Wait a minute! I'm coming out with you, old chap!"

Lord Mauleverer did not wait a minute. He did not wait a second. He accelerated. Apparently, he did not yearn for Billy Bunter's fascinating company in a walk after tea. Jimmy Vivian, grinning, disappeared down the stairs with his lordship.

The fat Owl blinked again into Study No. 1. Four juniors were standing there, with worried and serious faces. They were waiting for the outcome of Carter's complaint to his Form-master.

What the result was going to be they did not know. But there was no doubt that it would be a serious result for Bunter. It was quite possible that Mr. Quelch's views, as a beak, would approximate more to Carter's than to those of the chums of the Remove. Anyhow, he had to take official note of the matter if it was placed before him.

It was worrying and exasperating to the juniors. They were feeling strongly inclined to boot Bunter, and, at the same time, alarmed for him.

Bunter blinked inquisitively from face to face. He could see that something was wrong in the study, and he was always inquisitive.

"I say, you fellows, did you meet those Highcliffe cads? And did they whop you all round?" asked Bunter, with a cheery grin.

The four looked at him. Bunter, as he spoke, was dabbing at a smear of jam on his fat face. He had the fat and shiny look he generally had after an ample feed. If they had doubted before, they would not have doubted now. Bunter, evidently, had been parking foodstuffs on a generous scale. Jam on his face, cream on his fat fingers, crumbs on his extensive waistcoat were clues that did not need a Sherlock Holmes to spot them!

"Did they?" grinned Bunter. "You're looking like a lot of moulting owls! Sorry I couldn't come with you! I'd have handled them all right!"

"You fat ass!" said Harry. "I suppose it was you bagged Carter's tuck out of this study? It can't have been anybody else."

"Eh!" ejaculated Bunter. "What? Somebody bagged the tuck? He, he, he!"

"You did!" roared Johnny Bull.

"Oh, really, Bull!" Bunter blinked at the study table, and saw that it was bare, and chortled. "Oh crikey! Serve the cad right! He, he, he! Of course, I don't know anything about it! I'm not a fellow to bag a fellow's tuck, I hope!"

"Oh crumbs!"

"I never knew Carter had any tuck, if you come to that!" said Bunter. "No good trying to put it down to me."

"You saw Carter bringing it in!"

"I didn't!" contradicted Bunter promptly. "I haven't seen the chap at all this afternoon. Forgot he was at Greyfriars, in fact."

"He told us he dropped something on the landing, and you offered to pick it up for him."

"Well, why shouldn't I?" yapped Bunter. "A fellow can be obliging, I suppose. After all, he's my relation, though he acts like a rotten cad! Any fellow might have offered to help him pick up the things, mightn't he?"

"You've just said that you never saw him this afternoon!" roared Johnny Bull.

"I haven't, either," said Bunter, blinking at him. "I wasn't on the landing when he came up with that bundle,

and I never saw it. I don't know whether he had a bundle or not! Think I notice whether fellows are carrying bundles? Why should I?"

"Oh crikey!"

"If Carter says I've snaffled his tuck, he's telling whoppers!" said Bunter. "I should disdain to do anything of the kind, of course. You fellows were making out the other day that I had a cake from this study——"

"So you had, you podgy pirate!"

"Well, I told you I hadn't," said Bunter. "If you can't take a fellow's word, I can't help it. It's rather low! I must say that. As if I wanted to eat your measly cake! There were hardly any plums in it, too—not more than a dozen in a two-pound cake!"

"And—and—and you never had it!" gasped Wharton.

"Certainly not—or the doughnuts, either! You made out that I had half a dozen doughnuts in a bag——"

"So you had!" yelled Johnny Bull.

"I hadn't!" yelled Bunter. "There were only five!"

"Oh scissors!"

"Five measly doughnuts, and a cake with hardly any plums in it!" said Bunter, with withering scorn. "A fat lot to make a fuss about, especially as I never had them. I haven't tasted a doughnut since we came back from the holidays, or a cake, either, till to-day!"

"We'd better tip him I think," said Harry. "Quelch may be up here after him soon. If he rolls out lies to Quelch, it will make it worse for him. Look here, Bunter, Carter's gone to complain to Quelch!"

"Eh—what about?" asked Bunter.

"About his grub being bagged, fat-head!"

"Rotten trick!" said Bunter. "I wouldn't if a fellow bagged any of mine. Know who the fellow was?"

"You!" roared Wharton.

"Oh, don't be an ass! I've told you already that I didn't even know that Carter had anything in the study. I suppose a fellow saw it there—stacking it up on the table and leaving the door wide open! Think it was Bob Cherry?"

"Wha-at?"

"Well, Bob seems rather down on that cad Carter," said Bunter. "He might have bagged it. What do you think?"

The four juniors did not state what they thought. They only gazed at William George Bunter.

"Or was it you fellows?" asked Bunter.

"Us!" gasped Nugent.

"Well, you're here, and the grub isn't!" pointed out Bunter. "Looks a bit suspicious to me!"

"I'm going to boot him!" said Johnny Bull, breathing hard. "I'm going to boot him all over the shop!"

"Oh, really, Bull——"

"Bunter's got enough coming to him, old man, when Quelch blows in!" said Harry. "Look here, Bunter, you're booked for a row! Can't you understand that? For goodness' sake, don't tell Quelch any lies!"

"Oh, really, Wharton, I suppose you don't know that that's insulting!" said the fat Owl, with crushing dignity. "I

(Continued on next page.)

ask you fellows—all of you—have you ever known me tell a lie?"

"Oh crikey!"

"Some fellows are particular about such things, Wharton, if you could only understand it! Not you fellows, of course! But I——"

"Look here, Bunter——"

"Well, I can't stop!" said Bunter. "I'm going for a walk with Mauly. I'm keeping him waiting in the quad all this time. I——"

"Don't go, you fat dummy! Quelch will want you——"

"Rot! I can't keep old Mauly waiting like this!"

Billy Bunter turned from the study doorway and rolled off down the passage.

On the Remove landing he almost rolled into his Form-master. Mr. Quelch had just come up the Remove staircase with Carter.

"Bunter, where are you going?" rapped the Remove master.

"I—I'm going out with Mauleverer, sir."

"Come with me, Bunter!"

"I—I—I say, sir, it wasn't me!" exclaimed Bunter, in alarm. "If Carter says it was me, he's telling whoppers, sir! I never——"

"Come with me!" snapped Mr. Quelch.

"Oh! Yes, sir!"

Mr. Quelch rustled into the Remove passage. Carter walked after him. Billy Bunter gave his Cousin Arthur a glare of concentrated wrath and scorn, and rolled in his wake.

"You beast!" he hissed, at the back of Carter's head. "Sneaking to Quelch! Yah!"

Mr. Quelch glanced round.

"What did you say, Bunter?"

"Oh, nothing, sir!" gasped Bunter. "I—I didn't speak, sir! I—I only said to Carter that—that it was a fine afternoon, sir!"

Mr. Quelch gave him a look and rustled on. He swept into Study No. 1, and Carter and Bunter followed him in, the latter with great reluctance. And Harry Wharton & Co.—hungry as they were—forgot all about tea as they looked at Mr. Quelch's grim face. Only too clearly, the master of the Remove was taking a very serious view of the "pilfering" in the new junior's study!

THE EIGHTEENTH CHAPTER.

For It!

"WHARTON!"

"Yes, sir!" said Harry quietly.

His eyes gleamed for a moment at Carter as he answered his Form-master.

"It appears that pilfering—or, at least, the purloining of comestibles—has taken place in this study!" said Mr. Quelch. "I should have preferred you to bring this matter to my notice, as my head boy, instead of leaving it to the boy concerned—a new member of the Form!"

"There was nothing to report to you, sir!" answered Harry quietly. "If Carter calls it pilfering, he's the only fellow in the Form who would!"

Mr. Quelch gave him a sharp look.

"Do you mean that nothing has been taken, Wharton?"

"Nothing to speak of, sir!"

"I hardly understand you! If a person takes a pin that does not belong to him, the act amounts to pilfering," said Mr. Quelch. "The value of the article taken does not affect the issue at all."

"Oh, yes, sir, I know that. But——"

"You are not saying, Wharton, that Carter has made an untrue statement, and that nothing is missing here?"

"Oh, no, sir! Some grub seems to have been taken," said Harry. If it had been mine, any fellow in the Remove would have been welcome to help himself, if he dropped into the study and saw it. It was a bit thick to bag the lot, that was all!"

"It appears," said Mr. Quelch, "to have been a large quantity. Carter states that he spent the large and extravagant amount of twenty-four shillings on it, intending it for a party of schoolfellows. This is a serious matter, Wharton I am surprised that you regard it so lightly."

Wharton compressed his lips. He was being placed in the unpleasant position of finding excuses for a pilferer, which was extremely disagreeable.

"Bunter never meant to pilfer, sir," he said. "He's just a silly ass!"

"Oh, really, Wharton——"

"It was Bunter?" demanded Mr. Quelch.

"I never——" wailed Bunter.

"Answer me, Wharton!"

"I don't know, sir!" said Harry, at once. "We took it for granted it was Bunter, as he's the only fellow in the Form who is such a fool. But it happened before we came in, and we really know nothing about it—in fact, we don't know that there was anything in the study at all, except that Carter said so."

"Yes, that's so," said Nugent, taking his cue from Wharton, and glad to give Carter a thrust, in return for causing all this unpleasant trouble. "We only know that Carter said so, sir."

Carter's face crimsoned.

"If you ask Mrs. Mimble at the shop, sir, she will tell you exactly what I brought here," he said. "I can give you a list, if you like."

Mr. Quelch glanced from one to another.

"Come, come!" he said. "This is not a matter for recriminations! Carter has acted quite rightly in informing me, if pilfering has taken place—such a thing certainly cannot be permitted in the studies."

"Pilfering has not taken place, sir!" said Harry stubbornly. "At least, if it was Bunter! If it was any other fellow——"

"That is absurd, Wharton! I make every allowance for Bunter's well-known stupidity, but there is a limit to allowances that can be made. Bunter!"

"Oh dear! I never——"

"Did you, or did you not, take comestibles belonging to Carter from this study?" demanded Mr. Quelch.

"No, sir! Nothing of the kind! I wouldn't! Wharton knows I wouldn't, don't you, old chap? It was all a mistake about that cake the other day."

"Shut up, you ass!" hissed Johnny Bull.

"You need say nothing, Bull!" rapped Mr. Quelch. "I am quite acquainted with Bunter's ways, and I have punished him on several occasions for depredations in the pantry. Now, Bunter——"

"I never even saw the stuff, sir!" groaned Bunter. "I wasn't on the landing when Carter brought it up, and I never saw him drop anything out of the parcel."

"What?"

"I wasn't there, sir—I was in the quad! You can ask Carter himself! He saw me!" gasped Bunter.

"Upon my word!" said Mr. Quelch. "I do not know whether this boy's stupidity exceeds his untruthfulness, or whether his untruthfulness exceeds his stupidity. Bunter, if you tell me a single untruth again, I shall adjudge you guilty of this unscrupulous act."

"I—I wouldn't, sir!" gasped Bunter. "I——"

"Where were you when Carter left these—these comestibles in his study, Bunter?"

"In the quad, sir! A lot of fellows were with me, too."

"Give me their names!"

"Oh crikey!"

"Their names, at once, Bunter!"

"I—I—I forget, sir!" groaned Bunter. "N-now I come to think of it, I—I was in the—the Cloisters, sir, and—and there wasn't anybody with me."

"I warn you to be careful, Bunter."

"Oh! Yes, sir! May I go now, sir? Mauly's waiting for me in the quad! I—I can't keep him waiting, sir, if—if you don't mind."

"Bunter was on the landing when I went down, sir!" said Carter.

"I wasn't!" yelled Bunter. "You never saw me there, you beast! You never even looked at me, as you passed."

"Upon my word!" said Mr. Quelch.

Harry Wharton & Co. exchanged hopeless looks. Whether Bunter had bagged Carter's spread or not, he seemed bent on making Mr. Quelch believe that he had. Really, it seemed impossible for the fat Owl to tell the truth, even if he tried—and it never seemed to occur to him to try.

"You were on the landing, and saw Carter go down, after he had placed his—his property in this study, Bunter?"

"Oh crikey! I don't see how you know, sir!" groaned Bunter. "If—if you saw me, sir, I—I was there. I—I've just remembered that I was on the landing, sir."

Carter gave the fat Owl a curious look. If his object was to land the fat Owl into trouble, he seemed likely to get plenty of assistance from Billy Bunter himself.

"And what did you do, after Carter went down, Bunter?" demanded Mr. Quelch.

"I—I may have looked into this study, sir!" stammered Bunter. "No harm in looking into a chap's study. Wharton and Nugent wouldn't mind—they—they like me to—to look in sometimes! I—I used to be in this study with them, sir, only I changed out because of Wharton's beastly temper—didn't I, old chap?"

Wharton did not reply to that.

"You came to this study after Carter had left!" said Mr. Quelch. "For what reason, Bunter, unless to pilfer what Carter had left here?"

"I—I—I just looked in, that's all, sir——"

"And why?"

"Oh! I—I mean, I didn't look in! I wasn't looking at the tuck that that cad left on the table. I don't believe he left any on the table, either. I—I think most likely he scoffed it——"

"You need say no more, Bunter,"

Printed in England and published every Saturday by the Proprietors, The Amalgamated Press, Ltd., The Fleetway House, Farringdon Street, London, E.C.4. Advertisement offices: The Fleetway House, Farringdon Street, London, E.C.4. Registered for transmission by Canadian Magazine Post. Subscription rates: Inland and Abroad, 11s. per annum; 5s. 6d. for six months. Sole Agents for Australia and New Zealand: Messrs. Gordon & Gotch, Ltd., and for South Africa: Central News Agency, Ltd.—Saturday, January 15th, 1938.

said Mr. Quelch grimly. "You came to the study, for no reason, except that Carter had left food here; and the food is missing. You are so recklessly untruthful that I cannot believe a single word you utter——"

"Oh, really, sir! Not me!" exclaimed Bunter. "Do—do you mean Carter, sir?"

"Upon my word! Say no more, Bunter! I am bound to regard the matter as proved——"

"Oh crikey! But I never!" gasped Bunter. "Mauly knows I never!"

"That will do! Follow me——"

"Oh lor'!"

"One moment, sir, please!" exclaimed Harry Wharton. "What do you mean about Mauly, Bunter? Was Mauly up here at the time?"

"Of course he was, when he got hold of my ear and dragged me away," grunted Bunter. "Mind, I wasn't going to touch the tuck. I never even thought of it! I was just looking at it from the door—I mean to say, I—I wasn't looking at it at all—never noticed it! But Mauly thought——"

The four chums exchanged quick glances. Like Carter, they had taken it for granted that Bunter was the delinquent; and his prevarications had convinced Mr. Quelch of it. But this looked like a spot of hope for the fat Owl. And, just then, all their sympathies were with Bunter, and against the fellow who was making a mountain out of a molehill.

"I will listen to no further prevarications, Bunter!" said Mr. Quelch sternly. "Follow me to my study at once!"

"But, sir!" exclaimed Harry. "Bunter says that Mauleverer——"

"I have said, Wharton, that I will listen to no further prevarications!" snapped Mr. Quelch. "Bunter has already stated that he was in the quadrangle, that he was in the Cloisters, and finally admitted that he was on the landing. I will not waste further time listening to his untruthfulness."

"But——"

"That will do, Wharton. Follow me, Bunter!"

"But I say, sir——"

"Silence!"

Mr. Quelch rustled out. Billy Bunter gave the chums of the Remove a despairing blink, and rolled dismally after him.

"By gum, that chap can tell lies!" said Carter. "I can't understand you fellows standing up for him."

"You might understand, if you were a decent fellow yourself!" snapped Harry Wharton. "You've got that silly fathead into a fearful row now. This may go before the Head, for all we know."

Carter's eyes glinted for a second.

"At St. Olaf's, they would have booted a pilferer out of the school," he said.

"Rats to St. Olaf's!" growled Johnny Bull. "Don't bung St. Olaf's at us! I jolly well wish you'd stayed there, instead of coming here to make mischief."

Wharton gave the new junior a fixed look.

"Do you mean to say that you'd like to see that silly, helpless duffer booted out—and him your relation!" he said contemptuously.

"I'd like to see any pilferer booted out."

"Oh, shut up!" roared Wharton, his temper breaking out. "If you use that word again, I'll punch your cheeky head! And I'll tell you this—there's a chance for Bunter—I'm going to see Mauly about it, anyhow. He said——"

"You believe a word he says?" sneered Carter.

"Well, no; but there's a sporting chance, and if there's the ghost of a chance for the fat ass, he's going to have it."

And Harry Wharton cut out of the study and ran down the stairs. A minute later, Lord Mauleverer's graceful saunter under the elms was interrupted, and in less than another minute, Mauly —no longer sauntering—was heading for Mr. Quelch's study.

THE NINETEENTH CHAPTER.

Not Guilty!

"BUNTER!"

"Oh dear! I mean, yes, sir," groaned Bunter.

His apprehensive eyes were on the cane in Mr. Quelch's hand. Quelch was swishing that cane, with a thoughtful expression on his severe face.

"Dishonesty in small matters," said Mr. Quelch, "may lead to dishonesty in larger matters. Boys have been expelled from school for such things as you have done, Bunter!"

"But I haven't done them, sir! I never——"

"That will do!" said Mr. Quelch. "I shall deal with this matter myself, Bunter, but any recurrence of it will be placed before your headmaster!" He swished the cane again. "You will bend over that chair, Bunter!"

"But I never——" yelped Bunter.

"Bend over that chair at once."

"Oh crikey!"

Tap!

The study door opened, and Lord Mauleverer presented himself. His lordship came in a little breathlessly. Mauly seldom hurried—but on this occasion he had sprinted!

"If you please, sir!" gasped Mauly.

Mr. Quelch turned a freezing eye on him.

"Kindly do not interrupt me now, Mauleverer! If you have anything to say to me, you may wait until I have dealt with Bunter!"

"But it's about Bunter, sir!" exclaimed his breathless lordship. "Wharton's just told me about it, sir! Bunter never snaffled the prog——"

"What?"

"I mean he never bagged the fodder——"

"You mean what?"

"He never collared the tuck——"

"If you have anything to say to me, Mauleverer, kindly speak in the English language!"

"Oh! Yaas! Quite, sir! I mean Bunter never bagged—that is snaffled—never collared—never took the grub—I mean the food—Carter's stuff, sir—he never touched it."

"Indeed! And how do you know this, Mauleverer?"

"I was there, sir——"

"I told you Mauly knew, sir——"

"Silence, Bunter! I will not listen to another word from you! Mauleverer, you are a boy I can trust! Kindly give me your account of this matter."

"Certainly, sir! I went up to tea, and saw Bunter looking into Wharton's study, and a regular mountain of tuck on the table, so I grabbed his ear and led him up the passage, sir! I mean to say, I took him to my study to tea. Bunter tea'd with Vivian and me."

"But afterwards, Mauleverer——"

"We all three came away from my study together, sir, after tea—and the fellows were in Study No. 1 then! Bunter stopped to speak to them, and I went down into the quad with Vivian. The stuff must have been taken before

the fellows came in—they missed it when they came. Bunter was in my study all that time. He wasn't out of my sight, till I left him talking to Wharton at the door of Wharton's study—and that was the same time that Carter was down here telling you about it, sir."

Mr. Quelch gave Mauleverer a very keen look.

"You give me your word on this, Mauleverer?" he said.

"Yaas, sir; and Vivian will say the same, if you ask him. I can't imagine who cleared off the stuff in Wharton's study—but it wasn't a Remove man, I know that. It wasn't Bunter, as I know; and no other fellow in the Remove would do it."

"Oh, really, Mauly——"

Mr. Quelch pursed his lips.

"I am glad that you came here and told me this, Mauleverer," he said. "It is impossible to trust the word of so untruthful a boy as Bunter. I accept your statement, of course. I must conclude that this unscrupulous act was the act of a boy in another Form. Thank you, Mauleverer; you may go."

The Remove master turned to Bunter.

"I told you I never did, sir——" began the fat Owl.

"You need say nothing, Bunter! You have been punished for such acts before, and your word is worthless. However, it appears that you are innocent in this instance. It should be a lesson to you, Bunter, to see that I can accept Mauleverer's word without question, while your own carries no weight whatever. This should be a warning to you to speak the truth, Bunter."

"Oh, yes, sir, I always do."

"Wha-a-t! If you say another word, Bunter, I shall cane you! Leave my study at once!"

Quelch's hand strayed to the cane on the table—and Bunter made one jump for the door! He was only too glad to leave his Form-master's study at once. He fairly bolted down the passage, as if afraid that Quelch might change his mind and call him back.

THE TWENTIETH CHAPTER.

Tea in No. 13!

BOB CHERRY stared.

His study-mates, Mark Linley and Wun Lung, had gone down, and Bob was sitting at a solitary tea in Study No. 13, not in the best of spirits, when the door was hurled open, and his four chums presented themselves.

They tramped in, and Harry Wharton slammed a parcel on the table.

Bob blinked at them.

"What's this game?" he asked.

"Mind if we tea here?" asked Harry, laughing.

"Haven't you had tea yet?"

"No; a lot of interruptions." The captain of the Remove unwrapped the parcel. "Shove the kettle on, Franky. Slice up that loaf for toast, Johnny— it's Bob's loaf, but he won't report us to Quelch for pilfering it."

"Ha, ha, ha!"

"What the dickens——" exclaimed Bob in astonishment.

"We'd rather tea here," said Harry. "I don't know what you've got against that man Carter, Bob, and I dare say he means all right, according to his lights; but I feel that I can't stand any more of him just at present."

"Blessed if I see why he couldn't hang on at St. Olaf's!" grunted Johnny Bull. "No need to bung him into Greyfriars, that I can see."

Bob Cherry laughed. He knew the reason for that, if his friends did not.

"But what has he done?" he asked. "You seem to have got fed up with him mighty suddenly."

The four told him, all at once. Bob's face grew grimmer and grimmer, as he heard it.

"The cur!" he said.

"Well, he really has acted like a bit of a worm," said Harry. "Of course, he's new here, and he's got his own ideas! But——"

"He's right in a way," said Johnny Bull, "but——"

"The miserable cur!" said Bob. His eyes were blazing. Back into his mind came the words the new junior had uttered at Lantham, that he would "fix" his relation at Greyfriars somehow. "Oh, the cur! He meant to get Bunter kicked out, if he could—the cur!"

"Well, Bunter shouldn't do such things, of course," said Harry, "and any fellow might have got his back up. But he——"

"And it wasn't Bunter, after all!" chuckled Nugent. "Blessed if I know who can have snaffled the stuff—but Mauly yanked Bunter away by his ear before he could snoop it."

"We all thought it was Bunter, of course," said Harry, "and really Carter

was asking for it, sticking the stuff right under the fat bandit's nose——"

"Tha was his game!" said Bob savagely. "He knew Bunter would fall for it—and that's why he did it!"

"Oh, come, old chap, it's not so bad as that——"

"It is, and worse!" growled Bob. "I jolly well know——" He checked himself. "By gum, I'll keep an eye on the cur after this—he won't fix that fat frump so easily as he fancies!"

"My dear chap——"

"Oh, don't talk about him!" growled Bob. "He makes me feel ill. Hallo, hallo, hallo! Is that Bunter?"

A fat voice floated in from the passage.

"Yah! Rotter! Cad! Sneak! Thought you had me booked for a row with the Head, didn't you? Yah!"

"You fat rotter!" came Carter's voice in reply. "How did you manage to lie yourself out of it?"

"Yah! Cad! Sneak! Making out that a fellow snaffled your mouldy tuck! As if I'd touch it! Yah! Look here, Carter, don't you get bragging about the school that you're a relation of mine!"

"What?" yelled Carter.

"Ha, ha, ha!" roared Study No. 13.

"You're not the sort of relation that I want hanging about, Carter! I bar you! If I hear you bragging that you're a relation of mine, I'll jolly well punch your head, so yah!"

That defiance was followed by a swift patter of feet in the Remove passage. Billy Bunter bolted into Study No. 13.

"I say, you fellows, keep that beast off!" he gasped.

Billy Bunter hastily closed the door.

"Rotten cad, that chap!" he said. "If you fellows hear him swanking that he's a relation of mine, don't you take any notice. It's a very distant connection—very distant indeed! A rather low and disreputable branch of the family! In fact, we never mention them! I say, if you're having tea, I'll join you, if you like! I had a snack with Mauly, but if you fellows like——"

And without waiting to learn whether the fellows liked, Billy Bunter pulled a chair to the table.

THE END.

(Arthur Carter has failed to get Billy Bunter into trouble so far! Will he have better luck next week? You'll be surprised when you read: BUNTER THE BRAGGER! the second story in this exciting new series. Watch out for it in next Saturday's MAGNET!)

The Magnet

2D

Billy Bunter's Own Paper

MR QUELCH

AN UNINVITED GUEST!

DON'T WAIT FOR AN INVITE . . . JOIN UP RIGHT NOW with—

The GREYFRIARS GUIDE

A TOUR OF THE SCHOOL. The Remove Passage.

(1)

You won't find the calm of the Cloisters,
　No quiet seclusion is here,
The fellows aren't dumb like the oysters,
　Or like the old friars—no fear!
They like to make plenty of clatter
　To let people know they're alive,
If others object—what's it matter?
　At least, till the prefects arrive!

(2)

At times, Horace Coker comes charging
　Right into the place like a chump,
And then there is shouting and barging
　As Coker goes out—with a bump!
And often when Bunter's been bagging
　Some tuck from the study next door,
The noise of his subsequent ragging
　Is just like the Japanese war!

(3)

And yet, through the din and the
　　roaring,
　One fellow is calmly inert,
Old Mauly is peacefully snoring
　Till Cherry looks in—with a squirt!
With teacups and knives gaily clinking,
　The passage outside full of fun,
Oh, pity me, sitting here thinking
　And writing; but—Whoopee!—I'm
　　done!

AFTER SCHOOL HOURS

Chess Champions

(1)

Long years ago—well, more or less—
　When I was quite a fag,
A grand and thrilling game of chess
　Was started in the Rag.
Mark Linley challenged Hurree Singh
　To fierce and fearful fight,
And tried to checkmate Inky's king
　With bishop, pawn, and knight.

(2)

He moved a rook—we held our breath,
　And Inky lost his head;
With trembling feet, as pale as death,
　He tottered off to bed;
He tossed in anguish till the dawn,
　Then rose and sought the board;
With steady hand he moved a pawn!
　Jemima! How we roared!

(3)

But Linley, though he dared not speak,
　Was ready to attack;
He thought it over for a week,
　Then moved the castle back!
Just like a falchion from its sheath
　Flashed Inky's eyeballs keen!
He squared his jaw and set his teeth,
　And firmly moved his queen!

(4)

Term after term, night after night,
　Was finished and begun,
But never a moment ceased the fight
　Of the one and the—other one!
When bishops, rooks, and knights were
　　gone,
　The queens in combat met,
And still the game went dragging on—
　It hasn't finished yet!

THE GREYFRIARS ALPHABET

JAMES HOBSON,
Captain of the Shell Form.

H is for Hobson of the Shell,
A Form he captains very well;
Quite easy to get on with, he's
A very simple chap to please.
Good-tempered, rugged, rather plain,
He doesn't boast a lot of brain,

But Hobby's loyal all the while,
And meets misfortune with a smile.
The chief misfortune he endures
Is Hoskins and his overtures.
His music-loving study-mate,
Composing at a fearful rate
The most appalling serenade,
Makes Hobby listen while it's played!
He hears it to the bitter end.
Great jumping crackers! What a friend!

ANSWER TO PUZZLE

The second train would arrive first.
It's average speed is 45 m.p.h., while
the other train's is 40 m.p.h.

GREYFRIARS GRINS

Fisher T. Fish had a dud sixpence recently. But not for long.

Mr Twigg, after whopping a dozen inky fags, sends his cane to be decarbonised.

While Toddy was out, Bunter kindly kept his fried sosses warm by wrapping himself round them.

Wingate found his chimney smoking this morning. He gave it a hundred lines.

Something ought to be done about the behaviour in the French class. Mossoo talks so loud we can't hear ourselves speak.

Tom Redwing says that if there's anything in a fellow, the sea will bring it out. It often does!

Angel of the Fourth has been spotted coming out of the garden of the Three Fishers. His excuse, that he was trying to help a poor little robin with a broken wing, has not been well received. In fact, he got the bird!

PUZZLE PAR

Two trains run from Courtfield to London and back each day. The first goes up at 60 m.p.h. and back at 30 m.p.h. The second does 45 m.p.h. in each direction. Which gets back first?

Answer at foot of column 2.

Gosling denies that he takes whisky, except by doctor's orders. The expression of horror on his face when he takes his medicine would move a heart of stone. I don't think!

After niffing the fumes of Prout's cigars, we know what killed the grizzly bears! Not his rifle!

I see in the papers that steel-toughened glass, warranted not to crack in any circumstances, has just been invented. Now Bolsover major will be able to have his photograph taken.

WONDERS WILL NEVER CEASE! Mr. Quelch, a master at Greyfriars, has been the victim of a wild and reckless rag—and Billy Bunter, the fat and funky Owl of the Remove, not only admits that he's the guilty person, but brags of it!

BUNTER the BRAGGER!
By FRANK RICHARDS

"Who cares for Quelch?" said Bunter, as he strutted about the Rag with his fat little nose in the air. "I've made him sit up once, and I'll make him sit up again! Fat lot I care for beaks!"

THE FIRST CHAPTER
Lines for Two!

RAP!

"Woo-hooooh!"

Mr. Quelch jumped.

Really, it was quite a surprising occurrence in the Remove Form Room at Greyfriars.

The rap of the ruler on Billy Bunter's fat knuckles sounded almost like a pistol-shot, and the yell that followed fairly woke the echoes.

All the Remove stared round, as well as their Form-master.

Quelch had been about to point out some detail of interest—or otherwise—on a large map that hung over the blackboard on the easel. His back had been partly turned for the moment.

But at that sudden rap and that loud yell of anguish, the Remove master spun round and glared at his class.

"What——" he thundered. "Who——"

"Oh! Ah! Ow! Wow!" howled Billy Bunter, sucking frantically at his fat knuckles. "Beast! Ow! Oooogh! Wow!"

"Bunter——"

"Whooo-hoop!" howled Bunter.

"Shut up, you ass!" whispered Bob Cherry.

"Ow! Wow! Ah! Oh! Ooooh!"

"Bunter, what——"

Some of the Removites grinned as Micky Desmond was seen to slip a ruler under his desk. Micky, who was sitting next to Bunter, tried to look as if he knew nothing about rulers. Perhaps he regretted that hasty rap when Bunter's

frantic yell rang through the Form-room and drew Quelch's attention.

"Bunter," thundered Mr. Quelch, "what do you mean? What——"

"Ow! My knuckles!" howled Bunter. "Oh crikey! You beast, Desmond——"

"Desmond!"

"Yis, sorr!" mumbled Micky.

"Did you strike Bunter with a ruler?"

"I—I—I——" stammered Micky.

"'Yes,' or 'No'?" thundered Mr. Quelch.

"Sure, I rapped the fat baste's knuckles, sorr!" confessed Micky.

"Upon my word! How dare you do anything of the kind, especially in class! I shall cane you severely, Desmond, for such an act!"

••••••••••••••••••••••••••••••••••

Super School-Adventure yarn, starring HARRY WHARTON & CO., the Chums of GREYFRIARS.

••••••••••••••••••••••••••••••••••

Micky opened his mouth, and shut it again. Other fellows looked at him. Some of them had seen why Micky had rapped those fat knuckles So far as Mr. Quelch could see, it was a sudden thoughtless prank that had disturbed the serenity of the Form-room. Harry Wharton & Co. and three or four other fellows were aware that Bunter's fat hand had been sliding under Micky's desk, groping for something there—probably toffee!

But Micky was not going to tell Quelch so—for two good reasons. He was not going to "tell" on Bunter, and he did not want to reveal the fact that he had brought a packet of toffee into class.

As Micky did not choose to explain, it was nobody else's business to do so.

Mr. Quelch picked up the cane from his desk, and signed to Micky to step out before the Form.

Micky rose reluctantly to his feet.

"Yow-ow-ow-ow!" came from Bunter.

"Silence, Bunter!" rapped Mr. Quelch.

"Yes, sir! Yow-ow-ow-ow!"

"Will you be silent, Bunter?"

"Oh, certainly, sir! Yow-ow-ow-ow-ow!"

Micky was about to leave his place when another fellow rose to his feet. That fellow was Carter, the new junior in the Remove.

"If you please, sir——" said Carter.

"What—what have you to say, Carter?" snapped Mr. Quelch.

"I think, sir, that Bunter ought to tell you why Desmond rapped his knuckles," said Carter.

"Shut up, Carter!" whispered Harry Wharton.

"Fair play's a jewel!" answered Carter. "I don't see Desmond getting licked for nothing!"

"No bizney of yours!" muttered Frank Nugent.

"Silence in the class! You may sit down, Carter! Bunter, why did Desmond rap your knuckles?"

"Ow! Because he's a beast, sir!

THE MAGNET LIBRARY.—No. 1,562.

Wow! I wasn't after the toffee!" gasped Bunter. "I never knew he had any toffee!"

"Toffee!" thundered Mr. Quelch. "Did you say toffee, Bunter?"

"Oh, no, sir! I mean to say, I never reached under Desmond's desk for his toffee, sir! I never knew he had any! I—I was going to borrow a—a—a pennib!"

"Desmond, have you brought toffee into the Form-room?"

"Yis, sorr!" groaned Micky.

"Hand it to me at once!"

Mr. Quelch tossed the packet of toffee into the wastepaper-basket. Rather to Micky's relief, he laid down the cane. Carter's intervention had stopped the whopping, at all events.

"You should not have rapped Bunter's knuckles, Desmond! However, I shall excuse you, in the circumstances," said Mr. Quelch. "You will take a hundred lines from the first book of Virgil for bringing comestibles into the Form-room!"

"Yis, sorr!"

"Bunter——"

"I—I didn't!" gasped Bunter, in alarm. "I wasn't after the toffee, sir! It—it was all a mistake! I—I was simply reaching under Desmond's desk to borrow some blotting-paper, sir!"

"Upon my word!" exclaimed Mr. Quelch.

"I never knew there was any toffee there sir!" said Bunter anxiously. "I never saw Desmond put it there when we came in, sir! Besides, I don't like toffee, sir! It—it's one of the things I—I dislike most——"

"Will you be silent, Bunter?"

"Oh, yes, sir! But I never reached after that toffee, sir; I just wanted to get a pencil——"

"You will take a hundred lines, Bunter!"

"Oh, really, sir——"

"And if you utter another word, I shall cane you!"

Billy Bunter blinked at him through his big spectacles, and did not utter another word.

"You will both bring the lines to me before tea!" said Mr. Quelch. "If there is another interruption, I shall cane the offender!"

Geography was resumed in the Remove-room.

Billy Bunter turned his eyes and his spectacles on Carter. He gave the new junior a glare that bade fair to crack those big spectacles.

"You rotten sneak!" breathed Bunter.

Arthur Carter was a relative—a distant relative—of the fat Owl of the Remove. Bunter had rejoiced when he left his former school and came to Greyfriars, having told every fellow who wanted to hear, and still more who didn't, that Carter was a rich relation of his. But Carter, from his first day at Greyfriars, had barred Bunter, and not a single crumb from the rich man's table had come Bunter's way. So in a few days Billy Bunter's deep affection for his rich relation had turned to scornful dislike. But never had he disliked him so much as now.

Carter shrugged his shoulders.

"Sneaking beast!" hissed Bunter.

Mr Quelch looked round again.

"Are you talking in class, Bunter?" he asked.

"Oh no, sir! I never opened my mouth. I only said to Carter——"

"If you speak again, Bunter, I shall double your imposition!"

After which, William George Bunter was dumb.

THE SECOND CHAPTER.

Drastic Measures!

"BARGE!" said Harry Wharton. "Look here——" exclaimed Bob Cherry.

He had no time to say more.

The Famous Five of the Remove had come up to tea. As they reached the doorway of Study No. 1, Bob Cherry was about to walk on and leave his friends there.

Ever since Carter, the new fellow, had been in Study No. 1 with Wharton and Nugent Bob had avoided that study like a plague-spot.

On this occasion he was quite unable to avoid it; for at the word from the captain of the Remove, his four friends suddenly barged him into the doorway, and he went spinning in.

He spun headlong, stumbled over, and sat on the carpet, with a bump and a roar.

Four grinning faces looked at him from the doorway.

Bob sat up and glared at them.

Having barged him into the study, Harry Wharton and Frank Nugent, Johnny Bull and Hurree Jamset Ram Singh, were blocking the doorway, to bar him from escape—packing their goal, as it were.

"You silly asses!" gasped Bob Cherry.

"Ready for tea, old chap?" asked Nugent affably.

"Not here!" snorted Bob.

He scrambled to his feet, with a red and wrathy face. But there was no getting out of the study, without charging his friends like a bull. The doorway was well defended.

"Now, look here, Bob——" said Johnny Bull.

"Let me get out, you fatheads!" grunted Bob.

"No exit," said Nugent.

"You silly ass——"

"Now don't play the goat, Bob," said Harry Wharton soothingly. "We've always fed together in this study, and we're not going to chuck it because you don't like that man Carter. He doesn't bite——"

"I won't sit down to tea with Carter."

"Well, you can feed standing up like a horse, if you like that better," suggested Johnny Bull. "What about that?"

"Ha, ha, ha!"

Bob grinned for a moment. It was not easy for Bob Cherry to resist the blandishments of his friends. He had a sunny nature; and even if he disliked a fellow, his good temper and good nature generally got the upper hand. That made his deep dislike of Carter all the more puzzling and exasperating to his friends.

They were a little doubtful, perhaps, about the new fellow themselves. But on the whole they did not see any great harm in him. They saw no good reason why Bob should cut Study No. 1, simply because it was Carter's, as well as Wharton's and Nugent's. So now they were dealing with the difficulty.

"You see——" grunted Bob.

"The point is, that we don't," answered Harry. "Carter's come here from another school, and I dare say he's got his own ways; but we don't see any reason at all why you should bar him in this fatheaded way."

"The barfulness is not the proper caper, my esteemed and idiotic Bob," said Hurree Jamset Ram Singh, with a shake of his dusky head.

"Why not chuck playing the goat?" asked Johnny Bull. "After all, it's not your way to be a sulky ass, Bob."

Bob gave an angry grunt.

"I don't like the chap. I don't want to say anything against him, but I can't stand him!" he snapped. "Look what he did the other day—complaining to Quelch about Bunter bagging his tuck——"

"Well, yes, but——"

"And this afternoon," growled Bob, "sneaking to Quelch——"

"He might have held his tongue," agreed Harry. "Still, Bunter ought to have spoken out——"

"I know that, but——"

"He saved Desmond from getting a whopping," said Nugent. "Blessed if I know whether a chap should have spoken or not! I suppose Carter thought he ought——"

"Fat lot he cares about what he ought to do!" growled Bob. "He wanted to land Bunter into a row."

"Well, he doesn't seem frightfully fond of his relation," admitted Wharton.

"Oh, bother the cad!" grunted Bob. "I don't want to row with him. I want to steer clear of him."

"You're not going to cut this study!" said the captain of the Remove decidedly. "We don't cut Johnny's study because he's got Fishy there. And I suppose Carter's a bit better than Fishy."

"Worse!" grunted Bob.

"Oh, rot! The chap's quite ready to be friendly with you——"

"Let me catch him being friendly with me!" growled Bob.

"You're an unreasonable ass!"

"Well, if I'm an unreasonable ass, you don't want me in this study, so let a fellow get out."

"But we do, old bean. We're too fond of you to part with you," said Frank Nugent, laughing. "I say, we've got a cake for tea!"

"You silly chump!"

"And two kinds of jam——"

"Fathead!"

"And doughnuts——"

"Will you stop talking silly rot?" roared Bob Cherry. "Now, look here, I'm going out of this study before Carter comes up."

"'Charge, Chester, charge! On, Stanley, on!' quoted Frank Nugent.

And the four stood ready for a charge.

"Will you stop playing the goat?" roared Bob.

"That's what we're asking you to do."

"I've a jolly good mind to biff the lot of you over into the passage!" hooted Bob.

"Help!" exclaimed Johnny Bull.

"Ha, ha, ha!"

"I'm going out of this study!" bawled Bob. "Now shift!"

And he charged at the crammed doorway.

His friends did not shift. They staggered, under the hefty charge; but they rallied, and grasped their recalcitrant chum on all sides, and bore him back into the study.

Bob was a hefty fellow, but he was no match for the four, and, exasperated as he was, he did not think of punching. But he resisted fiercely, and there were two or three hectic minutes in Study No. 1 before he was dumped on the carpet again.

He sat there and gasped for breath.

The Co., gasping also after that strenuous tussle, packed the doorway again, and grinned breathlessly at him.

"You silly fatheads!" gasped Bob.

"We'll keep this up as long as you do, old chap," said Harry Wharton.

"You're teaing in this study with your old pals—Carter and all."

Bob staggered up. He set his collar and tie straight, and glared at the four. They smiled back at him.

There was a step in the passage, and the keen, penetrating eyes of Arthur Carter looked in, over the shoulders of the four.

"Hallo! You fellows scrapping?" exclaimed Carter. "I thought you fellows never rowed."

"Only a little friendly argument," answered Nugent.

THE THIRD CHAPTER.
Tea in Study No. 1!

"I SAY, you fellows!"

"Get out!" snapped Carter.

Billy Bunter blinked into Study No. 1, where six fellows sat at tea. As his "rich relation" spoke, Bunter turned his spectacles on him, with a glare of lofty and contemptuous scorn.

"Did you speak to me, Carter?" he inquired.

"Yes, I did, you fat ass!"

"I'm not in your study!" retorted Bunter. "A fellow can stand in the passage if he likes and speak to his friends. I'm not speaking to you—I bar you! If you fancy you're going to know me at Greyfriars, because we're distant connections, you're jolly well mistaken. Don't you fellows believe anything he says about that you know. At home, we don't know the Carters."

"You'd be jolly well glad to!" sneered Carter. "Now clear off!"

"Shan't! You make out you're fearfully rich," went on Bunter. "I haven't

As Billy Bunter's fat hand groped under Micky Desmond's desk, the Irish junior brought his ruler into play. "Ow! My knuckles!" howled Bunter. "Oh crikey! You beast, Desmond!" The fat junior's yell rang through the Form-room and drew Mr. Quelch's attention.

Bob Cherry gave the new junior a look. The chums of the Remove had not been scrapping, though certainly they had been struggling rather strenuously. But, it seemed to Bob, at least, that Carter always gave the most unpleasant turn he could to everything. Everything, in fact, that Carter did, seemed to get on Bob Cherry's nerves.

"What's the row about?" asked Carter.

Bob compressed his lips.

"Who said there was a row?" he snapped.

"Well, it sounded like one," said Carter. "Sorry to see you fellows falling out like this!"

"We're not falling out," said Harry Wharton sharply. "It's all right, Bob—have it your own way."

"Have it yours," said Bob. "It's all right. I'll make the toast, shall I?"

"Yes, old chap. You cut some bread, Johnny, while I put the kettle on and make the tea."

Toast and tea were soon ready. Bob Cherry sat down to tea with the Co. and Carter in Study No. 1, disliking the new fellow more than ever, but determined not to give him, at all events, the satisfaction of seeing a "row" on in the Co.

"Then don't," said Bunter. "I've told you before not to speak to me, Carter. I've told you not to presume on our relationship."

Five fellows grinned.

This was rather a new line for Billy Bunter to take with his rich relation. But Bunter had thought it out, and decided that if his rich relation was going to bar him, the least he could do was to bar him back. Having spent days and days in vain efforts to hook on to Carter, the fat Owl was now taking up an attitude of the loftiest disdain.

Carter did not grin; he scowled. Everybody in the Remove knew that he disliked that fat and fatuous relative. Nobody was really surprised by that. Few fellows, if related to Billy Bunter, would have boasted of it.

"I say, you fellows," went on Bunter, "if that chap makes out that he's a near relation of mine, don't you believe him. The actual fact is, that we never speak to the Carters."

"Will you get out?"

"Buzz off, old fat man!" said Harry Wharton.

"Oh, really, Wharton——"

"I've told you to get out of my study, you fat freak!" snapped Carter.

noticed you spending much since you've been here. I dare say old Carter, your uncle, isn't so rich as we supposed—I mean, as he made out! I've heard my pater say that he's been bankrupt more than once! Not that we ever talk about the Carters at Bunter Court! We never even mention them!"

Carter rose to his feet, and stepped to the door. He grasped it and hurled it shut with a sudden slam.

"Yaroooh!" came a roar from the passage.

Bunter was, as he had stated, standing in the passage. But his fat little nose was over the frontier, so to speak—it must have been, for the door banged on it! Bunter's wild roar rang far and wide.

"Yarooh! Yow—ow—ow! Beast! Oh crikey! My nose! Wow! My boko! Wow!

"Hallo, what's the row, fatty?" came another voice from the passage; that of Peter Todd.

"Ow! I say, Toddy, that beast Carter banged the door on my nose—I say, go in and kick him, old chap, will you? I say, he called you a bony freak the other day, Peter! I'd kick a chap who called me a bony freak!"

"Good egg: I will!"

"Yarooop! Wharrer you kicking me for, you beast! Stoppit!" roared Bunter. There was a sound of hurried retreating footsteps.

Five minutes later, the door of Study No. 1 opened again, and the fat face of Billy Bunter looked in. His fat little nose was red.

"I say, you fellows——"

"Will you clear off?" yelled the exasperated Carter.

"I've come here to speak to my pals!" said Bunter. "I say, you fellows, what do you think I'd better do about my lines?"

"Write them!" suggested Harry Wharton.

"Oh, don't be an ass!" said Bunter peevishly. That resource, apparently, had not occurred to the fat junior. "I say, Quelch said I was to take them in before tea. Desmond's done his already—I haven't had time. It's too late now, if I'm going to have tea with you fellows, now you've started——"

"That's all right—you're not."

"Oh, really, Wharton! I say, think Quelch would notice any difference, if I took in another chap's lines?" asked Bunter. "I mean to say, Desmond's writing is rather like mine, ain't it?"

"Quite!" said Harry. "Both like an inky spider crawling over the paper. But I can't see Micky doing your lines for you, as you got him his."

"Well, I daresay he wouldn't—he's selfish, like the rest of you," said Bunter. "But what I mean is, he's done his lines, and gone into the Rag with Morgan and Wibley. Well, suppose I borrowed his lines——"

"You fat villain!"

"I mean, I could write my name on the top, over his—Quelch wouldn't notice an extra smudge or so. Think Desmond would mind?" asked Bunter.

"Ha, ha, ha!"

"Well, I needn't mention it to him, after all," said Bunter. "He might get waxy about nothing—he's got an Irish temper, you know. Look here, suppose one of you fellows cut along to the study, and bag the lines! Then I can tell him I never went into his study, if he asks me—he might, you know! I don't want him to cop me there, if he comes in—I mean. I'm a bit more particular about the truth than you fellows——"

"If you touch Desmond's lines, you fat ass, Quelch will scalp you first, and Micky will scalp what's left of you!" roared Bob Cherry.

"Oh, really, Cherry——"

"Will you shut that door?" asked Carter.

"No! I say, you fellows, I'll chance it," said Bunter. "I haven't time to do the lines before tea—you fellows will be finished Quelch will wait a bit, too—blow Quelch!"

"Roll away to your own study, fathead!" said Nugent.

"There's nothing there," explained Bunter "Toddy and Dutton have gone to tea with Squiff. No good going to my study when there's nothing there, is it? I say, you fellows, if you could cash a postal order for me——"

"Scat!"

"I'm expecting it to-morrow——"

"Rats!"

"Well, look here," exclaimed Billy Bunter, warmly. "If you won't cash a postal order for me, after all I've done for you, the least you can do is to ask a fellow to tea! I must say that!"

Harry Wharton laughed.

"Oh, roll in, fathead!" he said. "Make room for the fat porpoise, you fellows!"

Carter rose from the table.

"I'll make room for him if you want him here," he said, curtly. "I'll cut!"

"Oh, rot!" said Harry "Look here, Carter, you ought to be able to stand your own relation, if other fellows can."

"Can't stand him at any price!" answered Carter. "But I'm not stopping you other fellows having him, if you want him. Anyhow, I've finished, or nearly."

"Nobody will miss you, you can bet on that!" said Billy Bunter disdainfully, as the new junior went to the door. "Your room's better than your company."

"Shut up, Bunter! Look here, Carter——"

Carter settled the matter, by walking out of the study, and shutting the door after him.

Billy Bunter grinned cheerfully, as he sat down in the chair vacated by the new junior. The fewer fellows there were to tea the more there was for those present: and as Bunter was present, that was important!

"Good riddance to bad rubbish!" remarked Bunter. "I say, you fellows, who's going to make some more toast?"

"You can, if you like."

"I don't care much for toast! Those sardines look all right—I'll have the lot if you fellows don't want any! Any sosses?"

"No fathead!"

"If I stood a fellow a treat, I should have some sosses! This isn't much better than tea in Hall."

"Try tea in Hall," suggested Nugent.

"Still, I see you've got a cake! I can fill up on cake! Don't open the jam yet, Cherry—I'm not ready till I've finished these sardines! Look here, don't you mop up all that jam, you know."

"Like Bunter better than Carter to tea, Bob?" asked Nugent with a chuckle.

"Yes!" answered Bob, unexpectedly. "I should jolly well think so!" said Bunter. "All the same, leave some of that jam for me! And dash it all, Wharton, you might wait for me, before you start on the cake! Tain't a big one, either."

If Bob Cherry preferred Bunter's company to Carter's, he was the only member of the Co. who did.

THE FOURTH CHAPTER.
Corn in Egypt!

"OH crikey!"

Billy Bunter rolled into his own study, after tea, and blinked in surprise. His eyes and his spectacles fixed on sheets of impot paper on the study table, covered with scrawled Latin

His eyes almost popped through his spectacles in astonishment.

It had not taken Bunter very long to clear the festive board in Study No. 1. Having done so thoroughly, Bunter had proposed that the Famous Five should all buckle to, and get his lines done for him. It would be, as he pointed out, only twenty each, for five fellows!

With the selfishness that Bunter might really have expected, the chums of the Remove had declined, and gone downstairs instead. After which, Billy Bunter had asked about a dozen fellows, up and down the studies, to lend him a hand, without getting a single offer.

Driven to his last resource, the fat Owl rolled, at last, into Study No. 7, to write the lines himself. It was high time that he tackled them, unless trouble was to accrue. By this time the lines were due, if not overdue, in Quelch's study: and the Remove master was rather particular about such matters.

It was doubtful, indeed, whether Bunter could have turned out a hundred lines in time, by setting to hard work. And setting to hard work was a thing that had never had any attraction for Bunter.

He was debating in his fat mind whether to drop in at Quelch's study, and explain that he had written the lines, but that Toddy had left the window open, and they had blown away. And then his eyes, and his spectacles, fell on that written impot, on the table. It was like a discovery of corn in Egypt in the lean years!

It was really astonishing. There before his popping eyes, lay a hundred lines from the first book of Virgil: beginning at "Arma virumque cano," and going on to "sub undis." Whoever had written those lines had done the exact hundred, and not bothered about making it a hundred-and-one, for the mere purpose of finishing at a full stop!

But who had done it?

Bunter had asked nearly ·half the Remove to help him with those lines: and not a man had offered. Some fellows whom he had not asked, apparently, had done the whole job unasked. seldom or never did such things happen!

"Oh crikey!" repeated Bunter.

He blinked, and blinked again, at those Latin lines! He counted them—exactly the hundred! The writing was a ragged scrawl, not unlike Bunter's own—but not quite so bad as Bunter's—few fellows in the school could write as badly as Bunter. That straggling, scraggy, round-hand might have been almost anybody's—it might have been Bunter's, if he had taken a little more care than usual.

Whosoever it was, the fellow had done Bunter a good turn. Amazed as he was to find his lines written for him, the fat Owl beamed with satisfaction.

This was all right. Quelch might have believed that Bunter's lines had been blown out of the study window—but it was much more probable that he mightn't! It was ever so much more satisfactory to take in the lines—as Bunter had not had the trouble of writing them.

He picked up a pen, to write his name on top of the top sheet, which was the rule. In the top corner was a thick black smudge. Bunter wrote his name under the smudge. It did not occur to his fat brain, at the moment, that the writer's name had been written there, and obliterated with ink. That was, really, natural enough; for finding the lines there, on his study table, he had no doubt that some good-natured fellow had done them for him. It was unusual, and it was surprising; still, there were the lines!

In a cheery and satisfied frame of mind, Bunter picked up the impot, and rolled out of the study with it. He found the Famous Five at the foot of the staircase, and they glanced at him, in surprise as they saw the impot in his fat hand.

"You haven't done your lines already!" exclaimed Bob Cherry.

"Looks as if I have!" grinned Bunter.

"You fat villain, if you've bagged Micky's lines——"

"Oh, really, Cherry! I hope I'm not the fellow to bag another fellow's lines!" exclaimed Bunter, warmly.

"Why, you frabjous, footling frump, you asked us, in the study, to cut along and bag them for you!"

"Oh! I—I mean—that is, what I really meant was, that I wouldn't have bagged his lines!" explained Bunter.

"Nothing would have induced me to do it! I'm rather more particular in such things than you are, Cherry!"

Bob Cherry made a movement with his foot—and Bunter scuttled on hastily.

He tapped at Mr. Quelch's door, and the Remove master bade him come in.

Bunter rolled in, and laid the imposition on the table.

"My lines, sir!"

"Oh! Very good!" said Mr. Quelch. "Wait a moment, Bunter!" He picked up the lines and glanced at them.

Bunter waited, rather uneasily! It was one of Quelch's maddening ways, to examine an impot—as if it mattered a boiled bean how it was done! More than once, Bunter had been directed to write lines over again—Quelch objected to a jig-saw puzzle of blots and smears.

Bunter always waited, uneasily, in such circumstances. Now he was more uneasy than usual. There were fewer blots and smudges than his lines generally showed, it was true; but he wondered whether Quelch was going to notice the difference of the "fist." He quaked inwardly as he saw his Form-master scanning the lines very closely.

But, to his relief, Mr. Quelch gave a nod expressive of approval.

"Your handwriting is improving, Bunter!" he said.

"I—I—I've been trying very hard to improve it, sir!" stammered Bunter.

"It is still very bad—very bad indeed —a mere scrawl—but it is not so slovenly as usual, Bunter. It is more like Desmond's hand than yours."

Bunter wondered whether it was Micky who had written those lines for him. It was unlikely, as Micky had had a hundred to write for himself. Still, the Irish junior often did good-natured things.

"Is—is it, sir?" mumbled Bunter, "I —I thought my writing was—was rather better than Desmond's, sir!"

"On the contrary, Bunter, Desmond's writing is rather better than yours, though both are very bad indeed!" said Mr. Quelch. "However, you have done better than usual, Bunter. You may go. Kindly tell Desmond that I am expecting his lines, and that they must be brought to me at once."

"Yes, sir!"

Bunter went—gladly.

He rolled cheerfully down Masters' Passage. It was a relief to have got those beastly lines off his mind. He rolled into the Rag to look for Micky Desmond, but he did not find him there.

"Seen Desmond, you chaps?" squeaked Bunter.

"Gone to take his lines to Quelch," answered Wibley.

"Eh? He hasn't taken them—Quelch has just told me to tell him!"

"Well, he went up to fetch them."

"Well, look here, Wib, Quelch wants him—you go up and tell him," suggested Bunter.

"Bow-wow!" said Wibley.

"I say, Smithy, are you going up to the studies?"

"No!" answered the Bounder.

"Well, look here, you might go up and tell Desmond——"

"Rats!"

"Beast! I say, Mauly, you're not too jolly lazy to walk up to the studies, are you?"

"Yaas!"

"What about you, Redwing?"

"Fathead!"

"Lazy lot!" said Bunter, scornfully. "Anybody might think it was a mile up to the studies. I suppose I shall have to go myself."

And he went.

THE FIFTH CHAPTER.

Backing Up Bunter!

"HOWLY Moses! I tell you, they're gone!" roared Micky Desmond.

"Rot!"

"How can they be gone?"

"You forgot to write them, old bean."

"Phwat!" Micky Desmond was always a little more Irish when he was excited. "Think I'm a fool entirely?"

"Yes, rather, old chap!"

"Ha, ha, ha!"

Quite a crowd of Remove fellows had gathered outside Micky's study. In the doorway stood Micky, red with rage. His infuriated voice could be heard at both ends of the passage. He roared.

"I tell yez!" bawled Micky, "I wrote thim lines, and so I did intirely, and Wibley and Morgan, in the study, seeing me do it, by the same token, and left thim on the table when I wint down to the Rag—and Wib remoinded me of thim, and I came up for thim, and they were gone! And I want to know phwat spalpeen has lifted thim lines from my study."

"I say, you fellows, what's up?" Billy Bunter rolled up the passage.

"Micky says that somebody has lifted his lines!" answered Squiff.

"Sure, they're gone!" roared Micky. "And I lift thim on the table."

"You'd better find them, then!" grinned Bunter. "Quelch has just told me to tell you he's waiting for them."

"How can I find thim whin they're gone?" shrieked Micky. "Some omad-haun has lifted thim lines. How can I take thim to Quelch when I can't find thim at all, at all? Who's taken my lines? By the howly smoke, when I find that spalpeen, I'll rejuice him to powther intirely! I tell you my lines are gone!"

"That won't do for Quelch!" said Bunter, shaking his head. "Bit too thin, old chap!"

"It's the thruth!" roared Micky.

"Well, look here, tell him you left the study window open, and they blew away!" suggested Bunter. "That's rather thin, I know—but not so thin as saying that somebody took the lines away! That's no good at all."

"Listen to the man who knows!" chuckled Skinner.

"Well, I mean to say, if you're going to tell a whopper, tell a good one," said Bunter. "It's not the sort of thing I'd do myself, of course. Still, it's absolutely useless to tell Quelch that somebody's pinched the lines! He would never fall for that."

"But I tell yez, some spalpeen has pinched them intirely!" howled Micky.

"Sure, I'm not going to tell Quelch any loies, yer fat omadhaun. Somebody wint in and lifted thim after I wint out of the study."

"Well, if Quelch believes that, he will believe anything!" said Bunter. "If you get away with it, I'll try it myself, next time."

"Ha, ha, ha!"

"But who the dickens could have done it?" asked Carter, who was in the little crowd in the passage. "Was it you, Bunter?"

"Oh, really, Carter——"

"You were saying something of the kind in my study, at tea-time!" said Carter. "A lot of fellows heard you."

"Beast!"

"Oh crumbs!" exclaimed Hazeldene. "Was it Bunter! I remember once he bagged Toddy's lines, and used them——"

"I didn't!" roared Bunter.

"You jolly well did!" exclaimed Peter Todd. "You fat brigand, have you bagged Desmond's lines?"

"Of course I haven't!" roared Bunter, indignantly. "I told Wharton I wouldn't because Desmond might come in and cop me in his study. I never even thought of doing anything of the kind! Not the sort of thing I would do."

"Oh crikey!"

"Ye thafe of the worruld!" roared Micky. "Where are my lines?"

"I don't know anything about your silly lines!" roared back Bunter. "I haven't been in your study, and none of those rotters would fetch them for me."

"Ha, ha, ha!"

"Have you taken in your own lines, Bunter?" grinned Snoop.

"Yes, I jolly well have, and I've got no use for anybody else's!" snorted Bunter. "As if I'd touch his lines!"

"Sure I'll mop up the passage wid ye!" bawled Micky, shaking a fist under Bunter's little fat nose. "I want those lines."

"Beast! I never——"

"Hallo, hallo, hallo! What's the thumping row?"

The Famous Five came up the Remove passage.

"Bunter's snaffled Micky's lines!" said Tom Brown.

"I haven't!" yelled Bunter.

"Oh, my hat! We saw him taking in his lines, and he never had time to write them!" exclaimed Harry Wharton. "Did you bag Desmond's lines, you fat bandit?"

"No!" shrieked Bunter.

"Then where did you get them? You never wrote them!" said the captain of the Remove. "Hold on, Micky! Don't slaughter Bunter till he's had time to answer—dead men tell no tales, you know."

"Ha, ha, ha!"

"You see," gasped Bunter, "it was like this! A pal wrote those lines for me——"

"Gammon! Who?"

"I—I don't know——"

"Ye gods and little fishes!" ejaculated Johnny Bull. "Does even that fat Owl expect anybody to believe that?"

"It's true!" roared Bunter. "I went to my study to write my lines, and found them on the table, all ready written. I don't know who did it, but somebody must have. Anyhow, I found them there, and took them to Quelch."

"Oh crumbs!"

"That's the jolly old limit!"

"It's true!" howled Bunter.

Even Bunter realised that it sounded improbable—especially with an impot missing from Desmond's study! Still, it was true!

"True!" gasped Nugent. "Oh, my hat!"

"If that be truth, where is untruth to be found?" inquired Skinner.

"The truthfulness is not terrific!" chuckled Hurree Jamset Ram Singh.

"I say, you fellows, it's really true!" gasped Bunter. "I say, if you ask all the fellows you'll find out who did those lines for me. I—I thought perhaps it was Desmond."

"Me!" roared Micky.

"Well, Quelch said that the fist was like yours, old chap——"

"Phwat!" shrieked Micky.

"He—he—he said that the fist was like Micky's—and you make out that you never snooped Micky's lines!" gasped Harry Wharton.

"I never did! I—I wouldn't!" gasped Bunter. "You might do such a thing, Wharton, but I—I wouldn't! Never!"

"Well, my only summer hat!" said Peter Todd, gazing at the fat Owl in

wonder. "You benighted bandersnatch, can't you see that every fellow here knows that they were Micky's lines you took in to Quelch?"

Billy Bunter blinked round at the juniors. It was dawning even on his fat mind that it was Micky Desmond's impot that he had found in his study.

"I—I say, you fellows, I—I never knew it was Micky's!" he gasped. "How was I to know, when I found it on my study table? Of course, I thought some fellow had done it for me."

"It walked to your study?" asked Carter.

"Beast!"

"You'll have to go to Quelch and own up!" said Peter Todd. "You can't leave Micky in the soup after sneaking his lines."

"Faith, and I should say not intirely!" gasped Micky.

"I'll watch it!" squeaked Bunter. "I found the lines in my study!"

"You did not!" roared Peter.

"I did!" yelled Bunter.

"Oh, fan me!" exclaimed Johnny Bull. "You piffling porker, are you asking us to believe that some fellow snooped Micky's lines and put them in your study for you to find?"

"I—I suppose so——"

"Ha, ha, ha!"

Bob Cherry did not join in that roar of laughter. His face set strangely, and his eyes turned on Carter, with a gleam in them.

But he did not speak. The suspicion that had flashed into his mind came with almost the force of certainty; but it was only suspicion! He set his lips hard.

"Are you going to Quelch, Bunter?" demanded Peter Todd.

"No; I jolly well ain't!"

"Then we'll jolly well bump you till you do!"

"Hear, hear!"

"Bag him!"

"I—I—I say, you fellows," gasped Bunter. "I—I never—I didn't—I—I wasn't—— I—I—I say—I—I——"

"You took Micky's lines!" said Harry Wharton. "You've played that trick before, and now you've played it again. You've got to own up, or get a ragging."

"I tell you—" yelled Bunter.

"Bag him!"

"Bump him!"

"Hold on!" rapped Bob Cherry. He stepped suddenly in front of Bunter, and the fat Owl, surprised but greatly relieved, dodged thankfully behind the sturdiest figure in the Greyfriars Remove. "Hands off Bunter!"

"What the dickens——" exclaimed Wharton.

"Don't be an ass, Bob!"

"Bunter says that he found the lines on his study table!" said Bob.

"Do you believe him, you fathead?"

"Yes, I do!"

The crowd of Removites stared at Bob Cherry blankly.

Nobody in the Remove thought of taking Billy Bunter's word, even if he made a probable statement. And his present statement was utterly improbable. That any fellow would have snaffled Micky's lines, to save Bunter the trouble of writing his own, was simply an absurd idea. It really sounded like the most fantastic of Billy Bunter's many and various "whoppers"

"You—you—you believe him?" gasped the captain of the Remove.

"Yes, I do!"

"Bob knows I wouldn't tell a lie, don't you, old chap?" gasped Bunter.

"I know you never tell anything else, you fat chump, or hardly ever! But I believe you're telling the truth this time!"

"And why?" demanded Wharton.

"Well, I do!" said Bob. "Bunter's had this landed on him. It's not fair to make him go to Quelch when he was diddled into taking those lines in."

"What utter rot!"

"Silly ass!"

"Look here——"

"Let us get at that fat frog!"

"You'll have to walk over me first!" said Bob Cherry quietly, but with a glint in his steady blue eyes. "I'm standing by Bunter!"

Harry Wharton compressed his lips.

"Well, nobody's going to walk over you, fathead!" he said. "If you really believe Bunter you're the only fellow here who does! But what's Micky going to do? Quelch will be after him, and he's got no time now to write the lines again."

Trotter, the House page, came up the passage from the House stairs.

"Master Desmond, please——"

"Oh, howly Moses!" groaned Micky.

"Mr. Quelch's study at once, please, sir!" said Trotter.

Micky Desmond drew a deep breath. He gave Billy Bunter one look of terrific deadliness, and followed Trotter down the passage to the stairs.

"That's a licking for Micky," said Johnny Bull. "And that fat blighter bagged his lines because he was too jolly lazy to do his impot."

"Beast! I never——"

Some of the juniors made a movement towards Bunter.

Bob's hands clenched hard, and he stood like a rock.

Harry Wharton hastily interposed.

"Chuck it!" he said. "You're a silly ass, Bob——"

"Same to you, with knobs on!"

"Oh, rats!"

Bob Cherry took hold of a fat arm and led Bunter into his study.

Billy Bunter was glad to get on the safe side of the door of Study No. 13. Just at present the hapless fat Owl was hardly safe among the Removites.

THE SIXTH CHAPTER.
After Bunter!

"STOP!" yelled Billy Bunter. "Bob, stop!"

It was the following afternoon.

Harry Wharton & Co. were going out of gates after dinner when that sudden yell reached their ears, and they looked round.

After them, cutting along at unaccustomed speed, came Billy Bunter.

After Bunter, running like a deer, came Micky Desmond.

The Famous Five grinned. Seldom, or never, had Billy Bunter been seen to put on such speed.

He came through the gateway almost like a stone from a catapult. Micky shot out after him. Bunter, breathless, dodged round the Famous Five in the road.

"Hould him!" gasped Micky, coming up, panting. "Hould that thafe of the worruld!"

"I say, you fellows, keep him off!" gasped Bunter. "I ain't going to do his rotten lines for him!"

"Hold on!" said Harry Wharton. "What's the row, Paddy?"

But he hardly needed to ask. It was that mysterious affair of the lines that was still causing trouble.

Micky's impot, not having been handed in at the due time, had been doubled. He had two hundred lines on hand now, instead of one hundred. And Quelch, though he would double an

"Yarooh! Yow-ow-ow! Beast!" Billy Bunter's wild roar rang far and wide. "Ow! I say, Toddy, that beast Carter banged the door on my nose—go in and kick him, old chap, will you? He called you a bony freak the other day, Peter! I'd kick a chap who called me a bony freak!"

impot that was not handed in, seldom redoubled—his next step was to hand over a whopping. That afternoon was a half-holiday; and Micky had many more attractive occupations for a half-holiday than writing lines. But it was lines or a licking!

Which, undoubtedly, was hard cheese, for Micky had done his lines in the first place, and they had been handed in by Bunter. Had he cared to tell Mr. Quelch so, he would have been all right —though certainly Bunter would have been in serious trouble.

But he had not told Quelch. All the fellows thought it was up to Bunter to own up to his trickery. But Micky had no idea of giving him away, if he did not. His idea was to set the matter right by leaving those two hundred lines to Bunter. Bunter did not seem to see it.

"I say, you fellows, he makes out that I had his lines yesterday, you know!" gasped the fat Owl.

"So you had!" grunted Johnny Bull.

"I never——"

"Oh, chuck it!" said Harry Wharton. "You had Micky's lines! If Quelch had spotted you, you'd have gone to the Head for a flogging!"

"Sure I couldn't tell Quilch!" said Micky. "I'm not going to be a snake!"

"A snake?" exclaimed Wharton. "What the dickens——"

"I wouldn't snake about him, and sind him up to the Head——"

"Oh! A sneak! I see!"

"I said a snake, didn't I? It would serve him right, afther snaking my lines, but I wasn't going to snake to Quilch. But I'm not going to write two hundred lines because that fat baste snaked my impot. Bunter's going to write them, see? If Quilch took my fist for his, he will take Bunter's fist for mine!"

"That's fair," said Nugent. "Up to you, Bunter!"

"Oh, really, Nugent——"

"The fairfulness is terrific!" declared Hurree Jamset Ram Singh.

"But I never snaked the lines!" howled Bunter. "I keep on telling you that I found them in my study——"

"You can keep on telling us that, till you're black in the face, and nobody will believe you!" growled Johnny Bull.

"Bob does—don't you, Bob?"

"Yea!" said Bob Cherry.

"'Twasn't my fault some fellow snaffled Desmond's lines, and put them in my study!" said Bunter.

"Gammon!"

"I don't know who did it," said Bunter, "unless it was Bob——"

"What?" roared Bob Cherry.

"You needn't yell at a chap," said Bunter, blinking at the curly-headed Bob. "I think it must have been you, as you're the only fellow who knows I didn't do it. If you did, you might as well own up to it."

Bob looked at him. The other fellows chuckled—even Micky, wrathy as he was. The expression on Bob's face at that moment was worth a guinea a box!

"You—you—you fat rotter!" gasped Bob. "It was a dirty trick to take Micky's lines, and leave them in your study!"

"I know it was! If you did it——"

"Ha, ha, ha!"

"That's what you get for standing up for Bunter!" chuckled Johnny Bull. "It's what you might have expected, too, you fathead!"

"Oh, really, Bull! If it was Bob, I——"

"You fat freak!" hissed Bob. "You ought to have done your lines, and then that cad, whoever he was, couldn't have played that trick on you. And if you'd

had the sense of a bunny rabbit, you'd have known it was a trick, when you found the lines in your study."

"Well, I was jolly glad to find them there, of course," said Bunter. "And if you put them there, Cherry, I think you ought to admit it. You're making all the fellows think I pinched them, at this rate."

"I did not!" roared Bob.

"Well, I take your word, of course, old fellow. Still, if you did——"

"Ha, ha, ha!"

"Blessed if I see anything to cackle at! Somebody put those lines in my study, and it looks——"

"Anyhow, you had Micky's lines," said Bob. "You ought to do at least a hundred for him, as you had them."

"So I would, if—if I had time! I—I mean, I—I would, only—only it would be like taking Quelch in, you know—deceitful, in fact! I—I couldn't do anything deceitful," said Bunter, shaking his head. "I dare say you could, Cherry, as you suggest it, but——"

"Ha, ha, ha!" yelled four members of the Co.

Bob Cherry gave the fat Owl a glare, and tramped away up the road.

His comrades followed him, laughing. Backing up Bunter was rather a thankless task.

"I say, you fellows, don't walk away while a chap's talking!" yelled Bunter. "I say——"

"Now, you fat baste——" roared Micky.

"Keep off, you beast! Oh crikey!" Billy Bunter broke into flight again.

After him flew Micky. His grasp was on Bunter's collar, when the fat Owl, in desperation, kicked backwards.

Micky gave a yell, as he caught a heel with his shin, and hopped.

Leaving him hopping, Bunter darted

in at the gates again, and disappeared.

For two or three minutes Micky hopped on one leg, and rubbed his hacked shin. Then he limped in after Bunter. The expression on his face was quite alarming.

It was fortunate for Billy Bunter that he had had time to disappear. It is related that the man who struck O'Hara was picked up afterwards in so many pieces that they could not be numbered. And something like the same fate loomed over the fat junior who had hacked Micky Desmond.

Fortunately, Billy Bunter had disappeared and he stayed disappeared!

THE SEVENTH CHAPTER.
Bob Cherry's Problem!

HARRY WHARTON & CO. stopped at the corner of Oak Lane, near Courtfield Common. There the five separated.

The chums of the Remove were taking that walk, that afternoon, to look for Ponsonby of the Fourth Form at Highcliffe. On a half-holiday, it was very likely that Pon would be taking a walk abroad, and very likely indeed that his footsteps would lead him in the direction of the Three Fishers, the disreputable inn on the river.

There were two ways of reaching that delectable resort—one by the back gate on Oak Lane, the other by the gate on the towpath by the Sark.

So, while Harry Wharton and Bob Cherry sauntered in the lane, the other three members of the Co. walked on to the towpath.

Frank Nugent, Johnny Bull, and Hurree Jamset Ram Singh disappeared from sight. Wharton and Bob sauntered at a leisurely pace, keeping in sight of the Three Fishers' fence, which bordered the lane for some distance.

Bob's face was rather grim and glum in expression.

It was far from being Bob's way to nourish a grudge; but he was very keen to get within hitting distance of Cecil Ponsonby.

It was a week since Pon & Co. had ragged him at Lantham Station, and left him tied up in the waiting-room there—and generally Bob forgot an offence in much less than a week. But Pon's rag had had unexpected consequences, which kept its memory green, as it were.

"I'm blessed," said Bob, breaking a long silence, "whether I know what a fellow ought to do!"

"And I'm blessed," said Harry, with a smile, "if I can make you out the last few days, old bean. First you take a dislike to a new fellow, for no reason that anybody can see—then you stand up for that fat villain Bunter against the whole Form——"

"The two things are connected!" grunted Bob. "It was Carter planted those lines in the fat fool's study for him to find!"

"Carter?" repeated Harry. "How do you know, Bob? If you've got any proof of anything of the kind, that alters the case, of course. But how——"

"Think that cunning rascal would let anybody get proof?" grunted Bob.

Wharton's face became grave.

"If there's no proof, Bob, you oughtn't to think so. Just because you dislike the fellow——"

"It's not that, ass! Carter was in the study when that fat idiot came in gabbling about Micky's lines. He left before we finished tea——"

"Because he can't stand his relation—and no wonder!"

"No—because Bunter's gabble had put the idea of that trick into his head. Only Bunter's fool enough to fall for it. But he knew Bunter was. What chance has that silly fathead against a clever rogue?"

"Blessed if I make you out. You're not quite fair to Carter," said Harry. "He doesn't like Bunter hooking on to him as a relation—and precious few fellows would, if you come to that. He knows perfectly well that the fat ass is only after his money."

"I know that! I'm not blaming him for that! If it were only that, do you think I should care a boiled bean?" grunted Bob. "He's here as Bunter's enemy, that's what's worrying me. That blithering ass can't take care of himself, and he's so fatheaded, and so beastly unscrupulous, he keeps on giving the cad chances."

"That's bosh!" said Harry. He stopped, and stood looking at Bob's flushed, troubled face. "Look here, you've said that when those Highcliffe cads left you tied up in that waiting-room, with a hanky stuffed in your mouth, the day Carter came, you heard something——"

"I couldn't help hearing it."

"I know, if they came into the waiting-room and jawed, while you were tied up behind the door. I saw that man Gooch, Carter's cousin, who brought him to the school that day. They changed trains at Lantham, I suppose, and came into the waiting-room while they waited for the Courtfield train. You heard what they said. You've told us that, but not what you heard——"

"I can't repeat what I heard from behind a door, can I—though it was those Highcliffe cads who fixed me up behind the door."

"Well, no; but——" Wharton paused. "It seems that what you heard there made you take a dislike to Carter. You said that he was a cad, and that the man with him was a rascal! Now you say he's Bunter's enemy. Does that mean that they were talking about Bunter?"

"Yes, it does!"

"But they can't have talked any harm," said Harry, utterly mystified. "Carter didn't know Bunter, I remember, when he got to Greyfriars——"

"That was gammon. He knew him all right! Look here," said Bob, with a deep breath, "I'd better tell you—only don't jaw about it, for goodness' sake. I want your advice what to do. Mind, it's in confidence. I can't repeat things about a chap that I heard in such a way. But—but—there's some rascality afoot, and it's up against that fat idiot, Bunter. How can I leave him to take what's coming to him?"

"I'll keep it dark, of course—and I dare say it will turn out to be next to nothing, after all," said Harry. "I know Carter's seen Bunter only once, before he came, and that was a long time ago, so he can't be his enemy, as you put it. He can't stand him, that's all!"

"If you'd heard——"

"Well, get it off your chest!"

"I don't remember every word, of course," said Bob, "but that fat ass, Bunter, thinks Carter a rich relation. Well, he isn't. Bunter doesn't know why he left St. Olaf's to come here—I do! He was kicked out of his last school as a bad hat——"

"What rot! The Head wouldn't have let him into Greyfriars——"

"The man Gooch mentioned that

Carter's uncle had a lot of difficulty in fixing it."

"Must have had—if it's correct!" said Wharton dryly.

"Well, never mind that—that's no business of mine, anyhow," said Bob. "I shouldn't dream of saying a word about that part But the rotten part is that old Carter got so annoyed with the young rascal that he cut him off: he's paying his school fees here, and that's the limit. He's altered his will, leaving his cash to another relation."

"Even if that's so, what is there to bother you about it? Blessed if I make you out."

"Fathead! The new name in the old bean's will, according to what they said, is the name of Carter's relation at Greyfriars."

"Oh!" said Harry.

"They never mentioned the name! But the only relation that Carter's got at our school, so far as I know, is Bunter."

"It's quite likely there might be another chap related to him, out of two or three hundred. Bunter's only seen the old man once, and it doesn't look likely——"

"Oh, I know—I know! But they said more than that! Carter's to play a reform game, to get back into old Carter's good graces, and, at the same time, to do all he can to disgrace the other fellow, making the old man think that the new heir is no better than the old heir—see?"

"Oh, my hat!"

"Well, from the very start, Carter's been on Bunter's trail, and that looks as if Bunter's the victim—especially as he's the only fellow, as far as we know, related to Carter. That's why he reported that grub raid to Quelch, last week. That's why he spoke out in class yesterday. That's why he's fixed Bunter over those lines. He banked on Bunter being shown up for snaffling them."

"Um!" said Harry.

"Twice, since Carter's been here, Bunter's had a narrow escape of going up to the Head! Well, a fellow can't keep on going up to the Head! A fellow who's always being sent up to the Head gets sacked, in the long run."

"I know. But——" Wharton shook his head. "Look here, Bob, a fellow can't be sent up to the Head, or sacked, either, for anything he hasn't done! It's all very well to say that Carter's on his trail: but Bunter does snoop tuck in the studies, and he does grab another fellow's lines if he gets a chance. Carter can't make him do it."

"He can take a rotten advantage of it when he does it."

"Well, that's Bunter's look-out; the fat ass should run straight."

"Yes, I know that. But that time he reported Bunter for a grub raid the fat ass hadn't done it. It turned out to be some fag or other. And this time Bunter never knew they were Micky's lines. I tell you I know that cad got them out of Micky's study and left them in Bunter's, as sure as if I'd seen him doing it!" said Bob irritably.

Harry Wharton stood silent.

"Well, what do you think?" asked Bob, at last. "I can't be certain it was Bunter those two rotters were talking about, as they never mentioned the name. But it looks pretty clear, the way he's been on the fat duffer's trail. It's a fool against a rogue. And from what they said, there's a lot of money at stake."

"I don't see how they could know that——"

"That man Gideon Gooch is a solicitor, and I suppose he nosed it out somehow. Anyhow, that's what he said. Carter said he would fix the fellow who had cut him out. I remember those words."

"It's all jolly queer!" said Harry slowly. "If you've got it right, it looks as if Old Man Carter has cut his nephew off and made a new will in Bunter's favour, and they're out to get it changed again. But—if you said a word about this, Bob, you couldn't prove a single syllable."

Bab flushed crimson.

"Does that mean that you don't believe me?" he exclaimed.

"Don't be as ass, old chap! I believe every word, of course, but you might very likely be mistaken—have misunder-stood something. If Carter was turfed out of his last school for playing the goat, it's odd that he's shown no signs of it here, in over a week."

"Bunter's said that he's caught him smoking."

"Bunter will say anything. Nobody
(*Continued on next page.*)

LEARN TO PLAY FOOTBALL!
OUR INTERNATIONAL COACH

PROFESSIONAL DODGES

I PROMISED you some more corner kick "secrets." I must be careful what I tell you, or I shall have players and managers on to me, accusing me of giving away private information. But so long as you remember the things I tell you, and they do you good, I don't mind taking the risk.

Look at any newspaper which prints photographs of football matches in progress—one of the big Sunday or Monday newspapers, for example—and you are almost sure to find some sort of picture of a corner kick. Either the goalkeeper saving, a goal being scored, or the players bunched together waiting for the ball to come over. Notice what an unruly jumble of players there seems to be.

Believe me, there is more thought put into that "jumble" than you think. Every player has his eye on a particular opponent; no one is allowed to stand unmarked. One or two defenders are ready to fall back on to the goal-line to cover up the goalkeeper in case he makes a slip. And the attackers are busy positioning themselves in the places where they think they will stand the best chance of getting to the ball as it comes across.

Neither does the player taking the kick merely slam the ball into the middle without any regard for the colleague to whom he wants it to go. Very often he has an arrangement with one of the players in the middle to put the ball across in a certain place, or in a certain way.

If you get a chance to see the Arsenal in action, watch carefully when they are awarded a corner kick. You may see Ted Drake, their "giant" centre-forward, stand well away from the goal, and then, as the ball comes over, dash in with a huge leap in an endeavour to head the ball into the net. Or watch the Arsenal when they are not doing too well—perhaps a goal down. As soon as a corner kick is awarded they bring up one or two of their tall defenders—Jack Crayston or Les Compton, for example—to try to force a goal that way. In the game against West Bromwich Albion, earlier this season, Compton, a full-back, saved the game by coming up for a corner kick when there were only five minutes left for play.

But remember this: If your defenders advance for a corner kick, other players must be sent back to act as defenders in the case of a quick breakaway by the other side.

> The subjects of this week's "lesson" by our special sporting contributor are corner-kick secrets—and a warning about heading the ball.

HEADING IS IMPORTANT

OTHER clubs adopt their own dodges to help them to score goals from corner kicks. Grimsby Town work one, and I have occasionally seen Chelsea try it on this season. Instead of banging the ball into the middle, the player taking the kick passes it gently to a colleague who is running up about half-way between the touchline and the centre of the field. From there the player with the ball can have a shot at goal. The point is, you see, that the fellow taking the kick must not play the ball again until it has been played by another player. He couldn't run in from the corner to have a shot, so he passes the ball to a colleague, who is at liberty to do as he likes.

In the foregoing you have a few of the dodges which first-class players "try on" in their efforts to improve that average of "one in eighteen" goals from corner kicks. Now let us take our corner kick and see how we get on. The ball went out on the left of the goal—that is on our right wing. We decided that, because we wanted our corners to be taken with the "wrong" foot, we would let our outside-left take the corners on the right wing. He must place the ball in the "arc" and, without moving the corner flag, take the kick as per the instructions which I have been giving you.

Now then, you forwards, position yourselves with some intelligence; don't all crowd in the goalmouth. The ball is coming over—a nice corner kick, not too high, and about four yards out from goal. Our centre-forward jumps, gets his head to the ball, but sends it over the bar, and the game must be started again by a goal kick.

I don't know who taught our centre-forward about heading the ball. It certainly wasn't me. You may have thought it queer that I haven't said anything about heading up to now. Don't think I have forgotten, or that I think heading doesn't play an im-portant part in football. Heading is important. Several players have failed to reach the top rank because they have not been able to head a ball properly.

WATCH THE BALL

I HAD reasons for not mentioning this heading business earlier. First of all, I remember telling you at the beginning of this series of "lessons" that football should be played on the ground If the game is played properly there should be no need for a great deal of heading.

The real reason, however, why I have left heading out of these notes up to now is that I don't advise you young footballers to get into the habit of heading a football. During a game a football can become very heavy. A soft skull, which isn't used to taking bangs, may easily be damaged if you head the ball in the wrong way. Don't think I am suggesting that you wrap yourselves up in cottonwool, or that you shouldn't do the things which might hurt you. But there is no point in running the risk of getting knocked out, or, at the best, going about for days with a severe headache. The head is a very delicate part of the anatomy, which needs looking after. For the time being, let us make it a rule that there shall be no heading in our games.

That doesn't mean that you must forget about this important part of football. Heading practice with a small dry football can do no harm and will do a great deal of good. Even a tennis ball will teach you the right and wrong ways to use your head. The most important thing to remember is that you never head a ball with the top of your head; always with the front or the side. The other thing to remember is to keep your eye on the ball all the time, even when it is just striking your head. It is a great temptation, I know, to shut your eyes as the ball gets nearer. Force yourself to keep them open, or you will never be able to head a ball accurately—like "Dixie" Dean, the Everton and England centre-forward, can, for example.

That is as much about heading as I am going to bother you with now. Watch how the first-class players head a ball, and practise yourself with a light ball. But, for the time being, forget about heading so far as actual games are concerned, and see that your feet go in the right places.

THE MAGNET LIBRARY.—No. 1,562.

else has—and even if he had, smoking is a silly trick, but not exactly a crime. Smithy smokes, and we're all friendly enough with Smithy. Don't be an ass, Bob!"

"He knows those Highcliffe cads, Pon & Co.——"

"So do we, if you come to that! Anyhow, he's only met Pon in the holidays. St. Olaf's is a couple of hundred miles from Highcliffe, so——" Harry Wharton shook his head again. "Look here, Bob, the chap's keen on football, and plays a jolly good game. That doesn't sound like a smoky ass and a bad hat."

"Smithy's as good a footballer as any man in the Remove, and he's a smoky ass and a bad hat!" growled Bob.

Harry Wharton laughed.

"Well, if he's no worse than the old Bounder we can stand him," he said. "We're not sitting on the bench to judge fellows. Anyhow, what he does is no bizney of yours or mine."

"I know that. It's about Bunter that I'm worried. I'm not even sure that Bunter's his game, but it looks like it. It might be only dislike that makes him rough on the fat chump. I've told you that because I want to know what you think. Well, what do you think?"

"I think it all sounds jolly steep, and that you may have got a wrong impression from what you heard that day at Lantham," answered Wharton frankly. "Still, in the circumstances, we might keep an eye on him and Bunter."

"Yes, that's all I've been able to come to!" grunted Bob.

"If the chap came a mucker at his last school, and is trying to make good at Greyfriars, it's to his credit," added Wharton. "He has a right to try to get his uncle's good opinion back, if he can—in fact, it's his duty. If he's trying to blacken Bunter, though, that's a dirty game, and we'll jolly soon put a stop to it. But I've seen no sign about him of what Inky would call badhatfulness."

Bob Cherry burst into a laugh.

"Look——" he said.

"What——"

"Oh, just look!"

Bob pointed down the winding lane.

The two chums were there, to see if Ponsonby came along to the gate of the Three Fishers. From the direction of the Courtfield road Ponsonby came up the lane, and stopped at that gate. But he did not come alone. Another fellow was walking by his side. That fellow was Arthur Carter, the new junior in the Greyfriars Remove.

THE EIGHTH CHAPTER.

Punches for Pon !

HARRY WHARTON stared. Bob Cherry broke into a rapid sprint.

Ponsonby had put his hand on the gate to open it, and it was plain that his Greyfriars friend was going to follow him in.

But the gate had only started to open, when Bob arrived, with a rush.

Pon, glancing round, received a shove on the chest, which sent him staggering back into the middle of the lane, where he sat down.

Carter stared at Bob, a flush coming into his face. Bob gave him no notice. He faced Ponsonby, standing between the Highcliffe fellow and the gate. He was giving Pon no chance to dodge into the grounds of the Three Fishers, where he could not have been followed.

Harry Wharton was on the spot by the time the dandy of Highcliffe had scrambled to his feet.

"You—you hooligan!" panted Pon. "What——"

"I've got you, this time!" said Bob, grimly. "Keep away from that gate, Ponsonby—banker and billiards can wait a bit!"

"You rotten ruffian, stand aside!" said Ponsonby, his voice thick with rage.

"Look here——" began Carter.

Bob gave him a look.

"You can shut up!" he snapped. "Cut into that den if you like—nobody's stopping you! Pon's not going till I've licked him!"

"I'm not going in!" muttered Carter. "I walked as far as this with Pon! That's all! Look here, if you've got a row on with Pon, you can leave it till he's not in my company"

"It's not so easy to catch Pon!" answered Bob scornfully. "He got me at Lantham, with three other fellows to help him. Now he's on his own, and he's going to have what he's asked for!"

"It was only a lark, that day at Lantham!" muttered Ponsonby. "I suppose it did you no harm to lose your train."

"It did more harm than you fancy! You ragged me and tied me up—four of you! You'd be glad enough to rag again, if you had a Highcliffe crowd with you!" said Bob contemptuously. "Are you going to put up your hands, Ponsonby?"

"No!" said Pon between his teeth.

"Look here, Wharton, you ought to stop this, as captain of the Remove," exclaimed Carter. "I've not been long at Greyfriars, but I've heard that Quelch is down on this rowing with Highcliffe. You've got friends at that school, too! Keep that silly fathead quiet!"

"Pon shouldn't ask for it, if he doesn't want it!" answered Wharton. "I'm here to see him get what's coming to him."

"Well, I shall stop it, if you won't!" snapped Carter. "Keep your paws to yourself, Cherry, or you'll have me to deal with, as well as Pon."

"Back me up," muttered Ponsonby.

"I certainly shall!"

"You won't!" said Harry Wharton. "I don't want any trouble with you, Carter, as you're in my study at Greyfriars, but if you chip in here, you'll have a scrap on your hands! Pile in, Bob!"

Bob Cherry, heedless of Carter, was already advancing on Ponsonby, his hands up, and his eyes gleaming over them.

Pon cast a hunted look at the Three Fishers gate; but he was barred off from it, and he backed away to the opposite side of the lane.

Carter made a forward step, and Harry Wharton immediately stepped into his way.

Carter had to stop.

"Keep clear," said Harry quietly. "It's man to man—and it was four to one when those cads tackled Bob at Lantham. You'll have to wait for Pon to join you in that den."

"I've said that I wasn't going in!" muttered Carter.

"Well, I hope it's true!" said Harry dryly. "Anyhow, Pon's going to be busy now—and you're not going to interfere."

Carter stood undecided. He was intensely irritated and angry, and keen to go to his Highcliffe pal's aid. But it was clear that he could render Pon no help; a fight with Wharton would not help Pon. And the captain of the Remove stood ready for him.

Meanwhile Pon, very unwillingly, was getting busy. A tap on his lofty nose

decided him to put up his hands, and as there was no escape for him, the dandy of Highcliffe threw himself into the fray with all the courage he could muster.

Wharton and Carter looked on.

For two or three minutes there was a wild and whirling combat in the lane. Twice Bob staggered under hefty blows—and twice Pon went down in the mud, with deplorable results to his elegant clobber.

When he went down for the third time, he stayed down, gasping.

"I give in!" he panted.

"You don't!" answered Bob coolly. "You're going on till you're licked, you rotten funk. Get up!"

"I—I can't!"

"Then I'll roll you into that ditch!"

Pon, evidently, could get up—for he jumped up like a jack-in-the-box at that.

Hammer and tongs they went again—Pon backing, and dodging, giving all the ground he could, and cunningly circling round, to get nearer and nearer to the gate in the fence.

Suddenly he made a fierce attack, pressing Bob so hard that the Greyfriars junior had to give a foot or two. Then, as Bob rallied, Pon spun round, ran for the gate, put his hands on the top bar, and vaulted over.

He was gone almost like a lightning flash.

Bob, red with wrath, made a fierce rush after him.

Pon dropped on the inner side of the gate, and cut off at a breathless run towards the red-tiled building that showed at a distance through the leafless trees.

"Hold on!" shouted Harry, as Bob put his hands on the gate, with the intention of leaping over after Ponsonby. In his excitement, Bob rather forgot that the Three Fishers was strictly out of bounds.

Harry Wharton ran to him, and caught him by the arm.

"You can't go in there, Bob!" he exclaimed.

"That cur's not getting away!" roared Bob. "I mayn't see him again this term—think he'll give me another chance if he can help it? I'm going to thrash him——"

"You've given him a good allowance, old chap——"

"Rot! I'd hardly started——"

"Look here, you're not going over that gate, so chuck it!" said Harry. "If you got spotted, it wouldn't be much use telling the Head you only went in for a row with a Highcliffe cad! Stop, I tell you!"

Bob Cherry grunted angrily, but he listened to reason. He turned away from the gate, and dabbed his nose, where one of Pon's knocks had landed.

"After all, he had a few!" he muttered.

"More than a few!" said Harry, laughing. "You can call it a day, Bob, so far as Ponsonby is concerned. Come and bathe your nose in the pond—and let's get after the other fellows."

"Oh, all right."

Harry Wharton glanced at Carter.

"You've said that you were not going into the den with Ponsonby, Carter," he said. "What are you waiting for?"

"I suppose I can wait here if I like!" yapped Carter.

"Oh, certainly; but as you're new to Greyfriars, I'd better tell you that a chap spotted at the Three Fishers is booked for a flogging, and might be sacked. And the beaks and prefects at Greyfriars are not so slack as at Highcliffe—Pon may be safe, but you wouldn't be."

"I give in!" panted Ponsonby, as he went down in the mud, with deplorable results to his elegant clobber. "You don't!" answered Bob Cherry coolly. "You're going on till you're licked, you rotten funk! Get up!"

"Thank you for nothing!" sneered Carter.

"Oh, come on!" snapped Bob. "The fellow's only waiting for us to turn our backs before he follows Ponsonby in."

"I'm waiting for Pon to come out," said Carter. "He's only gone in to speak to a man for a few minutes, I—I think."

"Oh! In that case, I'll wait, too!" said Bob sarcastically.

"He's not likely to come out while you're hanging about."

"No—nor for a couple of hours, anyhow. Come on, Wharton, you don't want to see Carter going in, I suppose?" growled Bob. "He's a bit more careful than Smithy—he doesn't want any Greyfriars man to spot him."

Carter gave Bob a bitter, and at the same time, curious look.

"You seem to have made up your mind that I'm a bad hat!" he remarked. "Any special reason?"

"I know you're a bad hat!" retorted Bob. "You wouldn't pal with that Highcliffe blackguard if you weren't."

"I've seen you very friendly with Vernon-Smith, and I've heard that he carries on exactly as Pon is doing! Are you a bad hat?" asked Carter.

Harry Wharton smiled, and caught Bob's arm.

"Come on!" he said.

They tramped away up the lane, heading for the wayside pond, for Bob to bathe his nose—which rather needed it. The pond was past a winding turn of the lane, and when they reached it the Three Fishers gate and Carter were out of sight behind.

"Bet you that cad's over the gate before this!" grunted Bob, as he dipped his handkerchief into the water.

Wharton made no reply. He did not feel sure, in his own mind, about Carter, and it was useless to argue the point. But he wondered.

Bob's damaged nose having been bathed, they walked on to the Sark, and joined the other members of the Co. on the towpath.

Whether Arthur Carter had followed Pon into the Three Fishers, as soon as their backs were turned, Harry Wharton did not know—and he was willing to give the new junior the benefit of the doubt. But there was no doubt in Bob's mind.

THE NINTH CHAPTER.
Quelch Comes Down Heavy!

"LEGGO!" roared Billy Bunter.

"Ye thafe of the worruld!" roared Micky Desmond.

"Beast!" howled Bunter. "Will you leggo?"

Billy Bunter had remained in a disappeared state for most of the afternoon. But towards tea-time it was impossible for Bunter to continue disappeared. He was very keen to miss Micky—but missing a meal was not to be thought of.

He hoped that Micky had got over the hack on his shin by that time. He hoped, also, that Micky had done those lines. Anyhow, he had to risk it, or miss his tea—which was unthinkable.

But it was rather a certainty than a risk, as he found when he rolled into the Remove passage. Micky Desmond pounced on him, before he even saw that the Irish junior was in the passage at all.

Micky had recovered, more or less, from the hack. But he had not done the lines. He had made up his mind that he was not going to do them. It was up to Bunter—and in that all the Remove fellows agreed with Micky. Even Bob, who believed that the lines had been "planted" on Bunter the day before, considered that it was up to the fat Owl to do half. Everybody else

considered that it was up to him to do the lot.

With, of course, the exception of Bunter himself. Bunter never considered that it was up to him to do anything involving exertion.

A dozen fellows in the Remove passage looked on, grinning, as the hapless fat Owl was collared. He wriggled and shook like a fat jelly in Micky's grasp.

"Now, ye podgy omadhaun," hissed Micky, "are you going to do the lines? They've got to be handed in by tay-time."

"No!" roared Bunter. "I say, Smithy, make him leggo!"

"I'll watch it!" grinned the Bounder.

"I say, Hazel, old chap——"

"Fathead!"

"Bolsover—I say, Bolsover, old chap——"

"If you 'old chap' me, I'll boot you!" said Bolsover major. "You pinched Desmond's lines, you fat burglar——"

"I didn't!" wailed Bunter. "Desmond, you beast, leggo! I've got to see Mauly—I'm going to tea with Mauly—— Yaroooop!"

Billy Bunter roared and howled as Micky yanked him along the passage to the tap and sink at the end, and put his fat head under the tap.

"Yow-ow-ow! If you turn that tap on me," shrieked Bunter, "I—I'll—I'll—— Gurrrrrggh!"

Holding Bunter's head under the tap with his right hand, Micky turned on the tap with his left!

Splash!

Billy Bunter gave a suffocated roar as the water streamed over his head. He struggled frantically.

"Now, you fat baste——" gasped Micky.

"Gurrrrggh!" gurgled Bunter.

"Ha, ha, ha!"

(*Continued on page* 16.)

A FISHY AFFAIR!

Spasm No. 2. of—
"*THE FORM-MASTER'S SECRET!*"
—a Sensational Serial, featuring Jack Jolly & Co., the Cheery Chums of St. Sam's.

By DICKY NUGENT

"Goodness grashus!" Doctor Birchemall made that remark.

The Head of St. Sam's was on his way to take the Sixth, and he had just caught site of Mr. Lickham.

It was a bright and frosty morning, and the Head was feeling full of life; but as soon as he saw Mr. Lickham he stopped dead.

"Goodness grashus!" he repected.

He could hardly beleeve his eyes!

The master of the Fourth was a most neat and tidy person, as a rule. But not on this occasion. For some reason which the Head did not understand, Mr. Lickham was now dressed without the slitest regard for his appearance. His shirt was dirty and he had no collar on his neck. His mortar-board was stuck on his head at a rakish angle. He had a day's growth of beard on his chin.

But what took the Head's eye most of all was a bundle which he carried on his sholder at the end of a stick. It was tied up in a red spotted handkercheef and it gave the last touch of untidyness to the appearance of the master of the Fourth.

"Lickham!" gasped the Head, in horrified axxents. "Lickham! My dear sir!"

"Wotcher, old covey!"

Doctor Birchemall jumped.

"What! What did you say, Lickham?" he gasped.

"Wotcher, old covey!" grinned Mr. Lickham. "'Ow's the gime?"

Doctor Birchemall gazed at the master of the Fourth in sheer amazement.

"What in the name of hevven is the matter, Lickham?" he cried. "Your appearance! Your axxent! What has happened to you?"

"Nothink's 'appened to me, old covey!" chuckled Mr. Lickham. "I'm as right as ninepence! Yuss! Comin' along of me as fur as my class-room?"

The Head nodded dumbly. He had to pass the Fourth Form Room to get to the Sixth, anyway, and it did not occur to him that he was serving a very useful purpuss to the Fourth Form master by showing him where his Form-room was.

Naturally, the Head did not dreem for a moment that the man

he took to be Mr. I. Jolliwell Lickham was, in aktual fakt, "Dusty" Lickham, the cuzzin of the real Fourth Form master and a member of the tramp class. "Dusty" Lickham was the living image of his cuzzin, and even the braniest fellow mite have been eggscused for failing to tell them apart; so, of corse, the Head stood no earthly chance of spotting the frawd!

"Here's your Form-room, Lickham!" he said brethlessly, when they reached the Form-room. "Before you go in, mite I ask you one or two questions? First, why are you speaking in

such a low, common voice?"

Dusty Lickham looked serprized.

"My voice hain't low an' common, old covey!" he said. "My mates allus say 'ow posh I speaks!"

"D-d-dear me! But your dress!" gasped the Head. "Why ain't you —I mean, why aren't you wearing a collar?"

"'Cause I 'ates collars—they stops me breethin' proper!"

"Good hevvens! But the bundle, Lickham— the bundle on your sholder! What is in it?"

"Fish for me breakfast!" replied Dusty Lickham. "Which I hain't 'ad time to 'ave me breakfast yet. So 'ere it is! See yet later, old covey!"

With these words, the bogus Form-master walked into the Fourth Form Room — leaving Doctor Birchemall to stagger on to the Sixth Form Room hardly knowing whether he was on his head or his heels!

The Fourth all rose to their feet respectively, when Dusty Lickham strolled in. They blinked when they saw how he was dressed and what he was carrying.

"Good-morning, sir," they mannidged to say.

"'Ow do, yung masters!"

The Fourth gasped.

"Eggscuse me, sir," said Jack Jolly feintly. "Did you say ''Ow do, yung masters?!"

"Yuss!"

"My hat!"

The Fourth farely flopped into their seats! These amazing words from the lips of a man

they had always known to be very partickular about his grammar and pronunciation simply nocked them all of a heap.

"Wot's the lesson?" asked the false Form master, cheerfully. "Is it readin', writin' or arithmetick? Wotever it is, I'm 'ot at it, you bet! Yuss!"

"G-g-grate pip!"

"As a matter of fakt, sir, it's Latin," grinned Jack Jolly. "But please yourself, of corse!"

"Wotto! I'll do that orlright, yung covey!" chuckled the freekish beak. "I'll make it arithmetick, see? Wot's two an' six?"

"Eight, sir!"

"Wrong!" larfed Dusty Lickham. "Two-an'-six is 'arf-a-crown! Get me?"

"Ha, ha, ha!"

The Fourth simply could not understand what had happened to their Form-master. But whatever it was, they found him in his present mood a distinkt improvement on the stern tirant who usually held the rains of offis in the Fourth Form Room.

Dusty Lickham deposited his bundle on his desk.

"Well, yung coveys, that's enuff of arithmetick!" he said. "The next thing as fur as I'm conserned is breakfast. 'Cause why? 'Cause I hain't 'ad none!"

"Ha, ha, ha!"

The Fourth larfed again. Then they gasped.

To their utter amazement, Dusty Lickham had unwrapped his bundle and brought to light a large collection of fresh herrings!

"Haw, haw, haw!" he chuckled, gloatingly, as he spread them out on his desk. "They ain't 'arf prime, ain't they? They make me fare smack my lips to look at 'em!"

"Beg pardon, sir, but are you going to eat them raw?" asked Frank Fearless.

"Not me, yung master!" grinned Dusty Lickham. "I'm a-goin' to cook 'em

---

HARRY WHARTON CALLING!

Br-r-r-r-r!

That's how we feel at Greyfriars at the time of going to press!

The temperature is something below zero and the School House system of central heating, such as it is, has ceased to function owing to a burst pipe.

For heat we're relying entirely on coal fires, and though coal fires are all very fine and large when you're near them, they cut no ice when you're not! And believe me, chums, there are a good many cold spots in the School House just now!

You might think that our recreations under these circumstances are confined to roasting chestnuts and playing chess. But, strange as it may

seem, most of us are spending as much time out of doors at present as we normally do in the summer term.

Footer is off owing to the frozen state of the playing fields. But we're putting in plenty of practice at cross-country running in readiness for the Open Cross-country Handicap which takes place later in the term. And when we're not running, we're skating!

The skating has been topping since we returned to school, and it doesn't stop when darkness sets in, either. On the contrary, it's then that the fun really begins, for while the frost lasts they are having the broad stretch of water on

the other side of Courtfield Common lit up by fairy lamps.

The Head has been a real sport. Knowing how few and far between are our chances of skating, he has been giving us late leave to go skating every evening. Miss Primrose having granted the same concession to the Cliff House girls, we've been meeting Marjorie & Co. on the ice and altogether we've been having a ripping time.

But all good things must come to an end. The English climate being what it is, I dare say that by the time I come to pen next week's chat, we shall be sweltering in a minor heat wave. Here's to our next merry meeting, chums, anyway—whatever the weather.

HARRY WHARTON.

HERALD

ARTON. January 22nd, 1938.

'ere fire!

help, sir?"
"We'll
or you, if
e can use
s for toast-

good idea,
" said the
rm-master.
s 'ere cane
he rest of
your pen-
wants to

a rush.
likely to
on sitting
lesk while
chance of
in front
room fire;
y felt that
ngs was a
etter than
lay.
could say
lf-a-duzzen
neeling in
re, holding
on the end
lders. The
m crowded
while Dusty

Lickham took up a place of honner in the centre, and toasted a large herring on the end of Mr. Lickham's cane with an eggspert hand.

Very soon the oader of frying herrings filled the Form-room. It was not long before it penny-trated other Form-rooms.

Just when the herrings were sizzling nicely, the door bust open. The Head looked in, his nose twitching and a look of sheer disbeleef on his skollerly dial.

"*Fish!*" he shreeked. "Bless my sole!"

"It ain't sole, old covey!" chortled Dusty Lickham, cheerfully. "It's herrin'!"

"Ha, ha, ha!"

Doctor Birchemall's eyes rolled feercely in their sockits. He seemed on the verge of an apolojettick fit.

"Cooking fish in the Form-room!" he gasped. "Why, it's simply unherd-of! What has happened to your branes?"

"They kep' them at the fish shop," grinned Dusty Lickham. "But I've got some nice soft roes!"

"Ha, ha, ha!"

"Why not 'ave a taster while you're 'ere?" went on the bogus Form-master. "Try this one, old covey! It looks a good 'un!"

So saying, he turned to the gaping Head, and rammed a large herring into his open mouth. Doctor Birchemall collapsed on the floor.

"Groooo! Yuroooo! Gug-gug-groooo!" he shreeked.

"My heye! The old covey don't seem to like it!" remarked Dusty Lickham, in serprize. "'Ere! Lemme get it hout for yer!"

He got it out with one terrifick wrench. A moment later, the Head was on his feet and making for the door at top speed.

Doctor Birchemall had had enuff of the supposed Mr. Lickham for one morning. And before long, Dusty Lickham was to lern that he had had enuff of him altogether!

(*What will happen when Dusty Lickham gets marching orders? For the answer, see next week's rib-tickling instalment!*)

HIS "CANDIED" OPINION!

Desmond has received a birthday cake from his native Ireland from which raisins have accidentally been omitted. In expressing his feelings about it in a rich Irish brogue, he is understood to have said that the gift was most un-"raisin"-able!

Fisher T. Fish, walking in the quad, found a shilling, another shilling, and yet another shilling. His beaming smile lasted till he discovered the hole in his trousers pocket!

MY FORM IS THE BEST AT GREYFRIARS!

Says P. P. PROUT, M.A.

Every Form in a school reflects the personality of the Form-master.

If the master is weak and slack, the Form will be weak and slack, too. If the master is strong and efficient, the Form will surely be the same.

It is for this reason that I claim, without fear of contradiction, that the Fifth Form—my Form—is the best Form at Greyfriars.

The logic of it is unanswerable. I am, without doubt, the best Form-master. Ergo—which, for the benefit of the more ignorant of my young readers, means "therefore"—my Form is the best Form!

If I were asked why it is that I am such an excellent Form-master, I should be inclined to say that it is my wide and varied experience of the world that has given me such an advantage over my less successful colleagues.

Unlike those gentlemen who have been content to spend all their time in the sheltered seclusion of a school, I have journeyed abroad and seen strange lands and strange customs with my own eyes.

The result is reflected in my pupils. See their eyes flash when I tell them stories of my big-game-hunting exploits! Why, I have known them follow my yarns with such concentration that the effort has caused them to fall asleep from sheer exhaustion!

When I think of Blundell, Bland, Fitzgerald, Potter, Greene, and others, I feel proud of my lads—but not half so proud, I am sure, as they feel of me! As for Coker, he is the exception that proves the rule—the rule that the Fifth is the best Form at Greyfriars!

IS THIS WHAT HE MEANT?

Coker tried out a second-hand car from a Courtfield garage last week and drove it straight into the river. It was well lined with wetness when hauled out again—which makes us suspect that Coker did it on purpose.

He has always maintained he'll never be satisfied with a car unless it's "stream"-lined.

S A JAPER—NOT A USIC-MAKER!

es CLAUDE HOSKINS

t!
my mind to do it, and
I've played an instru-
hnny Bull's so-called
s I promised myself I

ll may boast that he
t before the rehearsal.
will. Bull is a japer—
maker! It's just the
he would boast about!
mains that I played in
band without his know-
moral victory rests with

sk what possible motive
for wishing to play
motley crew of music-
isten to explain my

s Bull's band may be,
hat one musician of
ting an example to the
uide them in the right
his was my reason for
and, and I still stand

to you "Greyfriars
ers to judge whether I
thing or not in going
I did over it. I had
mfortable time I can

Knowing well that the one thing Bull could not stand in the band was the presence of one single musician of note, I went to young Wibley, swore him to secrecy, and asked him to disguise me.

Wibley, as you know, is really hot stuff at make-up. After I had told him I wanted to be disguised as any Remove chap who was not a member of Bull's band, Wibley walked round me and sized me up from all angles. Then he snapped his fingers and nodded.

"You'll make a perfect Tom Brown," he said. "By the time I've finished with you, Browny's own mother won't know you from her son!"

The kid was as good as his word, too. When I walked out of his study nobody would have taken me to be anybody but young Brown of the Remove.

My plans were well laid. I went along to my study and fetched the big French horn which I have recently been learning. Then I marched boldly down to the Rag, where Johnny Bull's band was just beginning a rehearsal.

Bull simply beamed at me when I marched in with my French horn slung over my shoulder.

"Good old Browny!" he yelled. "That's just the thing we needed to give us a bit of background! Sit down and get busy, old bean!"

I couldn't very well speak, or my voice would have given me away, so I tootled on the French horn instead. Everybody seemed to think this awfully funny, though what there is funny in a couple of notes on the French horn I entirely fail to see.

Well, I sat down and, as Bull vulgarly put it, "got busy."

The difference that my French horn made to that band had to be heard to be believed! I gave them tone and verve and all sorts of things. But, of course, the ignorant kids took it all the wrong way. They seemed quite resentful because I drowned their hideous din!

Even so, I think things would have gone well if Brown himself had not arrived. Unfortunately, he did arrive! Although up to this time he had not belonged to the band, it seemed that he played the concertina and had chosen this particular day to join up!

The young ass walked in with his concertina and the rest of the band stopped playing.

I didn't know that. I was too immersed in my music to notice it.

In fact, the first thing I knew about it was when I paused for a breath and had the strange and unpleasant experience of receiving a discharge of blue-black liquid against my lips from the mouthpiece of the French horn.

I dropped the instrument and leaped to my feet with a wild shriek. Only then did I realise that my secret was a secret no longer and that Bull had avenged himself on me by filling a water-pistol with ink and squirting it into the French horn!

I know that the sympathy of all musical readers will go out to me in this inglorious end to my bold attempt to create a real band out of Johnny Bull's noise-makers.

I intend to be worthy of your sympathy, dear readers—by trying yet again to put Bull's band on the right road to musical success! You wait and see!

BUNTER the BRAGGER!
By FRANK RICHARDS

(Continued from page 13.)

"Are you going to do the lines intoirely?" roared Micky.

"Hoooooogh!"

"Bunter's getting a wash," grinned Skinner. "Your first this term, old fat man! It will do you good!"

"He's changing already!" remarked Hazel.

"Gurrggh! Oooooooch! Woo-hoooch!" gurgled the hapless fat Owl. "I say, you fellows—— Goooooooooooooogh!"

"Sure, I'll hould yez here till yo say yis!" bawled Micky Desmond. "Will ye do the lines, ye fat spalpeen?"

"Grooooooogh!"

"Ha, ha, ha!"

"Cave!" called out Kipps of the Remove, from lower down the passage. "'Ware beaks!"

Bunter's frantic yells had been heard. Up from the stairs came Mr. Quelch, with rustling gown and frowning brow. He gave a thunderous glare up the passage towards the crowd at the end.

"Will ye do the lines for me?" roared Micky Desmond. "Sure I'll dhrown yez if ye don't, intoirely."

"Shut up!" breathed Smithy. "Here comes Quelchy, you ass!"

"Grooogh! I say, you fellows—— Oooogh!"

"Desmond!" came in a voice of thunder. "Release Bunter this instant! How dare you!"

"Oh, howly mother av Moses!" gasped Micky in dismay, and he let go Bunter as if the fat Owl had suddenly become red-hot to the touch.

"Oooooooogh!" gasped Bunter.

He sat down with a bump when he was released, streaming with water, and gasping and gurgling for breath.

Micky spun round to his Form-master, his face the picture of dismay. In his fixed belief that Bunter had deliberately "snooped" his impot for the day before, he had been deeply exasperated; but he realised that he had handled the fat Owl in rather a drastic manner, all the same.

"This is absolutely outrageous!" exclaimed Mr. Quelch. "I have never heard of such a thing! I heard what you said, Desmond—and I am very glad that I heard it! I shall take very severe measures to see that nothing of this kind recurs in my Form."

"I—I—I——" stammered Micky.

"You were drenching Bunter with water, to force him to write your imposition for you!" thundered Mr. Quelch. "I heard you, Desmond!"

"Yis, sorr, but—but——"

"I should cane you severely merely for asking another boy to write your lines, if it came to my knowledge! But you have actually bullied Bunter to compel him to do so!"

"Oh, no, sorr! You—you see——"

"I have the evidence of my eyes and my ears, Desmond! I do not think I have ever heard of anything so utterly outrageous!"

Micky stood blinking at him.

The rest of the Removites were silent. Few, if any, would have blamed

Micky if he had blurted out the whole story. But he said nothing. Whatever came of it, he was not going to "snake."

But Mr. Quelch's expression was really terrifying. He had, as he supposed, come upon a particularly obnoxious case of bullying. Certainly it looked like it —a fellow holding another fellow's head under the tap till the victim agreed to do his lines for him!

"Bunter! Go to the dormitory and dry yourself at once!" said Mr. Quelch. "Desmond, follow me to my study!"

"I nivir mint——" stammered the unfortunate Micky.

"I know what I have seen and heard, Desmond! You need say nothing! I will make it very clear to all that bullying is not permitted in my Form!"

"Sure I wasn't bullying!" gasped Micky. "You ask any of these fellows, sorr, whither they've iver seen me bullying——"

"Desmond wasn't to blame, sir!" said Vernon-Smith. "He could explain——"

"Have you anything to say, Desmond?"

Micky hesitated a moment. The Bounder's intervention gave him a chance and he was strongly tempted to tell the story of the "snooped" impot. But he hesitated only a moment.

"No, sorr, only that I wasn't bullying," he said. "Sure, I wouldn't touch the baste with me little finger if he hadn't asked for that same."

"You will take a hundred lines, Vernon-Smith, for your impertinent remark. Bunter, go to the dormitory at once. Desmond, follow me."

Billy Bunter, drenched and dripping, tottered away to the dormitory staircase.

Micky followed his Form-master down the lower stairs.

In his study, Mr. Quelch, with a grim brow, selected a stout cane.

Micky breathed hard through his nose.

"You have not written your lines, Desmond?" rapped the Remove master.

"No, sorr——"

"You were relying, no doubt, on coercing Bunter into writing them!" exclaimed Mr. Quelch. "I have never heard of such a thing. I shall cane you with the utmost severity! Bend over that chair!"

It was a harrowing scene that followed —for Micky!

Mr. Quelch felt it his duty to be severe; and he did his duty to the full! There were only six swipes—but every one of them rang like a pistol shot—and louder still rang the recipient's anguished yells.

"Now," said Mr. Quelch, laying down the cane.

"Ow! Ooogh! Howly Moses! Wow!" groaned the wriggling Micky.

"Be silent! You will be detained on Saturday afternoon, Desmond, and you will take five hundred lines, in addition to your caning."

"Howly smoke!" gasped Micky.

"In the event of any further bullying coming to my notice, I shall report you to your headmaster!" said Mr. Quelch sternly.

"I nivir bullied Bunter——"

"Silence! Leave my study!" rapped Mr. Quelch. "Another word, and I shall cane you again!"

"I don't care!" howled the exasperated Micky, reckless between anguish and indignation. "I nivir did bully anybody, and so I nivir did, and——"

"Upon my word!"

Mr. Quelch grasped the cane again. Three hefty swipes landed on Micky's shoulders before he escaped from the study.

In the Remove passage he was received with sympathy. But sympathy was not of much use to the suffering Micky.

"The baste!" he said. "The baste! Whipping a man for bullying, and I niver did—sure, I niver did intoirely! I'll make the baste sit up for it! Ow! Yow! Wow! Sure I shan't be able to sit down for a wake! Wow! Wow!"

And for a long, long time sounds of woe and tribulation were heard from Micky's study.

THE TENTH CHAPTER.

Bunter Puts Both Feet In It!

"I SAY, you fellows!"

"Turn out, you fat slacker!"

"I can't! I'm ill!"

The rising-bell rang in the dewy morn.

The Greyfriars Remove turned out to the familiar, unwelcome clang—with the exception of Billy Bunter. Bunter lifted a fat head from a pillow, and blinked at the other fellows.

"I'm ill!" he repeated firmly. "I caught a cold yesterday when that beast Desmond held my head under the tap——"

"That the latest?" asked Carter.

"You can shut up, Carter! I'm not speaking to you! No need for you to butt in!" snapped Bunter. "I say, Wharton, you tell Quelch I've caught a bad cold——"

"And all for ten minutes extra in bed!" said Skinner. "Think Quelch will swallow it, you fat ass?"

"I've said I'm ill!" answered Bunter, with dignity. "I was drenched with water—soaked all over! It stands to reason I've caught a cold! I'm not exactly coughing or sneezing—it's internal, see? I feel absolutely unable to get out of bed."

"Shall I help you?" asked Bob Cherry.

"No, you beast!" roared Bunter. "Can't you take a fellow's word that he's ill? I've been feeling ill all night! I haven't just thought of it because I want to stay in bed——"

"Ha, ha, ha!"

"Oh, cackle!" said Bunter. "Cackle while a fellow's lying——"

"Well, your lying is enough to make a cat laugh!" said Skinner.

"While a fellow's lying ill, I mean!" hooted Bunter. "I've got a temperament!"

"A which?" gasped Bob.

"A very serious temperament——"

"Oh, my hat! Do you mean a temperature?"

"Is it temperature? Well, whichever it is, I've got it—bad! It may turn to measles or—or plumbago, for all I know! I simply dare not put a foot out of bed! Tell Quelch, when you go down, Wharton, old chap!"

"You howling ass!" said Harry. "If you make Quelch believe you've got a cold, you'll be hiked off to sanny."

"It's not so bad as that," said Bunter hastily. "I—I may feel better shortly. At the present moment it's simply awful! Tell Quelch I'm suffering fearful agonies, will you, old fellow? That may touch his heart, you know."

There was a chuckle along the Remove dormitory. Billy Bunter's excuses for getting a few extra minutes in bed were many and various. This, nobody doubted, was one more of them.

Still, it was possible that Bunter had caught a cold, for that drenching under the Remove tap on Wednesday afternoon had been very thorough. The bare possibility saved him from having his bedclothes hooked off him.

If he claimed to be ill, he had a right to take the risk of disregarding rising-bell; it was his own affair! But if he were spoofing, nobody envied him his interview with Quelch.

Bunter laid his fat head on the pillow again. He was prepared to recover by the time the breakfast-bell rang. But this, he considered, was good for nearly an extra half-hour in bed. The fact that he hadn't a cold did not bother Bunter in the least. Truth and he were strangers.

He grinned on his pillow when the Removites had gone down. Now that all those noisy fellows were gone, there was a chance for a fellow to get another forty winks. That drenching under the Remove tap had been fearfully uncomfortable at the time; but the fat Owl was rather glad of it now. It was coming in useful.

Bunter's eyes closed and his mouth opened. He was about to glide off into happy slumber, when there was a footstep in the Remove dormitory.

The fat Owl's eyes closed and his mouth opened. He did not lift his head from the pillow, but he yapped out irritably:

"Aren't you all gone yet? How long are you going to hang about keeping a fellow awake? I say is that you, Wharton? Look here, you go and tell old Quelch I'm ill—why, if he isn't told, the old ass may come up here to see why I haven't gone down——"

"BUNTER!"

"Oh crikey!" gasped Bunter.

All desire for slumber vanished at the sound of his Form-master's voice. Bunter fairly bounded.

"Oh lor'!" he stuttered.

He fixed his terrified eyes on Mr. Quelch. It was not one of the Remove fellows who had not gone down—it was the Remove master who had come up! Bunter blinked at him in as much horror as if he had been the grisly ghost of a Form-master.

Mr. Quelch advanced towards the hapless Owl's bed. His gimlet eyes almost bored into Bunter.

"Bunter, as you did not come down with the rest of the Form, I came up to ascertain why. What expression did I hear you apply to me, Bunter?"

"Oh crumbs! I—I—I never called you an ass, sir!" gasped Bunter, in terror.

"I heard you!" thundered Mr. Quelch.

"Oh, no, sir! I—I was speaking of another old ass, sir!" gasped Bunter.

"Bunter!"

"I—I—I was, really, sir! You—you ain't the only old ass at Greyfriars, sir," babbled the fat Owl.

Mr. Quelch gasped.

"Get out of bed at once, Bunter!"

"Oh, yes, certainly, sir!" gasped Bunter, and he rolled out.

He quite forgot to be ill! Quelch's look did not encourage illness, at the moment!

"Now bend over that bed, Bunter!"

"Oh lor'!"

Mr. Quelch had brought his cane up to the dormitory with him; doubtless guessing that it might be needed! He swished it in the air as the hapless fat Owl bent over the bed.

Whack!

Pyjamas were a very poor protection against a cane. Billy Bunter's wild yell woke all the echoes of the dormitory.

Whack, whack, whack!

"Now, Bunter——"

"Yarooh! Oh crikey! Yarooop!" roared Bunter. "Oh dear! Ow!"

"If you are not down in five minutes, Bunter, I shall come up again!" said Mr. Quelch, in a voice resembling that of the Great Huge Bear.

And he tucked the cane under his arm and left the dormitory.

Billy Bunter was down under the five minutes. He was very anxious not to give his Form-master the trouble of coming up again!

He rolled out into the quad, wriggling.

"Hallo, hallo, hallo!" roared Bob Cherry. "Did you get away with it, old fat man?"

"Ow! The beast walloped me!" groaned Bunter. "Fancy a Form-master pitching into a chap when he's ill! That's how fellows are treated here!"

"Ha, ha, ha!"

"Blessed if I see anything to cackle at!" howled Bunter. "I've a jolly good mind to go to the Head about it! That beast Quelch——"

"Shut up, ass!" exclaimed Frank Nugent, as Mr. Quelch came out of the House, just behind Bunter.

"Shan't! The beast whopped me!" roared Bunter. "Whopped me for nothing! Think I'm going to be whopped for nothing? I came jolly near chucking a pillow at his head, I can tell you! I'd a jolly good mind to stick in the dorm, and chuck a pillow at his cheeky head when he came up again! I—— Leggo, you beast!" added Bunter, as a hand fell on his fat shoulder. "Is that you, Desmond, you rotter—— Oh crikey!"

Bunter's eyes popped through his spectacles at Mr. Quelch.

Early as it was, Bunter had done it twice that morning! Often and often did the fatuous fat Owl put his foot in it! Now he had, as it were, put both feet in it!

Mr. Quelch did not speak. But his face was eloquent as he led Billy Bunter back into the House.

A minute later, the sounds that echoed from Mr. Quelch's study might have touched a heart of stone.

THE ELEVENTH CHAPTER.

Getting Quelch!

WILLIAM WIBLEY took Micky Desmond by one arm, David Morgan took him by the other, and, between them, they walked him to his study—gently but firmly.

Micky had a large, heavy hassock in his hand—and the light of battle in his eye. They had grabbed him on the Remove landing after prep.

Umpteen times that day Micky had confided to his study-mates that he was going to make Quelch sorry for himself "entoirely"! Micky's wrath was transferred, it appeared, from Bunter to Quelch. The affair of the "snooped" impot had been washed out of his mind by that severe whopping in Quelch's study, from which he was still feeling twinges.

Worse than that, was detention on Saturday afternoon, with five hundred lines to write. Likewise, the imputation of bullying made Micky feel very sore—very sore indeed!

Bunter's delinquencies—or supposed delinquencies—had been washed out by that drenching under the Remove tap. Quelch's remained to be washed out—and until Micky recovered his usual good temper his friends were rather anxious about him.

As Mr. Quelch was standing below the staircase in conversation with Prout,

Wib and Morgan guessed what Micky was thinking of doing with that hassock. For which reason they grasped him and walked him off—Micky energetically protesting Heedless of protests, they walked him into the study and slammed him into an armchair.

"You howling ass!" said Wibley.

"Asking for the sack, look you!" said Morgan.

Micky glared at them—without a sign of gratitude for their friendly offices. Just at present what Micky wanted was vengeance.

"Ye cheeky, fatheaded spalpeens!" gasped Micky. "Sure, I'd have dhropped it right on his napper!"

"And what would happen afterwards?" inquired Wib.

"Sure, he'd be sorry for himself intoirely"

"You potty Celt!" said Wibley. "You balmy Hibernian! Lucky for you you've got friends to keep you from getting sacked!"

"If you think you're going to stop me——" hooted Micky.

"Sort of!" grinned Morgan. "You try to get out of this study till Quelch has cleared off, and we'll bung you on the floor and sit on your head!"

Micky glared wrath. In moments of excitement there was no doubt that Micky needed a restraining hand, and he was wildly excited now. Wibley and Morgan stood between him and the door, watchful.

"I tell you I'm going to get Quelch!" hissed Micky. "You thry to stop me, and, sure, I'll knock both of yez into the middle of nixt wake! You could no more stop me than you could stop the divil whin he was going through Athlone! Now get away from that dure!"

Micky jumped out of the armchair. "Collar him!" exclaimed Wibley.

Micky's friends closed in on him. Obviously he had to be kept in the study for his own good.

But Micky at the moment was quite blind to his own good. Making Quelch sorry for himself was the urgent business on hand, to his mind.

He gripped the hassock and swung it round his head.

William Wibley gave a howl as he caught it with his nose and went staggering across the study, to fall in the corner.

The next swipe landed on Morgan's ear, and he rolled over on the carpet with a roar.

Micky shot to the door.

In a moment or two his friends would have been up again and jumping at him—but a moment or two were enough for Micky.

He tore the door open and rushed out into the passage.

The Remove had gone down after prep, only three or four fellows remaining in the studies. Nobody was in the passage, or on the landing.

Micky Desmond shot down the passage to the landing.

By the time Wibley and Morgan were on their feet in the study Micky was shooting across the landing to the balustrade.

He looked down over it.

Quelch was still there, still in conversation with Mr. Prout.

Micky's eyes gleamed down at the top of his mortar-board.

He lifted the hassock over the balustrade, calculated carefully, and let it drop. Down it went like a plummet, landing fair and square on Mr. Quelch's mortar-board.

Plop !

Never had the Remove master been so surprised.

He staggered, tottered, gasped, and sat down with a bump.

Prout stared at him blankly.

Instantly Micky backed away from the balustrade. Micky was not much given to caution, but he realised that he needed to keep out of sight and remain undiscovered. The penalty for dropping a hassock on a Form-master's head was likely to be fearfully severe.

Grinning, he backed across the landing—as Wib and Morgan came cutting breathlessly out of the Remove passage.

He grinned at them as they came.

"Sure, I've done it!" he chuckled.

Loud exclamations from below told only too surely that Micky had "done it." Excitement reigned below.

"You mad ass!" gasped Wibley.

"You potty chump!" hissed Morgan. "Get away—quick! Quick!"

Up to that point Wibley and Morgan had been anxious to restrain their excited chum, but now that the deed was done their anxiety was to save him from the consequences.

They grasped him by the arms once more and rushed him away, but they did not return to the Remove studies. Obviously there would very soon be investigation in that quarter. They rushed Micky away by the Fifth Form passage and down a back staircase. In a very few moments all three of them were safely off the scene.

THE TWELFTH CHAPTER.

A Mystery !

"OOOOOH !" gasped Mr. Quelch.

"My dear Quelch——" stuttered Mr. Prout.

"Ooogh !"

"Goodness gracious ! What——"

"Something—something fell on—on my head, I—I think," gasped the Remove master dizzily.

Mr. Quelch sat in a dizzy state, gasping. A crowd gathered round at once. The Remove master's mortar-board had been knocked sideways, and now it slanted on his head at an intoxicated-looking angle. Beside him lay the hassock.

Quelch's first dizzy impression was that Greyfriars was collapsing on his head. Fortunately, it was not so bad as that.

"It was—was—was this !" exclaimed Prout, turning the hassock over with his foot. "Where, in the name of goodness, can this have fallen from ?"

"It must have dropped over the banisters, sir," said Wingate of the Sixth. He stared up.

"Extraordinary !" ejaculated Prout.

"It must have been done intentionally," said Mr. Hacker, the master of the Shell. "It cannot have been an accident."

"Pray let me help you, sir," said Loder of the Sixth officiously. He gave the Remove master a helping hand.

Mr. Quelch tottered to his feet.

He glanced at the hassock that had banged on his head. He put his mortar-board straight. His lips set in a tight line.

That hassock had been dropped on his head. Obviously it could not have got over the banisters on its own. Someone had done this—intentionally, as Hacker said. Quelch's face was almost pale with wrath. His gimlet-eyes glinted with a deadly glint.

"By gum !" came the voice of Coker

of the Fifth from the gathering crowd. "Some Remove kid larking with his beak ! By gum !"

"What silly ass——" murmured Bob Cherry.

The alarm had drawn a crowd of juniors from the Rag.

"Who's up in the studies ?" asked Carter.

"Oh crumbs ! Look !" breathed Harry Wharton.

Fifty pairs of eyes were turned upward—and all of them beheld a fat face adorned by a large pair of spectacles blinking over the balustrade of the Remove landing.

"Bunter !" breathed Nugent.

"That potty porpoise !"

"Bunter !" muttered Carter, his eyes gleaming.

"Rot !" said Bob Cherry. "Even Bunter wouldn't be ass enough to stay there if he'd done it !"

"Isn't he ass enough for anything ?" grinned the Bounder.

Mr. Quelch was already ascending the stairs. After him went a whole army of Greyfriars fellows.

If Bunter had done it he was certainly displaying uncommon nerve or uncommon obtuseness, for he did not go; he remained where he was, blinking down, apparently not in the least alarmed.

"I say, you fellows, what's up ?" he called out, as the crowd came swarming up to the landing.

"Bunter !" said Mr. Quelch in a voice that was not loud, but very, very deep. "Bunter, did you drop a hassock over the banisters ?"

Bunter blinked at him.

"Eh ? Oh, no, sir !"

"What are you doing here, Bunter ?"

"Eh ? Standing on the landing, sir," answered Bunter, puzzled.

There was a suppressed giggle among the crowd of fellows who had followed Quelch up. It was an awfully serious matter, but the fat Owl could always be relied upon to supply a little comic relief.

"Is that intended for impertinence, Bunter ?" roared Mr. Quelch. He was not in a mood to be patient with Bunter's obtuseness.

"Eh ? Oh, no, sir ! I—I haven't done anything," gasped Bunter in alarm. "I've been in my study, sir."

"Wingate ! Will you ascertain if any other Remove boys are in the studies ?"

"Yes, sir !"

The Greyfriars captain hurried up the Remove passage, to look into the studies. He found only two Remove fellows—Lord Mauleverer, yawning over unfinished prep in Study No. 12, and Fisher T. Fish counting his money in Study No. 14. He shepherded both of them along to the landing, where Billy Bunter was standing before his Form-master in a state of quaking alarm.

"These are all, Wingate ?"

"Yes, sir !"

"Have you been out of your study, Mauleverer, before Wingate came ?"

"No, sir !" answered Mauly, in wonder. "I haven't quite got through my prep yet, sir."

"And you, Fish ?"

"Nope !" answered Fish promptly.

Mr. Quelch glared at him.

"Answer me in English, Fish !" he rapped. "Yes or no !"

"Nope—I mean nunk—that is, nix—no, sir !" gasped Fish.

"I say, sir, I was in my study, too !" squeaked Bunter. "I never came out till I heard something going on. I came to see what it was. I never——"

Mr. Quelch fixed a penetrating glare on Bunter. Only that morning Bunter

had been whopped twice ! Only that morning Quelch had heard him declare that he had a "jolly good mind" to chuck a pillow at his Form-master's head ! And a hassock had actually been "chucked" at that majestic head !

"Someone," said Mr. Quelch, in a grinding voice, "dropped a hassock over the banisters, to fall on my head. You were here, Bunter."

"I—I wasn't, sir !" groaned Bunter. "I'd only just come. I shouldn't have waited for you if I'd done it, sir."

"Safe bet !" murmured Skinner.

"This morning," said Mr. Quelch, in the same grinding tone. "I heard you utter a threat, Bunter, which has now been carried out."

"Oh crikey ! I—I never meant it, sir !" groaned Bunter. "I—I wouldn't chuck a pillow at your head, sir ! Besides, it wasn't a pillow, sir, if it was a hassock."

"That is immaterial," said Mr. Quelch. "I suspect you very strongly, Bunter. Why did you remain in your study after preparation was over ?"

"I—I—I—I was mugging up Latin, sir ! I—I—I'm rather keen on it, sir, as—as you may have noticed."

"That statement is untruthful, Bunter. If you cannot tell the truth, I can only conclude——"

"Oh crikey ! I—I—I mean——"

"I will give you one more opportunity, Bunter, to explain why you remained up here after the rest of the Form had gone down."

"I—I—I'd rather not tell you while Toddy's here, sir !" gasped Bunter, with an anxious blink at Peter Todd, who was staring at him from the crowd.

"What has Todd to do with it ?" snapped Mr. Quelch.

"Well, he might make a fuss about the toffee, sir !" gasped Bunter. "He might think I'd had it."

"Ha, ha, ha !"

"Silence ! Bunter, tell me at once what——"

"Never mind the toffee, Bunter," put in Peter Todd. "That's all right."

"Oh, all right, then," said Bunter. "The fact is, sir, Toddy left some toffee in the study, and I—I ate it, sir."

"Do you mean to say, Bunter, that you remained after your study-mates had gone down, in order to consume comestibles belonging to Todd ?"

"Oh crikey ! N-n-no, sir ! I mean, Toddy didn't mind me having the toffee. Did you, Toddy, old chap ? Toddy knows that I shall stand him some toffee when my postal order comes. I'm expecting a postal order, sir——"

"That will do, Bunter ! You deny having committed this outrageous act ?"

"Oh, yes, rather, sir ! I—I wouldn't !"

"Very well !" said Mr. Quelch, between his closed lips. "In such a very serious matter as this, there must be absolute proof. The boy concerned will be reported to Dr. Locke for a public flogging. The facts will be ascertained before long. You are under suspicion, Bunter."

"Oh, really, sir——"

"You need say no more !"

Mr. Quelch turned and rustled away down the stairs. The expression on his face as he went was very eloquent. Nobody envied the hassock-hurler when he was discovered.

"I say, you fellows, fancy Quelch thinking it was me, you know !" gasped Bunter, as the Remove master disappeared. "Of course, I'd like to drop a ton of bricks on his napper, after whopping me for nothing. But——"

"You must have been a silly ass to stick there after doing it !" said Carter.

"Eh ? I've said I didn't do it, you beast !"

Carter laughed.

"I say, you fellows!" said Bunter, sitting up in bed and blinking at his Form-fellows. "I've been feeling ill all night! I haven't just thought of it because I want to stay in bed! I've got a temperament!" "A which?" gasped Bob Cherry. "A very serious temperament!" hooted Bunter.

"I say, you fellows, I never did, you know!" exclaimed Bunter. "I say, I wonder who did? Did you, Mauly?"

"Oh, gad! Hardly!"

"Was it you, Fishy?"

"I guess not, old-timer!" grinned Fisher T. Fish.

"Well, nobody else seems to have been up in the studies," said Bunter. "It's a bit of a mystery, ain't it?"

"Not fearfully mysterious, as every fellow here knows you did it!" answered Carter.

"I say, you fellows, I think most likely it was Carter!" said Billy Bunter. "He would like to land it on me. He's always trying to get me into a row, because I won't take him up as a relation——"

"Ha, ha, ha!"

"Carter was in the Rag, with us, when it happened, fathead!" said Harry Wharton.

"Oh, was he?" said Bunter. "Then I'm blessed if I know who it was. I know it wasn't me!"

"Quelch knows it was, old bean!" grinned Skinner.

"Beast!"

Until dorm, the matter was discussed in the Rag, and fellows were quite unable to make up their minds whether Bunter had done it or not. It was a reckless act, which did not look like Bunter. On the other hand, it was a fatheaded act, which did look like Bunter! Bunter's own statement, of course, did not weigh a feather's weight, one way or the other!

Three fellows in the Remove knew that it was not Bunter. But those three said no word on the subject.

If, indeed, the charge was officially fastened on the fat Owl, and Bunter was up for punishment, Micky Desmond had only one thing to do, which was to own up and take his gruel, and he would not have hesitated a moment to do so.

But unless it came to that, obviously, the least said was the soonest mended. So the matter remained, for the present, a mystery.

THE THIRTEENTH CHAPTER.

Loder Takes a Hint!

LODER of the Sixth glanced round. Loder was standing at his study window, looking out into the sunny, frosty quad, after class the next morning, when two Remove juniors strolled by, talking as they passed. One of them was Carter, the new fellow in the Remove, the other Skinner. Carter's voice floated clearly to the prefect's ears.

"Well, we all know it was Bunter! Of course, nobody's going to give him away—not that the fat ass needs much giving away. Quelch knows, all right."

"Quelch is like the jolly old schoolmaster in the story—a beast, but a just beast!" chuckled Skinner. "He won't skin Bunter without proof."

"Easy enough to prove."

Loder fixed his attention on Carter as the new junior made that remark.

As a Sixth Form prefect, it was Loder's duty, if he could, to discover the reckless young rascal who had dropped that hassock on Quelch's majestic napper. Loder was not a whale on duty; and though the other prefects were "prowling" on the subject, Gerald Loder had given the matter no thought at all. He did not, as a matter of fact, like Quelch, and was not in the least sorry that a hassock had banged on his head.

Still, Loder was a prefect, and he was keen to show what a zealous and capable prefect he was, if it could be done without taking any trouble. So he was quite keen to hear what Carter had

to say. Most Greyfriars prefects would have jibbed at getting information by overhearing talk among the juniors, but Loder was not particular. He lent Carter a very attentive ear.

Skinner had not noticed the prefect at his window. If Carter had, he did not reveal the fact.

"Blessed if I see it!" said Skinner. "Bunter was on the spot, but that doesn't really look as if he did it. He would have bolted. How's Quelch going to prove it?"

"There's the hassock," said Carter. "They've got that! Can't they find out whom it belongs to?"

"Dozens of them knocking about the studies," said Skinner.

"Oh, yes; but I fancy there's one missing from Bunter's study to-day," grinned Carter. "If I were Quelch, I should ask Bunter whether he had one, and whether he still has it."

The two juniors passed on, Loder looking after them curiously as they went.

It was clear that both of them believed that Bunter was the unknown hassock-hurler, and Carter's suggestion struck Loder as useful. He had a suspicion that Carter had spotted him at the open window, and had intended his words to be heard by official ears. If the fellow had chosen that surreptitious method of "sneaking," it did not matter to Loder; he was going to act on the suggestion.

He left his study and went to the doorway of the House. Most of the Removites were out in the quad after class. He called to Peter Todd.

"Where is Bunter, Todd?"

"He went up to the study after class," answered Peter.

Loder turned and went to the stairs. Peter whistled. That inquiry, from a prefect, looked as if they were on the track of the hassock-hurler.

The bully of the Sixth found Bunter in Study No. 7 in the Remove, travelling slowly but surely through a packet of butterscotch.

The fat Owl blinked round in alarm at the sight of a prefect looking in.

"I say, Loder, it wasn't me!" he exclaimed in a great hurry.

"What wasn't?" grinned Loder

"Oh! Anything! I mean, nothing!" stammered Bunter.

"I've come here to ask you a question, Bunter! You'd better tell me the truth!" said Loder, adopting his most bullying expression "There used to be a hassock in this study, I understand?"

"Eh? Oh, yes!" Bunter blinked at him. "I used to have it on my chair, Loder, because the table's so beastly high. I use a cushion now."

Loder laughed. Really, there was not much need for investigation in dealing with a fellow like Bunter.

"Where is it now?" he demanded.

"Eh? I don't know! You see——"

"Is it in this study?"

"Nunno! You see——"

"Yes, I see!" grinned Loder. "Follow me, Bunter. I fancy your Form-master would like to hear something about that hassock!"

"I—I don't suppose Quelch cares about it, Loder! A chap's allowed to chuck away an old hassock if he likes."

"That depends on where he chucks it!" said Loder. "Are you coming, Bunter, or do you want me to lead you along by your ear?"

"I—I'm coming! But——"

"Sharp's the word!" snapped Loder.

Billy Bunter rolled out of the study after Loder, and followed him down the stairs to Masters' Passage. He was feeling uneasy—Bunter always felt uneasy when he approached his Form-master's study. At the same time, he did not look so alarmed as Loder might have expected.

Loder tapped at Mr. Quelch's door. He entered, followed by the fat Owl.

Mr. Quelch glanced at the prefect inquiringly.

"What is it, Loder?"

"I've been making some inquiries, sir, into what happened last evening," explained Loder, with a dutiful smirk. "As the prefects were asked to investigate, I've been giving the matter a good deal of attention. I think there can be no doubt now that it was Bunter, sir, from what I have ascertained."

"You have made some discovery, Loder?" exclaimed Mr. Quelch.

There was no doubt that the Remove master was keen on news.

"I think so, sir! I thought of inquiring whether such a thing as a hassock was missing from a Remove study. It appears that one is missing from Bunter's study, so I have brought him to you, sir."

"Oh crikey!" gasped Bunter.

"Thank you, Loder!" said Mr. Quelch. "I had not thought of that line of investigation. It was very thoughtful of you. Bunter, you had a hassock in your study?"

"Oh! No, sir!"

"He admitted to me a few minutes ago, sir, that he had!" said Loder.

"I didn't!" howled Bunter. "It wasn't mine; it was Toddy's——"

"It was in your study?" rapped Mr. Quelch.

"Oh, yes, sir! Toddy keeps all his

THE MAGNET LIBRARY.—No. 1,562.

things in my study, as it's his study, too——"

"Is it in the study now?"

"No, sir!"

"What has become of it?"

"I don't know, sir! I chucked it away——"

"You—you threw it——"

"Yes, sir!"

"Upon my word! Then you admit, Bunter, that you were guilty of the assault upon your Form-master last evening?" thundered Mr. Quelch.

Bunter jumped.

"Oh, no, sir! Oh crikey! I mean, I chucked it away, sir—I didn't chuck it at your napper, sir—— Oh lor'! It wasn't the same hassock, sir! Oh crumbs! Nothing of the kind, sir! I—I chucked it away because it was worn out, and all the stuffing coming out all over the floor, sir, and——"

"That will do, Bunter! You had a hassock in your study, and it is no longer there! Last night a hassock was dropped on my head, and I have retained it in my possession. Nothing could be clearer——"

"But, sir, I never——"

"Bunter, you will come with me to your headmaster! Loder, I am very much obliged to you!"

"Not at all, sir!" said Loder, with another smirk.

"Follow me, Bunter!"

"Oh lor'!"

Bunter rolled after his Form-master. At the corner of the passage they passed Carter of the Remove. Carter glanced at them and smiled a cat-like smile as he watched them arrive at Dr. Locke's study.

———

THE FOURTEENTH CHAPTER.

Passing It On!

"VERY good!" said Dr. Locke. "Very good indeed!"

Bunter was entirely unable to see anything good in the matter at all.

He stood quaking, while his Form-master explained to Dr. Locke that the author of the unexampled outrage with the hassock has been discovered.

Why Quelch supposed that he was the hassock-hurler, Bunter did not know. But he could see that Quelch did. If the Head took the same view, it was all up with Bunter. Already the Head's eye was swerving towards his birch.

Everybody knew that the man who had bonneted Quelch was booked for a Head's flogging, if spotted. Dr. Locke seemed ready to get on with it at once. Billy Bunter was far from ready. Bunter's objections were deep and strong.

He had only one hope—in the fact that "old Locke" was well-known to be a "downy bird," with an almost superhuman faculty for getting at the truth!

Seldom was the truth a resource of Bunter's! But in this instance only the truth was of any use to him. For, in point of fact, he had not hurled that hassock, and had no idea who had.

"Very good!" repeated Dr. Locke. "I am very glad, Quelch, that a discovery has been made. Such an episode could not be suffered to pass without serious detriment to the discipline of the school. Bunter——"

"I didn't!" wailed Bunter.

"If you have anything to say, Bunter——"

"Oh, yes, sir! I didn't! I wasn't——"

"I should explain, sir," said Mr. Quelch grimly, "that I myself heard

this boy utter a threat to hurl a pillow at my head——"

"Is it possible, Mr. Quelch?"

"That—that was only gas, sir!" wailed Bunter "I never meant to! I—I—I shouldn't dare! Lots of fellows would like to chuck a pillow at your head, sir—but they never do——"

"What?" roared Mr. Quelch.

"Fellows have often said such things, sir! They never do it! I've heard a chap say he would chuck Mossoo across the detention-room—but nobody's ever chucked him——"

"Be silent, you foolish boy!" said Dr. Locke. "Mr. Quelch, you have other evidence beside foolish talk on the part of this stupid boy?"

"Naturally, sir. Bunter was on the spot when investigation was made. In view of his denial, I allowed the matter to remain in abeyance. But a Sixth Form prefect has now discovered that a hassock is missing from his study——"

"Bless my soul!" said the Head. "There could hardly be more conclusive evidence than that, I think."

"I quite agree, sir."

"I will hear you, Bunter, if you have anything further to say! The hassock missing from your study, it can hardly he doubted, is the one that was flung over the banisters at your Form-master. Did you——"

"It wasn't, sir!" howled Bunter. "It couldn't be, sir! You see, it's impossible!"

"And why so?" demanded Dr. Locke. "Where is your hassock now, Bunter, if it is not the one in Mr. Quelch's study?"

"It wasn't mine, sir; it was Toddy's."

"Answer my question—where is it?"

"I don't know, sir! How could I know?" wailed Bunter. "I don't know what the dustmen do with the things."

"The—the—the what?"

"Dustmen, sir."

"What do you mean, Bunter? What can the dustmen have to do with this matter?" exclaimed the Head.

"Well, I suppose they took it away, sir!" said Bunter. "They take all the rubbish away. I don't know what they do with it. You see, sir, Toddy grumbled about that old hassock bursting and dropping stuffing all over the shop, so I threw it away."

"Where did you throw it, Bunter?"

"Into a dustbin, sir."

"And when did this occur?"

"Last term, sir."

"Last term!" ejaculated Mr. Quelch blankly.

"Yes, sir! Toddy made out that I wore it out, because I used to sit on at prep in the study, and then he groused because I chucked it away, because it was his and——"

"Has there been a hassock in your study this term, Bunter?"

"Oh, no, sir! This term I've used a cushion on my chair. Toddy can't grumble about that, because I borrowed it from Mauly's study——"

Mr. Quelch gazed at Bunter a good deal like a gorgon. He had taken it for granted—he had had no doubt whatever—that the hassock missing from Study No. 7 was the one that had been dropped on his head. Really it was pretty good evidence. Still, if the hassock in Study No. 7 had been thrown away last term, it clearly wasn't the same hassock, and couldn't be!

"If this is true, Bunter, why did you not tell Mr. Quelch so?" exclaimed the Head.

"He never asked me, sir."

"Do you believe this statement, Mr.

Quelch? The boy Todd can be sent for to corroborate it or otherwise."

Mr. Quelch breathed hard and deep. "I think, sir, that it is unnecessary! If this boy had had the common intelligence to mention that he had had no hassock in his study this term, I should not have supposed——"

"Quite so," assented the Head. "Bunter should have made that statement immediately. He could hardly have supposed that you were inquiring about an article that was thrown away before the Christmas holidays. But——" He coughed. "If it was not the same hassock——"

Mr. Quelch breathed harder and deeper.

"I still suspect Bunter very strongly, sir. But it is a matter for proof, and the proof appears to be lacking. I regret, sir, having wasted your time."

"Not at all, Mr. Quelch! I am only too anxious for this matter to be cleared up," said the Head politely.

"M-m-may I go now, sir?" gasped Bunter.

"You may go, Bunter."

The fat junior made almost a bound for the door.

Mr. Quelch followed him more slowly, with a spot of colour in either cheek. The Head was always courteous, but Quelch knew perfectly well what he was thinking—that the matter should have been probed a little deeper before a busy headmaster's time was wasted on it.

That, Quelch realised, was the case—he should have elicited all these details before taking Bunter to the Head.

On the other hand, Loder, who had taken up the clue of the missing hassock in the first place, should have elicited the details before bringing Bunter to Quelch. Had not Loder acted hastily, jumping to conclusions, Mr. Quelch would not have followed his example.

Loder of the Sixth was loitering at the end of the passage. Perhaps he expected a word or two of commendation from Mr. Quelch for his zeal and perspicacity. If so, a disappointment was coming to him.

"The matter is now cleared up, sir, I trust," said Loder, with his dutiful smirk.

Quelch's eyes glinted at him. "The matter is not cleared up, Loder," he answered icily. "You have wasted my time and your headmaster's by your thoughtless carelessness."

"Wha-a-at, sir?" stuttered Loder.

"It transpires that Bunter's hassock is missing from his study, Loder, because it was thrown away last term. You should have ascertained this fact before making a report to me. You have been very remiss, Loder."

With that, Quelch stalked on, leaving Gerald Loder staring. Evidently there was no commendation coming Loder's way.

"By gad!" breathed Loder.

He went to his study and picked up his ashplant. With that instrument of punishment under his arm he walked out into the quadrangle and looked round over the fellows there.

He was looking for Carter.

He had taken a hint from Carter, with the result that he had made a fool of himself, and received the sharpest edge of Mr. Quelch's tongue as a reward. He could not handle Quelch, but he could handle Carter. Quelch had passed on his annoyance to Loder; Loder was going to pass it on to Carter.

He soon spotted the new Removite. Arthur Carter, in the quad, was watching Bunter with a puzzled expression on his face.

Bunter had been up before the Head, with the certainty of a flogging, and a sporting chance of the "sack." Yet he had rolled out of the House looking quite cheery and satisfied.

Naturally it puzzled Carter, and Loder, catching the expression on his face, knew beyond doubt that the young rascal had intended him to hear those words spoken under his study window. Carter had been surreptitiously sneaking, and was perplexed to see no result accrue therefrom.

Loder had no particular objection to "sneaking," on principle; but in this instance it had led to Loder making a fool of himself and getting "jawed" by a beak, which made a lot of difference.

As Carter stood staring at Bunter, Loder came up behind him. The ashplant slipped from under his arm into his hand.

Whop!

Carter gave a sudden yell and a bound, as that unexpected whop landed on his trousers.

"Oh! Ow!" he yelled. "What——"

Whop!

"Oh crumbs!" Carter leaped away and spun round, staring at Loder. "Look here, what the thump do you mean? What——"

Whop!

Carter bolted without waiting to ascertain why Loder was whopping him. Whatever the reason, there was no doubt about the fact, and Carter just dodged a fourth whop, and flew.

THE FIFTEENTH CHAPTER.

Glory for Bunter!

"WHERE he got the nerve from beats me!" said the Bounder.

"Me, too," agreed Skinner.

"He's not such a funk as he's always made out!" remarked Bolsover major.

"Fools rush in where angels fear to tread!" grinned Hazeldene.

"Well, yes, but fancy Bunter——"

"Beats me hollow!"

"And he's got by with it. They'll never spot him now!" said Smithy. "Fancy that fat ass ragging a Form-master, and getting by with it!"

"Jolly old wonders will never cease!"

Billy Bunter, listening with all his fat ears, grinned. Bunter was sprawling in an armchair in the Rag, after tea, when the other fellows came in.

They did not notice him there as they discussed the matter that was still a thrilling topic in the Remove—the bonneting of Henry Samuel Quelch with a hassock from the landing.

After the lapse of a day, it certainly looked as if the hassock-hurler was going to get by with it. No discovery had been made, except Loder's, which had turned out to be a mare's-nest.

It was known that Bunter had been up before the Head; but it was also known that he had escaped unscathed.

Few fellows doubted that Bunter had "done it." The three fellows who knew better were keeping it fearfully dark. And it was a matter of surprise and keen interest in the Remove. First, that Bunter had ever found the nerve to do it; and second, that he had not been bowled out.

Smithy, who was

a reckless ragger, would hardly have ventured to bonnet Quelch with a hassock. or anything else. Bunter, never supposed to be reckless, had done what the Bounder would never have ventured to do. So it was no wonder that the Removites wondered.

Bunter, as he sprawled unnoticed, and listened to the talk, grinned, with a sly gleam in his little round eyes, behind his big round spectacles.

At first Bunter had only been anxious to prove that he hadn't done it. At the same time he was rather elated at being regarded as a bold, bad ragger, who had the unheard-of nerve to rag such a man as Quelch.

Now, the danger being past, the great idea germinated in Bunter's fat intellect, of claiming the credit of that bold, bad rag.

Often and often had Bunter envied Smithy, who swanked as a fellow who did not care a boiled bean for beaks or prefects. Bunter would gladly have trodden the same reckless path, but for the awkward fact that he hadn't Smithy's nerve to carry out a rag, or Smithy's hardihood to endure the consequences if they came home to him. It was not of much use for Billy Bunter to set up as a devil-may-care desperado when the mere knitting of Quelch's brows made him quake.

Now, however, his bold, bad reputation was, as it were, ready-made for him.

Who had bunged that hassock at Quelch, Bunter had not the faintest idea. Whoever it was he was keeping it frightfully dark—as it behoved him to do. He, whoever he might be, was not likely to cut in and rob Bunter of the credit, if he laid claim to it.

Bunter did not, of course, think of laying claim to that distinction, so far as Quelch was concerned. He was thinking of spreading himself in the Remove as a bold, bad Bunter who feared no foe.

For which reason he grinned cheerfully as he heard the discussion going on behind the high back of the arm-chair in which his lazy, fat limbs sprawled.

He rose from that armchair, and blinked over the back at the group of juniors through his spectacles.

"I say, you fellows——" he squeaked.

"Oh, here he is!" said Vernon-Smith. "What did the Head want you for to-day. fatty?"

"What do you think?" grinned Bunter. "I pulled his leg all right! He, he, he!"

"Not so jolly easy to pull the Head's leg!" said Skinner, staring at him.

Bunter chuckled.

"Was I flogged?" he asked complacently. "Sacked—what? No fear! All you want is nerve, you know, dealing with the beaks! I was all right!"

"Then it was you?" exclaimed Bolsover major.

"Didn't you think it was?" asked Bunter calmly.

"Well, yes; but——"

"Of course, I rely on you fellows to keep it dark," said the fatuous fat Owl. "I don't want Quelch on my track. All the same, I fancy he'll be

(Continued on next page.)

a bit more careful after this. I told him to his face that I'd chuck a pillow at his head! You wouldn't have had the nerve to tell Quelch that, Smithy!"

"Hardly," agreed the Bounder. "Nor you, either, you fat fraud! Quelch heard you gassing by accident."

"Well, did I bung a hassock at him or not?" demanded Bunter "I said I would—and did I or not? By gum, if I have any more of his old buck, I'll let him have an inkpot next time—and the ink in it, too!"

"Yes, I can see you doing it!" grinned Smithy.

"Well, I can't see you dropping a hassock on his head," sneered Bunter, "and then waiting, as cool as an iceberg, for him to come up! You'd have cut off if you'd done it, Smithy!"

"Like a shot!" assented Smithy.

"Well, did I?" grinned Bunter. "No fear! Just stood there and waited for him to come up! I'm not afraid of Quelch, I can jolly well tell you! You fellows may be! Not me! You see, I've got nerve!"

The Bounder laughed.

"Well, old fat bean, you'll want all your nerve if Quelch gets on your track!" he said. "I shouldn't brag of it too much, if I were you."

"Who cares for Quelch!" said Bunter valorously. "Let him whop me again, that's all! I'll make him sit up again —see? I don't mind all the fellows knowing I did it! In fact, I'd rather they knew! They'll jolly well see that I'm not the man to stand any nonsense! Fat lot I care for beaks!"

With which, Billy Bunter rolled out of the Rag, with his fat little nose in the air. He was feeling tremendously bucked. Even the reckless Bounder had to take second place as a wild ragger to the fellow who had bonneted Quelch. This was glory!

Before very long the news spread in the Remove that Bunter had admitted it.

Most of the fellows had already believed so, though they still wondered where he had found the nerve. So few were surprised. But one member of the Remove was surprised—in fact, astonished. That one was Micky Desmond.

Micky had been in his study after tea getting some of his lines done. He heard the news when he came out, finding a dozen Remove fellows in the passage discussing it.

"Heard?" called out Skinner.

"Phwat?" asked Micky.

"Chap who bonneted Quelch," grinned Skinner. "No secret about it now."

Micky stared at him. He had had time to reflect since his wild and reckless act the night before, and from the bottom of his heart he wished that he had not done it. All he could hope for now, since it was done, and could not be undone, was that it would remain a secret and gradually be forgotten. So Skinner's statement that it was no secret now rather alarmed him.

"Phwat do ye main intoirely?" gasped Micky. "Sure they haven't found out—"

"Oh, no! Bunter's only told the Remove so far!" chuckled Skinner. "It won't get out till he spins the yarn outside the Form. No sneaks in the Remove."

"Bunter doesn't know——"

"He jolly well knows he did it! We all knew he did it, and now he's owned up to it."

Micky Desmond blinked.

"Owned up to it?" he gasped.

"Yes; told all the Form."

"Howly Moses! Bunter's owned up to dhroppin' that hassock on Quilch's napper!"

"Bragging of it right and left!" chortled Skinner. "The only man in the Form who ever got away with a rag on Quelch—if he has got away!"

"Bet you Quelch will nail him sooner or later!" said Carter. "Quelch is no fool. He knows Bunter did it as well as we do."

"Yes, but he's got to prove it."

"If he hears that Bunter has been bragging of it up and down the Form, he won't want much more proof!"

"The fat omadhaun!" exclaimed Micky. "He niver did it! Phwat is he saying he did for whin he didn't?"

"He did, you ass! We all knew he did!" answered Skinner. "He's let it out now because he thinks it's safe."

Micky Desmond, with quite a dazed expression on his face, made his way along the passage to Study No. 7. He heard Bunter's voice as he looked in.

"You see, it was like this, Toddy. I told him I'd heave a pillow at his head, and he whopped me. So I jolly well let him have it—right on his napper, you know! He, he, he! Did you guess I'd done it, Toddy?"

"Yes, I did," answered Peter Todd. "But now you say you did, I've got my doubts."

"Oh, really, Toddy——"

"You fat spalpeen!" gasped Micky Desmond. "Are ye saying ye bonneted Quilch with that hassock?"

Bunter blinked round at him.

"That's it, old chap!" he said complacently. "Got him right on the napper over the banisters! You wouldn't have had the nerve—what? He licked you as well as me, but I'll bet you'd never have bunged a hassock on his napper! He, he, he! It wanted some nerve, I can tell you!"

Micky gazed at him blankly.

"You—you—you did it?" he gasped, like a fellow in a dream.

"Little me!" said Bunter. "The only chap in the Remove who had the nerve to do it, too!"

"Oh, howly smoke!" gasped Micky.

He almost tottered away.

That evening, in the Rag, Billy Bunter was the cynosure of all eyes. He enjoyed it thoroughly. For the first time in history the fat and funky Owl of the Remove was able to show off as a wild and reckless ragger who had brought off the wildest and most reckless rag of the term. It was unaccustomed glory for Bunter, and he fairly revelled in it. Indeed, he seemed likely, like the classic gentleman in Horace, to strike the stars with his sublime head!

THE SIXTEENTH CHAPTER.

Bob Does his Best!

BOB CHERRY frowned.

Saturday afternoon was fine and bright, and most of the Greyfriars fellows had cheery faces when lessons were over. But there was one member of the Remove who looked as if most of the troubles in the universe had descended on his young shoulders. That one was Micky Desmond.

All the Form agreed that it was fearfully hard cheese on Micky. He had detention for the half-holiday and innumerable lines, and all because of that fat owl Bunter bagging his impot early in the week. Plenty of fellows would have regarded Micky as fully justified in letting Quelch know how the matter really stood; but Micky did not take that view, and so there was no help

for it. He was feeling disposed to hang, draw, and quarter William George Bunter, but not to give him away to a beak.

It was all the harder because there was a Form match on that afternoon with the Fourth. In that match the leading spirits of the Remove football world stood down to give the lesser lights a look-in, and Micky was one of the lesser lights in Soccer. He was not only losing his half-holiday, but losing his chance of playing football for the Form, which was really the limit.

Bob Cherry's frown was caused by the sight of Micky's doleful and dolorous countenance. As the only fellow in the Remove who did not believe that Bunter had snooped that impot, Bob did not lay the blame on Bunter, being the only fellow who did not. But he had been thinking the matter over, with the result that he looked for Bunter to put it to him.

Had Bunter "snooped" Micky's lines, certainly nothing would have induced him to reveal that fact to Quelch. The consequences would have been too painful But what had really happened was much less serious; he had found the impot written for him, as he supposed, by another fellow doing him a good turn. Quelch had been a schoolboy himself once upon a time, and he would surely realise that, in such circumstances, a fellow would make use of the lines. Bunter's punishment, if any, would be light—much less severe, at any rate, than what was coming to poor Micky.

True, Bunter was not, as a rule, the fellow to face any music, howsoever light. But, in view of his recently developed boldness and badness, it seemed more probable. Bob, like all the Remove excepting three, believed that Bunter had bonneted Quelch. The fellow who had done that would surely not be afraid to own up to a small fault.

He found Bunter blinking through his big spectacles at the window of the tuckshop. He was outside, instead of inside, because his celebrated postal order had not yet arrived.

Bob tapped him on the shoulder.

"Looking for you, old fat man!" he said amicably.

The Owl of the Remove gave him a hopeful blink.

"I say, old chap, if you've got a half-crown you don't want——" he began.

"Sorry, I haven't."

Grunt from Bunter! He turned back to his contemplation of the tuckshop window, with a total lack of interest in Bob Cherry.

"Look here, Bunter, about Desmond——" began Bob.

"Blow him!" grunted Bunter.

"He's got detention this afternoon! It's going to keep him out of the football," said Bob.

"I'd take his place, if Wharton asked me. I shouldn't mind playing for the Form! He would have to ask me civilly, of course."

Bob breathed hard.

"Look here, you could get Micky off," he said. "If Quelch knew that he had really done his impot the other day, and lost it, it would make a lot of difference. You're not to blame, as you found it stuck in your study. If Quelch knew, he would go easy with Micky——"

"He held my head under the tap——"

"Well, yes, but he thought you'd snooped his impot——"

"As if I would!" said Bunter indignantly. "Drenching a fellow all over like that! Blow him!"

"Suppose you go and let Quelch know——"

"I'll watch it."

"Look here, Bunter, it's up to you!" exclaimed Bob. "Quelch won't do more than give you lines, and I'll help you with them."

"More likely to whop me."

"Well, you're not afraid of a whopping, old bean, even if he did!" said Bob, encouragingly. "Why, the fellow who bunged a hassock on Quelch's head oughtn't to be afraid of anything!"

"Eh!" Bunter blinked at him. "Oh, yes! I'm afraid of nothing of course! You know my pluck!"

"Ah! Um! Yes! Well, look here, go and tell Quelch that you found those lines in your study, and thought a pal had done them—that's the truth! Quelch is no fool—he knows when a chap is telling the truth. Very likely he will let you off, for coming and owning up in a manly way. See? If he gives you the lines over again, I'll do them for you."

"Um!" said Bunter doubtfully.

"It will show that you've got the pluck to do the right thing!" urged Bob.

"Um!" said Bunter. "You don't think Quelch will whop me?"

"Not at all likely."

"And if there's lines, you'll do them?"

"Honour bright!"

"Oh, all right then," said Bunter, "I'll go to Quelch! Presently," he added cautiously.

Billy Bunter was quite willing, indeed keen, to show that he had plenty of pluck, if there was no danger involved. But he wanted to feel quite sure about that. That was rather important.

"No time like the present," said Bob. "Look here, I'll come with you." He slipped his hand through a fat arm, and led Bunter off towards the House.

Billy Bunter went willingly enough—until the House was reached. But at the door he paused.

"I—I—I say, I—I think I'll leave it till later——" he stammered.

"Come on, old bean."

"But I say——" mumbled Bunter feebly.

"This way!"

Bob almost dragged Bunter into the House. They got as far as the corner of Masters' Passage, and then Bunter jibbed like an obstinate horse.

"Look here, leggo my arm!" he hissed. "I'm going all right, but—but I don't want you to come to Quelch's study! Leggo my arm!"

Bob jerked at the fat arm. Bunter hung back. Really, it was not easy work, getting Bunter up to the scratch.

Obviously, if Bob let go the fat arm, Bunter was not going to proceed in the direction of Quelch's study. He was going to proceed in exactly the opposite direction! Bob did not let go.

"Now, look here, Bunter, if Micky has to cut the footer, you'll very likely get a ragging," he said. "You don't want that."

"Oh, no! But——"

"Well, come on, then!"

Bunter came on—reluctantly.

They arrived, at long last, at Mr. Quelch's study door.

Bob tapped at the door with his free hand.

"Come in!" said the deep voice from within.

Bunter gasped. The sound of his Form-master's voice did it. All the boldness and badness of bold, bad Bunter departed on the spot! One thing was fixed in Bunter's fat mind—he wasn't going into that study! But the grip on his fat arm was like steel! Bunter had to use strategy.

He grasped the door-handle and turned it.

Bob, under the impression that he

Micky Desmond's eyes gleamed as from the landing above he looked down at Mr. Quelch, who was in conversation with Mr. Prout. Then he lifted the hassock over the balustrade, calculated carefully, and let it drop. Down it went, like a plummet, landing fair and square on Mr. Quelch's mortar-board. Plop!

was going into the study, released the fat arm at last.

Bunter would have cut—but there was no doubt that Bob would have grabbed him before he was out of reach. He had to prevent that!

He made a quick step back and gave Bob a sudden shove. Taken by surprise, Bob Cherry crashed against the door. The door being unlatched, it flew open under his weight, and Bob toppled backwards into the study. At the same moment, Bunter cut down the passage.

Mr. Quelch started up from his chair, staring. It was enough to make him stare, the sight of a member of his Form knocking the door open, crashing into his study, and rolling on the carpet!

"Cherry!" gasped Mr. Quelch.

"Oh!" stuttered Bob.

He bounded to his feet, his face crimson.

Mr. Quelch, from the other side of his writing-table, glared at him.

"Cherry! What does this mean? What——"

"Oh! Sorry, sir!" stammered Bob. "I—I—I—somebody pushed me, sir—I—I fell against the door——"

"Take a hundred lines, Cherry! If you play such an absurd prank again, I shall cane you! Go!"

Bob Cherry went—with deep feelings! He spent the next ten minutes looking for Billy Bunter, with the intention of booting that fat youth all over the quad. But he did not find him. Billy Bunter was very careful not to be found!

THE SEVENTEENTH CHAPTER.

Bribing Bunter!

"SURE it's harrd lines, and so it is!" groaned Micky Desmond.

"We'll rag Bunter!" said Morgan.

"That won't get me oft detention."

"It won't!" said Wibley thoughtfully. Fellows were going into the changing-room. Micky watched them, with a gloomy brow. It was time for him to go into detention. Detention, never attractive, was less attractive than ever now. It was not even a detention class, which was bad enough. Micky had to sit in the Form-room on his lonely own, and write lines. And the other fellows would be playing football, and Micky might have been playing, too! It was hard lines!

Carter was in the Remove team. He came in to change, with the others, and glanced at Micky at the doorway. He smiled slightly at the expression on Micky's dismal face.

"You're out of it?" he asked.

"Yis!" groaned Micky.

"Well, you're an ass! Nobody would blame you if you let Quelch know about your impot being snooped. Ten to one Quelch would let you off."

"Think I'm a snake?" snorted Micky.

Carter shrugged his shoulders, and went in.

Micky gave a deep, deep sigh, and turned to make his way to the Form-room.

"If that fat chump owned up about snooping the impot——" muttered Wibley.

"Catch him!" grunted Morgan.

"Well, he might!" said Wibley thoughtfully. "Bunter will do anything for a feed! I've got an idea."

Wibley hurried away in search of Bunter. He found him in the Rag, frowsting over the fire. He was busily occupied in searching through all his pockets, one after another, in the hope of unearthing a forgotten bullseye!

"Oh, here you are!" said Wib cheerfully. "Come up to my study, Bunter! I've got a toffee-tin—one of those seven-pound tins——"

Bunter fairly bounded out of the arm-chair.

"What-ho!" he said.

He rolled joyfully up to the Remove after Wibley. In Wib's study he blinked round for the toffee. Wibley lifted a large tin out of the study cupboard, and placed it on the table.

Bunter's eyes, and spectacles, fairly gloated over it. It was a seven-pound tin, and the inscription on it was "Blunt's Super-Cream Toffee!" A packet of toffee would have delighted Bunter. A seven-pound tin quite dazzled him!

"Oh crikey!" gasped Bunter.

He stretched out a fat hand to the tin. Wibley pushed it back.

"Hold on!" he said "Don't touch! If you'd like that tin, Bunter, you can have it—if Micky's let off detention."

"Oh, really, Wibley——"

"You got him into a row with Quelch!" said Wibley. "Snooping his impot——"

"I didn't! I've told you——"

"Well, there's the tin!" said Wibley. "If Micky's let off to play Soccer this afternoon, it's yours. Otherwise, buzz off!"

Billy Bunter did not buzz off. He seemed unable to take his eyes off that tin! Only Wibley's intervention kept his fat hands off it.

"I—I—I say, let—let's talk it over!" suggested Bunter. "I—I'll have some of the toffees while—while we talk it over, old chap."

"You won't!" said Wibley. "You can have the whole tin if Micky's let off. It's up to you, and you know it."

Bunter paused. Bob Cherry had failed to get him up to the scratch. But seven pounds of toffee was seven pounds of toffee! He paused—he hesitated—but he made up his fat mind.

"I—I—I'll do it!" he gasped.

"Do!" said Wibley.

And Bunter did! He rolled away down the Remove passage.

Wibley, grinning, watched him over the banisters as he went downstairs. The fat Owl headed for Masters' Passage.

For the second time that afternoon Billy Bunter arrived at Mr. Quelch's door. There, for a long minute, he paused. But the lure of toffee was too strong, and he tapped and went in.

Mr. Quelch looked up from Latin papers.

"What is it, Bunter?"

Bunter blinked at him. Under the gimlet eyes he wished himself out of the study again. But he thought of that magnificent tin of toffees, and took his courage in both hands, as it were.

"I—I—I——" he began.

"Be brief!" rapped Mr. Quelch.

"Oh, yes! It—it's about Desmond, sir," stammered Bunter. "I—I think I—I ought to tell you, sir, as Micky's got detention and he wants to play football, and—and Bob thinks you won't be very waxy——"

"What?"

"I—I mean, that—that impot, sir," gasped Bunter. "It was really Desmond's, sir, that—that impot last Tuesday, sir——"

"It was Desmond's!" repeated Mr. Quelch blankly. "What? I remember that I remarked on the writing! Have you come here to tell me, Bunter, that you deceived me by using another boy's lines as your own?"

"Oh, no!" gasped Bunter. "I—I—I——"

"You took Desmond's lines!" thundered Mr Quelch.

"Oh, no! I—I found them in my study, sir!" gasped Bunter. "Some beast—I mean, some fellow—took them and put them in my study, and—and I thought a chap had done them for me, and—and so—so I brought them to you, sir!"

"Upon my word!" exclaimed Mr. Quelch.

"Only Desmond thought I had pinched them, sir, and—and that was why he wanted me to write the next lot, and held my head under the tap——"

"Upon my word!" repeated Mr. Quelch. "If this is true, Bunter, who was it that placed Desmond's lines in your study?"

"I don't know, sir! It was a rotten trick—it's made all the fellows think I pinched the lines, except Bob Cherry! Of course, I thought a chap had done them for me when I found them in my study."

Mr. Quelch gazed at him.

"Even if this statement is correct, Bunter, you are very well aware that you should not have brought the lines to me as your own!" he said sternly.

"Oh, yes! I mean, no, sir!"

"And why have you come to confess this to me now, Bunter?"

"I—I thought I ought to—to own up, sir! Bob Cherry thinks you wouldn't be very waxy if I came and told you the truth, sir."

"You utterly absurd boy! Desmond should have told me that he had written his lines if he had really done so. As you have told me this of your own accord, Bunter, I shall not punish you for having used another boy's lines."

"Oh, good! I—I mean, thank you, sir!"

"But if it should occur again——" said Mr. Quelch in a terrifying voice.

"Oh, no, sir! If I ever find lines in like my study again I shan't be taken in like that!" gasped Bunter. "I never knew that they were Desmond's——"

Mr. Quelch gave him an extremely penetrating look.

"It is very singular, Bunter, that some boy should have taken Desmond's imposition and placed it in your study!" he said slowly.

"Yes, sir! When you said the fist was like Micky's I thought it was Micky who'd done them for me. But it turned out that they were his lines, that he had left in his study, and some beast——"

"I believe your statement, Bunter, extraordinary as it is!" said Mr. Quelch. "I am glad that you have come and told me this. You may go."

Bunter shot out of the study.

Mr. Quelch remained some moments in puzzled thought. Then he left the study and went to the Form-room.

Micky Desmond was there, with a face as long as a fiddle. He gave his Form-master a dismal look.

Mr. Quelch smiled faintly.

"Desmond, I have learned from Bunter that your imposition was written last Tuesday, and taken from your study——"

"Oh!" gasped Micky. "Yis, sorr!"

"You should have told me so, Desmond!"

"Sure I'm no snake, sorr, and I couldn't give the fat baste away—I—I mean——"

"You supposed that Bunter had taken the lines?"

"Yis, sorr."

"I believe Bunter's statement that the lines were placed in his study by some unknown person. I shall make an inquiry into this. But you supposed that——"

"Oh, yis, sorr!"

"I should not have doubled the imposition if I had known. Nevertheless," said Mr. Quelch sternly, "you should never have thought of making Bunter write the second imposition for you, and most certainly you should never have used such methods, Desmond. You deserved the caning you received."

"Oh! Yis, sorr!"

"However, in the circumstances, I shall cancel the rest of your punishment," said Mr. Quelch. "You may leave the Form-room, Desmond."

Micky's dismal face brightened.

"Thin I can go and play futball, sorr?" he gasped.

"You may!" said Mr. Quelch.

Micky scudded out of the Form-room. At the corner of the passage he found Wibley and Morgan waiting for him.

"Have they started yit?" gasped Micky.

"No—they're still in the changing-room!" grinned Wibley. "You've got off?"

"Yis! Sure I wish I'd niver bonneted Quilch! Come on!" gasped Micky, and he careered away to the changing-room, just in time to catch the footballers before they came out.

Billy Bunter watched the three, as they went, with a cheery grin. He had earned that toffee-tin! And he rolled up to the Remove to bag his reward!

The seven-pound toffee-tin stood on the table in Wibley's study, where he had left it. It was Bunter's now! The fat Owl of the Remove gave it one joyous blink, and grabbed it. He tore off the lid and grabbed at the toffees within—and grabbed vacant space!

He blinked into the tin!

Then, as the poet has remarked, a change came o'er the spirit of his dream!

The tin was empty!

Bunter gazed at it! He blinked into it! He gasped.

Only bribery and corruption had induced Bunter to do the right thing! Wibley had bribed and corrupted him to go to Quelch! And he had bribed and corrupted him with an empty toffee-tin!

THE EIGHTEENTH CHAPTER.

Boots for Bunter!

"THAT cad!" muttered Bob Cherry.

"He can play football!" answered Harry Wharton.

"So can all the Remove!"

"We can't leave a man out of games, Bob, because you've got a feud on with him!" said the captain of the Remove. "Don't be an ass, old chap!"

Bob grunted.

Bob was one of the mighty men of the Remove who were standing down that afternoon to give the lesser lights a look-in. But as Micky Desmond was out of the team there was a place to be filled, and Bob was going to fill it. He was keen enough to play, though a match with Temple, Dabney & Co. of the Fourth was not much of a game. But his cheery face darkened when Carter came in to change.

Deeply as he disliked the new junior, Bob admitted that he could play Soccer. Carter was, or affected to be, keen on the game, and there was no doubt that he had shown up remarkably well in games practice. Harry Wharton, in fact, had an eye on him for the Remove eleven, and he was going to "try him out" in the Form match. Whether Carter was, or was not, the "rotter" that Bob believed him to be, the football captain had to consider him from the point of view of Soccer.

"Well, look here, you won't want me," said Bob at last. "Lots of fellows will jump at the chance as Micky's standing out."

"Now, look here, Bob," said the captain of the Remove quietly, "this game with Temple's lot doesn't matter much, but if Carter goes on as he's started he will have to be played for the Remove in big fixtures. You can't carry your rows with him into Soccer."

"Well, no; but——"

"Well, then, chuck it!" said Harry. "You can punch his head after the game if you like, but until then wash it out—see?"

Bob grunted again. He was not the fellow to carry private feuds into football, but it irked him to play in the same team with Carter. He stood undecided, with a football boot on and the other in his hand.

"If that fat ass Bunter had played up Micky would have got off," he muttered.

"Well, he hasn't, and won't! And so——"

"Hurrrooo!" came a sudden roar in the doorway. "Here I am, in toime—phwat? Hurrroo!"

Micky Desmond careered into the changing-room, collided with Bob Cherry, and sent him staggering.

Bob dropped his boot, staggered against Wharton, and sent the captain of the Remove tottering against the wall.

"You mad ass!" he gasped.

"Sure I'm in toime," grinned Micky. "Hould on a minute or two, Wharton darling, while I change. Hurroo!"

"Has Quelch let you off?" asked Harry.

"Sure, and he has intoirely! Where's me shirt? Where's me boots? Has innybody seen me boots?"

Carter glanced across at the Irish junior.

"So you told Quelch?" he asked.

"Tould him, is it?" snapped Micky.

"Sure I tould him nothing! Bunter wint and tould him."

"Bunter did!" exclaimed Carter blankly.

"Faith, and he did, and it's a broth av a bhoy he is, too!"

"Bunter told Quelch he had snooped your lines the other day!" exclaimed Johnny Bull.

Micky chuckled.

"No; he tould him he found thim in his study. Quelch belaves him—and sure so do I now. I belave innything, now I'm let off to play futball. Where's me boots? Who's got me boots?"

Bob Cherry laughed. As Micky had turned up in time, he was not wanted, after all. He was glad of it, not only for Micky's sake.

"Well, Bunter's coming out, and no mistake!" said Frank Nugent. "Bonneting Quelch with a hassock, and then going and owning up about snooping a fellow's lines. Where's Bunter getting all this nerve from?"

"The nervefulness is getting truly terrific," remarked Hurree Jamset Ram Singh.

William Wibley, in the doorway of the changing-room, chortled. He knew how Bunter had screwed up his courage to go to Quelch. And he was greatly entertained by the thought of Bunter's fat face, when he looked into the toffee-tin in the study.

The Fourth Form footballers were already in the field, and the Remove fellows were ready to join them there; but they waited for Micky to change. Micky was ready at last, when a fat figure loomed up at the doorway.

"I say, you fellows, is Wibley here?" squeaked Billy Bunter. "I say, where's that beast Wibley? Where's that rotter Wibley? Where's that cad Wibley?"

"Hallo, hallo, hallo! What's the row?" asked Bob.

"Where's that swab Wibley?"

"Here!" grinned Wibley.

"Beast! There weren't any toffees in that tin!" roared Bunter, shaking a fat fist under Wibley's nose. "Rotter! You said you'd stand me a seven-pound tin if I went to Quelch, and there weren't any toffees in the tin!"

"What?" exclaimed Harry Wharton.

"I say, you fellows, what do you think?" gasped Bunter, breathless with indignation. "He took me up to his study, and showed me a seven-pound toffee-tin, and said I could have it if I got Desmond off detention, and I went to Quelch, and got him off, and then there weren't any toffees in the tin."

"Ha, ha, ha!"

"So that was why——" exclaimed Bob Cherry.

"Not a single toffee!" yelled Bunter. "Fancy that! Pulling a fellow's leg, you know. He said seven pounds of toffee——"

"I didn't," chuckled Wibley. "I said a seven-pound toffee-tin. I never said there was anything in it."

"Ha, ha, ha!"

"You can have the tin," added Wibley. "I said you could have it, and you can have it."

"What's the good of an empty tin to me?" roared Bunter. "Of course, I thought it was full of toffees."

"Now I wonder what put that idea into your head," remarked Wibley.

"Ha, ha, ha!"

"You—you—you beast!" gasped Bunter. "I wouldn't have gone to Quelch if I'd known. I might have got whopped—you never know—with

a beak. And there wasn't any toffee in the tin——"

"Ha, ha, ha!"

"Blessed if I see anything to cackle at! An empty tin——"

"So you had to be bribed to go to Quelch, you fat villain!" chuckled Harry Wharton. And you know you deserve to be booted——"

"Oh, really, Wharton——"

"And you've come here to be booted——"

"Eh? I haven't!"

"Your mistake; you have! All together!" called out the captain of the Remove.

"Ha, ha, ha!"

"I say, you fellows, stoppit! I say —— Yaroooh! Why, you beasts, I—-—Yoo-hoop! Leave off kicking me, you rotters! I say—— Ow! Help! Fire! Murder! Wow! Yaroooop!"

The Remove footballers crowded out of the changing-room, and what seemed to Bunter like an infinite number of football boots landed on him. As a matter of fact, it was only eleven, but it seemed to Bunter like scores, if not hundreds.

Bunter's view was that he was a fellow with a grievance, and he was far from realising that he deserved to be booted. But it was clear to the other fellows, and booted he was. When the Removites passed on, chortling, the fat Owl was left sitting and gasping.

He was still sitting, and still gasping, when the game started on Little Side. For quite a long time Bunter sat and gasped. It was a dismal and breathless Owl that tottered away at last—still gasping.

THE NINETEENTH CHAPTER.

The Secret Out!

"HEARD about Bunter?"

"What about Bunter?"

"Bonneted his beak!"

"Not Bunter?"

"Yes, Bunter!"

That sort of talk was going the rounds, up and down Greyfriars School. At first it had been heard only in the Remove, but, naturally, it spread to other Forms Such an item of news could not fail to spread.

Investigation into that startling happening was still going on. Mr. Quelch was not likely to let it rest. The prefects were supposed to be fearfully keen on tracking down the offender. Loder, certainly, was not bothering about it any further, but the rest of the prefects were doing all they could.

So far, no discovery had been made; but while beaks and prefects remained in blissful ignorance, all the Remove knew—or—at least, thought that they knew—and fellows in other Forms knew—more and more of them.

Bonneting a beak was a rather unusual exploit It was the sort of thing that the Bounder might have done, from reckless swank, though even Smithy would have thought twice, or thrice, before dropping a hassock on Quelch's august napper That a hot-headed Irish youth had done it in haste, and repented of it at leisure, nobody thought of guessing. It was supposed to be the deed of a specially mad ragger. But that that mad ragger was Billy Bunter, was most amazing.

Fellows in the Remove had supposed that it was Bunter, amazing as it was, and when he openly admitted it, there could hardly be any doubt on the subject.

THE MAGNET LIBRARY.—No. 1,562.

Bunter not merely admitted it, he swanked about it. He bragged of it. He gloried in it.

It was sheer satisfaction, to the fat and fatuous Owl. to be stared at in the quad, as the wild and reckless ragger who had bonneted his beak. By Monday, his fame had spread far and wide.

They knew all about it in the Fourth and in the Shell. Cecil Reginald Temple of the Fourth stopped Bunter in the quad to ask him about it. Hobson of the Shell came to his study to get particulars. They talked about it in the Third and the Second. Even in the Fifth Form it was heard of, and on Monday afternoon Coker of the Fifth stopped Bunter, and asked him if it was so.

"You bunged that hassock on your beak's napper last week?" asked Coker.

Bunter grinned happily.

"Sort of," he answered airily.

"Well," said Coker. "you've got a nerve!"

Which filled the cup of Bunter's satisfaction. A Fifth Form man had stopped him in quad, and told him that he had a nerve. Bunter felt, at least, an inch taller when Coker, whistling, left him. A few minutes later he saw Coker pointing him out to Potter and Greene of the Fifth; and Potter and Greene stared round at him.

Rolling happily away, Bunter caught the voice of Tubb of the Third, speaking to Paget and Bolsover minor of that Form.

"That's Bunter—chap who banged a hassock on his beak's napper! Some nerve—what?"

"Cheeky ass!" said Paget.

"Yes; but what a nerve!"

Billy Bunter grinned cheerfully. By that time Bunter had ceased to wonder who really had bonneted Quelch. Obviously the genuine culprit had too much sense to talk about it. Sense was not Billy Bunter's long suit. He

had acquired a new and reckless reputation, outclassing even Smithy in that line, and he revelled in it.

Indeed, by this time, Bunter almost believed that he really had bonneted Quelch! Anyhow, his glory, such as it was, was safe; nobody else was likely to claim such a dangerous distinction.

It was rather an extraordinary situation, that while masters and prefects were trying to spot that reckless ragger, almost the whole of the Lower School knew who the ragger was, and discussed it freely

But nobody, of course, thought of giving Bunter away to the powers; and widely and freely as his exploit was discussed, fellows were careful to say nothing about it within hearing of official ears.

It was quite probable, however, that a topic discussed all through the Lower School, and even in Fifth Form studies, would reach, sooner or later, official ears.

It was, if Bunter had only known it, a certainty! On Tuesday morning, in break, Carter joined the fat Owl in the quad.

Billy Bunter greeted him with a disdainful and inimical blink: but his expression changed when Carter spoke.

"Did you drop half-a-crown under the elms, Bunter?" he asked.

"Yes," answered Bunter promptly. He held out a fat hand. "If you've picked it up, it's mine!"

"I didn't pick it up, as it wasn't mine," answered Carter. "I thought I'd ask you——"

Bunter did not wait for him to finish. He rolled away by the Elm Walk. If half-a-crown had been dropped there, Bunter was prepared to believe, on the spot, that he had dropped it.

Carter followed him under the elms.

Bunter, blinking anxiously along the path, did not observe the portly figure of Mr. Prout in the offing. Carter did.

"I say, Bunter!" Carter did not speak loudly, but he knew that his voice

reached the Fifth Form master. "I say, I wouldn't talk so much about bonneting Quelch, if I were you. If it got out——"

"Rot!" answered Bunter. "Think any man in the Remove would give me away? The fellows would scrag a sneak, I can jolly well tell you! I say, where did you see that half-crown?"

"It was about here somewhere. Now, if you'll take a tip from me, Bunter, you'll shut up about dropping that hassock on Quelch's napper——"

"Rats!" retorted Bunter. "Think I'm funky?"

"If Quelch heard——"

"Who's afraid of Quelch?"

"Well, if you're not, all right!" said Carter. "But, look here, Bunter, honest Injun, did you really drop that hassock on Quelch?"

"You jolly well know I did—the only man in the Form who'd have had the nerve, too!" said Bunter. "Smithy swanks about not caring a bean for the beaks—but Smithy wouldn't have had the nerve. You wouldn't, either! A Fifth Form man told me I'd got a lot of nerve to do it! So I have! Fat lot I care for beaks, or prefects, either!"

Carter laughed.

Mr. Prout, at a short distance, had turned his head, and was staring blankly at Bunter.

"But, I say, where did you see that half-crown?" asked Bunter. "It's mine, you know—I remember hearing it drop."

"Oh, my hat!" gasped Carter. "Well, if you heard it drop, you know where to look for it!"

And he walked away, Bunter blinking after him in great annoyance.

"Beast!" hooted Bunter. "I don't believe there was any half-crown at all! Rotter!"

And Bunter rolled away to the school shop, in the hope of finding Lord Mauleverer there.

Mr. Prout gazed after him as he went.

"Goodness gracious!" gasped Prout.

And the Fifth Form master walked to the House, with news for Mr. Quelch.

When the bell rang for third school, and Billy Bunter joined the Remove going in, he little dreamed of what awaited him. He had seen nothing of Prout under the elms, and had not the remotest idea that his brag was, as it were, coming home to roost.

The Remove gathered at their Form-room door, and when Mr. Quelch came along to let them in, the expression on his face caught many eyes.

"Mind your step, you fellows!" whispered Skinner. "Quelchy's got his rag out over something."

"Henry looks shirty!" murmured Bob Cherry.

"The shirtiness is terrific!"

That something was "up" was clear to all the Remove. Mr. Quelch's face, always severe, was extremely grim, and his eyes glinted. Like the young man in the Alpine poem, his brow was set, his eyes beneath, flashed like a falchion from its sheath. Trouble, it was clear, was coming to somebody; and the Removites wondered uneasily whom.

They took their places in the Form-room in silence, every fellow on his best behaviour for once. Nobody knew, so far, where the thunderbolt was going to fall—only that it was coming.

Mr. Quelch stood facing his class, and the Remove waited almost breathlessly. It was coming now!

"Bunter!"

Printed in England and published every Saturday by the Proprietors, The Amalgamated Press. Ltd., The Fleetway House, Farringdon Street, London, E.C.4. Advertisement offices : The Fleetway House Farringdon Street, London, E.C.4. Registered for transmission by Canadian Magazine Post. Subscription rates: Inland and Abroad, 11s. per annum; 5s. 6d. for six months. Sole Agents for Australia and New Zealand: Messrs. Gordon & Gotch, Ltd., and for South Africa : Central News Agency, Ltd.—Saturday, January 22nd, 1938.

The name was rapped out like a rifle-shot. And the other fellows breathed more freely. It was Bunter who was "for it." And most of them guessed at once why. Something had leaked out about Bunter's exploit with the hassock.

The fat Owl gave a jump as his name was rapped out. His eyes popped at his Form-master.

"Oh! Yes, sir!" gasped Bunter. "It wasn't me!"

"Stand out before the Form, Bunter!"

"Oh lor'!"

Bunter almost tottered out.

THE TWENTIETH CHAPTER.
Self-condemned!

"**B**UNTER!"

"I—I didn't, sir!" gasped Bunter. "It—it wasn't me!"

Bunter did not know yet of what he was going to be accused. Every other fellow in the Form-room had guessed. But Billy Bunter's powerful brain was not quick on the uptake.

But he could see that he was going to be accused of something, and he was prepared, on general principles, to deny anything and everything. On any and every subject the fat Owl was prepared to tell anything but the truth.

"It has come to my knowledge," said Mr Quelch, in a deep voice, "that it was you who committed a disrespectful and outrageous attack on your Form-master one day last week, Bunter. I had the very strongest suspicion of you at the time; but in so serious a matter, I felt bound to wait for absolute proof. That proof is now in my hands."

"Oh crikey!"

"I shall take you to your headmaster to be dealt with," pursued Mr. Quelch. "Whether Dr. Locke will administer a flogging merely, or whether you will be expelled, I cannot undertake to say. The decision rests with your head-master"

"Oh crumbs!"

"Howly Moses!" breathed Micky Desmond. He sat in his place, looking on in dismay.

"Wharton, I shall leave you in charge here for a few minutes, while I take Bunter to his headmaster."

"Very well, sir!" answered Harry with a glance of commiseration at the hapless fat Owl.

Bunter did not look much like a bold, bad, mad ragger now. His eyes were popping, and his jaw dropping. His fat face was the picture of woe and terror. His podgy knees knocked together.

"But, I—I say, sir!" squeaked Bunter desperately. "I—I didn't! I never did, sir! I was in my study——"

"I will listen to no further untruths from you, Bunter!" said the Remove master sternly. "I have said that proof is now in my hands! Not only is it known to me that you are the culprit, but I have reason to believe that the fact is known to the whole Form." Mr. Quelch cast a very severe glance over the Form. "I have no doubt that every boy here present is aware of it!"

Every boy there present tried to look as unconscious as he could. But it was quite easy for Quelch's gimlet eye to read that they all knew

"But I never did, sir!" wailed Bunter. "It can't be proved when I never did, sir! How can it?"

"From what I learn, you were not only guilty of that outrageous act, Bunter, but you have actually boasted of it!" said Mr. Quelch sternly. "In

break this morning, you were heard boasting of it to another Remove boy."

"Oh crumbs! I—I say, sir, if—if Carter says——"

"Carter has said nothing, Bunter! I should not be likely to listen to information given by one boy against another."

Bob Cherry gave a start, and his eyes flashed round at Carter. The latter sat with his eyes fixed on Bunter.

Bob drew a deep, hard breath. Carter could not have gone to Quelch with the story. Mr. Quelch was not a master to whom a sneaking story could be told. But it was plain that Carter was mixed up in it somehow. Bob knew, at least, he was certain, that the schemer of the Remove had contrived, somehow, to give the wretched Owl away.

"No boy has given me information!" said Mr. Quelch. "No boy would be permitted to do so. Your foolish and boastful words were heard by a member of Dr. Locke's staff, Bunter, who reported them to me."

"Oh lor'! But I—I never——"

"In break this morning, Bunter, you were heard to state, indeed to boast, in speaking to another Remove boy, that you threw the hassock——"

"I—I wasn't, sir!" gasped Bunter. "Nobody was there, but Carter. At least, I didn't see anybody."

"Mr. Prout heard you from a short distance Bunter."

"Did he, sir! Oh crikey! But—but I never said anything to Carter, sir! He made me go there, making out that there was a half-crown, and I never saw Prout! Oh crikey! But—but I never said anything to Carter, sir! I never said a word to him, sir! You can ask him, sir—he will remember all I said——"

"That will do, Bunter! Not only were you guilty of that outrage, on your own statement, but you have actually made it a matter of boasting!" said Mr. Quelch, sternly. "How any boy could find matter for boasting, in a foolish, reckless, and disrespectful act, passes my comprehension : but you have done so. You will now go with me to Dr. Locke——"

"But I never, sir!" yelled Bunter, in desperation. "I—I—I made out I did, sir, but I—I never did! It was only swank, sir!"

"You need say no more, Bunter!"

"But I didn't, sir!" wailed the unhappy Owl. "All the fellows thought so, and I let them think so, just for swank, sir! I never did it really! I—I wouldn't! Oh dear! I wish I hadn't said I did! Oh crikey!"

"Follow me, Bunter!"

"I—I don't want to go to the Head, sir!" groaned Bunter. "He—he—he might think I—I did it——"

Mr. Quelch dropped an iron hand on the fat Owl's shoulder, and led him out of the Form-room.

Bunter gave a squeak of terror as he went.

If ever a braggart repented him of his brag, the hapless Owl of the Remove did at that moment.

For several days Bunter had gloried in the reputation of a bad, mad ragger, and enjoyed it thoroughly. Up and down the Remove had Bunter swanked as a devil of a fellow who would bonnet a beak as soon as look at him!

He did not look very much like a devil of a fellow now! He quaked, as Mr. Quelch led him out. He seemed hardly able to drag his fat limbs along. After the feast had come the reckoning, and repentance came too late! Out of his own mouth he was condemned, and there was no hope for Bunter! His dragging footsteps and dismal squeak died away down the passage.

In the Remove, the juniors looked at one another. Wibley and Morgan looked at Micky Desmond. Micky looked at his desk.

"Well, it's out now!" said Harry Wharton. "Poor old Bunter! If he'd had the sense to hold his tongue about it——"

"The sensefulness of the idiotic Bunter is not terrific!" said Hurree Jamset Ram Singh. "The bragfulness is too preposterous."

"Isn't it just like him, to spout it out with a beak standing at his elbow!" said the Bounder. "Bunter all over——"

"Well, it was bound to come out sooner or later, with that fat ass swanking about it all over the shop!" said Johnny Bull.

"Poor old Bunter!"

"Dash it all, you might have stopped him, Carter, if Prout was in the offing," exclaimed Peter Todd. "You're not a blind Owl like Bunter—you must have seen Prout, if he was near enough to hear."

"Never noticed him!" answered Carter coolly. "Other side of a tree I expect. I haven't the faintest idea——"

"That's a lie!" roared Bob Cherry, starting to his feet, his face crimson, and his eyes flashing. "You pulled Bunter's leg into making him give himself away where a beak could hear him."

Carter spun round.

"What?" he gasped.

"Bob!" exclaimed Wharton.

"Chuck it, old man!" said Johnny Bull "As if any fellow would be cad enough—rotter enough——"

"Draw it mild, Cherry!" said the Bounder.

"Oh, don't talk to me!" roared Bob, flaming with angry indignation. "This isn't the first time that cad's tried to land that fat idiot in the soup; and he's got away with it this time. And I'll tell you this, Carter—if Bunter gets a flogging. I'll give you the biggest hiding you ever had in your life."

Carter sneered.

"I'm not the only fellow he's bragged to, am I?" he asked "He's told every fellow who would listen to him, in the Remove and out of it. He's told fellows in the senior Forms. He's shouted it out all over the school. He happened to be bragging to me when Prout heard it, that's all. He will get a flogging, and he jolly well deserves it for dropping a hassock on Quelch's head! You know that as well as I do!"

"Yes, I know that!" snapped Bob. "But it wasn't your business to get him a flogging, you rotten sneak! You wangled this——"

"Sure Bunter ain't going to get a flogging!" said Micky Desmond, rising to his feet. "I'm going to stop it intoirely."

"How can you stop it, fathead?" grunted Bob Cherry.

"Sure I'm the wan that did the thrick!"

"Wha-a-t?"

"You!" roared a dozen voices.

"Yis! Me!" groaned Micky "And a thumping fool I was, too, and by the same token I was sorry afther I'd done it: but sure I ain't going to let that fat omadhaun take my gruel for me!"

All eyes fixed on Micky Desmond, as he left his place, and went to the door.

His announcement utterly amazed the Remove. Not a fellow, excepting Wibley and Morgan, had dreamed of suspecting the real culprit Least of all had Carter!

Carter's eyes seemed to start from his head, as he stared at the Irish junior.

"You!" he gasped "You! Why, you

fool, what do you mean? It was Bunter——"

"Sure it was meself intoirely," answered Micky, over his shoulder, "and if Bob's right, and you mint to get Bunter a flogging, you spalpeen, you've got me one instead, and afther the Head's done with me, I'll sure make shavings of ye, and so I will!"

And Micky tramped out of the Form-room, leaving the Remove in a buzz.

THE TWENTY-FIRST CHAPTER.

The Way of the Transgressor!

"HAD it bad?"
Groan!
"Poor old chap!"
Groan!
"You did the right thing, Micky!"
Groan!
"Still feel it!"
Groan!

After third school Micky Desmond was surrounded by sympathisers. He had not returned to the Form-room for the lesson, and when the Remove were dismissed, they found him in the Rag —groaning. He wriggled, he writhed, and he groaned—dismally—eloquent evidence that the Head had not spared the rod.

Everybody was sympathetic. Everybody agreed that Micky had done the right thing in going to the Head and owning up. Sympathy and approval were no doubt grateful and comforting to the sad sufferer. Still, they did not soothe the pangs and twinges left by the Head's birch.

"Sure and bedad he laid it on!" groaned Micky. "And would ye belave it, he said that he would have made it more severe, only I'd owned up in time to get Bunter off. So he said he would only give me twilve sthrokes! Howly Moses, I wonder what it would have been like if he'd give me twinty! Wow!"

"Buck up, old chap!" said Billy Bunter. "It might have been worse, you know. I mean, it might have been me that got it."

"You blithering idiot! Wow!"

"After all, what's a whopping?" said Bunter. "Bear it, you know! Keep a stiff upper lip! Bite on the bullet, and all that! No good making a fuss about it, you know! I shouldn't!"

Micky look at him.

"It's all through that fat baste's bragging that it had to come out!" he said. "And now, Wibley, you spalpeen, Morgan, you baste, you call yourselves pals, and why don't you boot Bunter entoirely? Can't you do a little thing like that for a friend?"

Wibley and Morgan obeyed the call of friendship promptly. Two boots landed, at once, on the tightest trousers at Greyfriars School, and Micky's groans were drowned by a fiendish yell from Billy Bunter.

"Yarooh! Oh crikey! Keep off, you beasts! I say, you fellows—whoop!"

Bunter dodged for the door. After him rushed Wibley and Morgan. They landed three each before the fat Owl escaped from the Rag, and fled yelling down the passage.

Micky was feeling a little better at dinner. But he squirmed a good deal on his seat, and uttered little squeaks every now and then.

After dinner, however, he was better still. And when the juniors came out, he joined Bob Cherry in the quad.

"Ye remimber what ye said in the Form-room, Cherry?" he asked.

"Yes," said Bob, looking at him.

"You think that spalpeen Carter was snaking?"

"Whatting?" gasped Bob. "Oh, sneaking! Yes, I do! He thought it was Bunter, and he made the fat ass give himself away."

"And landed me instead of Bunter?" said Micky. "Well, I'm not sure ye're right, but, in case ye are, I'll give him snaking, the spalpeen!"

And he went to look for Carter.

"Ye thafe of the worruld!" he exclaimed, as he came up to the new

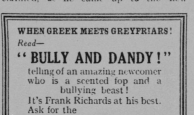
junior. "Ye got me a flogging with your snaking about Bunter——"

"You can thank Bunter for that!" answered Carter, with a scowl. "If you'd had sense enough to keep your silly mouth shut, you'd have got off all right."

Micky blinked at him.

"Keep me mouth shut, is it, and let another man take my gruel!" he exclaimed. "That's the sort of spalpeen ye are, is it?"

"Oh, go and eat coke!" snarled Carter.

"Bob Cherry thinks you gave Bunter away, ye baste——"

"Bob Cherry's a fool!"

"Well, perhaps ye did, and perhaps ye didn't!" said Micky. "But in case ye did, and me getting a flogging afther it, ye can take that—and that— and that——"

The next moment a fight was in progress. There was a rush of juniors at once to surround the combatants. Micky was going it hammer and tongs, and Carter had no choice but to play up. It was quite terrific for five

minutes at the end of which Carter lay on his back, winded to the wide, his nose streaming crimson.

Micky Desmond danced round him, urging him to get up and come on. Carter got up—but he did not come on; he tottered away to bathe his nose, which needed it badly!

.   .   .   .   .   .

"I say, you fellows!"

The Famous Five were in Bob Cherry's study at tea-time, when the door opened, and Billy Bunter blinked in.

Grim and unwelcoming stares greeted Bunter, regardless of which he rolled cheerfully in.

"Teaing here?" he asked breezily. "Fed-up with that cad Carter, what? Fancy the cad giving me away like that, you know—pulling my leg to make me tell Prout! If Desmond hadn't made out that he bonneted Quelch, I should have bagged a flogging! Of course, it was me, you know!"

"What?" roared the Famous Five together.

"Me, of course," said Bunter cheerfully. "Micky was only bragging, making out he did it! There are fellows who will brag about things they've never really done! Not the sort of thing I could do! Of course, I was jolly glad to get off a flogging! But it was me all the time!"

Harry Wharton & Co. gazed at Bunter.

They had been taken in by Bunter's brag—they had believed him to be a bold, bad ragger! Now that everybody knew the real facts, however, they had expected Bunter to "chuck" it.

Bunter, apparently, was not thinking of chucking it! He was not willing to part with his bold, bad reputation!

He winked at the staring five.

"Just brag, you know," he said. "Micky never did it! I did! Fat lot I care for beaks! I'd bonnet Quelch as soon as look at him! Or the Head, either, if you come to that! I'm the man for it! I'd— Yaroooh! I say, you fellows, leggo! Wharrer you at?"

"Bump him!" said Harry Wharton.

"I say——"

Bump!

"Yarooop!"

"Now, did you bonnet Quelch?"

"Ow! Yes!"

Bump!

"Stoppit! Wow! Ow! I say——"

"Did you bonnet Quelch?"

"Yes—I mean, no!" roared Bunter. "No! Never! Not at all! Not a bit! Yow-wow-ow! Never thought of it! Oh crikey!"

A last bump landed Bunter in the passage. It was the end of Billy Bunter's bragging!

THE END.

(The next yarn in this rattling fine series is better than ever. It's entitled: "RIVALS FOR RICHES!" You can only make sure of next Saturday's MAGNET *by ordering it to-day!)*

The Magnet

2ᴰ

Billy Bunter's Own Paper

BILLY BUNTER'S BOLT!

INSIDE INFORMATION ABOUT GREYFRIARS by the Man Who Knows—

The GREYFRIARS GUIDE

A TOUR OF THE SCHOOL. The Recreation Room—or Rag.

(1)

We've finished prep, and with cheerful
  step
We make our way to the Rag.
This homely room is no place for
  gloom—
Our tongues begin to wag;
While Bunter sits in a chair that fits
His figure like a glove.
The jokes are played and the plots are
  laid
With many a push and shove.

(2)

Then Temple's crowd are, of course,
  allowed
To use the Rag as well,
And many a scene we've had between
The Upper Fourth and the Shell.
When war breaks out we can thump and
  shout
And fight to our hearts' content,
Till prefects stroll in the door and dole
Out capital punishment !

(3)

Some fellows read, and there's some,
  indeed,
Like Mauly who sit and doze;
While some play chess, and I must
  confess
I'm frequently one of those.
There's "footer jaw," which is sure to
  draw
An argument in its train,
And the whole room hums until Wingate
  comes,
And—it's bed-time once again !

AFTER SCHOOL HOURS
Tom Brown's Wireless

Browney has a wireless set,
  A cottage radio,
And sometimes he's been known to get
  That wireless set to go !
In general, it seldom cares
  To let its voice be heard;
It likes to mind its own affairs
  And never says a word.
When fellows, full of interest,
  Are waiting in the room,
That wireless set is like the rest—
  As silent as the tomb.
But now and then the thing emits
  A most appalling squeak,
Which gives a nervous fellow fits
  That last about a week.
The reason why it should produce
  These squeaks, I can't explain;
But Browney says a screw is loose
  Inside the creature's brain.
Last night, for instance, after tea
  I heard a fearful squeal,
And what effect it had on me
  I simply can't reveal !
Peter Todd collapsed with grief;
  We carried him to bed,
And left him with the firm belief
  That blood was being shed.
Then Prout, complete with gun,
  rushed in
To stop a fearful crime,
And prefects added to the din—
  We had a lovely time !
Meanwhile, the set burst into speech
  In German dialect.
A book was lying within my reach—
  That's why the set is wrecked !

THE GREYFRIARS ALPHABET
CLAUDE HOSKINS,
the Musical Genius of the Shell.

H is for HOSKINS of the Shell,
And let me say, unless I dwell
Upon his talents (?) musical,
I needn't write of him at all.
For Hoskins you can only see
When playing some dashed rhapsody,
Or else composing for a lark
Far greater melodies than Bach,

Or even Mozart, let alone
Such men as Grieg and Mendelssohn.
If Hoskins studied music—well,
They might not chortle in the Shell.
He doesn't study it; he'll look
On music as an open book
Whose secrets are so clearly seen
By a great master—aged sixteen !

ANSWER TO PUZZLE

A blank notebook. If there were
1,000 books in the library, the largest
of them could not contain more than
999 words and, as they all had a
different number, one (at least) must
have been blank.

GREYFRIARS GRINS

I've just heard of a man who stood
quite still upon the corner of a street
for nine days. He must have been
having a chat with Prout !

Skinner, accused of eating toffee in
class, was ordered by Mr. Quelch to
turn out his pockets. Luckily, however,
he had only a packet of cigarettes and
some marked cards on him at the time !

Quelchy said recently that no sensible
boy would ever gamble, and I bet you
anything you like he's right !

Fisher T. Fish has decided to stop
giving offence to others. He is going
to charge for it !

Loder's face is covered with pimples.
Good job it's covered with something !

PUZZLE PAR

In the school library there are
a lot of books, no two of which
have the same number of words,
and there are more books in the
library than words in the largest
book. What is one of the books?
Answer at foot of column 2.

Don Ogilvy brought his bagpipes to
school this term and started by playing
"The Campbells are Coming !" First
time I've heard the prefects called
Campbells !

When Tubb of the Third spilled some
acid on his hands in chemistry class, he
smiled bravely, and said it might have
been worse ! Sure ! It might have been
soap and water !

In the last snowfall we thought
someone had built a snowman in the
quad, but it turned out to be Gosling,
sweeping it up.

When Inky saw Coker on his motor-
bike he turned pale with fright. Pale
black, of course.

MAKING GOOD at Greyfriars is a hard enough task for Arthur Carter, a " bad hat " who has been turned out of his last school—but " dishing " Billy Bunter, who has cut him out of his uncle's will, is more difficult still !

RIVALS for RICHES !

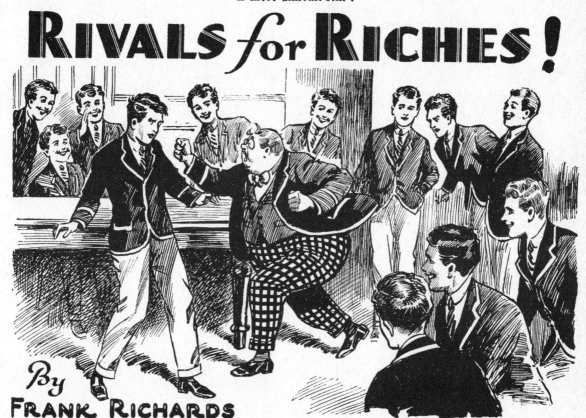

By FRANK RICHARDS

Billy Bunter faced Carter, a threatening frown on his fat face and a warlike gleam behind his spectacles.   He brandished a podgy fist under the new junior's nose !

THE FIRST CHAPTER.

Something Like a Surprise !

"SEEN my gold pencil?"

"No!"

"Well, I want it!" said Carter.

The new fellow in the Greyfriars Remove spoke in so significant and unpleasant a tone, that the other fellows in the study all turned their heads to look at him.

Harry Wharton and Frank Nugent were listening to Wun Lung, who was telling them about a Japanese air-raid that had knocked to pieces his father's "hong" at Canton. Billy Bunter was in Study No. 1—not because he was interested in the Chinese junior's description of Far-Eastern atrocities, but because he was in hopes of staying to tea.

Bunter was waiting impatiently for Wun to come to a finish.   Air-raids were thrilling, but sosses and chips were filling; and Billy Bunter would rather have been filled than thrilled.

Arthur Carter came into the study, looked over the table, looked over it again, and then addressed his question to the study generally.

"I left my gold pencil on the table when I went down!" said Carter.   "I want to know where it is."

"Look for it!" suggested Harry Wharton.

"I've looked!"

"Look again!" said Frank Nugent.

"Don't talk rot!   Where is it?"

Wun Lung ceased his narrative, and his slanting eyes dwelt curiously on the new member of the Remove.

Billy Bunter blinked at Carter, through his big spectacles, with an inimical blink.

Harry Wharton fixed his eyes on Carter.

"What do you mean?" he asked quietly.   "You don't suppose that anybody in this study has bagged your silly pencil, do you?"

"I know I left it on the table, and that it's not there now!   If you've shifted it, you can say so."

"I've not seen it," said Harry curtly.

"Nor I!" said Nugent.

"What about you, Bunter?" asked Carter.

"Don't talk to me, Carter!" answered

A Super-Quality School Story, featuring HARRY WHARTON & CO., of Greyfriars, by our Star Author.

Bunter disdainfully.   "I've told you I bar you.   If you think I'm going to know you here, because you happen to be a distant relation of mine, you're mistaken!   Just shut up, see?"

"You fat ass," exclaimed Harry Wharton, "tell the fellow whether you've seen his silly pencil or not."

"Well, I haven't seen it!   But I'm not going to tell Carter so; I'm not going to speak to him," retorted Bunter.   "He can jolly well find out whether I've seen it or not!"

"Me lookee!" said Wun Lung.

He came across to the table, brushing against Carter.

"Don't shove me, you Chinese image!" rapped Carter.

"Plenty solly me shovee nicey feller Cartee!" said Wun Lung amicably.   "No see pencil along table."

"Go on, Wun!" said Nugent.   "You were telling us——"

"You can cut that out!" interposed Carter.   "I can't afford to lose a gold pencil.   Who's got it?"

"Who's got it?" repeated Harry Wharton.   The captain of the Remove looked at Carter with glinting eyes.   "Did you say who's got it?"

"Don't you understand plain English?" asked Carter.   "I said exactly that, and I want an answer."

"You won't get any answer from me, unless it's a punch on your cheeky nose !"

"Don't get on the high horse, old bean—your favourite mount, from what I hear in the Remove!" said Carter coolly.   "I don't suspect your High Mightiness of pinching my pencil. There's a fellow in this study who pinches and pilfers up and down the Remove, and I want to know if he's got it."

Billy Bunter's fat face became as red as a newly boiled beetroot with wrath. His little round eyes flashed through his big, round spectacles.

"You—you—you cheeky cad!" he gasped.   "You toad!   You worm! You—you—you swab!   Do you think I'd touch your rotten pencil?"

"Quite!"

THE MAGNET LIBRARY.—No. 1,563.

"Beast!" roared Bunter.

"I've seen you with that gold pencil of yours, Carter," said Frank Nugent. "It looks fearfully expensive and frightfully swanky. But it's not eatable, is it?"

"What do you mean, you ass?"

"I mean that if it were eatable, Bunter's eaten it—but if it isn't, he hasn't touched it, and you know it as well as we do."

"I don't know it!" said Carter. "I know I left it on this table, and it isn't there now! I know that if I left a cake, or a bun, Bunter would pinch it —I've seen you fellows booting him for pinching tuck in this study. A fellow who would pinch a cake would pinch anything else."

"As if I'd pinch a cake!" roared Bunter indignantly. "I suppose you're making out that I had Bob Cherry's cake. So far as I know, it's still in his study cupboard. If it isn't, I don't know anything about it."

"Will you hand over that gold pencil, Bunter?" asked Carter. "It was a birthday present from my uncle, and cost some guineas, and I'm not going to lose it. I want it—at once."

"I advise you to chuck that, Carter!" said Harry Wharton. "What you say about a cake or a bun is true enough, but you know perfectly well that Bunter would not touch your things. You wouldn't dare to say so, if he could handle you as you deserve for your cheek."

"I say, you fellows, I'll jolly well boot him!" gasped Bunter. "I say, you hold him while I boot him!"

"I'm waiting!" said Carter.

"Beast!"

"Very well!" said Carter compressing his lips. "I've lost an article of value in this study, and I'm bound to report it to my Form-master! I'll go down to Quelch!" He turned to the door. "Unless Bunter turns out his pockets, this minute, I'm calling Quelch in! He can take his choice."

"Hold on!" said Harry Wharton. "Bunter, you fat ass, you ask for this sort of thing by snaffling tuck in the studies——"

"If you're trying to make out that I snaffle tuck in the studies, Harry Wharton——"

"Oh, shut up, fathead! Look here, nobody here except that suspicious cad believes that you would touch his mouldy pencil. We don't want Quelch up here! Turn out your pockets and satisfy the cad!"

"You're calling me some pretty names!" sneered Carter.

"I'm calling you exactly what you are!" said the captain of the Remove contemptuously. "If you fancy that Bunter would pinch your mouldy pencil, you're a suspicious cad."

"Hear, hear!" said Frank Nugent.

"Well, let us see the pockets turned out!" sneered Carter. "I left the pencil in this study, and it's gone."

"Beast!" roared Bunter. "Look here, then!"

And the fat Owl of the Remove began turning out his pockets.

He gave a sudden jump.

"I say, you fellows! My watch is gone!"

"Bother your watch!" snapped Harry Wharton.

"But it's gone!" yelled Bunter. "I've nearly lost it two or three times, since I sold the chain to Fishy. I say, you fellows, have you seen my watch?"

"Plaps Cartee gottee!" suggested Wun Lung innocently.

Carter glared round at the Chinese junior.

"What's that?" he roared.

THE MAGNET LIBRARY.—No. 1,563.

"You tinkee Buntee gottee pencil—plaps you gottee watchee blong Buntee!" grinned Wun Lung.

The Removite made a stride at the Chinese junior, his fists clenched and his eyes blazing.

Wun promptly dodged behind the captain of the Remove.

"You can chuck that, Carter!" said Harry. "You lay a finger on Wun, and you go out of this study on your neck!"

"You heard what he said!" yelled Carter.

"Yes—just what you said of Bunter! Sauce for the goose is sauce for the gander! If you don't like it, lump it!"

"He, he, he!" from Bunter.

Arthur Carter breathed hard.

Wun grinned at him cheerfully, from behind the sturdy defence of the captain of the Remove.

"Get on with it, Bunter, and get it over!" said Harry.

"But my watch——"

"Bother your twopenny rolled gold watch! Get on with it, before that cad starts a yarn up and down the Remove that there's been pinching in this study!" exclaimed Wharton, impatiently.

Bunter grunted, and resumed turning out the lining of his pockets.

There was a sudden gleam of gold in the wintry sunlight from the window.

"Oh crikey!" ejaculated Bunter.

His eyes almost popped through his spectacles as he dropped a gold pencil on the table.

Harry Wharton and Frank Nugent stared at it blankly, and Arthur Carter's lip curled in a bitter sneer.

"What about that?" he asked sarcastically.

But Wharton and Nugent did not reply. They could only stare at the gold pencil turned out of Billy Bunter's pocket in dumb amazement.

THE SECOND CHAPTER.

Only Wun!

BILLY BUNTER stood blinking at the gold pencil.

He blinked with bulging eyes.

If the other fellows in the study were amazed, Billy Bunter seemed more amazed still. He seemed hardly able to believe his eyes or his spectacles as he stared at the gold pencil.

"Oh!" gasped Bunter. "Oh crikey!"

Carter looked at him with a hard, grim look. Bunter looked amazed, but he was not likely to believe that that amazement was genuine. The gold pencil could not have got into the fat Owl's pocket of its own volition.

"That does it!" said Carter. "I knew it, and I suppose you fellows admit it now! This is going before the Head! I'm not going to keep this kind of thing dark!"

"I—I say, you fellows, I—I never touched it!" gasped Bunter.

"It jumped into your pocket!" sneered Carter.

"Beast!"

"You—you—you utter ass!" gasped Harry Wharton, finding his voice at last. "You—you benighted idiot! What——"

"Oh, really, Wharton——"

"Did you take it for a joke, or what, you thumping chump?" exclaimed Frank Nugent.

"I—I never took it!"

Carter laughed.

"You can tell Dr. Locke that!" he said. "I'm going down to report this to Quelch, and he will take it before the Head! You fellows will have to speak up as witnesses!"

Wun Lung made a swift scuttle across the study, turned the key in the door, jerked it out, and scuttled back behind Wharton.

It was done before Carter could raise a hand to stop him.

The new junior stared at Wun.

"Unlock that door, you Chinese idiot!" he snapped.

"No hully!" said Wun coolly. "You goey 'long old Quelch; say Buntee pinchee pencil! P'l'aps Buntee likee goey; say you pinchee watchee!"

"Give me that key, you heathen ass!"

"Don't be a duffer, Wun!" said Harry Wharton. "You can't keep the fellow here."

"Turnee out pockee, all samee Buntee!" said Wun. "Me tinkee watchee blong Buntee stop along pockee blong Cartee!"

"Rubbish!" said Harry.

"No tinkee lubbish! Me savvy plenty too much!" declared Wun. "You makee Buntee turnee out pockee blong him; makee Cartee samee!"

Carter clenched his hands almost convulsively. Only the fact that Harry Wharton was between them prevented him from hammering the Chinese junior right and left.

"Will you let me out of this study?" he hissed.

"You turnee out pockee!"

"I—I say, you fellows, you make him turn out his pockets!" gasped Billy Bunter. "I—I shouldn't wonder if he's got my watch! He's making out that I pinched his rotten pencil——"

"Look here, Wun, if you've got any reason to believe——"

"Me savvy."

"Now, look here, Carter," said Harry Wharton quietly, "Bunter's the biggest fool at Greyfriars, and he must have picked up your pencil for some idiotic idea of a joke on you——"

"He can tell the Head that!" sneered Carter.

"I never——"

"Shut up, you fat chump! But Wun says you've got Bunter's watch," said Harry, his eyes gleaming. "We've made Bunter turn out his pockets; now turn out yours before you go down to Quelch about Bunter!"

"I shall do nothing of the kind!" exclaimed Carter fiercely.

"You will!" retorted Wharton. "What's good for Bunter is good enough for you! You'll turn out your pockets before you leave this study! And if you refuse, I'll hold you by the neck while Nugent turns them out!"

"What-ho!" said Frank. "Blessed if it doesn't look as if he's got the watch!"

Carter gritted his teeth.

"You're two to one!" he said. "I'll turn out my pockets, if you like. But you know perfectly well——"

"Turn them out!"

Carter, with a savagely angry face, turned out his jacket pockets.

But the expression on his face changed strangely as a large timekeeper, obviously of the kind of gold called "rolled," came into view.

It thudded on the table as he dropped it there, with blank amazement in his face. There was a squeak from Billy Bunter.

"I say, you fellows, that's my watch! He had it!"

"Oh crumbs!" gasped Nugent.

"That's Bunter's old turnip, Carter!" said the captain of the Remove. "And it was in your pocket! How did it get there?"

"I—I—I——" Carter gasped. "I—I don't know!"

"It jumped into your pocket!" grinned Nugent.

Carter gazed at the watch. He seemed as amazed by the sight of the watch as Bunter had seemed by the sight of the gold pencil. He looked as if he could hardly believe his eyes.

"Well, you're a precious pair, and no mistake!" said the captain of the Remove. "I don't and can't believe that Bunter meant to keep your pencil, Carter; but you're not a fool like Bunter——"

"I—I never——" stammered Carter.

"You can go down to Quelch together!" said Harry. "Unlock that door, Wun, and let them get out!"

Wun Lung, grinning, unlocked the door. But Arthur Carter was no longer eager to leave the study.

"Look here," he said hoarsely, "this is some kind of a trick! I never knew that that watch was in my pocket. It must have been slipped in!"

"I never knew the pencil was in my pocket!" hooted Bunter. "I dare say you slipped it in when you pinched my watch!"

"Why, you fat rotter——"

"You skinny beast——"

Harry Wharton gave a sudden start, and his eyes turned on Wun Lung, who was almost doubled up in an excess of merriment.

A sudden suspicion shot into the mind of the captain of the Remove. He remembered the little Chince's weird sleight-of-hand trickeries. There had been an incident something of the same kind in that very study last term. Wharton suddenly remembered it now.

"Wun!" he roared. "You young rascal!"

"Wun——" repeated Nugent.

"Allee light! Only little jokee!" gasped Wun, gurgling with laughter. "Me makee you laugh plenty too much!"

"Oh!" gasped Nugent. "That blither-ing little Chinese idiot—at his potty tricks again!"

"Tinkee velly funnee!" chuckled Wun. "Me puttee pencil blong Cartee long pockee blong Buntee; watchee blong Buntee long pockee blong Cartee! Plenty too funny!"

"What?" gasped Carter blankly.

Harry Wharton almost gasped with relief. It was, after all, only one of the weird trickeries of the Chinese junior.

"Hankee blong Flanky stop along pockee blong you!" went on Wun, chortling. "Pockee-knifee blong you stop along pockee blong Flanky!"

Harry Wharton and Frank Nugent, in silence, made an exchange of a handkerchief and a pocket-knife.

"Oh crikey!" gasped Bunter. "That little Chinese beast playing tricks all the time!"

"But what," gasped Carter—"what——"

"Oh, you're new here!" snapped Wharton. "You haven't seen Wun at his mad tricks! He got such a booting for it last term I thought he'd chuck it. Wun put your rotten pencil in Bunter's pocket, and Bunter's mouldy watch in your pocket! Now do you understand—or do you want to go down to Quelch, and accuse your relation and yourself of stealing?"

"Oh!" gasped Carter.

He understood now, and he gave the chuckling Chinese junior a glare of concentrated rage.

Wun, evidently, regarded that extraordinary practical joke as extremely funny. Nobody else in the study took that view.

"Boot him!" said Harry Wharton.

Wun made a jump to the door.

Billy Bunter landed one as he jumped, and Wun gave a yell.

Carter rushed after him, and landed kick after kick as the Chince flew, yelling, up the Remove passage.

A dozen fellows stared out of the studies as Wun flew by, waking the echoes, Carter pursuing him with a savage face, kicking and kicking again.

"Hallo! What's this game?" exclaimed Vernon-Smith.

"What the thump——" exclaimed Peter Todd.

Wun flew on. Carter flew after him. He landed a dozen, at least, before the Chinee reached his study, No. 13 in the Remove.

Wun Lung hurled the door open and tore in, yelling frantically.

"Hallo, hallo, hallo!" roared Bob Cherry, as Wun Lung burst into the study. "What the merry dickens——" "You stoppee that fellee Cartee, nicey old Bob Chelly!" yelled the Chinese junior. "Plenty too muchee kickee 'long tlousers b'long me!"

"Hallo, hallo, hallo!" came Bob Cherry's voice from within the study.

"What the merry dickens——"

"You stoppee that fellee Cartee, nicey old Bob Chelly!" yelled Wun Lung. "Plenty too muchee kickee 'long tlousers b'long me."

Bob Cherry jumped up.

Carter was pursuing the Chince into the study, when Bob's stalwart figure stood in the way.

"Stop that!" rapped Bob.

"Do you know what he's done?" yelled Carter furiously.

"No; and don't want to! Get out!"

Bob slammed the door on Carter's nose.

Carter grabbed the door-handle, but he let it go again. Perhaps he concluded that Wun Lung had had enough. Wun had certainly come to that conclusion.

THE THIRD CHAPTER.
Gummy!

HENRY SAMUEL QUELCH, master of the Greyfriars Remove, sat in his study and frowned.

Five minutes ago, Mr. Quelch had sent

for a member of his Form to come to his study

That member of the Remove had not yet arrived.

Wherefore did Mr. Quelch frown, and with each succeeding minute his frown intensified, till at length it really seemed to resemble that "frightful, fearful, frantic frown" of the Lord High Executioner.

Quelch's time was valuable. Not perhaps so valuable as he believed it to be; still, very valuable. And Bunter was wasting it!

Quelch had work to do. There was a pile of Latin papers on the table, over every one of which Quelch's conscientious eye had to rove. But he had to get through with Bunter before he settled down to work: Bunter was keeping him waiting.

Trotter, the page, had been sent for Bunter. Quelch was perfectly well aware that Bunter was not out of gates, or even out of the House. He had actually seen Bunter as he came along to his study from Common-room. Bunter had been in Masters' Passage, and Quelch would have called him had not the fat junior vanished too swiftly round the nearest corner. So he had rung for the House page and sent him to call Bunter, and Bunter, though evidently not far away, had not yet arrived.

Mr. Quelch stretched out his hand to begin on Latin papers. He breathed hard as he did so. Then there was a sound of footsteps in the passage—slow and lagging footsteps that came reluctantly towards his door. He heard a grunt outside that door, a sure sign that Bunter was there. Still there came no tap, and the door did not open.

The Remove master stared at the door,

puzzled as well as irritated. It really seemed as if Bunter regarded his Formmaster's study as Daniel might have regarded the lion's den.

It was true that Quelch had caned him in class that morning, but that was no reason why the fat Owl should regard his study as a danger-zone. Unless, indeed, he had some sin on his fat conscience, and fancied that he was sent for for punishment.

Mr. Quelch nodded as that suspicion came into his mind. It was quite probable, for Bunter's sins, though not of a very serious kind, were numerous—as numerous as the sands on the seashore. Indeed, Mr. Quelch recalled that he had scuttled off in a very suspicious manner when he had seen him in the passage. Possibly he had been up to some mischief there before Quelch came along from Common-room. Quelch's frowning brow approximated still more to that of the Lord High Executioner.

"Bunter!" he rapped out, like a bullet.

"Oh!" came a gasp outside the door.

"Yes, sir! I—I was just—just going to knock, sir!"

The door opened at last, and Billy Bunter came in.

He gave Quelch a very uneasy blink through his spectacles. Obviously the fat junior was in a state of apprehension.

"I have sent for you, Bunter—" began Mr. Quelch.

"It wasn't me, sir!" interjected Bunter. "I know absolutely nothing about it, sir! Besides, I never had any gum!"

"Gum?" repeated Mr. Quelch blankly.

"Yes, sir—I mean, no, sir! As for taking Toddy's bottle of gum, I should

never have thought of it. Besides, he hadn't one."

Mr. Quelch fixed his gimlet-eyes on that hopeful member of his Form as if he would bore into him with them.

"Have you been playing some trick with gum, Bunter?" he rapped.

"Me, sir! Oh, no, sir!" gasped Bunter. "It was some other fellow, sir! I—I hope you don't think it was me, sir!"

"I have heard of no occurrence of the kind, Bunter——"

"Oh!" gasped Bunter. "I—I thought——"

The fat Owl broke off, and Mr. Quelch smiled faintly.

Evidently Bunter's tardy arrival in the study had been due to a conviction that he was sent for in connection with some matter involving gum.

Gum sometimes found its way into places where it had no business. It was not unknown in inkpots, and even in the seats of armchairs.

Billy Bunter breathed more freely as he realised that he had had a false alarm. Quelch had not sent for him about gum.

"Please do not talk nonsense, Bunter," went on Mr. Quelch. "I have sent for you because I have received a letter from a relative of yours."

"I—I think my father was awfully pleased with my report last term, sir!" ventured Bunter. "He—he—he was very satisfied, sir."

"Your father expressed no such satisfaction to me, Bunter. But it is of another relative that I am speaking—a Mr. Carter."

"Carter!" ejaculated Bunter.

"The uncle, I understand, of the new boy in my Form," said Mr. Quelch. "A distant relative of yours, Bunter."

"Oh, awfully distant, sir!" said Bunter. "We hardly know the Carters. A rather low lot, sir."

Mr. Quelch stared at him.

"I have told you not to talk nonsense, Bunter," he said. "Mr. Carter has written to me, as your Form-master, to ask some questions concerning you."

"Like his cheek, sir!" said Bunter warmly. "I've only seen the old josser once."

"The what?"

"I—I mean the old bean, sir—that is, old Mr. Carter!" stammered Bunter. "I'd only seen young Carter once before he came here. I don't like the Carters, sir."

"Your relative seems to take an interest in you, Bunter, though he has never displayed it before, so far as I am concerned. He desires me to make a report of you, and intimates that if it is a favourable one, it may be to your advantage in the future."

"Oh!" gasped Bunter.

His fat face brightened.

"I—I say, sir, he—he's not a bad old bean!" he exclaimed. "Young Carter is a beast, but old Carter's all right. I remember he treated me very decently the day I visited him, a long time ago. I found his specs for him——"

"Wha-a-t?"

"I believe young Carter hid them," said Bunter. "That's the sort of thing he would do. Anyhow, the old josser—I mean, the old bean—was in a fearful state of stew—I mean, he was upset—and I found his specs, and afterwards young Carter chucked a cushion at me, and——"

"That will do, Bunter! Precisely what Mr. Joseph Carter means by it, I cannot undertake to say; but he states that if you prove yourself worthy it may be to your future advantage. I am telling you this, Bunter, so that you may

do your best to earn the good opinion of a relative who takes an interest in you, and is, I understand, very wealthy."

"Rolling in it, sir!" said Bunter eagerly. "Just caked with oof!"

"Oof! Really, Bunter——"

"Spondulics, sir. You know——"

"Spondulics!" Mr. Quelch could hardly believe his ears. "Bunter, what do you mean by——"

"Brass, sir! The old bean's got tons of it, wallowing in it, in fact!"

"Upon my word, if you use such expressions, Bunter, I shall cane you! Now, listen to me. I cannot refuse to send this report to Mr. Joseph Carter, and you understand, I presume, that I can state only the exact facts in it. For your own sake, therefore, I advise you to make some effort at amendment this term."

"Me, sir!" exclaimed Bunter, in surprise.

The fat Owl did not appear to realise that he was in any need of amendment.

Bunter did not, perhaps, regard himself as a perfect character. But he was, he had no doubt, as near perfection as frail human nature could get. At all events, he could see no room for improvement, even with the aid of his big spectacles.

"You are aware, Bunter, of what I had to put in your last term's report," said Mr. Quelch sternly. "Laziness, untruthfulness, carelessness——"

"Oh, really, sir——"

"Slovenliness, both in classes and in person," said Mr. Quelch. "But most serious of all—untruthfulness."

"Not me, sir!" gasped Bunter. "Are —aren't you thinking of some other fellow, sir?"

"I shall now," said Mr. Quelch, "reply to Mr. Carter's letter. I advise you, Bunter, to do better this term than last, in order that the report, when I send it, may be as favourable as possible."

Mr. Quelch picked up his pen and drew notepaper towards him.

Billy Bunter's eyes and spectacles fixed upon him as he did so.

The pen dipped into the inkpot and came out again, with a straggle of something sticky adhering to the nib.

Billy Bunter backed rapidly to the door. Quelch had not told him to go, but in the circumstances Bunter thought it judicious not to wait to be told.

Mr. Quelch gazed blankly at the sticky substance streaming from his pen.

"Gum!" he ejaculated.

Bunter's fat hand was on the door-handle.

Mr. Quelch bounded to his feet.

"Bunter!"

"Oh crikey! It—it wasn't me, sir!" wailed Bunter. "I—I—I never knew there was any gum in your inkpot, sir! I never put it there because you whopped me this morning, sir! I—I haven't been near the study——"

Mr. Quelch laid down the gummy pen and picked up a cane; the expression on his face was terrifying.

"Bunter, you young rascal, bend over that chair!"

"Oh crumbs!"

Whack, whack, whack, whack!

"Yarooo-ooooh-ohh-ooooop!" roared Bunter.

"Now go!" thundered Mr. Quelch.

"Ooooooooh!"

Bunter scuttled.

The Remove master, breathing hard, sat down to write to Mr. Joseph Carter —with fresh ink. And it was probable, at least, that the incident of the gum in the inkpot would not add favourably to his description of old Mr. Carter's young relative at Greyfriars School.

THE FOURTH CHAPTER.
The Wrong Man!

"THAT ass Smithy!" grunted Johnny Bull.

"Asking for it, as usual!" remarked Nugent.

"The askfulness, as usual, is terrific and preposterous," remarked Hurree Jamset Ram Singh.

"Silly ass!" said Harry Wharton. "Come on!"

"Hold on a minute!" said Bob Cherry, with a glimmer in his eyes.

The Famous Five had been in the gym after lock-ups. Coming out of the gym, they were supposed to go directly back to the House; but Greyfriars juniors, like other mortals, did not always do exactly as they were supposed to do. It was a fine, clear, frosty evening, and the chums of the Remove saw no reason why they should not trot round the quad before going in.

So they trotted round.

That was how they came to spot the fellow who was climbing out over the school wall. Between the tall old elms and the school wall was deep dusk, but in the glimmer of winter stars they saw the clambering figure and had no doubt that it was Herbert Vernon-Smith, the Bounder of Greyfriars. Breaking bounds after lock-ups was one of Smithy's little ways, well known to all the Remove—though, fortunately for Smithy, not so well known to the school authorities.

"Oh, come on!" said Harry. "No bizney of ours, Bob! Smithy's own pal Redwing can't keep him straight, so it's not much good our trying."

"Redwing doesn't go the right way to work," said Bob cheerily. "He just argues with Smithy. I know a better way."

"Well, what's that?"

"There's a big puddle under that wall. If Smithy rolled in it, I don't suppose he would want to go out after that, even if Bill Lodgey is waiting for him at the Three Fishers."

"Think Smithy's the chap to fall down in a puddle, fathead?"

"Yes—if we pushed him in."

"Oh!" gasped Wharton. "But——"

Bob Cherry evidently had no use for "buts." He cut off towards the wall, rapidly approaching the climber.

The breaker of bounds had his arms over the top by this time and was about to pull himself over to drop on the outer side.

Just in time Bob Cherry got a grasp on his ankles.

There was a startled, terrified gasp from the fellow on the wall.

Probably he thought for the moment that some watchful prefect had spotted him—in which case he would have been marched in to see his headmaster.

The Co. followed Bob, chuckling. They were all more or less friendly with Smithy, in spite of that blackguardly kink in his character—having, like most schoolboys, a wide tolerance, and no desire to set up in judgment on other fellows. Still, it was a friendly act to keep the bad hat of the Remove from breaking bounds and taking the risk of a Head's flogging or the "sack."

The fellow clinging to the top of the wall struggled frantically to draw his feet up. He did not speak and he did not look down, in fear of being recognised if it was a prefect that had collared him.

His struggle to get loose and get away was desperate, but it was of no avail; Bob Cherry had possession of both his ankles—and he kept possession of them.

A moment more and the rest of the

Co. were grasping the wriggling legs; then the breaker of bounds had to let go his hold as they all pulled together, and he came down bumping.

He sprawled, panting, among the five, and the next moment Bob had tipped him over into the puddle. It was quite a large puddle, left by recent rain, and there was a loud splash as the junior's face plunged into it.

"Oooooooch!"

"Ha, ha, ha!"

"Roll him over!" said Bob cheerily. "He won't want to go out smothered with mud! Do him a good turn!"

And the Famous Five did that good turn—rolling the spluttering, gasping junior over in the puddle till he had gathered up most of the mud in it.

Horrible gurgles and gasps came from the wretched victim as he rolled and splashed and collected mud. When the Famous Five released him he sat up in the middle of the puddle, still gurgling breathlessly and glaring at them from a face thick with mud.

"You—urrgh—you—you—urrggh!" he gasped.

"Done you a good turn, old bean!" chuckled Bob. "You can't call on your bookmaking friend in that state— what?"

"Ha, ha, ha!"

"Lucky it wasn't Wingate, or Gwynne, or Loder spotted you, old thing!" chortled Nugent. "You'd have got something worse than mud."

"Gurrggh! You—you meddling fools! You mad cads! Gurrggh!" spluttered the wretched object in the puddle.

Harry Wharton started.

"That doesn't sound like Smithy!" he exclaimed. "That's not the Bounder!"

"Oh, my hat!" ejaculated Bob.

All the Famous Five had taken it for granted that the breaker of bounds was the reckless Bounder, but really they had taken rather a lot for granted. "Bad hats" were few and far between, no doubt, at Greyfriars, but undoubtedly Smithy was not the only one. Skinner and Snoop of the Remove sometimes followed the Bounder's bad example; and there were fellows in other Forms, such as Angel and Kenney of the Fourth.

"Is it Skinner?" asked Nugent, peering at the muddy face. "Serve him right if it is!"

"You fools! You rotters! You meddling cads!" The muddy junior staggered to his feet, his eyes gleaming with rage from the coating of mud. "You—you—you—— Oh, you rotters!"

"Carter!" exclaimed Harry Wharton.

"Oh crumbs! Carter!" repeated Nugent.

The muddy fellow's voice was husky with rage, but all the five recognised it now; the breaker of bounds was Arthur Carter, the new fellow in the Remove.

The grin faded from Bob Cherry's face.

"That worm!" he said. "I wouldn't have touched you if I'd known it was you, Carter! You're not nice to touch! The sooner you get yourself sacked the better for the Form!"

"You meddling fools!" hissed Carter. "What's it got to do with you? Can't you mind your own business?"

"Sorry we didn't!" said Bob. "We thought it was Smithy——"

"You fool, are you blind? You never thought it was Smithy; you did this on purpose, you fool—you cheeky rotter!" Carter seemed almost beside himself with rage.

No doubt he had cause to be exasperated. He was smothered with mud from head to foot, and certainly in no state to keep an appointment outside the school. On that subject, however, the Famous Five had no sympathy to waste on him.

"Oh, chuck it, Carter!" said the captain of the Remove contemptuously. "You deserve what you've got, anyhow! You've kept this sort of thing pretty dark since you've been here——"

"Is it your bizney?" snarled Carter.

"No; but you ought to be jolly well booted, all the same! Come on, you fellows, we've got to get in."

The Famous Five walked away to the House, leaving Carter still gasping and dripping mud.

"Blessed if I knew Carter was that kind of goat!" said Johnny Bull.

"I did!" growled Bob Cherry. "I told you he was a rotter the first day he came. Still, I wouldn't have yanked him down if I'd known it was Carter. I never thought of him—though I might have. The fellow ought never to have come to Greyfriars"

"Well, I suppose he's no worse than Smithy," said Nugent.

"Yes, he is—tons!" grunted Bob. "Smithy's a bad hat, but he's got some jolly good qualities; but that toad—— Pah!"

Bob Cherry went into the House frowning, his chums following him smiling.

Arthur Carter certainly, was not feeling grateful, as he panted for breath and scraped off mud. He was still breathless, and still muddy, when he crept in at a back window and sneaked away to the Remove.

THE FIFTH CHAPTER.

Peter is Pally!

"TODDY, old chap——"

"Stony!" said Toddy old chap, regretfully.

"Don't be a beast, Toddy! Can't a fellow open his mouth, without you thinking that he wants to borrow something off you?" demanded Billy Bunter, warmly.

"Not a fellow named Bunter!" answered Peter Todd.

"Beast!"

The Remove had come up to prep; and in Study No. 7, Peter Todd and Tom Dutton were sorting out their books.

Billy Bunter was reposing more or less gracefully in the armchair, apparently occupied by matters more important than prep! There was a deep wrinkle of thought in Bunter's fat brow.

"I say, Toddy, I want you to do something for me!" said Bunter. "I say, you've heard me speak of old Carter—that cad Carter's uncle?"

"Often!" assented Peter. "Too often, in fact!"

"Oh, really, Toddy! He's our rich relation, you know—I mean, one of our rich relations. I've always thought that the stuff was all going to that cad Carter—I know the old bean sent him to St. Olaf's and he had a big allowance there—sticky with oof. I told you he was a rich relation of mine when he came here, Toddy——"

"You did! Fifty times at least! Don't tell me again for the fifty-first!"

"But look here, he doesn't seem to spend a lot of money here," said Bunter. "He doesn't seem to be rolling in oof here, Peter, like he did at his last THE MAGNET LIBRARY.—No. 1,563.

school. That's rather surprising, ain't it?"

"Not at all!" answered Peter. "You see, old fat man, nobody believes in your rich relations excepting yourself—if you do!"

"Beast! I mean to say, old Joe Carter's fearfully rich! Looks to me as if he may be turning his nephew down!" said Bunter. "After all, he may have found out what a rotter he is! I found it out soon enough, after he came here. He is a fearful rotter, isn't he, Peter?"

"Well, there's one thing in his favour."

"What's that?" demanded Bunter, warmly.

"He can't stand you!"

"You silly ass!" roared Bunter. "Look here, Peter, I was going to take the brute up when he came here, and be kind and friendly, and all that—but you know how he's treated me——"

"I thought the trouble was that he wouldn't treat you!"

"I don't mean that sort of treating, you fathead! You're dense, Peter! Now, look here, old Carter's written to old Quelch, asking him about me. He says something about a good report being to my advantage. That might mean that he's fed up with that cad Carter, and means to shell out in my direction. He might leave me the oof. Even a tenner on a chap's birthday ain't to be sneezed at!" said Bunter. "What about prep?"

"Never mind prep now! Look here, Peter, I want to get a good report this term! Quelch is prejudiced against me, in a lot of ways: still, he's a fair man: he will tell the truth. The difficulty is, that he can't see that I'm the most decent chap in the Remove——"

"Oh crikey!" gasped Peter. "Now, I wonder why Quelch can't see that!"

"Prejudice!" said Bunter, shaking his head. "Schoolmasters have these prejudices, you know! Often they don't have much judgment! Why, Quelch thinks more of you, Toddy, than he does of me! That shows what a fool he is."

"D-d-does it?" stuttered Peter.

"Well, be reasonable, old chap!" said Bunter. "Are you in the same street with me, in anything! Uprightness, straightforwardness, manliness—that sort of thing, I mean."

"Ye gods!" murmured Peter.

"But the truth is, that Quelch has a lot of prejudice," said Bunter. "You'd hardly believe that he put untruthfulness in my last report, Peter! Me, you know—untruthful! Makes you stare a bit, what?"

Peter was undoubtedly staring at Bunter! He was staring at him quite blankly. He continued to stare.

"Well, I've got to set that right, somehow, and get a good report from Quelch this term," said Bunter. "Now, if I've got any faults, Peter——"

"If!"

"Yes, and if you notice them——"

"I—I—I might!" gurgled Peter.

"It's just barely within the bounds of possibility that I might notice a few."

"Well, if you do, point them out to me!" said Bunter. "I don't mind your being quite frank. Quelch says I'm lazy and untruthful—goodness knows why! But you know, when a schoolmaster gets an idea into his head, it takes a lot of shifting. I want to shift that idea right out of Quelch's head, though. You see, it's important, if old Carter's thinking of coming down handsome. The fact is, Peter, that fellows sometimes have little faults, without noticing them themselves—and that's where a

real pal comes in, to point them out. See?"

"I see!" gurgled Peter. "I'll borrow a microscope from the lab, and see if I can spot any faults in you, Bunty."

"Point out any you notice, quite frankly," said Bunter. "I mean to say, we've all got our faults: I don't make out that I'm faultless, though I suppose I'm a cut above any other fellow in the Remove. I want to get right with Quelch, before he sends off that report. A fellow might slack a bit, sort of unconsciously—he might draw the long bow a trifle—see? Well, if you ever spot me doing either, Peter, just let me know, quite plain, and I'll set it right."

Peter Todd gazed at the fat Owl.

If Billy Bunter's pal was to point out to him when he was lazy, and when he was untruthful, it seemed to Peter that that pal was going to be a little man with a busy day! Still Peter was ready to oblige.

"Well, what about prep?" he asked.

"Oh, blow prep!" said Bunter, peevishly. "I'll have a shot at it presently. If Quelch begins on me in the morning, I can tell him I lost a book or something."

"Ha, ha, ha!" yelled Peter.

Bunter blinked at him.

"What are you cackling at now?" he demanded.

"Looks to me as if I shall have to work overtime!" remarked Peter. "Still, here goes! Get out of that armchair!"

"Eh? What for?"

"Prep!"

"Blow prep! I'm tired! I say, leave that chair alone! Why, you beast, wharrer you at?" roared Bunter. "I say—yarooooop!"

Peter grasped the armchair by the back and tilted it.

The fat Owl rolled on the carpet with a bump and a roar.

He sat there, gasping, set his spectacles straight on his fat little nose, and blinked at Toddy with a petrifying blink.

"What do you think you're up to, you idiot?" he bawled.

"Pointing out to you that you're lazy!" explained Peter. "Quite unconscious on your part, I've no doubt, old fat bean: but it's generally considered lazy to squat in an armchair and cut work! See?"

"You silly ass!" howled Bunter, staggering up. "Look here, I'm not going to do any prep, see?"

"If you don't, I shall keep on pointing out to you that you're lazy—in the same way!"

"Beast!"

Billy Bunter drew a chair to the table, and sat down.

Peter, grinning, sat down also to his books.

Bunter gave one blink at Virgil—and another blink at the Latin dictionary—and pushed back his chair.

"I can't do any prep, Toddy! I've got a fearful headache!"

Peter picked up a ruler from the table. There was a sound like a pistol-shot in Study No. 7, as it cracked on Bunter's fat knuckles.

Bunter's frantic yell ran the length of the Remove passage. He sucked his knuckles and squealed wildly.

"You mad ass, wharrer you up to?" he shrieked.

"Pointing out to you that you're untruthful!"

"You—you—you beast, can't you take my word that I've got a tooth-ache!" roared Bunter

"Oh, my hat! As well as the headache?"

"I—I mean a headache! I've got a

"You fools—you rotters—you meddling cads !" The muddy junior staggered to his feet, his eyes gleaming with rage. "You—you—you—oh, you rotters !" "Carter !" exclaimed Harry Wharton, recognising the muddy junior's voice. "Oh crumbs ! Carter !" repeated Nugent.

dreadful headache in a double-tooth—I mean a frightful toothache in the back of my head—that is, I mean to say—— Yarooooop!"

Crack !

"You beast, keep that ruler away !" raved Bunter. "Look here, you beast, I'm sorry I asked you now—I don't want you to do it—mind your own business, see? Just mind your own business, and leave a fellow alone, you beast !"

Peter shook his head.

"Now I've started, I'm going to carry on the good work !" he declared. "I'm going to help you clear Quelch's mind of those prejudices. You slack any more, or tell any more lies, before we go down, and you get the ruler."

"Look here——" roared Bunter.

"You asked me to be pally, didn't you?" demanded Peter. "Well, I'm playing up ! Get on with your prep !"

"I've got a—a—I mean, all right, you beast ! Keep that ruler away ! I'm getting on with it, ain't I ?" yelled Bunter.

And he got on with it. He paused, every now and then, to give Peter Todd an infuriated blink. But he did not pause long—the ruler was ready, at Peter's elbow, and Peter was evidently going to be pally !

Not for the first time, Billy Bunter was dissatisfied at getting what he had asked for !

— — —

THE SIXTH CHAPTER.

Putting It Plain !

"WHAT'S up?" asked Frank Nugent.

"Blessed if I know."

"Is the upfulness terrific?" inquired Hurree Jamset Ram Singh.

"What the dickens——" grunted Johnny Bull.

Four members of the famous Co. came into Study No. 1 after class.

Arthur Carter was there, working at a Latin exercise. He was working in a slow, desultory, unwilling way at a book of Suetonius.

Since he had been at Greyfriars, the new junior had had spasms, as it were, of swotting. It was clear that he wanted to get on in class, and earn the good opinion of his Form-master; and at the same time, it was clear that he did not like work, and had no taste for learning anything. He seemed like a fellow who had made up his mind to do, somehow, what he most emphatically did not want to do.

He glanced up, irritably, as the four juniors came in. However, he could hardly complain of the fellows who shared the study coming in and bringing their friends with them. He dropped his eyes to his work again, and ploughed on.

"Bob's got something to say !" said Harry Wharton. "He asked me to round up you fellows here. That's all I know."

Carter looked up again.

"Cherry coming here?" he asked.

"Yes," answered Harry.

"Not much use a fellow trying to work, then," grunted Carter. "I'll chuck it, and get out !"

Bob Cherry appeared in the study doorway at that moment. He heard Carter's words, but he stepped in, and closed the study door behind him.

"Hold on, Carter," he said quietly. "I've got something to say to these fellows that I want you to hear."

Carter stared at him.

"I'm not interested in your chin-wag !" he answered.

"I think you will be, when I get going. Anyhow, I want you to hear."

"You can want !" said Carter, with a scowl. "You've cut this study, ever since I've been here ! Now you can

keep your jaw for your friends—I don't want to hear it."

"Well, you're going to hear it !" said Bob. He put his back to the door. "I shan't keep you long, Carter."

"You won't keep me at all !"

"You're staying here till I'm through !" said Bob. "I'm standing by the door till I've finished. If you want a scrap on your hands, you're your own master—but you're not going out of this study till I've said what I've come here to say."

Carter looked at him in mingled anger and astonishment. He did not, certainly, want a scrap · with the heftiest fighting-man in the Remove. His eyes gleamed, as he looked round at the Co.

"What does this foolery mean ?" he asked.

"Haven't the foggiest," answered Harry Wharton. "Bob asked us to come here, and I suppose from what he says he wants you, too ! Keep your temper—it won't hurt you to hang on for a few minutes."

"Do you fancy I'm going to be bullied like this?"

"Well, look here, Bob, this is rather thick, you know," said Johnny Bull. "I don't see making Carter stay here if he doesn't want to."

"Lots of things you don't see !" answered Bob. "Carter's got to hear me—but if he calls this bullying, he can go down, if he likes—and I'll say what I've got to say before a whole crowd. I fancy he will be rather sorry to have his private affairs known all over the Remove, that's all."

Carter gave a start.

"What the thump do you know about my private affairs ?" he exclaimed.

"More than I want to know !" retorted Bob. He stepped away from the door. "Go out, if you like—and if you want all Greyfriars to hear about your rotten treacherous scheming against your relation Bunter."

Carter caught his breath, and the colour wavered in his cheeks.

Three members of the Co. stared blankly at Bob, and Harry Wharton compressed his lips a little.

"Look here, Bob——" he began.

"I'm going to have this out!" said Bob. "It's been on my mind ever since that day at Lantham. I've heard what happened in this study the other day when Wun Lung was here, and that settles it. Carter's got to stop it, and it's only fair to warn him."

"I can't imagine what you're talking about!" muttered Carter. "Everybody knows that I bar that fat cad Bunter. Any fellow would bar him for trying to stick on as a relation! But——"

"If that was all, it would be no bizney of mine!" said Bob. "But that's not all. Bar him as much as you like—but you're not going to play treacherous tricks if I can stop you."

"You're simply talking in riddles!" said Carter, with a shrug of the shoulders. "Looks to me as if you're wandering in your mind."

"Can't say I make you out, Bob!" said Frank Nugent.

"Well, I'll clear it up!" said Bob Cherry. "I've told Wharton—and nobody else, so far. I'm going to tell you fellows—before Carter! You know how Ponsonby and his gang ragged me at Lantham Station a couple of weeks ago—tying me up, with a hanky stuffed in my mouth, behind the door in the waiting-room——"

"What on earth's that got to do with Carter?"

"It was the day Carter came. He came with that man Gooch, and they changed trains at Lantham, and waited in the waiting-room."

Carter gave another start.

"They never knew I was stuck there behind the door, and I couldn't make them hear me," said Bob. "I never got loose till some Cliff House girls came in, a long time afterwards, as I've told you. Well, Carter and that man Gooch jawed in the waiting-room, and I couldn't help hearing what they said."

"Oh!" gasped Carter.

He knew now, in a flash, why it was that Bob Cherry had barred him from the day he came to Greyfriars. It had puzzled him, but it puzzled him no longer.

"Hold on, Bob!" said Johnny Bull quietly. "You couldn't help hearing what was said, the way you were fixed, but that doesn't give you a right to repeat a private conversation."

"That's why I've said nothing," answered Bob. "I never told Wharton till a few days ago, to ask his advice. But I tell you, it's got to come out now—Carter's got to stop."

"I don't see——"

"You will when I tell you. The long and the short of it is, that Carter acted like a blackguard at his last school, and his uncle turned him down in consequence of——"

"It's false!" hissed Carter, white to the lips now.

Bob did not heed him.

"Old Mr. Carter's cut him off, and he and that man Gooch have found out somehow that he's leaving his money to another relation," he went on. "They never mentioned names, but they said that the relation was at this school. That can only be Bunter."

"No business of ours, or yours!" said Johnny.

"I've not finished yet. Carter's playing a double game here, from what he and Gooch said to one another—he's

going to play good, to get back into old Carter's good graces——"

"Why shouldn't he?"

"No reason why he shouldn't! But that's not all. The other half of his game is to blacken his relation here, to make the old man think that he's no better than the rotter he cut off. They said all that quite plain. Carter's own words were, that he would fix the cad who had cut him out."

Carter sneered. He had had the shock of his life, but he had pulled himself together very quickly.

"Did you go to sleep in that waiting-room?" he asked.

"No!" answered Bob quietly.

"Then how did you come to dream all this?"

Bob Cherry did not answer that question.

"You fellows have seen how he's been on Bunter's trail, ever since he's been here," he went on. "He's as artful as a bagful of monkeys, and he always manages to be in the right, but he's landed Bunter in trouble time and again. You fellows have fancied that he dislikes him because he's a relation he'd rather keep at a distance, and the fat 'ass was trying to hook on to him because he believed him to be well off, as he used to be. Well, that wasn't Carter's reason—his reason was to dish Bunter with old Mr. Carter."

"It's a lie!" said Carter.

"Oh, shut up, Carter!" said Johnny Bull. "If Bob says so, it's the truth, and we all know it."

"It's been bothering me ever since it happened," said Bob. "I didn't want to talk about the cad or repeat anything I'd heard in such a way, and I thought at first I'd just keep an eye on him, and see that he never got away with any tricks on that fat chump. But what happened here the other day tears it. Wun Lung played a silly trick, and Carter jumped at the chance. He would have made Bunter out to be a thief if he could have."

"What was I to think when my gold pencil was found in his pocket?" sneered Carter.

"Anything but what you were glad to think!" snapped Bob. "Bunter raids a fellow's tarts or cakes, and he's been jolly well booted for it, but he would no more steal than I would. You don't know that because you don't want to know it. You fancied he would pinch your rotten gold pencil. I shouldn't wonder if you left it lying about on purpose!"

"Bob!" exclaimed Nugent.

"Anyhow, you fellows saw how he jumped at the chance. He watches that fat idiot like a cat to catch him napping."

"No fellow can be caught at anything if he keeps straight!" sneered Carter. "He's not going to pinch my things—I know that!"

"Well, you needn't talk too much about keeping straight when you're the fellow we caught sneaking out of bounds last night!" answered Bob Cherry scornfully. "If Bunter snaffles a tart or a bun, he doesn't go pub-haunting after lock-up!"

"I was going out for a ramble."

"Oh, yes! And the day we saw you with Pon at the gate of the Three Fishers, you weren't going in!" said Bob contemptuously. "You can cut that out! No bizney of mine if you're a blackguard here, the same as you were at St. Olaf's! that's up to the prefects, not to me. But you're going to leave Bunter alone. I'm putting it out plain now to warn you. Now you know that your game's known to five fellows in the Form, you may have sense to chuck it.

If you don't, you can bank on it that you'll be jolly well stopped!"

"Is that the lot?" sneered Carter.

"Yes, that's the lot; and if you chuck it, nothing will be said outside this study. But you've got to chuck it."

Carter shrugged his shoulders.

"If you're finished, I'll say my piece," he said coolly "I don't care a boiled bean for your opinion; but I'd like to set myself right with the other fellows, as two of them are my study-mates here. It's true—as you learned from behind a door—that I had some trouble at my last school—not my fault, by any means. It's true that my uncle's got his back up, and that he's given me another chance to make good at this school. I'm doing my best, and any decent fellow ought to wish me luck."

"That's all right" said Harry Wharton. "But the rest——"

"There isn't any rest. Bunter doesn't come into the picture at all. Your precious pal says himself that no name was mentioned when he was listening behind a door. Gooch and I were speaking of a relation—a much nearer one. I remember saying I'd fix the cad who had cut me out; what I meant was that I'd punch his nose if I met him in the hols. All the rest is bunk. I fancy Cherry must have been to the films that day, and it got into his head a little."

The Co. looked at him, and looked at Bob Cherry.

Carter's explanation was plausible enough, and they could not help feeling dubious.

"Leave it at that, if you like," said Bob quietly. "The proof of the pudding's in the eating. If you leave Bunter alone, all right! If you don't, every fellow here will know what to think."

"I've nothing to do with the fat rotter! I bar him, and he bars me since he's found out there's nothing to be borrowed. I'd be jolly glad if he left; so would you be if he claimed you as a relation. But that's all. Do you think I'm going to crack the Head's safe and hide the loot in his pockets?" asked Carter sarcastically. "If he chooses to be a lying, pilfering rotter, and gets landed for it, that's his look-out, not mine!"

"Quite," said Bob—"so long as you don't have a hand in landing him. That's what I'm going to stop, and that's why I've warned you."

With that, Bob Cherry opened the door and walked out of the study. His friends followed him.

Carter was left alone, to get on with his Latin exercise if he liked. But he did not look at it. He moved restlessly about the study, with a knitted brow and his hands driven deep into his pockets.

"Making good" at Greyfriars was a difficult task for the "bad hat" who had been turfed out of his last school; "dishing" Bunter had seemed a much easier one. But he realised that both parts of his peculiar double game were going to be full of difficulties now!

THE SEVENTH CHAPTER.

No Offers!

"I SAY, you fellows, don't come barging in now!"

"What?"

"I mean, Linley's going to do some Latin for me. Ain't you, Linley?"

"No!" answered Mark Linley.

The Famous Five had arrived at the door of Study No. 13—Bob Cherry's study.

Mark Linley was standing by the table, engaged in argument with Billy Bunter. Little Wun Lung was curled up in the armchair, grinning.

Bunter waved a fat hand at the five. He did not want a lot of fellows to come bothering just then, and, apparently, he had an idea that they could be waved away like chickens.

But they couldn't. They tramped cheerily into the study, regardless of Bunter.

"Now, look here, Linley, old chap," urged the fat Owl, "this is up to you, and you know it! You like that rotten Latin; you're a beastly swot. I've seen you reading Virgil just for pleasure. You needn't deny it—I have!"

The Lancashire junior laughed.

"Guilty!" he admitted.

"Well, then, this is simply pie to you!" said Bunter warmly. "It's fearfully hard to me. Mind, I could do it on my head if I could bring my mind down to the stuff."

"Better bring it down, then!" suggested Mark.

"Well, look at the waste of time!" argued Bunter. "It doesn't matter about you, as you're keen on the tripe. If that beast Quelch had set us Virgil I could manage all right! I've got a crib to Virgil. But it's Suetonius——"

"What's the trouble?" asked Harry Wharton.

Bunter blinked round indignantly.

"Would you fellows believe it?" he said. "That beast Linley won't do my translation for me!"

"Awful!" said Bob solemnly. "You'd learn such a fearful lot of Latin if other fellows did your translations for you!"

"Well, who wants to learn a lot of Latin?" asked Bunter. "I know I jolly well don't! Lot of good Latin will be to me later on, when I'm an air marshal!"

"Oh crikey!"

"It's no good arguing with Quelch, of course," said Bunter. "He's paid to ram it in, and I suppose he thinks he ought to earn his salary. I've thought once or twice that he even fancies there's

(*Continued on next page.*)

LEARN TO PLAY FOOTBALL!
BY
OUR INTERNATIONAL COACH

THE LAST LINE OF DEFENCE

WHEN I was giving my "lecture" last week on the dangers of heading in football, there was one player on our side who probably felt he was rather out of it—the goalkeeper. Goalkeepers don't head the ball, because the laws of the game allow them to use their hands. The hands are, of course, much more useful than the head, when it is a question of reaching a high ball. Therefore, we never see a goalkeeper, in football, using his head.

To make up to our goalkeeper for having to listen to me telling you all about heading last week, I am going to tell you now about the goalkeeper's job.

That doesn't mean that all the rest of you can take a nap while this lesson is going on. Forwards particularly should listen carefully to what I am telling the goalkeeper. After all, the question of the number of goals the attackers score depends, to a large extent, upon what the goalkeeper does.

You all realise, of course, that the goalkeeper is really the last line of defence of a football side. When the half-backs and full-backs have been beaten, he alone stands between the opposing side and the goal. If a full-back, for the sake of example, misses his kick, or makes some other mistake, a colleague may come to the rescue. But if the goalkeeper makes a mistake, there is no time for anyone to help him out of his trouble. Mistakes by goalkeepers usually mean goals.

Thus the goalie's job is a very nerve-wracking one. Unless you have "cast-iron" nerves, as they say, you will find it hard to stand up to the strain of an important match, in which your play may make all the difference between defeat and victory for your colleagues.

A TRYING ORDEAL

I CAN show you just how great that strain is, by the well-known story of Frank Swift, Manchester City's goalkeeper. Until Christmas-time in 1933, Frank had never played in a first-class football match. On Christmas Day, he had a fine present when he was told that he was to be given a chance

This week's interesting article by our Soccer master tells of the secrets of successful goalkeeping and the things the "man between the sticks" should do.

in Manchester City's first team. He did well, and kept his place. About four months later he had the tremendous good luck for which the footballer sighs—that of playing in a Cup Final at Wembley. He was the City's goalkeeper in their Final tie against Portsmouth. Frank came through that game with flying colours, and the City won. But so great was the mental strain which Swift had gone through, that when the whistle blew for the end of the match, he fell down in a faint—overcome by the ordeal of those ninety anxious minutes. That will show you that the goalkeeper's job really is nerve-wracking.

A cast-iron nerve is not the only thing a goalkeeper needs, of course. He must be always alert, quick in his movements, and sometimes he needs a great deal of pluck to throw himself at the ball when making a desperate save. Height will help him, of course, in saving high shots. But there are some people who say that the taller a goalkeeper is, the longer he takes to get down to the ground to save the low shots. That may be true. Anyway, there have been small goalkeepers in the past. Harry Hibbs, for years the best goalkeeper in England, is by no means a big 'un. It's the speed of movement which counts more than size.

But even when you have all these things—general alertness, speed, pluck, and, of course, a good eye—you aren't by any means a tip-top goalkeeper. There is one thing which makes the difference between an ordinary and a really good 'keeper. It is the art of anticipation—the ability to know where the ball will go before it actually arrives. That is the secret.

SOUND ADVICE

I HAVE mentioned Harry Hibbs, the Birmingham and England goalkeeper. If you get the chance to watch him play—or, for that matter, any of the really first-class 'keepers in the game to-day—notice how many times you get the impression that the forwards are shooting the ball straight at him. Instead of sending the ball wide of him, on one side or the other, they always seem to shoot just where he is standing. Why is that? Simply because Hibbs has an uncanny knack of anticipating where a forward will shoot. He makes up his mind that the ball will come to a certain place, and when it does, he is there to catch it, and you think the forward has shot straight at him.

If you see a goalkeeper making all sorts of flying saves, diving here and there, just tipping the ball wide of the goal, don't immediately make up your mind that he's a good goalkeeper. If he has to dive across to the ball at the last minute, that means that he hasn't been able to anticipate where it would come. The best goalkeepers are the ones who make the job look easy.

Harry Hibbs once told me how he sets about developing his powers of anticipation. When the Birmingham players are playing a private practice match during the week, Hibbs can often be seen playing the part of a forward. He says that by doing this he gets to know what the goalkeeper looks like to a forward who is trying to score goals. He also learns some of the tricks which forwards get up to in their efforts to beat him.

Hibbs gave me another tip to pass on to you young goalkeepers. When you are practising, don't always use a football. Get one or two of your mates to throw tennis-balls at you. It won't be such hard work for them, and you will get your eyes and feet in training, and your hands accustomed to the ball, just as well as with a football. There are two tips for you to try, straight from the mouth of a goalkeeper who makes a good model for all young hopefuls.

THE MAGNET LIBRARY.—No. 1,563.

some sense in it; schoolmasters are queer fish, you know. We had Suetonius the other day, and, of course, I skewed it, and he's set me a translation. And how can I touch it without a crib? I say, you fellows, have you got a crib to Suetonius?"

"Alas!" grinned Frank Nugent. "We crib not, neither do we slack!"

"You're getting jolly keen all of a sudden, Bunter," said Johnny Bull, staring at him. "Can't you hand over your usual rot? I suppose you're not worrying about turning Quelch's hair grey!"

"Oh, blow Quelch!" said Bunter. "You see, it's fearfully particular now. I've got to get a good report this term, if I can. Old Carter——"

"Who?" exclaimed the Famous Five together.

"Young Carter's uncle, you know," explained Bunter. "Distant relation of mine; oodles of oof, as I've told you. Well, yesterday Quelch called me into his study to tell me that old Carter wanted to hear about me. He's going to get a copy of my report this term, as far as I can make out. That looks as if he's got an eye on me, and it may be worth something. What I mean is, I'm not thinking of his money, but of pleasing a kind old gentleman——"

"Oh, my hat!"

"Very nice old chap!" said Bunter. "Quite different from his nephew. I've always liked him—not because he's rich, you know. I never give a thought to such things, as you fellows know. Still, if a rich relation's got an eye on me and wants to hear whether I'm doing well at school, of course a chap wants to play up. Sense of duty, and all that, you know."

The Famous Five looked very curiously at Bunter.

These remarks from Billy Bunter rather corroborated what Bob Cherry had been saying ten minutes ago in Study No. 1.

It was evident that Carter's uncle had an eye on Bunter if he had written to his Form-master at Greyfriars about him—which certainly looked as if Bunter was Carter's rival for the riches.

"Well, you'd better play up, old fat top!" said Bob Cherry. "Very decent of Quelch to give you the tip! Play up, old barrel!"

"That's what I want to do," explained Bunter. "Quelch has given me this translation. Well, I want to take it in to him in first-class style. No mistakes, you know—mixing up rotten ablatives with mouldy datives, and all that. I want it to be a real good thing."

"Good man!" said Harry Wharton. "Now cut off to your study and slog at it."

"Don't talk rot, you know," said Bunter peevishly. "I want to make a really good impression on Quelch! That's why I want Linley to do the translation for me."

"Oh, my summer hat!"

"Linley can do it on the back of his neck," explained Bunter. "You fellows have seen Quelch grin with satisfaction over Linley's translations! They've often put him almost into a good temper! Linley being a beastly swot, is just the fellow to do it for me."

"You put it so nicely, Bunter!" said Mark, laughing.

"I say, you fellows, you talk to him!" urged Bunter. "Make the silly ass understand that he can't let me down when there's such a lot at stake. If I take my usual stuff to Quelch, he will snort, as usual—you know him! I want to please him this time! I'm rather surprised at Linley not wanting to back

THE MAGNET LIBRARY.—No. 1,563.

up a chap in pleasing his Form-master."

"You fat ass——"

"All I want Linley to do is to translate the stuff!" said Bunter. "I can copy it out afterwards. I don't mind doing that—I'm not lazy, I hope! Besides, it would have to be in my fist! There's not much of it—only a few lines from old Suet-pudding. It would take Linley only ten minutes——"

"You howling ass!" said Mark. "Can't you see that that's not the point? I can't do your work for you."

"And Quelch called me lazy!" said Bunter. "Hark at him!"

"I'm not going to help you pull Quelch's leg!" hooted Linley.

"Eh? Why not?"

"Ha, ha, ha!"

"I'll go through it with you, if you like, and help," said Mark. "Quelch would be down on that—but I'll go that far! But can't you see, you blitherer, that I can't let you take my work in to Quelch and call it your own?"

"But it will be mine, if you give it to me!" argued Bunter. "You just make a translation, and give it to me. Then it will be mine."

"Oh, you blithering owl!"

"Well, I call it mean," said Bunter. "Quelch makes out that I'm lazy and slack, and he's even going so far as to put it in my report—me, you know! It might do me a lot of harm with old Carter."

"Why not stop being lazy and slack?" asked Nugent.

"Ha, ha, ha!"

"Look here, Wharton, you're not so jolly lazy as Linley, and your Latin is jolly nearly as good. Will you do it for me?"

"Can't be done, fathead! There's a limit to spoof!" explained the captain of the Remove. "Besides, Quelch is a downy bird—he would spot it, ten to one."

"I'll risk that!" said Bunter. "That's all right! If he asks me if any fellow helped, I can say no, can't I?"

"Well, I suppose you could, as you're a direct descendant of Ananias! I shouldn't like to."

"Has Quelch put anything in your report about telling whoppers?" asked Johnny Bull.

"Eh? Yes. I don't know why."

"Oh crumbs! He doesn't know why!" gasped Bob Cherry.

"Ha, ha, ha!"

"I wish you fellows wouldn't cackle when a chap's worried," said Bunter reproachfully. "I say, Bob, you're rather a dud at Latin—but you might try it on. I mean to say, you can't help being rather a fool, and I shall be satisfied if you do your best, see?"

"Some fellows," remarked Bob, "are born tactful."

"The tactfulness is terrific."

"Well, look here, what about you, Bull?"

"If you ask me to help you tell lies to Quelch, I'll jolly well boot you!" grunted Johnny Bull.

"Beast! I've got to take this translation in before tea!" howled Bunter. "What shall I do?"

"The translation!" suggested Nugent.

"Oh, don't be a silly ass! What do you think I'd better do, Wharton?"

"Some work!"

"Beast!" roared Bunter.

That suggestion, evidently, was of no use to William George Bunter. Work was a very, very last resource—only to be resorted to in the most desperate extremity. The case was not yet so desperate as that—there were other studies in the Remove, to which Bunter

could take Suetonius, in the hope of finding a translator.

He rolled to the door.

He paused there, to cast a disdainful and scornful blink at the grinning juniors in Study No. 13.

"Well, if you won't back up a pal, you won't!" he said. "I must say that I despise the lot of you. Letting a man down like this! And I can jolly well tell you, that if I get something decent from old Carter, I jolly well shan't lend you anything out of it, so yah!"

And with that crushing valediction, the fat Owl of the Remove rolled away—leaving Study No. 13 chortling.

————

THE EIGHTH CHAPTER.
Bunter Begs for It!

"GET out!"

"Oh, really, Carter——"

Arthur Carter had sat down again to his Latin; when the door of Study No. 1 opened, and a fat face looked in, and a big pair of spectacles glimmered. Carter gave his podgy relative the blackest of black looks.

It was not surprising, perhaps, that he did not like Bunter. Even nice-natured and good-tempered fellows sometimes got fed-up with Bunter. Even Lord Mauleverer, the most tolerant fellow ever, sometimes felt that he could not stand Bunter. Carter had neither a nice nature nor a good temper—and his feeling towards the fat Owl was a mingling of dislike and scorn.

Neither could he be expected to feel pleased, because Bunter was likely to take his place in the good books of old Mr. Carter.

He could not fairly say that Bunter had "cut him out," as Bunter knew little or nothing about the matter, and had certainly made no move in it. And Bunter, with all his faults—and their name was legion—was quite incapable of unscrupulous scheming like Carter's. Bunter often schemed—but his scheming was fatheaded and fatuous.

But whether he could justly blame Bunter in the matter, or not, made very little difference to Carter, if the fat Owl of the Remove's name replaced his own in old Joseph's will.

A better fellow than Carter might have set matters right by mending his ways, playing the game, and winning back the good opinion he had lost by bad conduct. But that was not Carter's way. He disliked and despised the fat Owl; and he cultivated those amiable feelings, as a sort of justification for scheming against him.

At the present moment, he was in the very bitterest of tempers, owing to Bob Cherry's plain talk, in that study; and the risk it meant for him in carrying on with his peculiar campaign. It was rather an unfortunate moment for Bunter to drop into the study.

Carter's hand reached to the inkpot. The fat Owl eyed him warily, but he did not depart. Apparently he had some special purpose in dropping into that study; which was hard to guess, as only Carter was there.

"Are you getting out?" snarled Carter.

"I can come into Wharton's study if I like, I suppose!" answered Bunter, with dignity. "Think it belongs to you, because it happens to be your study, too! I'm not going to look at your rotten Latin."

Carter, staring at him, withdrew his hand from the inkpot.

"My Latin!" he repeated.

"I know you're doing Suetonius," said Bunter. "But if you think I'd

Billy Bunter was leaning over Carter's shoulder in the hope of getting a "squint" at his translation, when the new boy rose suddenly. Bang! "Yaroooooh!" roared Bunter, in anguish, as the top of his relative's head came in contact with his fat chin. "Ow! Beast! Wow!"

take a hint from you, you're jolly well mistaken I can do it better than you can, any day, and chance it."

Carter eyed him, very curiously, for some moments, and then resumed work on his exercise.

Bunter came a little farther into the study.

"The fact is," he went on, "that Wharton's asked me to look for a pencil he left somewhere! You mind your own business, see?"

Carter gave him no further heed.

The fat Owl hovered round the table. If he was looking for a pencil, he did not find one. He blinked, stealthily and cautiously, at the paper that lay before Carter, and which the new junior was translating.

Several times he hovered behind the junior's chair and glanced over his shoulder. He was more and more encouraged by the fact that Carter paid him no attention.

"I say, Carter, what part are you doing?" he ventured to ask, at last.

"Find out!" answered Carter, over his shoulder.

"What I mean is, I might help you!" said Bunter. "You're an awful rotter, you know, but after all, you're my relation. If you happened to be doing the forty-ninth in Book Six, I've got the same stuff to do."

Carter grinned.

Billy Bunter fancied that he was being fearfully astute. As a matter of fact, his words revealed his true object. If Carter was working at that particular section of Suetonius, what Bunter wanted was a "squint" at his paper, to copy down Carter's translation!

Carter, though not a willing learner, was pretty good; but if he had been a dud at Latin, he could hardly have been such a dud as Bunter. His translation, whatever it was like, was certain to be miles better than Bunter's.

So the fat Owl had the happy idea of taking a copy of it if he happened to be doing the same section.

This would make a good impression on Quelch, as an improvement on Bunter's usual performance, and would save Bunter work, which was still more important.

As it happened, Carter was doing a section of Book Five, dealing with the Emperor Claudius. Bunter's "squints" over his shoulder, had, therefore, been of no use to the fat Owl, so far.

But while apparently turning a deaf ear to the fat junior's talk, Carter now turned to Book Six, which dealt with Nero. He turned the pages till he came to Section XLIX, the one that Bunter wanted.

Bunter hovered round the table, and finally came back behind Carter's chair, and blinked over his shoulder again.

His fat face brightened.

Carter had refused to answer him, but this was as good as an answer in the affirmative. Carter was now working on the very bit that Bunter required to see him through.

He had taken a fresh sheet of paper, and, as regardless of Bunter as if the fat Owl had not been in the study at all, was translating XLIX, descriptive of the last hours of the Emperor Nero.

Bunter winked at the back of his head.

This, Bunter considered, was all right. All he had to do was to see what Carter wrote, and copy it down. Quelch was going to be quite surprised by the excellence of Bunter's work this time!

That there was anything unscrupulous in this kind of thing did not even occur to Billy Bunter. He was so accustomed to adopting every trick and dodge to get out of exerting himself, that anything that saved work came as naturally as breathing to him.

Moreover, Bunter did not share his Form-master's opinion that fellows were

at school to learn. Bunter had no desire to learn. Indeed, he objected to it!

Latin, in Bunter's valuable opinion, was beastly stuff that a beak bunged at a fellow's head, and that a fellow dodged, if he could, like a snowball.

The question with Bunter was, not ought he, but could he? Now it seemed that he could, so that was all right.

Unfortunately Carter moved his head, blocking the fat Owl's view.

Bunter glared at the back of that head.

"I—I say, have you seen Nugent's pen?" he asked, hoping that Carter would look round, and thus remove his obnoxious head out of the light. "Nugent asked me to come here and fetch his fountain-pen."

Bunter belonged to the class of persons who proverbially required good memories; but he had a rotten one.

Carter did not answer or shift, and the exasperated Owl continued to glare at the back of his head. He leaned over Carter's shoulder in the hope of getting a "squint."

Carter rose suddenly.

Bang!

"Yaroooooh!" roared Bunter, in anguish, as the top of his relative's head came with a sudden crash on his fat chin.

He staggered back, clasping a fat hand to the fat chin.

"Ow! Beast! Ow!" roared Bunter. "You did that on purpose! Wow!"

Carter glanced round at him, grinning.

"Were you looking over my shoulder?" he asked.

"No, you beast!" hooted Bunter. "Of course I wasn't! I was looking for Wharton's pocket-knife that he left here. Ow!"

(Continued on page 16.)

DUSTY'S VISITORS!

Another Bright and Breezy Instalment of:
"THE FORM-MASTER'S SECRET!"

By DICKY NUGENT

GREYFRIAR[S]

No. 277.

EDITED BY HA[...]

"What's the matter with Lickham ? "

That was the question that was being asked up and down St. Sam's.

Inky fags were asking it in the Second Form Room. Jack Jolly & Co. were asking it in the Junior Common-room. Stately seniors were asking it within the sacred precinkts of the Prefects' Room.

Doctor Birchemall was asking it as he paced up and down the carriage drive in front of the Skool House with Mr. Justiss, the master of the Fifth.

"Really, Justiss, it's beyond a joak ! " he said, with a shake of his head. "In fakt, things have come to a pretty pass, as the centre-forward remarked when the outside-right kicked the ball in his face. There's simply no knowing what Lickham is going to do next ! "

"Indeed, sir ! " said Mr. Justiss pompussly.

"Yes, indeed, Justiss ! His refined Oxbridge axxent has vannished completely. Would you credit it, Justiss, if I told you that I caught him frying fish in the Form-room ? "

"Impossibul, sir ! I should say it was cod ! "

"It was herring, as a matter of fakt ! " snorted the Head. "Then again, he walks about the skool without a collar, and with a bundle tied up in a red spotted handkerchief and slung over his sholder ! "

"By Jove ! "

"I tell you, Justiss, Lickham seems a changed man to me ! " said Doctor Birchemall seriously. "Unless there's a dickens of an alteration soon there is only one corse open to me—to discharge him with ignominy ! "

"Who's he, sir ? " asked the master of the Fifth innersently.

"I mean, to send him off with a flea in his ear—or, as the vulgar mite put it, to terminate his engagement compulsorily ! " eggsplained the Head. "If things don't improve, Justiss, that's what I shall have to do and——"

Doctor Birchemall broke off as the sounds of rawcuss voices fell on his ears.

"We're a-comin in ! "

"No, no, you're not ! "

"Ho, hain't we ? 'Oo's a-goin' to stop us ? "

"Me ! "

"Haw, haw, haw ! "

Doctor Birchemall and Mr. Justiss looked over to the gates from whence this argewment was coming, and their eyes fell on two burly looking tramps trying to force their way on to the premises past old Fossil, the skool porter.

"Bless my sole ! How dare these common persons have the sawce to come to St. Sam's ? " eggsclaimed the Head. "What do they think they're doing of, Justiss ? "

"They are certainly not the tipe of visitor one eggspects at a skool for the sons of jentlemen ! " remarked Mr. Justiss, with a frown. "Shall we go and see what they want, sir ? "

"Yes, rather ! "

Doctor Birchemall and the master of the Fifth broke into a gallop and charged down to the gates. They were just in time to catch the two ruffians biffing Fossil ruffly to one side.

"Stop ! " cried the Head, as they turned away from Fossil and started to march up to the Skool House.

The two tramps stopped and leered at the newcomers.

"'Ullo, matey ! " they corussed.

The Head shuddered slitely; vulgar slang always filled him with horror.

"What's the big idea ? " he rapped out. "Are you aware that you are trespassing on privit property ? "

"Ho, no, we hain't ! " said one of the preshus pair. "'Cawse why ? 'Cawse we come 'ere to see an ol' mate of ours, hain't we, Charlie ? "

"Yuss, Joe ! "

The Head's eyebrows went up sharply.

"You mean to tell me that you have a friend at St. Sam's—two low, common raskals like you ? " he cried. "Impossibul ! Who is he ? "

Back came the answer from the tramp called Charlie.

"I'll tell you 'is name, old covey ! " he leered. "It's Lickham ! "

"WHAT ? "

The Head and Mr. Justiss recoiled as from a blow.

"L-L-Lickham ? " phaltered the Head. "You—you mean the master of the Fourth ? "

"Yuss ! "

"Oh, grate pip ! "

Doctor Birchemall looked at Mr. Justiss and Mr. Justiss looked at the Head. The meer thought of a St. Sam's master being on terms of friendship with this pair of grimy raskals was enuff to give them both a blue fit.

A week ago they would have refused to beleeve it. But after the amazing change that had come over the Fourth Form master recently, they had an uneasy feeling that it was only too troo.

The Head recovered his breth at last.

"Mite I ask how you come to know Mr. Lickham ? " he asked.

"Yuss ! " leered Joe. "If you want to know, matey, 'e useter be on tramp with us afore 'e come to this 'ere college. Come on, Charlie ! "

Doctor Birchemall glared. It was a shock to him to lern that Mr Lickham had been a tramp before he had come to St. Sam's ; but he was becoming used to shocks from Mr. Lickham, and he had no intention, anyway, of allowing these two grubby spessimens [...] skool.

"Take another step [...] peril, you low creetche[r...] cried. "Friends of Mr. [...] or not, you're barred ! T[...] gate ! "

"Ho, yuss ? " leered Joe [...] 'ere's a oner for your nose, [...] Plonk !

"Yarooooo ! "

Doctor Birchemall hit th[...] path with a sickening thu[...] ruffian planted his grimy [...] his face. Mr. Justiss u[...] gasp of horror.

"Stop, you villans ! [...] realise what you've done [...] nocked down the headm[...]

"Orlright, matey ! " sai[...] with a brootal larf. "Now [...] the same for you, an' t[...] won't be jellus ! "

Bang !

"Ow-ow-ow ! Resk[...] Sam's ! Wooooop ! "

Mr. Justiss collapsed, [...] feendishly ; and the i[...] galloped away, larfing cal[...]

Half-a-minnit later, wh[...] Jolly & Co. arrived on t[...] the two tramps had vani[...]

The heroes of the Fourt[...] blinked when they saw t[...] and Mr. Justiss and Foss[...] ting on the ground, rubb[...] anattermies and groaning.

Their faces darkened w[...] herd the Head's breef ac[...] what had happened.

"My hat ! We can't al[...] sir ! " said Jack Jolly. "[...] it's rather a lark to see [...] buffers nocked about—[...]

"Eh ? "

"But we're not letting [...] take liberties with anybo[...] Sam's, sir—even you ! W[...] them pay dearly for this, [...] you chaps ? "

"Yes, rather ! "

And Jack Jolly & Co. [...] off to find Mr. Lickham's [...]

Meanwhile, the two tra[...] found the man they were [...] just coming out of the tuc[...]

Dusty Lickham was lo[...] pleased as a dog with t[...] He had just lerned from a [...] tellyfone inquiry that the [...] Lickham—the cuzzin wh[...] dentity he had adopted—[...] sentenced to fourteen [...] chokey. That left Dus[...] than a week in which t[...] enjoying himself at St. [...] As he stepped out of the t[...] there was a smear of jam [...] mouth and a cheerful gri[...] face.

But that grin disappea[...] flash when he saw Joe and [...] A look of alarm took its [...]

"'Ullo, you coveys ! " h[...]

"Wotto, Dusty ! "

The bogus Form-master [...] uneezily.

"Not so much of the ' D[...] he said. "My name's [...]

MY FORM IS THE BEST AT GREYFRIARS!

Claims HORACE HACKER, B.A.

In expressing the opinion that the Shell Form is the best at Greyfriars, I wish it to be understood that I do not pretend that they are more than the best of a bad lot. (SNIFF !)

My experiences as temporary headmaster showed me plainly that a lamentably large number of the boys at Greyfriars are nothing better than defiant and insubordinate young hooligans. (SNIFF !)

That the Shell Form contains a large number of such undisciplined young wretches I do not deny. (SNIFF !)

But I think I am correct in claiming that there are not so many of them as in other Forms, and the reason for this (SNIFF !) is not hard to find. It is simply that I have, by my firm methods, brought most of them to a condition of comparative tractability.

What they think of me inwardly I do not know and do not particularly care. (SNIFF !) It is sufficient for me that most of them are outwardly respectful and obedient. In this respect I feel sure that they compare very favourably with any other Form and I feel quite safe therefore in asserting that my Form is the best at Greyfriars. (SNIFF !) SNIFF !)

(N.B.—We put in the sniffs ourselves to give you the right atmosphere !—Ed.)

HERALD

STOP PRESS NEWS

WHARTON. January 29th, 1938.

HARRY WHARTON CALLING!

Last week I told you what a lot of outdoor activity goes on at Greyfriars even in this wintry season of the year.

This week, so that you are not left under any misapprehensions, I would like to assure you that indoor recreations are also in full swing.

The frost mentioned last week has now broken, and, skating being over—only temporarily, we hope!—there is a boom in indoor fun.

In the course of the last five evenings, we in the Remove have got through quite an impressive programme.

Inky won the chess championship of the Lower School, beating Peter Todd in two out of three very keen games.

A team of six Remove boxers beat the Upper Fourth team, winning four out of six bouts. This was a rattling fine performance, our opponents being in most cases appreciably heavier than ourselves. Bob Cherry, Vernon-Smith, Johnny Bull and myself were the victors. Dick Russell and Bolsover major were licked—but both earn full marks for putting up a jolly good show.

On Wednesday we had a meeting of our Debating Society and decided by sixteen votes to ten that schoolboys should be allowed to govern themselves. It is to be hoped that the authorities will sit up and take notice!

Johnny Bull and his band have put in two evenings at practice, and this time they have managed to keep out Hoskins. There is a big future for Johnny's boys despite Hoskins' absence—or because of it!

Wibley started selecting a cast for his new play on Thursday evening. The play is a thriller written by himself. He has called it "The Screaming Mummy" and I understand that it deals with weird events in the house of an Egyptologist. Wib is taking it very seriously. He was not a bit amused when Kipps suggested that it would sound more grown up if it was called "The Hysterical Mater"!

The Remove also played two games of table-tennis—one against the Upper Fourth and the other against the Shell. Sad to relate, our lads lost on both occasions. Can't keep up this non-stop win bizney in all departments!

No time for more now. I think I have said enough, anyway, to show you that most of us keep pretty busy after we've closed our books for the day! Meet you again next week, chums!—

HARRY WHARTON.

Answer to Correspondent:

G. LODER (Sixth).—" What do you think of the fag who served my dinner all over my head ?"

He wanted to see you wearing your old school PIE!

---

this 'ere skool—Izaak Jolliwell Lickham."

"Ho, yuss ?" said Joe, with an unplezzant larf. " Well, you're still Dusty to us, an' our ol' pal Dusty's goin' to 'elp us hover a little job, hain't 'e, Charlie ? "

Dusty Lickham frowned feercely.

" A meer nothink, Dusty ! " leered Charlie. " 'Elp us to kidnap a rich yung bloke of the name of Bullion as 'angs out in this 'ere skool. That's hall. Wot's your answer ? "

" 'Ere it is ! " replied Dusty Lickham, with a grim smile.

Bang ! Crash ! Wallop !

" Yow-ow ! 'Elp ! "

" Woo-oop ! 'Ands hoff ! "

" Now git hout ! " snapped Dusty Lickham.

Charlie and Joe waited for no more. They ran—and Dusty Lickham returned to the tuckshop to refresh himself with another ginger-pop.

But the introoders had by no means given up hoap of bringing off their kidnapping stunt. As soon as they were out of site of the tuck-shop, they asked a gardener's boy where Bullion was. And, as luck would have it, Bullion was just walking across to them from the playing-fields.

The two kidnappers waited for him in the shelter of some bushes.

" Gotcher ! " growled the ruffians, as they sprang out on the welthy yung Fourth Former.

In a brace of shakes, the yungster had been gagged and bound and bundled into an old sack. Then Joe slung him across his sholder and the kidnappers sneaked out of St. Sam's by a side gate.

Five minnits later, the Head summoned Mr. Lickham to his study.

" Lickham ! " he said, sternly. " Much as it greeves me to part with an old and trusted servant, I have decided that it is impossibul to keep a master who hobnobs with common tramps. You are discharged ! "

Dusty Lickham's scrubby jaw dropped.

" Ho, crikey ! " he mermered. " But look 'ere, old covey, them blokes as you saw hain't really pals of mine. If you'll lissen to me——"

He got no further. At that moment, the door was flung open and Jack Jolly & Co. bust into the room.

" Bullion, sir ! " gasped Jack Jolly. " He's kidnapped ! Those tramps have kidnapped him ! "

Doctor Birchemall started violently. Then slowly his gaze returned to the bogus Form-master.

" Kidnapped, eh ? " he cried, grimly. " So that's the game—and I fansy I know who's responsibul ! There's the culprit—your Form-master, Mr. Lickham ! Stop him from getting away, boys ! I'm going to tellyfone for the perlice ! "

(Looks as if Dusty Lickham—not to mention his " cuzzin "—will shortly be in hot water ! Don't miss next week's " eggsiting " developments !)

COLD COMFORT FOR COKER!

Strange Sequel to a Speedway Race!

Whoopee ! Coker of the Fifth has won a cup for his motor-bike!

But if you think the scoffers are piping down, wait till you've heard the full story !

Coker heard there was going to be a race for amateurs at the Lanthum Speedway. He heard it from Potter, who heard it from Blundell, who heard it from Hilton ; so he received his information in rather a roundabout way.

But that didn't worry Coker. The time and day were definite enough even though the conditions of the race were a bit vague. Wednesday afternoon at three o'clock prompt, Potter said, and Coker made up his mind about it at once.

" I'm in ! " he said. " I'm phoning my entry right away. It will mean I shan't be able to turn out for the Fifth at footer, but that can't be helped."

This little difficulty was of no importance, as it happened, for it appeared that Coker had not been selected to play for the Fifth. So everybody was satisfied except the fellows who like getting a cheap laugh by watching Coker play footer !

He phoned through his name and address to the Speedway and his entry was accepted.

On Wednesday afternoon, he drove off in great glee. Ever since he's had a motor-bike, Coker has dreamed of racing it on a Speedway to the frenzied cheering of thousands of fans. Now, it seemed, his dream is at last coming true !

Coker's machine shone like burnished gold when he left Greyfriars.

It looked somewhat different by the time he reached Lanthum.

In the course of the journey he had collided with a tree and a haystack and landed twice in a ditch. The motor-bike looked slightly the worse for wear. Coker regretted it ; but it couldn't be helped.

Coker was relieved, anyway, when he arrived, to find that his machine looked quite a smart affair in comparison with others present. True, it was covered in mud, but its general outline looked businesslike, whereas most of the others looked as if they had come out of the Ark.

Coker was given a number and lined up for one of the heats. The race started and, to his great joy, Coker rapidly forged ahead and, in spite of occasional wobbles and continual zigzagging, ended up an easy winner ! Later he was lined up in the final and repeated the performance by licking the lot.

Amid loud cheers, Coker was presented with a silver cup.

Then came the unfortunate sequel.

One of Coker's rivals lodged a protest and the stewards scraped some of the mud off Coker's machine and had a look at it. Then they disqualified Coker and awarded the race to the second man.

When Coker started kicking up a dust about it, he made a remarkable discovery, and the discovery was this :

The race he had won was a race for old crocks guaranteed to be not less than 20 years old !

Cheers for Coker, anyway, lads ! He can, at least, say he has won a motor-bike race, though we seriously doubt whether he'll boast much about it. If you take our tip, Coker, old man, you'll make the most of it. It's the only speedway race you're ever likely to win !

RIVALS for RICHES!

By FRANK RICHARDS

(Continued from page 13.)

"Well, I can't let you see my translation, if you're doing the same stuff," said Carter. "Quelch would hardly like that."

"Who wants to see it?" hooted Bunter. "Yah! Beast! Wow!"

Carter shrugged his shoulders, gathered up his papers, and left the study.

Billy Bunter watched him with an infuriated blink. His chance was gone now.

The next moment he uttered an ejaculation of surprise and glee. Carter, apparently from oversight, had left one of his papers on the table. And it was the very one that Bunter wanted!

"Oh crikey!" gasped Bunter.

He blinked at it eagerly. There was no mistake about it. There it was, headed "Book Six XLIX." Carter had translated the paragraph from "Tunc" to "pereo," which was exactly what Bunter had to do.

The fat Owl could hardly believe in his good luck.

He was glad now that Carter had left the study, as he had left that paper behind him. It could not have happened better for Bunter. All he had to do now was to sit in Carter's chair, copy the paper before him, and take it down to Quelch. Then, he hoped, he would see that grin of satisfaction dawn on Mr. Quelch's crusty visage, as often happened in the case of Mark Linley, but never in the case of Billy Bunter.

Bunter dipped pen into ink, annexed a sheet of paper, and started.

Having the translation before him, he did not even trouble to look at the Latin! That would have been an unnecessary bother!

Bunter would have been well advised to do so, all the same. Had he taken a "squint" or two at the Latin, it might have dawned on him what a very remarkable translation Carter had left behind him.

Even Bunter, on his own exertions, would hardly have turned "Qualis artifex pereo" into "What larks!"

Carter had done so, and the rest of the translation was on the same lines. But it did not even dawn on Bunter that Carter was aware of his game, and was pulling his podgy leg.

Happily satisfied, Bunter copied down that astonishing translation, which was calculated, not to make Quelch grin with satisfaction, but to make him bound out of his chair and clutch the nearest cane! Grinning with satisfaction, the fat Owl rolled out of the study to take that translation down to Mr. Quelch.

THE NINTH CHAPTER.

The Vials of Wrath!

MR. QUELCH smiled.

He did not always, or often, greet Bunter with a smile.

But he smiled now.

For one thing, Bunter had brought in THE MAGNET LIBRARY.—No. 1,563.

his translation promptly to time, instead of handing over various excuses, as usual, all of them untruthful. That looked like a sign of improvement in Bunter.

Moreover, the fat junior entered the study quite briskly, instead of lagging in like a fellow going to execution. That looked as if Bunter had shown a little keenness, for once, and had a translation to show up, for which he expected commendation. As a rule, Bunter was completely satisfied if he escaped whopping.

"Ah, you have done your paper, Bunter?" asked Mr. Quelch, quite genially.

Bunter was a trial to him in the Remove, but he was the man to encourage a dense and backward fellow who did his best.

"Yes, sir!" answered Bunter brightly. "I—I've taken a lot of trouble over this, sir, and—and I think I've done it rather well."

"I hope so, my boy," said Mr. Quelch. He picked up a school Suetonius from the table. Suetonius in the Remove was not handled in the complete state; it was taken in chunks, like pineapple. "Now, let me see, Book Six, I think——"

"Section XLIX, sir."

"Exactly! You may read out the Latin, Bunter, and I will then look at your translation."

"Yes, sir!"

Bunter could read out Latin, if he could not understand it when read. He proceeded to read the description of the last hours of Nero, beginning with "Tunc uno quoque," and winding up at "Qualis artifex pereo."

Now, the translation of that passage, in brief, was to the effect that Nero's companions in his flight urged him to escape death at the hands of Galba's soldiers by suicide, whereupon Nero bade them make the necessary preparations, and gather wood for the funeral pyre, meanwhile weeping and repeating "What an artist perishes!"

Bunter, had he tackled it, would have made endless mistakes, but he would have had some shots at the meaning, even if some of them had missed the mark.

But Bunter's very worst effort would have been nothing like the translation he now handed over to Mr. Quelch.

Quelch received it with a benign expression, prepared to see something better than usual.

But when he looked at it his face changed remarkably.

His gaze became fixed, and he looked as if he could hardly believe his eyes. Indeed, he hardly could.

Bunter, watching him in the hope of seeing that expected grin of satisfaction, realised that something was wrong.

He did not yet realise how awfully wrong that something was.

Mr. Quelch did not speak. He gazed and gazed and was dumb.

Bunter grew more and more uneasy.

Obviously Quelch was not satisfied. Obviously he was not going to grin. Thunder was gathering in his brow.

Which, if Bunter had only known it, was not really surprising, considering that that translation ran:

"While his companions talked to him like Dutch uncles, Nero told them to go and eat coke, which they accordingly did, and meanwhile he chuckled and chortled, continually repeating: 'What larks!'"

Mr. Quelch was accustomed to all sorts of translations from Billy Bunter. It was Bunter who had set the Remove in

a roar by construing "Arma virumque cano" into "The armed man and the dog!" It was Bunter who had turned "Est in conspectu Tenedos" into "He was expecting a tenner!"

Bunter, really, was capable of anything, or almost anything.

But this was the limit!

Even from Bunter, Mr. Quelch had never had anything like this before.

This was no crass example of blundering—it was not even carelessness—this was a deliberate leg-pull!

It could not possibly have been anything else! It was that or nothing!

Mr. Quelch found his voice at last! When he found it, it resembled that of the Great Huge Bear.

"Bunter!" he thundered.

"Yes, sir!" gasped Bunter, quaking. "Isn't it all right, sir?"

"What?" roared Mr. Quelch. "What did you say, Bunter?"

"Is—is—isn't it all right, sir?" gasped Bunter. Only too clearly he could see that it wasn't.

"How dare you, Bunter!" boomed the Remove master. He jumped to his feet. "Hand me that cane, Bunter!"

"That—that—that kik-kik-cane, sir!" stuttered the hapless fat Owl.

"At once!" thundered Mr. Quelch.

In the lowest of spirits, Bunter handed over the cane.

Mr. Quelch swished it.

"Now, Bunter!"

"But I—I—I say, sir," stammered Bunter. "If—if there's any—any mistakes in it, sir——"

"Mistakes!" roared Mr. Quelch.

"Yes, sir! I—I took a lot of trouble with it—nobody helped me, sir—I never asked Linley to help me, and he never said he wouldn't——"

"Bunter!"

"I—I—I thought it was pretty good, sir!" gasped Bunter. "Carter ain't bad at Latin——"

"Carter?" repeated Mr. Quelch. "What has Carter to do with it?"

"Oh, nothing, sir! I never copied this down from Carter's paper—he wouldn't let me see his paper, sir—he's a beast—I mean, I never wanted to see his paper, of course, sir——"

"Had you brought me a translation, Bunter, full of your usual careless mistakes, I should, I hope, have dealt with you patiently," said Mr. Quelch. "But this act of deliberate impertinence——"

"Wha-a-t, sir?"

"You may consider it amusing, Bunter, to make a jest of a task given out to you by your Form-master! I shall convince you, I hope, that it is not a jesting matter." Mr. Quelch swished the cane again. "Bend over that chair, Bunter!"

"Oh crikey!"

Whack, whack, whack!

"Oh! Ow! Woooooh!" roared Bunter.

"Yow-ow-woooop!"

Whack, whack, whack!

"Now, Bunter, I shall expect that translation this evening. You will bring it to me, or I shall cane you again. If you venture to make another absurd jest of it——"

"I—I didn't—I never—oh crikey!"

"I shall cane you more severely! You will be detained on Wednesday afternoon, Bunter. Now you may go!"

The unhappy Owl crawled from the study.

His progress up to the Remove passage was punctuated by moans and groans. He tottered along that passage, and blinked into Study No. 13, where seven fellows were at tea.

Johnny Bull picked up a cushion but

at the sight of Bunter's woebegone face he laid it down again.

"What's up, fathead?" asked Harry Wharton.

Bunter groaned.

"That beast Quelch! That beast Carter! Oh dear! He was pulling my leg! Ow! I see that now! Wow! He meant me to copy that beastly translation—ow!—and he did it all wrong to get me into a row with Quelch—yow-ow-ow! He was pulling my leg—ow!—and Quelch thought I was pulling his—and so—yow-ow-ow-ow!"

There was a chuckle in Study No. 13.

"Blessed if I see anything to cackle at!" groaned Bunter. "I've had six! Ow! I've got that mouldy translation to do over again! Yow-ow! I've got a detention for Wednesday! Oh dear! Ow!"

"Serve you jolly well right for copying another man's paper!" remarked Johnny Bull.

"Beast! Ow! Beast! Wow! Ow!" Harry Wharton laughed.

"You fat ass! You'd better not copy other fellows' papers—but if you do, you'd better steer clear of Carter's."

"The betterfulness will be terrific, my esteemed idiotic Bunter."

"Ow! Oh crikey! Ow!" groaned Bunter. "I say, Bob, old chap, you go and wallop that cad—ow!"

Grunt from Bob Cherry.

"You silly ass, you asked for it! You jolly well know you oughtn't to have copied his paper, and if you'd had the sense of a bunny rabbit, you'd have known that he wouldn't let you, except to pull your silly leg!"

"Beast!" groaned Bunter. "The awful cad took me in, you know! I believe he wants to get me into rows with Quelch, for some reason. I say, you fellows, I've had six, I've got a detention, and I—I haven't had my tea!"

That pathetic appeal was irresistible.

"Roll in, barrel!" said Bob.

Bunter rolled in. He was still feeling bad, very bad indeed; but not too bad to clear up most of what remained in the eatable line on the tea-table in Study No. 13.

THE TENTH CHAPTER.

Billy Bunter on the Warpath!

ARTHUR CARTER stepped quietly into Mr. Quelch's study, and closed the door quickly when he was inside.

He stepped towards the table and looked round him with swift, furtive eyes. And, as he did so, the gleam of a bright steel key sticking in one of the table drawers, caught his eye.

Carter's visit to his Form-master's study was surreptitious, but he was not there, as some fellows might have been, to "jape" Henry Samuel Quelch. He was not likely to put gum into the inkpot, like the fatuous Owl. He was, in fact, after the evening paper.

Evening papers were delivered in Common-room, and some of the beaks carried off their papers to their studies. Quelch often did. Carter had a particular reason for wanting to see the paper that evening. He was deeply interested in the fate of Bobby Bangle, who had run in the three o'clock that afternoon.

He could not venture into Masters' Common-room, but he could penetrate into a study when the occupant thereof was absent.

Mr. Quelch had been called away suddenly by a message from the Head.

Carter had seen him go, and so here he was, looking for the newspaper.

But he forgot the newspaper, and even Bobby Bangle at three to one, for the moment, as he saw the steel key sticking out of the drawer.

Quelch kept private papers in that drawer, as plenty of fellows knew. He was very careful to keep that drawer locked, and the key on his ring.

But the most careful of men are careless at times. Quelch had had a sudden call from the study, and he had omitted to put that key back on his ring before he left, for once.

Carter stood looking at it.

Billy Bunter, in his place, would probably have unlocked the drawer and peered in — inquisitiveness being Bunter's besetting sin. But Carter, though he had worse faults, was not inquisitive, and did not think of looking into the drawer. Quelch's papers had no interest for him.

For a long minute he stood still, staring at that gleaming key. Then he whipped it out of the lock, slipped it into his pocket, and left the study—without even glancing round again for the newspaper he wanted. After what he had done, the sooner he was off the scene the safer he was.

He strolled into the Rag with the key in his pocket.

A half-formed scheme was in the back of his scheming mind, and he required time to think it out in its details.

A dozen or more fellows were in the Rag after tea; among them, Billy Bunter.

Bunter's eyes, and spectacles, turned on Carter with a glare of ineffable scorn.

"Beast!" he hooted across the Rag. "Cad! Rotter!"

"Talking about yourself, as usual?" asked Carter.

"I say, you fellows, what do you think that beast did?" squeaked Billy Bunter. "He let me see a translation, and I took it to Quelch, and it was all wrong!"

"Ha, ha, ha!"

"You shouldn't bag another fellow's translation, old fat thing!" grinned Carter. "Honesty is the best policy."

"You jolly well let me see it on purpose, you beast, and you translated 'Qualis artifex pereo' into 'What larks,' and I've found out since what it really means——"

"Into what?" yelled Vernon-Smith.

"'What larks'!" roared Bunter indignantly. "Of course, if I'd thought a minute, I should have known that Nero wouldn't say 'What larks' when they were after him. But——"

"But thinking's not your long suit, is it?" chuckled the Bounder. "Mean to say you handed that to Quelch?"

"Yes, and he whopped me!"

"No wonder! Oh, my hat! I'd have liked to see Quelchy's face when he read it!"

"Ha, ha, ha!"

"You can cackle!" roared Bunter. "I got six! I've got that translation to do before prep. I'm going to thrash that cad! I mean, I've a jolly good mind to!"

"Sure it was a dirthy thrick intoirely!" exclaimed Micky Desmond "I'll hould ye're specs while you punch him, Bunter, me bhoy. I licked him aisy enough the other day, and so I did. Now you lick the spalpeen."

Billy Bunter blinked at Carter. Bunter would have given a good deal to lick the fellow who had played that trick on him. But Bunter was no fighting man. It was true that Micky Desmond had licked Carter in a scrap, and done it with ease. But Bunter

doubted whether it would be easy to his fat self.

To his surprise, Carter seemed far from keen on putting the matter to the test. Any fellow in the Rag would have said that Carter could have made rings round Bunter, with one hand tied. But he did not seem keen on it.

"My dear porpoise, only a joke," said Carter amicably. "Look here, I'll do the translation for you, if you like. There!"

"Think I'd trust you?" hooted Bunter.

"You can show it round, and see that it's all right."

Bunter stared at him.

That offer was a sound one. But it only showed, so far as Bunter could see, that Carter funked a scrap. For no other reason that was imaginable by Bunter, could he have made such an offer.

That was all Bunter needed to screw up his fat courage. If the other fellow was afraid, Bunter wasn't.

The fat Owl rolled towards Carter, with a threatening frown on his fat face, and a warlike gleam behind his spectacles. He brandished a podgy fist under Carter's nose.

Had Carter made a forward movement, Bunter would have made a prompt backward one. But it was Carter who backed away.

That did it. Bunter charged after him.

"You funk!" roared Bunter valorously. "I'm going to lick you! Put up your hands, you rotter!"

Carter backed round the long table in the Rag.

Bunter charged round the table after him. Carter still backed.

All the juniors stared on in surprise. To Bunter this looked like arrant funk; but the other fellows could only suppose that Carter was pulling the fat Owl's leg. Really it was difficult for anyone but Bunter to fancy that any fellow funked a combat with him.

"I say, you fellows, stop him!" yelled Bunter. "I say, make the beast stand up to it! He got me six from Quelch. I'm going to wallop him!"

"Look here!" exclaimed Carter. "Chuck it! I'm not going to scrap with you, Bunter."

"Ain't you?" snorted Bunter. "You jolly well are! You should have thought of that before you pulled my leg, and got me six from Quelch. I'm going to alter your features for you!"

"I'll do the translation over again," exclaimed Carter, jumping back from the brandishing fat fists. "Make it pax, old fat man, and I'll see you through with Suetonius."

Billy Bunter paused. Thrashing Carter—if he could do it—was a satisfactory idea. Still, he wanted that translation done.

"No larks?" he asked suspiciously.

"Honest Injun!"

"Well, you jolly well sit down and do it now, with my eye on you, and I'll let you off the thrashing!" said Bunter.

"Done!"

A dozen fellows watched Carter as he sat down to Bunter's Suetonius. They could only suppose that he was going to produce another ridiculous translation for the fat Owl to take to Quelch.

But if that was his game, a good many fellows present were ready to put paid to him. A joke was a joke; but getting a fellow caned was rather more than a joke.

Vernon-Smith and Peter Todd

looked over Carter's shoulders as he worked. Both of them were better men at the classics than Carter, so they were able to judge easily what his work was like.

To their mystification, he produced a good translation of XLIX, Book Six. It did not take him very long, though it would have meant hours of slogging to Billy Bunter. Carter had, in fact, been through it before with the help of a "crib," so it did not present any great difficulties to him.

Billy Bunter watched him with a suspicious eye. He was prepared to carry on hostilities, if Carter pulled his fat leg again.

When the task was finished, he blinked at it. Then he blinked inquiringly at the Bounder.

"Is it all right, Smithy?" he asked.

"Right as rain," answered Smithy.

"Quite all right," said Peter Todd. "But if Quelch knew that Carter had done it for you——"

"Well, I'm not going to tell him that," said Bunter. "I'll jolly well make Carter do all my translations after this. I'll jolly well thrash him if he doesn't—see?" Bunter grinned at that happy prospect. "Now give me that pen, Carter, and you can get out."

Carter gave him the pen, and got out.

Bunter proceeded to copy out the paper. Then he dropped Carter's translation into the fire in the Rag, and carried off his own to Mr. Quelch's study.

Mr. Quelch was not there. He was with the Head, but that did not matter. It was the rule for a fellow to leave his impositions on the Form-master's table, if he was absent when they were taken in.

Bunter laid his Latin paper on the table and rolled away in a state of considerable satisfaction.

That wretched Suetonius was off his fat mind at last. And it certainly never occurred to his podgy brain, that Carter had had any object in getting him to enter Quelch's study during Quelch's absence.

THE ELEVENTH CHAPTER.

Wary Wun!

WUN LUNG'S slanting eyes opened warily as Arthur Carter glanced into Study No. 13.

The little Chinee was alone there. Harry Wharton & Co. had gone to the gym, and Mark Linley had gone with them. The junior from the Flowery Land preferred a warm study and a blazing fire.

Wun was curled up in the armchair, with a rather serious expression on his little yellow face, which generally wore a cheery grin. He was thinking of the tragic happenings in his far-away native land.

To most of the Greyfriars fellows the Japanese invasion of China was little more than news in the newspapers. But to little Wun it came very near. His father, Wun Chung Lung, his grandfather Ko, his little Wun San, were in Canton, where Japanese bombs were falling. Often and often Wun's thoughts wandered to the distant East, where his countrymen had little more than courage and devotion to oppose to deadly weapons.

Wun turned his head as the study door opened.

At the sight of the new fellow he was wary at once.

His last experience of Carter had been the chase up the Remove passage, and he did not suppose that this was a friendly visit.

To his surprise, Carter gave him a cheery nod.

"Oh, you're here!" he said.

"Me hele," assented Wun. "You wantee see Bob Chelly, old Bob Chelly, go 'long gym."

Carter came in and closed the door.

"I wanted to speak to you," he said.

"You speakee, sposes you likee," said Wun, his slanting eyes curiously on the new fellow's face; his own face child-like and bland.

The little Chinee was as keen and astute as any fellow at Greyfriars, but his face had an expression of lamb-like innocence.

"I got rather wild the other day when you played that trick in my study," said Carter. "Sorry; I lost my temper."

"Allee light."

"It was a jolly clever trick," said Carter amicably. "How the dickens you got away with it, beats me."

"This lill' Chinee velly clevee fellee," agreed Wun Lung. "Plenty muchee blains 'long nappee blong me."

"Eh? Oh, yes! Look here, as you're so jolly clever at that sort of game. I want you to help me in a jape," said Carter, his keen eyes on the innocent face of the little Celestial. "Look at this!"

He produced a packet of toffee from his pocket.

Wun Lung looked at it. It was a small cardboard packet.

"What you wantee do?" asked Wun, puzzled.

"You shoved my pencil into Bunter's pocket the other day," said Carter. "He never knew. You could shove this toffee in the same way."

"Easy, easy," assented Wun Lung.

"You shoved Bunter's watch in my pocket, too," said Carter. "I suppose you did it when you pushed against me in the study, but I never knew."

"This lill' Chinee velly clevee," said Wun complacently.

"It's really wonderful," said Carter. "You're a clever little beggar, and no mistake. Now, suppose that fat ass Bunter found a packet of toffee in his pocket, what do you think he would do?"

"Him eatee toffee plenty quick!"

"Exactly!" grinned Carter. "And suppose a fellow had bored a hole in the toffee, and put some mustard in!"

Wun Lung chuckled.

"Velly funnee jokee on ole Buntee!" he said.

"Well, that's the idea!" said Carter. "Pulling the fat duffer's leg, you know. If I gave him the toffee, he would smell a rat—but if he found it in his pocket, he would scoff it on the spot, and then——"

"Coughee and gurgle plenty!" chuckled Wun.

"And we'll watch him coughing and gurgling!" grinned Carter. "The fat ass will think he had the toffee, and forgot it—he will never guess that it was slipped into his pocket by a giddy conjurer. Anyhow, he's jolly certain to eat it. And then——"

The little Chinee chortled.

"Plenty funnee jokee 'long fat ole Buntee!" he said. "You leavee toffee 'long me, me puttee 'long pockee blong Buntee."

"Here you are, then!" said Carter. "The fellows will be coming up to prep soon, and you can bump against the fat

ass in the passage, or on the stairs, and the trick's done."

"Me savvy!"

Wun, with a cheery grin, slipped the toffee-packet into his pocket, and Carter left the study.

After he was gone, the little Chinee winked at the glowing fire. Then he took out the toffee-packet, and opened the end of the cardboard carton.

His bland and smiling face had expressed nothing to Carter but enjoyment of the jape on Bunter. But behind that bland and smiling face, there was an Oriental keenness of which Carter had no suspicion.

No doubt it was no end of a joke to set Bunter coughing and gurgling with a dose of mustard hidden in a chunk of toffee. But Wun Lung meant to know exactly what was in that packet before he landed it on the Owl of the Remove.

To all appearance, it was an ordinary packet of toffee, with nothing whatever suspicious about it.

But there was more in that packet than met the eye.

Wun removed the chunk of toffee, and a gleam of metal in the carton caught his eye.

It was a small steel key that was packed under the toffee—invisible until the chunk was removed.

Wun's almond eyes fixed on it, and widened.

Then he examined the toffee. There was no sign on it that it had been bored for the introduction of mustard.

The little Chinee sat in deep thought for a few minutes. He did not like Carter, or trust him, and he knew that he was down on Bunter. Now he knew that his sleight-of-hand skill was to be made use of to plant that key on the unsuspecting fat Owl.

He knew that key! All the Remove fellows had seen it dozens of times. It was the key of Quelch's specially private drawer in his table, which was always kept carefully locked.

Private correspondence and all sorts of documents such as copies of school reports, or notes for the same, were kept in that drawer. Few fellows at Greyfriars would have cared to nose into it —but Bunter was one of the few! Bunter could always be relied upon to nose into anything, if he had the ghost of a chance.

How Carter had got hold of that key, Wun could not guess. Evidently he had done so somehow, and he intended to land it on Bunter!

That was the true meaning of the "jape" in which Wun was to lend his sleight-of-hand assistance.

A rather grim look came over Wun's little yellow face. Having reflected for a few minutes, he replaced the toffee in the packet and closed it—putting the key in his own pocket!

After which, with a cheery grin, the little Chinee strolled out of the study, and loitered about the passage till the Remove came up to prep.

Carter, in the doorway of Study No. 1, had an eye on him. He grinned as Wun gave him a wink, and continued to watch.

The fat Owl of the Remove came rolling into the passage.

Wun Lung stumbled against him as he passed.

Carter, watching keenly, had a glimpse of a toffee-packet in the little yellow hand for a moment. It vanished instantly.

"Urrrrggh!" gasped Bunter, as he tottered. "You clumsy heathen, wharrer you bumping into me for?"

"Plenty solly!" said Wun. "Foot slippee——"

"Oh, get out, bother you!"

Bunter rolled on to Study No. 7,

"Gurrggh!" gurgled Carter, as a stream of water from Wun Lung's squirt caught him full in the face. He grabbed out his handkerchief to dab his streaming face. Clink! A key, which had evidently been in the handkerchief, dropped to the floor.

happily unconscious that there was now a packet of toffee in his jacket pocket.

Wun Lung closed a slanting eye at Carter, who turned into Study No. 1 grinning—happily unconscious that the key was no longer in that toffee-packet.

Wun trotted back to Study No. 13, where Bob Cherry, Hurree Singh, and Mark Linley, had gone in for prep. His little yellow face was wreathed in grins.

"Hallo, hallo, hallo!" exclaimed Bob. "You're looking fearfully amused, Wun! What fatheaded trick have you been playing now?"

"Pullee leg blong Cartee!" grinned Wun.

"Oh, blow Carter!" grunted Bob.

And they settled down to prep in Study No. 13—Wun Lung interrupting his work, every now and then, with a little squeak of merriment.

THE TWELFTH CHAPTER.
The Missing Key!

"BLOW prep!" said Billy Bunter peevishly.

"Lazy!" said Peter Todd.

"I've a jolly good mind to chance it with Quelch! After all, if I'm put on con, I can tell him I had a bad headache."

"Untruthful!" said Peter.

"Oh, shut up, will you?" roared Bunter.

Peter grinned.

"Don't you want me to be pally any more?" he asked.

"No, I don't, if that's what you call pally!" growled Bunter. "Blow prep! I've had enough to do, with that rotten Suetonius! Lucky I made that cad Carter do it for me!"

"You made him!" chuckled Peter.

"You were there!" snorted Bunter.

"You saw how funky he was! I jolly well made him—and I'll make him do the next, too, now that I know he's funky!"

"Is that how you're going to get a good report from Quelch this term?"

"Oh, rats!"

There was a tap at the door of Study No. 7, and Trotter, the page, looked in. "Mr. Quelch's study, Master Bunter, please!" he said.

"Oh crikey!"

Billy Bunter rose unwillingly to his feet. Interruptions to prep certainly were welcome. But he did not want to see Mr. Quelch again. He had a very painful recollection of their last meeting.

"I—I say, Peter, that filthy translation was really all right, wasn't it?" he asked anxiously. "You saw it, you know."

"Right as rain!" answered Peter. "Quelch will give you good marks, old fat man, unless he tumbles to it that another fellow did it for you! In that case you'll probably get marks, too—from his cane."

"Well, I don't want to see him about it," growled Bunter. "But I suppose I'd better go, as the beast has sent for me."

"Much better!" agreed Peter.

And Bunter went.

He arrived in Quelch's study in an uneasy frame of mind. Both Smithy and Toddy had said that the Suetonius was all right; so really he ought to have nothing to fear on that score. But with a beak, you never could tell! Quelch might fancy that it had been done for him—he was a suspicious beast!

Mr. Quelch's expression was far from reassuring, as he entered.

For the second time that day, Quelch's brow was heavy with frowns, as if he was again understudying the Lord High

Executioner. His gimlet-eye gleamed at Bunter.

"You came to my study during my absence, Bunter!" he rapped.

"Yes, sir!" mumbled Bunter. "I—I left my paper on the table, sir! I—I hope it's all right this time, sir! I—I've given myself quite a headache doing it over again, sir."

"Your translation is fairly correct, Bunter—unusually good for you," said Mr. Quelch. "So far as that is concerned, you have shown that you can do better work than you have done this term, and I shall expect an improvement, therefore, in your work in Form."

"Oh!" This was rather a drawback to "making" Carter do his translations for him!

"But I have sent for you," continued Mr. Quelch, "to speak of another matter, Bunter! A key is missing from my study."

"Is it, sir?" asked Bunter, blinking at him. He saw no reason why Quelch should confide this circumstance to him!

"It is, Bunter! I was called away rather hurriedly by the headmaster, and inadvertently left the key in the lock of the drawer. It has been taken away."

"Oh!" gasped Bunter. He caught on now. "I—I haven't taken it, sir! When I want a key, I ask Fishy—he keeps a bunch of keys, and——"

"You were in the study, Bunter, in my absence. The key was taken away during my absence. No other boy in the Form had any business here, and I cannot suppose that any boy came here without a reason. Did you abstract the key from the drawer, Bunter?"

"Oh, no, sir!" gasped the dismayed Owl. "I never saw it, sir! Oh lor'!"

"You are, apparently, the only boy who came to my study during my absence!" said Mr. Quelch. "You were here, Bunter——"

"I—I wasn't, sir !" gasped Bunter.

"What ?" thundered Mr. Quelch. "How dare you make such a statement, Bunter, when I found your Latin paper on my table !"

"Oh—I—I mean——"

"You were here !" said Mr. Quelch, with intensifying sternness. "You have been punished on several occasions for inquisitiveness—indeed, on one occasion I myself caught you prying into my desk ! Whoever has taken that key must have taken it with the intention of prying, at a convenient opportunity, into the private papers in that drawer. He can have had no other motive. You are capable of this, Bunter, and I think that no other boy in the Form is either so prying or so stupid !"

"Oh, really, sir——"

"In short," said Mr. Quelch, "it is perfectly clear to me, Bunter, that you saw the key in the lock when you brought your translation to my study in my absence, and that you abstracted it !"

"Oh crikey !"

"You will now place it on the table, Bunter !" said Mr. Quelch, taking up his cane.

"But I haven't got it, sir !" gasped Bunter. "I—I never saw it ! It wasn't there when I brought my paper in, sir. I—I should have seen it."

"It certainly was there, Bunter !"

"It wasn't, sir !" gasped Bunter. "I should have noticed it when I looked at the table drawers, sir——"

"You looked at the table drawers?"

"Oh, no ! Not at all, sir ! I never thought that any of them might have been open, and never looked to see !" gasped Bunter. "I hope I'm not the sort of chap to do anything of the kind. I—I never went round the table at all, sir. I—I just stepped in and laid my Latin paper down, and—and went out."

If Billy Bunter hoped that his Form-master would believe that statement, it showed that Bunter had a really hopeful nature.

"Place the key on the table at once, Bunter !" thundered Mr. Quelch.

"I—I can't, sir, as—as I haven't got it !" groaned Bunter. "You couldn't have left it there, sir, or I should have seen it when I went round the table— I—I mean, I shouldn't have seen it, as I didn't go round the table ! Perhaps you've got it in your pocket all the time, sir——"

"Bunter !"

"I mean to say, you might forget putting it back in your pocket, sir," said Bunter hopefully. "Very old people do forget things, sir. My great-grand-father——"

"Silence, Bunter !" hooted Mr. Quelch, with a petrifying glare. "Place the key on the table this instant !"

"I—I would, sir, if I had it !" gasped Bunter. "But I haven't ! I hope you can take my word, sir ! I—I should be very sorry for you to think me un-truthful, sir, especially if you're going to mention it to Mr. Carter !"

Mr. Quelch breathed hard and deep.

"Turn out your pockets on my table, Bunter !"

"Yes, sir !" said Bunter, quite cheerfully.

Bunter knew, if his Form-master did not, that he had not taken the key, so he had no objection to revealing the contents of his pockets.

He turned out all sorts of articles, among them a cardboard packet of toffee.

Bunter blinked at that in surprise. He had not been aware that he was the happy possessor of a packet of toffee. If it had ever happened that Bunter had

overlooked such a possession, such hap-penings had been very rare !

But it certainly seemed as if he had overlooked this, for there was the toffee.

Every pocket was turned out to the lining. Nothing in the nature of a key was revealed.

Mr. Quelch examined the articles on the table, some of which might have been receptacles for a key. He opened Bunter's tattered notecase — without seeing any notes therein ! Neither was there a key in it. He even opened Bunter's watch, which was big enough to have contained that missing key. But the big watch only contained the works that didn't work ! He opened the packet of toffee, Bunter watching him uneasily.

He did not exactly suspect that Quelch might eat that toffee. Still, he felt relieved when the chunk was pushed back into the carton. Nothing but toffee was revealed in the carton.

"You—you see, sir——" stammered Bunter.

Mr. Quelch eyed him. The missing key certainly was not on Bunter, and neither Quelch nor Bunter had the remotest idea how very nearly that key had been discovered in the toffee packet.

"What have you done with the key, Bunter ?" asked Mr. Quelch at last.

"Nothing, sir ! I haven't touched it !"

"I cannot believe that statement, Bunter ! But——"

Quelch paused. He had had no doubt that the key was on Bunter. But it clearly was not on Bunter.

A doubt crept into Mr. Quelch's mind. It was not a very strong doubt. He was assured that Bunter had taken the key. Still, there was now an element of doubt in the matter.

Mr. Quelch, to Bunter's immense relief, laid down the cane.

"For the present, Bunter, you may go," he said, after a long pause. "I shall make further inquiry into the matter."

"Yes, sir," said Bunter.

And he packed his possessions back into his pockets, and went.

Mr. Quelch's suspicious stare followed him till the study door shut.

Bunter rolled back to Study No. 7 in the Remove. He grinned at Peter Todd as he rolled in.

"I say, Toddy, what do you think the old ass wanted ?" he asked. "He's lost a key to his table drawer. He, he, he ! He had the check to fancy that I might have snooped it !"

"Didn't you ?" asked Peter.

"No, I didn't !" roared Bunter. "The old ass has got it in his pocket, I expect ! I know it wasn't sticking in the drawer when I took my paper to his study, because I had a look round, and I should have seen it. Making out that I took his silly key ! As if I'd look into his rotten papers and things——"

"So you would, if you had a chance, you fat villain !" said Peter. "If you've got Quelch's key——"

"I've told you I haven't !"

"I know that ! If you have, the sooner you get it back to his study the better ! If I see you with it, I'll wallop you !"

"Beast !"

Bunter sat down again to prep.

"I say, Peter, I'm rather glad old Quelch sent for me. He made me turn out my pockets, and, I say, I found a packet of toffee in my pocket. I'd for-gotten I had it. Blessed if I know how I came to, but I must have ! Look !"

Bunter displayed the toffee with great satisfaction.

"I'd whack it out with you, Peter——"

"Thanks !"

"Only I feel rather hungry !"

And the chunk of toffee was jammed into Bunter's capacious mouth, and there it comforted him during prep.

THE THIRTEENTH CHAPTER.
Wun's Weird Way !

THE door of Study No. 1 was hurled open, and Wun Lung rushed breathlessly in.

Wharton, Nugent, and Carter stared up at him in surprise.

"What the thump——" exclaimed Harry.

Wun Lung tore breathlessly in, stumbled against Carter, and caught at him for support.

Carter pushed him off, and jumped up.

"You young ass ! What——"

"Ole Bob Chelly aftee me !" gasped Wun Lung.

"Bob after you ?" exclaimed Nugent, in astonishment.

There was a heavy tread in the Remove passage.

Bob Cherry's ruddy face looked in at the doorway, streaming with water.

Then the three juniors in Study No. 1 noticed that the Chinee had a squirt in his hand.

"That potty heathen here ?" roared Bob. "I'm going to give him a licking ! You young idiot——"

Wun, grinning, dodged behind Wharton and Nugent.

"Me velly solly, nicey old Bob Chelly !" he gasped. "Me tinkee you laugh, 'long me squirtee watee along face !"

Carter chuckled. He, at least, was amused.

"You potty little ass !" exclaimed Harry Wharton. "Do you think it's funny to squirt water in a fellow's face ?"

"Tinkee plenty muchee funnee !"

"You—you—you——" gasped Bob. "I've a jolly good mind to lynch you, you potty heathen ! So I will if you ever do it again !"

Bob took out his handkerchief to dab his face dry. He was accustomed to tolerating all sorts of weird pranks on the part of Wun Lung ; but, really, this was rather over the limit.

"No do any more ; sposee you no likee, handsome ole Bob Chelly !" said Wun meekly. "Me velly solly, nicey ole Bob !"

"Bother you !" grunted Bob.

And he walked back up the Remove passage.

"Well, of all the blithering little idiots !" said Harry Wharton. "Lucky it was Bob. Any other Remove man would have scalped you !"

Wun Lung grinned cheerfully. Bob had chased him down the Remove passage, after that extraordinary prank, but he was well aware that he had no punching to expect from Bob.

He sidled out of the study, grinning. And certainly it did not occur to any of the three fellows in the study that, when the artful little Chinee had rushed in and collided with Carter, he had transferred a little steel key to Carter's breast pocket. That key was back in Carter's possession now—if he had known it !

But he did not know it—and was not likely to learn it, until he had occasion to take the handkerchief out of that pocket.

Prep was nearly over in the Remove. Carter finished his work, in a mood of considerable satisfaction. He had no doubt that Bunter had been sent for, to Mr. Quelch's study—for it was hardly possible that Quelch had failed to suspect Bunter, when he missed the key. It was a practical certainty that Bunter had had to turn out his pockets, and that the purloined key had been found—hidden in the toffee packet. Whether Bunter had been whopped, or not, Carter cared little—it was one more black mark against him, and that was what the schemer of the Remove aimed at.

Indeed, in Carter's peculiar campaign against his rival for a fortune, he was able to bank on unintentional assistance from Bunter himself! For what he had planned to make Bunter appear to have done, was exactly what the prying Owl might have done, had opportunity offered. That fact, being well known to the Remove master, made it hopeless for Bunter, if the key was found on him. And Carter had little, or no doubt that it had been found. He had heard Bunter pass the door of Study No. 1 during prep, and that settled it, to his mind.

That simple little Chinee would suspect nothing, even if he heard that Quelch had found his key in the toffee-packet in Bunter's pocket! The obvious supposition would be, that Bunter had put it there, to keep it safe.

It was rather fortunate that the little Chinee was not quite so simple as he looked, and as Carter supposed him to be!

Herbert Vernon-Smith looked into the study, when prep was over.

"You fellows know what's up?" asked the Bounder.

"Is anything?" inquired Harry.

"Looks like it! Quelch is on the landing, and a prefect with him! Bunter been gumming his inkpot again. I wonder?" The Bounder chuckled. "It would be like him to jape Quelch, and leave his Latin paper on the table to show that he had been there!"

"Just like him!" said Harry, laughing.

The Removites came out of the studies. Something, plainly, was "up" —for it was uncommon for Quelch to post himself on the Remove landing, to see his Form after prep. He stood there, with a frowning brow, and Wingate of the Sixth came along the passage, calling to the juniors.

"All of you out of the studies!" he called.

"What's up, Wingate?" asked several voices.

"Quelch will tell you!"

The Greyfriars captain shepherded the whole Remove down the passage to the landing. There, Mr. Quelch signed to them to stop, and they stood facing their Form-master, every fellow wondering what the trouble was.

Wun Lung insinuated himself near Carter. The squirt, full of water again, was in his little yellow hand. There was a sly grin on Wun's face. Nothing could have suited him better than this, as he had been pondering how to catch Carter in the presence of his Form-master!

"My boys!" said Mr. Quelch. "I have a question to put to the whole Form. A key has been taken from my study, which I inadvertently left in a drawer in my desk. So far as I can ascertain, no boy but Bunter went to my study during my absence, but Bunter denies all knowledge of it."

"Oh, my hat!" murmured Wharton.

All eyes, for a moment, turned on Bunter. There were few fellows in the Form who doubted that the fat Owl knew all about the missing key. It was exactly one of his fatuous performances.

"I can only conclude," went on Mr. Quelch, in stern tones, "that the key of that private drawer has been taken with a view to prying into the private papers kept in it."

"Bunter or nobody!" whispered Skinner.

"I sent for Bunter, and he turned out his pockets in my presence," resumed Mr. Quelch. "The key was not found on him."

"I never——" squeaked Bunter.

"Silence, please!" rapped Mr. Quelch.

Carter caught his breath. He had had to conceal the key, for transfer to Bunter's possession. But surely Quelch could not have been ass enough to overlook it, if Bunter had turned out his pockets! But it looked as if he had!

"I cannot, and will not, order the boys of my Form to turn out their pockets," went on Mr. Quelch, "Bunter is an exceptional case—for I had, and have now, very little doubt that Bunter abstracted the key, and he has been guilty of such foolish and unscrupulous pranks before. But the key must be returned to me. I require it at once. I must ask, first, whether any boy here,

apart from Bunter, entered my study after tea."

There was no answer.

"Very well!" said Mr. Quelch, compressing his lips. "Some boy here present has taken the key. It must be returned. Until the key is returned to me, the whole Form will be under detention for all half-holidays."

"Oh!" gasped the Remove.

"I am sorry for this," said Mr. Quelch. "But I see no other resource. Some boy here has the key."

Swiiiissssh!

Mr. Quelch jumped. There was a sudden swish of water from a squirt—a most extraordinary and unheard of interruption when the Remove master was addressing his Form.

Carter gave a yell.

Full in his face came the whizzing stream of water from Wun Lung's squirt! It splashed all over his face.

"What—what—" gasped Mr. Quelch. "Wun Lung, how dare you?"

"Is the kid mad?" gasped Bob Cherry. "Wun, you awful little ass——"

"Upon my word!" thundered Mr. Quelch. "Wun——"

"Gurrggh!" gurgled Carter. "Oh! You little idiot! Ooooh!" He grabbed out his handkerchief to dab his streaming face.

Clink.

A small steel key, which had evidently been in the handkerchief in Carter's pocket, clinked on the landing, under all eyes.

THE FOURTEENTH CHAPTER.

The Culprit !

MR. QUELCH was making a stride towards Wun Lung.

He stopped.

His eyes were glued on that steel key, which had clinked down within a few feet of him, and lay glinting in the light.

So were all the eyes of the Remove.

Most, if not all, of the fellows, knew that key by sight. They had often seen Quelch using it in his study. It was the missing key—there was no doubt about that! And it had fallen from Carter's pocket!

"I say, you fellows," squeaked Billy

(*Continued on next page.*)

Bunter, in great excitement. "I say, that's the key! That cad Carter had it!"

"Carter!" exclaimed Harry Wharton.

"By gad! Carter!" said the Bounder.

Carter, dabbing his face, ceased to dab, and stared at the key. He stared at it like a fellow in a dream.

Indeed, he almost wondered whether he was dreaming!

He had hidden that key in the toffee-packet, and he knew that Wun had slipped the toffee into Bunter's pocket! Yet the key was in his own pocket all the time! It had fallen out, when he took out his handkerchief, under all eyes!

His brain fairly reeled! Had he only fancied that he had put the key in the toffee-packet? Really, it looked like it! There was the key—fallen from his own pocket.

Wun looked on with a smile that was child-like and bland! His amazing action with the squirt was almost forgotten, in the excitement at the unexpected discovery of the key.

"Carter!" Mr. Quelch found his voice. "You! You young rascal! Pick up that key, and hand it over to me at once!"

Carter in a dazed state, picked up the key, and handed it to his Form-master.

Mr. Quelch slipped it on his key-ring. His brow was thunderous as he did so. Nobody envied Arthur Carter what was coming next.

"Carter!"

"Ye-e-es, sir!" gasped Carter.

"You abstracted the key from my study!"

"I—I—I——" stammered Carter, helplessly.

"Wun Lung, you should not have played that foolish trick. But in view of this, I shall not cane you. You will take a hundred lines, and hand me that squirt."

"Yes, sir!" murmured Wun, meekly. He handed over the squirt.

"As for you, Carter, your punishment will be exemplary!" said Mr. Quelch. "I am surprised and shocked to find you capable of such conduct. I did not believe that there was such a boy in my Form, with one exception, capable of such a despicable action! I could have found some excuse for Bunter, as he is a very stupid boy, but there is no such excuse for you."

Carter stood gasping. He could not begin to understand how it had happened, but he was fairly caught; he understood that.

"My boys," said Mr. Quelch, "I am glad that this unpleasant matter has been cleared up. There will, of course, be no detention for the Form, as the boy who abstacted the key has now been discovered! Carter, follow me to my study!"

Carter limped down the stairs after his Form-master. The Remove were left in an excited buzz on the landing.

"Carter, all the time!" said Vernon-Smith. "What the dickens did he want Quelchy's key for? He's not a Peeping Tom, like Bunter."

"Oh, really, Smithy——"

"Can't make the fellow out!" said Peter Todd. "He must have sneaked into Quelch's study and snaffled it—goodness knows why."

"By gum, what a cad, though!" said Bolsover major. "He was going to let the whole Form get detention—he wasn't going to say a word if that key hadn't happened to turn up."

"Jolly lucky it did, as we're playing football to-morrow afternoon!" said Harry Wharton, with a deep breath. "What a rotter!"

THE MAGNET LIBRARY.—No. 1,563.

"The rotterfulness is terrific!"

"But why——" said Nugent blankly. "He can't want to play Nosey-parker, like Bunter——"

"Look here, you beast——"

"He jolly well knew that Quelch would jump on Bunter!" snorted Bob Cherry. "It's just one of the fat chump's silly tricks—and Bunter had been to his study, too, as it happens."

"Oh!" said Harry. "You think——"

"I don't think—I jolly well know!" growled Bob.

"I say, you fellows, what an awful beast!" said Billy Bunter. "I'll bet he knew Quelch would think of me. You know, people do always think of me, somehow, if there's anything missing. I don't know why——"

"Ha, ha, ha!"

"Blessed if I see anything to cackle at! All you fellows would have thought it was me if that key hadn't turned up!" exclaimed Bunter hotly.

"Your own fault!" said the Bounder. "You shouldn't do such things, old fat man. Nobody else in the Remove would—until your jolly old relation came. I suppose it runs in the family."

"Beast!"

"Well, I don't envy Carter!" said Johnny Bull. "Quelch will take the skin off him. Serve him jolly well right, too!"

"That isn't all he's going to get," said Billy Bunter darkly. "I'm going to thrash him for this!"

"Ha, ha, ha!"

"You can cackle!" roared Bunter. "You should have seen him funking in the Rag, after tea! Fairly trembling under my eye! I made him do my translation, because he was afraid to put up his hands. You wait till Quelch has done with him. I'll give him worse than Quelch!"

And Billy Bunter pushed back his cuffs—in readiness! His eyes gleamed behind his spectacles with the light of battle.

"Fattee old Buntee velly funnee!" said Wun Lung.

"Yah!" retorted Bunter. "You wait and see! If Carter's got any pal here, he'd better stand ready to pick up what I leave of him."

"Ha, ha, ha!"

"You'd better give him a miss, old porpoise!" chuckled the Bounder. "He won't be in a good temper after Quelch is through with him."

"Fat lot I care for his temper!" jeered Bunter. "You all saw how he funked, in the Rag! I'll jolly well make him cringe!"

"Let's hang on and see the circus!" chuckled Peter Todd. "Bunter will need first aid when he begins thrashing Carter."

"Oh, really Toddy! You saw me make him do my translation——"

"I saw him do it," grinned Peter, "and I wondered why. Looks to me now as if he wanted to make you walk into Quelch's study about that time!"

"I tell you he was funky!" roared Bunter. "And I jolly well know that he pinched that key to make Quelch think it was me. And I tell you I'm going to mop up this landing with him."

"We will all stand round and watch the mopfulness!" chuckled Hurree Jamset Ram Singh. "But I think it may be a boot on the other leg."

"Yah!"

A few minutes later, Carter was seen coming up the stairs.

Many curious eyes turned on him. His face was quite pale, and his brow was as black as thunder. His look showed that he had been through it very severely in Quelch's study.

Nobody had any sympathy to waste on him, however. Whether he had abstracted the key for prying purposes, or whether, as some of the fellows suspected, to land Bunter in a row, he fully deserved what he had received.

He came scowling across the landing, to go to his study.

Billy Bunter rolled into his way.

"Hold on!" yapped Bunter.

Carter gave him a deadly look.

"You fat fool! Get out of my way!"

"I'll watch it!" grinned Bunter. "I'm going to wallop you, you cad! You wanted to land me in a row with Quelch, you beast! I'm going to mop up the landing with you, and then I'm jolly well going to boot you along the passage! I can jolly well tell you that I'm jolly well going to—yarooooooop!"

Carter smote only once; but it was a hefty smite!

Billy Bunter went rolling along the landing, amid a yell of laughter. He brought up against the banisters, and sat there spluttering.

"Ooogh! Oh crikey! Keep off, you beast! Yoooogh!"

"Ha, ha, ha!"

Carter, scowling, went on to his study, went in, and slammed the door.

Billy Bunter gurgled for breath.

"Go it, Bunter!" chortled Skinner. "Go for him!"

"Ain't you going to mop him up, Bunter?" giggled Snoop.

"Pile in, old fat man!" said Peter Todd encouragingly. "We're all waiting to see him mopped."

"Groogh! Urrrggh! Oh crikey!" gasped Bunter. He set his spectacles straight on his fat little nose and tottered to his feet. "I say, you fellows, keep that beast off! I say, where's that beast?"

"He's gone," chuckled Peter. "You're in luck, old fat porpoise!"

"Oh!" gasped Bunter. "If—if—if he's run away, I—I—I'm not going to soil my hands on the rotten funk!"

"Have him out of his study!" urged Bolsover major. "Come on!"

"I—I—I think I'll—I'll—I'll let him off!" gasped Bunter. "After all, he had it bad from Quelch. I—I don't want to be hard on him, really."

"Ha, ha, ha!"

"Look here, we haven't waited up here for nothing!" said Peter. "Collar him and walk him along to Carter's study!"

"Good egg!"

"Bag him!"

Billy Bunter gave the grinning juniors one blink, turned, and scuttled down the stairs like a fat rabbit!

Evidently, Bunter's warlike ardour had petered out, and he was no longer thinking of mopping up the landing with Carter! It had dawned on his fat brain that the mopping up would be, as Hurree Singh expressed it, a boot on the other leg!

The fat Owl flew down the Remove staircase, missed his footing in his haste, rolled, and bumped on the next landing. And his yell, as he landed, was answered by a yell of laughter from the Remove.

THE FIFTEENTH CHAPTER.

Not Wanted!

"OH, get out!" muttered Harry Wharton.

Fellows in the changing-room looked round.

On Wednesday afternoon the Remove footballers were getting ready for a match with the Shell.

Hobson & Co. of the Shell were a rather tough team for the Lower

" Ooocoogggggh ! " spluttered Sir Hilton Popper, as he grabbed hold of Billy Bunter's outstretched fat hand. " Hold on ! " gasped the fat Removite. " Oh crikey ! I say, don't pull me in ! Oooogh ! " The willow swayed and creaked as Sir Hilton's weight fell on Bunter.

Fourth to tackle, and the best men in the Remove had been picked for the game. But it had been generally understood that there would be a new recruit in the team—Carter, the new man.

Partly, perhaps, because of his somewhat irresolute resolve to do better at Greyfriars than he had done at St. Olaf's, and partly because he really was keen on the game, Carter had devoted himself to Soccer since he had been in the school. Bob Cherry admitted that that was one redeeming point in an unpleasant character. He would rather have expected Carter to loaf about on a half-holiday with Pon & Co. of Highcliffe than exert himself on the football field.

But Carter was keen, and had shown good quality, and the captain of the Remove had intended to play him in that match. His name, however, had not appeared in the list posted in the Rag, after all. And when he looked in at the little crowd in the changing-room Wharton told him to get out.

Carter coloured under the many eyes that were turned on him.

"What do you mean?" he snapped. "You as good as told me that I should be wanted this afternoon."

"I know that. If you're keen to play you've only got yourself to thank," said Wharton curtly. "We came jolly near having this match washed out through that rotten trick you played on Quelch. If that key hadn't turned up we should all be in detention now—through you."

"That's got nothing to do with Soccer."

"Oh, quite ! But we're all feeling rather fed up—see? You were going to have a chance in this game, because you're good enough; but there's other fellows just as good, so you stand out, and you can go and eat coke !"

Carter stood silent, biting his lip. He had no special claim to play. He

was not, like Bob Cherry or Squiff or the Bounder, one of the mighty men who could not be spared. He was good—but, as Wharton said, there were others as good, and it made no difference to the team whether he played or did not play. And that narrow escape, caused by Carter, of the match having to be scratched, had made him, for the time, at least, extremely unpopular among the footballers.

Carter's eyes gleamed round at Bob Cherry, who was sitting on a bench, putting his football boots on.

"I suppose I owe this to you !" he snarled.

Bob gave him a look.

"I'm not skipper," he answered. "But if I were I wouldn't play you."

"I say, you fellows——" Billy Bunter pushed past Carter and rolled into the changing-room. "I say, is Wharton here?"

"Here," answered Harry, laughing. He was only a few feet from the Owl of the Remove.

"Oh !" Bunter blinked round at him. "I say, old chap, I suppose you know I've got a detention this afternoon."

"Time you got along to it, then."

"Well, the fact is, I don't want detention !" explained Bunter. "I want you to get me off, old fellow."

"Pleased, if I could do it !" answered Harry. "If you think Quelch will take orders from me, go and tell him to let you off at once."

"Ha, ha, ha !"

"Oh, really, Wharton ! What I mean is, Quelch always lets a fellow off if he's wanted in a match—I mean, he's done it before more than once," explained Bunter. "He did with Smithy, as you know ! Well, if you put me in the team——"

"If I put you in the team——" gasped Wharton.

"Yes, and go and tell Quelch that

you're absolutely relying on me to see you through in this match——"

"Oh crikey !"

"Ten to one he would let me off !" said Bunter hopefully. "I don't mean to say I'm specially keen on barging about at footer, you know; but I'd rather play football than stick in detention ! Any fellow would."

"You would—really !" stuttered the captain of the Remove.

"Yes, old chap—lots !"

"No time, I'm afraid !" said the captain of the Remove, shaking his head. "You see, you'd have to learn to play Soccer first ! That would take you about thirty years ! We can't ask Hobby and his men to hang about on Little Side all that time !"

"Ha, ha, ha !" roared the footballers.

"Now, don't be a beast, old chap !" urged Bunter. "I'm really particular about this, you know ! Quelch is going to stick me in the detention class with Mossoo—he's got about a dozen for French. I hate French much more than I do football—really and truly, you know——"

"Ha, ha, ha !"

"I can stand football all right—anyhow, I could dodge off the field when I got tired—see? That would make it all right."

Billy Bunter did not seem to see anything entertaining in this happy suggestion. But the Remove footballers evidently did. They yelled.

Bunter blinked round at them, apparently quite surprised by the merriment.

"I say, you fellows, I wish you wouldn't keep on cackling whenever a fellow opens his mouth !" he said crossly. "I simply can't be detained this afternoon, Wharton. My sister Bessie's asked me to tea at Cliff House, and she's got a cake. So, you see, it's rather important for me to get off. My idea is this—you beg me off with Quelch, and I'll play footer till it's time to start for Cliff House, and then chuck it—see? That will be all right."

"Ha, ha, ha!" yelled all the changing-room.

"Is it a go, Wharton?" asked Bunter anxiously. "I'll put in all the goals I can before I have to leave. Of course, I couldn't stay for the finish, as I should be late at Cliff House. But——"

"No!" gasped the captain of the Remove. "It isn't a go, old walrus! You see, Soccer's Soccer, and we want to beat the Shell—even if you have to miss the cake at Cliff House! Awfully and fearfully sorry, and all that—but now roll away like a good barrel!"

"Well, look here, old chap!" said Bunter. "I needn't actually play—it will be near enough if you go and tell Quelch that I'm wanted to play and you can't do without me. I don't suppose he will ever find out. I believe the beast is going out this afternoon, so he won't see the game. You cut off to Quelch and say—— Leggo, you beast!"

"Ha, ha, ha!"

Harry Wharton took the fat Owl by a fat neck and twirled him round in the doorway of the changing-room. Then he planted a football boot on Bunter's tight trousers, and the Owl of the Remove departed with a loud howl!

Carter scowled after him as he went. Then he bestowed another scowl on the footballers and lounged away.

Angry and irritated, he loafed in the quad, and scowled again at the sight of Mr. Quelch.

He was still feeling some twinges from the licking of the previous day. There was no doubt that Quelch had laid it on uncommonly hard. It was probable that, had Mr. Quelch known his real reason for abstracting the key, he would have laid it on harder still! But it had been hard enough, and Carter gave his Form-master an evil look as he saw him in conversation with Mr. Prout.

Prout's booming voice reached his ears:

"I am walking to Courtfield, Quelch! If you would care——"

"I should be delighted, but I have to call at Cliff House this afternoon," answered the Remove master. "Miss Bullivant desires to consult me about her young brother—you may remember the boy; he was in my Form here last term——"

Carter heard no more as he walked on.

But his eyes glinted unpleasantly as he went down to the gates.

Quelch was walking over to Cliff House that afternoon. He was fairly certain to take the footpath through the wood, which was half the distance by the road. Carter had been only a few weeks at Greyfriars, but he had learned his way about. He knew that footpath —and the plank bridge over the stream in Friardale Wood. It came into his vengeful mind that there was an easy and safe way of making Quelch sorry for that severe licking.

When the Remove master was going to start he did not know, but not yet, it was clear, for he was still talking to Prout in the quad. Carter had plenty of time to get ahead of him and clear off again before his Form-master came along.

He went at a trot, and in a few minutes was scudding along the woodland footpath. He reached the stream in the wood—which was low in the summer, but filled to the banks in the winter. The water splashed on the under side of the heavy old plank that

crossed it, resting on stones on either bank. Chips of ice floated in the water.

Carter crossed the plank, stopped, and cast furtive glances round him. There was no one in sight—few passengers used that path through the cold, frosty woods in winter-time. Leafless trees, gleaming with frost, surrounded him.

He bent and grasped the edge of the massive plank. It was not easy to shift, but he exerted his strength and shifted it.

He left it with only the tip of the plank resting on a slanting edge of stone, in such a position that it was certain to slip under the weight of any-one crossing.

There was no danger of drowning; or, if there were, it did not occur to him. The water was not more than three feet deep.

But the idea of giving a middle-aged man a ducking in that freezing water was one from which even an unfeeling fellow might have recoiled.

But Carter was in an evil, bitter, and revengeful mood. Having made that preparation for Quelch, he cut off through the wood and reached Friar-dale Lane. He walked back to the school with an unpleasant grin on his face.

THE SIXTEENTH CHAPTER.
Bunter's Bolt!

"BUNTAIR!"

"Oh lor'!" mumbled Bunter.

"Zat you sit down!" snapped Monsieur Charpentier.

"Beast!" murmured Bunter under his breath.

A detention class was never a happy function. Fellows under detention were never merry or bright, and Mossoo, probably, did not enjoy his task as detention master.

There were a dozen fellows in Class-room No. 10, going through extra French. Skinner and Snoop, Micky Desmond and Wibley of the Remove, Fry and Kenney of the Fourth, Hoskins of the Shell, and a few others, shared Bunter's woe that fine and frosty after-noon. They suffered under French irregular verbs and gave Mossoo all the trouble they could, which was the nature of a detention class.

Bunter was not thinking of ragging Mossoo—he was thinking of escaping from detention if he could.

Mossoo's back being turned for a moment, Bunter rose to slip out. Un-fortunately Mossoo looked round just as he made a move.

Bunter sat down again.

Irregular verbs went on their irregular way. Billy Bunter was not absorbing much knowledge of Mossoo's beautiful language. His fat mind was concentrated on getting away.

It was not merely that Bunter dis-liked detention. It was not merely that he disliked work. But if he stayed in Mossoo's class he lost not only his half-holiday, but Bessie's spread at Cliff House.

That beast Wharton might have begged him off from Quelch by putting him in the Remove eleven and explain-ing to Quelch how indispensable he was there. Quelch was considerate in such matters.

But the unspeakable beast had re-fused to do it! Just as if a football match mattered a boiled bean, in com-parison with Billy Bunter's comfort!

It was rather a reckless idea to break out of detention. With any master but Froggy, Bunter would not have thought of it.

But Froggy was a kind and peaceable

little man, and never—if he could help it—reported a man to his Form-master. He endured almost any amount of rag-ging; and Bunter knew that Smithy had once slipped out of the detention-room, and Mossoo had affected not to notice that he was gone. Other fellows had played the same game and got by with it. Why not Bunter?

Even if he was reported to Quelch it meant only a licking—and the feed at Cliff House was worth it. At least, it seemed worth it to Bunter while the feed was near and the licking far.

But ten to one Mossoo would say nothing. Peace at any price was his maxim—a maxim which certainly did not make his life at Greyfriars School very peaceful.

Still, even Mossoo's good-natured tolerance had its limit; fellow could not venture to walk out under his eyes. At the very least he had to wait till the French master's back was turned.

Bunter waited wearily for it to be turned again.

Micky Desmond dropped a book with a loud bang and drew Mossoo's atten-tion. Up rose Bunter again.

"Desmond, zat you keep ze order!" rapped Mossoo. "I vill not have ze rag in ze class! Ecoutez, you verree bad one! Zat is zhree time zat you drop one book on a floor."

"Sure, it dhropped, sorr——"

"Taisez-vous! If you drop zat book vunce more—— Buntair! Vy for you leave your place, Buntair?"

"Oh crikey! I—I wasn't leaving my place, sir!" gasped Bunter, who was two or three yards from his Form. "I—I—I——"

"Go back viz you, Buntair!" roared Mossoo. "Is it zat you zink zat you go out from zis class-room vhile zat my back is turn?"

"Oh, no, sir! I—I wasn't going out!" gasped Bunter. "Nothing of the kind, sir! I—I—I wouldn't!"

"If you move one more time, Buntair, I frappe you viz ze pointair."

Bunter sat down again, in the lowest of spirits.

On the football field Harry Wharton & Co. were enjoying life. That beast Carter, who had got him a detention, was free to do as he liked—and Bunter had to stick in detention!

A dozen other fellows had to, it was true, but they did not matter; only Bunter mattered.

A dreary half-hour crawled by. Twice in that half-hour Bunter rose—and sat down again, under Mossoo's glittering eye.

But his chance came at last.

Monsieur was chalking on the black-board; his back was turned; he seemed to have forgotten Bunter.

The fat Owl rose once more.

On tiptoe he crept towards the door. All eyes in the class-room were fixed on him, except Mossoo's. All the fellows were grinning. They all wished Bunter luck.

Nearer and nearer the door crept Bunter, his fat heart thumping. Mossoo did not glance round.

He reached the door; his fat hand was stretched out to the door-handle.

It was quite a breathless moment of excitement in Class Room No. 10. A few moments more and Bunter would be gone. If Mossoo did not look round——

But he did!

Perhaps he heard the sound of the opening door, cautiously as Bunter turned the handle. Anyhow, he looked round and spotted the fat junior in the very act of escaping.

"Buntair !" shrieked Mossoo.

"Oh crikey !"

Bunter had one foot in the passage. The sudden shriek behind him startled him, but it did not make him draw that foot back. The other followed it. Under Mossoo's exasperated eyes the fat Owl bounded into the passage.

"Mon Dieu ! Zat Buntair !" roared Mossoo.

He rushed after Bunter.

Had the fat Owl escaped unseen, no doubt Mossoo would have let it go at that—and even, perhaps, would have forgotten to report it to Quelch afterwards. But even Mossoo could not let a detained fellow walk off right under his nose.

He rushed into the passage and waved wild hands after the scuttling fat Owl.

"Buntair !" he bawled. "Zat you come back viz you ! Verree baddest of all ze bad boys, zat you come back !"

Bunter flew.

It was in for a penny in for a pound now ! The fat Owl raced down the passage, turned a corner, and bolted for the door of the House.

Mossoo bolted after him.

He was going to grab Bunter by a fat ear and lead him back into the fold.

Bunter, hearing the pattering footsteps behind him, put on speed. Breathless, he reached the doorway.

A fellow was coming in as he reached it. It was Carter, just back from his walk in Friardale Wood. Carter, as he came in at the gates, had seen Quelch starting—with considerable satisfaction. Now he was coming into the House—just in time to meet Bunter in his flight.

"Gerrout of the way !" gasped Bunter.

Mossoo was close behind.

"Zat you stop him, Cartair !" shouted Mossoo.

Carter made a movement to obey, but he checked himself. If Bunter was breaking out of detention, and doing it in this reckless way, Carter was not the man to save him from heading into bad trouble.

He made a catch at Bunter, and was careful to miss him.

The fat Owl, gasping, barged through the doorway.

But Mossoo was right behind him now, his outstretched hand about to clutch. Bunter would infallibly have been caught—had not Carter been there. Carter stumbled in Mossoo's way in the nick of time.

Mossoo bumped on him, staggered, and missed his clutch at Bunter.

Bunter bounded into the quad and flew for the gates.

"You verree clumsy garcon, Cartair !" gasped Mossoo.

"Sorry, sir ! I was trying to help you. You called to me——"

"Buntair ! Zat you come back, Buntair !" roared Monsieur Charpentier. He stood in the doorway, gesticulating. He did not feel disposed to chase Bunter across the quad.

Bunter heard, but he did not heed. He fled for the gates and vanished.

Monsieur Charpentier gesticulated and gasped for breath.

"Mon Dieu ! Zat verree bad boy ! I report zat verree bad boy to Mr. Quelch !" he gasped. "Mon Dieu ! On en a assez—— I report zat verree bad boy for zis !"

And monsieur gasped his way back to Class Room No. 10

Carter winked at his back as he went. There was no doubt that Billy Bunter was giving him plenty of assistance in his campaign to land the fat Owl in trouble

THE SEVENTEENTH CHAPTER.

Not a Ducking for Quelch !

"OH crikey !" gasped Bunter.

He ambled on his way down Friardale Lane, gurgling for breath, but came to a sudden halt at the sight of a well-known figure in the lane ahead.

Fortunately, he had only a back view of Mr. Quelch, and the Remove master did not look round.

He had escaped the clutches of Mossoo, and it would have been simply awful to fall into those of Quelch outside the gates—like an ancient mariner weathering Scylla and coming to grief on Charybois.

Quelch, it seemed, was walking down to Friardale. Where he was going Bunter did not know, but he was glad to see only his back.

He slowed down, blinking anxiously after Quelch.

There were two ways of getting to Cliff House School—one by the road through the village; the other by the footpath through the wood. The road was much longer, but the footpath was much muddier; so it was a matter of personal taste. Bunter would have preferred the footpath, preferring mud to distance. Quelch, who was a vigorous walker, and liked long walks, preferred the road—a circumstance that Carter had never thought of guessing when he made his preparations at the plank bridge.

Quelch, much to Bunter's relief, walked on to the village. That Quelch was going to Cliff House School by the longer way never occurred to Bunter. He, of course, knew nothing of Quelch's intention to call on Miss Bullivant, the games-mistress of Cliff House, in reference to a boy who had been in the Remove the previous term. So far as Bunter could see, Quelch was going down to Friardale—and he was glad to see him go.

The Remove master disappeared round a turn of the winding lane; and Bunter, in great relief, rolled on to the stile that gave on the footpath.

He sat on that stile to rest. After a quarter of a mile Billy Bunter needed a rest. He had lots of time to get to Cliff House, and Bessie would not be expecting him yet.

He sat and rested and puffed and blew.

He was not feeling fearfully bucked. True, he was free for the afternoon now, and going to tea with Sister Bessie at her school, and he knew that there was a cake But the way he had got out of detention was far from satisfactory. Had he slipped out unseen, he could have hoped that Mossoo would say nothing about it, as had happened more than once before. But after bolting under Mossoo's nose, and being chased as far as the door of the House, he could hardly hope that even Mossoo would overlook the occurrence. No doubt the cake was worth a licking; still, Bunter did not want the licking.

It was Carter's fault for getting him that detention. It was Mossoo's fault for watching a fellow like a cat ! It was Wharton's fault for not begging him off ! It was, in fact, everybody's fault but Bunter's. He had the consolation, such as it was, of realising that he was entirely blameless. But he could not hope that Quelch would take the same view, if Froggy reported him.

Still, there was Bessie's cake to think of, and he thought chiefly of the cake.

He had been resting about a quarter of an hour on the stile, when a tall, angular gentleman came striding up the lane.

Bunter blinked at him rather uneasily. Sir Hilton Popper was a governor of Greyfriars School and had he known that Bunter was out of detention, it was very probable that Sir Hilton would have walked him into it again.

Still, it was quite impossible for the lord of Popper Court to guess that Bunter was out of detention. There were plenty of Greyfriars juniors about in a half-holiday, and Bunter was only one of them.

The fat junior capped Sir Hilton respectfully as he came striding up. His fat face did not reveal what he was thinking—that Sir Hilton was a fussy old ass whom he would much rather not have seen just then.

Sir Hilton gave him the briefest of nods in acknowledgment, and stopped.

"Nice afternoon, sir !" ventured Bunter, supposing that the old baronet had stopped to speak to him.

"Kindly allow me to pass over that stile !" grunted Sir Hilton.

"Oh, yes; certainly, sir !" gasped Bunter

He realised that Sir Hilton had not stopped for a little conversation with a particularly nice member of his old school. He only wanted Bunter to get out of the way.

Bunter got out of the way.

Sir Hilton Popper stepped over the stile, and strode on his way up the footpath through the wintry wood. Apparently he was walking to Pegg through Friardale Wood. Bunter blinked after him.

"Beast !" he murmured.

Having got off the stile to allow Sir Hilton to pass, Bunter rolled on his way. Sir Hilton's long legs covered the ground at a much more rapid rate than Bunter's short, fat ones, and the old baronet drew farther and farther ahead.

He reached the plank over the woodland stream, while Bunter had only a distant view of it.

But he was still in sight, though at a distance, and Bunter saw the tall, angular figure stride across the plank.

What happened next made Bunter jump.

One moment that tall figure was standing on the plank over the stream; the next, it was splashing headlong in the water.

A suffocated yell floated back to Bunter.

"Oh crumbs !" gasped Bunter.

He stood blinking through his spectacles. His impression was that Sir Hilton had clumsily slipped off the plank. But the next moment he saw that the plank itself had disappeared from its place, and was floating down the stream.

In the middle of the woodland stream rose the long, lean figure of Sir Hilton Popper, splashing wildly.

He was a tall gentleman, and the water was hardly up to his waist. Had he kept his footing he would have been all right.

But that sudden plunge in icy water had made Sir Hilton quite dizzy, and the current was swift and strong.

Under Bunter's horrified eyes, the tall figure went whirling over, with wild splashing.

Billy Bunter broke into a run. Sir Hilton was not merely getting a ducking; he was in need of help. He was splashing and snorting like a grampus, evidently unable to get out.

Bunter charged along the footpath breathlessly. He could not help thinking how lucky it was that Sir Hilton had gone over the plank first—otherwise it would have been Bunter that got that ducking. Still, he was more than willing to render any aid he could.

He arrived breathless on the bank, and blinked through his big spectacles at the struggling figure in the water.

Sir Hilton Popper had grabbed at a bunch of grass, but it tore away in his fingers. He whirled over in the middle of the icy stream, spluttering frantically, and grasping wildly in all directions. Though it had never occurred to Carter, for a moment, there was actual danger of drowning unless a man had his wits about him—and Sir Hilton's, never of the best quality, were scattered far and wide.

"Oooooogggggh!" came spluttering from the water, as the old baronet's head went under for the third or fourth time.

"Oh crikey!" gasped Bunter. "I—I say, sir, this way! This way! Catch hold of my hand! Oh crumbs!"

Sir Hilton's head came up again. His feet found a footing in the mud at the bottom of the stream, and he heaved himself up.

Bunter grabbed a willow-branch with one hand, to hold on, and reached out with the other. Sir Hilton was within easy reach if he retained enough of his senses to catch hold.

Sir Hilton was on his feet again, grabbing frantically at space. But the rush of the water tumbled him over again. But as he tumbled he grabbed hold of Billy Bunter's outstretched fat hand.

"Hold on!" gasped Bunter. "Oh crikey! I say, don't pull me in! Oooooogh!"

The willow swayed and creaked as Sir Hilton's weight came on Bunter. The fat Owl held on desperately with his other hand. He could not have held on long; but Sir Hilton was on his feet now, steadied by his grip on Bunter's fat paw, and he scrambled up the bank.

"Good gad!" gasped Sir Hilton Popper, as he stood at last among the frozen rushes, streaming and dripping.

"Oh crikey!" gasped Bunter.

THE EIGHTEENTH CHAPTER.
Meeting Mr. Quelch!

BILLY BUNTER gasped for breath. His fat arm felt as if it had been almost wrenched out of its socket. He was splashed from head to foot, his trousers were drenched, and he was spattered with mud.

But Sir Hilton Popper was in much worse case, if that was any comfort. He was soaked from head to foot, his hat had disappeared in the stream, and he stood in a pool of water that ran down his long limbs. He gasped and gasped and gasped.

"Good gad!" repeated Sir Hilton. "Ooough! Good gad! That dashed plank! The local authorities are to blame! Good gad! Urrgh! I shall catch a cold! Gurrgh! Thank you, my boy! Wooogh!"

"Oh dear!" gasped Bunter. "I'm all wet!"

"Thank you for coming to my assistance, Punter. I think your name is Punter. I have seen you before. Grogh! Thank you, Punter!"

"Bunter, sir!"

"Oh, yes, Bunter! I am much obliged to you Punter—I mean, Bunter! You had better go in at once and change, or you will catch cold. Urrggh!"

With that good advice, Sir Hilton turned and strode away, back the way he had come, dripping water as he went. Evidently he had given up his walk, and was thinking only of getting out of his wet clothes as quickly as possible.

"Oh lor'!" groaned Bunter.

He was glad, no doubt, that he had helped Sir Hilton out of the water. But he was wet and cold and horribly uncomfortable. He did not think of taking Sir Hilton's good advice, and getting in and changing. That meant getting back into detention, and no tea at Cliff

House. But it was a dismal Owl that tramped away from the spot.

The plank being gone, he could not cross the stream. He had to walk back to the lane and take the longer way round. It was more than two miles—a dismaying prospect to Bunter.

He plugged drearily on his weary way. Luckily the exercise warmed him, though damp trousers were still horribly uncomfortable. Bunter could not help feeling that he would have earned that cake by the time he began masticating it.

It seemed an age to the fat Owl before Cliff House School came in sight at last. Comforted by getting to the end of his journey, he rolled on hopefully to the gate. He cheered up at the thought of the warm fire in Bessie's study, and big hunks of cake going down like oysters.

And then——

He reached the gateway, and was about to roll in, when Mr. Quelch stepped out!

"Bunter!" ejaculated Mr. Quelch. "Is—is that you, Bunter?"

"Oh! No, sir!" gasped Bunter. "I —I mean, yes, sir! I—I—oh crikey!"

"You are out of detention, Bunter!"

Bunter would gladly have denied it! But there he was—a good two miles from the detention-room!

"What are you doing here, Bunter?"

"I—I—I came over to see my—my sister, sir!" gasped Bunter. "She— she's ill, and—and I was very anxious about——"

"I have just passed your sister in the garden, Bunter, and she did not look ill!" said Mr. Quelch, in a grinding voice.

"Oh crikey! I—I mean——"

"Well, what do you mean?"

"N-n-nothing, sir!" groaned Bunter.

"I am about to walk back to Greyfriars," said Mr. Quelch. "You will walk with me, Bunter."

"Oh lor'!"

"I shall take you to your headmaster immediately we arrive at the school. I shall request him to administer a flogging for this outrageous disrespect for disregard of authority, Bunter."

"Oh crikey!"

"Come!" hooted Mr. Quelch.

Billy Bunter tottered away by his side He could have groaned. After all the risks he had taken, he had not even entered Cliff House—he was not even going to see the cake. He was going to see his headmaster instead, and bag a flogging from that gentleman! If life was worth living, under these harrowing conditions, Bunter did not see it.

"We will take the short cut, Bunter," he said. "This way!"

That reminded Bunter.

"We can't, sir—the plank's gone!" he groaned.

"Indeed!" said Mr. Quelch. "Then we must walk through the village. Are you sure the plank is gone, Bunter?"

"Oh, yes, sir, I saw it!" Bunter had a gleam of hope. He wondered whether his eminent service to Sir Hilton Popper would make any difference, if he told Quelch! After all, he had hooked the old bean out of the water, and Sir Hilton was a governor of the school. "I—I say, sir, the plank fell in when Sir Hilton Popper was walking across it——"

"Indeed!"

"I—I saved his life, sir——"

"You—you—you did what?" gasped Mr. Quelch.

"I—I plunged into the stormy waters,

Printed in England and published every Saturday by the Proprietors, The Amalgamated Press, Ltd., The Fleetway House, Farringdon Street, London, E.C.4. Advertisement offices: The Fleetway House, Farringdon Street, London, E.C.4. Registered for transmission by Canadian Magazine Post. Subscription rates: Inland and Abroad, 11s. per annum; 5s. 6d. for six months. Sole Agents for Australia and New Zealand: Messrs. Gordon & Gotch, Ltd. and for South Africa: Central News Agency, Ltd.—Saturday, January 29th, 1938.

sir, at—at the risk of my life, and brought him ashore——"

Mr. Quelch came to a halt, and fixed his eyes on Bunter. Never had they seemed to Bunter so much like gimlets.

"Bunter"—Quelch's voice came like the filing of a saw—"how dare you talk such absurd nonsense to me, your Form-master! If you utter another word before we reach the school, I will box your ears!"

Quelch strode on again.

Billy Bunter trailed after him, in the lowest of spirits, and did not utter another word till they reached the school.

THE NINETEENTH CHAPTER.

Poor Old Bunter!

"HALLO, hallo, hallo!"

"That ass——"

"Wasn't he in detention?"

"Looks as if he wasn't!"

The football match was over, and Harry Wharton & Co. were feeling rather bucked by the fact that they had beaten the Shell by two goals to one. They came along from the changing-room in time to see a weary, dreary, dismal fat Owl trail in at the heels of a frowning Form-master.

To state the exact fact, they had forgotten Bunter's fat existence that afternoon. Still, had they thought of him, they would have thought of him sitting at extra French. It was quite a surprise to see him trailing in after Quelch.

Bunter gave them a sad and lugubrious blink. Seldom had the fat Owl looked so sorrowfully down on his luck.

Quelch left him waiting, while he went to take off hat and coat. That gave the juniors a chance of asking him what was up. He told them dolorously.

Carter, who was lounging by, chuckled as he listened. He had expected the hapless fat Owl to land in a row, but he had hardly expected him to walk right into Quelch's clutches. But he was puzzled, too. If Bunter had run into Mr. Quelch at Cliff House, it looked as if the Remove master had not, after all, captured the ducking planned for him by that dutiful member of his Form. Quelch would hardly have walked on, to call on Miss Bullivant, if he had been ducked.

But as Bunter proceeded with his tale of woe, the schemer of the Remove understood. The wrong man had walked into his trap, which was annoying to Carter—but the fact that Bunter was "for it" was a solace for the young rascal.

"I say, you fellows, Quelch wouldn't listen to me when I told him how I got old Popper out!" wailed Bunter. "I say, do you think the Head would? I mean to say, they ought to let me off when I saved a man's life, don't you think? I mean, it's no joke to plunge into icy water, and——"

"Was the water wet?" asked Vernon-Smith.

"Eh? Of course it was, you ass! Wharrer you mean?"

"I mean that it's jolly odd that it hasn't wetted your clobber if it was!" grinned the Bounder.

"Ha, ha, ha!"

"Better not tell the Head any lies, old fat man!" said Bob Cherry.

"Mauvais garcon!" Monsieur Charpentier came up. "Vous etes de retour—you are of return viz yourself, isn't it? You Buntair——"

"I—I say, sir, I—I'm fearfully sorry I cleared off," said Bunter, blinking at

him. "If you'd put in a word for me, sir——"

"Vat?" ejaculated Mossoo. "You verree bad boy, Bunter. I shall report you to Mistair Quelch——"

"I say, sir, while I was out this afternoon, I shaved a man's wife—I mean, I saved a man's life!" gasped Bunter. "If I hadn't gone out, sir, Sir Pilton Hopper—I mean, Sir Hilton Popper—would have been drowned——"

"Parbleau!" ejaculated Monsieur Charpentier.

"He fell in the water, sir," said Bunter hopefully. "I—I leaped in, sir, at the risk of my life, and got him out. My jacket isn't wet, because I took it off before I—I plunged in, sir."

"Oh, my hat!" murmured the Bounder.

Evidently Bunter had taken a tip from his remark on the jacket.

"After a fearful struggle, sir, I got him ashore," said Bunter. "If—if I hadn't gone out, I couldn't have done it. So—so perhaps you'll put in a word for me, sir. I—I hope you believe me, sir."

"Mon Dieu! I believe not vun vord!" exclaimed Mossoo. "I zink zat you are ze most untrootful boy zat ever vas, Buntair. Voici Monsieur Quelch!" The Remove master came back for Bunter, and Monsieur Charpentier greeted him with gesticulating hands. "Monsieur, zis Buntair, he go out viz himself in ze detention—he run, he fly, he bunk, and I also, I run, I fly, I bunk, and I catch him if zat Cartair do not get in ze vay. But zat Cartair he get in ze vay, and zat Buntair he go, and I do not catch him. And——"

"I am already acquainted with Bunter's conduct this afternoon, Monsieur Charpentier," said Mr. Quelch grimly. "He came to Cliff House School, where I had called. I am about to take him to his headmaster, to report him for a flogging."

"Oh crikey! I say, sir——"

"You need say nothing, Bunter. Follow me."

"Oh, lor'!"

The fat Owl trailed away dismally after his Form-master to the Head's study.

Bob Cherry gave Carter a dark look.

"So you got in Mossoo's way, and stopped him from catching Bunter," he said.

Carter shrugged his shoulders.

"Can't I do my relation a good turn if I like?" he asked. "Wouldn't any fellow help a chap, with a beak after him?"

Bob gave an angry grunt. Had Mossoo caught Bunter before he escaped the matter would have ended there. Carter's intervention had been intended to help the fatuous fat Owl land himself in serious trouble. Bob had not the slightest doubt on that point. Nevertheless, almost any man in the Remove would have said that it was a good turn, to help a fellow who was dodging a beak. Bob Cherry grunted, but he said no more.

"Poor old Bunter!" said Harry Wharton. "He's up for a flogging this time. Of all the howling asses he's——"

"The fat chump walked out right under Mossoo's nose," said Wibley. "Bolted like a rabbit, with Mossoo after him. Even Froggy couldn't stand for that. And then to walk into Quelch's claws——"

"Bunter all over!" grinned the Bounder.

"Poor old Bunter!"

There was plenty of sympathy for

the forlorn fat Owl. Unfortunately, sympathy could not save him from receiving that for which he had asked so emphatically.

Billy Bunter was looking and feeling as if the sum total of the troubles of the universe had landed in a heap on his fat shoulders, as he trailed after his Form-master into the Head's study.

The door of that dreaded apartment closed behind him, and his well-wishers listened for the loud howls which would announce that Dr. Locke was getting busy with the birch; but, contrary to expectation, they did not hear the Owl howl.

THE TWENTIETH CHAPTER.

Luck for Bunter!

DR. LOCKE frowned at the sight of Bunter.

That term he had seen that particular member of Mr. Quelch's Form oftener than he was accustomed to see a Lower Fourth junior. Attractive fellow as Bunter was, his headmaster did not want to see him again.

"What is it this time, Mr. Quelch?" he asked.

He glanced as he spoke towards the birch. Evidently it occurred to him that that instrument might have to be featured in the scene.

"I am bound to report this junior to you, sir," said Mr. Quelch. "Bunter has always been troublesome, but this term he seems determined to give more trouble than ever. You will hardly believe, sir, that when I gave him a translation to do—a short and simple translation from Suetonius—he actually ventured to bring me a paper written in a spirit of mockery."

"I—I didn't!" gasped Bunter. "I mean, I never meant——"

"Silence! For that offence, sir, I thought of reporting him to you, but I decided that a caning and a detention would meet the case. This afternoon, sir, Bunter actually walked out of detention; he actually had the audacity to run, when Monsieur Charpentier followed him and called him back. In the circumstances, sir, I feel that only you can deal with him."

"Quite so, Mr. Quelch," said the Head. "No doubt a flogging——"

"I hope, sir, that a flogging may make this foolish and troublesome boy realise that he is not here to disregard all authority."

"I have no doubt of it," said Dr. Locke. "Bunter——"

"If—if you please, sir——" gasped Bunter.

"You can have nothing to say in extenuation of such an offence, Bunter," said Dr. Locke sternly. "I shall now administer——"

"But, sir, if I hadn't gone out, old Popper would have been drowned!" gasped Bunter.

It was the only card he had to play, and he played it, in the desperate hope that it might prove a trump.

"What?" ejaculated the Head. He withdrew his hand from the birch, and stared at Bunter. "What is the boy saying?"

"Some ridiculous story, sir, of which I do not believe a word," said Mr. Quelch grimly. "Bunter is, I am sorry to say, an absolutely untruthful boy."

"Oh, really, sir! It's true!" groaned Bunter. "You can ask old Popper, sir——"

"Who?" exclaimed the Head.

"I—I mean Sir Hilton Popper, sir! I—I saved his life, sir——"

"Do not talk nonsense to your headmaster, Bunter!" rapped Mr. Quelch.

"I—I—I ain't!" gasped Bunter. "I really did, sir, and as old Popper—I mean Sir Hilton Popper—is a governor of the school, sir, I thought very likely you'd rather he wasn't drowned, sir——"

"Bless my soul!" said the Head, blinking at Bunter. "If there is any truth in this, Mr. Quelch—certainly it is no excuse for breaking detention—nevertheless, Bunter, you may tell me what has happened."

"Yes, sir. Old Popper—I mean Sir Hilton Popper—I never call him old Popper, sir, like some of the fellows—I'm too respectful——"

"Proceed at once, Bunter!"

"Yes, sir. Old—Sir Hilton Popper fell off the plank in Friardale Wood, sir, and—and I rescued him, sir. Hearing his cries for help, I rushed up, sir, and—and, without thinking of the danger, plunged in, and—and swam with him to safety, sir."

"Do you believe this, Mr. Quelch?"

"I do not, sir!"

"Oh, really——" gasped Bunter.

"Bunter is a very poor swimmer," said Mr. Quelch. "What he states is quite impossible. I do not believe for one moment that anything of the kind occurred."

Not for the first time, Billy Bunter had reason to wish that he could have told a plain tale without trimmings.

"But—but it's true, sir!" wailed Bunter. "I—I fought for my life in the raging flood, sir——"

"Bunter is describing the woodland stream in Friardale Wood, sir," said Mr. Quelch grimly. "I regret that your time should be wasted with such nonsense."

"I shall certainly listen to no more!" said Dr. Locke, frowning. "How dare you make statements, Bunter, which are obviously untruthful?"

"I—I—I mean I—I didn't exactly plunge in, sir——" stammered Bunter. As the Head clearly did not believe in the heroic rescue, Bunter was prepared to moderate his transports, as it were. "What I really mean is, sir, that I—I got hold of a willow and reached out my hand to—to Sir Hilton Popper, sir, and got him, and—and dragged him out, sir."

Headmaster and Form-master gazed at Bunter.

Had the hapless Owl told the truth to begin with, doubtless he would have received credence. But the facts came too late to be of any service to Bunter. As he had started with fabrication, it was not surprising that the two masters regarded the whole story as fabrication.

"Upon my word!" said Mr. Quelch.

"Bless my soul!" said the Head, almost dazedly. "You have told me that you plunged into the water,

Bunter, and now you tell me that you reached out a hand to someone in the water. Mr. Quelch, I fear that this boy would say anything that came into his head to escape a just punishment."

"I fear so, too, sir!"

"Bunter, I shall now administer a flogging, all the more severe because of your reckless and unscrupulous prevarications——"

Buzzzzzzzzz!

The telephone bell interrupted Dr. Locke.

"Pray excuse me a moment, Mr. Quelch!" He picked up the receiver. "Yes, Dr. Locke speaking."

Billy Bunter cast a longing blink towards the door. To bolt from the Head's study, as he had bolted from the detention-room, was hardly to be thought of. But, really, Billy Bunter was capable of almost anything when a flogging impended over his fat head. Mr. Quelch's eye gleamed at him.

"Yes—Sir Hilton Popper!" the Head was saying into the transmitter. "Yes, what——"

The barking voice of the lord of Popper Court came back, audible to Quelch and Bunter, as well as the Head.

"I have rung you up to inquire after the boy, sir—a boy named Punter——"

"Punter! I do not think I know the name——"

"Oh!" gasped Bunter. His fat face brightened. "He—he means Bunter, sir——"

"Do you mean Bunter, Sir Hilton?" inquired the Head.

"Bunter? Yes, perhaps so—Punter or Bunter—it is quite immaterial—a very plump boy in glasses——"

"Yes, Bunter——"

"I shall be glad to hear, sir, that the boy has not caught a cold, or suffered any ill effects——"

"But what—what——"

"The boy Punter—I mean, Bunter—gave me very material assistance, sir, when I fell into the stream in Friardale Wood this afternoon. The plank, sir, fell in—owing to the crass carelessness, I presume, of the local authorities. I intend to take the matter up with the Rural District Council——"

"Yes, yes, but what——"

"I do not think, sir, that I was in actual danger, but I might have been —I might have been, sir, had not Bunter run up and assisted me. I can assure you, sir, that I was very glad of a helping hand out. The boy got very wet, but I shall be glad to hear that he suffered no ill effects——"

"None, I think, Sir Hilton!" gasped the Head.

"I am very glad to hear it, sir! I am very thankful that the boy was there. I should be glad, sir, if you will convey my thanks to Punter."

"Oh, certainly!"

Dr. Locke put up the receiver and turned back to Bunter, with a rather uncertain expression on his face.

"Er—Sir Hilton Popper desires me —er—to—to convey his thanks to you, Bunter," said the Head. "It—it appears that a—a part of your story, at least, is veracious! Mr. Quelch——"

He looked at the Remove master.

"Sir!" said Mr. Quelch. He looked at the Head.

"In these circumstances, Mr. Quelch——"

"Hem!" said Mr. Quelch.

"An accidental occurrence is, of course, no excuse for breaking out of detention. Nevertheless——"

"Nevertheless, sir——"

"Perhaps, in the circumstances, Bunter may be pardoned—no doubt he will take warning from his very narrow escape from a flogging——"

"I trust so, sir!"

"Bunter, you may go!"

Bunter made one jump to the door!

* * * * *

Harry Wharton & Co. gathered round Bunter when he reappeared. They were prepared to hand out all the sympathy that the sad circumstances required. But the fat Owl did not seem to be in need of sympathy. He was grinning from ear to ear.

"I say, you fellows," chuckled Bunter, "what luck! I say, I've never been nearer a flogging! Not that I care much about a flogging, you know —I can take my gruel I hope, without making a fuss, like some fellows! But——"

"You've got off?" exclaimed Bob Cherry.

"What do you think?" chortled Bunter. "Old Popper phoned up the Head while I was there, and told him how I saved him. After that, of course, it was all right! Dr. Locke patted me on the head and said 'Gallant lad!' Those very words!"

"Gammon!"

"Beast! And Quelch said he was proud to have me in the Form! His actual words were 'Bunter, I am proud to call you a member of my Form! If only the others were more like you!' Those were his words."

"Rats!"

"Yah! I say you fellows, wasn't it jolly lucky that old Popper took that dip? Somebody must have shifted that plank, you know, and if he hadn't, I should have had a flogging, safe as houses. I wonder who did it?' Jolly glad he did, anyhow."

Which Arthur Carter, perhaps, was glad to hear—though more probably not!

THE END.

(Billy Bunter plays the most prominent part in the next yarn in this exciting series. It's entitled: "BUNTER'S BIG BLUFF!" Amusing and amazing situations you'll find in plenty. Order your copy of next Saturday's MAGNET at the earliest opportunity! —ED.)

The Magnet

2D

Billy Bunter's Own Paper

AN EXCHANGE OF COATS!

Information You May or May Not Know About Greyfriars, By—

The GREYFRIARS GUIDE

A TOUR OF THE SCHOOL.   The Remove Box-Room.

(1)
Up the little staircase creeping
  Many sinful chaps have been,
While a wary eye they're keeping,
  Hoping that they won't be seen.
Safe inside the dusty box-room
  Where we keep our trunks and bags,
Skinner and his hearties have their
      little parties,
  With their little box of fags!

(2)
Up the little staircase grunting
  Billy Bunter takes his way,
While an angry schoolmate's hunting
  For a pie he bought that day !
Sitting on a pile of luggage,
  Bunter finds the pie A1.
Like a bloated eagle, wolfing his illegal
  Plunder till the deed is done !

(3)
Up the little staircase stealing
  In the silent hours of night,
Smithy comes, in darkness feeling,
  For he dares not show a light.
Dropping through the box-room window,
  Smithy's breaking bounds again,
Though he may be scorning every
      friendly warning,
  One day he'll repent in vain !

*   *   *

Hush ! Hush ! Whisper who dares,
When there's a tread on the box-room
      stairs !

AFTER SCHOOL HOURS
The Snowfight

Hurrah, the snow is thick and white
  Upon the hills and valleys,
And we can have a snowball fight
  With sudden darts and sallies.
Our side is led by Peter Todd,
  Who Wharton's crowd opposes,
And snowballs fly around the quad
  To crash on chins and noses.

*   *   *

The uproar spreads, and other Forms
  Come up to swell the battle;
The foemen may attack in swarms,
  We'll mow them down like cattle !
We've built a rampart in the snow,
  And stoutly we'll defend it,
While prefects, smiling, watch the show
  And have no wish to end it.

*   *   *

But Coker comes upon the scene,
  And frowns at us like thunder,
While Potter and his henchman, Greene,
  Move quickly off—no wonder !
"Stop that !" roars Coker. "Stop the
      din !
  It's perfectly disgraceful !"
A snowball crashes on his chin
  And gives the fool a face-full !

*   *

While Coker roars and hops about
  As though he were demented,
"Unparalleled !" says Mr. Prout,
  "Indeed, unprecedented !"
By "accident," an avalanche
  Of snowballs sends them sprawling.
And quickly they vamoose the ranch,
  And leave us still snowballing !

THE GREYFRIARS ALPHABET
OLIVER KIPPS,
the conjurer of the Remove.

K is for KIPPS, a conjurer clever,
He'd go on conjuring for ever.
It's one of Kipper's little habits
To find a topper full of rabbits.
From pockets which he swiftly rifles
He brings out eggs and other trifles.

Then quickly takes from Fishy's collar
A greenback banknote or a dollar !
It seems that Bolsover's breast pocket
Contains a rolled-gold lady's locket,
While from the ear of poor old Skinny
He swiftly wrings a golden guinea !
And postal orders in big batches
From Bunter's overcoat he snatches!
He's often bumped for being brilliant,
But, luckily, he's still resilient !

ANSWER TO PUZZLE
A pound of mixed nuts weighs one
pound.

A WEEKLY BUDGET OF FACT AND FUN
By
THE GREYFRIARS RHYMESTER

GREYFRIARS GRINS

At a debate on which period in history
the fellows would have preferred to live
in, the Remove voted solidly for the
year 50 B.C.—because at that date Virgil
was alive, and a fellow could get at
him !

Lecturing on the habits of rare butter-
flies, Mr. Capper said many of them
preferred to haunt black, dusty soil in
which there was little growth. Fellows
with butterfly-nets are now narrowly
watching the Second Form juniors'
necks.

Coker boasts that one of his ancestors
was eight feet tall and broad in pro-
portion. A great-great-grandfather !

PUZZLE PAR
If a chestnut weighs as much
as two brazil nuts, a brazil nut as
much as two walnuts, a walnut as
much as two almonds, and an
almond weighs $\frac{1}{4}$-ounce, what
would be the weight of a pound
of mixed nuts in which there
were an equal number of each
kind ?
Answer at foot of column 2.

It costs sixpence to see the live gorilla
in Courtfield Circus. Luckily for hard-
up fags, they can see Bolsover major for
nothing.

The School Museum wishes to acknowledge with thanks a gift from Mrs.
Mimble of the slab of hardbake which
has been in her window since Tudor
times.

Gosling, who doesn't like cold morn-
ings, has asked the Head for permission
to shift his bed into the main lobby,
immediately under the rope of the
rising-bell.

Mrs. Kebble's cat has just had six
kittens. Wun Lung is cleaning out his
stewpot.

CAN YOU STAND A SHOCK ? GOOD !   THEN LISTEN TO THIS—Billy Bunter, who is always broke from one year's end to the other, has got a fiver! The question is: HOW AND WHERE DID HE GET IT ?

BUNTER'S BIG BLUFF!

By FRANK RICHARDS

" Anybody here change a fiver ?" asked Billy Bunter, opening a tattered notecase. The Famous Five stared at a portion of a banknote that was visible.

THE FIRST CHAPTER

Not for Bunter !

"HAS Quelch gone out ?"
"Blessed if I know !"
"Oh blow !" said Billy Bunter crossly.
"What does it matter, fathead ?" asked Bob Cherry.
"Oh, nothing ! I mean—that is—well, nothing !" said Billy Bunter lucidly. "All the same, I think you fellows might have noticed whether he's gone out or not, sticking round the door !"

Harry Wharton & Co. were standing by the steps of the House, talking football, when Billy Bunter blew along.

They were not in the least interested in the movements of Mr. Quelch, the master of the Remove, after class.

"He hasn't come out this way, anyhow," said Harry. "Cut along to his study, fathead, and see if he's there if you want him."
"Eh—I don't want him !"
"Then what the dickens——"
"Besides, I've been to his study already," said Bunter, shaking his head. "He was there, and I had to ask him a question about prep, or he would have smelt a rat ! If I go again, he will get suspicious ! You know Quelch !"

The Famous Five of the Remove, at that, fixed their eyes on Billy Bunter. Evidently, the fat junior had some particular, peculiar, and personal reason for wanting to know whether his Formmaster had gone out or not.

"You fat chump !" said Bob Cherry. "Are you after something in Quelch's study ?"
"Oh, no ! Nothing of the kind !" said Bunter hastily. "I—I just want to know

whether he's gone or not, because I heard him tell Prout he was going out. I'm not going to his study when he's gone. Why should I ?"
"You'd better not, at any rate !" grunted Bob. "You've been in rows enough this term without asking for more !"

Skinner of the Remove came across the quad, and Billy Bunter, disregarding the Famous Five, turned inquiring spectacles on Skinner.

"I say, seen Quelch go out ?" he asked.
"Yes," answered Skinner.
"Oh, good ! Was he carrying a parcel ?"
"No; a bundle of Form papers," answered Skinner—"Latin papers."

Spanking Fine School Yarn of HARRY WHARTON & CO., of GREYFRIARS.

"Latin papers ?" repeated Billy Bunter, blinking at Skinner in astonishment. "What rot ! It must have been a parcel. Look here, when did you see him go out ?"
"Half an hour ago."
"You silly ass !" hooted Bunter. "I saw him in his study a quarter of an hour ago !"
"Well, that was a quarter of an hour after I saw him go out," smiled Skinner. "He generally goes to his study after he goes out of the Form-room."
"You — you — you idiot !" gasped

Bunter. "I wasn't asking you whether you saw him go out of the Form-room ! We all saw him go out of the Form-room ! Have you seen him go out ?"
"Only out of the Form-room !" grinned Skinner.
"Beast !"

Skinner went into the House, laughing.

Billy Bunter cast an irritated blink after him, and then turned his spectacles on the Famous Five again.

"I say, you fellows, one of you cut along to Quelch's study, and see whether he's gone out or not, will you ? You go, Wharton ! You can ask him something, as head boy of the Remove, you know. He won't think you're after the cake."
"The cake ?" repeated Harry Wharton.

If there was a cake in the Remove master's study, Billy Bunter's interest in his movements was fully explained. But what a cake was doing in Quelch's study was quite a mystery.

"You fat, frumptious fathead !" said Johnny Bull. "How can there be a cake in Quelch's study ? Think Quelch scoffs cakes like you do ?"
"Well, I saw it," said Bunter. "It was delivered from Chunkley's this afternoon. I fancy Quelch is going to send it to somebody—I mean, I saw him tying a label on the box, so I guessed he was going to send it by post. I can put two and two together ! Brains, you know !"
"That beats Sherlock Holmes !" remarked Frank Nugent gravely. "Fancy Bunter guessing that Quelch was going to post it, you fellows, simply from seeing him tie a label on the box !"

THE MAGNET LIBRARY.—No. 1,564.

"Ha, ha, ha!"

"Well, it stands to reason," argued Bunter. "He wouldn't label it if he was going to eat it—see? Besides, Quelch doesn't eat cakes. He's got a lot of nephews and nieces and things, and he often sends them something. Well, this time he's sending a cake. If he has a parcel with him when he goes out, it will be a cake. But he's more likely to leave it for Trotter to post. Only a fellow wants to know, you know."

Obviously, the fat Owl of the Remove had designs on that cake!

"My esteemed, idiotic Bunter," murmured Hurree Jamset Ram Singh, "if Quelch misses that cake——"

"He won't miss it!" grinned Bunter. "That's all right! You see, it's in a box on his table, all wrapped up ready for post. Well, suppose a fellow hiked the cake out of the box and put in something else—say, a hassock, or a lump of coal or something—what—and wrapped it up again?"

"Oh crikey!"

"Quelch would never know," said the astute Owl. "Of course, his nephew or niece would be a bit surprised, getting a hassock or a lump of coal by post——"

"Ha, ha, ha!"

"But it would be all right this end," said Bunter sagely. "Nothing for me to worry about—see? So long as I don't get copped, it's all right—that's important, of course. Safe as houses, I think—if only Quelch leaves that parcel in his study for the page to post. What do you fellows think?"

The Famous Five gazed at Bunter. Then they told him what they thought!

"I think you're a fat, foozling, pilfering pig!" said Johnny Bull.

"I think you're a gorging, greedy gargoyle!" said Bob Cherry.

"I think you want booting!" said Harry Wharton.

"I think I'll boot you!" said Frank Nugent.

"My absurd thinkfulness is that you should keep your idiotic hands from the pickfulness and the stealfulness!" said Hurree Jamset Ram Singh.

Billy Bunter blinked at them.

His fat mind was so fully occupied by the problem of getting hold of the cake that he seemed to have had no time to consider the moral aspect of the matter.

"I say, you fellows, I mean to whack it out!" he said reassuringly. "That's all right; don't you worry. It's a big cake—enormous—and it will go round! I'm not the fellow to keep it all for myself!"

"Do you think we want Quelch's cake?" gasped Harry Wharton.

"Eh—don't you?" asked Bunter. "What do you think's the matter with it, then? I tell you it's a ripping cake—from Chunkley's. You know what Chunkley's cakes are like! It's a good cake—take my word for that! I know something about cakes!"

Arthur Carter the new junior in the Remove, came out while Bunter was speaking. He cast a curious glance at the fat Owl.

Bunter blinked round at him. He was on the worst of terms with Carter, but that mattered nothing when he wanted information.

"I say, Carter, do you know if Quelch has gone out?" he asked.

"Yes," answered Carter. "He went out at the Common-room door with Prout."

"Wa he carrying a parcel?" asked Bunter eagerly.

"No!"

"That does it!" said Bunter. "That's

all right! Sure he wasn't carrying a parcel, Carter?"

"Quite!" answered Carter; and he walked away across the quad.

Billy Bunter rolled back into the House. The coast was clear now—the cake in Quelch's study, and Quelch gone out

The Famous Five exchanged a glance, and walked into the House after Bunter.

The fat Owl was heading for Masters' Passage A grip on the back of his fat neck brought him to a sudden halt.

He blinked round, in surprise and annoyance, at Bob Cherry.

"Leggo!" he howled.

"Come up to the studies, old fat man!" said Bob.

"I can't come now, you ass!" yapped Bunter "I'll come up in a few minutes!"

"You won't come now?"

"No!" howled Bunter.

"Will you, if I boot you?"

"Beast!"

Bob Cherry lifted his right foot.

One of the two largest feet in the Remove landed on the tightest trousers at Greyfriars.

Thud!

"Yoo-hoop!" roared Bunter.

"Coming up to the studies?"

"Ow! No!"

Thud!

"Ow! Wow! I'm coming, you beast!" gasped Bunter. "Leave off kicking me, you swab! Ow! I—I—I want to come!"

"Well, if you want to come, come along!" grinned Bob.

And Bunter came.

THE SECOND CHAPTER.
Catching Coker!

HORACE COKER, of the Greyfriars Fifth, left off talking.

As Coker had been talking football, that was a relief to Potter and Greene.

It was true that they were not listening; still, it was a relief. Silence was never so golden as when Coker left off talking.

The three men of the Fifth were walking down Friardale Lane to the School. Coker was explaining to his friends, at great length, what an absolute idiot Wingate, the Greyfriars captain, was. Wingate's idiocy consisted in putting Potter and Greene into the first eleven, and leaving Coker out. Coker thought that that was the limit, and apparently expected Potter and Greene to agree.

But Coker ceased to speak at the sight of something going on in the lane. Apparently there had been an accident.

A shabbily dressed man stood with an empty basket in his hand. At his feet was a little heap of smashed eggs.

A young man in cycling attire stood with his hand on a bicycle. He was speaking as the three Fifth Formers of Greyfriars came up.

"Certainly, certainly, my man, I will pay for the eggs!" he said. "My fault entirely! I did not see you in time! If you had change——"

"I ain't got no change, sir!" grunted the man with the basket. "'Ow'd I 'ave change for a fivepun note?"

"No doubt, no doubt; but as I have nothing smaller——"

The young man glanced round at the three Greyfriars fellows.

"Excuse me, young gentlemen," he said, very politely. "Perhaps you would be kind enough to stop a moment."

"What's up?" asked Coker.

"There has been an accident here, as you see. It was entirely my fault—I collided with this good man's basket, and upset his eggs. I am willing to pay for the damage, but have no change."

"Them eggs have got to be paid for!" said the shabby man, with a threatening growl in his voice. "You ain't going on till you've squared for them eggs. Five bob it will corst yer Running into a bloke on a blooming bike——"

"My good fellow, I have already said that I will pay for the damage."

"Well, 'and it over, then, and not so much gas! I got to get back to my work, I 'ave."

"Could you young gentlemen assist me?" asked the young man with the bicycle. "It is merely a matter of changing a note."

There was a notecase in the young man's hand, open. Three or four bank-notes could be seen within.

"Sorry!" said Potter politely.

"Sorry!" said Greene, with equal politeness.

Between them they could have made up the change for a five-pound note. And they quite sympathised with the young man in this disagreeable position. Still, they did not want to change bank-notes for strangers. It was not the sort of thing that a sensible fellow would do. The young man was well dressed, and looked quite respectable; still, you could never tell!

"Come on, Coker!" added Greene.

Coker did not come on

Coker was a kindhearted fellow, and a first-class fathead. He was, in fact, the very fellow that that young man wanted to meet.

Had Potter or Greene suggested obliging that young man, probably Coker would have told them that they were asses, and dismissed the idea. As they did not take that view. Coker took it! That was Horace Coker's way! Coker only needed to hear an opinion expressed, to express an opposite one.

"Hold on!" answered Coker. "We can manage it!"

"That's very kind of you, sir!" said the young man with the bicycle. "If this good man would wait till I rode on to Courtfield, and returned with change, I——"

"You ain't going till I'm paid for them eggs!" growled the shabby man. "I'll lay 'old of that blooming bike, I tell yer!"

"That will do, my man! If the young gentleman will kindly change a note for me, you shall have your five shillings." The young man extracted a five-pound note from the notecase.

Coker was feeling for his wallet.

Potter nudged him.

"Look here, old man, come on!" he whispered. "How do you know——"

"Rot!" said Coker. "The chap looks all right!"

"Yes; but——"

"Don't jaw!" said Coker.

"You'd better not——" began Greene uneasily.

"Don't jaw, Greene!"

Coker extracted four pound notes, and two for ten shillings, from his wallet. There were plenty of both there. Coker's Aunt Judy seldom left her dear Horace short of that necessary article, cash.

"I will put my name and address on the note," remarked the young man. "Hold my bicycle a moment, my good man."

The shabby man held the bike, while the young man took out a fountain-pen. He spread the fiver on the saddle and wrote on the back: "George Johnson,

16, Bank Buildings, Courtfield." If Coker had needed reassuring, that would have reassured him. That address was only a few miles from Greyfriars, and Bank Buildings was quite a good and respectable address.

He handed over four pound notes and two for ten shillings, and received the fiver in exchange.

"I am very much obliged, sir !" said the young man with the bicycle. "Now, my good man, you can change a ten-shilling note——"

The shabby man went through his pockets.

Coker & Co. walked on, leaving the young man holding out the ten-shilling note to the owner of the broken eggs.

Coker got back to the original theme, and talked on till the three reached Greyfriars.

Coker turned in the direction of the school shop when he went in Coker, as usual, was standing tea in the study; that was, indeed, the whole and sole reason why his friends had not told him their true and genuine views on football subjects !

In the tuckshop he drew that five-pound note from his wallet. He was going to change it there, just to show Potter and Greene what silly asses they were.

Having ordered his usual lavish supply of provender, Coker handed over the fiver in payment.

"And why not ?" grunted Coker.

"I is not a good one ! Mr. Mimble says you had better take it to the police station, sir."

Coker drew a deep, deep breath as he received back the "dud" note. Potter and Greene looked at him. He looked at them !

"You fatheads !" he said.

"Eh ?"

"What ?"

"You silly asses !"

Coker crumpled that banknote into his pocket and strode out of the school shop.

Potter and Greene were left staring, and wondering when they were going to have tea.

" Excuse me, young gentlemen," said the cyclist, as Coker & Co. came up. " Perhaps you would be kind enough to stop a moment." " What's up ? " asked Coker. " I collided with this good man's basket and upset his eggs," said the cyclist. " Could one of you young gentlemen assist me by changing a fiver ? "

Potter and Greene exchanged a glance behind Coker's burly back, as he walked in the middle. They did not really doubt that polite young man with the bicycle themselves; still, on general principles, they would not have changed banknotes for strangers.

Coker gave them a sarcastic look each.

"You fellows wouldn't have obliged that chap !" he said. "Look what a fix he was in—that rough-looking brute threatening to collar his bike ! I suppose a fiver's as good as currency notes when I change it at the school shop for tea."

"Yes—if——" said Potter.

"If what ?" grunted Coker.

"If it's a good one !" said Greene. "I jolly well know that I wouldn't take banknotes from a man I'd never seen before."

"They take them in shops, fathead !" said Coker.

"Yes; but——"

"Oh, you're an ass, Greeney !" said Coker. "You're another, Potter ! But that silly chump Wingate——" And

Mrs. Mimble looked at it. She put on her glasses and looked at it again. Then she gave it a third and very scrutinising look.

Coker frowned ! Potter and Greene exchanged a look ! Something about that fiver seemed to make Mrs. Mimble dubious.

"That note's all right, Mrs. Mimble," said Coker gruffly.

"Oh, yes, Master Coker, it must be, if you had it from home," said Mrs. Mimble. "But——"

"I didn't have it from home," grunted Coker. "I changed it for a man in Friardale Lane."

"Oh !" said Mrs. Mimble. "Please wait a moment, Master Coker."

She took the banknote into her back parlour, obviously to consult Mr. Mimble on the subject.

Potter and Greene gave one another still more expressive looks.

Coker's frown intensified.

Mrs. Mimble came back in a few minutes with a very grave face.

"I'm afraid I cannot take that note, Master Coker," she said.

Coker was not thinking of tea. He was cutting across to the gates as fast as his long legs could whisk.

Carter of the Remove was standing in the gateway—and he hardly knew what had happened to him. He sprawled as Coker barged him out of the way and flew on.

Back down Friardale Lane went Horace Coker, breathing wrath and vengeance. It had dawned even on Coker's powerful intellect that that little scene in the lane, with the bike and the broken eggs, had been a little comedy specially got up to enable a spoofing rascal to land a "dud" note on an unsuspecting stranger. Probably that polite young man had tried it on half a dozen times before Coker came along and obliged him.

Coker, in hot haste, flew along the lane. He was looking for those two rascals, his big fists clenched in readiness for dealing with them.

He was not likely to find them ! The well-dressed young man with the bike and the shabby man with the basket having happily shared Coker's currency notes, were already at a distance, travelling fast.

THE THIRD CHAPTER.
Looking After Bunter!

"I SAY, you fellows!"

"Shut up!"

"Look here, you beasts, what's this game?" roared Bunter, in breathless wrath.

Heedless of Billy Bunter's objections, the Famous Five had marched him up to the Remove passage, and into Study No. 1—the study that belonged to Wharton, Nugent, and the new fellow Carter.

Having arrived in that study, Bunter was plumped into the armchair, with a heavy bump. Bob Cherry stood between him and the doorway.

Four members of the famous Co. were grinning. But Bob's ruddy face was serious. All five of them were quite agreed that Bunter was going to keep a safe distance from that parcel in Quelch's study.

Bunter was quite without scruple where foodstuffs were concerned. It was sufficient for a cake to exist for Bunter to think that he ought to have it! Naturally, other fellows took different views. But, apart from the fact that grub-raiding was barred, it was altogether too dangerous for Bunter to scoff a cake belonging to a Form-master.

In the Remove they booted him for such things. But Mr Quelch was sure to take a much more severe view. For his own sake, if for no other reason, the fat Owl had to be stopped. And the chums of the Remove were pre-pared to boot him, as much as might be required, for his own good.

"Now," said Bob Cherry, "listen to me, you fat freak——"

"Shan't!" roared Bunter. "If you want to jaw, you can jaw to your pals. You can't expect me to listen to your chin-wag! Look here, lemme gerrout of this study."

"You're not going after Quelch's cake!" bawled Bob.

"Beast!" bawled back Bunter. "You're jolly well not going to have it! I'm offering to whack 't out! That's fair!"

"Oh, boot him!" said Johnny Bull.

"Beast! I say, Toddy, come in here and make these beasts let me go!" yelled Bunter, as Peter Todd passed the doorway.

Peter stopped and looked in. As Bunter's study-mate in Study No. 7, he was not deaf to that appeal.

"What's up?" he asked. "What are you doing with my prize pig?"

"Oh, really, Toddy——"

"All right, Toddy!" said Harry Wharton. "Quelch has left a cake in a box on his study table and that chump wants to raid it. We're trying to stop him from asking for a Head's flogging."

"I say, Toddy, 'tain't like that at all!" howled Bunter. "I—I've got to go and see Wingate. I—I can't keep a prefect waiting——"

"Oh, Wingate won't mind waiting!" said Peter. "He's gone down to footer."

"Ha, ha, ha!"

"I—I mean, I—I've promised to see Coker of the Fifth! I'm going to help him with some Latin——"

"Oh crikey!" gasped Peter. "Never mind, Coker old fat man—we can't have Fifth Form men getting their work done in the Remove."

"Well, look here, Toddy, the Head's waiting for me! A chap can't keep his headmaster waiting—it's not the thing!"

"Not as a rule!" chuckled Peter Todd. "But in the present circumstances I think the Head may as well wait, along with Wingate and Coker of the Fifth!"

And Peter Todd walked on to the stairs, laughing.

"Beast!" yelled Bunter after him.

Bob Cherry gave the fat Owl a glare.

"Now, you old fat Owl, listen!" he rapped. "All this term you've been in rows—ever since that relation of yours, Carter, came here. Now——"

"Oh, boot him, and let's get out!" said Johnny Bull. "There isn't much light left for footer."

"You fellows can cut," said Bob. "I'll follow you along. I've got to talk to Bunter."

"Oh, all right!"

Four members of the Co. left the study. Bunter was safe in Bob's hands, and they were keen to get a little footer before dark.

Bob slammed the door and turned to Bunter again.

The Owl of the Remove eyed him with an infuriated blink through his big spectacles. Never had Bunter regretted so much that he was no fighting-man! Gladly would he have pitched Bob across the study and cut out while there was yet time to snaffle that cake!

"Now, listen!" growled Bob. "Silly fathead as you are, you've got sense enough to see that that relation of yours, Carter, is getting you all the trouble he can, and you know why, I think."

"Blow Carter!"

"You've told us that his uncle, old Mr. Carter, has written to Quelch, to ask about your report, and that it may be a good thing for you if he's pleased with it."

"No bizney of yours!" yapped Bunter.

"Shut up! Carter has landed you in all the trouble he could, ever since he came here. You know that, and know why."

"The beast doesn't want me to get a good report, of course!" said Bunter. "I dare say old Joe Carter's found out what a cad he is, and may be thinking of leaving his money somewhere else. Looks like it, to me. I know he doesn't make him a big allowance here, like he used to at St. Olaf's. I shouldn't wonder if it comes my way."

"Well, then," said Bob, "haven't you sense enough to knock his game on the head? Carter can't do a thing to you if you keep straight. But if you don't, he will take care every time that Quelch knows about it. Can't you see that you should keep straight for your own sake?"

"I like that!" sneered Bunter. "If you were as straight as I am, Bob Cherry, you'd do!"

Bob breathed hard.

"Now, look here, fathead," he said, "I'll tell you something, as a tip! I know that Carter's game is to make things look as rotten as he can for you, to dish you with that old relation of yours. Never mind how I know—I heard something the day he came, and I do know! You're playing into his hands by being a lying, pilfering un-scrupulous little beast! See?"

"You cheeky beast!" roared Bunter.

"If you've got the sense of a bunny rabbit, you'll run straight, and then that scheming cad won't have a chance at you!" urged Bob. "If you snaffle

that cake out of Quelch's study, you can bank on it that you will be spotted. That cad daren't sneak openly; but he will see that you get nailed! Got that?"

"I know he's a sneaking beast!" said Bunter. "But I'm not afraid of him. He can't land anything on a fellow who's absolutely straightforward and straight as a die! I'm all right."

"Well, stick to that and you're O.K.," said Bob. "First of all, leave Quelch's cake alone."

Billy Bunter cast a longing blink at the door. But Bob Cherry was standing between him and the door.

"Oh, all right!" he said. "The fact is I wasn't going after that cake! In fact, I don't know anything about a cake in Quelch's study! So far as I know, Chunkley's never delivered one here this afternoon. I'm going to Quelch's study to get a—a Latin exercise——"

"You're not going to Quelch's study at all!" roared Bob.

"I—I—I mean, I ain't going to the study! Not at all! I—I'm going down to watch the football! Now, let me out of this, you beast!"

"All serene," said Bob. "I'm going down to the footer, and you can come with me."

"I—I—I mean, I—I've got to go to Wingate first—I mean, Coker—that is, the Head——"

"Yes, I know what you mean," said Bob. "I've a jolly good mind to let you go ahead and get yourself booted out of Greyfriars, you fat freak! But I suppose you can't help being a silly idiot! I shall leave you in this study——"

"The sooner the better, you beast!"

"With the door locked——"

Bunter bounced out of the armchair.

"You leave that door alone!" he howled. "I say, Wharton and Nugent may want to come in—and Carter, too—it's his study——"

"He had his coat on when he passed us downstairs," said Bob. "He must have gone out. You needn't worry about Carter, you fat fraud."

"I'm not staying here!" roared Bunter.

"You are," answered Bob grimly.

He drew the key out of the lock and put it in the outside of the door.

Billy Bunter eyed him with speechless wrath. Locked in that study, it was clear that his nefarious designs on Mr. Quelch's cake would have to be abandoned. It was rather a desperate measure for the fat Owl of the Remove to tackle Bob Cherry. But clearly it was a time for desperate measures! Bunter charged!

A fat fist landed on Bob's ribs, and another on his ear! Taken by surprise, he staggered away from the door.

Bunter shot past.

"Why, you—you—you——" gasped Bob.

He bounded after Bunter.

The fat Owl flew for the stairs. He was grabbed before he had covered three yards! A finger and thumb closed like a vice on a fat ear, and Bunter was jerked back.

"Yarooh!" roared Bunter. "Leggo my ear, you beast! You're pulling my ear off, you rotter! Yow-ow-ow!"

With that vice-like grip on the fat ear, Bob led him back to the study! Bunter yelped at every step—but he went!

In the doorway Bob halted, shot out a foot, and Bunter went into the study roaring. Then Bob Cherry slammed the door, locked it on the outside, and put the key in his pocket.

"Beast!" came a yell from within. "I say, lemme out! You're not going to

have that cake, you beast! I know your game, you rotter! Look here, I told you about that cake! I say, I'll go halves! I say——"

But answer there came none! Bob Cherry was going downstairs, with the key in his pocket—going, as Bunter had not the slightest doubt, after that cake!

As a matter of fact, he was going to the changing-room, and in a few minutes he joined his comrades at football. Talking to Bunter was useless; but locking him in a study seemed an efficacious method of keeping his fat paws off Quelch's cake! Billy Bunter was left in Study No. 1—raging!

THE FOURTH CHAPTER.
Too Late !

ARTHUR CARTER picked himself up in the school gateway, gasping for breath.

He stared blankly after Coker of the Fifth, vanishing down Friardale Lane.

"The silly ass!" gasped Carter.

Coker, of course, had no time to waste on a mere Lower Fourth junior. Carter having got in his way, Coker had barged him out of it, and that was that.

Carter had been standing in the gateway some time. He was, as Bob Cherry had remarked, in coat and hat, and had been going out. But he had stopped at the gates to think it over. He was curious—very curious—to know how Billy Bunter had got on with that parcel in his Form-master's study. He decided, at length, to ascertain—and turned to walk back to the House.

To the Remove generally Bunter was a fellow whose insignificance was unlimited. But all the fatuous proceedings of the Owl of the Remove were of interest to his distant relation, Carter. The fellow who had been turfed out of his former school in disgrace had been told plainly that he had nothing more to expect from old Mr. Carter. That wealthy old gentleman was considering another relative in his place, to be named in his will; and Carter knew, though Billy Bunter did not, that that other relative was the fat Owl of the Remove.

All Bunter knew was that old Mr. Carter was taking a sudden interest in him, and that it might be worth his while to make a good impression on the old bean!

Carter's idea was that the worse impression Bunter made, the better! He had displeased his uncle by bad and reckless conduct at St. Olaf's, where he had come a "mucker." He was going to be much more careful at Greyfriars; and he was going, if he could, to make the "old bean" see that his relative and rival was, at all events, no better a fellow than himself!

If that relative and rival had been a fellow like Bob Cherry or Harry Wharton, there would have been nothing doing! But with a fellow like Billy Bunter it seemed an easy game.

It was true that there was no real harm in Bunter. But his manners and customs were all his own!

Bunter and the Famous Five had disappeared when Carter came back into the House.

Carter walked down Masters' Passage and looked into Mr. Quelch's study.

On the table lay a box, wrapped up, tied, and labelled. That box, evidently, contained the cake on which Bunter had a nefarious eye! Clearly, he had not raided it yet!

Carter shut the door and departed.

At the corner of the passage Peter Todd passed him.

He noticed that there was a grin on Toddy's face, but gave him no other heed. He went to the Rag, to see whether the fat Owl was there.

Peter Todd, still grinning, walked down Masters' Passage, to the door of Mr. Quelch's study. He opened that door—but did not merely glance in, as Carter had done. He stepped into the study. He grinned more widely as he looked at the parcel on the table.

"The blithering idiot!" murmured Peter.

Obviously, if that parcel remained where it was during Mr. Quelch's absence, there was trouble ahead for Bunter. That was why Peter was there.

He lifted the parcel from the table and placed it underneath, in front of the legs of Mr. Quelch's chair. Under the table, it was quite out of sight; but Mr. Quelch would discover it as soon as he sat down, because his feet would bang against it! Bunter, of course, was not likely to look under the table.

Leaving it thus invisible, Peter left the study, and went out into the quad.

Carter, from the door of the Rag, saw him go, but certainly did not guess how he had lately been occupied.

A few minutes later Harry Wharton and Frank Nugent, Johnny Bull and Hurree Jamset Ram Singh came down and went to the changing-room. And after a few more minutes Bob Cherry appeared and followed in the same direction.

Carter wondered where Bunter was.

He went up to the Remove at last. Then, rather unexpectedly, he learned where Bunter was.

From the keyhole of the first study in the passage—his own study—came a hissing, infuriated voice:

"Are you there, you beast? Have you gone away, you rotter? Look here, you swab, if you don't let me out of this study I'll jolly well yell! I'll bring up the prefects! I'll bring up the Head! Do you hear me, you beast? Are you there, Bob Cherry, you rotter? Will you unlock this door, or won't you unlock this door, you cad?"

"Oh, my hat!" ejaculated Carter.

He understood now why Bunter had disappeared. He had guessed that the Famous Five were arguing with Bunter on the subject of that cake! Evidently Bob Cherry had used the irresistible argument of a locked door!

"Is that you, Cherry, you rotter?" squeaked Bunter, as he heard Carter's voice. "Will you let me out, you rotter?"

"What are you doing in my study, you fat freak?" asked Carter.

"Is that you, Carter? I say, Bob Cherry's locked me in! I say, get the key off him and let me out, will you?" howled Bunter.

Carter chuckled. Harry Wharton & Co. might take measures to prevent the fat and fatuous Owl from landing himself in serious trouble—but that was not Carter's object. The more Bunter hunted for trouble the more his amiable relative was pleased.

"I'll let you out all right," answered Carter. He had a bunch of keys, one of which fitted the study lock.

He unlocked the door and threw it open, much to Billy Bunter's relief.

"Get out!" said Carter.

"Beast!" retorted Bunter, doubtless by way of thanks. And he got out promptly.

Carter, grinning, followed him down the stairs.

Bunter, in breathless haste, rolled away for Masters' Studies. Carter did not need telling what he was going to do there!

With a grin on his face, he walked out of the House, and went down to the gates again. He still had plenty of time to meet Mr. Bill Lodgey, and get a "quid" on Simple Simon for the three o'clock on Wednesday! Arthur Carter was the same "bad hat at Greyfriars that he had been at St. Olaf's, the only difference being that he was more wary and cautious about it.

Meanwhile, the fat Owl of the Remove rolled up Masters' Passage. Bunter rolled into his Form-master's study and shut the door hastily, lest any beak should come along.

Then he rolled across to the table. And then——

"Beast!" hissed Bunter.

The parcel was gone.

"Rotter! Cad! Beast! Swab! Oh crikey!" gasped Bunter.

He was too late.

That unspeakable beast Bob Cherry had locked him in Study No. 1 while he cut down and snooped the cake! Bunter had not the slightest doubt of it! The thing spoke for itself. The parcel was gone.

Sadly and sorrowfully the fat Owl rolled away from Quelch's study. There was no cake for Bunter. It did not occur to his fat brain that it was fortunate for him. Bunter was not thinking of the consequences; he was thinking of the cake. Like Rachel of old, he mourned for that which was lost, and could not be comforted.

THE FIFTH CHAPTER.

Bunter's Whack!

"HALLO, hallo, hallo!"
The shades of night, as the poet has expressed it, were falling fast.

Harry Wharton & Co. came in fresh and ruddy after football practice, and more than ready for tea. They stared at the open doorway of Study No. 1. Carter and Skinner were in the room, the latter kneeling at the fire making toast. Bob had a key in his hand—but it was evidently not needed.

Carter glanced round at the five.

"Coming in here?" he asked. "I've got a fellow to tea——"

"No; we're teaing in Bob's study," answered Harry Wharton. "But——"

"I left this study locked, with Bunter in it," said Bob.

"Like your cheek!" answered Carter. "What the thump do you mean by locking a fellow out of his study?"

Bob coloured a little.

"You were gone out," he said. His brows knitted. "At least, you were going out when you passed us downstairs. Did you come back and let Bunter out, because you knew what he was up to?"

"I let him out because I didn't want him in my study. Don't take that key away again. I couldn't have got in if I hadn't happened to have one that would fit."

Bob Cherry stood in the doorway looking at him for a moment or two, but he turned away without speaking to Carter again.

"Come on, you men!" he said. "That fat fool's for it now, and it can't be helped. If I'd known that cad had another key to the study——"

"Well, old man, a fellow has a right to have a key to his own study," said Johnny Bull. "I don't see that Carter's to blame."

THE MAGNET LIBRARY.—No. 1,564.

"I do!" growled Bob. "Still, if Bunter keeps on asking for it he will have to take what comes to him. Bother the fat ass!"

The Famous Five walked on to Bob's study—Study No. 13.

As Mark Linley and little Wun Lung were teaing out they expected to have that study to themselves, but they found it occupied. A fat figure was reposing in the armchair; it sat up as the five juniors came in.

"Oh, here you are!" grunted Bunter. "You're jolly late for tea! Keeping a fellow waiting!"

"Did anybody ask that fat foozler to tea here?" inquired Johnny Bull.

"Not that I know of," answered Bob.

"I've asked myself," said Bunter, with a fat sneer. "If you think you're going to have all that cake, Bob Cherry, you're jolly well mistaken! See? Where is it?"

"Where's what, fathead?" snapped Bob.

"Quelch's cake!" hooted Bunter.

"You ought to know, if anybody does!" said Bob, staring at him. "Didn't you snaffle it when Carter let you out? That's what he let you out for, you benighted idiot!"

"Don't talk rot!" said Bunter. "Look here, where's the cake? I'm willing to whack it out, as I said before. But if you fancy you're going to have the lot——"

"What on earth is the fat ass talking about?" asked Harry Wharton in wonder.

"Quelch's cake!" hooted Bunter. "Perhaps you fellows don't know! That beast locked me in your study, Wharton, while he went down and snooped the cake——"

"Wha-a-t?"

"Mean, I call it!" said Bunter bitterly. "Not the sort of thing I would do myself! You'd never have heard of that cake if I hadn't told you! I don't suppose you even knew that Quelch had a cake at all until I mentioned it. You never noticed that it was delivered from Chunkley's. You fellows never notice anything! A man might carry a cake by, right under your noses, and you'd never notice that it was a cake at all. That's the sort of silly idiots you are! Then you go and lock me in a study while you bag the cake——"

Bob Cherry gasped.

"Does that blithering idiot think I bagged Quelch's cake?" he stuttered.

"I know you did, if that's what you mean!" sneered Bunter. "I jolly well knew that was why you locked me in Wharton's study! Dirty trick! I knew it all the time. But, mind, I'm having a whack in that cake! Where is it? You haven't scoffed it yet, I suppose? I've been waiting for you to come in."

The Famous Five gazed at Bunter. That Carter had let him out of the locked study to hunt for trouble Bob Cherry had no doubt, and the other fellows had no doubt—at all events, that he had scudded off to Quelch's study the moment he was loose. So his present remarks and his evident indignation quite puzzled them.

"I say, you fellows, make him shell out that cake!" appealed Bunter. "Fair play's a jewel! I told you about the cake in the first place! You know that."

"You fat villain, have you snooped Quelch's cake or not?" roared Bob.

"No, I haven't!" roared Bunter. "You have!"

"You fat, frumptious, frabjous, footling fathead——"

"Beast! It was gone when I got

there!" howled Bunter. "Who had it if you hadn't? Locking a fellow in a study while you pinch his cake——"

Bob Cherry crossed to the study cupboard.

Bunter blinked after him.

"It's not there!" he said. "I've looked all over the study! What have you done with it, Cherry? That's what I want to know. I tell you it's not in that cupboard; I've looked."

"I've got something here for you!" answered Bob over his shoulder.

He groped in the cupboard and drew out a cricket stump.

Bunter dodged round the table.

"I say, you fellows, keep him off!" he roared. "I say, it's only fair to let a fellow have a whack in the cake when I told you about it! Cherry couldn't have pinched it if I hadn't told you. Could he? I say, all I want is a fair whack——"

Whack!

"Yaroooop!" roared Bunter as he received the whack—apparently not the one he wanted.

Whack!

"Ow! Beast! Stoppit! You can keep the cake!" yelled Bunter. "You can have it all if you like, greedy pig! Ow!"

"Whack!

"Yoo-hoooop!"

"Ha, ha, ha!"

Billy Bunter bolted for the door. After him rushed Bob Cherry, brandishing the cricket stump.

Four fellows stood roaring with laughter; Bunter was roaring, too, though not with laughter!

Whack! rang again on his trousers as he dodged out of the study. A yell answered from the passage.

"Hold on!" gasped Harry Wharton, catching Bob by the arm. "'Nuff's as good as a feast, old man!"

"I—I—I'll burst him!" gasped Bob. "I—I—I'll——"

Frank Nugent shut the door.

Bob threw down the cricket stump; his face was crimson with wrath.

However, he calmed down; and the Famous Five sat down to tea.

It was about ten minutes later that the door opened, and a fat face and a big pair of spectacles glimmered in.

Billy Bunter shot a rapid blink at the tea-table—evidently in expectation of spotting a cake there.

Bob Cherry gave him a glare.

"I—I say, you fellows, haven't you started on the cake yet?" asked Bunter.

"You fat chump!" exclaimed Harry Wharton. "Don't you know you're the only grub-raider in the Remove? There isn't any cake."

"Well, what's Bob done with it, then?"

"Ha, ha, ha!"

"You—you—you——" gasped Bob. "You fat scoundrel, if you haven't pinched Quelch's cake it's still in his study! Do you think I would touch it?"

"Eh? You couldn't pick it up without touching it, I suppose!" said Bunter, blinking at him. "Wharrer you mean?"

"I haven't even seen Quelch's cake!" roared Bob.

"Well, you must have seen it when you picked it up! Blessed if I make you out!" said Bunter. "Look here, aren't you even going to whack it out with your own pals? I say, it's pretty thick to keep the whole cake for yourself! Not the sort of thing I would do!"

Bob made a grab at the cricket stump. The door slammed.

Billy Bunter vanished.

'I'm afraid I cannot take that note, Master Coker," said Mrs. Mimble gravely. "Mr. Mimble says it is not a good one!" Coker drew a deep breath, as Mrs. Mimble handed the "dud" note back.

This time he was gone for good—giving up, at last, his hope of a "whack" in that cake. And the chums of the Remove finished their tea in peace.

THE SIXTH CHAPTER.

Smithy Asks for It!

"SMITHY!" exclaimed Tom Redwing.

"Rats!" retorted Herbert Vernon-Smith, over his shoulder.

"Stop!"

"More rats!"

Smithy was at Mr. Quelch's study door, when his chum, Tom Redwing, suddenly appeared in the passage, and called to him.

Unheeding Redwing's call, the Bounder of Greyfriars opened the study door, stepped in, and shut it after him.

Smithy was in need of a telephone. His Form-master being out, he was going to borrow Mr. Quelch's. Smithy had rather an urgent call to put through. He was, in fact, interested in Simple Simon, as well as Carter of the Remove.

According to Ponsonby of Highcliffe, who had an extensive and expensive knowledge of gee-gees, Simple Simon was a "sure snip" for the three o'clock on Wednesday. Smithy was anxious to be "on." He was probably the only fellow at Greyfriars who would have had the nerve to use one of the school telephones for such a purpose. But the Bounder had nerve enough for anything.

A remonstrance from his chum, Redwing, was not likely to stop him. Smithy shut the study door, and crossed over to the telephone. It was deeply dusky in the study; but he did not need a light neither would he have ventured to turn one on. He picked up the receiver, and a voice came through:

"Number, please?"

Smithy was about to give the number of the Three Fishers, when footsteps came up the passage.

He looked round towards the door, with a knitted brow. If that cheeky ass, Redwing, was following him to the study——

Then, with a start, he realised that those footsteps were certainly not Redwing's. It was a steady tread that was familiar to his ear.

"Quelch!" breathed the Bounder.

"Number, please?" came again, from the exchange.

Herbert Vernon-Smith did not give the number. He was not likely to do so, in the circumstances.

He replaced the receiver hurriedly, and stepped away from the telephone. Quelch was almost at the door.

The Bounder realised now why Redwing had called to him so anxiously, from the corner of the passage. No doubt he had seen Mr. Quelch coming in, and had been anxious to warn his reckless chum in time.

But that knowledge came too late to be of any use to the bad hat of the Remove. Smithy was fairly caught.

All that he could do was to step well away from the telephone, so that Quelch would not guess that he had been going to use that instrument. Swiftly he cudgelled his brains for some excuse to account for his presence in the study, when his Form-master entered.

He had little time. But the Bounder had a quick wit, and, in dealing with "beaks," he had little more scruple, in regard to veracity, than Billy Bunter himself.

The door opened, and Mr. Quelch stepped in, switching on the light as he did so.

He gave a little start at the sight of Vernon-Smith standing there. His eyes fixed suspiciously on the Bounder.

"Vernon-Smith, what are you doing in my study?" he asked.

"I hope you'll excuse me, sir," said Smithy meekly. "Some fellow has hidden my Latin dictionary for a silly joke, and I came to ask you if you would mind lending me one. As you weren't here, sir, I thought you wouldn't mind if I borrowed a dictionary for a little while."

Mr. Quelch paused before replying.

He would willingly have excused any junior for entering his study without leave, for the object stated; but he did not quite trust that member of his Form. It seemed much more probable, to Mr. Quelch's mind, that the scapegrace of the Remove was there for some much less innocent purpose—such as playing some trick on his Form-master.

"Very well, Vernon-Smith," said the Remove master, after that long pause. "If that was your object in coming here, I shall certainly excuse you. You may, however, remain for a few minutes."

The Bounder suppressed a grin as his Form-master's keen eyes shot a searching glance round the study. He knew what was in Quelch's mind. But he had done nothing there; he had not even used the telephone, so he was feeling quite safe.

So he was startled, when a deep frown gathered on Mr. Quelch's brow. The Remove master looked at the study table, apparently in search of something that was not there. Then he fixed his eyes on Vernon-Smith again.

"What have you done with the

parcel from this table, Vernon-Smith?"

"The—the what, sir?" stammered the Bounder.

"I left a parcel on this table, ready for the post in the morning," said Mr. Quelch. "It is gone, and I find you here. Tell me at once, Vernon-Smith, what you have done with that parcel?"

The Bounder caught his breath.

Of Quelch's parcel, and Quelch's cake, destined for a distant niece, he knew nothing whatever. But it dawned upon him that that study had had an earlier visitor during Quelch's absence. Someone, evidently, had been there before Smithy.

"I—I haven't seen it, sir," stammered Vernon-Smith.

"You will hardly expect me to believe that statement, Vernon-Smith," said the Remove master dryly. "The parcel was left on this table, and it is gone. You are here."

"I—I came to borrow a dictionary," muttered the Bounder sullenly.

"I fear, Vernon-Smith, that that statement was the first pretext that came into your head, when I caught you here," said Mr. Quelch, in the same dry tone. "I have no doubt whatever that you were here for another purpose; and as the parcel has been removed, I can have no doubt of that purpose. What have you done with it?"

"You can see that I haven't a parcel, sir."

"I can see that, Vernon-Smith, and, as you are still here, I presume that you have not removed it from the study. No doubt you have concealed it in this room. I remember that you played a similar trick with some Latin papers last term, and I caned you for it."

"I—I haven't——"

"You need say no more, Vernon-Smith. Replace that parcel on the table at once!" snapped Mr. Quelch.

The Bounder stood looking at him. He had never heard of Mr. Quelch's parcel till his Form-master mentioned it; and he had not the faintest idea what had become of it.

Mr. Quelch sat down at his table—to wait for the Bounder to sort that parcel out of the spot where he was convinced Smithy had hidden it.

But it was unnecessary for Smithy to search for the missing parcel. As Mr. Quelch put his legs under the table, his foot banged against something, and he uttered a startled ejaculation:

"What——"

He bent down, peered under the table, and then, with a thunderous brow, lifted out the parcel. He placed it on the table, and turned his eyes on Vernon-Smith.

"So this is what you consider a practical joke, Vernon-Smith," he said, in a grinding voice. "Do you dare to deny further that you concealed this parcel under my table, and that that is why you were in the study?"

"I've never even seen it before," said the Bounder sullenly. "I've told you why I came here."

Mr. Quelch's gimlet eyes almost bored into him. Really, the evidence was strong enough to convince any Form-master. But Henry Samuel Quelch was a just man. He did not trust Smithy, and he was sure that that statement about the Latin dictionary was a glib excuse—the first that had come into Smithy's head when he was caught. But if there was a doubt, Quelch was the man to give a culprit the benefit of it.

THE MAGNET LIBRARY.—No. 1,564.

"Very well, Vernon-Smith," he said, at last, "I cannot rely upon your word; but there is a bare possibility that you are speaking the truth. Come with me."

He rose from the chair, put a cane under his arm, and went to the door.

The Bounder, puzzled, followed him. What Quelch had in his head now, he could not guess. He followed his Form-master down the passage.

Redwing was loitering at the corner, with a worried look on his face. He had tried to warn his wayward chum in time, and had failed.

Mr. Quelch gave him a glance, but passed on without speaking. He ascended the stairs, the perplexed Bounder at his heels.

A fat voice was heard as he crossed the landing to the Remove passage.

"I say, you fellows, that beast Cherry had it, and——"

"Shut up, fathead! 'Ware beaks!"

Billy Bunter shut up, blinking round at Mr. Quelch through his big spectacles.

Unheeding the juniors in the passage, the Remove master walked on to Study No. 4, which belonged to Smithy and Redwing.

"What's up, Smithy?" whispered Hazeldene, as the Bounder passed.

Smithy shrugged his shoulders.

"Only Quelch paying me a friendly call," he sneered.

And he followed into the study, leaving the fellows in the passage, grinning.

In Study No. 4 Quelch's gimlet eyes glittered round. Then, suddenly, the Bounder understood. The story he had told would have passed muster, had there been nothing wrong in Quelch's study! Now Quelch was investigating that story, and as the Bounder's Latin dictionary was not missing, the game was up. The gimlet eyes ran over the bookshelf, and Mr. Quelch lifted down a book—a Latin dictionary! He opened it, to reveal the name "H. Vernon-Smith" on the fly-leaf.

"This," said Mr. Quelch, "is the book that you stated was missing from your study, Vernon-Smith! Have you anything further to say?"

The Bounder was silent.

Mr. Quelch slipped the cane down from under his arm into his hand.

"Bend over that chair, Vernon-Smith!" he said. "I should have punished you lightly for a foolish trick in my study, but unscrupulous untruthfulness calls for severe punishment. I shall cane you severely, Vernon-Smith."

The fellows in the passage exchanged glances, as they listened to a sound from Study No. 4 that was like unto the beating of a carpet.

Six times the swipes rang like shots! There was no sound from the Bounder; he was tough all through, and could take his gruel in silence.

Mr. Quelch emerged from the study again, with a knitted brow, and the cane under his arm. Smithy was left wriggling.

THE SEVENTH CHAPTER.

A Banknote for Bunter!

"ROT!" said Coker.

"But——" urged Potter.

"I said rot!" Coker pointed out.

Billy Bunter blinked round, with his usual inquisitiveness.

It was morning break, and Bunter had suffered a disappointment that morning. He had been expecting a postal order. It had not come!

In break, many of the fellows felt a need of a little refreshment, to see them through third school. The tuckshop was open, for that purpose. But the tuckshop was of no use to a fellow who had been disappointed about a postal order.

Bunter, in fact, would have had nothing in break that morning, had he not fortunately discovered a packet of toffee in Wibley's study.

Whether that toffee belonged to Wibley, or Morgan, or Micky Desmond, the three fellows in that study, Bunter did not know. Neither did he bother about it. It was quite immaterial, for to whomsoever that toffee had once belonged, it belonged to William George Bunter now and was disappearing inside Bunter, chunk by chunk.

That was why Bunter was leaning against an elm, which obscured him from the general view of fellows in the quad. He did not want to meet the eyes of William Wibley, David Morgan, or Michael Desmond, until that toffee had been disposed of.

Three men of the Fifth were arguing, as they walked along. They did not notice Bunter, and had they noticed him, would probably not have heeded the fat Owl of the Remove. Billy Bunter had no concern with Fifth Form affairs, and Coker & Co.'s discussion had nothing to do with him. No doubt that was why he lent a fat ear to the discussion. Billy Bunter took a deep and abiding interest in everything that did not concern him.

"I said rot, and I mean rot!" added Horace Coker. "See?"

"That's all very well," said Potter tartly. "But a dud banknote ought to be handed over to the police."

"Suppose you passed it by mistake, old chap?" urged Greene.

"Am I the fellow to make mistakes?" asked Coker.

"Oh!" gasped Potter and Greene together. As Horace Coker, the day before, had allowed a spoofing rascal to land a "dud" fiver on him, that question really was difficult to answer.

"I'm not going to the police station with it!" said Coker. "Think I'm going to have old Grimes thinking me a silly fool to be taken in with a counterfeit note! Likely!"

"Oh!" repeated Potter and Greene helplessly. In view of the circumstances, they really did not see what else Inspector Grimes was to think!

"It was all your fault, really!" went on Coker accusingly.

"Our fault?"

"Yes, rather! If you hadn't let that spoofing rotter impose on you, I shouldn't have exchanged the banknote for him! I don't expect you fellows to be very bright—but of all the silly fools——"

"But it was you——" howled Greene.

"Don't yell at me, Greene!" Coker of the Fifth came to a halt, and fixed a frowning stare on Potter and Greene. "You can jaw as much as you like, but I'm not going to old Grimes about that note! I prefer to keep the matter in my own hands! I haven't much faith in the police! They can't do anything! They want brains in the police force! Brains like mine, if they could get 'em! Then they might be of some use."

"Oh dear!" moaned Potter.

"I shall keep an eye open for those scoundrels," went on Coker. "If I see them again, I shan't want a policeman to deal with them! I'll deal with them all right!"

"But look here, Coker——" urged Greene. "You can't carry a counterfeit note about with you. Suppose it turned up some time! People might think you were going to pass it——"

"If anybody thought that, I know I'd jolly well hit him in the eye!" said Coker.

"Um! Oh! Yes! But——"

"But I'm not going to keep the rotten thing," added Coker, with the air of a fellow making a concession. "I'm not going to Courtfield with it, and have that old ass, Grimes, making out that I'm the sort of fool they pass dud notes on! No fear! But I certainly don't intend to carry a spoof banknote about. Think I'm a fool?"

Potter and Greene refrained from stating what they thought on that point!

"I've chucked it away!" Coker condescended to explain. "I'd have chucked it into the fire, if you fellows hadn't let it out! Well, I've chucked it into the wastepaper-basket in the study. That's that! But as for taking it to Courtfield, and having that old ass Grimes looking at me as if he thought me a silly fool like you, Potter, or like you Greene——"

Coker & Co. walked on, and Billy Bunter's fat ears heard no more.

The fat Owl grinned after them.

Evidently, Horace Coker had had a bad banknote passed on him—he was the kind of fellow who would!

Very sensibly, his friends urged him to take it to the police station, which Coker, of course, ought to have done.

But Coker, as usual, had no use for advice from lesser mortals.

He was not going to have a fatheaded policeman thinking that he was the kind of silly fool to have a bad banknote passed on him! Not Coker!

Bunter grinned, as he finished Wibley's toffee.

Had that bad banknote come Bunter's way, he could have found a use for it! Not, of course, to pass as a good one; such an idea would never have occurred to him. But it would have been very useful to pack in a fellow's note-case, Bunter thought, and reveal to other fellows' eyes, in a careless sort of way!

So long as they did not look at it too closely, the effect would be good!

Coker had no such use for it—he had real banknotes, if he wanted to swank with such things. Bunter hadn't!

A thoughtful look came over Bunter's fat face. Coker had thrown that useless banknote—useless to him, but useful to Bunter—into the wastepaper-basket in his study according to what he had said.

In the natural course of things, that wastepaper-basket would be emptied, the banknote would be transferred to a dustbin, and the dustmen would remove it with the other rubbish. That would be the end of it.

But it occurred to Billy Bunter's fat brain to interrupt the natural course of things!

If that dud banknote was still where that ineffable ass, Coker, had thrown it, Bunter had only to sort it out!

It was nobody's now, and there was no reason why it should not be Bunter's! Fellows who made silly jokes about his postal order would be a bit surprised when Bunter showed a banknote in his wallet!

That brilliant idea had germinated in Bunter's podgy intellect, when the bell rang for third school.

Fellows crowded away to the Form-rooms, but Billy Bunter did not follow the Remove.

Bunter rolled into the House and headed for the stairs.

Bob Cherry, seeing him go, called after him.

"This way, fatty! Can't you hear the bell?"

Bunter did not heed.

He rolled on his way! Being late for

class meant lines, but that could not be helped. While everybody else was in class, that was Bunter's golden opportunity for rooting in Horace Coker's wastepaper-basket!

While the rest of the Remove went in with Quelch, therefore, and while Coker & Co. were going in with Prout, Billy Bunter rolled along the deserted Fifth Form studies.

He rolled into Coker's study and shut the door.

One blink round the study revealed the wastepaper-basket, half full of torn and crumpled papers.

Bunter lost no time. He had to be late for class, but he did not want to overdo it.

His fat hands groped in the wastepaper-basket, and he blinked eagerly through his big spectacles.

That banknote was not easy to find. Fragments of torn exercises and old letters were there in plenty. They strewed the floor as Bunter turned out the basket. But no banknote came into view.

Then suddenly Bunter spotted a little crumpled ball of paper, and pounced on it! With eager, fat fingers he uncrumpled it!

It was the banknote! There were the magic words "Bank of England" and the figure "£5." It was fearfully crumpled—it looked as if Coker had crumpled it up in an angry fist before throwing it away, as no doubt he had! Crumpled or not, there it was!

Bunter smoothed it out, grinning! Having smoothed it, he packed it into his note-case! He grinned again at it. In the note-case it partly showed—just enough of it to show that it was a fiver! Fellows who made out that Bunter never had any banknotes, like Smithy or Lord Mauleverer, would have to sing to a different tune when they saw that! Bunter was going to have at least one banknote for the rest of the term! Real notes, in Bunter's possession, never remained long in his keeping; but owing to the peculiar nature of that particular banknote it had to be a permanent possession!

Happily satisfied with his astuteness, the fat Owl repacked Coker's wastepaper-basket in order to leave no clues behind him, and rolled out of Coker's study! He rolled into the Remove Form Room ten minutes late for class.

A gimlet eye fixed on him as he appeared.

"Bunter, you are late for class!" rapped Mr. Quelch. "You will take fifty lines, Bunter."

"I never heard the bell, sir!" gasped Bunter.

"You will take an additional hundred lines for untruthfulness, Bunter!"

"Oh!" gasped Bunter.

Even Bunter realised that he had better say no more! He went to his place, richer by a dud banknote and a hundred and fifty lines.

THE EIGHTH CHAPTER.

Swank!

"WHARTON, old chap, I——"

"Yes, old barrel?"

"Change a fiver for me?"

It was quite a safe question to ask. Few fellows in the Lower Fourth were sufficiently well-provided with cash to change a fiver for anybody.

Billy Bunter rolled into the Rag to ask that question. He wanted, naturally, to ask it before a good many fellows. Now that Bunter was a chap with five-pound notes, like Mauly and the Bounder, he wanted all the Remove to be aware of it.

The captain of the Remove glanced at him and laughed.

"You don't mean a tenner?" he asked.

"No, I don't!" retorted Bunter. "I say a fiver, and I mean a fiver! I want to change one of my banknotes—see? Can you change it?"

"Only one of them?" grinned Bob Cherry.

"Yes, only one of them!" assented Bunter calmly. "Got the change, Wharton?"

"About as much as you've got the fiver, old fat bean!" answered Harry, laughing.

"Oh, really, Wharton——"

"Have they sent you a fiver in mistake for a postal order from Bunter Court?" inquired Bob. "I seem to have heard that you were expecting a postal order!"

"Ha, ha, ha!"

"Well, the fact is, the pater weighed in with a fiver this time!" explained Bunter. "If one of you fellows could change it for me——" Bunter put a fat hand into his pocket for his note-case. "The fact is, I've run out of currency notes, and I want this fiver changed."

"He's run out of currency notes!" gasped Bob Cherry. "Generally he's plastered with them, you know! But just for once he's run out of them."

"What does it feel like to be short of currency notes, Bunter?" asked Frank Nugent. "First time it's ever happened —what?"

"Oh, really, Nugent! Look here, can you change this note or not?" asked Bunter. And he opened the tattered note-case and revealed the edge of a banknote in a compartment otherwise empty.

Whether Bunter had banknotes or not, there was no doubt that he was short of currency notes!

The Famous Five glanced at the portion of the banknote that was visible —and then stared at it.

They were not, of course, thinking of "dud" notes. They knew nothing whatever about Coker's adventure with the

(Continued on next page.)

plausible young man in Friardale Lane. They naturally would not have supposed that there was such a thing within the walls of Greyfriars School.

They gazed at that banknote in great surprise.

Banknotes were unusual in the Remove. Smithy had them, and let fellows see that he had them! Lord Mauleverer had them, and had even been known to use one as a bookmark! Monty Newland probably had them, as his people were fearfully rich, but if he had they were never seen. But, apart from those three fellows, any Remove man who had a banknote was in a state of rare and happy prosperity. Pound notes were far from common in the Remove—fivers were very rare birds. Most of the fellows counted their cash by the half-crown or the shilling.

But if it were unusual for the average Remove man to possess a fiver, it was remarkably and surprisingly unusual for Bunter to possess one.

Bunter was always hard up.

It was true that he was generally expecting a postal order, but it was equally true that these expectations were seldom or never fulfilled. It was true that he told everybody who would listen, and, indeed, everybody who wouldn't, about the vast wealth of Bunter Court. But few if any signs of that vast wealth had ever reached Greyfriars.

In fact, only that morning, before he discovered the toffee in Wibley's study, Bunter had been trailing Remove fellows to borrow a humble bob.

So Bunter's banknote was not merely surprising—it was astonishing!

Harry Wharton & Co. regarded it with great interest.

Bob Cherry, indeed, shaded his eyes as if it dazzled him!

"Is it real?" he gasped.

"Oh, really, Cherry——,"

Bob laughed. His question was only a joke! Not for a moment did it occur to him that the banknote was not real!

"Gratters, old man!" he said. "Jolly good luck! Take a tip from me and don't spend it all on one feed! They'll shove you in sanny if you do."

"Well, the fact is, I'm thinking of standing a bit of a spread if you fellows can change this note for me!" said Bunter. "You chaps have stood me a spread at times! Got the change?"

"Not unless you'll take eightpence for it!" said Bob.

"I can go to eighteenpence!" said Nugent.

"I'll make it half-a-crown!" grinned Johnny Bull.

"Nothing doing, old fat man!" said Harry Wharton. "We haven't called on our bankers lately."

Other fellows in the Rag were gathering round now. They were all interested in Bunter's fiver.

Most interested of all was Arthur Carter. He did not speak, but he came along to the spot and looked on.

Bunter had no objection to the banknote being seen. Indeed, he wanted it to be seen—so long as it was not seen too closely!

What it was that marked off a bad banknote from a good one Bunter did not know, and, in fact, that dud note looked good enough to him. But he knew that it was a bad one and that there were sharper eyes than his own in the Remove. So he did not take it out of the tattered note-case. He carefully allowed enough of it to be seen, to show that it was a five-pound note, that was all.

"Where the dickens did you get it, Bunter?" asked Skinner.

"Tip from my pater," answered Bunter airily.

"And where did he get it?" further inquired Skinner.

"Yah!" was Bunter's elegant retort to that.

"I guess that's the goods," remarked Fisher T. Fish, "and I'll sure remind you, Bunter, that you owe me a bob."

"Do I?" said Bunter carelessly. "Well, you can't expect me to remember such trifles; but I'll take your word for it, Fishy! Give me four pounds nineteen change, and here you are."

That was a safe offer! Fisher T. Fish's financial resources fell far short of that sum!

"I guess you can change it at the school shop, though!" said Fishy. "I'll sure amble along with you, Bunter."

"I'll come, too!" said Skinner amicably. If Bunter were going to change a banknote in the tuckshop, Skinner considered that it was worth while to be on the scene.

But Bunter shook his head.

"No fear!" he answered. "Quelch might spot it! We ain't allowed to have so much as this in the Remove! Quelch wouldn't let me keep it if he knew."

"Smithy changes fivers there!" said Hazeldene.

"Yes; and Quelch spotted him once, and there was a row!" said Bunter. "I know once Quelch made Mauly send banknotes home again!"

"That was a tenner," said Skinner.

"I'm not taking any risks!" declared Bunter. "I dare say I can get it changed in the House some time."

"Better not let Quelch see it, anyhow!" said Bob Cherry.

"I'll watch it!" grinned Bunter.

Bunter had very good reasons, unknown to the other fellows, for not seeking to change that banknote in the school shop!

Still, the reason he had given was good enough. It was true that there was a rule on the subject of pocket-money, and that no fellow in Mr. Quelch's Form was allowed to have so much as five pounds at a time, if Quelch knew it. All the fellows knew how Quelch had made Mauleverer send home the ten-pound note his lordship had used as a book-mark!

"Well, look here, Smithy can change it for you, I guess!" said Fisher T. Fish. "Smithy's got tons." Fisher T. Fish was very anxious to see that "bob" which Bunter had owed him for whole terms. Fishy had almost despaired of ever collecting that shilling. But he had never forgotten it. Though lost to sight, it was to memory dear!

"Oh, never mind!" said Bunter, hastily, and he shoved the note-case back into his pocket. "I can trot down to Courtfield to-morrow and change it. After all, there is no hurry."

And Billy Bunter rolled out of the Rag—his banknote in his pocket—rather anxious, at that point, to let the matter drop! "Swank" was all very well, and the dud banknote answered that purpose admirably, but that banknote was like the laws of the Medes and Persians, it could not be changed. He left a good many of the juniors staring after him. Bunter had surprised them with the banknote—and he surprised them still more by not being keen to get it changed and expended! Generally Bunter's cash, when he had any, went to the tuckshop, by the shortest route in the shortest time.

"Why the dickens doesn't he want Smithy to change it?" said Skinner. "I suppose it isn't Smithy's?"

"Oh, my hat!"

"Ha, ha, ha!"

"Don't be a rotter, Skinner!" growled Bob Cherry.

Arthur Carter drew a deep, quick breath. Skinner's suggestion was only one of his malicious jests. The Remove fellows, though surprised, did not think of being suspicious. But there was a deep suspicion in the mind of the schemer of the Remove.

THE NINTH CHAPTER.

Play Up, Bunter!

"LOOK here!" said Peter Todd. Tom Dutton glanced round at him.

It was tea-time in the Remove: and Peter and Dutton were in Study No. 7—Billy Bunter not having yet arrived in that apartment.

No. 7 was not a lavish study at tea-time. Billy Bunter preferred to tea out, when he could. Lord Mauleverer was honoured with his fascinating company, as often as the fat Owl could inflict it on him. The Bounder's study was equally attractive—but nothing but a boot was likely to welcome Bunter there. The Famous Five often had the pleasure, or otherwise, of having Bunter to tea.

When other resources failed, Bunter rolled into his own study to tea—and often turned up his fat little nose thereat!

As Bunter seldom or never contributed to the festive board, any fellow who did not know him might have expected him to take what he could get and be thankful. But not any fellow who did know him!

"Look here——" repeated Peter. He seemed thoughtful.

"Eh?" Tom Dutton was deaf. "What?"

"Look here——"

"There's a lot of books here," answered Dutton. "Which one do you want?"

"Look here," roared Peter. Talking to Dutton was talking to half the Remove passage, but that could not be helped. "Look here, why shouldn't Bunter——"

He broke off, as the door was pushed open and Billy Bunter blinked in through his big spectacles.

"Come in, Fatty!" said Peter.

Bunter stood in the doorway, blinking at the table. It was a disparaging blink. Half a loaf, a pat of butter, and a tin of sardines, were not gratifying to Bunter's view at tea-time.

"That the lot?" he asked.

"That," said Peter, eyeing him, "is the lot, so far."

"Oh! Anything more coming?" asked Bunter brightening.

"I fancy so!"

"Right-ho, old chap, then!" said Bunter, and he rolled cheerfully in.

Peter Todd eyed him, rather grimly. He had not been in the Rag, after class, when the fat Owl swanked with the banknote. But he had heard about it. All the Remove had heard about it. And Bunter being, for once in a way, in funds, Peter saw no reason why he should not, like any other fellow, stand his "whack."

Bunter, to do him justice, would have seen no reason why not, either, had that banknote been changeable! With five real pounds in his possession, Bunter's study would have been like unto a land flowing with milk and honey, so long as the five pounds lasted.

Peter, knowing nothing about the fixed immutability of that banknote, naturally considered that the time had come for Bunter to play up.

Bunter, when he was hard up, as he

" I left a parcel on this table ready for the post in the morning," said Mr. Quelch, sternly. " What have you done with it, Vernon-Smith ? " " I—I haven't seen it, sir ! " stammered the Bounder. Neither Mr. Quelch nor Vernon-Smith were aware that the parcel was concealed under the table.

generally was, sponged on the study without mercy. So, when he was in funds—great funds—the least he could do was to do the decent thing ! Indeed, Peter rather expected him to roll in with a bundle of tuck under his fat arm. But there was no bundle about Bunter. Peter had been about to confide his opinion to Tom Dutton, that it was time for Bunter to play up, when the fat Owl arrived. So now he confided it to Bunter instead.

"How often have you stood your whack in this study, this term, fatty?" inquired Peter.

Bunter blinked at him.

"I may have missed once or twice !" he said, with dignity. "When a fellow's been disappointed about a postal order you——"

"Oh, quite !" agreed Peter. "But when a fellow's in funds, he's expected to stand his whack, see? You're a greedy little beast, Bunter—but there's no need for you to be a mean little beast, too ! Play up !"

"Just what I want to do !" said Bunter cheerily. "But, you see, I can't change my fiver at the shop—Quelch might get wise to it. Besides, Mrs. Mimble would very likely want to keep her old account out of it—you know what women are, Peter—unreasonable ! Another time, old chap ! I say, what else have you got for tea?"

"Nothing else—so far."

"Well, that's not much for three fellows !" said Bunter. "You said there was going to be something else, Toddy."

"Yes—you're going to stand it !"

"Oh ! Ah ! Yes ! To-morrow, old chap, or—or the day after——"

"No time like the present !" said Peter Todd, firmly. "I'm surprised at you, Bunter ! You're almost every kind of a worm——"

"Oh, really, Toddy——"

"But I shouldn't have expected you to be stingy, like Fishy. If you're taking Fishy as a model, you can chuck it, right now ! See? You're standing your whack this time. Smithy will change that note like a shot, if you ask him."

"I'm not going to speak to Smithy ! He kicked me this morning—I bar the cad !" said Bunter. "He made out that it was my fault that Quelch whopped him yesterday—as if I asked you to hide that beastly cake under the table ! I had a row with Bob Cherry about it, and all the time——"

"Never mind that—Mauly will change it."

"Mauly's got his study door locked— I've just been there ! I believe he's keeping out some barging cad he doesn't want in his study—anyhow, I couldn't get in."

"Oh, my hat !" gasped Peter. "Yes, I've no doubt he is—and I think I could guess the bargee's name, too ! Well, there's Newland——"

"I can't go to Newland !" said Bunter. "He's got his back up with me—just because I called him a Jew when he wouldn't lend me a bob this morning—"

"Well, there's that relation of yours, Carter," said Peter. "You've told all Greyfriars that he's a rich relation, so I suppose he can change a fiver."

"I—I fancy I was mistaken about that, Toddy ! I believe old Carter's turned him down. In fact, I think the old bean's got an eye on me instead. Carter's no good, Peter."

Peter's look grew grimmer and grimmer. He had named four fellows, one after another, and in each case Bunter had a reason why the fellow should not be asked to change the fiver. Really, it looked as if the fat Owl was

developing miserly ways, out-doing even Fisher T. Fish in that unattractive line.

"Well, what about Coker?" asked Peter, after a pause.

Bunter fairly jumped.

"Kik-kik-Coker !" he gasped.

"Yes, Coker. He's got tons of oof; and he would do it like a shot if you asked him civilly !"

"Oh crikey !" gasped Bunter.

He turned almost faint, at the idea of letting Coker of the Fifth see that banknote again—the dud banknote he had crumpled up in an angry fist and pitched into the wastepaper-basket ! Coker of the Fifth was the very last fellow at Greyfriars, to whom Billy Bunter would have liked to display that banknote !

"I—I can't ask a Fifth Form man !" gasped Bunter. "He—he'd think it cheek, Peter ! Besides, Coker's ratty with me, since some of the things went out of his hamper ! He made out that I'd been to his study, because Potter saw me coming out of it, you know ! I—I'm not going to Coker !"

"Angel of the Fourth might do it !" said Peter.

"I'm not going to speak to Angel of the Fourth, Peter ! He's a bad hat ! I'm not going to get mixed up with that sort of chap !"

Peter Todd drew a deep breath. Whatever Bunter's motive, one thing was quite clear—he was not going to change that banknote !

"Well," said Peter at last, "that's that ! Get out !"

"Eh ?"

"Get out !" roared Toddy.

"I haven't had my tea——"

"Dutton and I," said Peter, in measured tones, "have blued our last

(Continued on page 16.)
THE MAGNET LIBRARY.—No. 1,564.

MR. LICKHAM'S DILEMMA!

*Another Smashing Instalment
of Our Great Serial:*
"THE FORM-MASTER'S SECRET!"

By DICKY NUGENT

THE GREYFRIARS

No. 278.

EDITED BY HA

"I never 'ad no 'and in it!"

Dusty Lickham waved his hands dramatick-ally, as he spoke these words to his accusers.

Doctor Birchemall, the headmaster of St. Sam's, put down his tellyfone and larfed a skornful larf.

"Better tell that to the perlice when they come, Lickham!" he sneered. "Perhaps they'll beleeve you. On the other hand, they mite not!"

Dusty Lickham's face turned pail under its outer covering of grime.

"Look 'ere, old covey, don't be 'ard on a bloke."

"If you're thinking of pleading for mersy, Lickham, you may as well save your breth!" said the Head. "You had no mersy on yung Bullion of the Fourth when you plotted with your dastardly friends to have him kidnapped."

"I never done it!" gasped the bogus Form-master despritly.

"Ratts! Stand by that door, boys, in case your tretcherous Form-master attempts to escape!" added the Head, addressing Jack Jolly & Co., who were still lined up at the door.

"I, I, sir!" corussed the heroes of the Fourth.

Jack Jolly & Co. had always regarded their Form-master with grate respect and esteem. Even his recent ineggsplicable change from a refined and skollarly jentleman into a coarse creetcher with low and vulgar habits had not shaken their faith in him. They had no idea whatever, of corse, that the new Mr. Lickham was really Dusty Lickham, cuzzin and dubble of their real Form-master and pro-fessional tramp. Yet still they remained loyle to the Lickham they had known.

But if Mr. Lickham has dessended to the depth of assisting in the kidnapping of yung Bul-lion, then Jack Jolly & Co. were willing to admit that no fate could be too vile for him.

They lined up grimly in the doorway of the Head's study, prepared to bar the way if Lick-ham was so rash as to try to escape.

"Give a cove a charnst, yung jents!" wined Dusty Lickham.

"No fear," said Jack Jolly. "If you're innersent, as you say you are, you've nothing to fear when the perlice arrive!"

"But the perlice won't beleeve me!" gasped Dusty Lickham. "Knowin' as I'm a tramp——"

"A whatter?"

"A tramp!"

"But you're not a tramp!" yelled Frank Fearless. "You're a skoolmaster!"

Dusty Lickham started. In his eggsite-ment he had forgotten that.

"Ho, yuss. That's what I meant—a skool-master!" he mermered. "Knowin' as I'm a skoolmaster, the perlice are bound to think I'm a crook to begin with——"

"WHAT?" yelled the Head, indignantly.

"So I won't be given a charnst! Lemme pass, yung jents!"

"Not likely!"

Dusty Lickham groaned. But he was not beaten yet. If his pleas fell on deff ears, he was ready to fall back on cunning.

With a crafty gleem in his eyes, he edged towards the winder. He glanced down into the quad, as though re-fleckting on his unhappy fate, and then he gave a violent, spasmoddick start.

"My heye!" he cried. "Look at wot's a-goin' hon down there!"

Dusty's ruse sux-xeeded beyond his wild-est eggspectations. In an instant the Head and the Fourth Formers had herled themselves across the room and were struggling for front places at the winder—certain that something eggstraordinary must be happening in the quad.

An instant later, Dusty slipped back to the door, wrenched it open, and ran for his life.

"Haw, haw, haw!" he roared, as he ran down the passidge. "Ever bin 'ad? Haw, haw, haw!"

"It's a hoaks, boys!" gasped Doctor

Fearless. "You're a skoolmaster!"

Dusty Lickham started. In his eggsite-ment he had forgotten that.

"Ho, yuss. That's what I meant—a skool-master!" he mer-mered. "Knowin' as I'm a skoolmaster, the perlice are bound to think I'm a crook to begin with——"

"WHAT?" yelled the Head, indignantly.

"So I won't be given a charnst! Lemme pass, yung jents!"

"Not likely!"

Dusty Lickham groaned. But he was not beaten yet. If his pleas fell on deff ears, he was ready to fall back on cunning.

Birchemall. "Stop him!"

"Oh, grate pip!"

Jack Jolly & Co. could have kicked them-selves when they found how easily the sus-peckted kidnapper had diddled them. Woop-ing fewriously, they tore after him.

But although Dusty's start was short, his legs were long. He ran like a deer—and soon took all the hart out of Jack Jolly & Co. By the time they had reached the end of the passidge, he was at the other end of Big Hall; by the time they had reached the end of Big Hall, he was at the bottom of the School House steps; and by the time they were at the bottom of the School House steps, he had reached the gates!

And so it happened that when the perlice arrived at St. Sam's, it was only to find that the bird had flown and their task been made a lot more difficult. For now they had to look for the suspeckted arch-criminal himself in addi-tion to his fellow-plot-ters, Charlie and Joe, and, of corse, the missing Fourth Former, Bullion.

"There's no doubt about it, you fellows, the whole thing's a mistery," remarked Jack Jolly, as the heroes of the Fourth returned to their study. "Why should Lickham have changed like he did, in the first place?"

"Echo answers 'Why?'" said Bright, with a shake of his head.

"And why should those tramps have called for him?" asked Frank Fearless. "They were a cupple of villanous carrickters, by all accounts; but they seemed to know Lick-ham right enuff. What's the eggsplanation?"

"Give it up!" grinned Jolly. "It's an intreeg-ing mistery, and no mis-take. Whatever the solution is, anyway, I hoap that old Lickham will be proved innersent. I can't help feeling sorry for him now—persewed by perlice with blud-hounds, most likely, through lonely woods and perilous marshes——"

Tap, tap, tap!

The kaptin of the Fourth broke off. A tapping had suddenly become ordible on the winderpane.

The Co. looked round in grate serprize, for their study was quite a dickens of a distance from the ground. When they saw the reason for the tapping, a cry of sheer amazement went up from them.

"LICKHAM!"

"Grate pip! He must have climbed up the ivy!"

"My hat! He'd be safer in those woods and marshes you mentioned than up here, Jolly!" gasped Fearless. "Lend a hand, you fellows!"

"Yes, rather!"

Jack Jolly & Co. rushed to the winder and flung up the sash. The man they had reckernised as their Form-master was cling-ing to the winder-ledge by the skin of his teeth. He was also clinging to the ivy with his fingers. He was keyed up to a high pitch of eggsite-ment—and his eyes almost bolted out of their sockits!

"Hold on for a cupple of jiffies, sir!" said Jack Jolly. "We'll hawl you in, sir!"

"How can we do it?" asked Bright.

MY FORM IS THE BEST AT GREYFRIARS!

Claims Mr. WIGGINS, master of the Third Form

Is my Form the best at Greyfriars? Oh, yes—decidedly!

Other masters have told me that their pupils are very promising. Mine have no need to promise. They do what is required of them without promises—not to mention a lot that is not required of them!

Unfortunately, as you may know already, I am a little forgetful, or I would support my point with many factual ex-amples. I can remember one or two off-hand, though, which will give you an idea.

There was one occa-sion, for instance, when Tubb did something or other. I cannot recollect details, but the example proves my point up to the hilt.

Then there was that singular achievement of Bolsover minor. What it was exactly eludes my memory now, but it was a notable illustration of the truth of my conten-tion.

As for the time when Paget and Wingate minor—or was it Conrad and Bolter?—performed some rare and difficult feat (I have forgotten precisely what), I was filled with genuine en-thusiasm for my Form.

Unquestionably, the Third is the best—or was I saying the worst?—Form at Greyfriars. Oh, yes!

(Thanks, awfully, Mr. Wiggins! Now, of course, we know!—ED.)

Jack

fugiti
eager
gest

"I
by th
sudde

"G
The
leane
Jolly
one
while
grabb

"F
Jolly.
Th
and a
the n
sill fl
with
and
Jolly

B
Wallo
"Y
"A
grinn
safe
Feelin

"C
Yes,
Reall
how
boys

Jac
farely

The
accus
Lickh
his ai
coars
that
larly

The
week
been
trium
thou

No
he wa
But f
our
medic
Skinn
ning i
one!
the ti
at a
expla
to wi

"I
it?"
asked
had t
to th
cheer
graph

Sk
wink
drew
sinist

"H
know

I a

HERALD

HARTON.   February 5th, ...

HARRY WHARTON CALLING!

This morning I have received a letter from Tubb, of the Third.

"I admit that the 'Greyfriars Herald' is a pretty good paper from the point of view of the average reader," he says. "But we in the Third feel we don't get featured prominently enough in it. What's more, there are several much-needed improvements we could think of in the way you serve up Third Form news when you do trouble to print it. WHY DON'T YOU INVITE SUGGESTIONS FROM US ?"

The capitals at the end are mine. I think that this sentence really deserves them!

If Tubb saw a tenth part of the flood of suggestions that reach us every week, uninvited, he would no longer wonder why we don't go out of our way to invite suggestions!

The fact is, apart even from the countless readers we have outside Greyfriars, that nearly all our readers have ideas for "improving" the "Greyfriars Herald." And most of them are not backward in coming forward with them, either!

In the same post as Tubb's naive missive, for instance, were the following letters :

From Billy Bunter, threatening to start a rival paper called " The Grub-Fancier's Gazette " unless we print more about eating and cooking.

From Fisher T. Fish, offering to take over the paper entirely and run it for all the schools in the country instead of primarily for Greyfriars.

From Hurree Singh and Wun Lung, criticising our grammar and phraseology, and offering to re-write the entire paper each week in good English!

And this, my esteemed pals, is only a meagreful small bunch, chosen selectfully from others written in a likeful manner.

Now you savvy why we not invitee suggestions. Suggestions come plenty quick without invitee, see ? Me hopee Tubb understandee!

Don't mind me, chums—I'm just imagining how the " Herald " might read if I let Inky and Wun Lung have their way!

All the best till next week !

HARRY WHARTON.

---

scanned the
m - master
ad the big-
bout him.
—grab him
!" he said

! "
h Formers
the winder.
ight seezed,
ween them
s and Merry
ther.
" sang out

a long pull
pull ; and
the winder-
agh the air
est of ease,
in Jack
n his neeze.
Crash!

! "
en, sir ! "
. " You're
und now.
ght ? "
! Groooo !
you, Jolly.
rdly know
k you, my

y & Co.

become so
to a Mr.
o dropped
ad spoke in
on axxents,
ined, skol-
f the new-

comer fell on their ears like a bombshell.
" My hat ! You're speaking like you used to speak, sir ! " cried Fearless. " For the last week you've been talking like a tramp. And now you've changed back again ! "
Mr. Lickham gave a violent, spasmoddick start.
" You—you say I've been talking like a tramp, Fearless ? " he stuttered.
" Yes, rather, sir ! And acting like one, too ! "
" Surely you remember, sir ? "
With a mitey effort, Mr. Lickham conkered his impulse to say " No." He realised now what had happened. His cuzzin Dusty—the black sheep of the Lickham fambly—had yewsurped his place when he was taken off to prison for failing to keep up his instalments on his new cap and gown !
It was the real Mr. Lickham, the old original master of the Fourth. He had earned a remission of his sentence of 14 days becawse of good conduct and he had sneaked back to the skool in this manner to escape observation—hoaping later to invent

some plawsible eggscuse for his absence.
Now that Mr. Lickham lerned for the first time that his cuzzin Dusty had been filling his place as master of the Fourth, he simply did not know where he stood. He had enuff sense, however, to see that it would not do to give the game away completely. So when he was asked whether he remembered the events of the past week, he didn't say " No." Instead, he said :
" Yes, rather ! I remember it all now. It was just a joak. Awfully commical, boys, what ? Ha, ha, ha ! "
Jack Jolly & Co. looked rather dewbious.
" Well, it's commical in a way, sir ; but this bizziness of your pals, Charlie and Joe, kidnapping yung Bullion, isn't so funny," said Jack Jolly. " In fakt, the proper thing for us to do now is to tell the Head so that he can recall the perlice."
Mr. Lickham gasped.
" K - k - kidnapping ? Oh—er—yes, eggsactly ! " he stammered. " I can eggsplain all that, boys. Please don't tell the Head yet. I must have time."

" The judge will give you that before you're much older ! " broke in a voice from the doorway. " About five years, I imagine ! Lickham ! You're my prisoner ! "
" The Head ! " gasped Mr. Lickham.
Doctor Birchemall stalked into the study, a triumfant smile on his face.
" So this is where you were hiding, Lickham, eh ? " he cried. " A lucky thing I came along at the right moment ! I am going to take the liberty of locking you up for the nite now. To-morrow, you will be handed over to the perlice ! This way ! "
A groan burst from Mr. Lickham's lips. He simply longed to tell the Head the truth. And yet, to have done so would have meant laying bare the terribul secret that he had just returned from spending seven days in jail.
Never before in the history of St. Sam's had a Form-master been faced by such a dreadful dilemma !

(*Don't miss the next hair-raising instalment of Dicky Nugent's unique serial !*)

WON WALKING RACE IN A CANTER!

New Champ's Frank Admissions

se of the
letics has
Skinner's
the mara-
race.
ren knew
running !
at he told
cative im-
er the race,
n the run-
enses than
t, most of
' walked "
and this
he came
unter !
you do
resentative
Skinner
the tape
of much
l clicking
photo-
cras.
estowed a
rep. He
de, with a

hen you
he said.
in walking

races the same way—by running ! "
" Oh, scissors ! "
" Of course, I can't do it while there are judges and stewards about," Skinner hastened to explain. " Winning walking races by running calls for a good deal of discretion and judgment, I can tell you. You have to run when nobody's watching you."
" Is that so ? "
" Pretty obvious ! " grinned Skinner. " Fortunately, the course is too long for the judges to be watching a chap all the time."
" Quite ! " nodded our representative. " They leave it to your honour."

" Honour ? Never heard of it ! " said Skinner, with a shake of his head. " All I know is, you choose your spots carefully. There are quite a number of places where you can break into a run without being seen by the stewards ! "
" But don't the other competitors object ? "
" Oh, rather ! That's the funny thing about it ! " laughed Skinner. " They object strongly ; but for some obscure

reason they never report me. They tell me it's some barbarous taboo that stops 'em—sneakin' I fancy they call it ! "
" Great Scott ! "
" It gives me a big

advantage, of course," went on Skinner cheerfully. " It seems that I'm the only one who ignores this weird taboo of never bein' allowed to sneak. The rest just grin an' bear it—an' I walk off with the prize ! Ha, ha, ha ! "
" My hat ! Are you equally skilled in other forms of athletics ? " asked our representative. " Any good at cross-country running, for instance ? "
" Not a bit ! But all the same, I'm goin' to win the Junior event this season ! "
" How the thump will you do that ? "
" By gettin' lifts in lorries an' cars ! " explained the walking champion. " It ought to be even easier than this walkin' race bizney. Ha, ha, ha ! "
" Skinner ! " bawled out somebody just then, Skinner turned away.

" You'll have to excuse me," he grinned. " That's Wingate. I expect he's goin' to pat me on the back."
But Skinner was slightly mistaken. It appeared that Wingate had been quietly watching Skinner at one of the spots where Skinner had thought that he was unobserved.
And instead of patting him on the back, Wingate started whacking him on the rear part of his anatomy ! So Skinner's rivals reached the winning-post to find their victor touching his toes and yelling under the lashings of an ashplant !
If anybody is thinking of betting a few doughnuts on Skinner's chances in the Junior Cross-country run this year, we have one word of advice to give him : DON'T !

BUNTER'S BIG BLUFF!
By FRANK RICHARDS

(Continued from page 13.)

eighteenpence on this tea. And you're going to sit down and scoff it, with a five-pound note in your pocket!"

"Yes. You—you see——" stammered Bunter. "I—I say, Peter, what are you going to do with that cushion?"

There was no need for Peter to answer the question. Bunter, the next moment, knew!

Swipe!

"Ow!" spluttered Bunter. "I say——"

Swipe!

"I say—— Wow!" roared Bunter.

Swipe!

"Yaroooop!"

Bunter bounded for the door.

Peter bounded after him, still swiping with the cushion. Twice he got the fat Owl before Bunter escaped from the study. Then the Owl flew.

"Come back and have a few more!" roared Peter, brandishing the cushion in the doorway of Study No. 7.

Billy Bunter did not come back. It was not much of a tea in Study No. 7, but the most lavish of spreads would not have tempted Bunter back just then!

THE TENTH CHAPTER.
Whose Fiver?

ARTHUR CARTER sat at prep in Study No. 1, with Harry Wharton and Frank Nugent.

The three worked together fairly well. Bob Cherry's "feud" with Carter had lasted unchanged from the day he came; but Bob's friends did not share in it.

Several times, it was true, there had been sharp words in the study—Carter had ways that the other fellows did not like—but the Co. could not quite make up their minds that he was the scheming outsider that Bob believed him to be.

That he was "down" on Bunter, with a very heavy down, all the Form knew. But, really and truly, Billy Bunter was not the sort of relative to inspire affection. And if, as seemed to be the case, they were rivals for the riches of an undecided old gentleman who did not seem to know his own mind, mutual antipathy was not a thing to cause surprise.

Carter had, at least, one redeeming quality; he was keen on Soccer, and showing such form at the game that Wharton was thinking of playing him in the fixtures. And if, as Bob believed, he lost no opportunity of making things bad for Bunter, it was certain that he could have no chance, unless Bunter gave him one.

So, though his study-mates did not like him much, they pulled together more or less, and generally there was peace. On this particular evening Carter seemed unusually thoughtful—and that unusual thought was not all concentrated on prep.

When at last the books were closed and prep was over, Wharton and THE MAGNET LIBRARY.—No. 1,564.

Nugent prepared to leave the study. Since Carter had been there, they no longer heard Bob Cherry's cheery bang on the door after prep But if the mountain would not come to Mahomet, it was easy for Mahomet to go to the mountain! But as they were about to leave the study Carter spoke.

"Hold on a minute, Wharton, will you?"

"Fire away!" answered Harry.

"It's about Bunter——"

The captain of the Remove held up his hand.

"Chuck that!" he said tersely. "I don't want anything from you on that subject, Carter! You can row with your relations without my help."

"Or mine!" said Frank Nugent.

"I think it's a matter you should take up, as head boy of the Form," said Carter. "As Bunter's a distant connection of mine—a very distant one—it rather worries me. Your pal Cherry fancies that I should be glad to see the fat idiot turfed out of the school——"

"I don't think you'd be sorry if he left!" said Harry dryly.

"Neither would you be, I think, if he were your relation instead of mine!" retorted Carter. "But that's not the point. I shouldn't like a relative of mine, even a distant one, sacked for stealing."

"Oh, do chuck it!" exclaimed Wharton. "Has the fat ass snaffled a bun or a doughnut?"

"Or an aniseed ball?" grinned Nugent.

"Put it as you 'ike!" said Carter. "But if he'd got away with Quelch's cake yesterday, I fancy there would have been bad trouble for him."

"Yes, and that's why we all tried to stop him," answered Harry. "He's such a fool, that it's up to more sensible chaps. Bob locked him in this study to keep him out of mischief—and you let him out It turned out that Toddy had put the plunder out of sight or Bunter would have bagged it. Your fault if he had."

Carter shrugged his shoulders.

"Hardly my fault, if he can't keep his fat paws off what doesn't belong to him!" he answered. "But never mind that. It's that banknote that's in my mind."

"Well, what about that?" asked Harry, with his hand on the door-handle. He did not want to discuss Bunter with Carter, and his manner showed it plainly enough.

"Where did he get it?" asked Carter.

Wharton stared at him.

"I think he said his father sent it to him. What do you mean?"

"I mean, that I don't believe anything of the kind!" answered Carter coolly. "You ought to know Bunter by this time! I've been here only a few weeks, and I've never seen him with any money without seeing him bolt to the school shop with it. But nothing will make him change that fiver in the school."

"What rot!" said Harry uneasily.

"If Quelch got on to it——" said Nugent.

"Quelch might, if he changed it at the shop, though Smithy's changed banknotes there and nothing said!" retorted Carter. "But Quelch would hear nothing if he changed it in the Remove. Two or three fellows would do it for him. Bunter tea'd in Hall to-day—with five pounds in his pocket! Is that his usual way?"

"No," said Harry slowly.

"They've had a row in his study," said Carter. "I've heard a dozen fellows chortling over it. Toddy turned

Bunter out because he wanted to scoff tea there without standing his whack. Toddy offered to get the note changed for him, with half a dozen fellows. He refused."

Wharton made a gesture of annoyance.

"It's his own bizney," he said. "I've heard him say that he's taking the dashed thing to Courtfield to change to-morrow."

"Outside the school!" said Carter significantly.

"What do you mean by that?"

"I think the meaning's pretty clear. It looks to me as if that banknote belongs to somebody in the school, who might spot it if it was changed here."

Wharton compressed his lips.

"In plain English, you mean you suspect Bunter of having pinched somebody else's banknote?" he rapped.

"What does it look like?"

"I don't care what it looks like!" snapped the captain of the Remove.

"But I'll tell you what your rotten words look like—they look as if Bob had it right, and you've come here to make all the trouble you can for that fat ass!"

"Then you don't think you ought to look into it, as head of the Form?"

"No, I don't! If that's your rotten game, you won't get me to play it for you!" said Harry angrily.

"Cut it out, Carter!" said Frank Nugent. "Fellows don't often get fivers—but it does happen! As a matter of fact, this isn't the first that Bunter's had—I remember he had one before, once——"

"Whose was it?" sneered Carter.

"Oh, shut up!" said Frank roughly. "Come on, Wharton—I've had enough of this, if you have!"

"More than enough!" said Harry; and they left the study together, leaving Carter biting his lip.

The other members of the Co. joined them in the passage to go downstairs.

Billy Bunter rolled after them, and Harry Wharton glanced at him.

"Changed your fiver yet, old fat man?" he asked.

He would have been glad to hear that Bunter had, after what Carter had said in the study.

"Eh? Oh, no!" answered Bunter.

"If you've got change——"

"Smithy has!" said Harry.

"Oh, blow Smithy!" answered Bunter, and he rolled away across the landing and went down the stairs.

Harry Wharton's face clouded a little as he followed him with the Co. He had not thought of it before, but now that Carter had pointed it out, he realised that Billy Bunter's proceedings with that fiver were rather singular. He was, at all events, acting quite contrary to his usual manners and customs.

And the captain of the Remove could not help remembering what an unmitigated ass Billy Bunter was. That he would "pinch" a banknote was simply not to be thought of—by any fellow but Carter, at least. But if he had happened to find one, he was fat-head enough to fancy that "findings were keepings." Yet it was extremely improbable that he could have found one. Nobody, as far as Wharton had heard, had lost one.

"Anything up?" asked Bob Cherry, glancing at Wharton's face as they went down the Remove passage.

"Only that fellow Carter getting on my nerves!" said Harry. "I wish he'd never come here!"

And with that, he dismissed the matter from his mind, though it was to be recalled before long.

THE ELEVENTH CHAPTER
Bunter Explains !

BILLY BUNTER, in the Rag after prep, noticed that a good many eyes turned on him.

He was pleased thereby.

He had asked five or six fellows to change a fiver for him, only carefully avoiding asking Smithy, Newland, or Mauleverer, who could have done so.

Had a fellow unexpectedly produced the necessary change, the fatuous fat Owl would have been in rather a difficulty. But the unexpected did not happen. That "dud" fiver was still in the tattered notecase—useless in itself, but as useful as ever for the purpose of "swank."

Often and often had the fat Owl yearned to be a fellow like Smithy, who could show off banknotes. Now he could! In fact, owing to the peculiar nature of that banknote, he was going to be able to show off a fiver for the rest of the term.

Not for ten times its nominal value would Bunter have changed it. Not, indeed, for any consideration whatever would he have done so. Bunter had never seen Borstal, but he was quite sure that he did not want to go there.

Carter, when he came into the Rag, took no notice of Bunter. But nearly all the other fellows did—in fact, the general interest in Bunter was much greater than could be accounted for by the fact that he was in funds. No doubt it was very unusual for the impecunious Owl of the Remove to be in funds, and still more unusual for him to keep those funds intact, instead of exchanging them, at the earliest opportunity, for edibles. But there was something more than that. Harry Wharton, as he caught a word here and there, knew that Carter had been giving a hint on the subject to other fellows.

Nobody but Carter, it seemed, had thought of suspecting that that fiver was not Bunter's own. But nothing more than a hint was needed. The fat Owl was, in fact, asking for it.

Peter Todd joined the Famous Five, with a worried look on his face.

"I suppose you haven't heard of anybody missing a fiver?" he asked.

"No, ass!" said Harry.

"Well, I haven't, either. But——"

"Fathead!" said Nugent. "If anybody lost a banknote, there would be a notice on the board about it. There isn't."

"Oh!" said Peter. "You've looked?"

"Well, yes, after what Carter said in the study," admitted Frank. "Has he been jawing to you in the same strain?"

"He hasn't spoken to me, but—— Look here, it looks jolly queer," said Peter. "I swiped that fat ass for not standing his whack in the study, with a fiver in his pocket! It's not like him, really. It looks as if he's afraid to change it inside the school. Well, why?"

"The whyfulness is terrific, my esteemed Toddy!"

"I don't know whether it started with Carter, but there's a lot of jaw going on," said Toddy. "Of course, it's all rot. But Bunter's such a silly idiot—— Look here, do you fellows know where he got it?"

"From his pater, he said," answered Harry.

"Well, a lot of fellows know that he never had a letter to-day. He was seen looking for one, as usual; but he never had one."

"Might have had it yesterday."

"And said nothing about it."

"Um!"

"At this rate," said Peter, "we shall have all the Form fancying that the blithering idiot has pinched it I don't know who started it——"

"Easy enough to guess!" said Bob Cherry, with a snort.

"Well, anyhow, it's going the rounds," said Peter. "I think Bunter had better put it plain where he got it, for his own sake. As he's holding a one-man exhibition with the fiver, he may as well say where it came from. Better have it out now all the fellows are here to hear it—what?"

"No harm in asking him," said Harry.

Peter nodded, and went over to Bunter, who was sprawling in an armchair, with a cheery and satisfied grin on his fat face.

A score of fellows exchanged glances and gathered round, many of them grinning. Bunter's fiver was a matter not only of interest, but almost of excitement, in the Remove now. The bare possibility that he had a banknote that was not his own was startling, and it looked more and more like it. Anyhow, if it were his own, he could, of course, state exactly where it had come from. Peter's idea was to extract that statement in the presence of all the Form, and thus knock on the head the rumours on the subject.

"Where did you get that fiver, Bunter?" asked Peter Todd, coming directly to the point.

"Eh? My pater sent it, of course," answered Bunter, blinking at him.

Truth and Bunter were total strangers. But, really, he could hardly have explained that he had got it from a Fifth Form man's wastepaper-basket!

"By post?" asked Peter.

"Eh? He didn't walk in with it!" answered Bunter. "Wharrer you mean, Toddy? No bizney of yours, is it?"

"It happens that it is," said Peter. "Some of the fellows seem to have noticed that you never had a letter to-day—see?"

"Oh, it came yesterday!" said Bunter.

"And you kept it dark?" asked Vernon-Smith, with a grin.

Bunter blinked at him.

"Oh, really, Smithy, I'm not a chap like you, you know, to swank all over the shop with a banknote! I just shoved it in my pocket and forgot it."

"I can see you doing it!" remarked Skinner.

"So it came by post yesterday, did it?" chuckled Hazeldene. "And after we got our letters yesterday, you tried to touch me for a bob because your postal order hadn't come!"

"It came by the afternoon post," explained Bunter calmly. "Quelch sent for me to his study and handed it to me."

"Quelch did?" yelled Peter.

"Certainly!"

"Quelch went out with Prout after class, and never came back till nearly calling over!" roared Peter.

"Oh!" gasped Bunter. "I—I forgot that! I—I mean, I—I—I mean, he sent for me just before he went out, and handed me the letter—see?"

"Just about the time when you asked me whether he had gone out or not?" inquired Skinner.

"Yes—I mean, no!"

"Ha, ha, ha!"

"You fat ass!" exclaimed Bob Cherry. "Can't you ever tell the truth? You were asking all of us whether Quelch had gone out!"

"That—that was after I saw him in his study. I—I told you I saw him in his study."

"Yes; and you told us you were after his beastly cake, and that you'd asked him a question about prep, as he was there!" snorted Bob. "What are you telling lies for, you fat chump? You'll make fellows believe you've got hold of somebody else's banknote at this rate."

"Oh, really, Cherry——"

Peter Todd was eyeing the fat Owl very doubtfully now. He had brought this matter out before all the Form to prove that the banknote really was Bunter's. It began to look now as if he were going to prove something quite different.

"Now, look here, Bunter," said Peter, "I suppose you can't help telling crammers—it's your nature to! But you've got to cough up the truth this time—for your own sake, you fatheaded Ananias! Where did you get that fiver?"

"Oh, really, Toddy, anybody might think that my uncle never sends me a tip at this rate!"

"Your uncle?" gasped Peter.

"Yes," said Bunter warmly. "I've had tips from my uncle before, lots of times. He happens to have sent me a fiver this time, that's all."

"You said it came from your pater!" shrieked Peter.

"Oh—I—I mean——"

"Let's hear what you mean, by all means!" grinned Skinner. "By gum, I wonder whose fiver that is?"

"Oh, really, Skinner, it's mine, of course!"

"And your pater and your uncle sent it together?" chortled Snoop.

"Well, it was like this," explained Bunter—"it was really a tip from my uncle, but my pater sent it, as he was writing—see?"

The Remove fellows gazed at Bunter. Any other fellow might, or might not, have had letters, and nobody would have been the wiser. But it was well known that Bunter had had none. That day and the previous day he had scanned the rack with his big spectacles, in the delusive hope that his celebrated postal order might have arrived, and there had been no letters for Bunter. Nobody was likely to believe that he had tried to borrow "bobs" and "tanners" up and down the Remove with a banknote in his pocket.

"Will you tell the truth for once, you blithering chump?" hissed Peter. "Every fellow here knows that you haven't had a letter this week."

"Oh! I had it on Saturday!"

"You—you—you had it on Saturday, when you've just told us that you had it yesterday afternoon, when Quelch handed it to you in his study!" stuttered Peter.

"I—I forgot!" Billy Bunter sat up in the armchair and blinked at the crowd of fellows indignantly. "Look here, it's my bizney, ain't it?" he demanded. "What does it matter to you, I'd like to know? Asking a fellow a lot of impertinent questions!"

Peter Todd breathed hard.

"You never had that fiver by post at all," he said. "Will you tell us how you got it?"

"For goodness' sake, Bunter——" urged Bob Cherry.

Bob was backing up Bunter automatically, as it were, because he saw in this a new move of Carter's! But he was quite dismayed now.

Only too clearly Bunter was unable to account for the possession of that five-pound note! And if a fellow was in possession of a banknote for which he could not account, what did it and could it mean? Nobody, of course, could guess that it meant that a fatuous ass had sorted a dud banknote out of a waste-paper-basket, wholly and solely for purpose of swank!

"Bunter, old man," said Harry Wharton, "cough it up! Don't tell any more silly fibs! You're making fellows believe you pinched that banknote."

"Not much doubt about it now!" said Skinner. "Whose is it, Bunter?"

"It's mine!" yelled Bunter, indignantly.

"Yes, we know it's yours, Bunter!" said Bob. "But do tell the fellows where it came from."

"I don't mind telling you," said Bunter. "Why should I? I—I didn't exactly mean that it came by post, you know! I meant——"

Bunter paused.

"Now he's making up the next one!" remarked Skinner. "He's got it into his head that we know it never came by post. Give him time—even Bunter wants a minute or two to make up a good one!"

"Oh, shut up, Skinner!" growled Bob. "Now, Bunter, old man——"

"The fact is——" Bunter paused again.

"Trot out the fact!" chuckled the Bounder. "Listen-in, everybody! We don't often get facts from Bunter!"

"Ha, ha, ha!"

"The fact is," said Bunter at last, "that fiver never came by post at all. I—I happened to meet my Uncle George in Courtfield on Saturday, and he—he gave it to me."

"Let's have it clear!" said Skinner. "Did he give it to you before Quelch handed it to you in his study, or after?"

"Ha, ha, ha!"

"Beast! He—he gave it to me!" said Bunter. "A fiver's nothing to my uncle! My Uncle William's fearfully rich——"

"Your Uncle William!" gasped Bob.

"Yes, rolling in it," said Bunter. "More money than he knows what to do with really! He just handed me that fiver, as your uncle, Wharton, might have handed you a ten-shilling note!"

"You blithering idiot!"

"His Uncle William!" almost sobbed Skinner. "It was his Uncle George a few minutes ago!"

Bunter started.

"I—I mean my Uncle George!" he stammered. "I—I mean, to be exact, my Uncle William George! Sometimes I call him Uncle George, and sometimes Uncle William! That—that's how it is."

"Jolly odd that you met him, or them, in Courtfield on Saturday afternoon!" remarked Skinner.

"Eh! Why was it odd?" demanded Bunter.

"Because it was raining on Saturday afternoon, and you never went out of gates."

"Oh!" gasped Bunter.

"Liars should have good memories, you know!" said Skinner. "Try again, old fat man!"

"I—I meant Friday——"

"You meant Friday!" roared Peter Todd.

"Yes! I remember now, it was Friday, after class, that I met my Uncle Maurice in Friardale——"

"Oh crikey!"

"I—I mean, my Uncle George in Courtfield! That is, my Uncle William —I mean, William Maurice—that is, George!" Bunter seemed to be getting a little confused. "He—he came up to me and said 'Fancy meeting you, Billy! Here's a fiver for you!' Just like that! I said 'Thank you, Uncle Herbert'—I mean, William—that is, George!"

"Where did you get that fiver?" roared Peter.

"Haven't I just told you?" roared back Bunter. "Mean to say you don't believe me, you beast?"

"Believe you!" gasped Peter. "Be-

lieve that you got it on Monday, and on Saturday, and on Friday, and that it came by post from your pater, and that your Uncle William-George-Maurice-Herbert gave it to you in Courtfield, and in Friardale, too! No, I don't quite believe all that! Whose is it?"

"Mine!" yelled Bunter.

"You unspeakable idiot!" said Bob Cherry. "If it's yours, tell us how you got it?"

"I've told you!"

"Oh crikey!"

"Gentlemen, chaps, and blokes," said Skinner, "get ready to see a Remove man bunked from Greyfriars! I'll say good-bye now, Bunter, in case I don't see you again!"

"Ha, ha, ha!"

"Beast!"

"Bunter, old man," said Bob anxiously, "for goodness' sake——"

"Yah! Making out that a fellow's telling crammers!" said Billy Bunter, with deep indignation. "If you were as truthful as I am, Bob Cherry, you'd do! You never get a fiver for a tip—a half-crown is nearer your mark! Yah!"

Bob Cherry looked at him—and turned away in silence! He was resolved, so far as he could, to befriend the fatuous fat Owl against the machinations of his rival for riches. But there was no doubt that Bunter was a difficult fellow to befriend!

Bunter sat in the armchair, frowning, when he was left to himself! He was deeply annoyed. Fellows were as good as making out that he had pinched that fiver—which certainly he hadn't done! They had doubted his word, which was fearfully insulting! The fat Owl sat and frowned with indignation, while most of the fellows wondered how long it would be before he was spotted with somebody else's fiver, and sacked!

THE TWELFTH CHAPTER.
Bob Butts In!

"CHEEKY cad!"

"Ha, ha, ha!"

Six or seven fellows were in the lobby on Wednesday afternoon, and they were all grinning when Billy Bunter rolled in for his coat.

Bunter was—or was supposed to be—going to Courtfield that afternoon, as it was a half-holiday, to change that fiver, now famous in the Remove.

He had, as a matter of fact, no intention of walking anything like so far as Courtfield, as he had no banknote to change. He was going to change his mind instead of changing the fiver!

A very short walk was enough for Bunter at any time. It was a cold and windy afternoon, with a drift of mist from the sea, and Bunter rolled into the lobby for his overcoat.

Why the fellows there were grinning he did not know, till he went to hook down that coat! Then he glared.

Pinned to the coat was a card, and on the card was written in large letters:

"IN THIS STYLE!
3/11."

Bunter's coat was a little uncommon in the Remove. He had brought that overcoat back new that term, and was very pleased with it. Mr. Quelch had been seen to give it a grim glance.

It was a rule at Greyfriars that fellows dressed in dark, or, at least, inconspicuous colours. Smithy disregarded that rule sometimes, and it was known that he had been called to order for some of his waistcoats! But the Bounder had never ventured to dis-

regard it so recklessly as Bunter with that new overcoat.

It was of a light grey, with a rich purple stripe. Bunter had rather a gorgeous taste in colour, and his idea was that that coat looked really nobby! Other fellows had grey coats, though not such a conspicuous light grey; but no fellow excepting Bunter had a purple stripe.

When Bunter had that coat on he could be spotted from one extremity of the quad to the other, and after the term was a week old Bunter was tired of that coat and the jests of the other fellows about it.

He still thought that it looked very nobby and fearfully dressy, but he did wish that, on the whole, he had selected a rather less striking pattern.

But—though Quelch had regarded it with a grim eye, and the rest of the Remove jested about it—there was no help for it. It was the only overcoat Bunter had, and, in spite of the immense wealth of Bunter Court and the Bunter clan, the only one he was likely to have that winter.

For which reason Mr. Quelch, though he glared when he saw it, made no remark on the subject, though the Remove fellows made innumerable remarks.

This card stuck on the coat was evidently one of Skinner's little jokes. That coat, though far from expensive, had certainly cost more than three shillings and elevenpence.

"Cheeky cad!" repeated Bunter; and he jerked the card off the coat. "I say, you fellows, my tailor in Savile Row charged me ten guineas for that coat."

"He did you out of nine and a half, then," remarked Squiff.

"Nine and three-quarters," said Ogilvy.

"Ha, ha, ha!"

"I don't believe Bunter bought that coat at all," said Skinner. "More likely won it in a raffle."

Snort from Bunter. He was fed-up with jokes about the coat. However, he crammed his podgy person into it and rolled out, leaving the juniors chortling.

He passed his relative, Carter, near the door, and gave him an inimical blink.

He suspected that it was Carter who had started that talk about his fiver—as indeed it was. That talk was intensely annoying to Bunter. He wanted every fellow in the Form to know that he had a fiver, but he certainly did not want them to suspect him of having "pinched" the same.

In Carter's mind, it was not a suspicion, but a certainty. Perhaps the wish was father to the thought.

What puzzled him was, that nothing had been heard of a five-pound note being missing in the school.

How and where Bunter had got hold of it, Carter could not begin to guess; but that it did not belong to Bunter, he was assured. And it was really surprising that the owner had not missed it yet.

It was, however, bound to be missed, sooner or later, and then the young rascal would be "for it." Really, it was hardly necessary to scheme against a fellow like Bunter, who hunted so assiduously for trouble on his own.

"Changed your fiver yet?" asked Carter, with a very curious look at his fat relative.

"I'm going down to Courtfield to change it," answered Bunter, with dignity. "And I jolly well shan't

" Look 'ere," said the billiards-marker, as Wingate took the coat from the hook and looked at the tag that bore the name
" W. G. Bunter," " you leave that coat alone! " " This coat belongs to a Greyfriars boy," said the captain of Greyfriars,
" and if you don't stand aside, I'll knock you down ! "

lend you anything out of it, either."

And he rolled on, disdainful.

Carter stared after him, shrugging his shoulders. If that fat ass was really ass enough to change a bank-note that did not belong to him, he was done for, with a vengeance.

That he would not change it in the school, Carter knew, and from that he could draw only one conclusion. That he would not change it anywhere, Carter did not know, and could not guess.

Billy Bunter rolled down to the gates.

Harry Wharton & Co. were standing there, and Bob Cherry's eyes fell on Bunter as he approached. He was very visible to the eye in that coat.

"Here's that fat ass," muttered Bob. "Look here, we can't let him ——" He paused. "What do you fellows think? Is that fiver his or not?"

"Blessed if I know what to think!" confessed Harry Wharton. "Bunter wouldn't pinch—that's rot!—but he's fool enough to keep a fiver, if he picked it up."

"It's not his," said Johnny Bull. "He wouldn't have rolled out all those lies about it, if he came by it honestly."

"But nobody seems to have missed one," said Frank Nugent. "We should have heard by this time."

"It's not Bunter's," said Bob. "Goodness knows how he got hold of it, but it can't be his. He would tell lies about it, I suppose, if he'd borrowed it. But who'd lend Bunter a fiver?"

"Nobody would," said Johnny Bull. "If he borrowed it, the owner wasn't looking."

"He ought not to change it," said Bob uneasily. "He won't change it

in the school, and that looks—well, you know what it looks like. It just can't be his, and we can't let him land himself in awful trouble by changing it."

Grunt from Johnny Bull.

"Bunter knows whether it's his or not," he said. "If it isn't, he will be sacked as soon as he's spotted. And serve him jolly well right!"

"That's all very well," said Bob; "but he's such a fool Suppose he picked it up, and fancied that find-ings were keepings? He could hand it over, so long as he's got it; but if he changed it, it would be too late. That's stealing, though that fat idiot mightn't understand it. Look here, he's not going to take that fiver to Courtfield this afternoon."

"We can't stop him."

"I can; and I jolly well will!" said Bob.

"Games practice at two," said Harry.

"I shall have to cut it, then."

Billy Bunter rolled past the group of juniors in the gateway. Their eyes followed him, and they saw him start for the Courtfield road.

That settled it, for Bob Cherry.

He gave his friends a nod, turned away, and walked after Bunter.

The two of them disappeared up the road, and the Co. went in for games practice.

Bob was far from keen on cutting games practice that afternoon. But he was anxious about Bunter, and deter-mined, as it were, to save the fat Owl from himself.

He put on speed, and overtook the fat junior at a little distance from the school.

Bunter blinked round at him.

"Come for a walk this afternoon?" asked Bob.

"Eh? No!"

"Your mistake; you will," said Bob cheerfully; and he hooked hold of Bunter's fat arm, and turned him off the road by the first turning.

Bunter blinked at him in astonish-ment and wrath.

"Leggo my arm!" he roared.

"Rats!"

"What are you up to, you silly ass? What are you butting in for, I'd like to know?" bellowed Bunter.

"Taking you for a walk, old fat man," said Bob. "Anywhere you like but Courtfield. What about going along the towpath, as far as the bridge, and then home by Pegg and the woods? What?"

"You—you—you silly idiot!" gasped Bunter.

Bob was describing a ten-mile walk. Ten furlongs were too many for Bunter.

"Like the idea?"

"I'm not coming!" roared Bunter.

"You are!"

And Bunter did. So long as Bob Cherry had hold of his fat arm, there really was no choice in the matter.

THE THIRTEENTH CHAPTER.

Muddy !

BOB CHERRY swung cheerily along the towpath by the bank of the Sark.

He would have preferred footer, but he enjoyed a walk in keen, cold air.

Billy Bunter would not have pre-ferred footer, but he did not enjoy the walk. At almost every step, he turned a ferocious blink through his big spectacles on his companion. Why

Bob Cherry was butting in in this extraordinary manner, Bunter did not know; but he knew that he was not going to stand it, if he could help it.

"Will you leggo my arm, you beast?" he hissed, for the tenth time.

Bob let go the fat arm at last.

With the river on one side, and thick, wet woods on the other, Bunter had no chance of dodging. If he ran, he had no chance in a foot race, up or down the towpath. So Bob released the podgy arm.

"You cut, and I'll cut after you," he said. "I want your company this afternoon, old fat man."

"I don't want yours," hooted Bunter.

"Why not? You're in better company than I am."

"Beast!"

A figure appeared on the towpath. It was the Bounder, strolling up the river. Bob Cherry gave him a glance of disfavour.

Smithy was not out on a walk, as he could easily guess. There was a gate to the Three Fishers in the towpath farther on, and Bob could easily guess that that was the Bounder's destination. He more than suspected Carter of haunting the same disreputable spot; but if that were the case, Carter was a good deal more careful and cautious about it than the reckless Bounder.

Billy Bunter was lagging, or rather, crawling, and Bob had to accommodate his pace to the crawl of the fat Owl. So Smithy, coming up the towpath, soon passed them, though he had left the school a good deal later.

Bob's disfavouring glance did not affect the "bad hat" of the Remove. But he slowed down, and glanced from one to the other of them. It was evident that Billy Bunter was being taken on an unwilling walk.

"I say, Smithy," exclaimed Bunter, "hold that beast while I clear off, will you?"

"What on earth's this game, Cherry?" asked Vernon-Smith.

"I'm taking Bunter for a walk."

"I don't want to go!" howled Bunter.

"Why the thump are you taking Bunter for a walk, if he doesn't want to go?" demanded the Bounder.

"Oh, just to keep him out of mischief!" answered Bob. "Like to come along? We're going to do ten miles."

"We're not!" shrieked Bunter.

"Oh, my hat! You'll have to roll him like a barrel for the last nine," said Smithy. "You're an ass, Cherry. If you stop him to-day, you can't stop him for ever."

"Well, I'm going to stop him to-day, at any rate!" grunted Bob.

"What rot! If he chooses to do these things, why not let him take what's coming to him?"

"Rats!"

The Bounder laughed and walked on. He guessed without difficulty why Bob was taking Bunter for that walk—to keep him from changing the banknote at Courtfield.

That had not occurred to Billy Bunter's fat brain. As he had not, in point of fact, the remotest intention of changing the banknote, he was not thinking about that at all, and Bob's butting-in was inexplicable to him.

The fat Owl was paying rather dearly for his swank. Had Bob been aware of the real nature of that banknote he would not have butted in, and Bunter would not have been landed with that walk

Now he was landed with it, unless he could escape—but he was going to escape if he could.

He lagged more and more. Bob slowed down. Billy Bunter's eyes gleamed behind his spectacles.

He was no fighting-man—and, had he been, Bob was not the adversary he would have selected as a matter of choice. But he was getting desperate. He had to get away from the beast somehow.

"Buck up!" said Bob cheerily.

"Beast!" roared Bunter.

"Shall I help you with my boot?"

"Rotter!"

Bob dropped behind Bunter and lifted his foot; he stood for a moment on one leg. That was Bunter's chance—and he whirled round suddenly on Bob, and a fat fist thumped.

"Oh!" gasped Bob, as that thump with Bunter's weight behind it landed on his chest.

He went over backwards and crashed.

"Oh crikey!" gasped Bunter.

For an instant he blinked at Bob sprawling on his back, terrified at what he had done, but only for an instant; then he flew.

Bob sat up dizzily.

Bunter flew up the towpath like a runaway car. Seldom did Bunter put on speed, but he put it on now; he fairly whizzed.

Vernon-Smith had disappeared round a winding turn of the river bank ahead.

Bunter came round the curve like a locomotive.

He was not thinking of Smithy. He had forgotten Smithy. He was only thinking of getting away from Bob Cherry. Anyone on the towpath would have been in danger with Bunter charging along at top speed. Smithy happened to be there—and he got it! Billy Bunter whizzed round the bend and crashed in the middle of Smithy's back like a thunderbolt.

The Bounder gave a gasping howl and pitched over He splashed at full length in a muddy puddle.

Bunter bumped down on him.

"Oooooogh!" came a gurgle from the hapless Bounder.

"Oh crikey!" spluttered Bunter. "What—what—— Was that somebody? Oh crikey!"

He staggered off the Bounder.

Vernon-Smith sat up in the puddle. Smithy was wearing a very handsome overcoat, but it did not look very handsome now; from collar to tail it was wet and smothered with mud. Mud clothed him like a garment, and the expression on his face was terrifying.

"Oh crumbs!" gasped Bunter, blinking at him. "Is—is—is that you, Smithy? I say, it was that beast Cherry's fault——"

Vernon-Smith tottered out of the puddle. He looked down at his coat—streaming with water, and caked with mud—with the look of a demon in a pantomime.

"You—you—you——" he gasped. "Look what you've done! You—you——"

Probably it was fortunate for Bunter that Bob Cherry came cutting round the bend of the towpath. He was not far behind Bunter.

Vernon-Smith, with a furious face, was about to hurl himself at the fat Owl.

Bunter dodged promptly behind Bob. Bob Cherry was the lesser of two evils now.

"I—I say, keep that beast off, old chap!" gasped Bunter. "I say, he got in my way, you know——"

"Steady on, Smithy——" gasped Bob.

"Look at my coat!" yelled the Bounder. "I'll smash him! I'll mop him all over the towpath! I'll——"

"Well, it does look a bit muddy," agreed Bob. "But——"

"Let me get at that fat fool!" roared Vernon-Smith

Bob made soothing gestures, with Bunter behind him.

"You can't punch Bunter, old chap! He would burst if you punched him. Look here, we're only a mile from the school; you can cut in and change your coat——"

"I've got an appointment to keep, you fool!"

Bob's lip curled.

"I can guess what it is. All the better for you if you don't keep it!" he retorted.

The Bounder gave him a black look.

"I don't want any sermons from you, you dummy! I can't go into a place like this! Let me have your coat."

"Guess again!" grinned Bob.

"Then I'll have Bunter's. I can't keep this on!"

"Oh, really, Smithy——"

"Are they fearfully particular at the Three Fishers?" inquired Bob Cherry sarcastically.

"Oh, shut up!" snarled the Bounder. He whipped off his mud-drenched overcoat. They were not particular at the Three Fishers, but the Bounder had no intention of walking in dripping mud.

"Here you are, Bunter. You can put this on if you like; I'm having yours."

"You're jolly well not!" roared Bunter. "It's all muddy——"

"That's why you're going to have it!"

"Beast!"

The Bounder flung the muddy coat at Bunter. It fell on the towpath.

Billy Bunter eyed it with disdain. Not if he could help it was Bunter going to don that mud-caked garment.

"Well, that's only fair," said Bob Cherry. "You did it, Bunter. Let Smithy have your coat."

"Shan't!" roared Bunter indignantly.

"Then you can argue it out with Smithy," said Bob, stepping aside.

"I—I—I mean you—you—you can have my coat, Smithy, old chap!" gasped Bunter in a great hurry. He was not disposed to argue it out with the enraged Bounder. Smithy looked rather too dangerous for argument.

"Get a move on, you fat fool!" snarled the Bounder. He was by no means pleased at the idea of wearing Bunter's remarkable coat, but he had to have a coat.

Billy Bunter unwillingly stripped off his overcoat.

Vernon-Smith, with a scowling face, put it on and tramped away up the towpath.

Bunter picked up the mud-drenched coat and eyed it in a very gingerly manner. Bunter was not very particular about his garments, but that coat was really in an awful state. But there was a chill winter wind blowing along the river, and the fat Owl put it on.

Then he turned his spectacles on Bob Cherry with a ferocious blink.

"Look here, you beast, I can't go for a walk in this! You know I can't! I'm going back to the school! See?"

Bob Cherry laughed.

"You can go back to the school if you like, old fat man," he answered. "I'll come along with you. You can go anywhere you like but Courtfield."

"Eh? I wasn't going to Courtfield!" said Bunter.

"Oh, chuck it. you fat Ananias!"

"I mean——"

"Never mind what you mean! Get a move on, one way or the other."

Bunter got a move on—in the direction of the school. He grinned as he got the move on.

It dawned on his fat brain what Bob was thinking. Bunter had talked about going to Courtfield to change that fiver, simply to keep up the impression that it was a real fiver that he could change

if he liked. He had intended to walk about for a while, and return with some unveracious explanation why he had not changed it. Now Bob Cherry had provided him with an explanation ready made, as it were. He hadn't been able to go to Courtfield because Bob had butted in. So the fat Owl grinned cheerily as he rolled back to Greyfriars with Bob Cherry.

THE FOURTEENTH CHAPTER.
Soccer for Bunter !

"WHERE'S your boots?"
　　　"I don't want my boots!"
　　　"Do you want mine?"
　　　"Beast!"

If Billy Bunter had been exasperated when Bob Cherry started him on a long

(Continued on next page.)

LEARN TO PLAY FOOTBALL!
OUR INTERNATIONAL COACH

COMPLETE UNDERSTANDING IS NECESSARY !

IF I could have taken an aeroplane and flown all over England during this past week, I wonder on how many football grounds, or in how many back gardens or quiet streets I would have seen young goalkeepers trying to improve their job by practising with a tennis ball? I am not a schoolmaster, and therefore cannot watch over you all the time to make sure that you do the "lessons" which I set you. But I should be very disappointed if I thought that there were not a great number of you who try to do the things I suggest by way of practice.

Those of you who have been practising along the lines I suggested will have learned a good deal about goalkeeping that you didn't know before. Now I want to show you how really good goalkeepers take a part in the general defensive scheme of a football side. This defensive scheme is probably the most frequently discussed and the most highly developed phase of Soccer tactics.

I expect you noticed a great deal of discussion, in the newspapers earlier in the season, about a secret defensive plan which Charlton Athletic had devised, and which was helping them to win their matches. I can't give you any inside information about Charlton's secret plans, but I can assure you that great trouble is taken by the first-class clubs in the organisation of their defences.

The first important thing is that the goalkeeper should have a complete understanding with the full-backs who play in front of him. This can be brought about largely, of course, by constantly playing together, but a great deal can be done in a little "pow-wow" together before the match starts.

AND CO-OPERATION, TOO !

IN many teams it is an agreed thing, for example, that when the ball comes inside the goal area—that is, the six yards line—the goalkeeper shall deal with it. Whether the ball is in the air or on the ground, the full-backs can be certain that when the ball is inside that area, the goalkeeper can be left to do his clearance job. Occasions arise, of course, when there is some doubt in the mind of a full-back or the goalkeeper as to who should take a certain ball. How do they get over

With complete understanding with his partner and the goalkeeper, coupled with a keen sense of positional play, a full-back should be able to hold up most attackers who come his way.

that sort of difficulty? Next time you see a big football match, listen carefully, and I guarantee that in the course of the game you will repeatedly hear the goalkeepers yelling at their full-backs, or vice-versa: "O.K., Joe!" "Leave it!" "Let it come!" or such-like. You see if I am not right. And those shouts are most essential.

Defenders can't afford to make mistakes—they must know all the time what their colleagues are doing. Nor must there be any question of doubting the wisdom of a colleague's shout. If a full-back tells the goalkeeper to come out to take the ball, the goalkeeper must come out, without hesitation, as hard as he can. Complete understanding and co-operation. They are the essentials if the goalkeeper and full-backs are to make up a really strong defence.

Don't think that the helping is all done by the goalkeeper, however. The full-backs must always be ready to help the goalkeeper when he is in trouble. How often do you see, in reports of matches, that such-and-such a side were unlucky not to score a goal when a full-back kicked the ball off the goal-line after the goalkeeper had been beaten? Don't be so sure that it was all luck. The full-back went into the goalmouth because he saw that there was trouble coming, and he wanted to be there to help.

Take a look at the Arsenal defenders when their goal is being attacked. You will often see both full-backs as well as the goalkeeper, standing on the goal-line. And if the 'keeper leaves his goal, the full-backs are always there in case he misses the ball, and a shot comes in. Literally, dozens of goals must have been prevented in this way. Remember, too, that when the goalkeeper is taking a goal-kick, one of the full-backs should fall back into the goalmouth, in case the kick is a bad one, or the ball is blown back. I have seen that happen before now.

POSITIONAL PLAY !

SPECTATORS at football matches shout many funny things—some sensible, some absolutely ridiculous. I always think that the silliest people are those who make a habit of shouting "windy" when a full-back, to get himself out of a tight corner, passes back to his goalkeeper. These people, in my opinion, show that they don't know much about football. There are times when the only really safe course is to pass back to your goalkeeper. If you are hard pressed by attackers, it is far better to pass back to the goalkeeper, who can take an uninterrupted punt down-field, than to run the risk of losing the ball. So please, when you watch a football match, don't shout "windy" at a pass-back to the goalkeeper. And remember this very useful dodge when you are playing yourselves.

In addition to helping and covering their goalkeeper, it is the duty of full-backs to cover one another, and, most important, to cover their centre-half. Full-backs are usually told to mark the opposing wingers. That means they must play fairly near the wings—wide apart. They must always have an eye open for a slip by the centre-half, however, which will let the opposing forwards through down the centre of the field. Or, in extreme cases, they must be prepared to go right across to the other side of the field to help one another.

The full-backs' duties, perhaps more than those of any other player, require a great deal of concentration and an ability to anticipate. That is why some of the best full-backs in the game are the "old men," the fellows who have had years of experience. Positional play is the important thing for a full-back. Speed is not absolutely essential. I don't mean that speed is not useful. There aren't many better full-backs in the world to-day than Bert Sproston, of Leeds, and Eddie Hapgood, of Arsenal. These two players can sprint as fast as most wingers.

But if a full-back has complete understanding with his partner and his goalkeeper, and a keen sense of positional play—and by positional play I don't mean keeping in the same position all the time, but being in the right position at the right time—he will be better able to hold up attacks.

walk, he was doubly and trebly exasperated when they got back to Greyfriars. Bob had walked him straight to the changing-room.

As he was back in the school Bob saw no reason why he should not join his friends at games practice. As he had resolved to keep an eye on Bunter all that afternoon, Bunter had to join up at games practice also; there was nothing else to be done, so far as Bob could see.

But the idea of joining up for games practice when it was not a compulsory day simply infuriated Billy Bunter. Compulsory days were bad enough, but to play footer when he might have slacked in an armchair and frowsted over a fire was the limit and a little over.

Bunter's very spectacles gleamed with rage.

"Look here, you beast!" he roared. "I know what your game is. You want to keep me from changing my banknote."

"Here's your shirt!"

"I won't go to Courtfield. I'll give you my word! There!"

"I'd take it, if it was of any value," agreed Bob. "As it isn't, you can keep it. Get that shirt on!"

"I wasn't really going to change that banknote!" hissed Bunter. "I—I'm going to save it up for—for the holidays!"

"Here's your boots!"

"Can't I change my own banknote if I like, you beast?"

"You can't change anybody else's. Are you going to change for footer, or do you want me to boot you round the room?"

Billy Bunter gave him an infuriated blink. At that moment he came very near admitting the truth—that the celebrated banknote was a "dud," which Coker of the Fifth had been ass enough to throw into the wastepaper-basket!

That, of course, would have explained the whole matter, and Bob would have been concerned about him no longer.

But it was not easy for Bunter to part with his swank. The facts, if known, would cause one tremendous yell of laughter in the Remove. Bunter was not keen on setting the Remove in a roar by admitting that he had rescued a worthless slip of paper from a wastepaper-basket wholly and solely for the purpose of showing off!

Even games practice, awful as it was, was better than that.

"How long are you going to be?" demanded Bob impatiently. "If you want me to help you with my boot——"

"Beast! I'm not going——"

Thud!

"Ow!" roared Bunter. "Stop kicking me, you beast! Where's my shirt? Ow! I'm changing, ain't I, you rotter?"

The largest foot in the Greyfriars Remove was an unanswerable argument. Bunter changed for footer.

"Now come on, you fat, lazy slacker!" growled Bob, "and, mind, if you try to dodge away we'll jolly well use you for a football!"

"Beast!"

Bob marched the exasperated fat Owl down to Little Side, where a good many of the Remove were at practice, Bunter's objection to the same not being general in the Remove.

Harry Wharton & Co. stared at Bunter in surprise as he arrived on the scene with Bob. Even on compulsory days it was often necessary for a boot to help Bunter down to games practice. On other occasions he was never seen there.

"Bunter keen on footer for once?" asked the captain of the Remove.

"Oh, fearfully keen!" said Bob. "At any rate, he prefers it to a ten-mile walk. Don't you, Bunter?"

"I say, you fellows, I'm not staying here!" howled Bunter. "Look here, Wharton, that beast's dragged me down here. 'Tain't a compulsory day——"

"Why not play up for the love of the thing?" suggested Harry Wharton, laughing. "Show us how you can beat Squiff in goal!"

"I'll show you another time. The fact is, I've got a pain! You know that cad, Carter, hacked me in practice the other day. And he'd do it again if he got the chance, too——"

"That's all right. Carter's not here to-day. He's gone out of gates."

"Yes; but I've still got a fearful pain in my leg——"

"Which leg?" asked Bob Cherry.

"I forget——"

"Ha, ha, ha!"

"I—I mean the right leg—an awful, excruciating pain——"

"I'll give you one to match, in the other!" said Bob, drawing back a foot.

"Keep off, you beast!" Bunter dodged promptly. "Look here, Wharton——"

"Oh, shut up, and play up!" said the captain of the Remove. "You're no use, and you're no ornament; but Bob's taking the trouble to keep you out of mischief—and that's that! You'll be jolly glad you haven't changed that banknote when the owner turns up and asks for it."

"The gladfulness will be terrific, my esteemed idiotic Bunter!" grinned Hurree Jamset Ram Singh.

"I say, you fellows——"

"'Nuff said!" interrupted Harry Wharton. "Shut up, and play up! All you fellows keep an eye on him, and boot him back if he tries to bolt."

"Ha, ha, ha!"

There was no help for Bunter! During the next hour the fat Removite was able to learn from experience what a Soccer ball felt like! About a dozen times he essayed to flee, but there was always an eye on him, and a boot ready to stop him!

Gasping and spluttering, panting and gurgling, Bunter had to go through with it, and when the practice was over he tottered off the field, certainly not in a state to walk to Courtfield—if he had wanted to! He could hardly walk to the changing-room!

The Remove footballers had long changed, and gone, when Billy Bunter crawled out at last. He crawled as far as the Rag, where he collapsed in an armchair, and did not stir again until a sudden grab at his fat shoulder caused him to blink round with a squeak of indignant protest.

THE FIFTEENTH CHAPTER.

Carter Sees It All!

ARTHUR CARTER stopped suddenly and caught his breath.

He stared, as if he could hardly believe his eyes.

Indeed, he hardly could!

The new fellow in the Remove had emerged from a woodland path, on to the towpath by the Sark, at a little distance from the gate of the Three Fishers.

That delectable resort was Carter's destination, but he was a good deal more cautious about it than the Bounder. Not only from beaks and prefects, but from his Form-fellows in the Remove, he concealed his shady ways, so far as he could. He had no intention of changing the ways that had caused him to be turfed out of his last school; but he was not going to suffer the same fate at Greyfriars as at St. Olaf's if caution and cunning could save him

He had walked out of the school as if going to Courtfield, dodged into the wood at a distance from Greyfriars, and followed secluded and winding tracks to reach the towpath. No one, he was assured, had seen him on his way—and no one was going to see him go into the riverside inn that had such a lurid reputation. He had to take the risk of meeting there some other young rascal like himself; but even that he would have avoided, if he could. He knew nothing of the Bounder's plans for that afternoon.

Emerging on the towpath, he looked quickly up and down the river. He was not more than a dozen yards from the end of the Three Fishers' fence.

The gate was farther on; but he did not intend to go in openly by the gate. There was a gap in the palings nearer at hand, through which any fellow could squeeze—a gap he knew well. His game was to stroll slowly past that spot, and when he was quite sure that no eye was on him, squeeze through the gap in the palings and vanish within.

But what he saw as he looked up the towpath towards the fence quite changed his ideas. He stood and stared.

Some fellow ahead of him was in the very act of squeezing in through that gap in the Three Fishers' fence.

And that fellow, unless he was dreaming, was Billy Bunter!

As the fellow had his head and shoulders inside the fence when Carter spotted him from the rear, he could not, of course, see his face.

All he could see of him was a disappearing overcoat!

But he knew that overcoat.

Every fellow in the Remove knew that light-grey overcoat, with the purple stripes!

It was Bunter's, and there was no other coat like it in the school!

True, fellows did borrow one another's overcoats occasionally. But no fellow was likely to borrow that overcoat of Bunter's unless he was very hard pushed for a coat! And that it had not happened Carter knew, for he had seen the fat Owl walk out of the House in it!

He had not seen Bunter since, or thought about him! But he saw him now—at all events, he saw his overcoat, and had no doubt that Bunter was inside it. How could he have, when he had seen Bunter walk out in that coat?

He stood as if spellbound, watching that overcoat as it squeezed through the fence, and finally disappeared!

"By gum!" breathed Carter.

He stepped back quickly into the wood. If Bunter looked out, he did not want Bunter to see him—that fat ass, that pincher of banknotes, had gone into the Three Fishers—a place strictly out of bounds for all Greyfriars fellows. He was doing what Carter had been sacked from St. Olaf's for doing! Old Mr. Carter had turned his nephew down, with grim sternness, and was thinking of making Bunter his heir if he had good reports of him! And here was Bunter, doing exactly what Carter had done, with the same penalty to face if he were spotted!

Carter's eyes glittered.

He had never suspected Bunter of this! He had suspected him of every-

" Every fellow in this room knows that you pinched that banknote, Bunter ! " said Carter, knowing full well that Mr. Quelch was passing the open window at that moment. " You can shut up, Carter ! " bawled the fat Removite. " Don't speak to me, you cad—you know I bar you ! "

thing of which he was, so to speak, suspectable ! But this kind of thing he had never suspected !

But Carter could believe the evidence of his own eyes ! He had noticed nothing of the kind before, but, after all, he had been only a few weeks at Greyfriars. The fat Owl was always short of money, and that, no doubt, kept him from kicking over the traces. But he had five pounds in his pocket now !

Carter saw it all.

At least, he had no doubt that he did ! Bunter had pinched that fiver, to expend in blackguardly occupations, among the sporting set at the Three Fishers !

It was clear as noonday to Carter !

"The fat rotter !" breathed Carter. "And I never knew ! I'm pretty keen, I fancy, but I never knew this ! By gum ! If he were spotted there——"

His thoughts were moving rapidly now.

The fellow in that overcoat had just gone in. He was not likely to come out yet—especially if he had five pounds to blow. More likely than not, he would remain at the Three Fishers till it was time to return to the school for calling over. At any rate, he was sure to remain there some time.

Carter threaded his way back through the wood to the Courtfield road. His mind was quite made up.

This fellow, no better than himself, probably worse, was the fellow who was cutting him out with the "old bean." Well, the old bean would not get good reports of a fellow spotted pub-haunting ! If Bunter was caught, he might be expelled, or only flogged, but in either case, he was done for with old Mr. Carter ! Having disinherited one young blackguard, the "old bean" was not likely to take another into his

favour ! Carter's game was won— Bunter had won it for him, if he were spotted where he was now !

Carter did not turn his steps in the direction of the school when he reached the Courtfield road. He was not thinking of giving information to Bunter's Form-master. His life would hardly have been worth living at Greyfriars if he had, and neither was it likely that Mr. Quelch would have listened to a sneak. He had formed a much more cunning scheme than that.

At the corner of Oak Lane, he caught the motor-bus, which dropped him in Courtfield High Street. There, he walked into the post office, to use the telephone to speak to Dr. Locke at Greyfriars.

With perfect coolness, he rang up Greyfriars School.

He felt a slight tremor as the voice of his headmaster came back over the wires. He could not help wondering what Dr. Locke would have thought, had he known that it was a Greyfriars junior who had rung him. But the Head was not going to know that.

"Dr. Locke——" said Carter, making his voice as deep and husky as he could, to give the impression that it was a man speaking.

"Dr. Locke speaking !" came back the Head's voice.

Carter paused a second. Perhaps he felt a twinge of remorse for what he was going to do. If so, it did not last long.

"Pray excuse me, sir !" he said, in the same deep tones. "I feel it my duty to tell you that I saw a Greyfriars boy entering an exceedingly disreputable resort a short time ago——"

"Who is speaking?"

"George Smith, sir ! Furniture-remover, at Courtfield !" answered Carter, with calm assurance. "I was

passing the place called the Three Fishers, on the towpath, when I saw a boy in a Greyfriars cap entering the place. I felt that you ought to know."

"Can you tell me the boy's name ?"

"I have never seen him before, sir !" said Carter calmly. "I knew by his cap that he belonged to Greyfriars, that is all."

"You are sure of this, Mr. Smith ?"

"Quite, sir ! I trust you will not think me interfering, but in view of the dreadful reputation of that resort——"

"I am much obliged to you, Mr. Smith ! I shall inquire into the matter immediately."

Carter smiled sourly as he left the post office. Dr. Locke might regard "Mr. Smith" as an officious person, but he could hardly disregard such information.

Dr. Locke, in his study at Greyfriars, sat for some moments in frowning thought after he had replaced the receiver. Then he rang, and sent Trotter to call Wingate of the Sixth to the study.

THE SIXTEENTH CHAPTER.

Smithy's Narrow Escape !

CLICK !

Herbert Vernon-Smith smiled —and Ponsonby, of Highcliffe, scowled. It was the Bounder's sixth cannon in succession.

There were three people in the dingy, smoke-scented billiards-room at the Three Fishers. Smithy was playing— Pon resting the butt of his cue on the floor and watching him; and a shabby, boozy-looking marker chewing a cigarette. With a "quid" on the game, the dandy of Highcliffe was anxious for Smithy to score a miss—

while Smithy, on the other hand, looked likely to run out

The Bounder of Greyfriars had a skill, in the game of billiards, that was no credit to him. He could, as a matter of fact, play Pon's head off as easily at billiards as at Soccer. He had given Pon thirty in the hundred, and was still easily ahead, and winning. With Pon at sixty, and the Bounder at ninety, and still making cannons, it looked as if Pon's "quid" was a goner.

For which reason, Pon frowned, and Smithy smiled. The "quid" mattered nothing to Smithy, who had more money than was good for him, but he was always keen to win any game to which he set his hand, and he liked to defeat an opponent. He ran on with cannon after cannon.

The "bad hat" of the Remove was enjoying his half-holiday, in his own way. He was quite well aware that he would have done better to join his chum Redwing, who was with Harry Wharton & Co. at games practice that afternoon. He knew, too, that he liked football better than billiards, and fresh air much more than a smoke-laden atmosphere. But when the urge of blackguardism was on him, he was not the fellow to resist it.

It was the risk, as much as anything else, that appealed to the reckless Bounder. The fact that he would be expelled, if he were spotted, would have stopped another fellow—but it added a sort of zest to the Bounder's enjoyment. He liked to feel himself at war with beaks and prefects, and getting the best of it.

Bunter's overcoat hung on a peg, Smithy's cap lay on a chair. His half-smoked cigarette lay in an ash-tray, burning away. Intent on his game, the Bounder was thinking for the moment only of his play. But reckless as he was, he would have thrown aside his cue fast enough, had he been able to guess how Carter of the Remove had been occupied in the post office at Courtfield. But he was not, of course, thinking of Carter; neither, if he had thought of him, would he have thought of him as a sneak who would give a fellow away to punishment.

Click!

Pon's eyes glittered unpleasantly. His "quid" was as good as gone now, with Smithy at ninety-eight, and the balls left for another easy cannon. To his surprise, the Bounder missed the next shot.

Smithy grinned, as he propped the butt of his cue. He could have carried on quite easily, but he had muffed a shot, simply to give Pon a chance. Ponsonby was quite unaware of it; it was not a thing he would have done himself.

Ponsonby chalked his cue.

The Bounder lighted a fresh cigarette, and strolled across to the french windows, which gave on the ragged, ill-kept gardens, stretching away to the fence on the towpath. One side of the window stood open, and Smithy put his head out for a breath of fresh air.

The next instant, his head popped back, like that of a tortoise into its shell.

In that instant, Smithy had had a glimpse of an athletic figure coming up the path to the french windows of the billiards-room.

He recognised Wingate, of the Greyfriars Sixth; but he popped back too swiftly for the prefect to see him.

For a second, the Bounder's brain was in a whirl.

It was a Greyfriars prefect, coming directly to that door—which meant, and

could only mean, that he knew that a Greyfriars fellow was there, and was coming solely and specially to nail him.

Smithy had reason to be glad that he had given Pon that chance. Had he gone on playing, Wingate would have walked right in and caught him in the very act. As it was, he had a few seconds—no more!

Pon, taking his shot, gave a jump, and the marker turned round, staring, as Vernon-Smith made a bound back from the window. He passed the chair on which his cap lay, snatched it up in passing, and darted through an inner doorway, almost with the speed of lightning.

He did not speak—there was no time for speech, no time to snatch his coat; no time for anything, but to cut instantly, and there was barely time for that.

As the inner door closed behind the escaping Bounder, Wingate of the Sixth appeared in the open french windows. It was the narrowest escape of the Bounder's reckless career at Greyfriars.

"What the dooce——" snapped the Highcliffe junior, staring. Then, as he saw the Greyfriars prefect, he understood.

The marker gave Wingate a bleary stare, and moved to place his back against the door by which Vernon-Smith had escaped.

The Greyfriars Sixth Former stepped in.

His glance shot swiftly round the room. He was acting on his headmaster's instructions; if a Greyfriars fellow was there, it was the prefect's duty to collar him. And collared the Bounder certainly would have been, had he acted a little less swiftly.

Ponsonby stared at Wingate with cool impudence. The Highcliffe fellow had nothing to fear from a Greyfriars prefect; and he was quite indifferent to what Wingate might think of him.

The marker gave Wingate a beery grin.

"Table's engaged jest now, sir!" he said, "but——"

Wingate gave him a look of contempt.

"A Greyfriars boy was here, I think," he said, "where is he now?" Wingate had not failed to note the marker's movement towards the door that had shut, even as he looked in.

"Nobody here, sir, 'cept me and this young gentleman, 'aving 'undred up!" said the marker, with beery affability.

Wingate made no answer.

He had just missed his quarry. He could not, of course, think of looking through an establishment like the Three Fishers, in search of him. All that was left was to hurry out and nail the young rascal, if he could, before he had time to get clear. Then his eyes fell on the coat on the peg.

With a grim look he stepped towards it.

He had seen that coat before.

Neither Pon nor the marker knew that it was not Smithy's own coat.

Pon, watching the Greyfriars prefect, wondered whether there was anything in the coat to identify the wearer; in which case, Smithy's game was up! But the marker quickly interposed. The beery man did not want to lose one of his most open-handed patrons.

"'Ere, you leave that coat alone!" he said. "It belongs to this young gentleman—don't it, sir?"

Pon was by no means eager to admit the possession of such a coat as that! But he played up.

"Yes, that's my coat!" he said. "Leave it alone, please!"

Unheeding either of them, Wingate

took down the coat. It was possible, of course, that there were dozens of such coats; though there was none other like it at Greyfriars. But every garment, at Greyfriars, had to have the owner's name in it, and Wingate looked at the tag that bore the name.

"W. G. Bunter."

"Look 'ere, you leave that coat alone!" said the marker.

"This coat belongs to a Greyfriars boy, whose name is in it!" said Wingate coolly and contemptuously. "I shall take it away with me."

"You won't!" said the marker, and he came towards the Greyfriars captain, with a bullying, threatening air, stepping between him and the french windows.

Wingate put the coat over his left arm.

"Stand aside, or I shall knock you down!" he said quietly.

He advanced as he spoke, and the beery man backed out of the way.

Wingate walked out, the coat on his arm.

Ponsonby whistled.

"That does it!" he remarked.

"Anything in the coat, to give 'im away, you think?" asked the marker.

"They have their names in their coats, I believe."

"Oh crimes! That lets him in."

Herbert Vernon-Smith was already dropping on the safe side of a distant fence—coatless!

Wingate, with the coat over his arm, walked back to Greyfriars School; and as he entered the gates, he passed a Remove junior—who glanced at the coat on his arm, and smiled as he saw it.

THE SEVENTEENTH CHAPTER.

Carter is Pleased!

CARTER smiled.

He felt he had reason to smile.

Wingate did not notice him—but Carter's eyes followed the prefect as he went on towards the House, with Bunter's coat over his arm.

Carter had lost no time in getting back to Greyfriars, after his exploit on the post office telephone. He had been back some time; waiting in the gateway, eagerly curious to see what was to follow. That the Head would take some step in the matter, after receiving such information, he was fairly certain: but precisely what step would be taken, he could not know. But he had every hope of seeing William George Bunter marched in, with a prefect or a master in charge of him.

Bunter's coat, on Wingate's arm, told him all that he wanted to know. He had last seen that coat disappearing through the fence of the Three Fishers, so there was no doubt that Wingate had found it. The young rascal must have been very nearly caught at the Three Fishers, but if he had escaped detection, he had had no time to put on his coat: he had left an unmistakable clue behind him; it was as good as a catch.

Carter smiled, an unpleasant smile, as he strolled towards the House after Wingate.

A good many eyes, as well as Carter's, fell on the Greyfriars captain, as he was seen with that coat! It was an unusual sight for a fellow, wearing his own overcoat, to be carrying another on his arm!

Besides, most of the fellows knew that coat by sight—it was as well known as Joseph's celebrated coat of many colours. Dozens of fellows noticed that the Sixth Former was carrying Billy Bunter's coat on his arm, and wondered why.

Specially interested were two juniors, in a group near the House. One of them was Vernon-Smith—the other, Bob Cherry.

Vernon-Smith, after getting out of the Three Fishers over the back fence, had scudded as if he were up for the School quarter-mile. That Wingate had not seen him at the place, he knew; and he was anxious to be back in the school, and be prominently on view there, before Wingate got back. As Wingate walked back, and the Bounder had run like the wind, that was easy enough. He had been back a quarter of an hour before Wingate appeared.

The Famous Five were in the quad, after games practice, while Billy Bunter was reposing his weary limbs in the Rag.

Smithy joined them and started the topic of the forthcoming fixture with Highcliffe—a topic which all the Co. were quite willing to discuss—never guessing that Smithy's object was to keep them standing there with him, in full view, to meet Wingate's eyes when he came in.

Smithy, with all his keenness, had not given a thought to the coat he had left behind him at the Three Fishers. He had had enough to think about— and it had not occurred to him that Wingate would notice it hanging there.

He had to think of it now, however, as he saw it on Wingate's arm !

He stared at it !

So did Bob Cherry !

Smithy's first thought was, that it was a stroke of good fortune that he had changed coats with Bunter on the towpath. Otherwise, Wingate would have found his coat where he had found Bunter's.

But his next swift thought was, that that change of coats had to remain unknown.

"You ass, Smithy !" Bob Cherry spoke in a low tone. "That's Bunter's coat that Wingate's got there—look at it—did you——"

"Keep it dark, old man !" murmured the Bounder. "Look here, you were with Bunter this afternoon——"

"Yes—what——"

"That lets him out, then ! You can prove that he wasn't at that show."

"Of course I can—lucky for him, as you seem to have left his coat there !" growled Bob. "But as soon as they know that you changed coats——"

"Are you going to tell them ?" sneered the Bounder.

"Don't be a fool !" growled Bob.

"Anybody might have borrowed a coat—if you keep it dark !"

"Bunter will blab it all out first thing——"

"Where's Bunter ?"

"In the Rag, I think."

Vernon-Smith shot into the House.

Four members of the Co. had heard that whispered exchange of words, and were staring blankly.

"What——" began Harry Wharton.

"Mum's the word !" breathed Bob.

Wingate was passing the group. He went into the House, heading directly for Dr. Locke's study.

As soon as he was gone, Bob whispered an explanation to his friends.

Carter passed them, going into the House. He followed, at a distance, in Wingate's footsteps, and watched him enter the Head's study, with the coat on his arm.

A minute or two later the door reopened, and Wingate reappeared.

Seeing Carter at the end of the passage, he called to him.

"Carter ! Please go to Mr. Quelch,

and ask him to step into the Head's study."

"Yes, Wingate !"

Carter cut away to call Mr. Quelch. That gentleman rustled away to the headmaster's study at once—for what purpose, Carter did not need telling. He was to hear this charge against a member of his Form !

Carter wondered where Bunter was now, and whether he had got back to the school yet. Certainly he did not think of guessing that Billy Bunter was in the Rag—listening, with blinking astonishment, to eager whispers from the Bounder.

THE EIGHTEENTH CHAPTER.

All Right for Bunter !

"BEAST !" hooted Bunter.

Bunter was tired.

He did not intend to stir out of that armchair till tea-time ! But he had to stir when he was suddenly grabbed by a fat shoulder. He blinked through his spectacles at the Bounder.

"Beast ! Leggo ! Where's my coat, you beast ? Yours is in the lobby—and if you think I've brushed the mud off, you're jolly well mistaken, see ? I——"

"Shut up, you fat fool, and listen to me !" hissed the Bounder.

Bunter listened.

He listened in astonishment at first, but slowly a fat grin overspread his face.

"Oh crikey !" he ejaculated.

"You see ?" breathed the Bounder. "Somebody borrowed your coat—you don't know who it was——"

"Oh, really, Smithy ! If you think I can tell a lie——" exclaimed Bunter indignantly.

"What ?" yelled the Bounder.

"You might !" said Bunter, blinking at him. "I dare say you would ! Hardly the thing I could do !"

William George Bunter had a narrow escape, at that moment, of going across the Rag at the toe of Smithy's boot.

But the Bounder restrained his rage. It was no time for booting Bunter.

"If you give me away——" he breathed.

"Of course I shan't give you away ! I'm no sneak, I hope !" said Bunter with dignity. "I shan't mention that you had my coat ! I can prove where I've been all the afternoon, and that's good enough. But if you think I could tell an untruth, Smithy——"

"Keep it dark that I had your coat ! That's all that's needed—they'll never guess ! Might have been anybody, if you keep your mouth shut. See ?"

Bunter grinned cheerily.

"Right as rain, old chap ! Rely on me to keep it dark ! I'll see you through, old chap ! They won't get much out of me, I can tell you ! Think I shall have to go up to the Head ?"

"Most likely ! Keep cool—there's nothing to be afraid of, as a dozen fellows know you were here all the time——"

"He, he, he ! I ain't afraid of the Head like you are, Smithy ! I say, you jolly nearly got copped this time, old chap ! How did Wingate know ?"

The Bounder gritted his teeth.

"Some rotter must have sneaked—I can't guess who. By gum, if I find out who put them on my track—— Have you been gabbling, you fat fool ? You knew where I was going——"

"Oh, really, Smithy——"

"No—it can't have been your gabble —they think you were at the Three Fishers, from finding the coat there. They can't think anything else. That

fool Cherry wouldn't give a man away. But somebody——"

The Bounder's eyes burned. It was quite plain to him that Wingate had been acting on information; he had known that a Greyfriars fellow was there, though, fortunately, he did not know which fellow.

A voice was heard outside the doorway—that of Carter of the Remove.

"Quelch wants Bunter ! You fellows know whether he's come in ?"

"He came in long ago," answered Harry Wharton's voice. "Has Quelch sent for him ?"

"Yes, to the Head's study."

"He's in here."

Harry Wharton looked in.

"You're wanted, Bunter."

Vernon-Smith gave the fat Owl a last look.

Bunter favoured him with a fat wink in reply, and rolled out of the Rag.

Carter gave him a very curious look as he appeared. He had hardly expected Bunter to be back so soon.

"I say, you fellows," Bunter blinked at the Famous Five, "you'd better come with me. I may want you."

"We'll come as far as the corner, fathead !" said Harry Wharton. "We can't butt in on the Head !"

"Well, don't be too far off !" said Bunter anxiously "The Head mightn't take my word that I haven't been out of gates, you know ! He's doubted my word before—so has Quelch ! You know that !"

"Ass ! We're all ready to bear witness that you were on the football ground with us !" said Harry.

Carter gave a violent start. He was startled quite out of his self-possession as he heard that !

That Bunter would attempt to lie himself out of the scrape, he knew. But that fellows like Harry Wharton & Co. would back him up in it, he had never dreamed ! It was an utter surprise to him.

"What do you mean by that, Wharton ?" he exclaimed. "You've got the nerve to say that you're going to the Head to tell lies to get Bunter off ?"

The captain of the Remove stared at Carter.

"Who's going to tell lies, you cheeky fool ?" he snapped. "What do you mean ?"

"You're going to say that Bunter was on the football field with you——" exclaimed Carter. "You——"

"So he was !" snapped Harry.

"You know he was not !" almost yelled Carter. He was, for the moment, almost beside himself at this unexpected blow to all his scheming. "You're going to Dr. Locke to tell him a pack of lies——"

"You cur !" said Bob Cherry in a low voice of bitter contempt. "You'd like to see Bunter landed, wouldn't you ? Well, he won't be landed this time—he's got friends to see him through, see ? He hasn't been out of our sight all the afternoon, and we're ready to tell the Head so !"

"It's false !" shouted Carter.

Bob Cherry clenched his hands, his eyes flashing. But the captain of the Remove caught his arm.

"Hold on, Bob—leave the cad alone ! No time for rows now ! Come on, Bunter—you're all right, old fat bean !"

Bob nodded, and the Famous Five walked away with Bunter—leaving Arthur Carter rooted to the floor, staring after them.

From the doorway of the Rag, Herbert Vernon-Smith looked out at him with gleaming eyes. Somebody had given it away that a Greyfriars man was at the Three Fishers that afternoon —and Smithy could not think of a fellow who would have betrayed him. But he could think of a fellow who would have betrayed Bunter—and there was deep suspicion in his mind as he looked at Carter.

What did Carter know about the matter? Why was he so certain that Bunter had not been at football with the Remove fellows?

There was only one answer to that— Carter believed that Bunter had been at the Three Fishers! If that were so, the Bounder had not much farther to look for the fellow who had given information.

He stood looking at Carter's flushed, angry face, quietly and grimly. Carter did not notice him. After a few minutes he turned and followed Harry Wharton & Co.—leaving Smithy with very busy thoughts.

Billy Bunter, at the Head's door, hesitated.

He turned to cast a last blink along the passage at the group of juniors at the corner.

Bob Cherry gave him an encouraging grin.

"I say, you fellows, don't go away!" squeaked Bunter.

"O.K., fathead—get on with it!"

And Bunter, at last, tapped at the dreaded door and entered.

He felt an inward quake as he did so. For once the fat Owl of the Remove had a clear conscience—an unaccustomed possession! But the grave faces of the Head and Mr. Quelch were awe-inspiring, all the same. The grey overcoat, with its purple stripes, lay on the Head's table. Wingate stood by the window, his eyes on the uneasy fat Owl.

"Bunter!" The Head's voice was deep. "It appears that you have been out of school bounds this afternoon."

"Oh! No, sir!" gasped Bunter.

"That is your coat, Bunter?"

"Oh! Yes, sir! I—I wondered where it was!"

"That coat, Bunter, was found hanging in the billiards-room at the Three Fishers by a Greyfriars prefect, and brought back to the school by him."

"Was it, sir?"

"It was, Bunter!"

"I—I'm glad Wingate brought it back, sir! I—I shouldn't like to lose that coat! The fellows make a lot of silly jokes about it, but——"

"Do you deny that you were at that disreputable resort this afternoon, Bunter, and that you escaped almost as Wingate entered, leaving your coat behind?"

"Oh, yes, sir! I've been playing football this afternoon—I'm rather keen on games, and the fellows were very keen for me to play, and——"

"Upon my word!" breathed Mr. Quelch.

"You have not been out of bounds?" exclaimed the Head.

"Oh, no, sir!"

"I have told you where your coat was found, Bunter."

"Yes, sir. Somebody must have borrowed it."

There was a long pause.

"I suppose that that is possible, Mr. Quelch?" said the Head at last.

"It is possible, sir, but highly improbable!" said the Remove master, with a glance at the coat. "Very improbable indeed, I think."

The Head fixed his eyes on Bunter again.

"If your statement is true, Bunter, you can explain exactly how you have been occupied this afternoon, and where?"

"Oh, yes, sir!" said Bunter, quite cheerily. "After dinner I went for a bit of a walk with Bob Cherry, and we came in again for games practice. After that I went into the Rag. Lots of fellows about, sir."

"It was at half-past three that I received a telephone call, informing me that a Greyfriars boy had been seen to go into that low resort," said the Head. "Where were you from three o'clock till half-past, Bunter?"

"On the football ground, sir."

"Who else was there?"

"Wharton, Nugent, Bull, Inky, Redwing, Squiff—nearly all the Remove, sir."

"Upon my word!" repeated Mr. Quelch.

"If that statement is correct, Mr. Quelch, it is clear that some boy, at present unknown, must have borrowed Bunter's overcoat!" said the Head. "Will you kindly call some of the boys named, and we shall see whether they corroborate Bunter's statement."

"Certainly, sir."

Mr. Quelch had not far to go. He encountered five of the necessary fellows at once. They were in view at the corner of the passage when he stepped out.

"Wharton! All of you please come here!" called out Mr. Quelch.

"Yes, sir."

The Famous Five marched into the Head's study.

Billy Bunter gave them a fat grin as they came in. He was feeling quite reassured now.

"Wharton," said Dr. Locke, "kindly tell me, if you know, where Bunter was from three to three-thirty this afternoon."

"At games practice, sir," answered Harry.

"You were present?"

"Yes, sir. All these fellows were present and half the Form."

"Bunter came down to games practice with me, sir," said Bob Cherry. "That was before three. It was after half-past three when we chucked it—I mean, when we went back to the changing-room."

"All you boys saw him present there?"

"Oh, yes, sir!"

"You are satisfied with this evidence of boys of your Form, Mr. Quelch?"

"Perfectly so, sir!" answered Mr. Quelch. "It is absolutely clear now that Bunter's overcoat was worn by some other boy this afternoon."

"That boy must be discovered, Mr. Quelch. But I am glad, Bunter, that your friends have been able to clear you so completely. You may go, Bunter—you may take your coat with you."

"Yes, sir!" trilled Bunter.

He went—taking his coat with him—and the Famous Five followed him.

Dr. Locke, Mr. Quelch, and the head prefect of Greyfriars were left in discussion as to the identity of the utterly unknown fellow who had bagged Bunter's coat that afternoon. To that fellow there was—fortunately for the bad hat of the Remove—no clue.

THE NINETEENTH CHAPTER.
Brought to Light!

"I SAY, you fellows!"
Billy Bunter rolled into the Rag before tea.

A number of Remove fellows there were discussing a rather interesting topic—who had worn Bunter's overcoat that afternoon?

Bunter was not interested in that topic. For one thing, he knew, and, for another, it was close on tea-time, and Bunter's next meal always filled up all the available space on Bunter's horizon.

"I say, is that beast Cherry here?" asked Bunter.

"No!" called back Bob cheerily.

Printed in England and published every Saturday by the Proprietors, The Amalgamated Press, Ltd., The Fleetway House, Farringdon Street, London, E.C.4. Advertisement offices: The Fleetway House, Farringdon Street, London, E.C.4. Registered for transmission by Canadian Magazine Post. Subscription rates: Inland and Abroad, 11s. per annum; 5s. 6d. for six months. Sole Agents for Australia and New Zealand: Messrs. Gordon & Gotch, Ltd., and for South Africa: Central News Agency, Ltd.—Saturday, February 5th, 1938.

"There's a nice, attractive fellow of that name, if you want him."

"Oh, really, Cherry! I say, you fellows, I haven't changed my bank-note," said Bunter. "That beast Cherry stopped me, you know."

"Lucky for you, old fat man!" said Skinner. "You'd be in quod now, if he hadn't."

"Beast!" roared Bunter. "Look here, you men, I'm short of cash, owing to —to not changing my fiver. As that beast Cherry stopped me, it's up to you!"

"It hasn't come out yet who lost that fiver!" remarked Hazeldene. "Aren't you going to tell us whose it was, Bunter?"

"I've told you it's mine!" roared Bunter.

"Yes—we know whose it is now. I'm asking you whose it was!"

"Ha, ha, ha!"

"Bunter, old man," said Vernon-Smith. The Bounder spoke with an unusually kind note in his voice. He was not unmindful of the fact that Bunter had seen him through in that matter of the changed overcoats. "Look here, old fat lad, have a little sense! We all know that the fiver's not yours——"

"Oh, really, Smithy——"

"You've as good as told us so a dozen times. You must have picked it up somewhere! Well, findings ain't keepings, old podgy bean! Take it to Quelch, and tell him where you found it."

"That's good advice, Bunter!" said Harry Wharton.

Carter, who was lounging by the window of the Rag, looked round quickly. He, at all events, did not want to see the fat Owl take good advice.

The utter failure of his scheme that afternoon had filled the wretched schemer with bitterness. He had fully believed, at first, that the Famous Five were going to bear false witness, to see Bunter through. But it had not taken him long to learn that the fat Owl really had been at games practice, and that he could not, therefore, be the fellow he had seen in that conspicuous overcoat, squeezing through the gap in the Three Fishers fence. All the fellows knew now that somebody else had worn that overcoat—though only half a dozen knew the fellow's name.

It was an utterly unexpected blow to the schemer. It gave him a feeling that it was futile to lay the cunningest schemes, if something unexpected and incalculable, like this, was going to knock them to pieces.

In that he had, if he had only known it, discovered a lesson that might have been useful to him. For, in truth, there never was a treacherous scheme that did not contain within it the seeds of its own undoing!

But Carter, now, was pinning his faith, as it were, to the banknote! Bunter had got out of one scrape, only to tumble into a worse one—if he had, as Carter and nearly all the Form believed, got hold of a banknote that did not belong to him. He listened quite anxiously for the fat Owl's answer.

Whether the Bounder's advice was good or bad, however, Bunter had no use for it. He gave Smithy a scornful blink.

"If you're trying to make out that that banknote isn't mine, Smithy,——" he began loftily.

"You unspeakable idiot!" howled Smithy. "Every man in the Form knows that it's not yours!"

"The knowfulness is terrific, my esteemed, fatheaded Bunter"

"Look here, you cheeky beasts——" hooted Bunter.

"Have a little sense, you ass!" snapped the Bounder. "Look here, if you'll take that fiver to Quelch, and hand it over, I'll lend you a quid!"

"Jump at it, Bunter!" grinned Skinner.

"Jolly good offer, old fat man!" said Bob Cherry. "Do it, and do it now!"

Had it been a real fiver, and had Bunter, as the juniors supposed, found it somewhere, no doubt he would have jumped at the Bounder's offer. But he could not hand over to Quelch a "dud" fiver that he had picked out of Horace Coker's wastepaper-basket!

"I'll tell you what, Smithy," said Bunter—"I'll have the quid. But I can't take my fiver to Quelch, of course."

"Fathead!"

"You'll have to hand it over when they find out!" said Peter Todd.

"Oh, really, Toddy——"

Carter, at the window, gave a sudden start. Outside, on the gravel path, Mr. Quelch was coming along, pacing slowly and majestically in company with Mr. Capper.

Carter opened the window.

With the window open, voices in the Rag were audible to anyone passing on the path under it. Mr. Quelch was going to hear something as he passed that window!

"I say, you fellows, I think this is pretty thick!" said Billy Bunter, in tones of deep indignation. "Anybody would think that a fellow never had a fiver before! I've had lots and lots!"

"Every fellow in this room knows that you pinched that banknote, Bunter!" said Carter, speaking for the first time.

With the corner of his eye on the window, he saw Mr. Quelch's mortar-board give a sudden bob, as the Remove-master started His words, if not Bunter's, had reached Quelch's ears.

Billy Bunter blinked across at Carter with a scornful blink.

"You can shut up, Carter!" he bawled. "Don't you speak to me, you cad! You know I bar you! I say, you fellows, this sort of thing is insulting, you know. I've told you that I met my Uncle George——I mean my father William—that is, my Uncle Maurice—in Lantham—I mean, Friardale—that is, Courtfield—and he gave me that fiver on Saturday—I mean, Friday——"

"Ha, ha, ha!"

"Blessed if I see anything to cackle at!" hooted Bunter. "I've a jolly good mind to punch Carter's head! Only—only I won't soil my hands on the fellow. Shut that window, you beast—there's a draught."

Carter shut the window.

Mr. Quelch had left Mr. Capper, and was going into the House! Evidently he had heard enough to cause him to take action—prompt action!

"Well, look here, you fellows," went on Bunter, "here I am with a fiver in my pocket that I can't change owing to —to Bob Cherry! I'm expecting a postal order in the morning! Who's going to lend me half-a-crown till my postal order comes?"

"The who-fulness is terrific!"

"I say, Smithy——"

"Oh, go and eat coke!" grunted the Bounder. "I'll lend you a quid, as I said, if you take that banknote to Quelch and hand it over——"

"Think it ain't mine?" roared Bunter.

"I know it isn't!"

"Why, you beast!" howled Bunter. "Think I'm the fellow to touch a fiver if it isn't mine! Making out I'd pinch it! Why——"

"Hush!" said Harry Wharton hurriedly, as the door of the Rag opened and the master of the Remove stepped in.

"Shut up, Bunter!" breathed Frank Nugent.

"Shan't!" roared Bunter. "Making out that a fellow's pinched a fiver—as if I don't get lots from Bunter Court! I can jolly well say—— Oh crikey!"

Bunter broke off as he discerned Mr. Quelch!

There was a deep, deep silence in the Rag till the Remove master broke it.

THE TWENTIETH CHAPTER.
Only Swank !

"BUNTER!"

Mr. Quelch's voice was not loud, but deep.

"Oh! Yes, sir!" gasped Bunter.

Quelch's gimlet eyes seemed to be boring into the unhappy Owl.

The crowd of juniors stood silent, in dismay. In the Head's study the Famous Five had stood by the fat Owl and seen him through. But they could do nothing for him now. If Bunter was in possession of a banknote that did not belong to him he was for it, and his number was up at Greyfriars.

"I heard something said, as I passed the window of this room, a few minutes ago!" said Mr. Quelch. "I should not, as a rule, take cognisance of any remark heard by chance, but this appears to be a very serious matter. I must ask you, Bunter, whether you have a banknote in your possession, and where you obtained it?"

"Oh! No, sir!" gasped Bunter.

"You have not?" asked Mr. Quelch, raising his voice a little.

"I—I mean, yes, sir!" stammered Bunter.

"You mean yes?" said Mr. Quelch grimly. "Very good! You have a five-pound note, Bunter; a larger sum than any Remove boy is allowed to have at one time. That, however, is a minor point at the moment. It appears to be a general impression here that the bank-note does not belong to you. I must inquire into this at once. Your Form-fellows appear to think that you purloined it——"

"Oh, no, sir!" exclaimed Harry Wharton. "Nobody here thinks that Bunter would do that, sir!"

"I heard a boy here say so, distinctly, as I passed the window, Wharton."

"Well, if he thinks so, sir, he's got his opinion to himself!" said the captain of the Remove, with a glance of contempt at Carter.

"Does that mean that you believe the banknote to be Bunter's, Wharton?"

"Well, no, sir! I—I think he must have picked it up somewhere, and he's such a fool——"

"Oh, really, Wharton——"

"He's such a fool, sir, that he's idiot enough to think that findings are keepings! Not a fellow here believes that he would pinch a banknote. Every fellow here will say the same, sir."

The captain of the Remove was doing his best for the fat Owl. There was a murmur of approval from the other fellows. "Findings keepings" was a possible explanation. Bunter was well known to be an ass, but few fellows could think that he had actually taken

THE MAGNET LIBRARY.—No. 1,564.

a banknote that did not belong to him.

"Very well," said Mr. Quelch, "if that is the explanation it is serious enough—very serious indeed! Answer me, Bunter! Did you pick up that banknote somewhere?"

"No, sir!" gasped Bunter.

"Oh, you fat idiot!" hissed the Bounder. "Can't you tell the truth for once? Do you want to be sacked?"

"Oh, really, Smithy——"

"Do not speak to Bunter, Vernon-Smith!" rapped Mr. Quelch. "Bunter, answer me directly! Where did you obtain that banknote?"

"My—my pater sent it to me, sir——" Peter Todd made almost frantic signs to the fat Owl. So did five or six other fellows. But they had no effect on Bunter.

"Your father sent it to you?" repeated Mr. Quelch. "Very well, I will telephone at once to Mr. Bunter and make inquiries——"

"Oh crikey! I—I—I mean——"

"Have you anything further to say, Bunter?"

"Oh! Yes, sir! I—I mean my uncle——"

"You mean your uncle!" repeated Mr. Quelch in a terrifying voice.

"Yes, sir; my—my Uncle William, sir! He—he often sends me tips, and—and this time he sent me a fiver, sir, and—and—and that's all, sir."

Mr. Quelch breathed hard.

"Have you the letter in which the banknote came, Bunter?"

"I—I've lost it, sir."

"By what post did it come?"

"Oh crikey!" Bunter remembered that letters for the Remove passed through their Form-master's hands. So he tried a new tack. "I—I mean, it—it didn't come by post at all, sir!"

"It did not come by post—when you have just stated that you have lost the letter it came in!" exclaimed Mr. Quelch.

"Yes, sir! I mean, no sir! I—I meant that I hadn't lost the letter, sir, as—as there wasn't one!" stuttered Bunter. "I met my Uncle George in Courtfield, sir——"

"Your Uncle George?"

"Yes, sir, and he—he tipped me the fiver! He—he—he often does."

Mr. Quelch breathed harder. If Bunter hoped that he were going to believe those varying statements Bunter was booked for a disappointment.

"I—I happened to run into him, sir, in Lantham—I mean, Courtfield—on Saturday afternoon—I mean, Friday—and he just gave me the fiver, sir! My Uncle Herbert's very generous, sir."

"Your Uncle Herbert!" gasped Mr. Quelch.

"Yes, sir! No, sir—I mean, George—that is, William George! He said 'Here's a fiver for you, Billy!' Just like that, sir!"

Carter was grinning. All the other

fellows looked dismayed. Mr. Quelch's brow was growing like a thundercloud.

"Bunter"—his voice came like the grinding of a saw—"I will listen to no further reckless prevarications from you! Whether you found that banknote, or whether you have purloined it, in either case it obviously does not belong to you. In either case you will be expelled for your dishonesty!"

"Oh crikey!"

"You will now hand me the banknote, Bunter! I shall endeavour to trace its ownership——"

"It—it—it hasn't any owner, sir!" gasped Bunter. "It—it—it ain't real, sir!"

"It is not real!" repeated Mr. Quelch almost dazedly. "What do you mean, Bunter?"

"I—I mean, it's a—a—a dud, sir!"

"A what?"

"I mean, spoof—imitation, sir!" gasped Bunter. "I—I wasn't going to change it, sir! I—I was just keeping it in my note-case just to—to—to look like a banknote, sir!"

"Oh, my hat!" gasped Bob Cherry.

"A dud banknote!" stuttered the Bounder. "Oh gad!"

"Bunter, give me that banknote at once!" thundered Mr. Quelch.

Slowly, unwillingly, the fat Owl extracted the tattered note-case from his pocket and opened it. The banknote within could be partially seen, and it looked real enough.

Slowly Bunter drew it forth, and handed it to his Form-master.

Mr. Quelch examined it with minute attention.

The Removites watched him breathlessly. There was a silence—brief, but it seemed long to the juniors.

"This," said Mr. Quelch, "is a counterfeit note. It is a very skilful imitation, but there is no doubt that it is counterfeit. Bunter, how did a counterfeit note come into your possession? Where did you obtain this?"

"In a wastepaper-basket, sir," groaned Bunter.

"A wastepaper-basket!"

"Ye-es, sir."

"Where?"

"In Coker's study, sir."

"Coker—Coker of the Fifth Form!" exclaimed Mr. Quelch

"Yes, sir," groaned Bunter. "Coker had it passed on him, and—and I heard him tell Potter and Greene that he'd chucked it into his wastepaper-basket, sir. So—so I got it out."

"Bless my soul!" said Mr. Quelch blankly. "And why did you do such an extremely foolish thing, Bunter?"

"I—it—it was just to—to—to let the fellows see that I had banknotes sometimes, sir," groaned Bunter. "I—I was only keeping it in my notecase, sir, just—just to let the fellows see it. It—it looked all right, and—and they didn't know it was a dud."

Carter, who had been grinning when the other fellows were looking serious, was not grinning now. He was looking serious—indeed, utterly taken aback and flabbergasted—while the other fellows roared with laughter. There was a yell that made the Rag echo.

"Silence!" exclaimed Mr. Quelch. "Silence, please! Bunter, you incredibly absurd boy, you—you placed a counterfeit note in your notecase, for—for the purpose of—of absurd ostentation! Upon my word! Coker should have taken this banknote to the police station. I shall see that he does so. As for you, Bunter, I hardly know how to deal with you. You have exposed yourself to the suspicion of dishonesty; you have run the risk of being taken up by the police for possession of counterfeit money, and all for no purpose, but—— Upon my word! This is past belief! Bunter, follow me to my study! I shall cane you!"

"Oh, lor'!"

Billy Bunter left the Rag in a roar as he followed his Form-master. Carter left the Rag with set lips. Every other fellow was howling with laughter.

The Rag was still in a roar of merriment when Billy Bunter came back, wriggling. He did not look as if he had enjoyed his visit to Mr. Quelch's study.

"I say, you fellows!" squeaked Bunter dolorously.

"Ha, ha, ha!" yelled the Remove.

"Blessed if I see anything to cackle at! I say, Quelch gave me six, and he jawed me as well. 'Tain't fair to jaw a fellow, as well as giving him six. And I say, he's kept my banknote!"

"Ha, ha, ha!"

"Making out that I was showing off with it, you know," said Bunter. "As if I'm a fellow to show off! I say, Smithy, what about that quid?"

"Eh?"

"You said a quid, if I handed that banknote over to Quelch. Well, he's got it now."

Smithy stared for a moment; then, laughing, he handed it over. Bunter forgot to wriggle as his fat fingers closed on a pound note. The fat Owl had had to part with his swank; but a real pound note, after all, was better than a dud fiver. A roar of laughter followed him as he shot out of the Rag—unheeded by Billy Bunter, as he headed for the tuckshop.

THE END.

(The title of the next yarn in this spanking fine series is: "GETTING HIS OWN BACK!" You'll roar with laughter when you read it, chums. Take my tip and order a copy of next Saturday's MAGNET at the earliest opportunity!—ED.)

The Magnet

2ᴅ

Billy Bunter's Own Paper

A STICKY BUSINESS!

WHO SAYS ANOTHER RAMBLE WITH—

The GREYFRIARS GUIDE

A TOUR OF THE SCHOOL. The Fags' Common-Room.

(1)

There's a smell of burning kippers
From the kingdom of the nippers,
  What a stench !
There's a crowd of little creatures,
All with ink-bespattered features,
  On a bench !
And they shouldn't be inspected
Till they've all been disinfected !

(2)

What a shindy they're creating
As they sit there, congregating
  Round the fire !
And the fish, while slowly turning
Into charcoal, smells like burning
  Rubber tyre !
Here they live together gaily,
Here they start a dog-fight daily !

(3)

Toasted kippers, black and fuming,
Is the supper they're consuming—
  Rather "high" !
They enjoy each blackened ember,
And at one time, I remember,
  So did I !
It's a very gay existence,
But it's better at a distance !

AFTER SCHOOL HOURS
Bunter Minds the Shop

(1)

Mrs. Mimble, full of worry,
 Cried : "Oh dear, I cannot stop !
I must go out in a hurry.
 Who will stay and mind the shop ?"
Bunter, as he stood there hearing
 Mrs. Mimble's tale of woe,
Lost no time in volunteering,
 Took her place and watched her go !

(2)

Hardly could he trust his senses
 As he saw the piles of tuck,
Caring naught for consequences,
 Bunter murmured : "This is luck !"
Shakespeare said (or was it Bacon ?)
 "There's a tide in our affairs
Which, if well and truly taken,
 Leads us on to millionaires."

(3)

More to Bunter than mere money
 Was the stuff around him spread,
In a land of milk and honey
 Now he reigned supreme as head !
Swiftly to the door retreating,
 Bunter shut and turned the lock,
Swiftly then he started eating,
 Swiftly travelling through the stock.

(4)

Tarts or doughnuts—what's it matter ?
 Bunter meant to eat them all.
Steadily the Owl grew fatter
 Till he stretched from wall to wall !
Then he burst—Ah, dreadful slaughter !
 Burst !—and wakened with a scream !
Cherry, with a jug of water,
 Shattered Bunter's blissful dream !

THE GREYFRIARS ALPHABET
MR. "LARRY" LASCELLES,
mathematics and Games-Master.

L is for LASCELLES—our "Larry,"
Who makes the whole school "dot and
  carry" !
When teaching us cubes and quadratics,
That hideous tripe, mathematics !
His horrible tangents and angles

Tie me into terrible tangles,
But Larry is most sympathetic
Providing a chap's energetic,
He'll give you a hand with the questions
And make very helpful suggestions.
At games he's a popular figure,
He coaches us hard and with vigour,
He'll referee junior matches,
Emerging without any scratches.
At cricket and boxing a winner,
He's liked by us all—even Skinner !

CURIOUS EVENTS AT GREY-
FRIARS.—The Upper Fourth football
eleven scored a goal in a Form match
yesterday.

ANSWER TO PUZZLE

MORGAN.

GREYFRIARS GRINS

The Head has just gone into Big Hall
with a tape-measure. Looks as though
someone's going to be flogged within an
inch of his life.

A visitor to the district complains that
he couldn't find the school. Perhaps
Bunter was standing in front of it at the
time.

A reader asks if there is any fish in
the Greyfriars fountain ? Sometimes—
when he starts swindling the Remove.

Why is Bunter the bigger part of the
Remove ?
Because he is the "ass" of the
"class."

PUZZLE PAR

The initial letters of the following names, when put into the
right order, will make another
Greyfriars name. Can you find
it ? Greene, Redwing, Nugent,
Angel, Mauleverer, Ogilvy.
Answer at foot of column 2.

By an awful mistake Mrs. Mimble
used Gosling's bag of cement instead of
flour in her latest doughnuts. I thought
they seemed a bit softer than usual.

When Gosling overslept the other
morning there was a terrific rush to ring
a rising-bell under his window.

They are talking of putting a postage-
stamp machine in Hall to save fellows
going to the post office. After that, they
will no doubt put a postal order machine
to save the postman's daily tramp with
bulging sacks for Bunter.

Dicky Nugent was seen wandering
about in an aimless fashion yesterday.
He's forgotten what it's like to be out
of detention, and he doesn't know what
to do with himself.

When did Greyfriars begin with a G
and end with an E ?—Greyfriars always
begins with a G and "end" with an E.

ONE BAD TURN DESERVES ANOTHER ! And when Arthur Carter nearly brings about Vernon-Smith's expulsion, the Bounder goes all out for—

GETTING HIS OWN BACK!

By FRANK RICHARDS

In the gloom, Carter, the breaker of bounds, saw the face of Vernon-Smith at the window. The sarcastic grin on the Bounder's face alarmed him !

THE FIRST CHAPTER.
Too Late !

"BUNTER !"

"Oh ! Yes, sir !"

In the Remove Form Room at Greyfriars Billy Bunter's eyes —and spectacles—were on the clock.

Mr. Quelch's eyes were on Billy Bunter !

The lesson was near its end. Class that day ended at four, and towards four other eyes as well as Bunter's turned surreptitiously on the clock.

Harry Wharton & Co. were thinking of a spot of football before tea. Billy Bunter was thinking of a spot of tea—a large spot !

But if other fellows' eyes glanced at the clock, Bunter's did not merely glance at it—they turned on it continually ! The clock seemed to draw his gaze like a magnet. Had that clock been a thing of beauty and a joy for ever the Owl of the Remove could not have gazed at it more earnestly.

Quelch did not approve of this kind of thing.

What was the use of a Form-master handing out valuable historical instruction if his pupils, instead of listening attentively and absorbing the same, only counted the last minutes till he shut down ?

Quelch had given Bob Cherry a severe glance. He had frowned even at Harry Wharton, his head boy. But he glared at Bunter.

Bunter, gazing at the clock, was wondering whether it had stopped. It had indicated five minutes to four at his last blink. Now it indicated four and a half to four ! Bunter was sure that several minutes, at least, had passed since his last blink. It seemed like hours really !

It was rather rotten, Bunter thought, if that beastly clock was slowing down when a fellow wanted to get out.

Gazing earnestly at the clock to ascertain whether the putrid thing really had stopped, Bunter was quite startled by his Form-master's voice rapping out.

He gave a jump and transferred his gaze to Mr. Quelch.

"You were looking at the clock, Bunter !" said the Remove master.

"Oh, no, sir !" said Bunter promptly. "I—I wasn't wondering whether it had stopped, sir ! I—I was listening to you, sir ! I—I heard every word you were saying, sir."

"Very well, Bunter !" said Mr.

~~~~~~~~~~~~~~~~~~~~~~~~~~~~~~~~

Spanking Fine School-Adventure Yarn of HARRY WHARTON & CO., the Cheery Chums of Greyfriars.

~~~~~~~~~~~~~~~~~~~~~~~~~~~~~~~~

Quelch in a grinding voice. "I shall ask you a question, and if you fail to answer it correctly I shall cane you."

"Oh crikey !"

Remove fellows gave Billy Bunter sympathetic glances. Bunter had difficulties in class owing to an uncommonly bad memory, and still more uncommon laziness. And on this occasion all his attention had been concentrated for some time on the Form-room clock. Whatever question Quelch asked, it was fairly certain that Bunter was going to supply the wrong answer.

"The year of the Conquest, Bunter ?" said Mr. Quelch.

That was such an easy one that it ought to have been a relief to Bunter. But the easiest of easy ones was never easy to the fat Owl.

He blinked at Mr. Quelch.

"Well ?" rapped Quelch.

"I—I—I remember perfectly, sir !" gasped Bunter.

"Then answer me !"

"If—if you'll let me think a minute, sir——" groaned Bunter.

Bob Cherry, under his desk, pencilled "1066" on a fragment of paper and passed it along out of sight.

Which, of course, Bob ought not to have done ; but it was Bob's way to help any fellow out of a scrape first and think about it afterwards.

Unseen, under the desk, that fragment of paper passed along, by several hands, till it reached the fellow sitting next to Bunter.

That fellow was Carter, the new junior in the Remove.

"Bunter——" came Quelch's deep voice.

"Oh ! Yes, sir ! I—I know !" gasped Bunter.

He was aware, though Mr. Quelch was not, of the spot of information that was coming to the rescue.

It was only a matter of seconds.

The fragment of paper reached Carter.

He held it in his hand, under cover of the desk, where Bunter's eyes could drop on it.

Unfortunately, whether by accident or design, Carter held it upside down.

Bunter, dropping his eyes, saw it, and read :

"9901."

THE MAGNET LIBRARY.—No. 1,565.

No fellow in the Greyfriars Remove excepting Billy Bunter would have fancied that 9901 could be the date of anything that had happened in English history so far.

Even Bunter would have realised that it post-dated the Conquest very considerably, had he stopped to think for a moment.

But Bunter did not stop to think.

Thinking was not his long suit, anyway.

"If you do not answer me immediately, Bunter——" came Quelch's deep voice.

"Oh, yes, sir! Nine thousand nine hundred and one, sir!" said Billy Bunter cheerfully.

"What!"

"N-nun-nine thousand nun-nine hundred and—and one, sir!" gasped Bunter.

"Ha, ha, ha!" came a howl along the Remove. Really, they could not help it! This was too good even from Bunter.

"Upon my word!" exclaimed Mr. Quelch. "What do you mean, Bunter? How dare you make such an answer!"

"Ain't that right, sir?" stammered Bunter. "I—I—I thought it—it was nine thousand nine hundred and—and—and one, sir!"

"Are you not aware, Bunter, that the present year is only one thousand nine hundred and thirty-eight?" shrieked Mr. Quelch.

"Oh! Yes! Of course, sir!" gasped Bunter.

"Then what do you mean, Bunter?"

"I—I—I mean—— Oh lor'!"

"You will stand out before the Form, Bunter."

"Oh crumbs!"

Mr. Quelch picked up a cane from his desk.

Billy Bunter rolled out reluctantly to receive the same.

Arthur Carter crumpled the fragment of paper in his hand and dropped it under the desks. He was grinning—all the Remove was grinning.

It did not seem to have occurred to Mr. Quelch that Bunter had given the right number upside down! But it occurred to most of the juniors—especially to those who had passed the paper along.

Bob Cherry gave Carter a glare behind a row of heads. Evidently he had held the paper upside down, and, with an ass like Bunter, that had done it! Bob did not believe that it was an accident. Certainly any fellow but Bunter would have guessed that the paper was upside down. Bunter could be relied upon not to guess that, or anything else.

"Bend over that chair, Bunter!"

Whack!

"Wow!"

"Now go back to your place, Bunter! You will remain in the Form-room until half-past four! If I see you glance at the clock again I shall detain you until five."

"Oh lor'!"

Bunter rolled back to his place, wriggling.

A few minutes later the Remove were dismissed—leaving William George Bunter sitting in solitary state—and making manful efforts to keep his eyes and spectacles off the clock!

THE SECOND CHAPTER.

The Trail of Vengeance!

"HALLO, hallo, hallo!"

"What have you got there?"

"Nothing!" answered Billy Bunter.

THE MAGNET LIBRARY.—No. 1,565.

Harry Wharton & Co. were coming in to tea after their spot of football.

The Famous Five, Vernon-Smith, Carter, and several other fellows were coming up the staircase together when Billy Bunter was seen coming down.

Under Billy Bunter's jacket was a large bulge.

Bunter's jacket, like his other garments, fitted him tightly. He had more to pack in than most fellows.

The fat Owl could hardly have squeezed a bullseye under his jacket without the fact being revealed.

And it was something of much more considerable size that was packed under his jacket now. It bulged to such an extent that it would have caught the most casual glance. In fact, it leaped to the eye.

The juniors stopped half-way up the staircase and surrounded Bunter, with grinning faces.

They were not likely to believe that he had "nothing" there, when one side of his jacket was swollen, as if it had a bad toothache.

"I say, you fellows, gerrout of the way!" yapped Bunter. "I'm in rather a hurry——"

"Whose study have you been raiding this time?" asked Johnny Bull.

"Oh, really, Bull——"

"What are you hiding under your jacket?" asked Frank Nugent.

"Nothing, old chap! I—I mean, it—it's a Latin dictionary. I—I'm going to take it down to the Rag, and—and read it. See?"

"Ha, ha, ha!" howled the Removites. They could not quite "see" Bunter sitting in the Rag reading a Latin dictionary.

"You fat villain!" said Smithy. "If that's the box of chocolates from my study——"

"I haven't been in your study, you beast! I never knew you had a box of chocolates there——"

"You'd have been in, if you'd known!" grinned Carter.

"Yah! I say, you fellows——"

"Stand and deliver!" said Bob Cherry.

"Oh, really, Cherry——"

"Show up, you fat brigand!" said Harry Wharton. "You've been grub-raiding again, or you wouldn't be hiding the plunder."

"I haven't!" yelled Bunter. "I say, gerrout of the way—Quelch has gone over to the Head's house, but I don't know how long he will be. I tell you I'm in a hurry!"

"You howling ass, what have you got in your fat nut now?" exclaimed Bob.

"Nothing!"

"Ha, ha, ha!"

"I say, you fellows, do let a chap pass. This tin of treacle doesn't belong to any of you. I'm not going to mop it over the papers in Quelch's study. I wouldn't waste treacle like that! Besides, I haven't got a tin of treacle. Now let me pass."

"You priceless ass!" gasped Bob. "You're going to mop treacle over Quelch's papers?"

"Well, look what he did!" said Bunter warmly. "Caning a fellow for nothing, and keeping me in till five o'clock. He made out that I was looking at the clock again, just because he saw me, you know. That's the sort of justice we get here."

"Ha, ha, ha!"

"Besides, I ain't going to Quelch's study. Very likely he's there. I never saw him go over to the Head's house—you see, I wasn't keeping an eye on him. I've got this book of poetry to read in the Rag——"

"As well as a Latin dictionary?"

"I—I mean, a Latin dick! I say, do let a fellow pass. I never got it out of your study cupboard, Wharton! If you had a tin of treacle there, I don't know what's become of it. How could I?"

Harry Wharton laughed.

"Well, you're not going to get a flogging for mopping treacle over Quelch's papers, old fat man—especially my treacle!" he said. "Hand it over!"

"I haven't got any! Look here, you beast! I suppose I can carry a geography book under my jacket if I like!"

"Shake it out of him!" said Bob Cherry.

"The shakefulness is the proper caper!" grinned Hurree Jamset Ram Singh.

Three or four fellows collared Bunter.

They had not, perhaps, any objection, in principle, to treacle being mopped over a Form-master's papers. But such a jape on Quelch was altogether too dangerous—especially as Bunter was just the fellow to be caught at it. And there was the treacle to be considered—by the owner thereof.

"Leggo!" howled Bunter. He struggled in the grasp of many hands.

A whop from Quelch's cane, and an hour's detention, had made Bunter wrathy. Quelch had made it painful for him to sit down; so it was only just, from Bunter's point of view, to make Quelch sit up.

There was no doubt that the Remove master would have "sat up" very emphatically had he found the papers on his study table sticky with treacle.

The consequences would have been dire, had the perpetrator been found out. But that did not worry Bunter. He was not going to be found out!

He wriggled wildly in the grasp of the grinning juniors. That tin of golden syrup, naturally, slid from under his jacket as he struggled.

Bang!

It landed on a stair.

Smithy made a clutch at it, Hurree Singh made another, but both were too late. The tin rolled on to the next stair, and then on to the next, and went sailing merrily down.

Bump, bump, bump, bump! went the treacle tin, from stair to stair. There was no stopping it now.

"Oh crikey!" gasped Bunter. "Look what you've done, you dummies! I say, get hold of it—stop it—they'll spot it—oh crumbs!"

Bump, bump, bump! Bang!

Bunter wrenched himself loose, and rushed down the stairs after the treacle, as it landed, with a final bang, at the foot of the staircase.

"Bless my soul! What is that?" exclaimed Mr. Prout, the master of the Fifth, coming across to stare at the article that had crashed down.

"Mon Dieu! Vat is zat?" ejaculated Monsieur Charpentier, who had been standing near the staircase talking to the Fifth Form master—or, to be more accurate, listening to him.

Bunter jumped from the stairs, and bagged the rolling tin—under the eyes of the two masters.

"What——" boomed Prout.

"I—I—I dropped it, sir!" gasped Bunter. "It—it's mine!"

From the staircase a bunch of Removites watched breathlessly. Bunter had the treacle tin again—and, under the eyes of the beaks, they could not recapture Bunter. They wondered whether even the fatuous fat Owl would be ass enough to carry on, after it had been seen. There was no doubt that both Prout and Mossoo would remember that treacle tin, if it transpired later that Quelch's papers had been smothered with treacle !

But even Billy Bunter's asinine gifts had a limit.

He put the tin of treacle under a fat arm, but he did not start for Masters' Passage with it—under official eyes. He rolled away to the Rag—to wait there till the coast was clear. A fellow had a right to take a tin of treacle into the junior day-room, if he liked—so Bunter

had waited only two minutes out of the ten when the door of the Rag opened, and Harry Wharton & Co. came in and shut the door after them

Bunter gave them a wrathful blink through his big spectacles. He could see that those beasts were going to butt in again.

They were ! They surrounded the fat Owl in the Rag, as they had surrounded him on the stairs. A dozen fellows were in the room before tea, and they all looked round.

"Oh, shake it out of him again !" grunted Johnny Bull.

"I say, you fellows—— Yarooop !" Bump !

Billy Bunter sat down on the floor of the Rag, and the treacle tin rolled again.

Peter Todd pounced on it, and picked it up.

Bunter sat and spluttered.

"Now, you fat ass," said Harry Wharton, "you're not having that tin of treacle ! You're not going to play

"What was the year of the Conquest ?" asked Mr. Quelch. Whether by accident or design, Carter held the paper—on which was scribbled the date—upside down. "Nine thousand, nine hundred, and one, sir !" said Billy Bunter cheerfully. "What !" gasped Mr. Quelch.

saw nothing for a beak to be suspicious about

The Bounder chuckled.

"Well, that does it !" he said. "If that benighted Owl lands that treacle on Quelch now—ha, ha, ha !"

Smithy went on up the stairs, laughing. Harry Wharton & Co. exchanged a glance, and went down. Carter remained on the staircase, looking over the banisters—his eyes following the Famous Five far from pleasantly.

Carter, for reasons of his own, would have been very glad to see Bunter carry on with that jape on Quelch—but he was not going to carry on with it if his well-wishers could stop him. And the Famous Five thought that they could.

— — —

THE THIRD CHAPTER.

Sticky !

BILLY BUNTER waited in the Rag, the treacle tin parked under his jacket as before, and bulging.

He was going to give Prout and Mossoo time to clear off the scene—ten minutes, he thought, would do. He was anxious to get through before his Form-master came back from the Head's house—but it was only caution to wait a bit. But, as a matter of fact, Bunter

"Now, you fat ass——" said Bob Cherry.

"Beast !" roared Bunter. "Mind your own bizney, see ?"

"Hand over that treacle !" rapped Harry Wharton.

"Shan't !"

"Bag him !" said Johnny Bull.

"I say, Toddy, keep those beasts off !" roared Bunter.

Peter Todd came across to the group.

"What's up ?" he asked.

"Bunter will be up—for a flogging if we don't stop the silly Owl !" said Frank Nugent. "He's got that tin of treacle for Quelch !"

"I—I—I ain't, Toddy !" gasped Bunter. "I ain't going to take this treacle to Quelch's study and mop it over his papers—I ain't, really !"

"You're not !" agreed Peter, grinning. "You can bank on that, old fat ass ! We don't want any floggings in Study No. 7. Hand it over !"

"Look here, Toddy ! Don't you be a beast, like the other beasts !" exclaimed Bunter, in dismay. "Look what Quelch did——"

"Never mind that—you'd better think about what he will do, if he finds that treacle in his study !" chuckled Peter. "Hand it over !"

"Beast !"

tricks on Quelch ! Quelch is too jolly dangerous—see ?"

"Beast !" roared Bunter. He staggered to his feet. "Gimme that treacle, Toddy ! Look here, if you don't give me that tin of treacle——"

"No 'if' about it !" grinned Toddy.

"Then I'll jolly well go and mop the ink instead !" hooted Bunter. "See ? Think I'm going to be whopped and kept in an hour for nothing ? I'll jolly well go straight to Quelch's study and upset his inkpot over his papers—so yah !"

And Billy Bunter turned towards the door, his fat mind evidently made up.

"Hold on !" exclaimed Toddy. "If you mean that, you can have the treacle, Bunter !"

"Oh !" Bunter turned back. "Hand it over, then !"

"You fathead, Toddy !" exclaimed Bob Cherry. "He's not to have it ! The blinking Owl will get flogged——"

"You shut up, Bob Cherry !" howled Bunter. "Gimme that treacle, Toddy !"

"Look here, Todd——" exclaimed Harry Wharton.

"My dear chaps," said Peter, "my idea is that if I give Bunter the treacle, he won't go to Quelch's study at all. I think he will be too busy with the treacle ! Bag him !"

"Oh!" exclaimed the Famous Five together

They caught on to Toddy's idea—and they caught on to Bunter

"Leggo, will you?" roared the fat Owl. "Will you leggo, you beasts! Now, Toddy, will you give me that treacle?"

"Here you are!" smiled Peter.

He prised off the lid of the tin. Then he held the latter over Billy Bunter's head, and upended it.

There was a roar of laughter from the fellows in the Rag. From Billy Bunter there was a shriek of apprehension. He realised now in what manner Toddy was going to give him the treacle.

"I say, leggo! Stoppit! I say, take that tin away! I—I say, I shall be all sticky!"

"Better you than Quelch's papers, old fat man!" said Peter cheerily.

"Ha, ha, ha!"

"Hold him!" grinned Peter, as Bunter struggled frantically. "He doesn't seem to want it now he's getting it! Blessed if he seems to know his own mind at all! You heard him asking for it!"

"We did!" chuckled Bob.

"The askfulness was terrific!"

"Ha, ha, ha!"

Treacle, in a sticky mass, exuded from the tin It landed on Billy Bunter's fat head and flowed down his fat face. It felt clammy and sticky—horrid, in fact! Bunter rather liked golden syrup, taken internally He did not like it taken externally. But it was externally that he had to take it, and he took it in bulk!

"Urrggh! Gurrgh! Wurrggh!" gurgled the hapless fat Owl.

There was no escape for Bunter, and the sticky stream flowed down—down his face and down his fat neck.

That it was better for Bunter, in the long run, to get the treacle himself than to mop it over Quelch's papers was certain. Obviously, after that tin was emptied on him, Bunter was going to be too busy, getting the treacle off, to think of japes on Quelch He was going to be very busily occupied, and there was no doubt that Quelch would be back in his study long before Bunter had finished scraping off treacle. That was a sheer benefit to Bunter; Peter and the Famous Five were doing him a good turn, as every fellow but the fat Owl knew

But Bunter did not realise it, and there was no doubt that the treacle was sticky and horrid. He struggled, he wriggled, he squirmed, he spluttered, he howled, and he yelled.

But it booted not. Treacle streamed out of the tin and swamped him. Not till the stream was reduced to a mere trickle did Peter throw the tin into a wastepaper-basket.

By that time Bunter's state was really awful. He lived, and moved, and breathed, and had his being in golden syrup!

He clawed at it wildly, and his fat paws streamed with treacle.

"Ooooogh! I'm all sticky!" howled Bunter "Oh, you beasts! Wow! Look at me!"

The juniors looked at him, and roared.

"The stickfulness is terrific!" chuckled Hurree Jamset Ram Singh.

"You beast, Toddy!" shrieked Bunter. "I'll jolly well——"

He made an enraged rush at Peter. Peter Todd dodged round the table. Bunter was rather too sticky for a fellow to touch.

"Better get a wash, old man!" grinned Bob Cherry. "I know you hate

washing, but it's not so bad as the Head's birch."

"Ha, ha, ha!"

"A spot of washfulness, my esteemed Bunter——"

"This way, Bunter!" said Harry Wharton, opening the door of the lobby at the end of the room, where there were wash-basins. "Don't touch anything till you've washed!"

"Beast!"

"Ha, ha, ha!"

Even Billy Bunter, in that treacly state, realised that what he chiefly needed was a wash.

He rolled into the lobby, and Harry Wharton turned on hot water for him, and Bob kindly handed him soap. Then they left him to himself, gasping, spluttering, and gurgling, as he washed off treacle.

With cheery faces—happy to have done Bunter that good turn—the Famous Five went out of the Rag and up the stairs again.

Carter was still on the staircase, and he eyed them as they passed him.

They went on up to the Remove passage, leaving the new junior still looking over the banisters. But Billy Bunter did not emerge from the Rag; he was not likely to emerge for a good long time yet. Carter was driven to the conclusion that the fat Owl had abandoned the idea of that jape on Quelch, though he did not know why.

THE FOURTH CHAPTER.

Bunter is Wanted !

MR. QUELCH opened his study door, switched on the light, and stepped in.

There was quite an agreeable expression on Quelch's face. He had had tea and a pleasant chat with his chief, and forgotten temporarily the worries of a Form-master's existence. In a very good humour, he had come back to his study, to put in an hour going over Latin papers for his Form.

He sat down in his chair at the table, turned on the reading-lamp, and stretched his hand out to the pile of papers.

Then he gave a sort of convulsive start.

Naturally, he had not noticed that those papers were sticky. He had not expected them to be sticky. He did not discover till his fingers touched them. Then he discovered it.

The amiable expression faded from Quelch's countenance as if wiped off by a duster.

He stared at sticky fingers. Then he stared at sticky papers. Then he rose to his feet and fixed his eyes on that pile of Latin papers, with an expression that the fabled basilisk might have envied.

"Treacle!" said Mr. Quelch.

It was treacle. A whole tin of it must have been emptied on that pile of papers. They were almost swimming in it. Treacle flowed over them, and flowed in little streams from them about the table. One stream, as Mr. Quelch now discerned, had reached the edge of the table and was dripping to the floor.

Quelch gazed.

Tricks had been played in his study before—not often, for the results were generally very painful. Still, such things had happened. But this was rather the limit. Quelch gazed and gazed, his brow growing more and more thunderous as he gazed.

It was impossible to go through those Latin papers now. Careless mistakes in

any of those papers had to pass unrebuked.

That, perhaps, was the object of the japer. Possibly some fellow who had doubts about his paper had done this to keep his blunders from discovery.

Somebody, at all events, had done it. Quelch's looks indicated that there was a high old time in store for that somebody.

He had been an hour with the Head. During that hour some young rascal had surreptitiously entered the study and done this. The next item on the programme was to discover that young rascal. The next but one was to take him to the headmaster, with a request for a flogging to be administered. Quelch, with a bitter brow and set lips, wiped the stickiness from his fingers, stepped to the door, and looked out into the passage.

"Has anything happened, Quelch?"

Mr. Capper, the master of the Fourth, was coming along, and he glanced in surprise at Quelch's expressive face.

"A wretched trick has been played in my study, Capper!" answered the Remove master. "Have you seen anyone here during my absence?"

"I have been in the Form-room," answered Mr. Capper. "Perhaps Hacker——"

The master of the Shell was looking out of his doorway.

"Have you noticed anyone coming to my study, Hacker?" asked Mr. Quelch.

Hacker shook his head.

"No. I have been reading," he answered. "What has happened?"

"Someone has upset treacle over my papers, Mr. Prout!" Prout looked out at the sound of voices. "Have you seen——"

"Bless my soul!" exclaimed Prout. "Did you say treacle, Quelch?"

"Yes—a number of papers in my study have been swamped with it! If you have seen any boy of my Form here——"

"I have not!" said Prout. "But half an hour ago, Quelch, I saw a boy of your Form with a tin of treacle. He dropped it on the stairs, and it rolled down."

"Which boy, Prout?"

"Bunter?"

Quelch's eyes glinted. He had caned Bunter that afternoon. He had detained him for an hour after class. On the other hand, a tin of golden syrup was quite a natural possession for Bunter, if he was going up to his study to tea.

"Was Bunter going upstairs, or down, Prout?" he asked.

"He was coming down," answered Prout. "He went into the junior dayroom, Quelch, and I did not see him again."

"Taking the treacle with him."

"Certainly."

"Thank you, Prout!" said Mr. Quelch. "That leaves no doubt on the matter." He rustled away down the passage.

There could, of course, be no doubt now! Bunter might have been taking a tin of golden syrup, bought at the school shop, to his study for tea! He could have had no imaginable reason for bringing it downstairs, except one!

Mr. Quelch whisked away to the staircase, and mounted rapidly. On the Remove landing, several fellows glanced at him curiously. The Bounder was standing there, talking to his chum Redwing, and Carter was sitting on the settee by the balustrade, reading. They all looked at Mr. Quelch.

He passed them like a thundercloud, and went up the Remove passage.

The Bounder whistled.

"What's up?" asked Redwing.

Smithy glanced up the passage after Mr. Quelch, saw him stop at the door of Study No. 7, and grinned.

"Bunter's number, I fancy!" he answered.

"What has that fat chump been doing?" asked Carter.

"Treacling Quelch's papers, I rather think!" grinned the Bounder. "Quelch is after him!"

Mr. Quelch looked into Study No. 7 in the Remove, which belonged to Bunter, Toddy, and Tom Dutton. Only the last-named was there.

Dutton, who was deaf, was stirring the fire, and having his back to the door, did not see his Form-master step in. Neither, being deaf, did he hear him.

"Dutton!" rapped Mr. Quelch.

Dutton went on stirring the study fire.

"Dutton!" hooted Mr. Quelch. And as the deaf junior still did not turn his head, he rustled across the study, and clapped him on the shoulder. Dutton, startled, jumped.

"You silly ass, making a fellow jump!" he exclaimed. "Don't be such a thumping fool, Toddy—oh——"

Dutton jumped again, as he looked round. "I—I didn't know it was you, sir."

"Where is Bunter, Dutton? Do you know?"

"Do what now, sir?" asked Dutton, puzzled.

"What? Bless the boy! I desire to see Bunter at once! If you know where Bunter is, tell me at once."

"Wasn't my Latin paper all right, sir?" asked Dutton anxiously. "I did my best with it, sir. I—I try not to be a dunce, sir."

"What—what? I did not call you a dunce," gasped Mr. Quelch. "I told you to tell me at once where Bunter is. This is his study."

"Do you mean my boots, sir?"

"Your—your boots?"

"I wiped them when I came in, sir."

"I am not speaking about your boots!" shrieked Mr. Quelch.

"Oh, aren't you, sir? What did you mean was muddy, then?"

"I did not say muddy! Bless my soul! Can you tell me where Bunter is at this moment?" raved Mr. Quelch.

"Oh! Do you want Bunter, sir? I haven't seen him since class, sir."

Mr. Quelch, breathing hard, rustled out of the study.

Tom Dutton stared after him. He could see that Quelch was in a bait, and he wondered what was wrong with his Latin paper, to make Quelch come up and call him a dunce!

There was a sound of cheery voices from Study No. 1, and Mr. Quelch tapped on that door, and opened it, to inquire further for Bunter.

"Oh, here's the blithering ass!" said Bob Cherry's voice, as the door opened. "Had a wash, fathead? You needed one—in fact, you've needed one all the term."

"Cherry!"

"Oh crikey!" gasped Bob. He bounded. "I—I—I thought it was Bunter, sir——"

"I am in search of Bunter!" said Mr. Quelch, in a grinding voice. "Do you know where Bunter is, Wharton?"

"We left him down in the Rag, some time ago, sir!"

"I—I think he's been rather too busy to come up to tea, sir!" said Frank Nugent.

Snort from Mr. Quelch! Apparently he had mounted the stairs for nothing! He turned, and whisked out of the passage.

"What on earth's up?" asked Harry Wharton, rather alarmed. "Quelch

looks as if he's going to bite Bunter! That fat ass can't have——"

"He can't have treacled Quelch's study!" said Bob. "He couldn't have used that treacle, after he got it off."

"Ha, ha, ha!"

"He can hardly have got it off, yet," said Johnny Bull. "But something's up. Better go along, I think."

The Famous Five left the study, and hurried after their Form-master. Mr. Quelch was whisking down the stairs at a great rate.

On the landing, Carter was watching him curiously, over the banisters, the Bounder was grinning, and Redwing looking very serious.

"Know what's up, you fellows?" asked Harry.

"Looks as if Bunter got on with his treacle stunt!" said Vernon-Smith. "I thought you fellows were going to stop him."

"So we did!" said Bob Cherry. "Bunter jolly well never took that treacle to Quelch's study! What on earth's happened?"

The juniors hurried down the stairs. They sighted Mr. Quelch again, at the door of the Rag, and followed him in. The fellows in that apartment ceased speaking, all at once, as they saw Quelch's thunderous face.

"Is Bunter here?" snapped Mr. Quelch.

"Yes, sir," answered Peter Todd.

"I do not see him—where is he?" Quelch's gimlet eyes gleamed round the Rag, without discerning the fat Owl.

"He's in the lobby, sir, getting a wash——"

"Call him at once."

Peter pitched the door open.

"Bunter, you're wanted——"

"Beast!" came back a yell. "I'm all sticky! I haven't got all this filthy treacle off yet! Go and eat coke!"

"It's Quelch, fathead!" hissed Peter.

"Oh crikey!"

Billy Bunter emerged into the Rag. His collar and tie were off, and his fat face wet and soapy, and he had a towel over a fat arm.

"Bunter!"

"Oh! Yes, sir!"

"Did I hear you mention treacle?"

"Eh? Oh, yes! I got all sticky, sir——"

"No doubt!" said Mr. Quelch grimly. "No doubt at all! You may dry yourself, Bunter—I will wait a few moments! You will then follow me to your headmaster's study!"

Bunter jumped.

"Wha-a-t for, sir?" he gasped.

"To receive a flogging!" said Mr. Quelch grimly. "Lose no time, Bunter!"

THE FIFTH CHAPTER.

Not Bunter!

HARRY WHARTON & CO. followed Mr. Quelch into the Rag. Smithy and Redwing came in with them. The Famous Five were alarmed for the fat Owl. They had, as they supposed, left him too busy to think about japes on Quelch, when they went up to tea, but it was plain that something had happened—and something very serious.

Billy Bunter dabbed at his fat face with the towel, set his spectacles on his fat little nose, and blinked at his Formmaster.

"I—I say, sir, it—it wasn't me!" he gasped, in great alarm.

Bunter did not yet know of what he was suspected, not having the faintest idea that treacle had been spilt in THE MAGNET LIBRARY.—No. 1,565.

Quelch's study. But he was prepared to deny anything and everything.

"I have not the slightest doubt, Bunter, that you are guilty of the outrage in my study!" said Mr. Quelch sternly. "But I will hear you, if you have anything to say. You had a tin of treacle——"

"Oh! No, sir!"

"Mr. Prout saw you drop it on the staircase, Bunter! He has told me so! Now do you dare to deny that you had a tin of treacle!" thundered Mr. Quelch.

"It wasn't mine, sir!" gasped Bunter. "It was Wharton's."

"That is immaterial; it was in your hands."

"Oh, no, sir!"

"I have told you of Mr. Prout's statement, Bunter! Do you venture to deny that the tin of treacle was in your hands?"

"Yes, sir! It really wasn't, sir! You can ask all these fellows, sir! It was under my arm!"

"Under your arm!" repeated Mr. Quelch. In spite of the gravity of the situation, there was a chortle in the Rag. It died away, however, as the gimlet eyes glittered round. "Bunter, is that merely stupidity, or is it intended for impertinence?"

"It—it's true, sir!" gasped Bunter. "Wharton saw it, sir; so did Smithy. I say, you fellows, hadn't I got it under my arm?" appealed Bunter.

"Ha, ha, ha!"

"Silence! Bunter, when I say that it was in your hands, I mean in your possession!" shrieked Mr. Quelch.

"Oh, I—I see, sir! Of course I couldn't guess what you meant, if you didn't say so, sir."

"It is proved, beyond doubt, that a tin of treacle was in your possession half an hour ago. What were you doing with it, Bunter?"

"Oh, taking it up to tea, sir!"

"You were seen to bring it downstairs, Bunter, and to enter this room with it."

"Oh, yes! I—I mean I—I was bringing it down to—to—to this—this room, sir!" stuttered Bunter.

"Where is it now?"

"The—the treacle's been—been spilt, sir, but the tin's in the wastepaper-basket, if you want it!" gasped Bunter.

"The proof could hardly be more complete," said Mr. Quelch. "It was you, Bunter, who upset treacle over the papers on my study table."

Really it looked complete enough. Bunter had been seen with the tin of treacle. It was now empty in the wastepaper-basket, and Bunter had been washing off treacle. Few Form-masters would have wanted more proof than that!

Bunter's fat jaw dropped.

"In—in—in your study, sir!" he gurgled. "I—I haven't been to your study, sir! Oh crikey!"

"Great pip!" murmured Peter Todd. "Has some other silly fathead had the same silly fatheaded idea?"

"Now, Bunter——"

"I didn't!" yelled Bunter desperately. "I never went near your study, sir! I say, you fellows, you tell him——"

"It wasn't Bunter, sir!" exclaimed Peter Todd.

"What? How dare you say so, Todd, when Bunter, even now, has traces of treacle about him!" exclaimed Mr. Quelch.

"Bunter never took that tin of treacle to your study, sir!" exclaimed Harry Wharton. "We all know that, sir."

"How can you know anything of the kind, Wharton?" snapped Mr. Quelch.

"He came into this room with it, sir, and it got spilt over him," said the captain of the Remove.

"Spilt over Bunter!" exclaimed Mr. Quelch.

"I've been washing it off ever since!" gasped Bunter. "I haven't got it all off yet, but I've been washing and washing and washing——"

"Bunter's been here more than half an hour, sir, washing treacle off all the time," said Peter. "Every fellow here's heard him grunting and snorting—I—I mean, heard him at it, sir."

Mr. Quelch paused.

"Do you mean, Todd, that the tin of treacle which Mr. Prout saw in Bunter's possession was spilt over Bunter in this room, and that he has been here ever since?"

"Yes, sir. All the fellows here will tell you."

"Yes, sir, that's so," said Squiff and Tom Brown and Hazeldene and three or four more fellows, all at once.

"Upon my word!" exclaimed Mr. Quelch. "It is a very singular coincidence—very singular indeed—that Bunter should have been carrying a tin of treacle about the House, and that another boy should have played a disgraceful trick with treacle in my study at the same time."

"By gad, it is!" murmured the Bounder.

There was no doubt about that. It was a very remarkable coincidence.

It was so very remarkable that the Bounder, at least, suspected that there was something more than a coincidence in it. Some thought of the same kind was in Bob Cherry's mind.

"I am bound, of course, to believe what you tell me," said Mr. Quelch. "But it is very singular indeed. But for the accident of the treacle having been spilt over Bunter, it would have looked—certainly it would have looked, beyond doubt——"

Mr. Quelch paused. He realised that he had been within measurable distance of an act of injustice. That was a painful thought to the Remove master.

"I shall inquire very strictly into this matter," said Mr. Quelch, after a pause. "As the tin of treacle which Mr. Prout saw in your possession, Bunter, is now accounted for, you are not under suspicion."

Mr. Quelch left the Rag with that. Evidently he had to find some new line of investigation if he hoped to discover the treacler.

"By gum!" said Bob Cherry, when he was gone. "You can thank your lucky stars, Bunter, that we treacled you! You'd have been for it!"

"Who the dickens can have treacled Quelch's study, though?" asked Hazeldene.

Bob gave an angry grunt.

"Some cad who knew what that fat idiot was up to, and wanted to land him in a row with Quelch!" he growled. "As Bunter didn't do it, he did it for him, and left Quelch to think it was that potty porpoise."

"I say, that's rather thick!" said Skinner.

Bob gave another grunt, and walked out of the Rag with his friends. Bob, at least, had no doubt about it, though in the total absence of all proof he did not care to mention Carter's name.

"I say, you fellows, it wasn't me, anyhow!" said Billy Bunter. "I'm jolly glad some fellow did it, of course, after Quelch whopping me and keeping me in. Some pal of mine, I expect, paying Quelch out for me."

"Lucky Quelch didn't ask what you were going to do with that treacle if it hadn't got spilled over you by accident!" grinned Peter. "You'd better let this be a lesson to you, you fat chump!"

"I say, you fellows, think Quelch will go to the Head about this?" asked Bunter. "If he does he won't be in his study. I—I think I'll cut along to his study."

"You'll cut along to Quelch's study?" gasped Peter Todd. "What for?"

Bunter grinned.

"What about upsetting the ink over the treacle?" he asked. "Make him wild when he goes back and finds the ink mixed with the treacle. What?"

"You blithering, bloated bloater!" gasped Peter.

"Oh, really, Toddy! If he asks me about it, you can tell him I haven't left the Rag, same as before—see?"

Peter Todd gazed for a moment at William George Bunter. Then he seized him by a fat neck.

Bang!

Bunter's head smote the table in the Rag. The roar that came from Billy Bunter woke the echoes far and near.

"Yoo-hooooop!"

Bang!

"Yarooh! Leggo! Beast! Help! Rescue! Yaroooop!"

Bang!

"Ow! Wow! Oh crikey! Ow!"

"There!" gasped Peter. "Still thinking of japing in Quelch's study?"

"Ow! Yes! I——"

Bang!

"I mean no!" roared Bunter. "Nothing of the sort! Leggo! I—I—I won't go near Quelch's study! Yoohoop!"

"Ha, ha, ha!"

Billy Bunter did not go near Quelch's study. Between washing off the lingering remains of the treacle, and rubbing his bullet head where it had been banged, Bunter was too busy for some time to think of the trail of vengeance.

THE SIXTH CHAPTER.

A Row in the Changing-room!

"PLAYING Dutton?"

"Didn't you see his name in the list?"

"Well, yes, but——" said Carter.

"But what?"

"Seems rather rot to me."

Carter was speaking to Harry Wharton in the changing-room. He did not glance at Bob Cherry, who was sitting on a bench, with one boot on, and the other in his hand. Vernon-Smith, on the same bench, did glance at Bob, and grinned as he glanced.

All the Remove knew that Bob barred the new junior, though only Bob's friends knew why. Bob could be civil to a fellow, even if he barred him; but it seemed to be difficult for him to keep civil to Arthur Carter.

Everything that the new fellow did or said seemed to touch Bob on the raw. Now he was glaring at Carter as the latter talked to the captain of the Remove, and Smithy, grinning as he watched him, knew that Bob would have liked to pitch the boot in his hand at the new junior's head.

That Wednesday afternoon Highcliffe were coming over to play the Remove. The Highcliffe fixture was a big event in the Remove list, and men for that match were selected with care. Carter, who had only come to the school that term, was considered lucky to be picked out.

Billy Bunter blinked at Bob Cherry in surprise through his big spectacles. "You want to be a bit tough to play Soccer, you know! Don't you think you're a bit soft, old chap, to come off just for a hack?" Bob Cherry, who could hardly stand on his damaged leg, glared at the fat junior as if he could have eaten him.

But there was no doubt that he was showing great form at Soccer. Harry Wharton, who was getting more and more to share Bob's repugnance for the new fellow personally, did not think for a moment of allowing that to interfere with football matters. If he had disliked Carter as much as Bob did, or twice as much, he would still have put him in the team if he believed he could help to beat Highcliffe.

So Carter was in, on the right wing, Hurree Singh having been shifted along the front line, in a little rearrangement. Bob had nothing to say to that —he did not like Carter, but he had to admit that the fellow deserved a place, on the form he had shown. But Carter's talk, in the changing-room, made Bob's eyes gleam—much to the Bounder's amusement.

Tom Dutton was in the team at right-back, in the place usually taken by Mark Linley. Mark had a game knee, from an accidental kick, in games-practice, and had to stand down.

Dutton, who had already changed, looked a very active and sturdy fellow in football garb, keen as mustard. The fact that Dutton was deaf, was undoubtedly a handicap in any game. But he was a good player, keen and wary and watchful, and he could hear a shout, even if ordinary conversation was rather lost on him.

Bob would have stretched a point, or a good many points, in favour of a fellow who had to carry on under such a handicap. But that was evidently not Carter's view.

"I hear that this game is expected to be rather a tussle," went on Carter.

"Highcliffe are always good!" answered Harry shortly.

"You see, your pal Ponsonby isn't in their team!" said Peter Todd, with cheery sarcasm. Peter, who was by no means pleased by Carter's remarks. Tom

Dutton belonged to his study, and was also his pal. "You mustn't judge Highcliffe by your friends there, Carter!"

"Well, I wouldn't play a deaf ass, if I were skipper!" said Carter. "Don't you want to win the match?"

The captain of the Remove looked at him.

"You're not skipper!" he pointed out.

"And Dutton isn't an ass! And if he heard you say so, he would probably punch your cheeky head, so it's just as well for you that he's deaf."

Dutton, who was within a few feet of them, had a cheery smile on his face, evidently unaware that he was being discussed.

Carter laughed.

"Well, he hasn't heard me say so, and he won't hear anything you may have to say to him on the field!" he remarked. "Seems rot to me to put him in."

"Oh, shut up, Carter!" broke out Bob Cherry. "Nobody asked for your opinion! Keep it to yourself."

Carter glanced round at Bob.

"I don't think I was speaking to you!" he drawled.

"Well, I'm speaking to you," growled Bob, his face reddening. "Dutton's a decent fellow, deaf or not, which you will never be. Any fellow here would rather be deaf like old Dutton, than a scheming worm like you."

"Chuck it, Bob, old chap!" said Harry hastily. "No rows here, you know."

"Let him shut up, then," grunted Bob. "He makes me ill."

"I'll please myself about that, if it's all the same to you, Cherry!" drawled Carter. "Can't a fellow ask a question?"

"Oh, all right!" growled Bob, "I'll

ask one, too! Where were you when that treacle was mopped over Quelch's papers yesterday?"

Carter started a little.

"I hardly remember, at the moment," he answered. "What does it matter?"

"Oh, try to remember," retorted Bob, with savage sarcasm. "Then, perhaps, you'll call to mind that you were in Quelch's study, pouring out that treacle, to set him on Bunter's track."

"Did you see me there?"

"You took jolly good care that nobody saw you there!"

"Then do you think it quite fair to say that I was there, when you own up that you don't know anything about it?"

"I know it as well as if I saw you!"

"Draw it mild, old man!" murmured Squiff. "You're not a giddy magician, you know."

"Well I do know it!" grunted Bob.

"You don't," said Carter coolly, "and to put it plain, it's a lie!"

Bob Cherry bounded up from the bench. With one boot on, and one boot off, he jumped towards Carter.

Five or six fellows interposed at once.

Carter stood with a sneer on his face. He was in no danger. The footballers were not likely to let a scrap begin in the changing-room, when Highcliffe were expected almost any minute.

"Let me go!" roared Bob, struggling in the grasp of Harry Wharton, Johnny Bull, Hurree Singh, Tom Brown and the Bounder.

"Chuck it, fathead——"

"Cheese it, you ass!"

"Hold on, Bob——"

"Do you think I'm going to let that cad call me a liar?" roared Bob.

"Well, dash it all, if you say things you can't prove, what do you expect the chap to say?" exclaimed Tom Brown. "Anyhow, you're not going to scrap."

"Chuck it, Bob!" said Harry.

"Don't play the goat! Do you want Courtenay's crowd to see a fight on here when they blow in?"

Bob Cherry controlled his anger. He realised that it would not do.

"Oh, all right!" he grunted. "Let go, you duffers—I won't touch the fellow. He can go and eat coke!"

Bob went back to the bench and put on his other boot. Carter shrugged his shoulders. Tom Dutton looked round, from face to face.

"What's the row?" he asked. "What were you going for Carter for, Cherry?"

"Oh, nothing; it's all right!" answered Bob.

"A fight? This isn't the place for a fight, old chap!" said Dutton. "We're going to play football, you know."

"All right!" howled Bob.

"Oh, lots!" said Dutton. "What do you mean? It's only two o'clock now—of course there will be light—plenty of it."

"Ha, ha, ha!"

"Ring off, old chap!"

"Eh? I'm going to play with it on. What do you mean, fling off my cap?" asked Dutton, in surprise.

"Oh, help!" gasped Bob.

"Do you mean Carter? Look here, Cherry, I shouldn't call a chap a whelp, if I were you. It's not a nice thing to call any fellow, even if you do dislike him. I don't see that Carter's a whelp! He seems all right to me."

"Give us a rest!"

"Whose chest?" asked Dutton.

"Ha, ha, ha!"

Bob did not answer that question. He liked Tom Dutton, and he was ready to stand up for him at any time; but a little conversation with him went a long way.

THE SEVENTH CHAPTER.
Accidents Will Happen!

BOB CHERRY quite forgot irritation and annoyance, on the football field. His ruddy face was bright and cheery.

Highcliffe had come over in great form. Harry Wharton & Co. always expected a tussle with Courtenay's team, and they had it. The Highcliffe footballers were very different from Carter's friends at that school—Pon & Co.

Bob, who was at right-half, was accustomed to see Smithy and Hurree Singh in front of him. Now he had Smithy and Carter, the Nabob of Bhanipur being on the left-wing. It was quite possible that Carter, in Bob's place, would have failed to "feed the forwards": but Bob, once he was in the game, quite forgot that he barred Carter.

Carter, at the moment, was simply the Greyfriars outside-right, to Bob—and, in fact, in that position, the new junior played up brilliantly. He was at least as good as Hurree Jamset Ram Singh, and a good many fellows thought him better. He was quick and alert, keen on the game, and had pace—and Bob, if he had thought about it, would have admitted that the captain of the Remove was right in playing him. But Bob was not thinking about that—he was only thinking of the game.

It was hard and fast from the whistle. Highcliffe had come over for a victory—and the Greyfriars men were determined to greet them with a defeat; so the game was rather like the old story of the irresistible force brought to bear on the immovable object!

The first half ended without a score.

for either side. In the second half, both sides went all out for victory. But luck seemed with the Highcliffians. They came down like wolves on the fold. Squiff, in goal, was all eyes and hands and feet, and thrice he drove the leather away: and the third time, it sailed over Johnny Bull, who was on his back. The Caterpillar was on it, when Tom Dutton hooked it fairly away from his toe, and sent it to midfield. The game swayed back up the field.

"Good man, Dutton!" gasped Harry Wharton—his words quite lost on Tom.

Vernon-Smith had the ball, and the Bounder took it up the field. The Highcliffians had to fall back and defend, and there was a hot struggle in front of the visitors' goal.

But the leather went away again, and again Courtenay & Co. were attacking. There was a mix-up on the right wing.

Three or four fellows went down, and from one of the sprawling figures came a sudden yelp of pain. The Caterpillar had the ball again, and was racing on with it, the other Highcliffe forwards speeding on. Behind them, Bob Cherry staggered to his feet, reeled, and went down again on one knee.

"Goal!"

It was a Highcliffe shout.

The Caterpillar had passed to Courtenay, who slammed the ball in, beating Squiff this time. It was first blood to Highcliffe.

"Goal!"

"Cherry, old chap——"

"Bob——"

Bob was up again, but he was tottering. His ruddy face was white with pain.

Harry Wharton caught him by the shoulder.

"Hurt, old chap?"

"Ask Carter!" breathed Bob. "He knows whether he's hurt me. I—I—I can't carry on—awfully sorry, old man—I can't stand on that leg!"

"Carter——"

"Sorry!" said Carter. "If I fell on you——"

"You know you did!"

"I was barged over——"

Potter of the Fifth, who was refereeing the junior match, came up.

"What——" he began.

"All right—I've got a hack!" stammered Bob. "I shall have to totter off—sorry, you chaps!"

"I say, I'm awfully sorry, if it was me," said Carter. "I was barged right over, as you all saw. I never knew I'd given Cherry a knock——"

Bob took no further heed of him. It was possibly an accident.

Bob limped off the field, his football finished for that afternoon. He had had a cruel hack, and he could hardly put his right foot to the ground.

"You fellows can't imagine——" exclaimed Carter.

"Of course not!" said Harry. "Line up! We've got to put our beef into this, you men—a man short."

"Man hurt?" asked Courtenay, coming up.

"Yes, an accident——"

"One of ours——"

"Oh, no, one of ours—just an accident."

The sides lined up again, Greyfriars a man short.

The Bounder's eyes were curiously and keenly on Carter. He dropped a whisper in his fellow-winger's ear as they lined up.

"One accident is enough for one game, Carter."

"What do you mean, Vernon-Smith?"

"I mean, that if you have an accident with me, I'll have an accident with you!" answered the Bounder deliberately. "That's what I mean—and you'd better have none in my direction."

"You fool, do you think——"

"I don't think—I know! Shut it!" said the Bounder.

The whistle went, and the game was resumed after the Highcliffe goal.

Bob Cherry limped away to the changing-room, with a clouded face and a heavy heart.

It was difficult for a fellow like Bob to believe that a man had deliberately hacked him—a man on his own side, too, as good as throwing away the game to gratify personal malice. But he could not help thinking that Carter had done so. It might have been an accident—he hoped that it had been—but he did not believe so."

Billy Bunter met him on the way and blinked at him in surprise through his big spectacles.

"Finished already?" he asked. "Who won?"

"No, ass! I've had to get off!" grunted Bob. "Crocked!"

"Bagged a hack?"

"Yes."

"Does it hurt?"

"Idiot!"

"Oh, really, Cherry! I shouldn't have chucked it for that!" said Bunter, shaking his head. "You want to be a bit tough to play Soccer, you know! No good a fellow playing Soccer if he can't stand a knock or two! Don't you think you're a bit soft, old chap, to come off just for a hack?"

Bob Cherry, who could not even stand on his damaged leg, glared at William George Bunter as if he could have eaten him.

Bunter wagged his fat head seriously.

"Hardly what I should do!" he remarked. "Wharton made a mistake in not playing me. Don't you think so? I offered."

"You priceless idiot!"

"Well, I don't think you ought to call a fellow names because he can stand a knock or two better than you can!" said Bunter reprovingly. "You're as soft as putty, old chap!"

Bob made a frantic mental calculation whether he could stand on his damaged leg long enough to kick Bunter with the other. A fearful spasm of pain warned him that he couldn't!

"Look here, brace up, and get back to it!" said Bunter encouragingly. "They'll want you, you know. You're not much good, but they don't want to play a man short against Highcliffe! Brace up! That's my advice!"

Bob looked round.

"Here, Micky!" he yelled.

Micky Desmond looked round. He hurried up.

"Sure, if you want me to lind you a hand——" he said.

"No," gasped Bob, "a foot! Kick Bunter for me, will you? I can't."

"Yarooooh!"

If Micky was pleased, Bunter was not.

"Kick him again for me," gasped Bob. "I'll do the same for you another time."

Bunter fled. Micky landed two more as he went. Bob limped on his way, feeling a little better.

Meanwhile, the game was going on, ding-dong. It was close on the finish, when a roar from the Greyfriars crowd reached Bob Cherry's ears.

"Goal!"

"Good man, Carter!"

"Goal! Goal!"

The footballers came crowding into the changing-room—the game a draw. It was Carter who had kicked the equalising goal—the only one taken by the side. He seemed very popular with the other fellows as he came in—and Bob, as he sat, rubbing his damaged leg with embrocation, looked on—with very mixed feelings.

THE EIGHTH CHAPTER.

Smithy Wants to Know !

HERBERT VERNON-SMITH strolled into Study No. 13, after prep that evening.

Bob Cherry was alone there.

His study-mates, Linley and Hurree Singh and Wun Lung, had gone down, Bob remaining to give his bruised leg another rub or two.

He had it resting across a chair, and there was a perceptible scent of embrocation in the atmosphere when the Bounder lounged in.

Bob gave him a glance—not a very affable one. His usually sunny temper was not at its best. He hated to give in to an injury, and he hated to appear to be making a fuss about one. But there was no help for that! He was still in a limping state, and he had to limp whether he liked it or not.

"Still bad?" asked Smithy.

"Oh, a twinge or two!" answered Bob carelessly.

The Bounder grinned and shut the door. He sat on the corner of the table, looking at Bob.

"I know all about that twinge or two!" he agreed. "I can see the damage. That cur got you fair and square."

"Oh! You think——"

"Don't you?"

"Well, I did at first when I got it!" admitted Bob. "But it seems such a rotten thing—a fellow to foul a man on his own side, just because——"

"Don't you think so now?"

"Well, I'd rather not, anyhow! After all, he kicked a goal for the side—the only one we got. They'd have beaten us otherwise."

"He can play Soccer!" said the Bounder. "He's no sportsman, but he can play Soccer. I believe he did it on purpose, because of that row in the changing-room, and what you said. I suppose you meant what you said?"

"Yes, I did!" grunted Bob. "Perhaps I shouldn't have said it, but I did mean it, and do now."

Vernon-Smith nodded.

"There's been a lot of jaw in the Form about that fellow Carter, and his jolly old relation Bunter," he remarked. "Can't blame a chap for being down on a relation like Bunter. But, according to what's going round, there's some question of rivalry for some old bean's money-bags. Bunter makes out, at any rate, that Carter's uncle, who is a sort of uncle-three-times-removed to Bunter, has got an eye on our fat old Owl. It seems clear, anyhow, that the old bean's written to Quelch about Bunter, and wants to hear his report this term."

Bob made no answer to that.

He knew more than the other fellows about that rivalry between Carter and Bunter, but he was not disposed to discuss what he knew with the Bounder.

"You've been up against the fellow ever since he came," went on Vernon-Smith. "Sort of protector to Bunter—what?"

"The fat fool needs somebody to help him keep his end up!" grunted Bob.

"No doubt about that, if a cunning fox like that man Carter is on his track. Looks to me as if something may depend on Bunter getting a good report this term, and Carter's made up his mind that he shall get a jolly bad one."

Bob, in silence, rubbed a big black bruise.

The Bounder, now that he turned his thoughts to the matter, saw how things stood, with his usual keenness. But Bob could not help wondering why he bothered his head about it at all. Smithy had his good qualities; but he was not the fellow to go out of his way to back up a lame duck. Bunter was nothing to him.

"Exactly!" said Vernon-Smith, as if Bob had spoken.

Bob started, and looked at him.

"Readin' your thoughts, old bean!" explained the Bounder airily. "Right on the wicket! If Bunter chooses to be a mixture of fool and rogue, he can take the consequences, and be blowed to him! I'm not worryin' a lot about Bunter. But if that cad hits out wildly and hits the wrong man, he must expect the wrong man to hit back—if the wrong man's me."

"What on earth do you mean?" asked Bob.

"I'll tell you. A week ago I was nearly nabbed at the Three Fishers. It would have been the sack."

"Serve you right!"

"Oh, quite! But that isn't the point. You and Bunter knew that I was there, and neither of you would have given me away, for love or money—not even that fat, grub-raiding, frabjous Owl!" The Bounder set his lips. "But I was given away, Cherry—Wingate of the Sixth came straight there, acting on information received, as the bobbies say. I got out of sight so quick it made my head swim. No time to get hold of my overcoat. And if it had been my own coat, I should have been done for."

"I know But what——"

"You remember how it happened; that fool, Bunter, barged me over and made my coat muddy, on the towpath, and I made him change. Well, Wingate never got me—he got the coat, and brought it back, and Bunter was up before the Head! But as everybody knew he had been in gates, he was all right. They had to leave it that somebody had borrowed Bunter's coat that afternoon—and they never found out who."

"Lucky for you!" grunted Bob.

"I'm usually lucky—my long suit!" grinned the Bounder. "But it was the closest shave I ever had, old bean, and I've been thinking about it ever since. I had my eye on Carter that day. He seemed so jolly sure that Bunter had been nailed, through the coat. Now, why did he fancy that Bunter was at the Three Fishers that afternoon?"

"Might have seen you, at a distance, after you'd got Bunter's coat on. Everybody knows that coat by sight; it's some coat!"

"Exactly!" said Vernon-Smith, with a nod. "I've thought it over, and that's how I work it out. That purple-striped coat of Bunter's would be known half a mile off—and I had it on, as it happened. If Carter chanced to see me going in, from a distance, he would think it was Bunter."

"That accounts——" said Bob, slowly.

"I think it does. From what the Head said, when Bunter was up, he was warned by a telephone call that a Greyfriars man had been seen going into the place, and then he sent Wingate to investigate. Who phoned?"

"Goodness knows! Hardly Carter; the Head might have known his voice and——"

(*Continued on next page.*)

"I've talked on the telephone without my voice giving me away," said the Bounder "So could Carter."

"But—I can't believe—even Carter is——"

"Look at it! Carter gave it completely away that he believed that Bunter was at that den on the river. He even thought, at first, that you fellows were telling lies when you testified that the fat ass had been in gates all the time. That can only mean that he spotted Bunter's overcoat going in. Then comes a mysterious telephone call, warning the Head! If it's true that Carter wants to disgrace Bunter here, it's all plain enough."

"Well, it looks like it, but——"

"But," said the Bounder, "he was making a bungle, like scheming cads often do. He nearly got me sacked, getting after Bunter! One good turn deserves another—and the same applies to a bad turn! It might happen like that again. Carter doesn't seem to care where his shots hit, so long as there's a chance of one getting Bunter! If it were Carter gave me away that day, I don't care whether he was after Bunter or not; I'm going to hand him the same as he handed me. Sneaking to the Head, and betraying a fellow—especially the wrong fellow—is a little too thick for the Remove."

"Blessed if I know what you're telling me all this for, Smithy!" said Bob, rather restively.

"I'll put it in words of one syllable, suitable to your undeveloped intellect, old scout. It's come out lately that Bunter is Carter's rival for some old bean's cash—through Bunter's gabble on the subject. But you were up against Carter from the day he came, before there was any talk on the subject. So I work it out that somehow you knew something earlier. What was it?"

"I'd rather not talk about it."

"Then there is something——"

"Something I heard by accident. I can't jaw about it."

"All I want is to get it quite clear that Carter's after Bunter, and using any method that comes to hand. If I'm certain of that, I'm certain that he's the man who gave me away last week. Get it off your chest."

"I'm not talking about it."

"You're against him—so am I, if I get that clear! Two heads are better than one, in any sort of a tussle."

"I'm not against him, so long as he leaves Bunter alone! What does it matter to me who bags old Joseph Carter's cash!" said Bob, irritably. "All I care about is seeing that he doesn't play treacherous tricks on that fat fool. I'm jolly well going to stop that."

"I'd stop him faster than you! I've got about ten times your gumption, old bean! Will you spout it all out?"

Bob shook his head.

The Bounder shrugged his shoulders and slipped from the study table.

"Keep it packed up, then!" he snapped. "I'll find out for myself. And if I get it clear that the cad got me within an inch of the sack last week, let him look out! He may get nearer to it than I did!"

And with that, the Bounder of Greyfriars tramped out of the study and slammed the door after him.

THE NINTH CHAPTER.

Whose Cigarette?

"GOT a match, Skinner?" Carter of the Remove stared in surprise.

He was coming along the path under the old elms, the day after

the Highcliffe match, when he came on Billy Bunter.

Bunter had a cigarette in his fat fingers.

Carter himself smoked cigarettes, though he was careful to keep it as dark as he could. But he had never suspected Bunter of it.

Neither was Bunter ass enough to spend money on smokes. If Bunter were seen in possession of a cigarette, it was a safe bet that it belonged to somebody whose name was not Bunter.

But here he was, with a cigarette, and as Carter came along, he blinked at him through his big spectacles, addressed him as Skinner, and asked him for a match.

Only a minute or two before, Loder of the Sixth had passed along that path. Carter had seen him. He might turn back, for all Carter knew—or Bunter! In which case, he would assuredly spot the fatuous Owl with that smoke.

Loder was a prefect, and, though it was rumoured that he smoked, in quiet spots, himself, it was certain that he would not fail to do his duty if he caught a Lower boy smoking! It meant a swipe from an ashplant if Bunter were spotted with that smoke!

"Oh! You!" Bunter, at the second blink, recognised Carter. "I don't want a match from you, Carter! You can go and eat coke!"

He put his fat hand behind him, with the cigarette in it.

Carter laughed.

"Is that a fag you've got there?" he asked.

He spoke quite loudly. He was fairly sure that Loder of the Sixth was not far away.

"Eh? No. Certainly not!" answered Bunter. "If you think you're going to find out anything to tell tales about, Carter, you're mistaken. I've got a stick of toffee here——"

"You wanted a match for a stick of toffee?" asked Carter, laughing.

He spotted Loder of the Sixth, hitherto hidden from sight by an elm trunk. The prefect was coming towards the spot.

Loder was looking annoyed. It was rather a secluded spot, between the old elms and the wall, and perhaps Loder was not pleased to hear the voices of the juniors there. It was barely possible that Gerald Loder had strolled there to put on a quiet smoke himself!

"It's toffee, anyhow!" said Bunter defiantly. "I jolly well know you smoke, Carter. I've seen you in the Cloisters. You'd like to let out, where Quelch could hear you, that you'd seen me with a smoke, wouldn't you? Yah!"

"You've got a cigarette in your paw now, you fat ass!" said Carter, quite loud enough for Loder to hear. "Did Smithy give you one?"

"No, he didn't!" snapped Bunter. "This is a better sort of smoke than Smithy's. Much more expensive! Not that I've got one." added Bunter cautiously. "I've got a stick of toffee, as I said. If you can't take a fellow's word about that, it only shows what a suspicious cad you are!"

"Bunter!"

"Oh crikey!" Billy Bunter gave a jump and revolved like a fat humming-top at Loder's sharp voice.

As Loder had come along from behind Bunter he could hardly have failed to see the cigarette held behind him. But Bunter, as he faced round, kept it behind him, hoping that Loder hadn't seen it. Bunter had a hopeful nature.

"Smoking, you young rascal!" rapped Loder. He slipped his ashplant down from under his arm into his hand.

"Oh, no! I haven't lighted it!"

gasped Bunter. "I mean, I—I haven't a cigarette, Loder! Only a—a stick of toffee."

Carter, smiling, strolled away. Having drawn Loder's attention to the fat Owl and his cigarette, he was finished there. He wondered whether Loder would report this to Mr. Quelch. He hoped so; it would be another black mark against Bunter—and every black mark counted, in consideration of the report that was to go to old Mr. Carter later.

Billy Bunter backed away from Loder in alarm.

Really he wished that he hadn't been in possession of a cigarette. He rather liked to fancy himself a "bad hat," like the Bounder; but, in point of fact, Bunter would have given all the cigarettes in the wide world for one stick of toffee or packet of butterscotch. Had he lighted that cigarette he would not have taken more than a couple of puffs —just to prove to himself, as it were, what a gay dog and a bad hat he was! But he had not even lighted it when Loder came down on him like a wolf on the fold.

"I—I say, Loder, don't you take any notice of that cad Carter!" gasped Bunter. "He's always getting me into rows. He jolly well knew you were there——"

"You've been smoking?"

"Oh, no! I hadn't a match—I mean I haven't a cigarette——"

"Hand it over at once, and then touch your toes," said Loder. He swished the ashplant.

"I—I—I say, Loder, I—I—I only picked it up!" gasped Bunter. "I—I give you my word that I—I just picked it up——"

"Sounds likely!" grinned Loder. "Lots of cigarettes lying about Greyfriars, I dare say! I told you to touch your toes."

Bunter backed away farther. A flick from Wingate or Gwynne would not have worried him very much, but Loder always swiped! And Loder was evidently annoyed about something— Bunter did not know what. When Loder was annoyed he had a way of laying it on very hard.

"Stoop, you young ass!" rapped Loder.

"Look here, I'm not going to be whopped just for picking up a cigarette I saw on the ground!" gasped Bunter. "I—I was only going to—to throw it over the wall, Loder; nasty thing, you know! I wouldn't smoke it! I—I—I ain't going to be whopped!"

"By gum! I'll——"

Loder made a forward stride.

Billy Bunter fairly bolted. He flew— and after him strode Loder.

Mr. Quelch was walking in the quad after morning school, and Billy Bunter headed for Quelch. The Remove master, who was pacing majestically, in conversation with Mr. Wiggins, the master of the Third, stared at that plump member of his Form as he came gasping up.

Loder, at the sight of the Remove master, followed more slowly. But he followed—he was not likely to let a junior escape, having once bidden him "touch his toes."

"What——" began Mr. Quelch.

"I—I—I wasn't, sir!" gasped Bunter. "I didn't! I mean, I never did! It's all a mistake, sir!"

Mr. Quelch made him a gesture to be silent.

"What is it, Loder?" he asked.

"Smoking, sir!" answered Loder. "As Bunter has come to you, perhaps

" Unless you can give me the name of the boy who dropped the cigarette you hold in your hand, Bunter," said Mr. Quelch grimly, " I shall request Loder to give you six strokes ! "   " Well, if you must know, sir," said Bunter, " it was Loder ! "

you would prefer to deal with the matter."

"Upon my word !" exclaimed Mr. Quelch. "Bunter, you——"

"I haven't !" howled Bunter. "I didn't ! I wasn't ! I never——"

"Why, there is a cigarette in your hand at this moment !" exclaimed Mr. Quelch.

"I—I—I picked it up, sir !" groaned Bunter. "I—I saw a fellow drop it, sir, and—and just picked it up to—to see what it was, sir !"

"Indeed !" said Mr. Quelch grimly. "If that statement is correct, Bunter, you may give me the name of the boy who dropped the cigarette."

"Oh, I—I—I'd rather not, sir——" stammered Bunter, with an uneasy blink at Loder. "I—I hope you can take my word, sir——"

"I can do nothing of the kind, Bunter ! Unless you give me the name immediately, I shall request Loder to give you six strokes, for such a pernicious——"

"Oh crikey !"

"Loder, you will kindly——"

"I—I—I'll tell you, sir, if—if Loder doesn't mind !" gasped Bunter.

Loder stared at him.

"Why should I mind, you young ass ?" he snapped. "If you're telling the truth, tell Mr. Quelch at once."

"Oh, all right ! It was Loder, sir !"

THE TENTH CHAPTER.

Not According to Plan !

LODER gave a jump.

Mr. Quelch stared.

Mr Wiggins blinked, and then smiled.

Loder's hand shot to his pocket.

He had slipped a couple of loose cigarettes into that pocket, in his study,

to smoke in a secluded corner, secure from observing eyes. He had supposed up to that moment that they were still there.

But at Bunter's words he hastily groped. He caught his breath as he felt only one cigarette in his pocket—and a hole in the lining !

"Did—did you say Loder ?" exclaimed Mr. Quelch blankly.

"Yes, sir !"

"Why, you young rascal——" exclaimed Loder furiously.

"I—I say, you keep off, Loder !" squeaked Bunter. "You said you didn't mind ! You know you did ! You told me to tell Mr. Quelch."

Mr. Quelch gazed from one to the other.

Mr. Wiggins, with a lurking smile on his face, admired the scenery.

"Upon my word !" said Mr. Quelch. "You state that you saw Loder, a Sixth Form prefect, drop that cigarette, Bunter ?"

"Oh dear ! Yes, sir ! It dropped behind him when he went under the elms, sir," said Bunter. "I—I wasn't going to smoke it ! I just picked it up ! I was going to throw it away when I asked Carter for a match—I mean——"

"Hand it to me at once, Bunter !"

"Yes, sir ! I—I—- Shall I ask one of the fellows for a match for you, sir ?"

"You utterly ridiculous boy, be silent !" hooted Mr. Quelch. He scanned that cigarette. It was a large, fat, Turkish cigarette, hardly the kind that Bunter would have been likely to spend his money on if he spent money on smokes at all. "If Bunter picked up this cigarette, as he states, Loder, there is evidently no occasion for punishment, as it has not been lighted But——"

Quelch's eyes fixed on Loder like two pin-points.

"You will hardly suppose, sir, that I, a Sixth Form prefect, smoke cigarettes, against all the rules of the school !" said Gerald Loder, with all the dignity he could muster in the difficult circumstances.

"I trust not, Loder. In any case, the Sixth Form are not under my authority," said Mr. Quelch dryly. "But—— If you prefer this matter to be investigated by your headmaster——"

Loder breathed hard. At that moment he would have been glad to be dealing with Carter of the Remove, who had landed him in this. But Carter of the Remove had to wait.

It was quite clear that Bunter had seen Loder drop that cigarette and had picked it up. Quelch knew how to sift the wheat from the chaff, and he knew that that much was true. And Loder knew that he knew—and dreaded the possibility of the circumstances being mentioned to the headmaster.

"The fact is, sir," said Loder, pulling his wits together very rapidly—"the fact is, I think Bunter is probably telling the truth. If he had told me, I should have understood. In break this morning I took a couple of cigarettes away from a junior and put them in my pocket, intending to throw them into the fire when I went to my study. I forgot all about them."

"If the junior you refer to was a Remove boy, Loder, kindly give me his name."

"He was not a Remove boy, sir."

"If he was a Third Form boy, kindly give me his name, Loder," said Mr. Wiggins.

"He was not in the Third, sir."

Mr. Wiggins resumed admiring the scenery.

Mr. Quelch's eyes continued to be fixed on Loder's flushed face.

(Continued on page 15.)

No. 279. EDITED BY HARRY

DUSTY TO THE RESCUE!

Another Side-Splitting Spasm of Our Super Serial:
"THE FORM-MASTER'S SECRET!"

By DICKY NUGENT

Jack Jolly & Co. were given special permission from Doctor Birchemall, the Head of St. Sam's, to go out on their bikes looking for Bullion, the welthy yung Fourth Former who had been kidnapped from the skool.

The heroes of the Fourth beleeved in the old motter: "It's the early bird that catches the worm"—so they were up with the lark. Their eagle eyes were going to search the countryside around St. Sam's with hawk-like zeal. If they found the kidnappers, they were going to swallow no tale desined to put them off their stroak. They would at once take swift action to cook the kidnapper's goose.

Jack Jolly & Co. were very hoapful of a quick suxxess that would enable them to crow over the rest of the skool for weeks. Their faces were grim and determined, as they wheeled their bikes past the Skool House on their way down to the gates.

Suddenly they halted. From a hevvily barred winder at the top of the Skool House they had caught site of somebody waving to them.

It was Mr. Lickham, the master of the Fourth.

Mr. Lickham had spent a restless nite in the punishment-room where the Head had locked him until the perlice arrived in the morning. The prospect of being arrested for a crime he had never committed was one that simply appawled him.

He was tired and hungry—and completely fed up! His entire career was at steak; and arrest would simply send him off his onion.

The maddening thing about it was that this charge of being consernod in the plot to kidnap Bullion was one of which he could have cleared himself at any moment he wished.

He had only to reveel that his disreputable cuzzin Dusty had been impersonating him at St. Sam's for the last week to free himself from all suspishon!

But to reveal that meant also revealing that he himself had spent that same week in jail for falling into arrears with the instalments on his new cap and gown. And that revelation would disgrace him for ever in the eyes of the orthorities at St. Sam's!

No wonder, then, Mr. Lickham looked woeful and weery, as he pressed his face against the bars outside the punishment-room winder!

"Where are you going, boys?" he cried, as Jack Jolly & Co. halted on the gravel path beneeth him.

"Searching for Bullion, sir!"

"I wish I could join you!" sighed Mr. Lickham. "If you would only help me to escape, I could!"

"Some hoaps, sir!" larfed Jolly. "With all dew respect, you're locked up in that room for a very good reason—becawse the Head suspeckts you of having a hand in the kidnapping of yung Bullion!"

"Hear, hear!"

Mr. Lickham shook his head viggerously.

"I never did it, Jolly—honner bright! It's all a garstly mistake. Surely you know me better than that?"

"Well, I thought I did at one time," acknollidged the kaptin of the Fourth. "But you must admit that you've been a changed man during the last week. After the way you've carried on, I can quite imagine you doing anything!"

"Oh, bust it!" muttered the master of the Fourth. Once again he was in the unforchunit position of being unable to prove his innersence without giving away his secret!

"Sorry and all that, sir!" grinned Frank Fearless. "But there's nothing doing! Toodle-oo!"

The juniors mounted their machines and pedalled off; and Mr. Lickham was left to wrench and tug away at the bars that barred his way to freedom.

Jack Jolly & Co. put all their hart and sole into the search for Bullion that morning. Nothing escaped their keen eyes. They went through every yard of the woods, every foot of the hedgerows, and every inch of the fields.

They crawled on hands and neeze through ditches, they dessended dark, dank, dreery wells, they eggsplored the top of many a haystack.

But not a sine of the missing Bullion did they discover!

"Wherever those vilIans have hidden him, it must be a pretty good hiding-place!" remarked Jolly grimly, as they pedalled slowly away from a coppice they had just been scouring. "Some secret underground cell, perhaps, or a consealed room in some rambling old mansion!"

"I wonder if Lickham knows!" mermered Fearless thoughtfully. Then he gave a sudden violent start. "Grate pip! There he is!"

As he spoke, Fearless pointed to a field which they were passing. His pals glanced in the direction indicated, and, to their utter amazement, saw Lickham crawling across the grass on his hands and neeze, apparently eggsamining footmarks through a magnifying-glass!

"My hat! He must have escaped!" gasped Jolly. "And he's mannidged to get a change of clothing, too! Let's go and talk to him!"

"Yes, rather!"

The Co. dumped their bikes at the side of the road and dived through a gap in the hedge. But the noise they made evidently betrayed them.

By the time they arrived in the field, Lickham had vannished just as though the earth had opened and swallowed him up!

Discerning readers will hardly need to be told that the man they had seen in the field was Dusty Lickham, and not Mr. I. Jolliwell Lickham, the real Form-master of the Fourth.

Dusty was a low, common creetcher, but he had a conshance. The black sheep of the Lickham fambly did not intend to have the wool pulled over Doctor Birchemall's eyes if he could help it. If it was yewmanly possibul to track down the raskally Joe and Charlie, he was going to do it. After that, he would reskew Bullion and restore him to St. Sam's—thus delivering the Fourth Form master from the suspishons which he had unintentionally fastened on him!

While Jack Jolly & Co. were gazing blankly round the field, Dusty was watching them from some bushes where he had taken cover; and he took good care not to ventcher fourth again until the Co. had mounted their bikes once more and pedalled away down the road.

After they had gone, Dusty resoomed his interrupted work of tracking down Joe and Charlie even more keenly than before.

"I 'ope as 'ow I shan't see those yung jents again to-day!" he muttered to himself, as he continued to crawl across the field.

Little did he dreem how soon and in what dramattick circumstances he was to renew his ackwaintance with the Co.

Jack Jolly & Co. cycled on towards Muggleton. But they never reached that town.

What stopped them from doing so was a feint cry from an old barn at the side of the road.

"Help! Help!"

That cry was enuff for Jack Jolly & Co. With one accord they leaped off their bikes—their eyes simply blazing with eggsitement!

"Bullion!" hist Jolly.

"Not the slitest doubt about it!" said Fearless, between his clenched teeth. "This way, you fellows!"

"Yes, rather!"

They farely rushed over to the barn!

Jolly was the first to reach the door. It was bolted and barred; but one mitey kick from the

kaptin
bust i
other
of th
swarm
The
Bullio
on the
and f
For
chewe
and v
feint c
kidnap
farely
recker
boys,
faces
saw h
"Th
leave
cried
shall
before
older!
"Ho
out a
hind
Jack
wheel
that
had a
just
mome
The
burly
the t
dagge
mite
the b
Jolly
hezzit
With
cries
flung
riously
A la
alone
agains
scoun
flashe
whirle
of the
found
agains
genz!
Clin
Fear
to fall,
soon
finally
self, p
pulp,
a regu
blows.
But
hoaps
sunk
help
unegg
Throu
way
that
to th
Fourth
"L
gaspe
The
waded
nappe

MY FORM IS THE BEST AT GREYFRIARS!

Claims A. CAPPER, M.A.

Of course it is!

Frankly, I am amazed that there should be any question about it.

Have you never seen Temple's trousers with their immaculate crease? Or Fry's fancy waistcoat? Or Dabney's dinner-jacket?

Furthermore, look at their toppers! Is there another Form at Greyfriars that can wear toppers with the same easy, nonchalant grace of the Upper Fourth? I think not!

But their socks and ties are what really clinch it. Were I a sporting man I would wager any amount that for sheer artistry in socks and ties the Upper Fourth cannot be equalled — let alone surpassed—anywhere!

Without doubt, my Form is the best DRESSED Form at Greyfriars!

(*Capitals ours. We knew that Mr. Capper had got it wrong somewhere. We asked him if the Upper Fourth was the BEST—not the BEST DRESSED! But as their clobber is the only possible thing the Upper Fourth can boast about, his mistake was quite natural!—Ed.*).

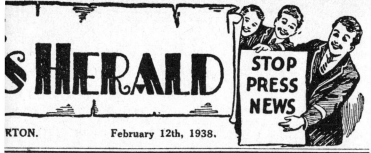

HERALD

STOP PRESS NEWS

...RTON. February 12th, 1938.

HARRY WHARTON CALLING

" Are the gay dogs of Greyfriars as black as they are painted ? " asks a reader in a letter I received this week.

This query, in various forms, is one I have put to me with surprising frequency. There seems to be a mysterious fascination about the more shady activities which sometimes go on in the school !

Well, personally, though I haven't much time for the bright young things who get their amusement out of puffing at cheap cigarettes and perusing pink sporting papers, I am inclined to believe that they are not half so villainous as they like to be thought !

Some readers seem to imagine that chaps like Loder of the Sixth, Hilton of the Fifth, Angel of the Fourth, and Skinner of our own Form, spend their entire time gambling and plotting dark plots against me and my friends.

Nothing of the kind, dear readers, I assure you !

Loder plays a good game of footer, Hilton is a topping boxer, Angel plays tennis very well, and Skinner is pretty hot at gymnastics. They can do many other things, but I mention these particularly to show you that a good deal of their time is spent in quite normal pursuits.

To imagine any chap at Greyfriars as an unmitigated rotter would, in my opinion, be very unjust. The four fellows I have mentioned have often in the past been at loggerheads with me. But I have also been at loggerheads with them and possibly the fault has not always been on one side !

Nobody is entirely bad—nor entirely good ! I am not exactly a saint myself. On the other hand, fellows whose code of conduct is not the same as my own are not necessarily the last word in villains !

I feel sure that the " gay dogs " of Greyfriars are not half so black as they are painted !

More chinwag next week, chums ! Cheerio !

HARRY WHARTON.

(Left columns — serial story)

...e Fourth ...n an- ...the heroes ...rth were ...the barn. ...iately saw ...was lying ...ound hand ...d gagged. ..., he had ...of his gag, ...to utter ...help. The ...ior's eyes ...when he ...e St. Sam's ...the Co.'s ...d as they

...ndrells, to ...ike this ! " ...ly. " They ...rly for it ...re much

... wrapped ... voice be-

...& Co. ...d, to find ...s captors ...n the seen ...e wrong

...those two ...armed to ...ith nives, ...cudgels, ...e dawnted ...But Jack ...did not ...moment. ...ging war-...ips, they ...ves few-...idnappers. ...r curridge ...ot enuff ...desprit ...Nives ...cudgels ...he heroes ...h quickly ...y were up ...th a ven-

...! Wallop ! ...s the first ...nd Bright ...him, and ...olly him-...lmost into ...wn under ...of cudgel-

...when the ...Co. had ...to zero, ...m a most ...quarter. ...pen door-...a figger ...y familiar ...s of the

...m ! " they ...Lickham ...the kid-...an eye-

opener to Jack Jolly & Co. He treated nife-stabs as if they were meer pinpricks, while as for cudgel-blows, he treated them with sheer disdain.

" Stop your tickling, Jock ! " was all he said about them !

But it was a different matter with the kidnappers when they reeeeved his fist in their faces ! Howls and shreeks of aggerny rent the air. Cudgels and nives dropped to the floor as though their owners had lost the power to hold them ! Evenchally, the kidnappers themselves followed their weppons and Lickham (Dusty Lickham, of corse, though the juniors did not know it !) was victorious !

" Good old Mr. Lickham ! " cheered Jack Jolly & Co.

Their wounds forgotten in their eggsitement, they jumped to their feet again.

" Shall we send for the perlice, sir ? " asked Fearless.

But Dusty shook his head.

" No, yung jents. Personally, I hain't got no use for the peelers. Let me give these blokes a talkin' to instead."

And, much to the Fourth Formers' serprize, he yanked the kidnappers to their feet and gave them a lecture on what bad lads they had been !

" Promiss you'll go straight in future ? " he finished.

" Yuss. We promiss ! " wined Charlie and Joe.

" Hoff you go, then ! "

And off they went and stuck to the straight path—till they reached the place where it turned into the road !

" Well, sir, after this there's no doubt about it being all right for you to come back to St. Sam's," said Jolly, as they released Bullion. " The Head will be jolly glad, in fakt, that you did escape from the punishment - room this morning ! "

Dusty Lickham started violently.

" Me hexcaped from the punishment - room ? Wot the dickens—— "

Then Dusty saw it all ! His cuzzin must have come back—and landed right into all the trubble that Dusty had left for him !

" My heye ! " mermered Dusty. " Heggs-cuse me, yung jents, but if you'll be orlright to go back to the skool on

your own, I think I'll go another way ! "

And, sure enuff, he insisted on leaving them before they reached St. Sam's. And Jack Jolly & Co. returned in triumf with Bullion — minus the man who had really reskewed Bullion !

(Don't miss the comical conclusion of this great serial in next week's " Herald " !

BE A CAKE-SNATCHER !

Fellows who are devoting thought to their future careers should consider the advantages of taking up cake-snatching as a profession. Pleasant and profitable ! For a course of instruction by the acknowledged expert, apply (with the Editor's compliments) to PRO-FESSOR BUNTER, care of GREYFRIARS HERALD.

WANT A FIGHT ?

Heavyweight Boxer seeks bouts with ambitious youngsters in need of experience. Applications considered from undersized weaklings who are willing to accept advertiser's own referee ! Write : BATTLING BOLSOVER, Box No. 233, GREYFRIARS HERALD.

SORROWS OF A SWOT

Mark Linley enjoys school work so much that he can hardly bear the thought of holidays.

The idea of " breaking up " almost makes him " break down " !

RAKE A WORTHY WINNER ON ROLLERS !

Says MONTY NEWLAND

A sprained ankle having finished my chances of winning the Lower School Roller-skating Championship, I was very glad to agree to Wharton's request to report on the race for the " Greyfriars Herald."

Roller-skating, in my opinion, is a great sport. I am always at home on a pair of rollers, whether I'm on a rink surface or on an ordinary road. I've won long-distance races on several occasions. I had hoped to win the silver medal that Mr. Lascelles put up for the winner of the Lower School Championship, too ; but fate in the shape of a learner who got in my way at the Lantham Rink decreed otherwise and landed me with a sprained ankle instead !

With my name out of it, the race was a pretty open one and a large crowd turned up in the gym. on the great night. Wingate and Blundell were

the judges, and they stood on a raised platform from which they could watch competitors all round the track. The presence of these two distinguished seniors, incidentally, has given a lot of prestige to the sport at Greyfriars. Fellows who have looked down on roller-skating as a kid's game in the past can hardly do so now that Wingate and Blundell have patronised it !

Ten skaters lined up for the start. The race was over 25 laps, and forecasts that it would be a close one were fully justified. For the first ten laps there was never more than a few yards between the first and last man, despite the fact that several fancied skaters were making great efforts to forge ahead !

An alarming incident occurred at this juncture, when Bunter, who had arrived too late for the start, careered into the gym. on skates at a hair-raising speed — unfortunately going the wrong way

round the track ! Bunter skated with both arms stretched outwards and succeeded in knocking down Bob Cherry and Don Ogilvy simultaneously before landing on the back of his neck. Stewards on skates rushed to the spot and stuck a " Danger " sign on Bunter to give due warning to approaching skaters.

Bunter took no further part in the race.

At twenty laps the field had extended out a bit and Bull led, with Brown second and Rake third. Rake was going well at this stage and went even better in the next few laps. Despite desperate efforts on the part of Brown and Bull, he passed each in turn, and eventually got home by the narrow margin of a couple of yards !

Mr. Lascelles himself presented the medal and a very enjoyable evening concluded with loud cheers.

Roller-skating at Greyfriars has received quite a fillip !

GETTING HIS OWN BACK!

By FRANK RICHARDS

(Continued from page 13.)

"I find now," went on Loder, "that there is a hole in the lining of my pocket. So Bunter's statement may be correct, sir !"

"In that case, Loder, the matter ends here," said Mr. Quelch in an exceedingly dry tone. "If you will take a word of advice from me, Loder, you will not on another occasion carry about with you cigarettes that you may take from juniors. Such proceedings are liable to misconstruction. Bunter, you may go."

Bunter gladly went.

Mr. Quelch snapped the Turkish cigarette in his fingers and threw away the fragments.

Loder did not stay to witness that destruction of one of his expensive smokes. He retired from the spot with feelings that he could not have expressed in words.

He went to look for Carter.

He was going to whop Carter for having landed him in that painful position. He felt that he had to whop somebody. He would have liked, indeed, to whop Mr. Quelch, had that been practicable

He could not, of course, whop Quelch. He could not, in the circumstances, whop Bunter! But he could think of some pretext or other for whopping Carter.

As it happened, he found his pretext ready-made for him. Carter had gone into the changing-room, and Billy Bunter, in the doorway of that apartment, was addressing him, in tones of the deepest scorn.

"Yah ! Cad ! Sneak ! You jolly well knew that Loder could hear you, when you gave me away ! Yah !"

"Shut up, you fat fool!" came Carter's voice, from within.

"Shan't ! I say, you fellows, what do you think that cad did ? Shouted out for Loder to hear, that I had a smoke——"

"Will you shut up ?"

"No, I won't ! You rotten swab—ow ! Leggo, you beast !" roared Bunter, as Carter stepped into the doorway and gripped a fat ear, just as Loder arrived in the offing. "Ow !. Leggo ! I'll hack your shins ! I say, you fellows, make him leggo ! Ow ! My ears ! Wow !"

Bump !

Bunter sat down—hard !

"Now will you shut up, you fat freak?" snarled Carter.

"Yaroooop !"

"Carter !" rapped Loder. Here was his pretext, and a good one !

"Oh ! Yes, Loder !"

"What do you mean by handling Bunter like that—a helpless fat duffer who cannot stand up for himself ?" said Loder sternly. "You're new here, Carter, but you'd better learn that this sort of thing won't do for Greyfriars ! Step back into that room, and bend over."

Carter, setting his lips, stepped back into the changing-room. The fellows THE MAGNET LIBRARY.—No. 1,565.

there looked on. Loder pointed to a bench with his ash.

"Bend over that bench !" he said. "I don't know what they let you do at your last school, Carter, but bullying isn't allowed here."

The Bounder, who was in the changing-room, winked at the other fellows. That was rather good, from the bully of the Sixth.

"Look here——" muttered Carter.

"I've told you to bend over that bench !" said Loder grimly, swishing the ashplant. "Now then."

Carter, setting his lips, bent over the bench.

Billy Bunter scrambled up, and stood blinking at the scene through his big spectacles, with a cheery grin on his fat face ! He was rather glad that Carter had bumped him over, in view of the result!

Whack, whack, whack !

"He, he, he !" from Bunter.

Whack, whack, whack !

It was a full "six," and every one a swipe. Carter was panting by the time Loder had finished.

Loder tucked the ashplant under his arm.

"Let that be a lesson to you !" he remarked, and he walked out of the changing-room.

Carter stood wriggling.

"He, he, he !" cackled Bunter. "I say, you fellows, he fancied he was going to get me six, and he's got six himself ! He, he, he !"

Carter, with a savage face, made a stride towards the grinning fat Owl.

Bunter blinked defiance at him.

"You touch me, and I'll call Loder !" he grinned. "I'm not going to lick you myself—you ain't worth it. But Loder——"

Carter decided not to "touch" Bunter—not at present, at all events. He swung away scowling—leaving the fat Owl of the Remove grinning.

THE ELEVENTH CHAPTER.

Spotted—by Smithy !

HERBERT VERNON-SMITH smiled sourly.

His eyes were on the new fellow in the Remove.

Carter was standing at the window of the Rag, looking out. Nobody else was taking any interest in that fact—but the Bounder was.

Since the episode the previous week, when Smithy had had so narrow an escape through some unknown person giving information, his interest in Carter had been very keen. Smithy's was not a forgiving nature ; and if it was Carter who had given him that narrow escape, Carter had trouble to come. "Sneaking" was barred in the Remove, and a fellow who had nearly landed Smithy in expulsion, by sneaking, was booked for the hardest knock that Smithy could hand back.

But Smithy wanted to be sure. If it was true, as he knew that Bob Cherry believed, that Carter was scheming and planning to land the fat Owl of the Remove in trouble after trouble, there was no doubt that he was the man who had given away the fellow who was wearing Bunter's coat on that occasion. Smithy wanted to know, and he was going to know.

Glancing from another window, he saw Mr. Quelch and Mr. Prout in the quad, in coats and hats. Quelch was going out, after class, in company with the master of the Fifth. Carter was watching them—and the Bounder had no doubt that he was waiting for his Form-

master to get clear of the school, for reasons of his own. But he had to wait, for the plump Prout progressed slowly towards the gates, and Quelch had to accommodate his pace to the Fifth Form master's

Leaving Carter at the window, Smithy strolled out of the Rag.

Tom Redwing called to him, as he went, but he took no heed.

He walked away to Masters' Passage.

Carter, he had no doubt, had something on hand, after Quelch had gone out. The episode of the treacle was not forgotten yet, and the Bounder had little doubt that Bob Cherry had stated the exact facts, in that row in the changing-room. If something of that kind was again in Carter's mind, his cunning was not going to save him from discovery this time. The Bounder, at least, was going to know.

He slipped quietly into Mr. Quelch's study.

There was a screen across a corner of that study. Vernon-Smith slipped behind it, and re-arranged it, so that it concealed him from view.

Then he waited !

If Carter came to that study in Quelch's absence, he would not come unseen. And if he played some similar trick to the treacle stunt, to be landed somehow on Bunter, the Bounder would know all he wanted to know.

He grinned, behind the screen, when, about five minutes later, the study door opened, and shut again quickly.

Someone had come in, and Smithy did not need telling who that someone was. Carter had waited and watched, for Mr. Quelch to get clear, in order to enter his study surreptitiously.

He heard the unseen fellow breathing quickly. Then, rather to his surprise, he heard the receiver taken off the telephone.

Smithy made a grimace.

If Carter had only been waiting for Quelch to get clear, in order to borrow his telephone, the Bounder was there for nothing. It was a thing he had often done himself, and he had no interest in Carter's private affairs, apart from Bunter.

But he was there now, and he certainly did not care to reveal himself to Carter He had to see it through. He heard a voice give a Lantham number. It was Carter's voice.

There was a pause, and then Carter spoke into the transmitter.

"That you, Gooch ?"

The Bounder knitted his brows with great discomfort. He knew the name of Gooch, the man who had brought Carter to the school, the first week of the term He had heard that the man was a solicitor, and a cousin of Carter's. Smithy did not want—very much indeed did not want—to play the eavesdropper. Carter's talk to Mr. Gooch was nothing to him. He would have got away, if he could have done so unseen.

But that was impossible.

Carter's voice resumed :

"That's all right, Gideon—this is the first chance I've had of phoning to-day —but it's all right ! I can't talk about it over the phone—I shall have to see you. Saturday's a half-holiday here— that all right ?"

Another pause.

"Saturday afternoon, then—say three: I'll be walking along the tow-path between the school and Friardale. No— I've had no luck at all—the fat fool seems to wriggle out of everything."

Smithy, behind the screen in the corner, gave a start.

The "fat fool" would hardly be anyone but Billy Bunter ! Did this mean that Carter had a confederate, outside the school, in his peculiar game at Greyfriars—and that confederate was his relative, Gooch?

It certainly sounded like it: and Smithy was no longer sorry that he was there to hear! He was listening, now, keenly.

But there was no more to hear.

"Saturday afternoon, then!" said Carter, and hung up the receiver.

But he did not immediately leave the study. The junior behind the screen heard him moving, with stealthy caution. He wondered what his occupation was—more and more convinced that his suspicion was well-founded, and that Carter had another object in the study, as well as calling Gooch on the telephone.

Then he heard the door open and shut.

Carter was gone.

The Bounder shifted the screen and stepped out. He started, and stared, at a paper that lay on Mr. Quelch's writing-table.

"Oh crumbs!" breathed the Bounder.

It was an ordinary sheet of impot paper—with a drawing on it. The artistic style revealed the handiwork of William George Bunter.

There were plenty of fellows in the Remove who could not draw, but no fellow could have depicted anything so utterly out of drawing as this—except the fat Owl.

But bad as the drawing was, its meaning was clear enough. A figure in cap and gown was whopping a junior who was bending over a chair. Behind that figure was depicted another junior, with his thumb and fingers to his nose.

This was Billy Bunter's brilliant idea of humour. Bunter did such drawings sometimes to show the other fellows, but certainly not to show Mr. Quelch. Had that work of art caught Quelch's eyes, the result for Billy Bunter would have been quite unnerving.

The Bounder grinned at the absurd picture. But his face became set and serious again. Quelch, when he came back, was to find that picture on his study table, and he could hardly doubt that Bunter had left it there for him. It would be easy enough to prove that it was Bunter's work. That that disrespectful drawing would get Quelch's rag out to an alarming extent, there was no doubt whatever.

"The cur!" breathed the Bounder.

He picked up the paper, folded it, and put it in his pocket.

Then, after peering out at the door to make sure that the coast was clear, he quitted the study.

There was a grim smile on Smithy's face as he went up to the Remove. He had learned now what he wanted to know—the schemer of the Remove was up against a fellow as keen as himself, or keener, and the probability was that there was more trouble coming to Carter than to Bunter.

THE TWELFTH CHAPTER.

Bunter is Annoyed!

STUDY No. 7 were at tea when Herbert Vernon-Smith looked in. On Billy Bunter's fat brow sat an expression of deep discontent. Having scoffed half the tea intended for three, Bunter had been stopped from further depredations by a rap on his fat knuckles, which annoyed Bunter, though not so much as it annoyed him to be stopped from annexing what was left.

"Beast!" he was remarking, when Smithy opened the door and looked in.

"Pig!" answered Peter Todd cheerfully.

Bunter blinked round at the Bounder hopefully.

"I say, Smithy, if you've looked in to ask a fellow to tea——" said the fat Owl, quite brightly.

"I haven't!" answered the Bounder.

Grunt from Bunter! He immediately lost all interest in Herbert Vernon-Smith.

"Shut that door, then, will you? There's a beastly draught!"

"Want anything, Smithy?" asked Peter Todd.

"Yes. That fat chump was showing off one of his idiotic drawings in the Rag this afternoon! What have you done with it, Bunter?"

"Oh! Like to see it, Smithy?" asked Bunter, bright again. "I say, it's awfully funny! He, he, he! There's old Quelch whopping a chap—he, he, he!—and another chap pulling noses at him behind his back! He, he, he! I'm going to do pictures for 'Punch' later on! I've got the gift, you know!"

"One of your many gifts, old fat man!" said the Bounder. "Well, let's see it. I'm quite keen to see it."

"All right! It's here."

Billy Bunter blinked round the study through his big spectacles.

"I say, Toddy, what did you do with that picture when you cleared the table for tea? I left it on the table."

"Never saw it," answered Peter.

"Then that ass Dutton must have moved it! I say, Dutton, what have you done with my picture of old Quelch?"

"Eh—who's Welsh?" asked Dutton. "Do you mean Morgan? He's Welsh all right. What about him?"

"I didn't say Welsh, you fathead! I said Quelch! Blow Morgan!"

"I'd like to hear you at it!" said Dutton derisively. "You couldn't play a tin-whistle, let alone an organ!"

"Oh crikey! You ask him, Peter!"

"He, ha, ha! Get on with it, old fat man! It will do your lungs good!"

"Have you seen the picture I left on the table?" roared Bunter.

"Rot!" said Dutton. "You're not able to do anything of the kind! It takes some brains to play the organ! You've got none that I've ever noticed!"

"Who's talking about playing the organ?" shrieked Bunter.

"Oh, Morgan! Yes, I dare say he can play the organ. He's Welsh, and music comes naturally to them. But you couldn't!"

"I left my picture of Quelch here——"

"Eh?"

"Here!" roared Bunter.

"Yes; I can hear all right when you don't mumble! What's that about Morgan playing the organ? I never knew he could."

"Oh crikey! Look here," Bunter roared, "I left my picture of Quelch on this table! Have you seen it?"

"Eh? Oh, no! You needn't shout! I'm not deaf!" said Dutton testily. "No need to yell at a fellow because he's a trifle hard of hearing! Look here, never mind about your picture! I'm rather interested in what you were saying about Morgan——"

But Billy Bunter had no more to say to Dutton. He proceeded to blink round the study through his big spectacles.

The Bounder watched him, with a sarcastic grin, while Peter went on with his tea.

"I say, it's not here!" said Bunter at last. "Some fellow must have bagged it—some chap going to make out that he drew it, I suppose!"

"Oh, my hat!" gasped Toddy. "You're quite safe there, Bunter.

Nobody will ever claim your artistic works as his own."

"Well, I don't know about that," said Bunter morosely. "It was a jolly good drawing—good enough for the comic papers, you know! They pay lots of money for comic pictures like that! I've often thought of drawing for the comic papers if I could find the time."

"Only the time necessary?" asked Peter blandly.

"Eh—yes! Sorry I can't show it to you, Smithy. It was really fearfully funny," said Bunter. "Somebody's bagged it."

"You think it safe to leave fatheaded tripe like that lying about the study?" asked Smithy. "Suppose Quelch saw it?"

"How could Quelch see it, fathead?"

"The fellow who bagged it might drop it in his study."

"What rot! As if any fellow would be sneak enough!"

"I shouldn't chance it, if I were you," said the Bounder. "Here's your tommy-rot, Bunter, and my tip to you is to shove it straight in the study fire!"

He took the folded paper from his pocket and threw it on the table.

Billy Bunter gave an angry squeak as he unfolded it.

"Look here, you beast, you've crumpled it all up!" he exclaimed. "What the thump did you want to crumple it in your pocket for?"

"Put it in the fire, fathead!"

"I'll watch it!" grunted Bunter. "Why, it took me half an hour to draw that picture, and there's lots of fellows I haven't shown it to yet! Like your cheek to bag it from my study and crumple it up like that!"

The Bounder laughed.

"Lucky for you I bagged it!" he answered. "I bagged that potty tommy-rot from Quelch's study, Bunter!"

"Rot!"

Peter Todd gave the Bounder a sharp look.

"What do you mean by that, Smithy?" he asked. "You're not saying that some fellow snooped that rot of Bunter's and left it in Quelch's study to land him in a row?"

"I'm saying exactly that!"

"Bit steep, old man! Pulling our leg, or what?"

Peter evidently had strong doubts.

Billy Bunter blinked at the Bounder in plain unbelief.

"Well, who was the man, if you know so much about it, Smithy?" asked Peter Todd tartly.

"Same man who did the treacling the other day, I fancy!" drawled the Bounder.

"Well, it never came out who did that."

"No. This wouldn't have come out, either, if I hadn't spotted it. Bunter's idiot enough to leave that in Quelch's study—at least, everybody would think so if it was found there. I know Quelch would. You don't believe that I got that out of Quelch's study, Toddy?"

"Not unless Bunter was ass enough to put it there. He might."

"Oh, really, Toddy, I thought of it, but it seemed rather too risky, you know."

"Did you actually see a fellow put that in Quelch's study, Smithy?" asked Peter Todd, with deep dubiousness.

"I can't say I actually saw him. I found it there just after he had been in the study, and I know he put it there."

"Um!" said Peter.

The Bounder laughed, and walked on to his own study. He had no intention of entering into a dispute in which it would have been his word against

Carter's. Neither was he keenly interested in the matter. He had saved Bunter from a serious row, and he had given him a warning, and he was quite satisfied to leave it at that.

"Cheeky ass!" said Bunter. "Bagging my picture, and crumpling it up in his pocket like that. Smithy's too jolly cheeky, Peter!"

"Did you stick that rot in Quelch's study, Bunter?"

"Eh! No! I left it here! I said so, didn't I?"

"Yes; that rather makes me think you didn't."

"Oh, really, Toddy——"

"Anyhow, it's safer in the fire, as Smithy said! Put it there."

"I'll watch it!" said Bunter warmly. "I'm going to show it to all the fellows! Smithy's jealous of my drawing—that's what it really comes to. I'm afraid you are, too, Toddy! I shouldn't be jealous, old chap! Some fellows can do things and some can't! It just happens that I can and you can't—see?"

Peter made no answer to that. He rose from the tea-table, grasped Bunter by the back of his fat neck, and jerked him over to the study fire.

"Chuck it in!" he said tersely.

"Beast! Shan't!" roared Bunter.

"Dutton, old man, hand me that poker."

"What's the joke?" asked Dutton. "Do you mean Bunter's a joker?"

"Poker!" roared Peter.

"Oh, poker! Here you are!"

"Will you leggo, you beast?" roared Bunter, wriggling with his fat neck in Peter's grip.

Peter took the poker in his free hand.

"Chucking that rubbish into the fire?" he asked.

"No!" roared Bunter.

Swipe!

"Why, you awful beast!" howled Bunter. "I'll jolly well punch your cheeky head, Toddy!"

Swipe!

"Ow! Leggo! There!" gasped Bunter, as he dropped the work of art into the fire. "There, you rotter! Wow!"

"Much safer there!" said Peter, with a cheery nod. "You've bagged enough trouble this term, old fat bean, and we don't want any floggings in this study. Don't do any more high art, Bunty—it's not your long suit. If I catch you at it again I'll swipe you again! I can't say fairer than that."

"Beast!"

Billy Bunter rolled out of the study in a state of great wrath and deep indignation. He passed Carter in the Remove passage and gave him an inimical blink. Carter glanced after him, with a rather sardonic smile. Had Bunter been able to read the thoughts in the schemer's mind he would have been glad that that picture of Mr. Quelch had been safely disposed of in the study fire.

THE THIRTEENTH CHAPTER.

Quite a Mystery!

MR. QUELCH went to his study when he came in after his walk with Prout!

He did not specially notice a Remove junior who was standing by the window near the corner of the passage.

But Carter was interested in Quelch, if Quelch was not interested in Carter.

He was very curious to see what would happen when the Remove master found that remarkable picture staring him in the face.

It was more than an hour since Carter

had left it there, but it did not occur to him, naturally, that anything could have happened to it. Nobody had been—or, at any rate, should have been—in the study during the Remove master's absence.

The scheme with the treacle had missed fire. But this little scheme could not, so far as Carter could see, miss fire. He waited for the sight of the Remove master's angry face appearing from his study doorway.

No such sight, however, met his eyes. Quelch had shut his door, and it remained shut.

He must have seen the picture. He could not have failed to see it. Carter concluded that he had rung for Trotter, to send the page to summon Bunter to the study. But Trotter did not arrive.

Minutes passed — five — ten—fifteen! Carter was more and more puzzled. Quelch had been a quarter of an hour in the study—yet he had not, seemingly, seen that picture staring at him from his study table. It was really extraordinary.

He had taken in an evening paper under his arm. Was it possible that he had sat down to read it without seeing the picture? It was scarcely possible; yet, if that was not the explanation, what was it?

Carter waited, his perplexity growing. Quelch's door opened at last, and the Remove master went up the passage in the direction of Masters' Common-room.

Carter, with puzzled eyes, watched him turn the corner in the distance.

Obviously he had not seen that disrespectful caricature of himself. Had he seen it there would have been thunder in the air. But how he could have failed to see it was a mystery.

Quelch having gone, Carter cut up the passage and stepped quickly into the study to ascertain how matters stood. It was unlikely, but it was possible, that some draught, perhaps when Quelch opened the door, had blown that paper off the table! If so, he had only to replace it.

He stepped in hurriedly and glanced quickly at the table. It was not yet dark, but it was dusky in the study. Quelch had switched on the light when he went in, and turned it off again when he left. But it was light enough for Carter to see that paper if it were there.

"Oh!" he breathed.

On the table lay the evening paper Quelch had brought in with him. It lay on the Remove master's blotting-pad, in front of his chair, where Carter had left the picture.

It looked as if Quelch had dropped that newspaper on the table, thus covering up Bunter's picture before noticing it.

Carter stepped across the study and picked up the newspaper, nothing doubting that he would see the picture underneath.

Only the blotting-pad met his view!

He stared at it blankly.

The picture was gone!

He stood gazing at the spot where it should have been, hopelessly perplexed. He could not begin to fathom it.

Quelch might have taken the picture and gone to see Bunter! But he had gone to Common-room, and there had been nothing in his hand. So it was not that. The picture seemed to have vanished of its own accord into thin air.

As Carter stood, with the newspaper in his hand, staring blankly at the vacant spot, there was a footstep at the door.

He gave a jump as Mr. Quelch stepped in again and switched on the light.

The Remove master stepped towards the study table, his hand outstretched as he came. Then he stared at Carter.

He had come back for the newspaper he had left there! Carter guessed that too late for it to be of much use to him. Carter was standing there, with the newspaper in his hand!

"Carter!" exclaimed Mr. Quelch. "What—what— How dare you come to my study to take the newspaper, Carter?"

"Oh! I—I——" stammered Carter.

"This is an act of impertinence, Carter!" said Mr. Quelch angrily. "Upon my word! I repeat, how dare you!"

"I—I—I was—was——"

"Give me that newspaper at once!" snapped Mr. Quelch. "If you desire to see the evening paper, Carter, you should ask permission to do so. You are perfectly aware of that."

Carter had nothing to say. Certainly he could not have told Mr. Quelch his real reason for having visited the study!

Quelch gave him a thunderous frown.

"I came back specially for this paper!" he exclaimed. "Did you intend to take it away, Carter?"

"Oh, no, sir!" gasped Carter. "I—I was just—just looking at the—the war news, sir——"

"You should have done nothing of the kind, Carter! Take two hundred lines and leave my study. If this should occur again I shall cane you."

Carter, in savage silence, left the study.

Mr. Quelch, with a frowning brow, watched him go, and then walked away with his evening paper, heading for Common-room again.

Carter went up to the Remove to get busy with lines. At Study No. 1 he sighted a fat figure in the doorway of that celebrated apartment, and scowled at it. Billy Bunter was addressing the fellows within.

"I say, you fellows, I can't show you my picture of Quelch now——"

"What a loss!" came a deep sigh from Frank Nugent.

"Well, it was fearfully funny, you know! I say, that beast Toddy made me stick it in the study fire! It's gone now."

"Best thing you could have done with it, old fat man!" said Harry Wharton.

"Oh, really, Wharton—— Beast! Who are you shoving?" grunted Bunter, as Carter pushed him aside and went into the study. And Bunter rolled on.

Carter sat down to lines. What he had heard from Bunter added to his puzzlement. Evidently the "picture" Bunter referred to was the one Carter had left for Quelch. How it had got back into Bunter's hands was a mystery.

But Carter had no time to expend on elucidating mysteries. Until prep that evening he had plenty to do grinding out lines for Quelch!

THE FOURTEENTH CHAPTER.

Catching Carter!

"COMING for a trot?" asked the Bounder.

"Games practice this afternoon!" said Harry Wharton.

"Lots of time for that! Do come!"

The Famous Five of the Remove regarded the Bounder rather curiously. On Saturday afternoon, which was a half-holiday, they had nothing special on—but as there was no match, they were going to put in some time at practice. They were not averse to a "trot" on a fine frosty afternoon; but

" Look here, you beast, you've crumpled up my drawing ! " exclaimed Bunter angrily. " It took me half an hour to draw that picture, and there's lots of fellows I haven't shown it to yet ! " " Lucky for you," said Vernon-Smith. " I bagged that tommy-rot from Quelch's study, Bunter ! "

they were rather surprised at Smithy asking them to join him in one.

Generally, when football did not claim the Bounder, he had occupations on his half-holidays that he was far from likely to ask Harry Wharton & Co. to share. They had no taste for smoking cigarettes at the Cross Keys, or playing billiards at the Three Fishers—and though they liked a spot of excitement now and then, the excitement of risking getting expelled from Greyfriars was not the kind that appealed to them.

"Look here ! What's the game ?" asked Bob Cherry.

"Carter's gone for a walk," answered Smithy.

"Blow Carter !" grunted Bob.

"Well, why shouldn't we go for a walk, too ?" urged the Bounder. "Feeling too old and tired for a walk ?"

"I'd walk your head off, ass !"

"Come on, then, and walk it off ! Just a trot along the towpath, down as far as Friardale Bridge."

"What for ?" asked Nugent.

"Just because I ask you, and I'm such nice company that you can't refuse."

Harry Wharton laughed.

"Oh, let's !" he said. "I can see that Smithy's got something on, though I'm blessed if I can see what it is !"

"Highcliffe cads about ?" asked Johnny Bull, with a little interest. "I'd like to boot Pon—haven't booted him this term, so far."

"No—just come on, because it's a nice walk in attractive company."

"Oh, all right !"

Somewhat puzzled, but willing to oblige, the Famous Five walked out of gates with Herbert Vernon-Smith. They turned into the towpath along the Sark, and sighted a well-known figure ahead of them—that of Arthur Carter, the new fellow in the Remove.

Carter was some distance ahead, walking in a leisurely way. The chums of the Remove had no desire to overtake him. It did not occur to them, at the moment, that Carter had anything to do with that walk along the river. They supposed that Smithy had chosen the same direction by chance.

When the village bridge came in sight in the distance, Carter looked round over his shoulder.

His eyes narrowed at the sight of six Remove fellows coming on.

He slowed down in his walk.

Smithy slowed down to the same rate of progress. There was a mocking glimmer in the Bounder's eyes. He knew—what the Famous Five did not think of guessing—that Carter was there to keep an appointment, which he would rather not have made known to Greyfriars fellows generally. His occasional meetings, and consultations with Mr. Gooch, were not a matter that he would have cared to have discussed in the Remove.

"Oh, come on, Smithy !" said Johnny Bull. "Call this a trot ! You're crawling !"

"What's the hurry ?" asked Vernon-Smith.

"Well, we haven't come out of gates to crawl along like Bunter, I suppose !" grunted Johnny.

"My dear man, you've come for a walk with me, and I'm setting the pace !" said Smithy. "Besides, Cherry's got a game leg."

"That's nearly all right now," said Bob.

"Can't be too careful, old man, when you've had a knock like that ! Take it easy !" said Smithy.

"Oh, rot !" said Bob. "Look here ! What are you up to, Smithy ? I'm beginning to think that it's got something to do with that chap ahead."

The Bounder chuckled.

"With a brain like that, old bean, you're wasted in the Lower Fourth !" he said. "You ought to be head of the Sixth."

"Look here ! I want to steer clear of that chap !" grunted Bob.

"That's all right—we shall pass him soon."

"Not if we crawl like this, fathead !"

"Oh, yes ! He will stop before we get to the bridge."

The Famous Five stared at the Bounder as he made that statement. It was growing clear to all of them, by this time, that he had something "on," and that it was somehow connected with the fellow who was dawdling ahead.

"How do you know he will stop, Smithy ?" asked Harry Wharton quietly.

"Because next time he looks round he will see that we shan't pass him at this rate !" answered the Bounder coolly.

"Do you mean that he wants us to pass him ?"

"Or else turn back !"

"Look here !" growled Bob. "If that cad's come out here to meet some shady rotter from the Cross Keys, I don't want to know anything about it."

"He hasn't !"

"Well, I jolly well don't understand you, then !"

"You can't expect to with an intellect like yours, old bean !" said the Bounder affably. "Keep cool—he will stop in a minute or two."

Somewhat curious to see whether the Bounder was right, the Famous Five walked on, at a snail's pace. Friardale Bridge was in sight in the distance, and the Bounder had not forgotten that it was between the bridge and the school that Carter was to meet that legal, or illegal, gentleman, Mr. Gooch. He was quite certain that Carter would stop soon, to allow the party to pass him, as the only means of getting rid of them before he met Gooch.

Carter glanced back again, and then came to a halt. He stood by the trees that lined the towpath, looking out across the shining river.

"He's stopped!" g r i n n e d the Bounder.

"Oh, come on!" grunted Bob.

There was no further reason for delay, and the Bounder stepped out. In a few minutes they passed the spot where Carter stood, and left him behind.

"Going as far as the bridge?" asked Nugent.

"Yes—then we'll turn back."

"Might walk back the other way, through Friardale."

"Oh, no, stick to the towpath."

"Why the stickfulness, my esteemed Smithy?" inquired Hurree Jamset Ram Singh.

"Easier goin' on the towpath than on the roads for Cherry's game leg!" said the Bounder airily.

"Oh, chuck that, you ass!" grunted Bob. "Look here! If you want to keep an eye on that cad Carter, I don't, and that's that!"

"Cherry, old man, you've got one fault in your otherwise perfect character —you jaw too much," said the Bounder. "come on!"

They turned at the village bridge and walked back along the towpath.

Carter was in motion again, coming on slowly.

From the corner of his eye he watched them furtively. It was past three, and at any moment now Gideon Gooch might come along from Friardale Station.

Smithy stopped as they met Carter face to face.

"Coming back to the school, Carter?" he asked blandly.

"No—I'm going on."

"Right-ho! Let's walk on with Carter, shall we, you fellows?" asked Smithy. "It's a ripping day for walking."

The expression on Carter's face as Smithy made that happy suggestion, caused the other fellows to grin. It was only too clear that Carter was anxious to be rid of the lot of them.

"Don't do anything of the kind," said Carter, far from pleasantly. "I prefer my own company, if it's all the same to you."

And he walked on more quickly.

"Rather a facer, what?" grinned the Bounder. "Nice fellows like us—turned down like that! Well, the towpath doesn't belong to Carter. Let's walk back to the bridge again."

"Look here——" hooted Bob.

The Bounder, unheeding, walked after Carter. The Famous Five, hardly knowing what to do, went with him.

A minute or two later, Carter glanced over his shoulder, and scowled blackly, as he saw them behind him.

"Hallo, hallo, hallo! There's that man Gooch!" said Bob Cherry, as a figure came in sight from the direction of the village—a thin, ungainly man, dressed in black, with a sharp nose, and sharper eyes glistening over it.

"That's the man who brought Carter to the school the day he came," remarked Johnny Bull. He stared at Smithy. "Look here! If Carter's here to meet that chap, it's got nothing to do with us, Smithy."

"Might have something to do with Bunter," said the Bounder.

"Bunter?" repeated Harry Wharton.

"Oh!" Bob Cherry drew a deep breath. "That's the rotten rascal I

heard——" He broke off abruptly. "How the thump did you know that Carter was meeting that vulture, Smithy?"

The Bounder laughed

"Did you know, Smithy?" asked Wharton.

"Sort of! I fancy Carter's seen him a good many times, but he keeps it dark. He's not keeping it dark this time! Look at his face—worth watchin', what?"

Carter's face was rather entertaining to watch. He glanced up the towpath at the group of juniors, and down the towpath at the approaching figure in black, evidently undecided. But he could see that the juniors had seen Mr. Gideon Gooch, and there was no help for it now. He hurried down the towpath to meet Gooch.

"Chuck it now, Smithy!" muttered Bob.

"Oh, come on!" urged the Bounder. "That cad's meeting the Gooch man to jaw over his next move against that fat chump Bunter. Let's go up and be introduced to the Gooch bird!" He chuckled. "Don't you think he'd be glad to know nice fellows like us?"

Harry Wharton laughed.

"Not quite! I'm going back!"

"Same here!"

The Famous Five walked back towards the school. They had had enough of the Bounder's peculiar game of catching Carter. And the Bounder, laughing, went with them—Carter, from a distance, scowling blackly after them as they went.

THE FIFTEENTH CHAPTER.

Hot Stuff!

"LOST something, Smithy?"

It was after prep on Monday evening, and the Famous Five were about to go down, with a crowd of other fellows, when they came on the Bounder, standing on the Remove landing, going through his pockets, apparently in search of something.

Bob Cherry stopped to ask the question. Billy Bunter, who was rolling after the Famous Five, stopped also. If Smithy had lost something, the good-natured Bob was ready to help him look for it. So was Bunter if it happened to be something eatable—though, in that case, if Bunter found it, it was never likely to meet the Bounder's eyes again.

"What the dickens did I do with it?" said the Bounder, in a tone of annoyance. "Nothing fearfully valuable—just a whipped cream walnut."

"I say, think you dropped it, Smithy?" asked Billy Bunter eagerly. "I'll help you find it, if——"

"No, ass, as if I should drop it! It was the last one in the bag!" said Vernon-Smith. "Did you see me lay a little paper bag anywhere, Reddy?"

"Yes, on the study table, just before you came away!" answered Redwing.

"Oh, that's all right, then—I shall find it there later!" said the Bounder carelessly.

Billy Bunter who had been heading for the stairs, now revolved on his axis and disappeared into the Remove passage again.

Harry Wharton & Co. grinned as he went.

"You fancy you'll find that cream walnut on your study table later, Smithy?" asked Frank Nugent.

"Why not?"

"I've got a sort of an idea that it's going to be found pretty soon, by some-

body else, if you don't hurry up," said Nugent, laughing.

"Think so?" asked the Bounder blandly.

"Look here, Smithy, what are you pulling Bunter's leg for?" grunted Bob Cherry. "The fat ass is always getting into trouble for grub-raiding—and that's really encouraging the blithering ass!"

"I hardly think so."

"Oh, rot! You know as well as we do that the fat chump's gone straight to your study for that cream walnut you left on the table."

"Yes, I know that!"

"Well, you can't make a fuss, then, if that fat blitherer bags it! You know him well enough."

"Not at all. I think Bunter will make the fuss," said the Bounder cheerfully. "You see, I'm doing Bunter a good turn. Don't you think he ought to have a lesson about grub-raiding in the studies, and that it would do him good?"

"Yes, ass; he gets booted often enough. If the fat chump had the sense of a bunny rabbit, he would chuck it, now there's a cad here watching him like a cat, to land him in trouble every time he gets a chance!" growled Bob.

"Exactly. I'm helping him."

"By leaving a cream walnut on your study table for him to gobble!"

"Just that! My belief is that Bunter won't enjoy that whipped cream walnut! Do you think he will look it over carefully before he scoffs it?"

"No Why should he?"

"Echo answers why. So he won't! He will take it down in one gobble! And he won't find out, till then, that there's mustard in it."

"Wha-a-at?"

"Mustard!"

"Oh crumbs!"

"Ha, ha, ha!"

The Bounder moved back across the landing and looked up the passage. The other fellows followed him.

If Billy Bunter snooped that whipped cream walnut and discovered the mustard in it when he crunched it in his capacious mouth, something like a volcanic eruption was to be expected.

"Oh, my hat! Listen!" exclaimed Bob.

From the open doorway of Study No. 4, up the passage, came a sudden, startling sound:

"Grooooooch! Ooooch! Currrggh!"

"He's got it!"

"The gotfulness is terrific!"

"Ha, ha, ha!"

"Urrggh! Gurrggh! Wurrggh! Oh crikey! Woooogh! I'm burnt! Yoooogh!" came a frantic splutter from Smithy's study.

"Ha, ha, ha!" yelled the juniors.

Evidently Billy Bunter had scoffed that deceptive cream walnut and discovered the mustard too late.

"Gurrgh! Beast! Rotter! Yooogh! Pulling a fellow's leg! Oooogh! Oh crikey! Aytishoo! Atchooooh! Ooogh!"

A wild and spluttering figure emerged from behind Smithy's study. Bunter's face was crimson, his eyes streaming water behind his spectacles, his mouth open, emitting frantic gurgles.

He did not look towards the group of laughing juniors on the landing. He bolted up the passage towards the tap, which was at the upper end.

He spluttered frantically as he went. Bunter seemed to be finding that mustard hot!

He turned on the tap, twisted his fat head under it, and opened his burning mouth wide to receive the water.

What Bunter wanted, just then, was something to cool his mouth, which felt like the crater of Vesuvius, and he let the water stream into it.

"Ha, ha, ha!" yelled the Removites.

"Urrggh! Gurrggh! Wurrggh!"

The juniors walked up the passage and gathered round the suffering fat Owl. He blinked at them with wet spectacles, spluttering.

"Anything the matter, Bunter?" asked Vernon-Smith blandly.

"Beast! Rotter! Ow!"

"What's up?"

"Cad! Swab! Beast!" roared Bunter. "Ow! I'm burnt! My tongue's burnt off! I can't use it—I mean, I nearly can't! Ooooogh!"

"Ha, ha, ha!"

"You should keep your absurd claws from the pickfulness and the stealfulness, my esteemed Bunter!" chuckled Hurree Jamset Ram Singh. "Honesty is the cracked pitcher that goes longest to the bird in hand."

"I say, you fellows—groogh—that cad Smithy—ooogh—— I'm all burnt!" wailed Bunter. "He put a lot of mustard in that—— Groooogh!"

"You've been raiding in my study?" asked the Bounder. "Did you find that whipped cream walnut? Wasn't it nice?"

"Urrggh! Beast! You stuck it there to pull my leg!" roared Bunter. "Think I don't know? You did it on purpose, you beast!"

"What a brain!" gasped the Bounder. "He's guessed it!"

"Ha, ha, ha!"

"Gurrggh! Wurrggh!"

Bunter had recourse to the tap again, and the juniors, yelling, left him to it. His gurgles and gasps followed them for quite a distance.

It was some time before Billy (*Continued on next page.*)

LEARN TO PLAY FOOTBALL!
BY OUR INTERNATIONAL COACH

THE PIVOT OF THE SIDE

I HAVE spent the last two "periods" dealing thoroughly with the things which are expected of the full-backs and goalkeeper of a football team. A little bird whispered to me as I sat down to think out this week's lesson. It said "Be careful, you will have the other fellows getting jealous." Perhaps the bird was right. Now that I have started going through the positions of a team I had better carry on until I have told you all there is to know about the position you may chance to occupy—or, at least, as much as I know myself, as nobody knows everything about football.

Next in order come the half-backs. It would not be right for me to treat the three half-backs all at the same time. I must take the centre-half and the wing halves separately. The centre-half certainly deserves individual attention. There are many teams in first-class football to-day which may truthfully be said to have been built up around the centre-half—he was chosen and made the "pole in the middle," and the rest of the "building" was put up round him, like putting up a tent.

I asked Mr. Jimmy Seed, the manager of Charlton Athletic, what he thought about the importance of the centre-half. Supposing, I said, that you had to start building the Charlton team all over again, which players would you look for first? Remember that no manager in the world to-day has done more for one club than Mr. Seed, who was an England player when he was younger and played for Tottenham Hotspur and Sheffield Wednesday, and then for Charlton. So he must be a pretty good judge. He told me that if he had to start building a football team to-day he would first of all choose the goalkeeper—because that is obviously a very important job—and after that he would look for his centre-half. Now you know how important the centre-half is.

STOPPERS AND ATTACKERS

YOU probably know, too, if you are a keen football follower, that there are two distinct kinds of centre-half. There is the one who has been nicknamed the "stopper"

When making up a football team be particularly careful when choosing your centre-half—it's one of the most important positions on the field.

centre-half, because the only thing he worries about is stopping the opposing centre-forward. Players like Herbert Roberts, of Arsenal, Alf Young, of Huddersfield Town, and Jack Allen, of Aston Villa, go under the stopper heading.

The other type is the fellow who is popularly called the attacking centre-half. As well as making it his duty to mark the opposing centre-forward, he gives some of his attention towards attacking and helping the forwards with their job of scoring goals. Jack Barker, of Derby County, and Stan Cullis, of the Wolves, are perhaps the best examples of the attacking centre-half in present-day football.

From my first description of the two kinds of centre-half you don't need to be very clever to realise that the fellows who play the stopper game have the easier time. They are sent on to the field with one instruction—stick to that centre-forward like glue and don't let him get a look at the ball. That roughly is what they are told. I don't say that it is always easy to "bottle up" the opposing centre-forward. He is often just as good a footballer as the centre-half, and, with the help of his colleagues, he works out tricks which will get him past the stopper. But the point is, that the defensive centre-half—that is another name for him—has only one duty to perform.

The attacking type of centre-half must carry out the defensive business to just the same extent, but he also has to think about helping his forwards. Thus, I think, it is true to say that the attacking centre-half must be more of a complete footballer than the stopper. The stopper will be all right if he has speed, plenty of weight, height to reach the ball when it is in the air, and the ability to head it safely and accurately. With all those things there won't be many centre-forwards whom he can't stop. But the attacker must have all those, and in addition be a good dribbler, so that he can take the ball up, and also be able to pass it accurately rather than just boot it.

Watch Jack Barker playing his attacking game. He gets the ball, takes it up a few strides, perhaps beating an opponent, and then sends a long pass, straight as an arrow, to one of his wing men. And yet he always seems to be back in his place to stop the opposing forwards when they come down.

THE MAN THAT COUNTS

I AM afraid I cannot help you to make the decision as to which kind of centre-half you would like to be. What I can tell you is that you will have to be exceptionally good, when you get a bit older, to hold your place in a football side as an attacking centre-half. Unfortunately, the stopper is more in favour nowadays.

Your decision about the style of centre-half game you want to play will have a big effect on the play of the wing half-backs in your side. As a matter of fact, I was rather surprised, when I popped the question to Mr. Seed about how he would set about building a football side, that he didn't put the wing half-backs next in importance after the goalkeeper. When I think of all the fine sides I have known in my time as a footballer it seems to me that the secret of all of them has been in the strength of their wing halves.

Yet I suppose it would be necessary to choose the centre-half first, because, if he is to play a defensive role, the wing halves must, between them, take over his attacking duties. If the centre-half is himself an attacker the wing halves must make doubly sure that no gaps are left in defence. Thus even the important wing half-backs are really built around the centre-half.

Nevertheless, wing halves are just as worthy of individual attention as the centre-half, so I will tell you about their job next week.

THE MAGNET LIBRARY.—No. 1,565.

Bunter appeared in the Rag that evening. The mustard kept him busy for a long time.

When he did appear, his fat face was red and damp, and his eyes still watering. Every now and then he gurgled —and every now and then he sneezed. The effect of the mustard seemed to be lingering. Smithy had prepared that whipped cream walnut thoroughly—perhaps a little too thoroughly.

Bunter was still in a state of woe and tribulation when the Remove went up to their dormitory.

THE SIXTEENTH CHAPTER.

After Lights Out !

ARTHUR CARTER sat up in bed in the dark dormitory and listened.

Half-past ten had chimed, and at that time the Remove fellows were—or ought to have been—fast asleep.

But Carter was very wide-awake.

He listened with intent ears to the sound of steady breathing from many sleepers and a rumbling snore from Bunter's bed.

That familiar sound in the Remove dormitory was not so regular as usual. Generally, Bunter's snore was an unending melody, from bed-time till rising-bell in the morning.

Now it was intermittent. The fat Owl was not sleeping soundly that night—doubtless owing to the effect of Smithy's mustard.

However, he was snoring at the moment.

Carter listened for two or three minutes. Then he slipped noiselessly from his bed, and dressed in the dark, almost without a sound. He slipped on a pair of rubber-soled shoes.

Bunter's snore died away—and he stirred. Carter stood quite still ! He did not want any Remove fellow to discover that he was breaking bounds after lights out—least of all, Bunter.

"Urrrrggh !" came a sleepy mumble from Bunter. "Urrggh ! Beast !"

He settled down again, and snored.

Carter trod lightly to the door. That any fellow was awake, in the long, dark dormitory, he could not see, and did not suspect. It did not occur to him that a pair of keen, mocking eyes were watching him over the edge of a blanket, fixed on his shadowy form in the gloom, losing no movement.

He turned the door-handle silently.

It was strange, perhaps, that the fellow who had been expelled from his last school as a "bad hat," and was being given a last chance at Greyfriars, should run such risks. But Carter, if he had really intended to reform, had soon fallen back into the old ways. It was, indeed, when on his way to the Three Fishers, on a half-holiday, that he had, as he fancied, spotted Bunter there, and played the informer, very nearly landing Smithy with the "sack." But he was quite unaware that the Bounder knew it, and was determined to give him back, as he expressed it, some of the same.

Gideon Gooch had advised him, and urged him, to keep as straight as a die at his new school, for reasons of common prudence. Getting Bunter a bad name would keep the fat Owl out of old Mr. Carter's good graces; but only a good name for himself could get Carter back into those good graces. But good advice was wasted on a young rascal who was a blackguard by nature. So far as Bunter was concerned, Carter was carrying on the scheme without scruple,

THE MAGNET LIBRARY.—No. 1,565.

but so far as he himself was concerned, he was taking the same risks at Greyfriars as at St. Olaf's. All he had learned was caution !

Softly he closed the dormitory door behind him.

There was risk, but it could only come by unlucky chance.

It was always possible that the Remove master might glance into the dormitory at a late hour, to be sure that all was as it should be with his Form. But Carter had left a dummy in his bed—a coat and rug, and blankets arranged to give the appearance of a sleeper.

That was an old game with him at his last school, and it was done skilfully enough to deceive a casual glance.

Not unless he was specially suspected was the Form-master—if he came—likely to look closely at the bed, and there was no reason why he should be suspected. He had been too careful for that, so far as masters and prefects were concerned—indeed, so far as his own Form were concerned, also.

In the Remove, only the Bounder knew him as he was, though Bob Cherry had much the same opinion of him. He was aware that Bob had a pretty clear idea what sort of a fellow he was; but he was aware, too, that nothing would have induced Bob to give a fellow away. Of the Bounder's knowledge he knew nothing. He was not thinking of either of them as he trod away silently by dark staircases and passages. He was thinking of a room at the Three Fishers, of cigarettes and banker with Bill Lodgey and one or two other sporting characters.

He would have felt less easy in his mind had he known that as the dormitory door closed after him another fellow slipped quietly out of bed.

The Bounder did not trouble to dress. He was not, like Carter, booked for a "night out." He drew on trousers and jacket over his pyjamas, and a pair of soft slippers.

Again Billy Bunter's snore intermitted. There was a grunt from the fat junior, and a sneeze. The mustard still lingered.

The Bounder glanced round angrily at the sound.

"Urrrrggh !" grunted Bunter.

He sat up in bed, groping for a handkerchief. He gave a sudden squeak at the sight of a shadowy figure between him and the starlit window.

"Ooogh ! Who——"

"Quiet, you fool !" whispered the Bounder. He did not want Bunter to wake the dormitory. "Quiet, only me !"

"Oh !" gasped Bunter. "That you, Smithy ?"

"Yes, ass ! Don't kick up a row !"

"Beast !" hissed Bunter. "It's your fault I've woke up ! That beastly mustard——"

"If you make another sound," said Vernon-Smith, in a low, concentrated voice, "I'll have you out of that bed and bang your silly head on the floor !"

Bunter did not make another sound.

He glared at Smithy with watery eyes, in mute wrath. But he did not want his head banged on the floor. He remained silent.

His fat head sank on the pillow again.

Vernon-Smith gave him a scowl and trod away softly to the door. He had no doubt that Bunter would be asleep again in a minute or two.

But Billy Bunter did not go to sleep again. As the dormitory door closed after the Bounder he sat up.

"Beast !" he breathed.

Of Carter's absence from the

dormitory Bunter knew nothing. He could only suppose that Smithy was going out of bounds after lights-out. All the Remove knew Smithy's manners and customs. Smithy, the beast who had caused him to swallow mustard, and spoiled his night's rest ! The Bounder was on the trail of vengeance—and Billy Bunter could be revengeful, too ! The fat Owl did not like getting out of bed, especially on a cold night. But he got out !

Smithy probably forgot his fat existence as he crept quietly down the dormitory passage.

He was going to be reminded of it !

THE SEVENTEENTH CHAPTER.

Measure for Measure !

CARTER stopped at the door of the Remove box-room, turned his head, and listened.

All was dark, silent, and still.

Downstairs, there were lights in some of the studies; masters had not yet gone to bed, and some of the Sixth were still up.

But in the Remove passage all was silent, and only a gleam of starlight from a window broke the darkness.

It had seemed to Carter that he caught a faint, stealthy sound, as if some other, as well as he, was creeping cautiously through the gloom.

But as he listened he heard nothing, and, reassured, he opened the box-room door, stepped in, and shut it after him.

He crossed to the window, which looked out on flat leads. It was the easiest way out at night, and Carter had not been long at Greyfriars before he learned it. He knew, from talk among Skinner & Co. in the Remove, that that was the way the Bounder went on such occasions. It was an easy descent, by a rainpipe, from the leads to the ground.

He pushed up the window, dropped out on the leads, and drew the sash down, leaving it an inch open, for his return.

Then he turned to grope across the leads, under the stars.

He stopped suddenly.

There was a sound from the window behind him. The sash, which he had pushed down, was pushed up again.

Carter spun round and stared at it blankly, his heart thumping almost to suffocation.

The opening of the window could mean only one thing—that he was discovered ! In sheer terror he gazed, expecting to see the light flash on and the face of his Form-master, or a prefect, looking out.

But no light came.

In the gloom he saw a head and shoulders at the open window. The glimmer of the stars revealed the face of Herbert Vernon-Smith.

Carter panted with relief.

He was not discovered ! It was not a master or a prefect ! It was a young rascal, like himself, on the same errand ! So he supposed, for the moment, at least.

But the Bounder did not drop from the window. And Carter noticed that he was not fully dressed. His pyjamas could be seen under the half-buttoned jacket he had thrown on. And the sardonic grin on the Bounder's face alarmed him. He had guessed already that Vernon-Smith did not regard him with friendly feelings. Now it dawned on his mind that the Bounder was not merely no friend, but an enemy.

"Smithy !" he muttered, his voice shaking. "What——"

Vernon-Smith picked up the bolster and stepped towards Bunter's bed. Swipe, swipe, swipe ! "Yaroooh ! I say, you fellows, stoppim !" shrieked Bunter, wildly dodging the swipes. "I say, it wasn't me, Smithy—honest Injun ! I never knew those chairs were in the passage till I heard you fall over them !"

He stepped back towards the window and put his hands on the sill.

"Don't try to climb in," said the Bounder, in a low, cool voice.

"Why not?"

"Because I shall slam the window."

Carter breathed hard.

"You cad ! What do you mean ? What are you playing this rotten trick for? What have I done to you?"

"I'll tell you," said Vernon-Smith. "Stand where you are, my pippin ! When I'm through, you can hike off to the Three Fishers as soon as you like—if you're in the mood for it !" He chuckled. "I fancy you won't be. But please yourself !"

"What do you mean to do?" breathed Carter.

"I'm going to shut you out of the House," answered the Bounder deliberately.

Carter caught his breath.

"And I'll tell you why. A Roland for an Oliver, you treacherous, double-crossing cur !" said the Bounder, between his teeth. "I've been waiting for this. I knew you were going to-night—I got a tip about that. I was watching you when you left the dorm. I came after you. And now I've got you exactly where I want you—on toast ! I'm going to give you exactly the chance you gave me—just that, and no more or less."

"What?" breathed Carter.

"A week or two ago you were going to the Three Fishers. You spotted a fellow in Bunter's overcoat, fancied it was Bunter, and gave him away."

"I—I did not !"

"Lies won't see you through !" said the Bounder contemptuously. "I knew it the same day; but I had to make sure, and I've made sure since. You're here to give that fat fool foul play, and you don't care what methods you use to diddle him with old Carter. I know all

about that. No bizney of mine, though I'd put a spoke in your wheel if the chance came my way. Well, you fancied you had landed Bunter that day, but it came out that another fellow had borrowed Bunter's coat——"

"What?" muttered Carter. "What about that, you rotter? Nothing to do with you."

"I happened to be the fellow !" said the Bounder grimly.

"Oh !" gasped Carter.

"I just got away by the skin of my teeth when Wingate came to that show," went on Vernon-Smith. "I had to leave the coat behind me. He brought it back to the school, and Bunter was up before the Head. If it hadn't happened that a crowd of fellows knew he had been in gates, he would have been for it—as you planned, you worm ! And then—can you guess what would have happened then?"

Carter did not speak.

"Bunter knew that I had his coat. I'd made the fat idiot give it to me, because he made mine muddy on the towpath. He would have given me away to save his own skin if it had been in danger. Not that it was much odds. I shouldn't have let another fellow take what was coming to me, if he had been willing to keep his mouth shut. I had the narrowest escape ever of getting it right in the neck."

Carter understood.

"If Wingate had been a minute sooner at the Three Fishers, or if I'd been playing billiards when he came, as I very nearly was, or if Bunter hadn't been able to prove that he was in gates, I should have been up before the Head, and bunked the same day."

The Bounder's eyes glittered down at the face looking up at him.

"Now you've got the lot. You nearly landed me, playing a dirty, treacherous

trick on that fat Owl. I'm giving you exactly the same back. I'm not going to give you away. I'm going to land you as you landed me, and you can get out of it, if you can, same as I did. Measure for measure—see?"

"Oh !" breathed Carter.

"Once this window is shut and fastened you're out for the night. I shall lock the door on the outside, too, in case you might get the window open. You'll be in the same fix that I was in that day, and you're welcome to get out of it if you can. If you can get back another way, if you can lie yourself out of it when you're found out of the House in the morning, go ahead and do it, and I wish you luck. You've got the same chance that I had—no more and no less—and I'll leave you to it !"

Carter's lips opened, but the Bounder did not stay to listen. He had said all that he had to say, and he shut down the sash.

The click of the catch within, as he fastened it, was like a knell to the ears of the young rascal outside.

He had a moment's glimpse of the Bounder's face, looking at him through the glass. It vanished.

Vernon-Smith was gone.

Arthur Carter leaned on the window-sill, his knees sagging under him. He made no attempt to open the window. Even had it been possible, it was futile, if the Bounder locked the box-room door on the outside. That the Bounder would relent he had not the slightest hope. The look on Smithy's bitter, scornful face washed out all hope of that.

He was done for !

He was not thinking of going on his way and getting to the Three Fishers now. Bill Lodgey & Co. were not going to see him that night. He leaned on the cold stone window-sill, overcome.

THE MAGNET LIBRARY.—No. 1,565.

At his last school he had come a
"mucker." The same ways had landed
him in the same fate at his new school.
There was no help and no hope. As he
had done, he was done by, and his game
was up!

THE EIGHTEENTH CHAPTER.

Bunter Hits Back!

HARRY WHARTON awoke. So
did six or seven other fellows in
the Remove dormitory.

There were sounds—unaccustomed sounds—at that hour of the
night. It seemed to the captain of the
Remove, as he awoke, that furniture
removing was going on—which was remarkable, to say the least, in a junior
dormitory at past half-past ten.

Wharton sat up in bed and stared
round in the dim shadows.

Bump! Thud!

"Oh, blow it!"

The sound seemed like that of a chair
tumbling over. The voice was the voice
of William George Bunter, the fat ornament of the Lower Fourth.

Bunter evidently was out of bed.
Equally evidently, he was shifting furniture. There were a number of light,
cane-seated chairs in the dormitory,
beside the beds. Why Bunter was up
and shifting them about was a remarkable mystery.

"Bunter!" came Peter Todd's voice.

"Hallo, hallo, hallo!"

"That fat ass—"

"What the thump——"

"Oh, I say, you fellows, don't wake
the House!" gasped Bunter. "Do you
want Quelch up here? I—I'm not out
of bed!"

"You blithering owl!" exclaimed
Harry Wharton. "What are you up
to?"

"Nothing, old chap—nothing at all!"

"What have you woke us all up for?"
hooted Johnny Bull.

"I haven't. I didn't want you to
wake up. You woke yourselves!"

"Is that fat chump potty?" exclaimed
Skinner. "He's pitching the chairs
about the dorm!"

"Mad as a hatter!" exclaimed
Ogilvy.

"The madfulness is preposterous."

"You potty porpoise!"

"You batchy bloater!"

"What are you chucking the chairs
about for?" shrieked Bob Cherry.

"I—I'm not, old chap! I just
dropped it, that's all. It's all right.
You fellows go to sleep!"

The Remove fellows did not take that
advice. Half the Form had awakened,
and they sat up and blinked in amazement at the shadowy figure of the fat
Owl.

Peter Todd lighted a match, and then
a candle-end, and the glimmer revealed
Bunter with a chair under either arm.
He was carrying them doorward.

In utter amazement they gazed.

A fellow who got up late at night to
carry chairs out of the dormitory was
surely off his "rocker"—if Billy Bunter
had ever been quite on it.

Bunter had not intended to wake anybody while he carried out this stunt. He
had done it without intending it.

The amazed juniors watched him open
the door, walk out with the two chairs,
and disappear. They just stared.

"Barmy!" said Bolsover major.

"Absolutely batty!" said Russell.

But Bunter reappeared in the doorway in a few moments. He reappeared
without the chairs. He came in and
shut the door, and the candle-light

THE MAGNET LIBRARY.—No. 1,565.

showed a fat grin on his face as he
rolled bedward.

For what reason he had taken two
chairs out of the dormitory and left
them in the passage, beat the Remove
hollow. Unless he actually was "potty,"
the reason was hard to guess.

Apparently the fat Owl's job was done
now. He rolled back into bed. He was
heard to emit a chuckle as he did so.

"You howling ass!" exclaimed Harry
Wharton. "Go and fetch those chairs
in. Suppose somebody came along in
the dark and tumbled over them?"

"He, he, he!"

"Is that the game, you potty ass?"
exclaimed Peter Todd. "Do you fancy
that somebody will be coming up the
passage?"

"Well, I don't fancy he will stay out
all night. He, he, he!" chuckled
Bunter. "I suppose he'll be back before twelve. He, he, he!"

"Who?" exclaimed Redwing, rather
sharply. If some fellow was out of the
dormitory the Bounder's chum thought
that he could guess the fellow's name.

"Oh, nobody!" said Bunter hastily.
"Nobody's gone out, old chap! Don't
you butt in! Nothing to do with you,
Redwing!"

"Smithy out of bounds?" exclaimed
Skinner.

"Oh, no! I never woke up and saw
Smithy going out! Nothing of the
kind! He—he hasn't gone! I haven't
laid those chairs across the passage to
catch him when he comes back, either.
It's all right, Redwing; nothing for you
to worry about."

"You fat fool!"

"Oh, really, Redwing——"

Tom Redwing jumped hastily out of
bed. He picked up Toddy's candle-end
and threw the light on Vernon-Smith's
bed. It was empty; the bedclothes
turned back, just as the Bounder had
left it when he followed Carter.

Evidently the Bounder was outside
the dormitory. Of his game to give
Carter "measure for measure," the
other fellows, of course, knew nothing.
They could only suppose that the bad
hat of the Remove had gone out of
bounds after lights-out.

The light of the candle glimmered
also on Carter's bed. But no one gave
that bed any attention. The dummy in
it was skilfully arranged, and no one
doubted that Arthur Carter was there
and fast asleep.

Redwing stared at his chum's bed, his
face setting.

Billy Bunter gave him an anxious
blink.

He had carefully arranged those two
chairs lying end to end across the passage outside to catch the Bounder when
he came back—late, as Bunter supposed.
A fellow coming along in the dark
would not see the obstruction, and
would not, of course, expect anything of
the kind. If the chairs were still there
when Smithy returned, he was booked
for a rather unpleasant tumble. This
seemed, to Bunter's mind, a jolly good
idea, in return for the mustard in the
whipped-cream walnut.

"So Smithy's out!" grunted Johnny
Bull.

"Looks like it," said Harry. "The
silly ass!"

"I say, you fellows, don't you let that
fathead Redwing butt in," said Billy
Bunter anxiously. "I say, you know
what that cad Smithy did—sticking a
dose of mustard inside a cream walnut
to catch a fellow——"

"Ha, ha, ha!"

"You fat idiot!" exclaimed Redwing.
"You've stuck those chairs out there

for Smithy to stumble over when he
comes back."

"Well, serve him right, for going out
of bounds," said Bunter. "He would
get more than that from Quelch if he
was spotted. I'm rather surprised at
you, Redwing, sticking up for a blackguard like Smithy. Let him tumble
over when he comes back at twelve,
smelling of smoke. You see, it will be
a lesson to him. Don't you think so?"

Redwing glared at the fat Owl.

If Smithy crashed in the passage in
the dark the noise was quite likely to
bring a master or a prefect on the
scene. And there was no doubt at all
that Smithy would collect some
damages. Redwing did not want either
to happen. He was angry and impatient with his chum's lawless ways,
but he was a loyal pal.

"Cut out and get the chairs in,
Reddy!" said Harry Wharton, laughing. "Lots of time; if Smithy's only
just gone, he won't be back yet."

"Not before midnight!" said Johnny
Bull, with a snort. "Serve him jolly
well right if Quelch got him!"

"I say, you fellows——"

"Shut up, Bunter!"

"Look here, don't you barge in, Redwing! See?" howled Bunter. "You
know what that beast Smithy did——"

Redwing made no answer to that.
He turned away towards the door, with
the intention of going out into the
passage and fetching in the chairs.

Billy Bunter glared at him with an
infuriated glare. He had turned out
of bed in the cold and taken a lot of
trouble to lay that trap for Smithy.
Now Redwing was going to spoil everything.

But, as it happened, Redwing was not
in time. It did not occur to him, or to
anyone, that Vernon-Smith would be
coming back hardly more than ten
minutes after he had left. All the
fellows who were awake supposed that
he was out of the House, never dreaming that he had gone no farther than
the box-room window for purposes of
his own.

Redwing had not reached the door
when there came a sudden terrific crash
and bump in the passage.

Crash! Bump, bump! Yell!

"Great pip!" gasped Bob Cherry.

"That's somebody——"

"Can't be Smithy yet!" exclaimed
Harry Wharton. "Don't go out, Reddy.
That can't be Smithy!"

"Who the dickens——" breathed
Nugent.

"Some beak making the rounds,"
grinned Skinner. "Bunter's made a
catch all right. Most likely Quelch!"

"Oh crikey!" gasped Bunter.

Peter Todd blew out the candle.
Redwing dived back into bed. Somebody, it was plain, had gone headlong
over Bunter's fatuous trap in the dark
passage. But that it was Smithy, returning so soon, no one supposed. The
Remove fellows could only wonder who
it was as they listened to the startling
sounds from the dormitory passage.

THE NINETEENTH CHAPTER.

A Mystery of the Night!

HERBERT VERNON-SMITH
hardly knew what was happening to him.

Having finished with Carter,
and left him to it, the Bounder crept up
the dormitory stairs, cut across the big
landing, and hurried up the passage
towards the door of the Remove
dormitory.

He had forgotten Bunter; but if he had remembered him, he would never have dreamed of the fat Owl's fatuous idea of "hitting back" for that hot cream walnut.

He came quickly up the passage in the dark, and all of a sudden something caught his knee, and he went headlong.

He had no chance of saving himself—he was over before he knew that he was falling.

He crashed!

Instinctively he threw out his hands, which was fortunate for him, or his face would have had a most unpleasant knock on hard old oak.

As it was, his nose tapped and both his hands banged and his chin jarred on the floor; his legs thrashed on the chairs, rolling him over. The crashing of the chairs, the bumping of the Bounder, and his wild, startled yell rang far and wide in the silence of the night. He yelled and spluttered and panted and rolled helplessly over.

Scrambling up, he caught his foot in one of the chairs and staggered and bumped over again, with another loud howl.

Groping in the dark, he picked himself up more carefully, in rage and astonishment, with aches and pains all over him. His nose was damaged, his chin was damaged, his hands felt as if he had had a severe caning on them; he had barked a shin on one leg and banged a knee on the other. He panted as he dragged himself to his feet.

Something had been in his way, and he had fallen over it—he could not imagine what. Gasping for breath, he grabbed a flash-lamp from his pocket and flashed on the light.

Then he saw the chairs lying on the floor. He had shifted them in falling over them, but he could see that they had lain end to end across the passage. He breathed fury as he realised that he had been caught in a trap. Someone had done this to catch him as he came back—and he did not need telling who. Only one fellow in the Remove had been awake when he left—and only one fellow in the Remove was idiot enough to play such a trick. With an assortment of pains from head to foot, the Bounder breathed fury.

But the next instant he forgot Bunter as he caught the sound of voices and footsteps. Instantly he shut off the light.

He realised that the sound of his crash had been heard. It would have been surprising had it not. The masters were not yet gone to bed; but even had they been, that crash would have been heard. There were footsteps on the big landing at the end of the passage.

"You heard, Quelch?"—it was Prout's boom.

"Yes. What——"

"Extraordinary!"

"Very! It sounded like a fall——"

"I heard a voice——"

The Bounder shut his teeth. A light flashed on on the landing. Any moment a light might flash on in the passage where he stood. He made a swift step up the passage, but even at that perilous moment the wary Bounder had his wits about him. He paused, grabbed up the two chairs, and carried them with him as he cut along to the dormitory door.

Those chairs belonged to the Remove dormitory, and he did not want investigation to be directed there. It would be a poor ending to his retaliation on Carter if he was caught breaking dormitory bounds himself at nearly eleven o'clock at night. Whatever Carter's

fate, the Bounder did not want to share it.

He reached the dormitory door and cut in, taking the two chairs; he shut the door, panting with relief.

There was a buzz of startled voices in the dormitory.

"Who's that?"

"Shut up, you fools!" hissed the Bounder. "Quelch is coming—and old Prout! Shut up, I tell you!" He was already hurrying to his bed.

"I say, you fellows, it's Smithy!" exclaimed Billy Bunter in astonishment. "I say, he's come back!"

"Quiet, you fat fool!"

"Oh, really, Smithy——"

"Where the dickens have you been, Smithy?" exclaimed Tom Redwing. "I thought, when I saw your bed empty, that——"

"Never mind what you thought! Shut up!"

"But what——" exclaimed Skinner.

"Will you be quiet? I tell you Quelch is coming!"

The Bounder was in bed now, pulling the bedclothes over him. Footsteps could be heard in the passage. Under the door came a gleam.

"They're coming here!" murmured Bob Cherry. "They'll find the chairs out there, and——"

"I brought them in with me!" hissed the Bounder. "Will you shut up? We're all asleep if they look in here."

"Oh, fast asleep!" chuckled Skinner. "Haven't opened our innocent eyes since we laid our dear little heads on the pillows! You'd better snore, Bunter, if you're going to be asleep!"

"Oh, really, Skinner——"

"Quiet!" breathed Harry Wharton.

There was a sound of the door-handle turning. The Remove fellows settled down in perfect stillness. If Smithy had brought the chairs in, there was no clue to trace the disturbance to the Remove dormitory. What the beaks were going to think did not matter very much to the juniors, so long as they did not think that a Remove man had been out. Hardly a man in the Remove approved of Smithy's manners and customs, but no man there wanted him to be caught.

The door opened.

In the light from the passage two figures were visible to cautious eyes peering over the blankets—the tall, angular figure of Quelch and the portly form of Mr. Prout, the master of the Fifth.

Quelch's gimlet eyes gleamed over the dormitory.

"All seems quiet here," he remarked.

"I am sure the noise was in this passage," said Prout. "Of that I am absolutely convinced, Quelch."

"My boys are all asleep."

"Apparently so," said Prout. "But, in the circumstances, I should not trust to appearances, Quelch. I am convinced that——"

"It is easy to ascertain whether any boy here is out of the dormitory," said Mr. Quelch. "Please speak quietly, Prout! I do not desire the boys to be awakened at this hour."

That remark caused quite a number of fellows to find some difficulty in repressing a chuckle. If any fellow in the dormitory was still asleep, he must have been a very sound sleeper.

But the juniors remained as still as mice.

Mr. Quelch did not switch on the dormitory light. As he had said, he did not want to awaken his Form at that hour. He stepped quietly in, and scanned the low row of beds in the light from the passage, which was sufficient to reveal whether a bed was occupied or not.

Every bed contained—or, at least appeared to contain—a sleeper. Only the Bounder knew that Carter was missing—and Carter's bed looked as if it had a sleeper in it.

Mr. Quelch stepped back to the passage.

"The boys are all present," he said. He was speaking low, but the Remove fellows—not being so fast asleep as Quelch supposed—could hear. "Nothing has occurred here. It is very singular that——"

"I am absolutely convinced, Quelch, that the noise came from this passage. Someone fell down, and cried out—indeed, I may say, yelled——"

"I heard it, Prout. But who——"

"Is it possible, Quelch, that some extraneous person is in the House——"

"Really, it is unlikely."

"A burglar?" breathed Prout.

"I can scarcely think so, with lights on downstairs."

"On the other hand, my dear Quelch, someone certainly was here. There is a window at the end of this passage; it might be reached by means of the ivy——"

"Very improbable."

"Let us, at all events, examine the window."

"Oh, certainly, Prout!"

The door closed.

Suppressed chuckles were audible in the dormitory as soon as it had closed. The Bounder laughed. He was more than willing for the beaks to go looking for an imaginary burglar.

"Narrow shave for you, Smithy!" chuckled Skinner. "What did you come back so early for? Somebody spotted you getting out, or what?"

"You can't have gone far, Smithy!" said Snoop. "Did you get out of the House at all?"

The Bounder grinned in the dark. He had no intention of revealing why he had left the dormitory. None of the fellows knew that Carter was absent, and they were not going to know until the morning. A dozen fellows would have been ready to intervene had they known how matters stood. Fellows who liked him least would not have left him to it, had the Bounder's deadly scheme of retaliation become known.

"The fact is, I never got out," drawled the Bounder. "I decided to come back, and go to bed like a good boy."

"You mean you spotted the beaks on the prowl?" asked Skinner. "Well, they jolly nearly got you this time."

"A miss is as good as a mile! I suppose they'll keep on prowling. I shall have to leave you till the morning, Bunter."

"I—I say, Smithy, it wasn't me put those chairs in the passage for you to fall over!" said Bunter anxiously. "I—I hope you haven't got that idea in your mind, Smithy?"

"Ha, ha, ha!"

"I have!" said the Bounder grimly. "I've got about a dozen bruises and bumps all over me! I'll give you twice as many to-morrow!"

"Beast!"

Some of the juniors wondered whether the beaks were visiting other dormitories, or whether they were looking for that burglar. They did not, at all events, return to the Remove dormitory, and the juniors settled down to sleep again.

The Bounder was the last to fall asleep; his aches and pains were rather painful, and he was thinking, with malicious satisfaction, of the wretched black sheep shut out of the House—probably making a frantic search for some door or window that might possibly give him admittance.

Not a twinge of remorse did the Bounder feel The fellow had brought him within an ace of expulsion, in furtherance of a rascally scheme against a fatuous ass. He had given him back what he had handed out—measure for measure. Smithy had escaped on that occasion by the skin of his teeth, as it were. Carter was welcome to do the same, if he could. And that was that! The Bounder of Greyfriars was feeling quite satisfied with himself and with what he had done when at last he fell asleep.

THE TWENTIETH CHAPTER.

Out in the Night !

ARTHUR CARTER had descended from the leads under the boxroom window. There was no ingress for him there, and there was little chance of finding ingress elsewhere, but that faint, hopeless chance was all he had left.

He groped round the buildings, keeping in the shadow of walls and buttresses and old trees; for it was a clear night, with a touch of frost, the sky like steel, and the stars shining brightly. In the open he might have been spotted by a master glancing from a window, especially now that a silvery crescent of moon was coming up over the clock-tower.

Such hope as he had was very faint, but he clung to it that all was not yet lost.

Shut out of the House, he had to get in and creep back to the Remove dormitory, or his game was up. "Breaking out at night" was a serious matter at any school, but in Carter's case it was more serious than in any other fellow's. Only after long hesitation had the headmaster of Greyfriars allowed him to come there at all, after what had happened at his last school.

The first clear evidence that he had not changed his ways—that he was the same black sheep that he had been at St. Olaf's—meant the finish for him, without the remotest hope of pardon. If it was discovered that he had been out of the House at night, he had his box to pack first thing in the morning; the train would bear him away while the Remove were going in to class. That was what he had risked in his dingy folly, and that was what was now booked to happen, unless unexpected good fortune befriended him.

But he did not give up hope—he dared not. The Bounder, that day at the Three Fishers, had been in equal peril, and had pulled out. Carter desperately hoped to pull out somehow.

By chance some window might have been left unfastened—some door unlocked. It was improbable, but it might have happened It was even possible that some young rascal like himself might have got out and left an unfastened window behind him—if he could find it. The chances were remote, but he dared not give up hope.

He had, at least, time. He knew that the Bounder did not intend to give him away beyond what he had done already. Exact "measure for measure" was the game, leaving him in the peril in which he had left Smithy, to get out of it if he could, as Smithy had done. He would not be missed from the House until morning; he had ample time, if only luck came his way.

Prout was still up. So was Quelch—his window glimmered, too. Other study windows showed light—as well as several of those of the Sixth Form. Carter gave them a glance from a distance—keeping in shadow.

He paused at an ivy-clad wall, and looked up. Above him was a window that gave on the dormitory passage, and the old ivy was thick and strong. That window had old sashes through which a penknife could be slipped, and the catch

on it was a simple one. If he could have climbed——

But he knew, with a sinking of the heart, that he dared not. A slip, or a breaking tendril of the ivy, at such a height, meant a fall that would end all things. He dared not take the risk. Even the Bounder, who had twice Carter's nerve, would hardly have tried it on—and Carter, though he thought of it, standing there and looking up, made no motion to attempt it. Suddenly, as he stood there, the window was illuminated.

He blinked at the light.

That illuminated window meant that the light had been switched on in the passage on which the Remove dormitory opened. What could that mean, but a visit to the Remove? If the dummy in his bed was discovered, it did not matter much about planning and contriving to get back into the House. Had it been discovered? Had that fool, Vernon-Smith, been spotted getting back to the dormitory! If they knew that a fellow was out——

He stood staring up at the high, glimmering window, with doubt and anxiety in his mind, miserable despair in his heart.

Two heads appeared at the lighted window. He saw the shadowy motion of an arm, as a hand groped over the sash.

He could make out only outlines at the distance, against the glimmer of light; but he fancied that the man groping over the window was the portly Prout—the other, a leaner man, might have been Quelch or Hacker. Prout seemed to be examining the window-fastening—why, Carter could not begin to guess. Certainly the beaks could not suspect that a fellow had got out that way.

Suddenly the window-sash shot up, and Prout's portly shoulder leaned out. He stared down. It flashed into Carter's mind that, standing there in the starlight, he was visible from the window. He had forgotten that—he realised it as the Fifth Form master leaned out. Instantly he darted into the shadow of the masses of ivy.

From above, Prout's boom reached him.

"Did you see him, Quelch?"

"I saw no one, Prout !"

"You were not looking ! I distinctly saw someone standing there—I am absolutely convinced that I saw someone."

Carter, hidden in the ivy, trembled. Prout had seen him—had he recognised him? It was not likely, at the distance, and in the dimness. But he trembled from head to foot.

Quelch leaned out to look.

"You are sure, Prout?" Carter heard the clear, sharp voice.

"Positive !" said Prout. "Someone was standing there—looking up at this window, Quelch. Who——"

"Gosling, perhaps——"

"It was certainly not the porter, Quelch. A much smaller person—and he was wearing a cap—Gosling does not wear a cap. I could not say for certain whether it was a boy or a man—but certainly nothing like Gosling. Either a burglar, Quelch——"

"Really, Prout——"

"Or a boy out of House bounds—at this hour of the night ! You are sure that no boy is missing from the Remove, Quelch?"

Carter, who heard every word in the

Printed in England and published every Saturday by the Proprietors, The Amalgamated Press, Ltd., The Fleetway House, Farringdon Street, London, E.C.4. Advertisement offices: The Fleetway House, Farringdon Street, London, E.C.4. Registered for transmission by Canadian Magazine Post. Subscription rates: Inland and Abroad, 11s. per annum; 5s. 6d. for six months. Sole Agents for Australia and New Zealand: Messrs. Gordon & Gotch, Ltd. and for South Africa: Central News Agency, Ltd.— Saturday, February 12th, 1938.

still night, listened in anguish for his Form-master's reply. He gave a gasp of relief when he heard it. It came short and sharp.

"Quite!"

Evidently the dummy in his bed had not been discovered!

"The noise we heard was certainly in this passage, Quelch! Possibly a Third Form boy——"

"Not at all!" chimed in another voice—that of Mr. Wiggins. "I have visited the dormitory, Prout, and no boy of my Form is missing."

"Nor of mine!" came another voice—that of Mr. Capper, the master of the Fourth.

There were now four masters at the open window above Carter. He realised that something must have disturbed them and set them "on the prowl." From what Prout said, Smithy must have made some sort of a row getting back to the Remove dormitory.

Four heads at the window looked out. Carter hugged deep cover at the foot of the wall in the thick ivy.

"You are quite sure, Quelch, that no boy is missing from the Remove?" came Prout's boom again.

"I have said so!" answered the Remove master tartly.

"Someone, Quelch, is out in the quadrangle. If you think it is a burglar, we——"

"I do not think so for one moment!"

"This w i n d o w, certainly, was fastened! But if it is not an extraneous intruder, Quelch, it must be a Greyfriars boy. There are certain unruly spirits in your Form——"

"I have said, Prout, that the Remove boys are all in bed, and fast asleep. Shall we investigate the Fifth Form dormitory?"

"If you suggest, for one moment, that a Fifth Form boy—a boy of my Form, is——"

"It is precisely the suggestion you have made in reference to my Form, Prout."

The voices were rising a little, and growing acid. Mr. Capper's mild tones intervened.

"Possibly you were mistaken, Prout, and saw no one—a moving shadow, perhaps—this light is very deceptive."

"I am positive that I saw someone, Capper, and that he darted into the shadow below—he may be there at this moment, listening to us."

"Call to him," suggested Mr. Quelch. "If it is a Fifth Form boy——"

"It is not a Fifth Form boy, Quelch!"

"It is certainly not a Remove boy!"

"It is somewhat cold here, with that window open," remarked Mr. Capper. "I shall return to my study."

"I shall go to bed," yawned Mr. Wiggins.

"And I," said Mr. Quelch, "shall return to my study."

"One moment, Quelch!" boomed Prout. "How do you account for the noise—the startling noise—that we all heard?"

"Some Fifth Form boy, perhaps," suggested Quelch, with acid politeness.

Snort! from Prout, and the window closed with a bang. Carter heard no more.

THE TWENTY-FIRST CHAPTER.

By the Skin of His Teeth!

THE junior hidden in the ivy below did not venture to stir until he heard the window close. Then he crept away, almost on tiptoe, carefully keeping in the shadow of the wall.

Of the four beaks who had been "prowling," three seemed to be satisfied that all was well; and Carter hoped that Prout would give it up also. The alarm over, he had his chance of hunting for a window or a door that might give access to the House

A sudden stream of light from an open doorway dazzled him for a moment, breaking into the dusky starlight. He blinked at it.

It was the door on Masters' Passage that was open. Framed in the lighted doorway was the portly figure of Prout, staring out.

The lighted passage behind him could be seen—no one visible but Prout. The others, evidently, had gone back to their studies, or gone to bed. Prout was still keeping it up.

Prout was, in fact, very much annoyed He did not, on reflection, think it possible that a burglar was hanging about the quadrangle, while many windows were still lighted. Burglars generally came later. But if it was not that, it was some Greyfriars fellow out of bounds that he had seen—and he had little or no doubt that it was one of Quelch's boys. He was assured of that, because Quelch had suggested that it might be a Fifth Form boy.

Prout's own Form—in Prout's opinion at least—was above such suspicion. Someone, Prout was sure, was out of bounds—and he would have derived a certain satisfaction from proving that it was a Remove boy.

He stared out into the dusky starlight, and gave quite a start, as he glimpsed a skulking figure backing quickly away.

"Stop!" roared Prout.

Carter was not likely to stop. He had very nearly come under Prout's vision—he knew that Prout had had a glimpse of him. He flew.

Prout rushed out.

Prout had intended to walk round the quad, with a keen and wary eye, looking for the delinquent, but locking the door after him, in case that delinquent dodged in behind his back. But now, having actually glimpsed the skulking form, he rushed, leaving the door wide open behind him.

Carter darted away, with thumping heart. That dismal and desperate hunt for a way in had to be postponed—escape was the immediate and pressing necessity. He dodged round ancient elms, Prout pounding on his track.

"Stop!" panted Prout. "I saw you—a junior, I am certain of that now! Stop! Oh, goodness gracious—— Ow!"

Prout stopped himself as he banged into an elm trunk. He came to quite a sudden stop.

"Oh! Ah! Ow! My nose! Ooooh!" came from Prout, in a series of gasps. "Oh! Woooogh! Ooogh!"

Carter, in terror, clamped himself behind a tree. He was hardly three yards from Prout.

Prout, at a standstill, clasped his nose with a large hand. Then he dabbed it with a handkerchief.

Carter cast a longing glance at the open doorway, in the distance, with the light streaming therefrom.

Had it been dark, he would have chanced it! But in the light from within, he would have been full in Prout's sight. He dared not stir.

For several long minutes—terribly long to Carter—the Fifth Form master stood dabbing his nose and gasping and grunting. Then he moved at last, going back towards the House.

The half-seen fugitive had dodged him and escaped. But there was absolutely no doubt on the subject now—some junior was out in the quadrangle, and there was going to be a search. If the other masters did not care to undertake it, Prout was going to call the Sixth Form prefects.

Carter watched him go.

Whether Prout was going in and giving it up, or whether he was going to rouse the House, Carter could not guess—but the latter, of course, was the most probable. Now that Prout knew, as a positive fact, that a junior boy was out of the House after eleven o'clock at night, he could not possibly let the matter drop. Apart from his personal desire to score over the Remove master, he had his duty to do. Instead of searching on his own, he was going to call in assistance—and Carter's heart sank at the thought of Wingate, Loder, Gwynne, perhaps all the Sixth Form prefects, rooting after him.

Prout, with his handkerchief to his nose, and red spots on the handkerchief, puffed and blew back to the open doorway.

Carter's eyes gleamed after him.

He was desperate now.

In a mood of sheer desperation, he tiptoed after the Fifth Form master. Prout did not look back—he did not think of looking back. He rolled on towards the door, grunting. Somewhere in the shadowy quad behind him was that young rascal—to be rooted out as soon as he had called the prefects. It did not occur to him how close behind him that young rascal was! Only desperation could have made Carter act as he did—and it was not surprising, perhaps, that Prout was taken quite by surprise.

He was hardly six yards from the doorway, when, Carter, lowering his head, rushed at his portly back and butted.

Prout went over like an ox!

He gave one gurgle and flapped down on his chest; his nose, already damaged on the tree, gathering further damages on the cold, unsympathetic earth!

"Gurrrggh!" came from Prout.

Carter flashed past him.

Prout's nose was still digging into the quad when the young rascal darted into the doorway and whipped behind the open door.

To reach the stairs, he had to cut along the passage, past Masters' Studies—and that he dared not do, unless he was sure that the doors were shut.

He hunted the first cover that came to hand—and that was the wide-open door! In the twinkling of an eye he was crammed behind it.

It was fortunate for him that he had lost no time. From the quad came a roar like that of the Bull of Bashan—from Prout, scrambling to his feet, in terrific wrath. Two or three study doors immediately opened—Hacker, Capper, and Quelch looked out. All three emerged, and came hurrying down to the door—behind which Carter hardly breathed.

Another bellow from Prout! Then he staggered into the doorway, his face purple, his nose red and raw, sprinklings of earth on his knees and his gown.

"What——" gasped Mr. Quelch.

"My dear Prout——" ejaculated Capper.

"You have fallen down?" asked Mr. Hacker.

"No, sir!" spluttered Prout. "I have not fallen down, sir! I have been hurled over, sir—attacked from behind, sir, and hurled over."

"Goodness gracious! Who—what —why——"

"I saw him, sir—I saw someone—a junior—and if I had not run into a tree—— Upon my word, are you laughing, Hacker?"

"Certainly not. I—I am sorry to hear——"

"I was coming back to call the prefects, when I was attacked—charged— butted—hurled over from behind!" gasped Prout. "Look at me!"

Prout tottered in and tottered away. Hacker shrugged his shoulders and went back to his study. Quelch and Capper exchanged a faint smile, and both of them stepped out of the doorway to look round.

Carter's heart beat. This was his chance! Prout would be at least a few minutes in the Sixth Form quarters— Hacker had gone into his study and shut the door—Quelch and Capper were outside. No other beak had appeared —the others, probably, had gone to bed. Carter gave the door a sudden push and slammed it Then he cut away like lightning.

He was on the staircase by the time the door reopened. From the distance he caught Quelch's voice:

"Was that the wind, Capper? Very odd that——"

Carter flew up the stairs. In less than a minute he was at the door of the Remove dormitory.

Faintly, from afar, he heard sounds —Prout, doubtless, gathering the prefects to the search! They were welcome to search now! Breathing in great gulps, Carter opened the dormitory door, stepped softly in, and shut it behind him.

He was safe back in his quarters now—hardly daring to believe that he really had escaped!

But he had. He stood in the sleeping dormitory, panting and panting. All the fellows were asleep. The Bounder, last to fall asleep, had dropped off by that time. Bunter's snore rumbled intermittently. For once Carter was glad to hear that familiar sound. He did not dream that it was through the fatuous fat Owl that he had escaped the peril that Smithy had left him in.

He gave Billy Bunter no thought. His eyes fixed, with a glitter in them, on the Bounder's bed. A glimmer of starlight fell on Smithy's face, and showed his eyes closed. He was sleeping. He could sleep, after what he had done! Carter's look was black and bitter.

But his expression changed, and a sardonic grin came over his face. He

made no sound. Swiftly he threw off his clothes, removed the dummy from his bed, and turned in. Smithy could see him there when he turned out in the morning—a pleasant surprise for the Bounder!

Below in the quad, Prout and the prefects were prowling, looking for that unknown junior who was out of bounds, and who had hurled Prout over. Perhaps they did not wholly believe in that junior out of bounds. Anyhow, they did not find anybody, though they were still searching when Carter, in his bed in the Remove dormitory, went to sleep.

THE TWENTY-SECOND CHAPTER.

A Surprise for Smithy !

BANG! Clang! Clang!

Bob Cherry bounded out of bed—the first out, as usual. His cheery voice woke the echoes of the Remove dormitory.

"Hallo, hallo, hallo! Turn out, you slackers!"

Snore!

"Out you come, Bunter!"

Snore!

Either Billy Bunter had not awakened, or he was not going to waken. But he had little choice when Bob Cherry was there to help Blankets were whipped off Bunter, and his snore was suddenly changed into a howl of protest.

"Ow! Beast! It's cold! Gimme my bedclothes, you rotter! I'm not getting up yet. Why, the bell hasn't stopped yet, you beast!"

Herbert Vernon-Smith picked up his bolster as he turned out. He stepped towards Bunter's bed.

Swipe!

"Yaroooh! Stop that, Bull, you beast!"

"Ha, ha, ha!"

Swipe!

"Ow! Is that you, Smithy, you rotter? Stoppit!"

Swipe, swipe, swipe!

"I say, you fellows, stoppim!" shrieked Bunter, wildly dodging the swipes of the Bounder's bolster. "I say, it wasn't me, Smithy—honest Injun, old chap! I never knew those chairs were in the passage till I heard you fall over them—and never heard you, old fellow. I was fast asleep!"

Swipe, swipe!

Bump!

Bunter rolled off the bed on the farther side.

Vernon-Smith scrambled over the bed and re-started after the brief interval.

Swipe, swipe, swipe, swipe!

"Yarooh! Help! Fire! Yoo-hoop!" roared Bunter. "I say, you fellows——"

Swipe, swipe!

Bunter rolled under his bed, yelling.

Harry Wharton & Co. rushed at the Bounder, grabbed him, and spun him away, and Bunter was able to crawl out, unbolstered.

All the Remove were up by that time

—with one exception. Arthur Carter had not stirred.

He could hardly have been asleep, after the bolstering of Billy Bunter, and the terrific yelling that accompanied the same. Several fellows glanced towards his bed—the Bounder with a sardonic smile.

Smithy had no doubt that what appeared to be a sleeper in the bed was the dummy Carter had left there. So far, he had no suspicion that Carter had got back into the dormitory in the night.

"Wake up, Carter!" called out Harry Wharton. "The rising-bell's stopped!"

No answer from Carter. He was grinning sourly under the edge of the blanket, quite aware of the thoughts that would be in Herbert Vernon-Smith's mind.

"I fancy Carter won't hear you, Wharton," said the Bounder.

"Eh? Why not?"

"Well, I wouldn't be certain, of course, but I've got a sort of idea that he's had a night out," grinned Smithy.

"What rot! There he is in bed!" said Harry, staring.

"Might be a dummy!" drawled the Bounder. "I've known of such things in my time."

"Oh!"

Attention was concentrated on Carter's bed now.

The Bounder stepped towards it.

"Look!" he said.

He whipped off the bedclothes. He had not the slightest doubt that a dummy would be revealed. He fairly staggered as Carter sat up and rubbed his eyes.

Carter gave him a glance.

"Thanks!" he said. "Rising-bell stopped? Thanks for calling me, Smithy!"

The Bounder could only stare.

"What on earth made you think that Carter was out, Smithy?" asked Harry Wharton.

Smithy did not answer that question. He did not speak again till the Remove were going down. Then he spoke to Carter on the stairs.

"So you squeezed through, somehow?" He burst into a laugh. "Well, I'm rather glad than not. You had as much chance as you gave me, and you seem to have got through, same as I did. Gratters! But if you'll take a tip from me, you'll chuck up your rotten, dirty, double-crossing tricks. You can bank on it that if I come into the picture again, you'll get measure for measure."

And the Bounder passed on, without waiting for an answer.

THE END.

(*Well, try as he may, Carter hasn't succeeded in getting Bunter in his Form-master's black books yet. But he's not given up trying, by any means, as you'll learn when you read: "THE SCHEMER OF THE REMOVE!" next Saturday's exciting story of Harry Wharton & Co.*)

The Magnet

2D

Billy Bunter's Own Paper

BUNTER'S BREAKAWAY!

NO CHARGE FOR ADMISSION, CHUMS! STEP RIGHT IN WITH—

The GREYFRIARS GUIDE

A TOUR OF THE SCHOOL. The Dormitories.

(1)

The dorms are similar, you know,
  For each is long and wide,
With beds and lockers in a row
  On either side.
There's very little to attract
  The chap who likes a circus,
It's rather bleak, in point of fact,
  And not unlike a work-'us!

(2)

No pictures, curtains, rugs or fire
  Or anything to make
A fellow sleepless with desire
  To keep awake!
But still, it's healthy, big and clean,
  And daren't be ornamental,
For pillow-fights have seldom been
  Conspicuously gentle!

(3)

We pillow-fight from sheer delight
  In being young and strong;
We'd like to keep it up all night,
  But don't for long!
The masters stop that little plan,
  Their arguments are stinging!
And hardly have we slumbered than
  The rising-bell starts ringing!

AFTER SCHOOL HOURS
Black Beauty

Regard it with wonder and awe,
  A sight that is pleasant to see!
Oh, Topper, that shinest on Temple, the
    finest
  Of verses are feeble for thee!
Behold its black body and brim,
  It's far too delightful for him!

But now the world rocks in despair,
  The stars in the heavens fall flat!
It's awful, unnerving! A turf has come
    curving
  And landed on Temple's top-hat!
That topper has rolled in the mud—
  A crime to be answered in blood!

Too stricken with horror to move
  Stands Temple, bereft of his sense!
In stupefied loathing that tricks upon
    clothing
    Are played in this college for
      gents!
Stands Greyfriars, he asks, where it
    did,
  When fellows can turf a chap's lid?

And now a vile scoundrelly boot
  Has lifted that topper a mile,
Astounding! Amazing! While Temple
    stands gazing,
    They're playing a game with the
      tile!
And Cherry—inhuman young brat!—
  Has scored a neat goal with the hat!

In gibbering rage and dismay
  He rescues that topper at last.
Too late, for its glory is only a story,
  A tale that is told and is past!
Bespattered and dented and creased,
  Black Beauty is now a Black Beast!

THE GREYFRIARS ALPHABET
MARK LINLEY,
the Lancashire Lad of the Remove.

L is for LINLEY, a Lancashire Lad,
At Learning his Lessons his Labours are
  glad;
He has quite a Liking for Latin and
  Lore,
Not Languid or Lazy, but ready for
  more!

His scholarship made him despised by
  the worms,
Like Skinner and Bunter for several
  terms,
But Marky was steady, good-humoured
  and cool,
And soon won a place with the best in
  the school!
At sport he is sound, never flashy or
  tame,
He plays for his school and the good of
  the game;
But please don't imagine that Marky is
  dull,
A "little tin saint" with a ring round
  his skull!
He may be a little more steady than
  some,
But that doesn't mean he is gloomy and
  glum;
He's always at home in a rag or a lark,
And fights like a Trojan—good health
  to our Mark!

GREYFRIARS GRINS

A reader asks why Bunter wears glasses in bed. Well, he's so short-sighted he wants to see what he's dreaming about!

Yesterday, Quelch sent Bunter out of class for half an hour to wash his neck. This morning, thirty-one fellows turned up with unwashed necks.

Fisher T. Fish is getting so absent-minded that he's just swindled himself out of fourpence.

The big mirror in the Remove dorm is cracked. We've warned Bolsover major dozens of times not to look in it.

Hurree Singh offers to teach any Remove fellow Hindustani free of charge. Well, it might help us to tell Coker what he really is.

Coker has just asked Mr. Prout to excuse him from classes in future because "his time is rather occupied." He must have foreseen that he would get 1,000 lines!

After Hoskins had finished one of his brilliant (?) piano studies, he asked the Shell what they thought of his execution. They were strongly in favour of it, at an early date.

David Morgan is collecting sea-shells. We're afraid this wild excitement will be bad for him.

ANSWER TO PUZZLE

They put the small pie on the big one and cut round it

The SCHEMER of the REMOVE!

By FRANK RICHARDS

Carter crammed Mr. Quelch's manuscript into the study fire, with the exception of one sheet which he slipped into an inner pocket!

THE FIRST CHAPTER.

The Heavy Hand!

KNOCK!

"Come in!" said Mr. Quelch irritably.

The master of the Greyfriars Remove had, as a rule, a calm, though severe temper. Sometimes he was wrathy. Sometimes he was quite fierce. But he was never irritable in the Form-room.

But Mr. Quelch, at the present moment, was sitting at the typewriter in his study, clicking off one more chapter of that celebrated "History of Greyfriars," which had been his constant companion for twenty years or so.

So he was, at the moment, not a schoolmaster, but an author. Authors are well-known to be an irritable tribe! Interruption of their literary labours makes them snap like dogs, or spit like cats!

That knock at his study door irritated Quelch. His fingers ceased to wander idly over the noisy keys, and he snapped "Come in!"

The door did not open.

Quelch glared round at it.

"Come in!" he repeated.

Still the door did not open.

Quelch breathed hard and deep! Some fool—some insensate fool—had tapped at his door by mistake, it seemed, and passed on!

He resumed typing.

Click, click, click, click!

The frown faded from his brow. His mind drifted happily back over the centuries. He became absorbed in the History of Greyfriars.

Knock!

"Upon my word!" said Mr. Quelch.

That was what he said; but his tone was more emphatic than his words.

"Come in!" he almost snarled.

The door did not open.

"Upon my word!" repeated Mr. Quelch.

It could not be a mistake this time! Such a thing could hardly ·have happened twice! Yet no one entered.

It seemed impossible—unthinkable—that any fellow could be "ragging" the master of the Remove. Wiggins and Capper were sometimes ragged. Quelch was about as safe to rag as a tiger in the jungle. Yet there had been two successive knocks at his door and no one had entered. It was a rag, or nothing.

An Amazing Story of Schoolboy Adventure, starring HARRY WHARTON & CO., of GREYFRIARS.

Mr. Quelch rose from his chair, leaving a half-written sheet in the machine, picked up a cane, and stepped to the door.

He opened the door suddenly.

No one was in sight in Masters' Passage. Whoever had knocked had vanished. Up the passage, down the passage, Quelch's gimlet eyes glittered. Like Moses of old, he looked this way, and he looked that way, but there was no man!

With feelings that could hardly have been expressed in words, but which were plainly indicated in his speaking countenance, Mr. Quelch shut his door and returned to the typewriter.

But he did not recommence clicking on the keys.

Inspiration had departed.

Interrupted authors cannot carry on regardless. At such moments, they are dangerous to approach. Quelch sat with knitted brows.

He did not expect that unknown practical joker to come again. But he rather hoped that he would! He wanted to catch him! He would have given half a term's salary as master of the Remove to catch him. It was quite pleasant to think of the cane ringing on that practical joker's trousers.

Knock!

Quelch started.

"Come in!" he gasped.

But the door did not open. Amazing as it was, it was that japer again. This time Quelch did not go to the door.

He knew that the young rascal would have vanished, as before, by the time he got the door open. He sat breathing hard. The expression on his face might have terrified any practical joker.

He waited!

If that young villain came again, Quelch was not going to say "Come in," and give him time to clear! He was going to make one bound to the door and catch him fairly in the act.

He listened intently.

Hitherto, he had heard nothing of the enemy's approach. The fellow, whoever he was, tiptoed cautiously to the door. But, straining his ears, the Remove master hoped to catch a sound that would put him on his guard! By this time he would have given a whole term's salary to catch the young rascal.

THE MAGNET LIBRARY.—No. 1,566.

He wondered which young rascal it was! Harry Wharton & Co. were sometimes given to japing, but they would not play tricks like this. More likely Vernon-Smith—he was almost the only fellow in the Form with nerve enough to rag Quelch. On the other hand, this kind of thing—runaway knocking—was rather beneath Smithy's usual style. Whoever was doing this was not merely disrespectful, but stupid as well. Thinking of stupidity naturally made Mr. Quelch remember Billy Bunter!

Was it Bunter? Bunter had been more than usually troublesome that term. Moreover, Bunter had lines, which he had to bring to his Form-master at tea-time. He was much more likely to turn up with some excuse for not having done them. If it was Bunter——

There was a sound in the passage. Mr. Quelch rose to his feet, his eyes glittering. Silently he stepped to the study door, cane in hand. If a knock come, the young rascal was not going to escape this time !

Knock !

Quelch grabbed the door-handle with his left, and the door flew open. His swiftness was really like lightning. In a split second more, his hand was grasping at a collar.

"Oh !" came a startled gasp.

It was Bunter! There stood the fat ornament of Mr. Quelch's Form—his eyes almost popping through his spectacles in startled surprise.

He stood there only for a moment ! Then the grasp on his collar whirled him into the study.

"I—I—I say——" gasped Bunter.

Whack !

"Yaroooh !" roared Bunter.

Whack !

Quelch did not tell him to bend over, as was the custom ! He seemed unwilling to let go of Bunter, now that he had got him !

Grasping him by the back of the collar with his left, he laid on the cane with his right.

Whack, whack, whack !

The whacks rang like pistol-shots ! Louder still rang the frantic roars of Billy Bunter! He wriggled and squirmed in his Form-master's grip! He roared, he howled, and he yelled ! But it booted not ! The whacks came hard, and the whacks came fast.

Whack, whack, whack !

Quelch was putting his beef into it.

Whack, whack !

"Ow! Wow! Yow! Yaroop! Help! Stoppit ! I say—yarooh !" roared Bunter. "Oh crikey ! Oh crumbs ! Oh scissors ! Oh jiminy ! Oh lor' ! Whoo-hoooop !"

Whack, whack, whack !

"There !" gasped Mr. Quelch. He was getting tired; though not so tired as Bunter ! "That will be a warning to you !"

"Yarooop !"

"Leave my study !" thundered Mr. Quelch.

"Yow-ow-ow-ow !"

Bunter was glad to leave the study. Quelch had stopped—but he looked like restarting after the interval.

Bunter bolted ! He did Masters' Passage at about 50 m.p.h.

Mr. Quelch sat down again ! He was feeling better ! He was assured that there would be no more runaway knocks at his door ! He was right—there were none !

Calmness and peace of mind returned, at last, and Mr. Quelch resumed literary clicking ! He dismissed the matter from his mind.

Bunter did not ! It was not so easy for Bunter to dismiss it !

THE MAGNET LIBRARY.—No. 1,566.

THE SECOND CHAPTER.

A Dog with a Bad Name !

"HALLO, hallo, hallo !"

"What——"

"What's that cad been up to ?" growled Bob Cherry.

The Famous Five of the Remove were walking in the quad after class. They were engaged in a rather warm argument.

The topic was the match with St. Jim's, which was booked to come along shortly. Bob Cherry, the best half-back in the Remove, did not want to figure in that match. He did not, at all events, want to do so if Carter, the new fellow in the Remove, was in the team.

Which was disconcerting to his friends, and extremely exasperating to one of them who happened to be football skipper.

Argument was waxing warm, when Bob Cherry suddenly changed the subject. He was staring towards the windows of Masters' Studies.

On a raw February afternoon, those windows, naturally, were closed. But one of them had opened, and from within, a junior dropped into the quad.

It was the fellow of whom they had been speaking—Arthur Carter, the new Removite.

The window from which he had dropped was that of Prout's study. Prout, the master of the Fifth, was out. During his absence, it seemed, Carter had some business in his study, and had preferred to leave by the window.

So swift was Carter's drop from the window, that few would have been likely to notice it. One instant he was at the window—the next, standing on the earth below the sill, looking quite casual, as if he had just strolled there in the most harmless way imaginable. Of the five juniors, only one saw him—Bob, because he had happened to be looking in that direction when Carter dropped.

The other four glanced round.

"That's Bunter's jolly old relation, Carter !" said Frank Nugent. "What about him? What do you mean, Bob?"

Grunt, from Bob Cherry.

"What's he been doing in old Prout's study ?" he snapped.

"Has he been in old Prout's study ?" asked Johnny Bull.

"I saw him drop from the window, just before you fellows looked round."

"Blessed if I saw him !" said Harry Wharton. "He doesn't look as if he's been up to anything, Bob ! Sure——"

"Think I'm blind ?"

Harry Wharton laughed.

"No—but you bar that new man, and you dislike him so much, old bean, that you seem to see something wrong in everything he does—or doesn't."

"The esteemed window is opened !" murmured Hurree Jamset Ram Singh.

"Prout might have left it open," said Johnny Bull. "I don't see what a Remove man would want in the Fifth Form beak's study. Still, if the chap's been japing old Pompous, where's the harm ?"

Bob Cherry's brow darkened.

"That cad has been up to something in Prout's study !" he said. "He won't get nailed for it—he hardly ever does get nailed for his dirty tricks ! If Bunter gets nailed for it, I shall chip in."

"Bunter ?" repeated Harry Wharton.

"Haven't I told you, and don't you know without being told, that that cad Carter has been landing things on Bunter ever since the term started ?" exclaimed Bob. "If he's ragged in Prout's study, he's left something to make it look as if Bunter's been there."

"Well, I know it's looked that way sometimes, but——"

"Oh, he makes me ill !" growled Bob. "Look here, I can't play in the St. Jim's match if that fellow plays. He hacked me in the match with Highcliffe last week, and I was limping for days afterwards. I had to go off the field. No good having to send a man off in the St. Jim's match."

"That was an accident, old chap——"

"Accidents will happen, sometimes, in Soccer !" said Johnny Bull. "Any man might get a hack."

"I know that ! Am I the fellow to do a song and dance about a hack ?" grunted Bob Cherry. "He fell on me, when a Highcliffe man barged me over, and hacked me as he fell—it was just deliberate. Smithy saw him, and he knows."

"Smithy bars him, like you do, so he's not an unprejudiced judge !" said Frank Nugent.

"And why does Smithy bar him? Because the cad gave him away to the beaks," snorted Bob.

"Smithy may think so, but——"

"Well, it's no good jawing !" said Bob. "That cad crocked me in the Highcliffe match, and he'd do the same again, if he felt like it. He loathes me, for standing up for Bunter, and stopping his tricks on that fat fool. Whatever it is that he's just done, nobody will spot him—if I don't ! He's been in old Pompous' study, and sneaked out by the window. What does he care about japing Prout? Not a thing—unless he's got some foul play on hand."

Four members of the famous Co. exchanged a smile.

It was not like cheery, honest old Bob to take deep dislikes; he had a kind-hearted toleration for everybody, from Smithy, the bad hat of the Remove, to Billy Bunter, the grub-raider of the studies. He could be friendly with Bolsover major, who was a good deal of a bully, and with Skinner, who was artful and malicious. He could even see some good in Fisher T. Fish ! But he barred the new man, Carter, thoroughly and whole-heartedly : and it was a fact that he could see no good in anything that Carter ever did or said. If Carter had said that it was a fine day, Bob would almost have suspected that there was some trick behind it ! To Bob Cherry, Carter was a dog with a bad name !

"Well, look here," said Harry, "let's ask him ! If he's gummed old Pompous' slippers, he can tell us."

"More likely to tell lies !" grunted Bob.

"Oh, rot ! Come and ask him."

Carter was strolling away with his hands in his pockets, his air careless and casual.

Harry Wharton & Co. cut after him, and he glanced round at them as they came up.

"What are you on Prout's track for ?" asked the captain of the Remove, directly.

Carter stared at him.

"On Prout's track? What do you mean? I've got nothing to do with Prout."

"I mean, what have you done in his study ?"

"In his study !" repeated Carter.

His eyes narrowed at the Famous Five. Up to that moment, he had supposed that his sudden and surreptitious exit from Prout's study had been entirely unobserved. He had noticed the chums of the Remove in the distance, that was all. But Wharton's question showed him that he had been seen.

"Are you going to tell us you haven't been in Prout's study?" asked Bob Cherry scornfully.

Carter gave him a dark look.

"Bob saw you drop from the window!" explained Nugent.

"He seems very interested in what doesn't concern him," drawled Carter. "Suppose I dropped into the Fifth Form beak's study, and dropped out again after looking at his newspapers, what about it?"

"His newspapers?" repeated Harry.

"Just that! My Uncle Carter has some property in China, so I'm rather interested to keep an eye on the newspapers to see whether the Japanese have bombed it to bits! Cherry got any objections?" asked Carter sarcastically.

"You haven't been japing old Pompous?"

"Not at all."

"Nothing happened in his study to make him go raging to Quelch, to call Bunter over the coals?" said Bob Cherry, with savage sarcasm.

Carter laughed.

"Still got that bee in your bonnet?" he asked. "Well, I don't want to get into a row for borrowing the newspapers in a master's study—but if you hear anything's happened in Prout's study, you can put it down to me, and you can go to Quelch about it, and I'll come with you! Can't say fairer than that, can I?"

"Hardly!" said Harry Wharton laughing.

"I'll keep you to that!" grunted Bob.

"Do!" said Carter. And he walked on, with his hands in his pockets.

Bob stared after him grimly.

"What the dickens was his game in that study?" he muttered.

"He's told us!" said Nugent.

"Oh, rats! You can believe him if you like!" snorted Bob. "I don't believe a word of it! If anything's happened there——"

"Nothing has!" said Harry. "You're making a hobby of being down on that man Carter, Bob. Chuck it and come in to tea!"

And the Famous Five went into the House—where a buzz of voices and a sound of laughter drew them to the Rag.

THE THIRD CHAPTER.

Startling News!

"I SAY, you fellows!"

"What the dickens——"

"Quelch has gone mad!"

"Wha-a-t-t?"

"Mad as a hatter!" gasped Billy Bunter. "Dangerous! Raving!"

Billy Bunter, in a state of great excitement, was in the Rag, surrounded by a crowd of juniors. Some of them were laughing. Some looked startled. All were interested. Bunter, evidently, had a startling tale to tell. As the Famous Five came in, he gave them a blink and an excited squeak. They joined Bunter's audience, in great surprise.

"Mad!" repeated Bunter. "Fancy a —a Form-master, you know, going right off his onion! And—and I went to his study, you know, not knowing that he had gone mad, and he got me! Grabbed me——"

"Grabbed you?" gasped Harry Wharton.

"Clutched me!" gasped Bunter. "Just like a clutching hand on the films, you know."

"Quelch did?" exclaimed Bob Cherry.

"Sprang at me!" spluttered Bunter. "Leaped at me like a—a leopard! Sprang at me like a—a tiger! Hurled himself at me like a—a-a——"

"Hippopotamus?" suggested Skinner. "Ha, ha, ha!"

"Blessed if I see anything to cackle at! I—I barely escaped with my life!" gasped Bunter. "I say, Wharton, now you're here, will you go to the Head about it? You'd better do it, as captain of the Form. Go to Dr. Locke and tell him——"

Harry Wharton stared.

"Go to Dr. Locke and tell him that Quelch has gone mad!" he ejaculated.

"What on earth's up?" asked Carter, as he peered into the study. "What's the matter with Bunter? Is he off his rocker?" "Oh!" Bunter popped his head out from under the table. "Is that Carter? You beast, Skinner, you said it was Quelch!"

"Yes; at once, old chap," said Bunter eagerly. "Don't lose any time about it."

"I can see myself doing it!" gasped Wharton.

"Ha, ha, ha!"

"But what's happened?" roared Bob Cherry. "Has anything——"

"Oh, really, Cherry——"

"It's jolly queer, from what Bunter says," remarked Peter Todd. "But Bunter's such a fearful fibber——"

"Oh, really, Toddy——"

"He's been whopped," said Vernon-Smith. "He says Quelch whopped him for nothing."

"Bunter always gets it for nothing," grinned Hazeldene. "Never was there such an innocent chap as Bunter."

"Hadn't you done your lines?" asked Nugent.

"You see, it was like this," gasped Bunter. "Do shut up, you fellows, and let me tell Wharton! He will have to go to the Head about it. Quelch will have to be collared——"

"Collared!" gasped Harry.

"Yes; and put under restraint, you know."

"Oh crikey!"

"I mean to say, he went for me with the cane; but suppose he got hold of the poker——"

"The poker! Great pip!"

"Or a bread-knife, or something !" said Bunter. "You can see the danger, now he's gone mad."

"Is the madfulness terrific?" chuckled Hurree Jamset Ram Singh.

"Well, listen. I went to his study— You see, I was going to ask him to let me leave my lines till after tea, owing to having a pain in my finger."

"Which finger?" grinned Johnny Bull.

"I don't know. I—I mean, what does that matter? Never mind that. I had a pain in my finger, and I couldn't do the lines. So I went to Quelch——"

"You might have expected a whopper like that to get his rag out, fathead !"

"But I never told him !" gasped Bunter. "I never said a single word. I hadn't time to speak. I only knocked at the door, and then—— Oh crikey ! I say, it makes me shudder now, really. Quelch was hiding inside the door——"

"Hiding !" gasped Harry Wharton.

"Lurking," said Bunter.

"Lurking ! Oh, my hat !"

"Lurking just inside the door, like —like a tiger waiting for his prey," said Bunter. "The instant I knocked, he tore the door open and seized me. He sawed me as soon as he seed me— I mean, he seized me as soon as he saw me——"

"Ha, ha, ha !"

"'Tain't a laughing matter !" hooted Bunter. "Fancy a chap knocking at his Form-master's door, and his Form-master grabbing the door open suddenly, springing on him, and dragging him into the study."

"What utter rot !" said Bob.

"That's what he did !" yelled Bunter. "I—I was fairly flabbergasted ! Quelch has always been a beast, of course, but he's never been a wild beast before— that I've noticed. Grabbing me with one hand, he pitched into me with the cane in the other—right and left, like billy-ho ! I hadn't said a word. He never even knew why I'd come to the study—never knew I hadn't done my lines, or anything ! 'Tain't time to take them in yet, anyhow. Not a word—nothing ! Just seized me like a raging lion, and whopped me right and left !"

Harry Wharton & Co. stared blankly at the fat Owl of the Remove. This tale sounded more incredible than usual—though Billy Bunter was well known for telling the tale.

That such a thing could have happened was simply impossible. And yet, impossible and incredible as it was, it was clear that Bunter, for once, was telling the truth—or as near to it as Bunter could be expected to get. No doubt he was exaggerating, and piling on the agony—that was Bunter's way. But his excitement and terror were evidently genuine. It was clear that the fat Owl had been scared almost out of his fat wits.

"I've had a fearful whopping," he went on breathlessly. "Quelch has hardly ever laid it on like that before. For nothing, you know ! I never did anything—never said anything ! I'd only just knocked at the door, when it flew open, and there was Quelch springing at me like a tiger ! What do you fellows think of that?"

"Blessed if I can make it out—if it happened !" said Harry Wharton. "Had you been playing any silly trick at the door?"

"I'd only just got there !" gasped Bunter. "I told Toddy I was going, didn't I, Toddy? I was here in the Rag. I wasn't sure I'd go, you know. Quelch mightn't have believed that I had a pain in my finger; he's doubted my word before, as you fellows know. That cad Carter ought to have done the lines for me, and I told him so. It was his fault I got them. You know the beast got me those lines in class— dropping a book, and making Quelch look round just as I was putting a bullseye into my mouth."

"Never mind Carter now !"

"Well, it was all his fault, and I told him he ought to do the lines; but the beast only laughed and went out. Then I asked Toddy to do them; but he was selfish, as usual—he wouldn't. So I decided at last to go and tell Quelch about the pain in my finger— see? Well, Toddy knows that I went straight to his study from here, don't you, Toddy?"

"Yes; that's so," said Peter. "And I know you came back five minutes afterwards, yelling like a Red Indian."

"You'd have yelled, I think, if a mad beak had clutched you, and pitched into you right and left !" howled Bunter indignantly. "Why, two or three of the other beaks looked out of their studies. I saw Capper and Wiggins and Hacker as I came away. They wondered what was up. I looked at it as soon as Quelch let go— you bet ! Sprinted ! I—I was afraid he might come raging after me, you know—perhaps with the poker in his hand !"

"You've done nothing ?"

"Nothing at all, except knock at the door. Instead of saying 'Come in !' as usual, I tell you he grabbed the door open, and sprang at me.'"

"Well, this beats the band !" said Bob. "I believe Quelch is doing his typing stunts. I heard the clicking from his window, I believe. He doesn't like being interrupted when he's on that typewriter of his. But——"

"But he wouldn't——" exclaimed Nugent.

"He couldn't——" said Johnny Bull.

"He did !" howled Bunter. "I'm not going to his study again, I can tell you. I shan't take in my lines—I—I daren't ! Suppose he got hold of the poker, and knocked my brains out——"

"Well, he could hardly do that," remarked the Bounder. "He might get hold of the poker, but he couldn't spot the brains."

"Ha, ha, ha !"

"Beast ! You can cackle !" exclaimed Bunter. "I jolly well shan't go to his study again—I know that ! I think Wharton ought to go to the Head about this. I mean to say, Dr. Locke ought to be warned. He ought to be told that Quelch is mad, before he does something awful. It happened to be me this time, but it might have been anybody. I say, you fellows, suppose he sprang at the Head ?"

"Oh crikey !"

"Well, he might. A maniac might spring at anybody. I can tell you he's as mad as a hatter ! Lurking just inside his study door, and springing at a fellow when he knocked——"

"Is that Quelch coming in here ?" asked Skinner, as the door of the Rag reopened.

"Ow ! Help !" yelled Bunter.

He made a dive for the table, and bolted underneath it. He disappeared like a ghost at cock-crow.

"Ha, ha, ha !" yelled the Removites.

It was only Carter who had come in. He stared round him in surprise.

"I say, you fellows, keep him off !"

came a squeak of terror from underneath the table.

"Ha, ha, ha!"

"What on earth's up?" asked Carter. "What's the matter with Bunter? Is he off his rocker?"

"Oh!" Bunter peered out from under the table. "Is that Carter? You beast, Skinner, you said it was Quelch——"

"Ha, ha, ha!"

Billy Bunter, reassured, crawled into view again.

Carter stared at him.

"I say, don't you go to Quelch's study, Carter!" exclaimed Bunter.

"Why not, fathead?"

"He's gone mad!"

"Wha-a-a-t?"

"Mad as a March hatter—I mean a March hare! He was lurking inside his study door, and sprang on me like a savage tiger when I knocked——"

The Famous Five left the Rag, and went up to the Remove to tea, leaving Billy Bunter telling the thrilling tale over again from the beginning. They no more knew what to make of it than the other fellows. That the calm, sedate, severe master of the Remove had suddenly gone out of his senses seemed very improbable—to say the least. But, if things had happened as described by Bunter, Quelch's actions were hard to account for, on any other theory. Not a fellow could understand what it all meant; but Billy Bunter, at least, remained convinced that his Form-master had gone dotty — stark staring, raving dotty! Really, it looked like it.

THE FOURTH CHAPTER.

Desperate Measures!

PETER TODD grinned.

Tom Dutton stared.

Billy Bunter quaked.

Tea was going on, in Study No. 7 in the Remove, as in other studies. Probably for the first time in history, Billy Bunter was not devoting his whole attention to the foodstuffs.

Bunter was pricking up his fat ears, like a rabbit alarmed by a dog. Every footstep in the Remove passage made him start and quake.

Starting and quaking, therefore, were almost incessant, as there were, of course, a good many footsteps in that passage at tea-time.

"I—I—I say, is—is that Quelch?" asked Bunter, for the umpteenth time, when Lord Mauleverer sauntered past the study door. "Oh dear!" He gave a gurgle of relief as the footsteps passed on. "I say, Toddy, ain't it awful?"

"Frightful!" agreed Toddy.

"I haven't taken in my lines," groaned Bunter. "I daren't go to a study with a raging maniac in it, Toddy!"

"I'll take them in for you, if you like, old fat man."

"Well, I haven't written them yet, you know! I say, Toddy, it's only a hundred; you might do them and take them in——"

"I'll watch it!" said Toddy.

"Still, he may forget all about the lines, being mad," said Bunter hopefully. "Do potty people remember things, Peter?"

"Dunno. You ought to know. What's your own memory like?"

"Beast!"

"I say, is anything up, you fellows?" asked Tom Dutton, who had been staring at Bunter in great surprise and curiosity.

Dutton, being deaf, was the only fellow in the Remove who had not heard Bunter's strange and startling tale.

"Quelch has gone mad!" answered Bunter.

"Eh?"

"Quelch—mad!" hooted Bunter. "Gone off his dot"!"

"Rot!" said Tom. "I should have heard it if a shot had gone off. I'm not so deaf as you make out."

"Not shot—dot!" shrieked Bunter. "Dot, not shot."

"Oh, draw it mild! A lot of shots. How could a lot of shots have gone off? Do you mean old Prout's rifle, that he keeps in his study?"

"Quelch!" yelled Bunter.

"Quelch doesn't keep a rifle in his study, does he? Old Prout keeps that old gun because he used to go hunting with it—though I've heard Price of the Fifth say that he bought it second-hand at old Lazarus', in Courtfield. But Quelch——"

"He's potty!" roared Bunter.

"Gammon! If he's potted anything with old Prout's rifle, what has he potted? Tell me that!"

"Quelch has gone barmy!" howled Bunter.

"I never knew that. I don't believe he was in the army! I've never heard of it before. When was he in the army?"

"Oh crumbs!"

"Trying to pull my leg, because I'm deaf?" asked Dutton crossly. "I'm not so deaf as you make out. I heard all you said. It's news to me that old Quelch was ever in the army—and I don't believe it, either."

Another footstep came along the passage. This time it was a heavier tread.

Bunter knew that tread.

He bounded.

"I—I—I say, Peter, that — that's Quelch!" he said faintly.

"He's come up to ask about your lines, fathead!"

"Help!"

"You blithering ass——"

"Don't tell him I'm here, Peter!" Bunter made a bound behind the back of the armchair and squatted, invisible. "I say, old chap, keep it dark! If he springs at you I'll rush out and help you—I will, really. Honest Injun! But—but d-d-don't you give me away!"

There was a sharp rap at the study door, and it flew open. The severe countenance of Henry Samuel Quelch looked in.

Peter Todd and Tom Dutton rose to their feet at once. Bunter did not! The fat Owl squatted out of sight, hardly breathing.

Peter looked very curiously at his Form-master. He could detect no signs of insanity in that severe and majestic countenance. Quelch looked the same as usual, only he was frowning. But his frown was accounted for by the circumstance that Bunter had not taken in his lines when due, and that Quelch had had to come to his study to see about the matter.

"Bunter!" said Mr. Quelch, in a deep voice. Then he glanced round the study. "Is not Bunter here?"

That was a difficult question for Peter to answer. He did not share Bunter's terrors on the subject of Quelch's alleged insanity, and he saw no reason why the fat Owl should not face his Form-master. But he could hardly let Quelch know that Bunter had hunted cover to dodge him. On the other hand, he had to answer Quelch.

"Bunter, sir?" he repeated. "I—I don't see him here, sir."

That answer was perfectly true, though it savoured, perhaps, a little more of the wisdom of the serpent than of the innocence of the dove!

"This is his study!" snapped Mr. Quelch. "Can you tell me which study Bunter is in at the moment, Todd?"

"I don't think he's in any of the other studies, sir!" answered Peter, again truthfully, and again with more wisdom than innocence.

"Dutton! Do you know where Bunter is?" asked Mr. Quelch.

"Certainly, sir!" answered Tom, in surprise. "A man who hunts, sir."

"What?" roared Mr. Quelch. "What do you mean, Dutton?"

"I suppose that's right, sir!" said Dutton, still more surprised. "A hunter is a man who hunts——"

"Bless my soul! I did not ask you what a hunter was, Dutton! Have you seen Bunter?"

"Only Mr. Prout, sir."

"Mr. Prout?" repeated the Remove master dazedly.

"I have heard that he used to be a hunter, sir. I don't know that I've ever seen any other hunter."

"Bunter!" bawled Mr. Quelch.

"Bunter!" repeated Tom. "Oh, no, sir; Bunter's no hunter! Fancy Bunter hunting! I shouldn't think so, sir."

Mr. Quelch, breathing hard and deep, turned to the door again. As he did so, his glance fell on the tea-table, with plain and obvious evidence that three fellows had been at tea. The frown on his brow intensified. If Bunter was not there, clearly he had been there very recently; and Quelch had not seen him leave the study as he came up the passage from the stairs. He fixed his eyes on Peter's face.

"Todd! Was Bunter in this study? Is it possible—is it even imaginable—that that reckless and disrespectful boy is deliberately eluding me, his Form-master? I have already caned him severely this afternoon. Apparently, I was too lenient with him, however. Is Bunter here?"

"I—I——" stammered Peter.

Mr. Quelch stared—or, rather, glared—round the study. It was really almost unimaginable, to Mr. Quelch, that a member of his Form could, or would, dare to dodge out of sight when he came along looking for him! But it certainly looked as if Billy Bunter had done so.

There was only one possible hiding-place in Study No. 7, and that was behind the high back of the armchair.

Mr. Quelch grasped the top of that high chair-back and twirled the armchair aside on its castors.

Bunter, squatting in terror, was revealed!

Mr. Quelch gazed at him.

"Bunter!" he gasped.

"I'm not here! I mean, keep off! Help!" roared Bunter. "Rescue! Hold him, Toddy! Keep him off! Help!"

"Bunter!" shrieked Mr. Quelch. "What do you mean? How dare you? Are you out of your senses, Bunter? Come here at once!"

"Ow! Keep off!" shrieked Bunter, springing up and dodging round the armchair. "Keep him off, Toddy! I won't be murdered! Help!"

"Bunter!" gurgled Mr. Quelch. "Boy! Are you mad?"

"No! You are! Help!"

"Boy!"

Quelch made a clutch. In the fixed belief that it was a maniac clutching at him, Bunter was desperate. He grabbed the cushion from the armchair and hurled it.

Bang!

The cushion landed on Mr. Quelch's scholastic gown, where that gown screened the third button of his waistcoat! It landed hard.

"Oooooop!" came from Quelch.

THE MAGNET LIBRARY.—No. 1,566.

He staggered.
He sat down.
There was a bump in Study No. 7.
Mr. Quelch sat, amazed, astounded, breathless, gazing at Bunter—indeed, almost gibbering at him.
Bunter did not stay to be gibbered at. Promptness and presence of mind aad saved him, for the moment, from the maniac's clutch. But he had no time to lose. He bounded to the door. He grabbed it, and slammed it after him as he fled.
"Bunter!" gurgled Mr. Quelch.
Slam!
Bunter was gone;

THE FIFTH CHAPTER.
Hunting Bunter!

"SAVE me!"
    "Hallo, hallo, hallo!"
    "Help!"
    "What——"
"Hide me! He's after me!"
Seven fellows were at tea in Study No. 13—the Famous Five of the Remove, and Mark Linley and little Wun Lung. Seven fellows bounded like one man, as the study door was hurled open and Billy Bunter shot in like a stone from a catapult, and banged the door after him and yelled.
"I say, you fellows, help!" roared Bunter. "He's after me! He nearly got me in my study! Help! Save me! Hide me! I say, back me up! Get hold of the poker, some of you! Have you got any cricket stumps or anything? I say——"
"You mad ass!" yelled Bob Cherry. "Who's after you?"
"Quelch!" shrieked Bunter.
"Quelch!" gasped Mark Linley.
"He's madder than ever!" panted Bunter. He gurgled for breath, his eyes popping through his spectacles, perspiration trickling down his fat face. "I say, he came up to my study after me, and nearly got me. If I hadn't bowled him over with a cushion he would have had me!"
"You bowled Quelch over with a cushion?" shrieked Harry Wharton.
"Yes, just in time; got him right in the bread-basket!" gasped Bunter. "He'd have had me. I say, he's madder than ever—grinding his teeth, and his eyes flashing fire! I say, if he comes to this study don't tell him I'm here. Tell him I've gone home."
"You blithering bloater!" yelled Johnny Bull.
"I say, where can I hide? He spotted me behind the armchair in my study. You know how sharp maniacs are!" groaned Bunter. "I say, I'll get under the table, and if all you fellows sit round close he'll never see me there. Mind you don't give me away!"
"You potty porpoise——"
"Fattee ole Buntee velly funnee!" chuckled Wun Lung. "Tinkee fat ole Buntee gone off lockee."
"Beast! Make room for a chap, will you?" hissed Bunter. "I believe I can hear him coming!"
There was not much room to squeeze under a study table with seven fellows sitting round it; but it was a case of any port in a storm, and Bunter plunged wildly among fourteen legs. He squatted, gasping, under the centre of the table, surrounded by legs and feet.
"I say, you fellows, can you hear him?" came a terrified squeak from under the table.
"Come out of it, you howling ass!" roared Bob.
"No fear! I say, you fellows, don't
THE MAGNET LIBRARY.—No. 1,566.

move; sit tight, and keep me out of sight. If Quelch looks in here, say I've gone to the Head—or—or say I've gone home—or—or say I've fallen downstairs! Say anything that will keep him off. I don't mind what, so long as you keep him off!"
"Quelch will want some keeping off if Bunter has really been biffing him with a cushion!" gasped Frank Nugent.
"I say, you fellows, get hold of something—the poker will do! Get him when he opens the door! Stun him!" gasped Bunter. "If you stun him, I—I'll help you tie him up——"
"Ha, ha, ha!" yelled the Removites.
"You howling chump——"
"You barmy bloater——"
"Don't let on that I'm here! I hardly got away alive!" groaned Bunter. "I say, you fellows, if you all grab him together, I could get away and go to the Head. The Head ought to know."
"Ha, ha, ha!"
"I say, is he coming? Can you hear mad yells or anything?" gasped Bunter.
There was a good deal to be heard from the Remove passage. Most of the Form were in the studies at tea, and most of them seemed to be turning out into the passage. Doors opened and voices called. The Remove seemed to have been disturbed like a hive of bees.
Through the hum and buzz came the sharp tones of Mr. Quelch, cutting like a knife.
"Where is Bunter? Has anyone seen Bunter?"
The Remove master's tread approached the door of Study No. 13.
"Come out of it, Bunter!" exclaimed Harry Wharton. "You can't stick there, you potty oyster, when Quelch wants you."
"Beast! Don't you give me away. I say, is he coming?"
"Sounds like it!" grinned Johnny Bull. "Seems to be looking in all the studies."
"Oh crikey!"
The door of Study No. 13 opened.
Harry Wharton & Co. rose respectfully to their feet. They stood as thickly round the table as they could, in the hope that a host of legs would screen Bunter. Quelch, it appeared, had come up the passage, looking into study after study, so he could not know that the fat Owl was there.
If Bunter had cushioned Quelch, as he stated, the penalty was awful to think of. There was no saving Bunter ultimately; still, it was something if he could keep doggo till Quelch had had time to cool down. Anyhow, the juniors in the study did not want to hand him over. A forest of legs hid the terrified fat Owl from Quelch's searching eyes.
"Linley—— Oh, you are here, Wharton! I am looking for Bunter!" exclaimed Mr. Quelch. "I fear that something has happened to the unfortunate boy. He does not seem in his right mind. Do you know where he is? I think he ran into one of the studies. I must find him immediately."
"Is—is anything wrong with Bunter, sir?" stammered the captain of the Remove, diplomatically avoiding a direct answer.
"I fear so, Wharton. His actions are so very strange. However, he does not seem to be here."
Quelch turned back into the passage.
The juniors looked at one another. If Quelch found out that Bunter had been in that study all the while it meant trouble all round; but that could not be helped.
There was only one more study for Quelch to search—Study No. 14. He looked into that study, and found Fisher

T. Fish alone there; then he turned back along the passage.
As he did so a fat squeak floated out of Study No. 13.
"I say, you fellows, shut that door! For goodness' sake shut that door before he comes back!"
Mr. Quelch jumped.
"Quiet, you potty ass!" hissed Bob Cherry.
"Beast! If that mad old ass finds me——"
"Bunter!" It was quite a roar, as Mr. Quelch reappeared in the study doorway. "Bunter!"
"Oh crikey!"
"Wharton, Bunter is here—I heard his voice. How dare you conceal his presence from me! Is this a conspiracy? Every boy here will take two hundred lines! Bunter, come out at once! Bunter, where are you?"
"I—I ain't under the table, sir!" gasped Bunter.
"Upon my word! Will you emerge, or will you not emerge?" thundered Mr. Quelch. "Bunter, emerge this instant!"
"I—I—I won't!" howled Bunter desperately. "I ain't going to be murdered!"
"What?"
"I say, you fellows, hold him—keep him off while I get away!" yelled Bunter, from beneath the table. "Catch hold of him, Cherry! Grab him, Wharton! All of you hold him while I bunk!"
"The boy is mad!" gasped Mr. Quelch. "He must be insane! Bunter, emerge from under that table immediately! Wharton, Cherry, remove that table!"
There was no help for it. The table was shifted aside. Once more a squatting fat Owl was revealed to Quelch's gimlet eyes.
"Now, Bunter——"
"Keep off!" shrieked Bunter, bounding. "Don't you clutch me, you maniac! I won't be clutched by a maniac! Keep off!"
"Bunter, you ass——"
"Shut up, you fathead!"
"For goodness' sake, Bunter——"
But appeals were lost on the frightened fat Owl. He was too terrified to heed. He bounded round the study as Mr. Quelch strode at him.
A sudden shove from Bunter sent little Wun Lung staggering in the way of the Remove master.
Bunter dodged out of the study.
"Bunter!" roared Mr. Quelch. He flew out of the study after Bunter, his gown streaming behind him.
"Oh, my hat!" gasped Bob Cherry.
"Oh scissors!"
The juniors rushed to the door to watch. In the Remove passage a score of fellows were buzzing with wild excitement. Bunter was doing that passage like the cinder-path. His feet seemed hardly to touch the floor as he flew. After him rushed Quelch. Quelch was not only angry; he was alarmed. He could only suppose that Bunter had taken leave of his senses. Bunter had to be secured at once. But Bunter was not going to be secured by a mad Form-master, if he could help it. Not Bunter!
"Bunter—stop!" roared Mr. Quelch. "Stop that boy! Do you hear? Stop him!"
Nobody stopped Bunter, he flew out of the passage, across the landing. He descended the stairs three at a time, bounding like a kangaroo. After him bounded Quelch, leaving the Remove passage in a roar.

Peter Todd made quick work of Billy Bunter's book. The pages, in bunches, were torn up and reduced to fragments. Bunter sat and gurgled for breath, as the fragments dropped into the empty bag on the table, glaring at Peter with a glare that almost cracked his spectacles.

THE SIXTH CHAPTER.

Merely a Misunderstanding!

DR. LOCKE gave so violent a start, that he dropped his pen, scattering blots.

He gazed in amazement—almost incredulous amazement—at a fat, breathless figure that dashed into his study. His eyes bulged at Billy Bunter! Never had the headmaster of Greyfriars School been so startled and astonished.

"What——" gasped the Head. "What — what does this mean? What——"

"Help!" gurgled Bunter.

"Boy!"

"He's after me——"

"Bunter——"

"He's mad!"

"Bless my soul! What——" Dr. Locke started to his feet, as pursuing footsteps reached his study door. "Mr. Quelch—what——"

Quelch panted for breath.

"I regret, sir, that you should have been disturbed by this boy of my Form—— I fear that the boy has lost his wits——"

"Goodness gracious!"

"Keep him off!" shrieked Bunter. "Oh, save me—save me! Keep him off, sir! He's mad!"

"Bunter," gasped Mr. Quelch. "Calm yourself——"

"Keep away! I won't be clutched by a lunatic! You keep him off, sir! Oh, help! Make him go away, sir! He's mad!"

Bunter in desperation, dodged round the Head's chair, as Mr. Quelch stepped into the study.

The Head gazed at him, dazedly, and gazed at Quelch.

Mr. Quelch shut the study door.

"I am sorry, sir——" he gasped.

"The boy appears to be out of his wits! It is most distressing! He actually hurled a cushion at me, sir, and fled—I have been in pursuit of him——"

"Bless my soul!" repeated the Head. "Bunter, calm yourself! Endeavour to calm yourself, my poor boy! A doctor shall be sent for immediately! You shall have every care! You have nothing to fear! Be calm, Bunter."

"Keep him off, sir!" moaned Bunter. "I ain't mad, sir—he's mad!"

"This is dreadful!" said the Head. "This unfortunate boy——"

"I will take him away, sir——"

"Keep him off!" shrieked Bunter. "Make him go away, sir! I won't be seized! I won't be murdered! I—I—I won't!"

"Pray leave him to me, Mr. Quelch!" said the Head, hastily. "He appears to be in dread of you, but not of me. Perhaps I can calm him! Bunter, be calm! You are quite safe with your headmaster, Bunter!"

"You won't let him spring on me, sir, like he did before?" gasped Bunter.

"No, no! Be calm! What an extraordinary delusion!" said the Head. "What can have made this unhappy boy imagine that you did anything of the kind, Quelch?"

"I have no idea, sir! An amazing delusion——"

"He did, sir!" babbled Bunter. "He's mad, sir! Oh crikey! Hid behind his study door, and jumped out at me—oh lor'!"

"Amazing!" said the Head, pityingly. "Poor, poor boy!" Dr. Locke was not likely to believe that a member of his staff had hidden behind a door, and jumped out at a junior!

"I didn't know he was mad, when I went to his study, sir," moaned Bunter, "I wouldn't have gone, if I'd known, sir! He sprang on me——"

"Poor boy!"

"He—he seized me, and dragged me into the study, sir, and pitched into me with a cane! Oh, dear! I told all the fellows he was mad, but they don't believe me, sir! I asked Wharton and Cherry to collar him, but they wouldn't! Oh lor'!"

"Extraordinary!" said the Head. "Have you noticed any delusions of this kind in the boy before, Mr. Quelch?"

Mr. Quelch did not answer that question. His eyes were fixed on Bunter, with a rather startled look. He recalled the scene in his study, following the series of runaway knocks that had interrupted his literary labours.

"Nothing of the kind has occurred, of course, Mr. Quelch!" said Dr. Locke, rather surprised by the Remove master's look.

"The boy is giving a foolish and wildly exaggerated account of something that did actually occur this afternoon!" gasped Mr. Quelch. "I had occasion to cane him for playing disrespectful tricks at my study door——"

"I never!" howled Bunter.

"Be silent, Bunter, please! What did the boy do, Mr. Quelch?"

"After class, sir, I was engaged on some literary work, and I was disturbed by a series of knocks at my study door!" explained Mr. Quelch. "I caught Bunter in the act, and caned him——"

"I never——"

Dr. Locke looked searchingly at Bunter's fat excited face. That fat face was wildly excited and alarmed; but that was all. It dawned on the Head that there was some strange misunderstanding here.

Bunter had, certainly, acted like a fellow out of his wits! But he was not out of his wits—it was only that he supposed for some extraordinary reason, that his Form-master was!

"I never, sir!" repeated Bunter. "That's because he's mad, sir! He sprang on me like a tiger, sir——"

"Be silent, Bunter! There is some extraordinary misapprehension here!" said the Head. "Possibly this stupid boy can explain it. You knocked at Mr. Quelch's door, Bunter——"

"We have to knock, sir——"

"Yes, yes, but you knocked more than once——"

"Oh, no, sir! The minute I knocked he jerked the door open and jumped at me, sir!" gasped Bunter. "I—I didn't know he was mad, or I wouldn't have gone——"

"You foolish boy, be silent! You are sure, Mr. Quelch, that there was more than one knock——"

"A whole series of knocks, sir—a miserable and disrespectful trick, to disturb me at my work!" said Mr. Quelch. "After it had happened several times, I did not call out 'come in,' but stood within the door, ready to open it as soon as the young rascal knocked again. I did so, and caught Bunter——"

"Oh crikey!" gasped Bunter.

"I understand," said the Head. "But——"

"It wasn't me!" howled Bunter. "I never knocked more than once! I'd just knocked, sir, to speak to him about my lines, and he grabbed the door open and clutched me——"

"It was you!" exclaimed Mr. Quelch. "At—at least——" He faltered a little, as a doubt crossed his own mind. "At least, I had no doubt, Bunter, as I found you knocking at the door, that—that——"

"It wasn't!" wailed Bunter. "I—I thought you'd gone mad, sir, when you grabbed me like that——"

"Upon my word!" gasped Mr. Quelch. "Is—is—is it possible—that—that that is why you have been acting in this insane manner, Bunter——"

"Ain't you mad, sir?" gasped Bunter.

"Bunter, be silent!" gasped the Head. "Bless my soul, what a very, very extraordinary boy! Is it possible, Mr. Quelch, that Bunter was not the boy who knocked continually at your door, but that he came to your study for some normal reason? In that case, of course, he must have been very much surprised when you—hem—when you——"

"Bunter had no occasion to come to my study, sir! He had lines to bring me at tea-time, but it was yet an hour——"

"I came to ask you to let me leave the lines till after tea, because I'd hurt my finger!" wailed Bunter.

"Oh!" gasped Mr. Quelch.

"Bunter! Were you, or were you not, the boy who knocked continually on Mr. Quelch's door for a foolish practical joke?"

"Oh crikey! No, sir! I went straight to the study from the Rag—all the fellows know, sir—I hadn't been there a minute—I just came straight up to the door and knocked, and then Mr. Quelch grabbed it open, and sprang at me——"

"I did nothing of the kind!" gasped Mr. Quelch. "As I have said, sir, I waited for another knock at the door, opened it quickly, and finding Bunter there, I took him by the collar, before he could escape."

"I quite understand," said the Head, his face twitching a little. "But if Bunter, as he states, came for a normal reason, and had nothing to do with the runaway knocks, he was naturally very

much surprised, and—and startled——"

"I thought he'd gone mad, sir! I told all the fellows——"

"Say no more, you foolish boy."

"Well, what was I to think, sir, when the door flew open, and he grabbed me, and dragged me in, and whopped me for nothing——"

"Silence!" rapped the Head.

He avoided looking at Mr. Quelch! Quelch's face was growing absolutely crimson.

It was plain that Bunter's amazing antics could only be accounted for by his belief that his Form-master had gone mad—which meant that he was not the runaway knocker! Had he been, he would have known why he was grabbed. But coming to the study, knowing nothing of the runaway knocks, Quelch's unexpected action was really enough to make him think that the Remove master had gone out of his wits.

Quelch stood crimson and dumb!

He had, he knew now, made a mistake. He had made a member of his Form think him insane, and he had punished that member of his Form for nothing! It was awful for Quelch!

Dr. Locke passed his hand over his mouth. He knew that his lips were twitching, and he did not want the dismayed and distressed Form-master to see him smile.

"If you are satisfied, Mr. Quelch, that it was not Bunter who——"

"I—I think, probably, that—that—er——" stammered Mr. Quelch.

"In that case, Bunter's extraordinary conduct may, perhaps, be overlooked," suggested the Head. "I leave the matter entirely in your hands, of course, my dear Quelch! Bunter, leave my study!"

Billy Bunter eyed his Form-master very uneasily as he obeyed. He kept as far from Mr. Quelch as possible as he made for the door. Even Bunter understood now that it was all a misunderstanding, but he seemed to have a lingering doubt of his Form-master's sanity. He kept his eyes—and spectacles—on Quelch, as he circled round to the door.

"Go at once, Bunter!" gasped the Head.

"Oh! Yes, sir!"

Bunter made a sudden bolt, and skipped out of the study.

Quelch breathed hard! He looked at the Head, his face red as a peony.

"I—I—I regret, sir——"

"Not at all, my dear Quelch!" said the Head courteously "Dear me, that foolish boy has caused me to blot my paper! I fear that Bunter must be somewhat of a trial to you in your Form, Quelch!"

Which was very nice of the Head, in the circumstances, and a little comfort to Quelch, as he backed out of the study.

But the hapless Remove master was feeling the biggest idiot ever, as he went; and he had only one consolation —the faint hope of discovering who really had delivered those runaway knocks at his study door that afternoon!

THE SEVENTH CHAPTER.

Spotting the Schemer!

IN the Rag that evening there were sounds of merriment.

Mr. Quelch did not regard it as a laughing matter; neither did Bunter! Quelch had caned a fellow for nothing, which was very worrying and distressing to a just man like Quelch. Bunter was the fellow who had been caned—which was, perhaps, more dis-

tressing still! But to the Remove generally it seemed no end of a joke!

Quelch, lurking in wait for the ragger and catching the wrong man, struck the fellows as fearfully funny. It was such an easy mistake to make—and really Bunter's fault, as he had no business at the study at that time, and was not expected there.

Anyhow, Quelch had made that mistake, and whopped the hapless Owl right and left, while the ragger, whoever he was, had got away safely, and was laughing in his sleeve. And Bunter's wild idea that Quelch had gone mad, as the only way of accounting for his actions, made the fellows yell!

Bumping Quelch over with a cushion, fleeing to the Head's study for protection—really, it was the limit! And Bunter was getting off scot-free, after all that—certainly the only Remove man who had ever cushioned Quelch and lived to tell the tale, as it were!

The Removites chuckled over it. They fairly chortled over it. They laughed and howled over it. Only Bunter's fat face was morose. Bunter had a grievance. He had been whopped for nothing! Likewise, he was still feeling many sharp twinges from the whopping.

Bunter did not bother about the dozens of whoppings he ought to have had, but never had had! He concentrated on that undeserved one, which he had had! He felt deeply injured.

Another fellow in the Rag was rather serious—Bob Cherry had a grimly thoughtful brow.

Nothing had been heard of any trouble in Prout's study; nothing in the way of a rag had occurred there, or certainly something would have been heard about it when the Fifth Form master came in. The Co., therefore, had no doubt of Carter's statement, that he had gone into "Old Pompous'" study to look at the newspaper, and had left by the window as the safest egress. Bob Cherry had not believed that statement at the time—and believed it still less now that he was thinking over the mysterious affair of the runaway knocks.

Inquiry had failed to reveal the runaway knocker. All that was known was that it was not Bunter, though Bunter had got the benefit of the vials of wrath. Bob Cherry thought that he could guess. Several times, his eyes fixed on Carter with a grim and scornful glare, which several fellows noticed —with smiles. Bob's dislike of the schemer of the Remove was well known, and it was rumoured in the Form that he was taking it to the length of refusing to play in the same football team with Carter.

Bob's friends were talking football, after prep. Bob was not listening. He was thinking, and frowning.

"Look here, Bob, about the St. Jim's match," said Harry Wharton, at last. "You can't be such an ass as to want to cut the match. If you really believe that Carter hacked you on purpose the other day——"

"I know he did!" said Bob gruffly.

"Well, I can't get it down, old chap, but, anyhow, I'll shift him off the right wing, and put Inky there—get him as far from you as possible——"

"Never mind that now!" said Bob. "Who do you think did that runaway knocking at Quelch's door this afternoon?"

"Haven't the foggiest!"

"I'll tell you, then—it was Carter!"

"Oh, my only hat!" exclaimed Wharton, in exasperation. "Does that new man do everything that's done these days? Really, Bob——"

"Well, I'm going to put it to the

cur!" said Bob grimly. "I'm rather curious to see what rotten lies he will tell about it."

"Oh, don't row with Carter now, for goodness' sake! You've done nothing but row with the chap ever since he came."

"I'm ready to chuck it as soon as he chucks playing dirty tricks! I'm going to stop him from landing that fat fool Bunter into rows, as far as I can."

"My esteemed Bob——" murmured Hurree Jamset Ram Singh.

Bob crossed over towards Carter, who was standing by the fire, in conversation with Skinner and Bolsover major. There was a general movement of interest in the Rag. This looked like a row coming!

Bob's friends followed him, looking, as they felt, worried and irritated. They did not like Carter much, but there was a limit. All the Remove knew that there was a sort of rivalry between Carter and Bunter, for the good graces of old Mr. Joseph Carter. Carter said nothing of it—Bunter had said much A lot, it was supposed, depended on what sort of a report Bunter got that term.

Bunter was, for that reason, awfully keen on getting a good report from his Form-master for the term. That keenness, however, did not make him show any desire to work in the Form-room, it did not make him cease to scamp his prep; it did not even make him wash his neck, if he could get out of it! Prospects from old Mr. Carter were uncertain; but had they been certain, they would hardly have made Billy Bunter anything but a fat slacker.

That was Bunter's own look out, of course! But if Carter was intervening to spoil Bunter's chance, such as it was, of getting a good report, and to get him a particularly bad one, it was a dirty trick, and Bob Cherry believed—indeed, was quite certain—that it was the case. And it was not surprising that such miserable trickery made Bob loathe the fellow.

In the affair of the afternoon he saw Carter's cunning hand again, though no one else did.

"I want to ask you a question, Carter,' said Bob abruptly.

The new junior looked round at him, with a curl of the lip.

"Don't you bar me?" he asked.

"You know I do!" growled Bob.

"Then hadn't you better keep your distance?" suggested Carter. "I'd really rather you didn't speak to me!"

"I'm going to speak, all the same! They're hunting for the fellow who banged on Quelch's door this afternoon. I'm not going to give you away to the beaks," added Bob scornfully, as Carter gave a start, "but it was you!"

"Think so, if you like," said Carter, shrugging his shoulders, "I'm really quite indifferent to what you think."

"Dash it all, draw it mild, Cherry!" said Bolsover major. "You're always accusing that man Carter of something."

"Only of what he does," said Bob. "Dirty trickery isn't good enough for the Remove."

"What's the latest, old bean?" grinned Skinner. "No fearful wickedness in ragging Quelch, is there? I've done it myself"

"No; but landing it on another fellow is a different story!" said Bob. "It was just after Quelch bagged Bunter at his study door that I saw Carter getting out of Prout's window. I know now how the ragger wasn't caught. Prout was out, and the chap hid in his study, crept out to bang Quelch's door, and ran back again. He was using Prout's study as a hide-out,

and after the row he left it by the window."

"Oh!" said Harry Wharton.

"Well, where's the harm?" asked Bolsover major. "Why shouldn't he?"

"I'll tell you why he shouldn't," said Bob. "He knew that that fool, Bunter, was going to Quelch's study with a lying tale about hurting his finger and being unable to do his lines——"

"Oh, really, Cherry!" squeaked Bunter.

"Quelch wasn't expecting Bunter, as he had no business there," went on Bob. "Carter got his rag out with runaway knocks, and parked himself in Prout's study when Bunter came along. It was a hundred to 'one that when Bunter knocked, Quelch would think it was the ragger again—as he actually did."

"Oh gum!" said Skinner. "It sounds thick! I don't suppose Carter knew anything at all about what the fat ass was going to do."

"He did," said Bob. "He was here when Bunter was gabbling about it to Toddy. Bunter wanted him to do the lines, like the fat ass he is. Wasn't Carter here then, Toddy?"

"Yes, he was," answered Peter Todd. "He cleared off about ten minutes before Bunter started for Quelch's study."

"And now I've told you why!" said Bob savagely. "What have you got to say now, you rotter? Are you going to deny that you were landing Bunter into another row with Quelch?"

All eyes turned on Carter. He was quite cool. Bob Cherry had worked it to his satisfaction, but there was, at all events, nothing in the nature of proof.

Arthur Carter laughed lightly.

"Quite a Machiavellian scheme!" he said. "You ought to be a detective, old bean! Sorry there's nothing in it. I went to Prout's study, as I said, to look at his newspaper. I got out of the window because I heard a row in the passage, and thought some beak might spot me leaving by the door. If Quelch thought it was Bunter hanging at his door I've no doubt he was right. Bunter's got out of it by lying, as he usually does."

"Why, you cheeky beast!" roared Bunter, "I never——"

"So you say it was not you who ragged Quelch?" said Bob.

"Not at all! Sorry if it disappoints you."

"Then who was it?" said Bob Cherry, looking round the circle of faces. "We're all here and nobody will give the man away. No harm in a rag on Quelch—if it wasn't a dirty trick on another Remove man at the same time. Nobody need be afraid of letting the Form know. Who was it?"

Carter set his lips. He had not foreseen that. There was, as Bob said, no reason why the ragger should not own up to the Form; indeed, he might have been expected to tell the story in the Remove as an exploit.

To Quelch it was a disrespectful prank; to the juniors it was just a jape. And a fellow who had japed Quelch, and got by with it, had no reason to conceal his exploit from the rest of the Form.

But Bob waited in vain for an answer.

"Who the dickens was it?" asked Hazeldene. "We're all here. It was one of us! Speak up, somebody!"

Nobody spoke up.

"Anything to say now, Carter?" asked Bob contemptuously.

"Is it my fault that the fellow,

whoever he was, prefers to keep it dark?" asked Carter.

"You're the only fellow who would keep it dark, because you did it as a dirty trick on Bunter," said Bob. "Any other fellow would have done it just as a jape on Quelch, and he would tell us so at once."

"Right on the wicket!" said Vernon-Smith. "Cherry, old man, you're getting quite bright. Sherlock Holmes was a goat to you."

"Blessed if it doesn't look——" said Harry Wharton slowly. "Look here, Carter, what were you in Prout's study for at that very time?"

"Looking at his newspaper," drawled Carter. "I've told you."

"Only a coincidence that you were on the spot when that runaway knocking was going on?" snorted Bob.

"Just that. I never knew anything about that till afterwards. Catch me ragging Quelch, when I specially want a good report this term," said Carter.

"And you specially want Bunter to get a bad one!" growled Bob. "Well, I can't fix it on you—you're too artful to let anything be fixed on you—but every fellow here with as much sense as a bunny-rabbit knows that you did it, and knows why. I fancy Quelch would know, too, if he knew that you were parked in Prout's study while it was going on."

"You can go and tell him if you like!" sneered Carter.

"That's a safe thing to say, as you know I won't. But I've shown up your rotten trickery to the Form, and I'll do the same every time I catch you at it—even if you hack me in Soccer afterwards for doing it!" added Bob savagely.

With that Bob Cherry turned his back on the new junior, and went out of the Rag. He left his friends looking very dubious.

But Billy Bunter was not dubious. He rolled up to Carter, fixed a withering blink on him through his big spectacles, and emitted a scornful squeak.

"Cad!"

"You fat chump!" growled Carter.

"I know your game!" snorted Bunter contemptuously. "Old Joe Carter's turned you down because he's found out what a rotten worm you are. He's thinking of putting you down in his will instead, because he wants to leave his money to a decent, honourable, straightforward fellow, the sort of fellow who's a credit to his Form and his school——"

"Ha, ha, ha!"

"Go it, Bunter!"

"Blessed if I see anything to cackle at! If I get a good report this term it may mean a lot to me," said Bunter. "Old Carter said plainly that it would be to my advantage. I've told you fellows so. Well, all I can do is to go on being upright and honourable and straightforward."

"When did you begin?" gasped Skinner.

"Ha, ha, ha!"

"Yah! That's all I can do," said Bunter, "and that cad is trying to dish me! Yah! Cad!"

(Continued on next page.)

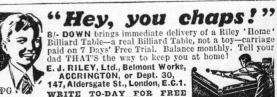

"Will you shut up, you fat fool?" snapped Carter.

"No. I won't!"

"Ha, ha, ha!"

"Worm!" roared Bunter. "Cad!"

"Ha, ha, ha!"

Carter made an angry stride towards the fat Owl of the Remove.

Billy Bunter promptly dodged behind Smithy.

"Cad!" he howled, over the Bounder's shoulder.

"Ha, ha, ha!"

"Will you let me get at that fat pig and shut him up, Vernon-Smith?" said Carter, between his teeth.

"No," answered the Bounder coolly, "I won't. If you want a scrap, get on with it. I'm more your weight than Bunter is."

"Swab!" roared Bunter. "Rats!"

"Ha, ha, ha!"

"Shut up, Bunter!" said Harry Wharton, laughing.

"Shan't! Swab! Cad! Worm! Beast! Sneak!" roared Bunter victoriously, over the Bounder's shoulder. "Yah! Rat! Pig! Worm!"

"Ha, ha, ha!" yelled the juniors.

Carter, with a crimson and furious face, walked out of the Rag. He did not want a scrap with the Bounder, and he did not want any more of Bunter's bright and genial conversation, so he had to leave the fat Owl victorious.

"Yah! Cad! Swab! Funk! Sneaking worm!" came Bunter's scornful squeak, as he went.

"Ha, ha, ha!"

Carter slammed the door. In the passage he passed Bob Cherry, and if looks could have damaged, Bob would have been left seriously crocked when Carter had passed him. Fortunately looks couldn't!

THE EIGHTH CHAPTER.

A Precious Pair!

M R. GIDEON GOOCH set his thin lips tightly, and the wrinkles on his forehead deepened in an angry frown.

Coming along the footpath in Friardale Wood, Mr. Gooch turned off, and followed a scarcely marked track which led through the thickness of the wood. Then his narrow slits of eyes fell on a Greyfriars junior who was waiting and lounging under a big oak-tree, with a cigarette in his mouth.

Arthur Carter did not remove the cigarette as Gooch came up. He gave the thin man in black a careless nod.

"You young fool!" was Mr. Gooch's cheery greeting.

"You old ditto!" was Carter's polite answer.

"You are smoking."

"Safe enough here. Don't be an ass, Gideon! If you've come along to give me sermons, the sooner you go back for your train the better."

"And it was you," said Gideon, "who was kicked out of St. Olaf's for bad conduct; you who hardly scraped into another school; you who have no prospects unless you can get back into Joseph Carter's favour. A bad report from your Form-master for your first term means that Mr. Carter will not even keep you on at Greyfriars. Yet you cannot behave yourself, with so much at stake."

"Cut it out! I'm careful," said Carter. "Nobody's been able to get anything on me, so far. I've learned a lesson from what happened at St. Olaf's. I'm as sharp as you are when you're diddling clients."

THE MAGNET LIBRARY.—No. 1,566.

Mr. Gooch looked at his schoolboy cousin with an expressive look. At that moment he would have liked nothing better than to have boxed the young rascal's ears soundly.

But he restrained that natural desire.

"Have you anything to tell me?" he snapped.

"Only rotten luck, all along the line!" growled Carter. "That fool I've told you of—a fellow named Cherry—makes a lot of trouble for me. He's wise to it, and some other fellows are getting wise to it, too, and if anything happens to that fat fool he shouts it out for everybody to hear that I had a hand in it. It's pretty awkward."

"It is an unlooked-for difficulty," said Gideon; "but, like other difficulties, it must be overcome. Your task should have been a perfectly easy one. From what you have told me of Bunter, it can be only necessary for old Joseph to know him exactly as he is to discard any idea of putting him in your place."

"I know; but——"

"A copy of Bunter's report this term will go to Mr. Carter. If it is a bad one—a very bad one—he will dismiss Bunter from his mind. You say that he is lazy, untruthful; that he pilfers food in the studies, slacks in class and slacks at games. A far from creditable boy, by your description."

"Yes; but I never have any luck. Cherry backs him up all along the line, and watches me like a cat. Another fellow—Smithy—has got his knife into me, too. And Cherry's friends are suspicious of me."

"I don't see how it concerns any of them——"

"It doesn't. They don't care a straw about my affairs or Bunter's," said Carter irritably. "The fat fool has gabbled it all over the shop since my uncle wrote to Quelch asking about his report. But they don't believe much, and don't care anything. It's their idea of fair play; it they think I'm landing that fat idiot in trouble in an underhand way they'll stand up for him like one man."

"I understand that. You must be cautious—doubly cautious."

"It's all very well to jaw!" grunted Carter. "But everything seems to go wrong. I thought I had him one day, and got another fellow by mistake—Smithy—and made an enemy of him. Not that he bothers his head about it much; he's not a fellow like Cherry. That fool Cherry would walk ten miles to help a lame dog over a stile. He sticks up for Bunter just because the fat idiot is a helpless ass."

"If you had been a little more like him, Arthur, you would never have been expelled from St. Olaf's," said Gideon. "You might do worse than take him for a model."

"Oh, don't be a fool!"

"The term is wearing on," said Gideon. "You know what is at stake. You must get a good report, and Bunter a bad one. If Bunter will not land himself in trouble with your help——"

"I help him all I can in that direction," said Carter, with a sour grin.

"You must help him more. Such a fatuous fool as you have described——"

"I believe there's such a thing as fool's luck," grunted Carter. "He keeps on asking for it, but never seems to get it—even with my help. The other day he drew an idiotic caricature of our Form-master that would have made Quelch hopping mad if he'd seen it——"

"You should have contrived that he saw it."

"I did. I got hold of it and left it on Quelch's table. Some other fellow

must have seen it there and snooped it in time. Anyhow, Quelch never saw it. And only yesterday I had him on toast, but——"

"What happened yesterday, then?"

Carter snarled out the story of the runaway knocking at the Remove master's door.

Gideon listened very attentively. His foxy face remained wrinkled in thought for some minutes after Carter had finished speaking.

"This may be useful," he said at last.

"I tell you it was a rotten fizzle. Bunter got a whopping, but that's no use; Quelch knew he got it for nothing."

"From what you have told me, he is the sort of fool to resent a caning and make some stupid attempt to get back on the master."

"Oh, that's Bunter all over!"

"This literary work you have mentioned—is Quelch very much concerned about it? Does he value the papers highly?"

"Eh? Yes. He would raise Cain if anything happened to any of his scribble."

"Something might happen to it," said Gideon. "Bunter might destroy some of the papers in revenge for that caning."

"Just what the silly idiot would do if he thought of it. That's the kind of benighted fathead he is. I suppose I can't suggest it to him!" snapped Carter. "What are you getting at, Gideon?"

"I will leave you to think that over."

"Oh, speak out plain!" snarled Carter. "You're not a solicitor in an office, pulling a client's leg now; you're in this game with me. Put it plain. Can't you ever be straight?"

"I make no suggestions," said Mr. Gooch calmly. "But it appears to me that if some of those papers were torn or defaced, and an odd sheet or two found in Bunter's study——"

"Oh!" gasped Carter.

Mr. Gooch looked at his watch.

"I must walk back to Friardale for my train now," he said. "Think it over, Arthur—and, above all, be cautious."

Carter stood looking after the man in black as he creaked away on his creaky shoes, then he lighted another cigarette.

There was a thoughtful frown on his brow when he took his way back to Greyfriars at last. The schemer of the Remove was, as Mr. Gooch recommended, thinking it over.

THE NINTH CHAPTER.

On the Scent!

T HERE was a sound of rending and tearing in Study No. 13.

In the middle of the room stood a large basket; round that basket sat the Famous Five, tearing and rending. Old newspapers, ancient exercises, all sorts of papers were being rent to fragments, and the fragments dropped into the basket—from which any observer might have guessed that the Remove fellows were making preparations for a paper-chase.

Five voices hailed Billy Bunter at once when he opened the door and blinked in through his big spectacles.

"Lend a hand, Bunter!"

Billy Bunter rolled into the study. But he had not, apparently, come to lend a hand; he rolled across to the armchair and plumped into it.

"Not looking for work?" asked Johnny Bull sarcastically.

Mr. Quelch's eyes glittered as, from the heap of paper fragments, he picked out a small piece of foolscap on which was written the word "Greyfriars." Bob Cherry and his friends, seeing that that fragment bore a word in Quelch's "fist," exchanged startled glances.

"I've come here to help——" said Bunter.

"Pile in, then!" said Bob Cherry.

"With a suggestion——" added Bunter.

"You can keep the suggestions and lend a hand tearing up these papers!" said Harry Wharton.

"You want a lot of paper for scent," said Bunter, unheeding. "I can tell you where to get lots."

"Oh? Fire away, then!" said the captain of the Remove. "We've been up and down all the studies and bagged all the old newspapers we can get hold of and we haven't got enough. I noticed a paper in your study, but Toddy said it was yours. The 'Burglars' Boarding-School,' I think it was called; I nearly had it——"

"You jolly well let that alone!" exclaimed Billy Bunter warmly. "I haven't finished reading that yet. I say, you fellows, it's a jolly good story —all about a boarding-school for burglars, with the headmaster a crook, and the assistant masters all convicts. A real-life story, you know."

"Oh, my hat!" gasped Bob Cherry. "It sounds a lot like real life!"

"Ha, ha, ha!"

"Thrilling, too," said Bunter. "I can tell you that the part where young Burglar Bill gets a gun on the headmaster in his study is ripping—realistic, and all that! I'll tell you about it. He walks into the study as cool as you please and says 'Hands up, headmaster——'"

"Oh crikey!"

"And just as he's making the Head hand over the loot another master comes in and slugs him on the back of the head with a gaspipe," said Bunter. "That's the sort of story I like— realistic!"

"Ha, ha, ha!" yelled the Famous Five.

"Eh? What are you cackling at?" asked Bunter. "'Tain't a funny story!"

"Sort of sounds funny!" chuckled Bob Cherry. "Look here, you'd better let us have that jolly paper for scent, Bunter."

"I'll watch it! I gave threepence for it!" said Bunter. "I borrowed the threepence specially from Toddy. I say, the part where the Head shoots the Scotland Yard man and hides the body behind the blackboard is fine! And the part where young Burglar Bill blows up the school with dynamite——"

"Fetch it along!" said Frank Nugent.

"You'd like to read it?" asked Bunter.

"No: I'd like to tear it up for scent!"

"Oh, really, Nugent! Look here, I can tell you where to get lots of scent," said Bunter. "That's why I've come here. I'd go and get it myself, only Quelch might think it was me——"

"Quelch!" repeated Harry Wharton, looking round.

"Well, I mean to say he whopped me for nothing yesterday," said Bunter. "He might think I was getting back on him. I prefer to remain clear of the matter personally."

"What has that fat idiot got into his silly head now?" asked Bob Cherry. "Are you thinking of bagging Quelch's Latin dictionaries and Greek lexicons, you benighted bloater?"

"No fear! What about his 'History of Greyfriars'?" asked Billy Bunter, with a fat and cheery wink.

"What!" yelled the Famous Five.

"Stacks of it; all the scent you want —and a bit over!" said Bunter. "He'd be rather wild, what, if it went?"

"Wild?" gasped Bob Cherry. "Yes, I fancy so—just a spot! You howling ass, Quelch would raise the roof if anything happened to his precious manuscripts! Have you gone quite batchy?"

"Well, I'd like to see him raising the roof, so long as he didn't get after me," explained Bunter. "That's important, of course. He gave me a fearful whopping, and all you fellows know it was for nothing. He's let me off my lines since—but what's that? I say, you fellows, wouldn't it make Quelch sit up if his History of Greyfriars went?"

The Famous Five ceased to tear and rend, and looked at Bunter almost in horror. Evidently he was in earnest. The fatuous grin on his podgy countenance revealed that much.

Any fellow but Bunter might have shuddered at the thought of what would follow if anything happened to Quelch's precious manuscripts. But fools rush in where angels fear to tread.

"Pay him out all right, what?" grinned Bunter.

"You—you—you unspeakable idiot!" gasped Bob Cherry. "Quelch would be as mad as a hatter!"

"That's what I want."

"He would go to the Head——"

"Let him!"

"And the Head would sack the fellow who did it!" shrieked Bob.

"Well, he couldn't, if he didn't know who it was!" Bunter pointed out. "He wouldn't know, you know! That's all right."

"Let me catch you going after Quelch's papers!"

"I'm not going after them!" said Bunter, shaking his head. "I've said that Quelch might suspect that it was me. You fellows go after them, see? Wharton would be best as he's head boy, and Quelch would never guess that

(Continued on page 16.)

THE HERO OF THE HOUR!

Last Laughable Instalment of
" THE FORM-MASTER'S SECRET ! "

By DICKY NUGENT

" Inspector of the perlice to see you, sir ! "

Binding, the St. Sam's page, made that brethless annowncement, as he shoved his boolit head into Doctor Birchemall's study.

The next moment a man in the uniform of a perlice-inspector walked briskly into the room. He had a hatchet face, well-chiselled feetchers, a pair of gimlet eyes and a voice like a rusty file.

" Name of Cutts—Inspector Cutts, at your serviss ! " he cried. " I understand that you have detained somebody in connection with the kidnapping of yung Bullion."

The Head rubbed his hands gleefully.

" Right on the wicket, inspector," he chortled. " His name is Lickham —I. Jolliwell Lickham. He is the missing junior's Form-master."

" The dickens he is ! " ejackulated Inspector Cutts.

" I suspeckted him right from the moment when I heard Bullion had vannished," grinned the Head. " You see, inspector, I have recently found out that, unbeknown to me, this Lickham has at some time in his career been hobnobbing with a lot of low, common tramps."

" Jumping truncheons ! Are you serious ? "

" Never more so, inspector, I assure you ! Just before Bullion disappeared, two villanous-looking raskals came to St. Sam's, claiming that they had come to see Lickham. I have it on the best orthority that they carried out their intention. In fakt, Lickham and his pals," said the Head, with a skornful curl of his lip, " were actually seen near the skool tuckshop with their heads together —obviously plotting the dastardly crime ! "

" My hat ! "

" Shortly afterwards, Bullion was seen walking towards the tuckshop. Shortly after that the two tramps were observed leaving St. Sam's, carrying between them a sack which obviously contained a farely weighty burden." The Head pawsed and shrugged: " Need I tell you, inspector, what was

undoubtedly inside that sack ? "

Inspector Cutts' eyes gleemed.

" I fansy I can make a pretty good guess, Doctor Birchemall," he rasped. " The sack contained tuck ! "

" Ass ! " grunted Doctor Birchemall. " I don't mean tuck. I mean yung Bullion."

The inspector started violently.

" Ha ! I see ! You are implying that this was how they kidnapped the yungster ? "

" Eggsactly ! "

The inspector wissled.

" Few ! If what you tell me is correct, sir, this man Lickham seems booked for a good long stretch ! Does he konfess to the crime ? "

" Not so far. But you'll soon be able to make him konfess if you put him through the third degree," said the Head eagerly. " We have an eggsellent collection of instruments of tortcher in the skool museum if they are of any use——"

" Thanks for the offer, but I'm afraid we are not allowed to use third degree methods," said the inspector rewfully. " I sujjest that you conduct me to the prisoner and allow me to talk to him myself."

" With plezzure, inspector ! This way ! "

Doctor Birchemall led the officer out of his study and up the stairs to the punishment-room where he had incarcerated Mr. Lickham.

Outside that dredded apartment, he dived into his trowsis pocket and projooced a key. He winked slyly at Inspector Cutts.

" Have your handcuffs ready, inspector," he wispered. " We'll take him by serprize and render him horse de combat before he knows we've arrived ! "

" Good wheeze ! "

Silently and stelthily the Head inserted the key in the lock ; then, with a swift movement, he turned it, flung open the door and bounded into the room—the inspector close at his heels.

An instant later the two came to a dead stop, uttering a simultaneous cry of amazement.

" GONE ! "

The bird had flown ! Mr. I. Jolliwell Lickham had vannished just as though the floor had opened and swallowed him up ! But the real eggsplanation was by no means so sensational as this, as the newcomers could see when they turned their eyes to the winder.

Two of the iron bars that barred the winder had been removed from their settings completely ! So any idiot could see that the prisoner had escaped by climbing out of the winder and down the ivy. Doctor Birchemall and the inspector could see it for themselves.

" Bust it ! " hist the Head. " He has slipped through our fingers— and I'm certain that he was the evil jeenius behind this kidnapping stunt ! Some people say he could never have done it becawse he had a hart of gold. But,

personally, I am convinced of his gilt."

" Really, this is most unforchunit," rasped the inspector. " With Lickham in our hands we stood some chance of finding Bullion. But now he has escaped I'm afraid that the question we shall never be able to answer is : Where is Bullion ? "

" Here I am ! "

It was a youthful voice from the doorway ; and the meer sound of it was suffishant to make the Head and his visitor nearly jump out of their skins.

" What the — who the—"

" How the — where the——"

" BULLION ! " shreeked Doctor Birchemall suddenly. " It's Bullion—or his ghost ! "

" I'm no ghost, sir ! " larfed Bullion. " I'm here in the flesh right enuff—thanks to Mr. Lickham ! "

" WHA-AT ? "

" Fakt, sir ! " grinned Jack Jolly, who, with Merry and Bright and Fearless, now appeared behind Bullion. " Mr. Lickham tracked down the kidnappers to their lair and reskewed the whole lot of us. He properly gave them beans, too, didn't he, you fellows ? "

" Yes, rather ! "

" But isn't Lickham the man who was sus-

peckted of doing the kidnapping himself ? " asked the inspector in astonishment.

" He may have been once," said Jack Jolly, " but not after what we saw to-day, sir ! "

" We—we have evvidently made a garstly mistake ! " stammered the Head, who hardly knew whether he was on his head or his heels. " But where is Mr. Lickham now ? "

" I know, sir ! " wined another newcomer from the doorway ; and Toadey minor appeared.

" You know where Mr. Lickham is, Toadey ? " wrapped out Doctor Birchemall. " Then tell what you know at once ! "

" Please, sir, he's in the woodshed, hiding amongst the wood ! " wined Toadey minor.

" Come on ! " said the Head.

There was a rush to the door.

Nobody, of corse, dreemed for a moment that the Mr. Lickham

who woo Mr. resh fron kidr

M had the tran Dus only for 1

T rush st a acro to shee

M was enu d i c whe fare the and the

" inne as qua nap

T at lodg

HARRY WHARTON CALLING !

Is the old custom of sending out romantic cards on Valentine Day really reviving or not ?

If Greyfriars can be taken as a reliable guide, it certainly is !

A distinct softening of the feelings of many prominent residents was noticeable this year, as Valentine Day drew near. On inquiry I learned that in each case the resident affected was either going to send or had sent already a beribboned card to some fair damsel whose charms had smitten him !

Take Bolsover major, for instance. I bumped into him in the quad wearing a sweet and soulful simper on his battle-scarred face. He was inhaling the fragrance of a daffodil.

He shyly confessed that he was on his way to post a valentine to one of the young ladies who show people to

their seats at the Courtfield Cinema !

Later on I spotted Bob Cherry sitting abstractedly in the Rag with a pencil in his hand and paper on the table before him. Blushing violently, he asked me if I knew a word to rhyme with " dimples." He looked awfully reproachful when I suggested " pimples."

Yes, you've guessed it ! He was composing a valentine of his own to send to Marjorie Hazeldene !

Other he-men similarly affected were Tom Brown, Rake, and Morgan in the Remove, Temple in the Upper Fourth, and Hobson and Stewart in the Shell. For a couple of days these fellows wandered about the school looking like lost sheep— and they all made a rush for the postman on Valentine Day !

Imagine their ex-

cite foun abo val then men rag out tinc

It ner othe seiz to s ma then thou bee spe poir tha to

I don way wer disc quil they Val year has I fa bit full

STOP THESE SLANDERS!

Roars GERALD LODER

I am a kind-hearted sort of chap, usually. (Great pip!—Ed.) It takes a lot to upset me. I am very patient and forgiving at that. (Ye gods!—Ed.) But there is a limit to my patience, and I am going to say here and now that this week the limit has been reached. Cruel and malicious slanders have been uttered about my private life—chiefly by members of the Remove Form. If these slanders are repeated, my patience and kindness will at last come to an end, and whatever little worm it is that slanders me will be torn to pieces and strewn all over the Sixth Form passage. So get that!

The tale that these tattling tongues have told is one which will be treated with the contempt it deserves by those who know my blameless character. (Phew! Fan me, somebody!—Ed.) Briefly, it is that I visited a low tavern called the Peal o' Bells in Courtfield, played cards with some very common fellows, and cheated (cheated, mark you! Me!) and finally got thrown out on my neck.

Admittedly, I did go to Courtfield; but as for the Peal o' Bells, perish the thought! The place to which I actually went was a milk bar.

As I sat down, quietly sipping my glass of milk, some quite refined fellows who were there asked me if I'd join them in a noughts-and-crosses tournament. With my customary politeness, I smilingly accepted and we played.

There was, I admit, a slight difference of opinion afterwards as to the rules of the game, and when we left the milk bar I was in a slight huff. But, of course, the suggestion that I was thrown out is simply absurd. I may have flicked one of the fellows lightly on the tip of the nose and he and his friends may have sniffed audibly and made restrained gestures of disapproval at me.

But nothing more than that!

These are the facts about the trivial incident on which slanderous tongues have based their ridiculous tales about me.

Now that I have revealed the entire truth about it, I hope that the slanderers will hide their diminished heads in shame and for ever hold their peace!

(What a hope! As we go to press news reaches us that Loder has been up on the carpet before the Head and received a dressing-down and a month's "gating." If our readers believe the Head gave Loder all that for getting involved in a noughts-and-crosses argument in a milk bar, they can do so. We know what we think about it ourselves!—Ed.)

HE LET THE SIDE DOWN!

Gatty, of the Second, is in disgrace in the Lower School.

We understand that he washed his hands before his Form-master gave him the order.

...ding in the ...as not the ...n who had ...he juniors ...tches of the

...rell Lickham ...ved ...his ...tin, ...un, ...well

...11 ...vn-...n d ...nad ...od-

...am ...ght ...he ...a y ...ted ...He ...om ...ned ...for

top speed! ...lone! I'm ...he yelped, ...across the ...never kid-...on!" ...im to earth ...ar Fossil's ...gates.

...when they ...there were ...a dozen ...or each of ...t excite-...changed to ...they found ...rt of valen-...were.

...that Skin-...number of ...orists had ...pportunity ...few home-...ntines of ...And, al-...have not ...o secure a ...prove my ...assure you ...ere not at ...entary!

...n to have ...good, any-...chaps who ...d with the ...e become ...ial since ...ed their ...ay post. ...ough this ...ntine Day ...ll records, ...ay prove a ...ost in the

...again next ...s! ...HARTON.

Then Mr. Lickham received a big serprize. For the first time he spotted Bullion.

"Bullion!" he gasped.

A moment later he had a still bigger ser-

prize, when, instead of seezing him and putting him in irons as he egg-spected, his persewers seezed him and lifted him shoulder-high!

"Hip, hip, hooray!" they cheered.

"Good old Lickham!"

"B-b-bless my sole!" stuttered Mr. Lickham. when they started carrying him back to the Skool House to the tune of "See the Conkering Hero Comes." "I must be dreeming!"

But it was no dreem, as Mr. Lickham realised in the end. Putting two and two together and making five, he came to the correct concloosion—that his cuzzin Dusty had turned up trumps at last and done something that was redounding to his credit!

The sellybrations ended at last. Inspector Cutts went away cmpty-handed, but happy in the nollidge that Bullion had been found. Mr. Lickham, in the privacy of his study, sank into an armchair and breeth-ed freely for the first time for many days.

But he had not been breething freely for more than a cupple of seconds before a tap on the winder set him gasping for breth once more!

It was Dusty Lickham who threw up the sash and let himself in—and at the same moment Jack Jolly & Co. entered

---

Mr. Lickham's study by the doorway!

The heroes of the Fourth had come to the concloosion that they would ask the master of the Fourth for an eggsplanation of all the strange happenings that had recently taken place in the St. Sam's Fourth. But when they spotted the two Lickhams they could see the eggsplana-tion for themselves.

"Grato pip! There are two of them!" gasped Jack Jolly.

"Quite correct, Jolly," groaned Mr. Lickham. "Come in, all of you, and close the door. This is my cuzzin—Dusty Lick-ham!"

"Don't worrit about introductions, Izaak!" grinned Dusty Lickham. "We've met afore, hain't we, yung jents?"

"Yes, rather!" grin-ned Fearless. "And we thought all the time that you were our own Mr. Lickham. We know better now!"

The skoolmaster-tramp larfed.

"Hall I 'ope, yung coveys, is as you'll keep hall this 'ere under your 'ats. 'Cawse why? 'Cawse I don't want my cuzzin 'ere to git into trubble. See?"

"All screen, Dusty!" grinned Jack Jolly. "We'll be as mum as oysters. Won't we, you fellows?"

"Yes, rather!" cor-

---

ussed Fearless and Merry and Bright.

A gleem of hoap came into Mr. Lickham's eyes. He knew that Jack Jolly & Co. were stawnch enuff; but what about his cuzzin Dusty? He glanced at Dusty, and, to his grate releef, found that there was a beeming smile on his grimy face.

"Er—do I gather from your remarks, Dusty, that you will no longer be staying at St. Sam's?" he stammered.

"Yuss, Izaak, that's right!" grinned Dusty. "Hall I come back for really was me bundle wot I left be'ind in this 'ere study. Gimme me bundle an' hoff I go!"

"Thank goodness!" mermered Mr. Lickham.

He picked up the bundle, tied up in a red spotted handkercheef that rested on the floor beside his desk. Dusty took it and carefully tied it to the end of his old stick. Then he slung it over his sholder and stepped out of the win-der again.

"Toodle-oo, you coveys!" he cried. "An' thanks to one an' hall for givin' me a blinkin' fine time at St. Sam's!"

"Don't mention it!" chuckled Jack Jolly.

"Mind you keep wot you know to your-selves!" grinned Dusty, as he vannished.

Needless to say, they did!

THE END.

MY FORM IS THE BEST AT GREYFRIARS!

By H. H. LOCKE, Esq., D.D., M.A.

As headmaster of Greyfriars, I suppose I should preserve a feeling of complete impartiality towards the various Forms in the school. I trust, therefore, that my readers will not regard it as a weakness on my part when I confess that the Form which I usually teach—namely, the Sixth—is, in my opinion, the best Form at Greyfriars.

I have read with great interest the articles which have pre-ceded mine, and it is gratifying to me to know that each Form-master has so staunchly advo-cated the claims of his own

Form. Nevertheless, I still feel that the Sixth is the best.

Surely this is only as it should be!

It is the aim of our education at Greyfriars to train the intelligence and faculties by gradual stages. It is not to be expected that the results of this training should reach maturity before the Sixth Form stage.

If the Sixth Form were not the best at Greyfriars, in fact, it would show that something had gone wrong with the pro-gramme!

The Sixth Form over which I preside at present is a Form of which any schoolmaster might be proud.

Wingate is an ideal head boy, possessing great strength of character and exercising a fine influence over the entire school. He is, in addition, a great classical scholar—which en-hances him considerably in my eyes!

Faulkner, Wynne, Hammers-ley and North support him nobly, as do most of the Sixth. And, though there are one or two weaklings who seek to make up for their lack of character by apeing the less desirable habits of grown-ups, they are in a negligible minority.

So I feel that I am justified in considering that the Sixth is the best Form at Greyfriars—and I hope that it will always be the same!

The SCHEMER of the REMOVE! By FRANK RICHARDS

(*Continued from page* 13.)

he did it! Besides, Quelch would take his word, if he said he didn't, so that's all right!"

"I—I—I—" stuttered the captain of the Remove. "I'm to pinch Quelch's papers, and tell him lies about it——"

"Well, I suppose you tell one or two now and then," said Bunter. "I wouldn't myself—it's not the sort of thing I could do; but you ain't so jolly particular, old chap!"

"You—you—you——" gurgled Wharton.

"Safe as houses," said Bunter. "We make Quelch sit up for giving me that whopping for nothing, see? You get a lot of scent for the paper-chase to-morrow—tons of it."

"Luckily, Quelch keeps his papers locked up, so that fat idiot wouldn't be able to get at them," said Nugent.

"He's always got some on his table, though," said Bunter, "and he might leave the drawer unlocked, and you could get the rest. Anyhow, you could snaffle those on his table. Every little helps, you know."

"That's the chap who wants to get a good report this term!" gasped Johnny Bull.

"Well, that's all right, as I'm not going to do it," said Bunter. "If Wharton's funky, you do it, Bob! You're not funky, old chap."

"I suppose," said Bob Cherry slowly, "that Bunter can't help being a born idiot! But he can help being a revengeful little beast! I think we ought to give him a lesson about that."

"Hear, hear!"

"Well, I got a whopping, didn't I?" argued Bunter. "An eye for an eye, and a nose for a nose, you know—I mean a tooth for a tooth! I believe in paying a beast out."

"Sure you do?" asked Bob.

"Yes, rather!"

"All right! A beast—a very greedy beast—snooped a bag of toffee out of this study yesterday——"

"Eh?"

"So I'll pay him out——"

"I—I say——"

"Ha, ha, ha!"

Billy Bunter—apparently repentant of having come to Study No. 1 with that valuable suggestion—jumped out of the armchair and bolted for the door.

He was grabbed in transit.

"Yarooh!" roared the fat Owl, as he was twisted over a chair in a hefty hand. "I say—leggo! I say——"

"Hand me that ruler, Nugent."

"Here you are!"

"I say, you beast, if you touch me with that ruler, I'll—yarooooop!" roared Bunter.

Whop, whop, whop, whop!

The ruler fairly rang on Billy Bunter's trousers. Bunter's frantic yells rang far beyond Study No. 13.

Whop, whop, whop!

"Leave off! Leggo! Help! Yaroop!" roared Bunter. "I say, you fellows, rescue! Make him leggo! Yoo hoop!"

"Now," gasped Bob Cherry, "do you still believe in paying a beast out?"

"Ow! Yes!"

Whop, whop, whop!

"Yarooh! No!" roared Bunter. "Not at all! I—I don't want to pip-pip-pay anybody out! Nothing of the kind! Never! Yarooooh!"

"Sure?" demanded Bob, lifting the ruler.

"Ow! Yes! Leggo! I—I don't want to pay out Quelch out! Nothing of the sort! After all, it was only a mistake! I—I wouldn't pay him out for anything!" howled Bunter.

"Ha, ha, ha!"

"Mind, if you get paying Quelch out for that whopping, I'm going on paying you out for snooping my toffee!" grinned Bob. "Sauce for the goose is sauce for the jolly old gander! Quite sure?"

"Ow! Yes! Wow! Ow!"

"Then you can cut, old fat ass!" said Bob. "Hold on a sec. I want to boot you into the passage!"

Billy Bunter did not hold on the fraction of a second. He made one frantic bound into the passage, and disappeared.

THE TENTH CHAPTER.

Beastly for Bunter!

"HOW much have you got?"

Peter Todd asked that question as Bunter came into Study No. 7. Peter and Tom Dutton were tearing up old papers for scent, and filling a bag that stood on the study table.

Bunter shook his head.

"Stony, old man!" he answered. "My postal order never came!"

"You fat chump! I mean, how much scent have you got?"

"Oh, scent!" said Bunter. "I haven't had time to find any old papers, Toddy, and if I had, I haven't time to tear them up. I'm pretty busy, you know, one way and another."

Billy Bunter plumped down in the study armchair, and picked up a volume that bore the thrilling and attractive title, "The Burglars' Boarding-School," perhaps to show how busy he was!

With his fat shoulders in the chair, his fat head on a cushion, and his feet on the table, Bunter fixed his eyes and spectacles on that thrilling literature, and was soon deep in the hectic adventures of "Young Burglar Bill."

Peter glared at him.

"You haven't time to lend a hand tearing up scent?" he asked.

"Eh? No! Don't interrupt a chap when he's reading!" said Bunter.

"Chuck that muck over here," said Peter.

"Oh, don't be an ass!" said Bunter. "I'll read some of it out to you if you like. I don't mind doing that! I never was lazy, I hope! This is the chapter where the Scotland Yard man comes to the school. Listen to this bit. '"Ha!" cried the Head. "A sleuth from Scotland Yard!" Springing at him like a tiger, he bore him——'

"He bored him?" asked Peter.

"No, you fathead—he bore him——"

"Not so much as you're boring me, old fat bean."

"Shut up! 'He bore him backwards, with a thundering crash, to the floor of the study!'" continued Bunter. "'Drawing a dagger from under his gown—' The headmaster always had a dagger under his gown, Toddy," explained Bunter.

"He would!" agreed Peter. "Sort of thing a headmaster would naturally carry about with him."

"'Drawing a dagger from under his gown,'" went on Bunter, "'he stabbed the sleuth to the heart——'"

"Some headmaster!" said Peter. "Can't see Dr. Locke treating visitors like that! But I suppose things are different at different schools."

"Do shut up, old chap! I tell you this is good!" urged Bunter. "Frightfully thrilling! 'He stabbed——'"

"Chuck it," said Peter. "That will do to go on with."

"Oh, do shut up and listen! 'Drawing a dagger, he slabbed the tooth—I mean he stabbed the sleuth—to the heart, and with a fearful yell, he expired. "Ha!" hissed the Head——' If you chuck that book at me, you beast——"

Bang!

Peter chucked the book, as Bunter was speaking, and it landed on a fat chin. The "Burglars' Boarding-School" fell on the floor, and Billy Bunter clasped his fat chin with both fat hands, and roared.

"Beast!"

"Now get on," said Peter cheerfully. "You've got to lend a hand, old fat frump! If you think you can stick in that chair, while other fellows are doing all the work, the sooner you get another idea, the better."

Billy Bunter rubbed his fat chin, and glared.

Tearing up paper for scent was not, perhaps, hard work. But it was work: and Bunter objected to work, on principle. Besides, he was fearfully interested in that thrilling story, the "Burglars' Boarding-School." There was bloodshed in every chapter. Dead bodies lay about that remarkable school like leaves in Vallombrosa. What could any fellow want more than that?

"If you can't let a fellow read a book in peace!" howled Bunter indignantly. "Look here, can't you let a chap have a little peace?"

"Never mind a little peace—what we want are little pieces!" said Peter. "Let's tear that rubbish up."

"Shan't!" roared Bunter.

Peter Todd rose to his feet and picked up the bag of scent from the table. It was nearly full. All the available supply of paper in the study had been reduced to fragments—except the "Burglars' Boarding-School!" Most of the fellows, in the other studies, had been busy, too; and it was arranged that the supply from every study should be taken along to Study No. 13, and tipped into the big basket there, as soon as the work was done. Peter had quite a handsome contribution to make—to which Bunter had not added one fragment.

"Come on, Dutton," said Peter. "Now look here, Bunter, I'm taking this bag along to Cherry's study, to put in the basket. I'll bring it back here and leave it empty for you."

"You needn't!" yapped Bunter.

"And if you haven't shoved into it your share of scent before prep, I'll bag that precious volume of yours, and it goes into the bag! See? Mind, I mean that!"

"Beast!"

"Look here, Toddy, Bunter's in the paper-chase to-morrow," said Tom Dutton, "he ought to be tearing up some scent. If he won't he ought to be kicked."

"Boot him!" said Toddy.

"Oh, don't be an ass—we can't shoot him! What do you mean? I think he ought to be kicked! What do you think?"

"Go it!"

"Well, you can say stow it, but I think so, anyhow," said Dutton warmly.

"What about shoving that silly book down his neck, then?"

"Good egg!" grinned Peter.

"Look here, get out!" howled Bunter. "You've got to take that scent along to Cherry's study before you go down, and—yar-ooh! Leggo! Will you leggo?"

Peter and Dutton did not let go! They grabbed the fat Owl and jerked him out of the armchair.

The "Burglars' Boarding-School" was crumpled and stuffed down the back of a fat neck—to an accompaniment of fiendish yells from Billy Bunter.

The fat Owl wriggled and roared. But the crumpled volume was stuffed down his back, and driven well home.

Then Peter and Tom left the study—leaving Billy Bunter wriggling like a fat eel, making frantic efforts to extract the "Burglars' Boarding-School" from the back of his neck.

Peter Todd walked along to Study No. 13, where the Famous Five were still busy, with Mark Linley and Wun Lung helping them on with the good work. He tipped the bagful of scent into the big basket.

"Good man!" said Bob Cherry. "How much has Bunter done?"

"None, so far!" said Peter. "But he's going to do some—or else he's going to be sorry he didn't!"

Peter carried the empty bag back to Study No. 7, where Bunter was still struggling at the task of extraction. He slammed it on the table.

"There you are, Bunty—empty, ready for your lot!" he said.

"Beast!" howled Bunter.

Peter, with a cheery grin, joined Tom Dutton in the passage, and they went down together to the Rag.

Bunter continued his wild struggle with the "Burglars' Boarding-School." It was a considerable time before that entrancing volume was extracted; and by that time, Bunter was crimson and breathless, and less inclined than ever to exert himself adding to the supply of scent.

Gasping, he plumped down in the armchair again; and the empty bag on the table remained empty.

Peter Todd was a man of his word; and there was no doubt that if Bunter failed to play up, Peter would collar the "Burglars' Boarding-School" and put it in that bag in small pieces. But Bunter, deep in the wild adventures of young Burglar Bill, forgot Peter and his dire threat.

He sprawled in the armchair and devoured page after page, till at long last he reached the thrilling conclusion of that thrilling volume.

It was not till he had finished it that he remembered that Squiff was going to bake chestnuts in the Rag, before prep.

The fat Owl heaved himself out of the armchair, threw the "Burglars' Boarding-School" on the table, and rolled out of the study. Luckily he was in time for the baked chestnuts! So all was calm and bright!

THE ELEVENTH CHAPTER.

Laying the Trap!

ARTHUR CARTER stepped quietly into his Form-master's study and shut the door without a sound.

He stood for a long moment, his breath coming thick and fast, his heart beating unpleasantly.

Mr. Quelch was in Common-room, with the other beaks; there was little danger of being caught in his study. Carter was not so much afraid of that as of what he was going to do.

But, uneasy as he was feeling, he proceeded to do it.

He dared not switch on the light; but he turned on a pocket flash-lamp, and it gleamed over the Remove master's writing-table.

There were many papers on that table. There was a pile of Latin exercises, and several letters pinned under a paper-weight.

Carter's eyes passed over these carelessly, and fixed on a little batch of manuscript, fastened by a clip at the corner.

This was what he wanted! It was a section of Quelch's celebrated History of Greyfriars.

It was Quelch's custom to make the first draft of his literary works with a pen, which, after being corrected, and corrected again, were transcribed on the typewriter, with final improvements.

The mass of typescript was kept in a drawer of the table, which was, fortunately, locked, and out of the young rascal's reach.

These half-dozen sheets of foolscap were covered closely with Mr. Quelch's clear, fine writing, with plenty of interlined and marginal corrections.

Those few sheets represented hours of labour, in sorting over black-letter manuscripts from the School library, and digging deep into dusty old tomes.

The loss of that batch was certain to cause Quelch to go off at the deep end, in the most emphatic manner.

Gum in his inkpot, jam in his armchair, would never have exasperated Quelch like damage to his precious manuscripts.

That the Remove master, when he missed those papers, would feel a painful shock, as well as deep anger, mattered nothing to Carter. He crumpled the little batch of foolscap and crammed it into the study fire, with the exception of a single sheet.

The single sheet he slipped into an inner pocket.

The papers in the fire, he carefully stirred, until every vestige of them was lost among the glowing cinders. He was very careful to leave no sign. Mr. Quelch was to suppose that the batch had been taken away—otherwise, of course, he would not search for them—and it was Carter's game to cause a search.

But Carter was not quite finished yet. From a pocket he drew a grubby, crumpled handkerchief, which he dropped on the floor near the table.

From its grubbiness, any fellow might have guessed that hanky belonged to William George Bunter. The initials "W. G. B." were in the corner, but they were no surer clue to the ownership!

Then Carter shut off his flash-lamp, opened the study door, and peered out. The coast was clear, and he slipped quietly out of the study.

It was getting near time for prep. Most of the Remove were in the Rag. But baked chestnuts had no interest for Carter, at the moment. He went up the stairs and strolled into the Remove passage.

Only one fellow was in sight there—Fisher T. Fish, going into his study at the other end of the passage.

Carter loitered in the doorway of Study No. 1 till Fishy disappeared into Study No. 14 and shut the door.

Then he cut along swiftly to Bunter's study, Study No. 7.

He did not need his flash-lamp there. Bunter, with his usual carelessness, had left the light on when he went down. Carter shut the door, and glanced quickly and keenly round the study.

As Study No. 7 was shared by three fellows, he had to be careful to land the "clue" to the missing manuscript on Bunter, and not on Todd or Dutton. Quelch was to suppose that the fat Owl had walked those manuscripts off; and the single sheet that Carter had brought away was to be the clue to Bunter as the depredator and destroyer! It had to lead to Bunter, and Bunter alone, of the three fellows who used Study No. 7!

Carter's eyes glinted as they fell on the paper-covered volume, with the startling title of the "Burglars' Boarding-School," lying on the study table where the fat Owl had left it.

A sour grin came over his face.

That volume was well known to be Bunter's. A dozen fellows had seen him reading it. Plenty more had heard him talking about it. Nothing could have suited Carter's purpose better.

He took the sheet of foolscap from his pocket, and tore it in halves. One half he threw into the study fire, where it was burned away at once. The other half he slipped between the leaves of the "Burglars' Boarding-School." Anyone seeing it there would have supposed that it had been used as a book-mark. Plenty of fellows marked a place in a book with a torn strip of paper, or a fragment of an old letter.

Leaving the volume where he had found it, Carter slipped quietly out of the study, and went downstairs.

He heard Billy Bunter's fat voice as he strolled into the Rag.

"I say, you fellows, any more chestnuts?"

"No, you cormorant!"

"Well, I've only had a dozen," said Bunter. "I say, Squiff, you can have one of my bullseyes, old chap. I've had your chestnuts."

Billy Bunter extracted three bullseyes from his trousers pocket. They were sticky, and, being sticky, had collected dust and fluff from his pocket. That made no difference to Bunter. A bullseye was a bullseye. But to any other fellow they did not look fearfully attractive.

Sampson Quincy Iffley Field glanced at the sticky lump in the grubby, fat paw, and grinned.

"Thanks, old bean!" he said. "Lots of thanks! But——"

"I mean it," said Bunter generously. "Take any one of them you like."

Squiff chuckled.

"I'm not awfully keen on bullseyes, old fat Owl," he said. "You scoff them."

"Oh, all right!" said Bunter.

And he scoffed them.

"Lend me your hanky, will you?" he asked. "I've made my fingers sticky."

"Can't you use your own, fathead?"

"I've dropped it somewhere. I believe I dropped it when that beast Carter ran into me after class—at least, I've not seen it since. Lend me yours, I say, don't walk away while a fellow's talking to you!" squeaked Bunter. "I say, lend me your hanky!"

But Squiff did walk away. Apparently he did not want sticky fingers wiped on his handkerchief.

"Beast!" grunted Bunter. "Lend me your hanky, will you, Bob?"

"I don't think!"

"Lend me yours, Wharton."

"What about stepping into the lobby and washing your paws?" suggested the captain of the Remove. "They could do with it. You haven't washed them since last term, you know."

"Yah!" retorted Bunter.

Extra washing had no attraction for Bunter. As nobody had a hanky to lend, he rubbed his sticky fingers on his trousers, and was satisfied. In some matters, Billy Bunter was not an easy fellow to satisfy, but in such matters as these, he was the most easily satisfied of all the Remove.

A little later the Remove fellows went up to the studies for prep. Carter's eyes followed Billy Bunter curiously as the fat junior rolled into Study No. 7 with Toddy and Dutton. With prep on hand, Bunter was not likely to open his book, and discover the book-mark. And before prep was over, Carter had no doubt that there would be a terrific row going on on account of Quelch's manuscripts.

He went into his own study, Study No. 1, with Wharton and Nugent for prep.

The three settled down to work, as usual—Carter with an ear on the alert. He, at least, expected prep to be interrupted that evening.

He was thinking a good deal more of his scheme for "dishing" the fat Owl of the Remove, than of prep. That hint from Mr. Gooch had fallen like seed in fertile soil. So far as Carter could see, nothing could go amiss with this carefully laid scheme.

Quelch, when he went back to his study, would discover what had happened to his precious manuscripts. He would find Bunter's handkerchief on the study floor.

That in itself would hardly be proof. Bunter might have dropped it there while in the study after class. But it would be a clue. It would draw Quelch's attention specially to Bunter; and certainly he would remember the whopping he had given Bunter the day before.

What would it look like?

It would look, of course, as if Bunter had wrought havoc with those precious sheets of foolscap, in revenge for that undeserved whopping—as he was quite fool enough to do.

Indeed, had Carter known it, that very idea had occurred to Bunter's fat brain, though Bob Cherry had discouraged it so energetically that the fat Owl had given up the idea.

Quelch would be after Bunter.

Obviously he would search Bunter's study, first of all, in the hope of discovering them yet unharmed.

There had to be proof—and there was proof. The manuscripts were gone; but the book-mark in Bunter's book would not escape discovery. Quelch was not the man to miss anything in a search. And, besides, a book was just the place to look for hidden papers.

His attention being concentrated on Bunter, he would search Study No. 7; he would find that torn sheet used as a book-mark, and he was not likely to want any more proof than that.

What would happen to Bunter, in the way of punishment, Carter cared nothing. What mattered was, that Bunter would be in his Form-master's black books—his very blackest books. His report that term would not only be bad, but the worst he had ever had, and he would, in consequence, be done for, in the direction of old Joseph Carter.

It seemed a certainty this time. On his own the rascal of the Remove had had little luck in his campaign. But with the help of that hint from Gideon Gooch, he looked like backing a winner at last. Thinking it over and over, Carter could see no loophole by which the fat Owl could escape from this cunning snare. He was caught like a fat rabbit in a trap.

THE MAGNET LIBRARY.—No. 1.566.

Carter had no doubt about that. Like many another schemer, he forgot that the most elaborate scheme is always at the mercy of chance. And it might have been useful to him to remember the ancient maxim, that "great is truth, and it must prevail."

THE TWELFTH CHAPTER.
Bunter's Contribution !

"BLOW prep!" grunted Billy Bunter.

He blinked morosely at the study table, where Peter Todd and Tom Dutton were sorting out books. Bunter did not like preparation.

It was true that preparation was rather necessary, if a fellow was going to learn anything from the subsequent lesson. But Bunter had no desire to learn anything from any lesson. So, from Bunter's point of view, prep was simply one of those worries which schoolmasters inflicted on fellows, who could have found lots of pleasanter occupations for their time.

However, prep had to be done. Like the hail and the rain, it fell alike on the just and the unjust.

Peter Todd glanced at the bag on the table. He hardly needed to glance at it to ascertain whether Bunter had added thereunto. He could guess that Bunter hadn't. One glance was enough. That bag was exactly as Peter had left it—not a single spot of torn paper in it. Peter's second glance passed to that great work of fiction, the "Burglars' Boarding-School," which lay near the empty bag.

"You lazy ass!" said Peter.

"Well, who likes prep?" grunted Bunter. "Lot of rot, if you ask me!"

"Never mind prep! What about the scent?" demanded Peter. "Didn't I tell you you had to put up your whack?"

"You jolly well know I've had no time!" yapped Bunter.

"And you jolly well know what I told you would happen, if you couldn't find time!" said Peter.

He picked up the "Burglars' Boarding-School."

There was a howl of alarmed protest from Bunter.

"You let that book alone, you beast! I'm going to read that again. Besides, I can sell it for a penny when I'm done with it. Fishy will give me a penny for it, and sell it to some fag for tuppence—see?"

"Fishy might give you a penny for it when you've done with it," admitted Peter. "But I don't think he'd give you a farthing for it when I'm done with it. It's going into this bag. Lots of room for it."

"Beast! Gimme my book!" yelled Bunter. "I say, Dutton, make that beast gimme my book!"

"Rot!" answered Dutton. "No time for cooking now. We've come up here for prep, you fat ass!"

"I didn't say cook—I said book!" howled Bunter.

"What's the use of a cookery-book now? We've got to get on with prep. Besides, I haven't any cookery-book. Think I'm always thinking about grub like you are?"

"Take my book away from that beast!" yelled Bunter.

"Well, I don't know about taking my book away from a feast—I like a spread, as much as any fellow! What feast do you mean?"

"My book——" shrieked Bunter.

"Look at what?"

"Oh, you deaf chump——"

"I'd jolly well like to see you do it! You give me a clump, and I'll jolly soon give you a clout!" retorted Tom Dutton. "What do you mean, you fat Owl? Talking about giving a fellow a clump, just because he hasn't got a cookery-book! How the dickens could I have a cookery-book?"

"Gimme that book, Peter Todd, you rotter!" yelled Bunter, and he rolled round the study table and grabbed at the "Burglars' Boarding-School!"

Peter held that entrancing volume over his head, out of Bunter's reach, in one hand. With the other, he gave the fat Owl a poke on his well-filled waistcoat.

"Gurrrrggh!" gurgled Bunter.

He sat down, suddenly.

Peter, with a cheery grin, proceeded to tear up the "Burglars' Boarding-School" for scent! He rent it, and rent it, again and again. He tore it limb from limb, as it were.

He made quick work of that volume. The pages, in bunches, were torn across and across.

As he reduced them to fragments, Peter dropped them into the empty bag on the table.

That there was a half-sheet of written foolscap tucked away between the leaves of that volume, naturally did not transpire. It was torn up along with the leaves that enfolded it.

Bunter sat and gurgled for breath, glaring at Peter with a glare that almost cracked his spectacles.

"Beast!" he gasped.

"Hear, hear!" said Toddy.

"Rotter!" panted Bunter.

"Go it!"

"Swosh!" hooted Bunter, "Tick!"

"Keep it up!"

"I'll jolly well make you pay for that book!" howled Bunter.

"I've paid for it once," grinned Toddy. "I'm not going to be a twicer! You can pay for the next!"

"I've a jolly good mind to boot you round the study!" yelled Bunter, as he staggered up. "I jolly well would, only——"

"Only you can't perform impossibilities, old fat man!" agreed Peter. "But I'll tell you what—I'll boot you round the study instead!"

"Ow! Beast! Keep off!" yelled Bunter, dodging round the table. "I say, leave off, will you! I say, old chap —leave off, you beast—look here, old rotter—I mean, old fellow—yaroooooh!"

"What are you kicking Bunter for, Toddy?" asked Dutton.

"For his good!" answered Peter.

"What food?"

"Oh crumbs!"

"Plums? Well, if he's got plums he's not whacking out in the study, I'll jolly well kick him, too!" said Dutton. "It's mean to hide food away from the other fellows in the study, Bunter. You have more than your whack here."

"Ha, ha, ha!" yelled Peter.

He picked up the bag, and left Study No. 7, leaving Tom Dutton booting the unfortunate Owl.

Peter carried the bag up the passage to Study No. 13, where the Famous Five had been busy after tea tearing up scent into the big basket.

Bob Cherry and Hurree Singh, Mark Linley and Wun Lung were in the study now, for prep. The big basket of scent stood in a corner.

"Hallo, hallo, hallo!" said Bob, looking round. "What——"

"Scent," explained Peter, as he tipped the bag into the basket. "The

**From somewhere in the thickets a lump of turf whizzed, hitting Mr. Quelch's hat fair and square, and knocking it off his head.
"Good gracious!" gasped Prout, as the Remove master staggered, with a startled exclamation. "Who—what——"**

'Burglars' Boarding-School'—Bunter contributed that."

"Best thing he could do with it!" said Bob, laughing. "He wouldn't contribute that when we asked him."

"Oh, he did it all right when I asked him," said Peter. "I persuaded him. One poke in the bread-basket did it."

"Ha, ha, ha!"

Peter Todd carried an empty bag back to Study No. 7. He was greeted there by a glare from a pair of big spectacles.

"Beast!" hooted Bunter. "Rotter! Cad! Swab!"

"Stop talking about yourself, and get on to prep!" said Peter.

"I've a jolly good mind——" roared Bunter.

"Gammon! If you've got one at all, it's a jolly bad one."

"Yah!" hooted Bunter.

And he settled down at last, to prep. The "Burglars' Boarding-School" was gone, and gone for good; and Billy Bunter little guessed how very fortunate it was for him that that priceless volume had gone for good.

THE THIRTEENTH CHAPTER.

Quelch on the War-path!

PREP in Study No. 7, was not destined to pursue the usual even tenor of its way that evening.

A quarter of an hour later it was interrupted.

Peter and Tom were working, and Bunter slacking and grousing—which was the usual way of doing prep in that study—when there was a sharp rap at the door, and it flew open.

Mr. Quelch appeared in the doorway.

Behind him appeared Trotter, the page, with a rather scared expression on his chubby face. That expression was reflected on three other faces, when the three juniors looked at Mr. Quelch.

Seldom had they seen their Form-master looking so intensely angry.

He was calm: but it was a deadly calmness. His lips were set in a hard line, and his eyes glinted like steel.

The three jumped to their feet at once. Peter and Tom looked a little alarmed—Bunter terrified. He blinked at his Form-master through his big spectacles with popping eyes. There was always some sin or other on Billy Bunter's fat conscience—and it was unusual for the Form-master to barge in, in prep, especially with that speaking expression on his face.

"Bunter!" said Mr. Quelch in a deep voice.

"Oh! Yes, sir!" gasped Bunter. "I mean, no, sir! It wasn't me, sir! If Coker says I've been to his study——"

"Look at this, Bunter!"

Mr. Quelch held up a handkerchief —an extremely grubby handkerchief. He held it up by the extreme tip of the corner, between finger and thumb. He did not seem to like touching that hanky!

"Is that your handkerchief, Bunter?"

"Eh? No! Yes! I—I dropped my handkerchief somewhere, sir!" stammered Bunter "I—I was going to look for it, sir, but—but I hadn't time—I—I've been so busy helping the fellows tear up scent for the paper-chase to-morrow, and——"

"Your initials are on that handkerchief, Bunter."

"Then—then it's mine, sir! T-t-thank you for bringing it here, sir! I—I'd have come down for it, if I'd known you'd found it, sir——"

"I found this handkerchief in my study, Bunter."

"Oh! I never knew I dropped it there, sir! I—I've been looking everywhere else for it, sir! Everywhere."

"You have been to my study, Bunter."

"Yes, sir, after class."

"And you removed certain manuscripts from my table!" said Mr. Quelch, in a voice like that of the Great Huge Bear.

Bunter jumped.

"Oh! No, sir!"

"I have no doubt that you did, Bunter."

"Oh, really, sir!" gasped Bunter. "You'd have seen me if I had, sir! You wouldn't have let me! How—how could I, sir, with you sitting at the table, glaring at me—I—I mean, looking at me——"

"I was not present when you visited my study."

"Oh crikey!" gasped Bunter. He wondered whether Mr. Quelch was, after all, "balmy," as he had supposed the previous day! "Don't you remember, sir, you were sitting at your table, and you jawed me——"

"What?"

"I—I—I mean, you pointed out the errors in my Latin paper!" gasped Bunter. "I didn't mean jawed, sir! I never say you jaw a chap, like some of the fellows. I—I don't call it jawing, sir. I—I like to hear you jaw—I mean——"

"I am not alluding, Bunter, to the occasion when I sent for you, after class, to speak to you about the disgraceful state of your Latin paper. You paid a later visit to my study, while I was in Common-room."

"I didn't!" yelled Bunter.

"Then how came your handkerchief there, Bunter?"

"It must have dropped when you were jawing me, sir—I mean, when you were speaking to me about the disgraceful state of my Latin paper——"

"That is, of course, possible!" said Mr. Quelch. "I shall not condemn you without proof, Bunter! Do you deny having removed some sheets of written foolscap from my study?"

"Oh! Yes, sir! I never touched them!" wailed Bunter. At that moment the fat Owl was glad, very glad, that Bob Cherry had discouraged him from carrying on with his great idea of "paying out" Quelch.

Somebody else, it seemed, had had the same bright idea, and had done it!

Bunter, looking at Mr. Quelch's expressive countenance, was glad that he was not the fellow!

"Certain papers," said Mr. Quelch, "have been taken from my study. If they are still in existence, the boy concerned will be flogged. If they have been destroyed, the boy concerned will be expelled from Greyfriars. I can hardly believe that any boy, however unfeeling and unprincipled, would venture to destroy my work! If you, Bunter——"

"It wasn't me, sir!" groaned Bunter.

"That is what I must ascertain, Bunter! Do you know anything of this, Todd?"

"No, sir!"

"Dutton! Do you know anything of this matter?"

"Do you mean Bunter, sir?"

"What! I was asking you if you know anything of this matter," snapped Mr. Quelch.

"Bunter's fatter than any other chap in the Form, sir. He can't help it, I suppose," said Dutton.

"Do you know anything of the matter to which I have been alluding, Dutton?"

"I haven't seen him with a pudding to-day, sir! Or any mutton, either! I don't think it can have been Bunter, sir!"

Mr. Quelch breathed very hard. He had forgotten, for the moment, that Tom Dutton was deaf. Now he was reminded of it. He gave Dutton up, and turned to the page waiting at the door.

"Trotter! Step into the study."

"Yessir!"

Trotter stepped in.

"You will search this study, Trotter, and hand me any paper written in my hand, with which you are acquainted."

"Yessir!"

The three Removites backed out of the way, and Trotter proceeded to make the search. Quelch's gimlet eye following every movement.

It was quite clear that Mr. Quelch expected Trotter to make a discovery in that study.

He simply could not believe that any boy would have had the nerve, or the audacity, to destroy his precious papers. Such an act of vandalism seemed unthinkable to him. The papers had been taken from his study, and if they had not been destroyed, they could be found. And as he believed that it was Bunter who had taken them, he had little doubt that they would be discovered in Bunter's study. It was, in fact, quite in keeping with Bunter's fatuous obtuseness, to take away the papers and hide them, to pull his Form-master's leg. He had done such things before, and it looked as if he had done such a thing again.

Billy Bunter's fat knees knocked together, as he watched Trotter search.

He knew, of course, that he had not touched Quelch's papers. But it was clear that his Form-master suspected him, and, only too well, he knew that Quelch would not take his unsupported word on that subject or any other.

Under Quelch's direction, Trotter took every volume from the bookshelf, and opened it, and shook it, to make sure that no papers were hidden inside.

Had the "Burglars' Boarding-School"

been in the study, it would have been subjected to the same test—with awful results for Bunter! For, had that torn sheet turned up, in Bunter's book, it could hardly have failed to turn Quelch's suspicion into a certainty.

But from the books in the study, no discovery was to be made. Every volume—even to the school books on the table—was examined. But the result was precisely nil.

Trotter looked inquiringly at the Remove master. Mr. Quelch, with tight-set lips, made a gesture of dismissal, and the House page left the study. There was nothing further to be done in the way of searching. Obviously, the missing manuscripts were not there.

Quelch's eyes fixed on the shivering fat Owl.

"Bunter!"

"Yes, sir!" groaned Bunter. "It wasn't me, sir!"

"What have you done with my papers?"

"I haven't seen them, sir."

"If you have hidden them, Bunter, I shall be more lenient with you, if you hand them over to me at once."

"I—I—I haven't, sir!"

"If you have destroyed them, I shall make a special request to Dr. Locke to expel you from the school."

"Oh crikey!"

"Have you anything to say, Bunter?"

"N-n-no, sir!"

"I believe," said Mr. Quelch, "that some preparations are being made for a paper-chase to-morrow, Todd! I handed Wharton a number of old papers to be torn up for the purpose."

"Yes, sir, we've got a lot of scent now," said Peter.

"No doubt some of the papers were torn up in this study?"

"Yes, sir."

"Bunter! Did you tear up my manuscripts with the rest?"

"Oh crumbs! No, sir!" gasped Bunter. "I—I never thought of such a thing, sir, and Bob Cherry never laid into me with a ruler——"

"WHAT!"

"I—I mean to say, I—I wouldn't!" gasped the hapless fat Owl. "I never went to Study No. 13 after tea, at all, sir! You can ask Wharton and his friends—they were there when I went in——"

"Todd! Cease making signs to Bunter this instant!"

"Oh! Yes, sir!" gasped Peter.

"I cannot believe, Bunter, that Wharton, or any other sensible boy, would permit you to commit such an act, with his knowledge!" said Mr. Quelch. "But if you suggested it——"

"Oh, no, sir! What—what I really said was, that—that I wouldn't dream of tearing up your papers for scent, sir, even if you offered them to me!" gasped Bunter. "That—that's what I really said, sir, and I never said anything about paying you out for whopping me for nothing, and it was—was because Bob Cherry misunderstood, that he pitched into me with a ruler——"

"Where is this torn paper, Todd?" thundered Mr. Quelch. "I must examine it. Where——"

"It's all collected in a basket now, sir," stammered Peter. "Some if it was torn up in every study in the Remove, and it was all put together."

"Where is the basket?" thundered Mr. Quelch.

"In Cherry's study, sir—Study No. 13."

"Very good! I shall examine it! I shall examine the whole of it, Bunter, and if I find even one fragment in my handwriting, I shall know what to believe."

"But I never——"

"What?"

"I never tore up any, sir——"

"You have stated, Bunter, that you did not look for your handkerchief because you were busy tearing up scent for the paper-chase to-morrow!"

"Oh crikey! I—I mean—I—I meant that——"

"That will do, Bunter! You will know what to expect, if I find a single fragment of my papers in the basket in Cherry's study!"

"Oh lor'!"

Mr. Quelch swept out of Study No. 7 like a thundercloud.

Billy Bunter and Peter Todd were left dismayed—Tom Dutton puzzled and curious.

"I say, what did Quelch come here for?" asked Dutton.

"He was after some papers."

"What rot! As if a man of Quelch's age would come here to cut capers! Besides, he wasn't cutting capers! He looked to me jolly bad-tempered," said Tom. "Is anything the matter?"

"Quelch has lost some papers," yelled Peter. "Papers!"

"Oh, tapers! Well, he couldn't expect us to have any tapers in our study! Blessed if I see what he wants tapers for, but he can't expect to find any in the Remove—we don't use tapers in the studies."

And Tom Dutton sat down to prep again.

But Bunter and Peter were too worried for prep—especially Bunter! The fat Owl of the Remove waited in deep and dismal trepidation for what was to come next.

THE FOURTEENTH CHAPTER.

The Scrap of Paper!

BOB CHERRY jumped, as a sharp rap came at his study door.

Mark Linley, Hurree Singh, and Wun Lung were busy with prep—but Bob was giving himself a few minutes' rest, while he added a little to the basket of scent in the corner of the study. Having found some old letters, he was tearing them up, dropping the fragments in the top of the basket, which was already nearly full.

Plenty of scent was wanted, and this was an agreeable change from prep, especially as the Remove were preparing Cæsar that evening, and Bob was always specially bored by that long-winded ancient Roman.

"What silly ass——" ejaculated Bob, as that sudden rap at the door made him jump and scatter fragments on the carpet instead of in the basket. "Oh!" he added, with a gasp, as a grim face looked in. "Ah! Oh! You, sir!"

Mr. Quelch rustled in.

The juniors seated at the table jumped up.

Bob Cherry coloured under his Form-master's eye. His occupation was evident—and plainly had nothing to do with Cæsar's Gallic War. In prep, fellows were supposed to devote themselves to prep, and nothing but prep.

It was quite frequent for fellows not to do as they were supposed to do—especially in junior studies! Still, no fellow liked to be caught.

"Is that how you do your preparation, Cherry?" inquired Mr. Quelch.

"Oh! Yes—no!" stammered Bob.

"Cherry left off only for a minute, sir, when he found some old letters in his pocket," said Mark Linley.

"You need not speak, Linley."

"Oh, very well, sir!"

Evidently Mr. Quelch was not in his bonniest mood.

The four juniors wondered why he

had come to the study, and what the row was, anyhow. Obviously, there was a "row" on. They soon learned!

"Is that the basket of scent to be used in the paper-chase to-morrow, Cherry?" asked Mr. Quelch, pointing to it.

"Yes, sir!"

"Is that all you have?"

"Oh, yes, sir! It will be quite enough, now that we've had it from all the studies," answered Bob, wondering rather dizzily why Quelch was making such an inquiry. "But if you've got any more old papers you don't want, sir——"

"Do not talk nonsense,. Cherry!"

"Oh, yes, sir! As you gave Whar-ton some this morning——" stammered Bob.

"You are sure that this basket contains the total supply of torn paper?" rapped Mr. Quelch.

"That's the whole lot, sir."

"Very well! Clear this table, please, and empty that basket in the middle. Take care to spill none on the floor."

The four juniors stared at their Form-master. Really, for a moment, they almost fancied that Billy Bunter had been right about his mental state. Such a command was absolutely astounding.

So astounding was it that they blinked at him, instead of obeying.

"Did—did—did you say empty the basket on the—the **table, sir**?" stuttered Bob blankly.

"I did! Do so **this** instant!"

"Oh, all right!"

Utterly amazed, the juniors cleared books and inkstand **off** the table, leaving it clear.

Bob picked up the basket and up-ended it on the table, the contents falling out in a very large heap.

It was such a stack of small fragments of all sorts of paper, that anyone less fiercely determined than Mr. Quelch might have hesitated to search through it for a clue.

But Mr. Quelch did not hesitate. His papers had not been found in (*Continued on next page.*)

LEARN TO PLAY FOOTBALL!
BY OUR INTERNATIONAL COACH

DEFEND AND ATTACK

I POINTED out last week the fact that nearly all the great teams of the past could point to strength in the wing-half positions as one of their most important secrets of success. When we think about the duties of the wing half-backs of a football side, we are not surprised that this should be so. I have explained previously that the wing-half has two distinct duties to perform—he must be a defender and an attacker. It is not possible to say which is the more important of these two. There are the jobs—the player must see that they are both done.

As a means of putting the duties of a wing half-back into a nut-shell, which all of you can crack without much trouble, let me summarise them. I like to think of the half-back line, and the wing-halves in particular, as a brick wall. In the first of my pictures the opposing side is represented by a hard ball, made of lead, or something like that. This hard ball keeps throwing itself at the brick wall, but the wall is too thick to break down, and the ball just drops to the ground, unable to get any farther. In that picture the brick wall is representing half-backs who are very good at the defensive part of their job, but are not well up in the attacking side. They can stop the ball—in 'other words the opponents—but they can't send it back the way it has come.

Now put that picture side by side with my second one. In this the half-backs are represented by a brick wall in just the same way. The opponents, however, are represented by a tennis ball. The tennis ball keeps on throwing itself against the brick wall. But this time there is a difference. The brick wall throws the ball back again. Do you see the moral of the pictures? The half-backs in the second one are stopping the opposition, and then sending the ball back again to their own forwards. That is what the complete half-back is doing all the time. Breaking up opposition attacks and backing up his own forwards both with actual support and accurate passes.

Speed, ball control and accuracy combined with heftiness and artistry go to make the perfect wing-half. Read what our special reporter has to say about this all-important position on the football field.

THE COMPLETE FOOTBALLER

YOU can see that to do the "brick wall" part of his job the wing-half will find height, weight, and strength a great advantage. I don't say these things are by any means essential. There was a player named Tommy Meehan, of Chelsea, who was well under five and a half feet in height, yet he played at half-back for England. Indeed, I am not so sure that height and weight are so important as the things which are needed to carry out the other part of the wing-half's duties—the supporting and attacking side. For this there must be real football ability—speed, ball-control, accuracy. In fact, everything which goes to make up the complete footballer.

If you can combine "heftiness" and artistry, all well and good. Players like Jack Crayston, of Arsenal, Don Welsh, of Charlton, and Bill Imrie, of Newcastle, are just about the ideal. Big and strong, really good dribblers, and first-class at sending passes up to their forwards.

As I explained to you last week it is impossible for me to lay down the law as to how much attacking and how much defending a half-back should do. He must change his style according to the play of his colleagues, and the way the game is going. Always, however, the half-back who can find time to go up amongst the forwards, and perhaps take a hand in the business of goal-scoring, will be the best sort to have on your side. I mentioned Bill Imrie just now. Do you know that in the early part of this season, Imrie scored more goals than any other Newcastle player?

ONCE IN A LIFETIME

I EXPECT you have all heard of Arthur Grimsdell. A lot of people say that he was the best wing-half who ever kicked a football. In one season in which he played at left-half for Tottenham Hotspur he scored fourteen League goals—more than most forwards score nowadays. I also mentioned Don Welsh a little way back. I wonder how many of you went to see Chelsea and Charlton play at Stamford Bridge on Christmas Day? The people who were there saw Welsh, the Charlton half-back, score the sort of goal which most of us see only once in a life-time. He dribbled the ball a good fifty yards before putting it into the net with a shot which Woodley, who, don't forget, is England's goal-keeper, probably didn't see. That goal would have been remarkable enough if it had been scored by a forward. But Welsh is a half-back. He was helping his forwards in the very best way.

While I was watching that game on Christmas Day, however, I made a little note on the back of my programme. It read like this: "Tell MAGNET readers—Welsh going up—the danger." Looks rather like double-dutch, doesn't it? This is what it means. Just after Welsh had scored his great goal, he tried to do it a second time. But he didn't manage it. He lost the ball to a Chelsea defender, who passed it on down the right wing.

In the normal way, Welsh, who was the left-half, would have been there to stop the inside-right getting away. But Welsh was still farther up the field, and the Chelsea winger had no one to stop him taking the ball down and putting in a centre—from which Chelsea scored a goal. When that happened, I made my little note to point out to you that when a half-back goes up amongst the forwards, perhaps to try a shot at goal, someone must fall back to take his place in case there is any defensive work to be done. Welsh's move was a very good one. The other players were at fault in not filling the gap which he had left in the defence.

THE MAGNET LIBRARY.—No. 1,566.

Bunter's study. Bunter denied all knowledge of them. He had as good as admitted that he had, at least, thought of tearing up those papers. Now Mr. Quelch dreaded that they were destroyed. If that was the fact, he was going to make it clear, if he could. If the fatuous Bunter had added fragments of the "History of Greyfriars " to the scent for the paper-chase, no amount of trouble was going to prevent Mr. Quelch from bringing it to light !

Standing by the table in Study No. 13, the Remove master proceeded to sort through that immense collection of torn fragments, of all shapes and sizes —watched in silence by the four juniors in the study.

Prep, as a rule, was regarded as an extremely important function by the master of the Remove. Now he seemed to disregard it entirely. Four juniors stood idle, while he sorted and sorted and sorted again.

Suddenly his eyes glittered.

From the heap of paper fragments he picked a small piece of foolscap with a single word written on it. The word was "Greyfriars "—and the hand-writing was his own !

It was a fragment of one of the papers missing from his study ! That was a certainty !

He needed to search no farther. It was a case of "ex pede Herculem "— from that single fragment he traced the whole of the missing manuscript !

Mr. Quelch held up that fragment between finger and thumb. His eyes glittered at it. And Bob and his friends, seeing that that fragment bore a word in Quelch's "fist," exchanged startled glances. The Remove master had given Wharton some old papers that morning to be torn up for scent; but none written in his handwriting. How this fragment came to be in the scent was, therefore, a puzzle to the juniors.

It was no puzzle to their Form-master. He had no doubt on the sub-ject now. Bunter had torn up those papers !

"You may replace the paper in the basket, Cherry !" said Mr. Quelch grimly. "I have found enough "

"Yes, sir !" said Bob.

"A 'quantity of that paper was brought from Study No. 7, I presume ?" said Mr. Quelch.

"Yes, sir, from all the studies——"

"I have asked you particularly whether any was brought from Study No. 7."

"Yes, sir."

"By Bunter ?"

"No, Toddy—I mean, Todd brought it here and tipped it into the basket, sir. He brought some more just be-fore prep, and——"

"Very well !"

Mr. Quelch rustled out of the study, leaving the four fellows perplexed and rather scared. He strode back to Study No. 7 with billowing gown.

Billy Bunter gave a gasp of alarm when he reappeared there.

Mr. Quelch held up the fragment of foolscap !

"Bunter ! That is a portion of one of the sheets of paper removed from my study !" he said. "That paper was torn up for scent. My papers have been destroyed, I have no doubt—I can have no doubt—that it was done by you !"

"I—I never——" gasped Bunter.

"You will be judged by your head-master, Bunter ! Dr Locke will be in his study in an hour's time. You will then go there——"

THE MAGNET LIBRARY.—No. 1,566.

"I—I say——"

"I shall be there !" added Mr. Quelch grimly. "I can hold out no hope to you, Bunter, that you will escape expulsion from Greyfriars. That you deserve it, for this act of wanton and unfeeling destruction, you must be well aware. That, for the present, is all."

Mr. Quelch thundered away.

Billy Bunter fairly gaped after him. "Oh crikey !" he gasped.

That was all that Bunter could say !

THE FIFTEENTH CHAPTER.
The Way Out !

HARRY WHARTON opened the door of Study No. 1 and looked out into the passage.

Frank Nugent joined him in the doorway.

Carter remained at the study table— a lurking grin on his hard face. He had expected prep to be interrupted that evening—! It had been inter-rupted !

"What the dickens is up ?" exclaimed Wharton.

In prep, fellows were supposed to keep in their studies. There were, indeed, penalties for leaving the same in prep. But that rule was disregarded now by nearly all the Remove.

More than half the study doors were open. More than half the Form were out in the passage. There was a buzz of excited voices.

From amid the buzz came the fat, dismal, dolorous squeak of William George Bunter.

"I say, you fellows, I'm for it ! I never did it, you know ! You know I never did it, don't you, Bob ?"

"I know I thought I'd stopped you, you fat chump !" answered Bob Cherry. "If you were idiot enough——"

"I wasn't going to do it !" howled Bunter. "You jolly well know I wasn't ! I asked you fellows if you'd do it ! That's quite different !"

"More in your line !" remarked Skinner.

"I knew Quelch would jump on me, if I did !" wailed Bunter. "I told you so. Cherry ! You know I did."

"I guess somebody did it !" grinned Fisher T. Fish. "I'll tell a man, you're the nigger in the woodpile, Bunter."

"Beast ! I never——"

"What's up !" roared Wharton along the passage.

A dozen voices told him. The cap-tain of the Remove joined the crowd, and Nugent followed him. Carter fol-lowed as far as the study doorway and stood looking out and listening.

"But why did Quelch fix on Bunter, Toddy ?" asked the captain of the Remove. "Every fellow in the Form had a hand in tearing up the scent, and it was all stacked into the same basket."

"That fat chump dropped his hanky in Quelch's study, and Quelch found it there !" answered Peter.

"That was when I saw him, after class, about my Latin paper !" howled Bunter. "It must have been, you see, because I never went to the study after-wards."

"Sez you !" grinned Fisher T. Fish.

"I tell you I never did——"

"Well, if Quelch found a bit of his manuscript in the scent, some Remove man must have torn up his papers," said Harry. "None of your larks, Smithy ?"

He gave the Bounder a rather sharp look.

Herbert Vernon-Smith laughed.

"Hardly !" he said. "I've got some nerve—but not nerve enough to meddle with Quelch's jolly old literary works ! Not guilty, my lord !"

"Fancy Bunter having the nerve !" said Hazeldene.

"Fools rush in where angels fear to tread !" remarked Squiff.

"I didn't——" yelled Bunter.

"Quelch seems to think you did, if he's going to take you to the big Beak to be sacked !" remarked Ogilvy.

"I don't see that it's proved against Bunter !" said Bob Cherry slowly. "He might have dropped that hanky there when he saw Quelch after class."

"The blithering Owl let out to Quelch that he had the idea in his silly nut," said Peter. "That did it !"

"Oh, my hat !"

"I didn't !" roared Bunter. "You heard me, Toddy ! I told Quelch that I never thought of such a thing, and that Bob never laid into me with a ruler——"

"Ha, ha, ha !"

"Blessed if I can see anything to cackle at ! I jolly well know I never did it—why, I jolly shouldn't have dared !" gasped Bunter.

"That bit sounds true !" remarked the Bounder.

Bob Cherry glanced along the passage to the hard face looking out of the doorway of Study No. 1. His lips set. Since he had learned of Carter's scheme against the fat Owl of the Remove, Bob was prepared to see Carter's hand in all the long tale of disasters that happened to Billy Bunter. That suspicion was in his mind now.

Yet he had to admit to himself that that was merely a suspicion, based on his knowledge of the fellow's tortuous trickery. There was not the remotest spot of evidence to connect Carter with the matter at all.

There was a rather strange expression on Carter's face.

He was as much surprised as any other fellow in the Remove, to hear that a torn fragment of Quelch's manu-script had been discovered in the basket of scent. He had expected that discovery to be made in Bunter's book in Bunter's study. But it did not take him long to guess that that book itself must have been torn up for scent, and that that was how it had happened.

"Look here," said Bob Cherry, amid a buzz of voices. "Bunter thought of that fatheaded idea, but he wanted other fellows to do it—he hadn't the nerve himself ! I don't believe he did it !"

"Better tell Quelch that !" grinned Skinner. "Quelch knows that Bunter thought of doing it—and knows that it was done ! Quelch can put two and two together ! He's quite good at arithmetic !"

"Ha, ha, ha !"

"Some Remove chap must have done it !" said Bolsover major.

"I don't believe Bunter did !"

"I jolly well didn't !" gasped Bunter. "I say, Cherry, was it you did it ?"

"What ?" roared Bob.

"I mean to say, if you did, you ought to own up, now I'm up for the sack, you know !" urged Bunter anxiously. "I know I suggested it—but if you did it, old chap——"

"You burbling idiot !"

"Oh, really, Cherry——"

"Where was Bunter, after I booted him out of my study ?" asked Bob. "If he can prove that he was nowhere near Quelch's study——"

"I was in my study, reading the 'Burglars' Boarding-School,' that that beast Toddy tore up for scent after-wards——"

" Bless my soul ! "exclaimed Mr. Quelch. " Are—are you sure that you have that dog safe, Bunter ? " " Oh, quite, sir ! "
chirruped the fat Removite. " He's all right with me ! I—I know how to manage dogs, sir ! "

"Then you can't prove——"

"Only my word !" said Bunter. "I think Quelch ought to take my word ! I could tell him anything if he would, you know ! But—he won't !"

"Ha, ha, ha !"

"Oh, don't cackle !" roared Bunter. "I've got to go to the Head ! Quelch says it will be the sack ! I say, you fellows, what can I do ?"

"Pack your box !" suggested Skinner.

"Beast !"

"Shut up, Skinner !" growled Bob Cherry. "This isn't a matter for joking ! That fat ass is for it, if he can't get out of this ! I don't believe he did it. For one thing, he was too jolly lazy to tear up any scent."

"I never had time, you know——"

"Shut up, fathead !"

"Beast !"

"Look here," said Bob, wrinkling his brows in thought. "Some Remove man did it—we don't know who, though I may have an idea. But whoever did it, tore the papers up as scent, and I jolly well know that none came from Bunter. I believe he was the only fellow in the Form who never lent a hand—but I know he didn't."

"Not a scrap !" said Bunter eagerly. "You see, I never had the time——"

"By gum," exclaimed Harry Wharton, "if Bunter never tore up any scent, he never tore up Quelch's papers——"

"I never did——"

"The basket was in my study," said Bob. "I know Bunter never brought any there ! Toddy did——"

"Not from Bunter !" said Peter. "I mopped up his gory literature, because he hadn't put a spot of scent in the bag."

"Then if Bunter did it, how did he do it ?" demanded Bob. "Quelch found that scrap of paper in our basket of scent. Bunter never contributed a single scrap ! So it never came from Bunter."

"My esteemed Bob, you ought to be an absurd detective !" exclaimed Hurree Jamset Ram Singh. "It is terrifically certain that the idiotic Bunter was too lazy to tear up any scent !"

"Beats Sherlock Holmes !" grinned the Bounder. "Blessed if I can see how Bunter can possibly have done it !"

"We'll tell the Head so, when Bunter goes !" said Bob. "We're all witnesses that the lazy fat snail never did any of the work."

"Beast !"

Carter turned back into Study No. 1 with a bitter look on his face. He had thought and thought over his cunning scheme, and had been able to detect no loophole of escape for Bunter. Chance—and Bob Cherry—had found one !

That unexpected chance, that Bunter's book had been torn up and added to the basket of scent, had done it ! Nobody knew that Quelch's paper had been in that book—but everybody knew that Billy Bunter had not added a single, solitary scrap to the basket of scent in Study No. 13.

The schemer of the Remove really began to wonder whether it was, after all, chance, or whether there was something in roguery itself that fore-doomed it to defeat !

THE SIXTEENTH CHAPTER.

Pulling Bunter Through !

DR. LOCKE raised his eyebrows. Mr. Quelch glared.

Bunter was expected in the Head's study ! An army of the Remove were not ! But quite an army marched in with Bunter.

The fat Owl rolled in first. After him walked the Famous Five. Then came Peter Todd, and Smithy, and Russell, and Ogilvy, and several more fellows. The Head's study was a spacious apartment; but it looked quite crowded.

"What——" began the Head.

"What——" rapped Mr. Quelch.

"I understood, Mr. Quelch, that Bunter alone was sent for !" said Dr. Locke.

"That is the case, sir ! I cannot imagine why all these other boys have come here with him. Leave the study at once !"

"If you please, sir——" began Harry Wharton.

"I have told you to leave the study, Wharton !"

"Yes, sir; but——"

"One moment," said Dr. Locke, raising his hand. "Possibly these boys have some knowledge of the matter, Mr. Quelch. It may be as well to hear what they have to say."

"Is that the case, Wharton ?"

"Yes, sir !"

"We all know, sir——" began Bob.

"You need say nothing, Cherry, until your headmaster questions you !" said Mr. Quelch acidly.

"Oh ! Very well, sir !"

"I will question Bunter first !" said Dr. Locke. "Bunter, do you deny having abstracted certain papers from your Form-master's study ?"

"Oh, yes, sir ! I never did——"

"You deny having torn them up for—for what I think is called scent, for a paper-chase ?"

"I never——"

"Had you any intention of doing so, Bunter ?"

"Oh, no, sir ! I wouldn't !" gasped Bunter. "These fellows know, sir—I told them I wouldn't, because Quelch would guess it was me, sir ! I mean, I never thought of anything of the kind, sir! It's not the sort of thing that I should think of."

"Shut up, you fat idiot!" breathed Peter Todd.

"Oh really, Toddy——"

"Silence! It is clear," said the Head, "that the thought occurred to this foolish boy of doing this very thing, and his statements are absolutely worthless. I will hear what these boys have to say. You will speak, Wharton."

"Yes, sir! It's true that Bunter thought of playing that silly trick——"

"Oh, really, Toddy——"

"Silence, Bunter."

"He thought of it, sir," said Harry, "but he never did it. He hasn't sense enough to understand how serious it was; but he never thought of doing it himself. And we all know that he never did it, sir, and we thought we ought to come here and tell you so."

"If you know this, Wharton, how do you know?" asked the Head.

"Mr. Quelch found his papers, or scraps of them, in the basket of scent in Cherry's study, sir. They had been torn up for scent. I suppose it must have been a Remove man that did it; but it certainly was not Bunter, for he never tore up any scent, and never went near the basket."

"Indeed!" said the Head.

Mr. Quelch compressed his lips.

"Is it not the custom for all the boys concerned in a paper-chase to assist in preparing the scent?" asked Dr. Locke.

"Yes, as a rule, sir; but Bunter was too lazy——"

"Look here, Wharton——"

"Will you be silent, Bunter?"

"Yes, sir; but I never had time——"

"Be silent! Proceed, Wharton."

"Bunter was the only fellow in the whole Form that never helped," went on the captain of the Remove. "He dodged it all the time. Todd left an empty bag in his study for Bunter to fill, and found it empty when he went up to prep. All the scent torn up in Study No. 7 was done by Todd and Dutton, and taken along to Study No. 13 by Todd. Bunter had nothing to do with it."

"Indeed!" repeated the Head.

"The only time he came to Bob's—I mean Cherry's—study was when we were all there, and after we went down Wun Lung stayed in the study. Bunter never went near the basket. He never put anything into Todd's bag. Not a single scrap came from Bunter."

"What do you think of this, Mr. Quelch?" asked the Head. "Wharton, I understand, is your head boy, and you can rely upon him."

"We all say the same, sir!" said Bob Cherry.

"I rely upon all these boys, so far as their knowledge extends," said Mr. Quelch. "But Bunter himself made the explicit statement to me, that he had been too busy tearing up scent for the paper-chase to have time to look for the handkerchief he had dropped in my study."

"Oh crikey!" gasped Bunter. "I—I never meant—— Oh lor'! Oh crumbs!"

Even the fat Ananias of the Remove realised just then that truth had its uses, and reckless prevarication its little difficulties.

"You hear this, Wharton?" said the Head severely.

"Bunter was talking nonsense, sir, as he always does," said Harry. "He never did any of the scent."

"May I speak, sir?" asked Peter.

"You may, Todd, if you have anything to say bearing upon the matter."

THE MAGNET LIBRARY.—No. 1,566.

"Bunter fancied that Mr. Quelch was angry with him for losing his handkerchief, and told the first silly lie that came into his head," explained Peter. "He always does, as Mr. Quelch knows, sir."

"Oh, really, Toddy——"

"Silence, Bunter!"

"I don't think Todd ought to make out that I'm untruthful, sir," said Bunter.

"Be silent, you foolish boy!"

"We're all witnesses, sir, that not a scrap of paper from Bunter went into the basket of scent," said Frank Nugent. "He couldn't possibly have put in what Mr. Quelch found there."

"If that is the case, Mr. Quelch, and these boys appear certain of what they say——" said the Head slowly.

Mr. Quelch's lips closed harder. Bitterly incensed as he was, he wanted to be just. Very much indeed he wanted to visit dire punishment on the young rascal who had destroyed his precious manuscripts, but he did not want to land it on the wrong man. There was a brief silence.

"In view of this, sir," said Mr. Quelch, at last, "I can only ask you to leave the matter open, pending further investigation."

"That appears to be the only resource," said Dr. Locke. "Boys, you may leave my study."

And the army of juniors marched out, Billy Bunter gasping with relief when he was once safely outside the dreaded door.

"I say, you fellows, I'm jolly glad that's over," he said. "I say, I wonder who ragged old Quelch's silly papers? Some pal of mine, I expect, paying him out for giving me that whopping for nothing. Was it you, Toddy?"

"Idiot!"

"Well, you can tell me, old chap," said Bunter. "I shan't give you away, of course. Was it you, Cherry?"

"Fathead!"

"Well, it must have been somebody," said Bunter. "One of you fellows, of course. I don't see why you can't tell me. If it was you, Cherry—— Ow! What are you grabbing my collar for, you fathead?"

Bob Cherry did not explain why he was grabbing Bunter's collar. Explanation was unnecessary, as Bunter knew the next moment.

Bang!

"Yarooh!" roared Bunter, as his bullet head established contact with the passage wall.

Bang!

"Ow! Wow! Yoo-hoop! Beast! Leggo!"

Bang!

"Yoo-hoo-hoooooop!" roared Bunter.

And the army of juniors marched away, leaving Billy Bunter rubbing his head and glaring after Bob with the deadliest glare of which his big spectacles were capable.

THE SEVENTEENTH CHAPTER.

The Paper-chase!

"YOUR boys, Quelch?" said Mr. Prout.

"Yes," said Mr. Quelch shortly.

He frowned.

It was the following afternoon—Wednesday, and a half-holiday. The Remove paper-chase was on.

The two Form-masters were taking a walk that afternoon by country lanes and woodland paths, and they were a good many miles from Greyfriars when they spotted the paper-chase.

Quelch was stalking, and Prout rolling, by a glade in Redclyffe Wood, when the note of a distant bugle reached their ears. Then two juniors came trotting in sight—Wharton and Bob Cherry—scattering scent from the bags of torn paper slung over their shoulders.

The two juniors looked bright and cheery and very fit, and were evidently enjoying the run across country—quite a pleasant sight to Mr. Quelch's eyes. But he frowned. He could not help thinking of fragments of the "History of Greyfriars" mixed with the scent the hares were scattering as they ran.

That morning, in class, Quelch had been sharp, indeed acid—like a bear with a sore head, as Skinner disrespectfully described it. Not a clue had been found to the vandal who had scrapped his papers. The one thing clear was, that it was not Bunter; but it might have been almost any other fellow in the Remove. Quelch's Form was a numerous one, so he had plenty to choose from.

The Remove fellows themselves could not guess who the culprit was. Bob Cherry suspected Carter; no one else had even a suspicion. But they all knew that Bunter was not the man.

Quelch had, more or less, to take the same view; but doubt lingered. Searching inquiry had revealed nothing. Certainly he was not going to risk giving Bunter another unjust punishment. One mistake of that kind was more than enough. But he was not satisfied that Bunter was not the man, and the fat Owl had found him quite unpleasant in class. Quelch was just, but Billy Bunter found strict justice rather an uncomfortable thing. Bunter was called to order for every fault that morning, and as the name of his faults was legion he had had quite a hectic time.

Fragments of paper scattered behind Wharton and Bob Cherry, left a trail through the wood; but the ring of the bugle behind showed that they had been sighted. They put on speed, and came racing past the spot where the two Form-masters stood.

"Hallo, hallo, hallo! There's Quelch!" ejaculated Bob, in passing.

They ran on, and disappeared into the wood. Then on the paper trail came the pack into sight—Vernon-Smith and Squiff leading, Mark Linley and Carter just behind, and a dozen more Removites strung out after them. The pack rushed on, and disappeared into the wood after the hares.

"A healthy sport, Quelch!" boomed Prout.

"Oh, quite!" said Mr. Quelch.

Stragglers of the pack came on after the main body, singly or in twos. Last of all rolled Billy Bunter, puffing and blowing.

Mr. Quelch gave Bunter a special frown as he passed.

The fat junior, spotting him, put on speed and vanished after the rest.

Then the two Form-masters resumed their walk.

Hares and hounds ran on, with a long run before they circled back to the school. But there was one member of the pack who was no longer running. That one was Billy Bunter. And there was another if Bunter had known it.

Bunter was not fearfully keen on paper-chases. In fact, he disliked heaving his weight along the paper trail as much as he disliked the labour of tearing up the scent.

Bunter had kept up with the pack, so far, for one reason, and one reason only. Peter Todd had been keeping an eye on him.

Peter's idea was that they did not slack in Study No. 7. This was rather hard on Bunter, whose fat existence was one perpetual slack, so far as he could make it so.

During that run, Bunter had stopped to rest three times, and tried to dodge away four times. Seven times had Peter's boot started him on the trail again, regardless of the loud howls of protest from Bunter.

So long as they were crossing open country, there was no help for it, and Bunter rolled, and plunged, and puffed, and blew, and gave Peter deadly blinks, and thought with longing of a study armchair and a study fire to frowst over. But in the intricate paths of Redclyffe Wood, Bunter's chance came at last.

Amid trees and thickets, Peter's eagle eye looked round for him—in vain. And he had to keep on minus Bunter!

Bunter's idea of a paper-chase was to "chuck" it at the earliest possible moment and pick the shortest route homeward. Now he was, at least, free to plod his homeward way, like the weary ploughman in the poem.

The shortest cut to Greyfriars, from that part of Redclyffe Wood, lay across the land of Redmay Farm. Bunter knew where to find a stile giving access to the farm—and he knew, also, that it was adorned by a large board— "Trespassers will be Prosecuted."

He did not bother about that. Mr. Redmay's objection to strangers rooting over his land, and disturbing his flocks and herds, did not matter so much as the more important fact that it saved a mile on the homeward way.

So, once safe from Peter's eagle eye and active boot, Bunter rolled in search of that stile, recklessly ready to trespass at the risk of being prosecuted—and happily ignorant that another member of the pack was following him.

A footpath led to the stile, and Bunter had almost reached it when he discerned two figures ahead of him, standing at the stile.

"Beasts!" murmured Bunter. And he halted.

He applied that disrespectful epithet to Quelch and Prout! The two Form-masters stood there, looking across at the attractive, sunny meadows beyond, dotted with sheep, their backs to Bunter.

Obviously, Bunter could not disregard that warning board under the eyes of his Form-master. He leaned on a tree to rest, and waited for the beasts to go.

Prout's boom reached his fat ears.

"Come, Quelch! A very pleasant walk across these meadows——"

"You see the notice, Prout?"

"Really, Quelch, we shall do no harm to the farmer's sheep if we walk across these meadows! Moreover, I have no doubt that it is an empty threat. How often are trespassers prosecuted?"

"Rarely, perhaps; but once would be too often, if the prosecuted person happened to be oneself," said Mr. Quelch dryly.

"I doubt very much whether the farmer has a right to put up that notice at all, Quelch."

"Possibly not. But I should prefer not to contest the matter in Courtfield County Court, Prout!"

Grunt, from Prout!

The portly master of the Fifth had more weight to carry than the long, lean master of the Remove, and short cuts appealed to him almost as much as to Billy Bunter.

"A bad example to the boys, Prout," added Quelch.

"If any were present, perhaps!" grunted Prout.

He glanced round—and spotted a fat figure on the footpath behind, at a little distance.

"Oh!" he ejaculated.

Quelch glanced round, and smiled faintly.

"That is Bunter," he said. "A schoolmaster cannot be too careful, as you see, Prout! If Bunter saw us disregard this board he would be encouraged to do the same. Indeed, it may be with that very intention that he is there! I had better speak to him. Bunter!"

Billy Bunter faded into the wood.

Perhaps he guessed what Quelch was going to say. Anyhow, he had had enough of Quelch for one day. He turned a deaf ear and backed out of sight.

Mr. Quelch frowned. He was almost sure that Bunter had heard him. Still, he could not be quite sure.

"He is gone!" said Prout, with a rather yearning eye on that short cut home.

"Probably not far!" answered Mr. Quelch.

"Really, Quelch, I think—— Why—what—what—what is that?" gasped Prout. "Good gracious! What——"

Whiz! Crash!

From somewhere in the thickets a lump of turf whizzed, hitting Mr. Quelch's hat fair and square, and knocking it off his head!

The Remove master staggered, with a startled exclamation. His hat dropped at his feet, accompanied by the turf.

"Good gracious!" gasped Prout. "Who—what——"

Mr. Quelch put a hand on the stile to steady himself! He gazed as if transfixed at his hat on the ground. Someone had hurled that turf from the thickets, and knocked his hat off—and only a minute ago he had seen Bunter!

The expression that came over Mr. Quelch's face was positively terrifying. For a moment or two he stood, then he grabbed up the hat, jammed it on his head, and rushed back into the wood in search of the turf-hurler.

He was not likely to find him. Arthur Carter was already cutting after the pack at top speed, leaving the Owl of the Remove to face the music!

— — —

THE EIGHTEENTH CHAPTER.

Quelch in a Quandary!

"OH crikey!" gasped Billy Bunter.

Peering out of the thickets, to ascertain whether Quelch and Prout were getting a move on, Bunter's eyes almost popped through his spectacles at the sight of Quelch's hat flying off under the crash of the whizzing turf.

Who had done it, Bunter had not the faintest idea.

He had not given Carter a thought. It was not likely to occur to his fat brain that the rascally young schemer, after seeing Mr. Quelch, had dropped behind the pack in the hope of spotting just such a chance. Had Bunter kept on the run no such chance could have come Carter's way; but, as usual, his own fat slacking was his undoing. As it was, he had played into the young rascal's hands as completely as Carter himself could have wished.

"Bunter!" he heard Mr. Quelch's voice, on a high note. "Bunter!"

"Oh crumbs!"

"Bunter! Where—oh! You are here! You young rascal—you disrespectful young rascal!" thundered Mr. Quelch. "How dare you?"

Billy Bunter blinked at him in terror.

"I—I say, I haven't done anything!" he gasped.

"You threw that turf——"

"Oh crikey! I didn't!" shrieked Bunter. "Oh lor'! It wasn't me! Oh lor'! I never——"

He jumped back, with unusual activity.

Quelch had a walking-stick in his right hand. With his left he reached at Bunter.

What he was going to do with the walking-stick in his right, after he had grabbed Bunter with his left, the fat Owl did not need telling.

Bunter did not stay to be grabbed! He dodged, and flew.

"Bunter!" roared Mr. Quelch. "Stop! I am going to punish you most severely! Stop!"

That really was not the way to make Bunter stop! Being punished most severely had no attraction for him whatever!

He bolted, and after him rushed Mr. Quelch!

Prout gave a gasp as a fat figure flew by him, bounded at the stile, and careered over it.

"Stop that boy!" shrieked Mr. Quelch.

Prout clutched—too late!

Bunter was over the stile, and speeding across the meadow, his fat little legs going like machinery! Bunter's one fixed idea, at that moment, was to get out of reach of Mr. Quelch and his walking-stick! Nothing else mattered.

"My dear Quelch——" ejaculated Prout.

Quelch did not answer him. His long legs whisked over the stile, and he rushed after Bunter. Boards announcing that trespassers would be prosecuted failed to interest him at that moment. He wanted to reach Bunter, just as keenly as Bunter did not want to be reached!

"Bless my soul!" gasped Mr. Prout as pursued and pursuer vanished across the green meadow.

Billy Bunter, as a rule, was no sprinter; but he put up quite a surprising speed at this moment. He fairly whizzed!

"Hi!" roared a voice, as he shot past a barn. "Hi! Stop!"

Bunter did not heed, even if he heard! A barking dog was heard in the barn. A red-faced man, in gaiters, and armed with a pitchfork, rushed out into Bunter's way, to stop him. Trespassers were a worry to Mr. Redmay, but he had really never beheld such a flagrant case as this—a schoolboy bolting by his barn, under his very eyes, and refusing to heed his call to stop! He rushed to stop him!

No doubt, the farmer expected Bunter to stop at once as he jumped into his way. But Bunter did not stop. With Quelch and his walking-stick behind, he dared not! Bunter charged wildly on, lowered his bullet head, and butted!

Taken by surprise, the farmer sat down suddenly, with a bump that almost shook his farm.

Bunter careered round him and charged on.

The farmer sat and spluttered. A big mastiff came scuttling out of the barn, and pranced round the sitting man, barking industriously.

Bunter scudded on. He was winded, and gurgling for breath; and though the February day was cold, perspiration clotted his fat brow.

Even with Mr. Quelch's walking-stick brandished behind, Bunter could not have kept it up much longer. He plunged through a gap in the hedge.

into the next field, and blinked back over a fat shoulder.

To his surprise, he saw no pursuer—neither Mr. Quelch nor the farmer!

It was an immense relief!

He tottered on, towards a cart that lay at rest with its shafts to the ground. It was the only spot where he could get a rest out of sight. There was straw in the cart, and Bunter rolled into it with a gasp of thankfulness. He could only hope that Quelch, when he came on, would pass that cart, without guessing that Bunter had taken cover in it.

But Quelch had Bunter only known it, was not coming on!

Quelch had arrived at the spot where the farmer sat spluttering; and it was a case of "thus far and no farther."

The stout man in gaiters clambered to his feet, picked up his pitchfork and glared at the Remove master, blocking his way! It was altogether too much for Mr. Redmay's patience! A schoolboy had bolted across his land, and knocked him over in transit. Now a man in a muddy hat and an overcoat was following on—regardless of the rights of property! The farmer was not standing this, at any price! He held the pitchfork threateningly in front of Mr. Quelch—and the Remove master halted and backed away a step or two.

"Off with you, you trespassing rascal!" roared the farmer.

"My good man——" gasped Mr. Quelch.

"Good man yourself!" retorted Mr. Redmay. "Get out, or I'll set the dog on you! Here, Toothy!"

"I am a schoolmaster—I am following a boy belonging to my Form—I must ask you to excuse me——" gasped Mr. Quelch.

"You a schoolmaster!" hooted the farmer. "If you're a schoolmaster, can't you read?"

"Eh! What? Yes! Certainly."

"Then you've read that board at the stile, and you know that this is private land, and you're trespassing!" snorted Mr. Redmay.

"Oh! Yes! But——"

"Trampling over my land, and disturbing my sheep! There's been a pitchfork missed from that barn! I dare say you had it!"

Mr. Quelch fairly gurgled. It was true that he was trespassing—he could not deny that! But to be suspected of having "pinched" a pitchfork from a farmer's barn, was really too much.

"How dare you!" he gasped. "You are insolent—I——"

"Seize him, Toothy!" roared Mr. Redmay. "Get him! Get that tramp, Toothy!"

There was a regular tornado of barking from Toothy, and he careered at Mr. Quelch.

Quelch was no coward; but a big mastiff rushing at him, with big jaws, was a serious proposition. He backed swiftly away, whacking out with his walking-stick! He stumbled in the stubble, and the stick slipped from his grasp as he threw out his hands to save himself. Leaping up, weaponless, the Remove master dodged wildly.

"Call that dog off, you stupid man!" he yelled.

"Seize him, Toothy!" roared Mr. Redmay, waving the dog on.

Quelch dodged, and hopped, and jumped! Close at hand was the barn—one of those ancient buildings with a thatched roof sloping down at one end, to within three feet of the ground. Mr. Quelch grabbed at it, and swung himself out of reach.

Toothy had to stop below the eaves, glaring up at him, and barking furiously. Mr. Quelch, clamped on the thatched slope, gasped for breath, and stared down at Toothy.

"Will you call your dog off?" he shrieked.

"No, I won't!" retorted the farmer. "You came on my land without leave, and I dessay you was after another pitchfork——"

"Fool!"

"Oh, all right! I ain't fool enough to 'ave my tools pinched, if I can stop

it! You get off my land, as soon as you like! Watch him, Toothy!"

"I cannot remain here!" shrieked Mr. Quelch, as the farmer turned to go.

"Who's asking you to?" retorted Mr. Redmay.

"Call that dog off."

"Watch him, Toothy!"

The farmer tramped away in the direction Billy Bunter had taken.

Mr. Quelch shouted after him, unheeded. Then he stared down at Toothy—watching him! The mastiff had ceased to bark; but he watched, with a steady eye. The more Mr. Quelch looked at that big, powerful mastiff, the less inclined he felt to come to close quarters with him.

He cast a despairing glance back the way he had come, wondering if Prout could help him. Redclyffe Wood was a dark line in the distance—the stile where he had left Prout was out of sight. Prout had not followed. There was no help for Quelch.

He looked at Toothy again! He liked the mastiff's looks less than ever. He glanced after the farmer—but Mr. Redmay had already disappeared beyond a hedge.

"Bless my soul!" gasped Mr. Quelch.

He remained on the slanting thatched roof. He had to remain there, till the farmer chose to return and call off the mastiff. Obviously, the farmer did not intend to return soon—if at all! He was giving that trespasser a lesson! It was awful for Mr. Quelch!

But there was no help for it! The cold winds of February blew round him, as he bunched himself on the slope of the barn, and watched Toothy, while Toothy watched him. The long, long minutes, weary and dreary minutes, passed, while Mr. Quelch, a helpless prisoner, squatted on the thatch like Patience on a monument!

THE NINETEENTH CHAPTER.

Bunter the Brave!

BILLY BUNTER hardly breathed. His fat person was only half-hidden by the straw in the cart, in which he had taken refuge. Anyone looking in, over the side of the cart, must have spotted him. So the sound of footsteps stopping close at hand, was a terrifying one to his fat ears!

Unaware of Mr. Quelch's dilemma, he expected the Remove master to come on in pursuit, any moment; and hoped fervently that he would pass that cart unsuspecting. But the footsteps stopped!

The hapless fat Owl suppressed his breathing! If this was Quelch, he was done for! But he soon learned that it was not Quelch, as he heard a deep voice from the man he could not see.

"Seen a boy crossing this field, George?"

"No, zur—I only just coom——"

"I dare say he's far enough away by this time, the trespassing young scoundrel! Well, I've got the other!"

Bunter heard a chuckle—apparently from George!

"I see un, Mr. Redmay, zur! Sticking on the roof of the old barn! Haw, haw, haw!"

Another chuckle—this time from Mr. Redmay!

"Let him stick there, George! P'r'aps he'll learn to keep off a farmer's land! He says he's a schoolmaster! If he is, how'd he like me to walk into his school any time I pleased? People

Printed in England and published every Saturday by the Proprietors, The Amalgamated Press, Ltd., The Fleetway House, Farringdon Street, London, E.C.4. Advertisement offices: The Fleetway House, Farringdon Street, London, E.C.4. Registered for transmission by Canadian Magazine Post. Subscription rates: Inland and Abroad, 11s. per annum; 5s. 6d. for six months. Sole Agents for Australia and New Zealand: Messrs. Gordon & Gotch, Ltd., and for South Africa: Central News Agency, Ltd.—Saturday, February 19th, 1938.
LL

seem to think that a farmer's property is everybody's property, George."

"They do so, zur."

"He can stick there as long as he likes! I've got to go over to Court-field. Don't you go near the barn, George."

"No, zur."

"Toothy's watching him! He won't guess that Toothy wouldn't bite a man for love or money, till he tries to get away!"

"Haw, haw, haw!"

"He won't try it on in a hurry!" chuckled the farmer. "Toothy looks as if he'd bite his leg off! He's frightened plenty of tramps, and they never know that he's as gentle as a young lamb, and takes the children for rides on his back! His looks do it! I fancy that trespasser won't risk it till dark, at the earliest! When he does, he will be all right— Toothy won't touch him!"

George gave a series of throaty chuckles.

He seemed greatly amused, by the idea of the trespasser remaining cornered on the roof of a barn, in terror of a dog that would not have bitten him for love or money!

No doubt it was funny, from the point of view of the farmer and his man— though far from funny to Mr. Quelch, who judged Toothy on his looks, which were formidable enough to scare the heftiest tramp.

"I'll send one of the children to take the dog away, at dusk, if he's not gone!" chuckled Mr. Redmay. "He can have a few hours of it, and learn to keep off other people's property! Schoolmaster indeed! P'r'aps he'd like me to turn my sheep into his school play-ground! Why not, if he can walk about my land whenever he likes? I'll learn him."

Another throaty chuckle from George!

"Get the horse, and take this cart over to Giles' Corner, George!" added Mr. Redmay. "Keep clear of the old barn!"

"Yes, zur."

There was a sound—a glad sound to Billy Bunter's ears—of retreating footsteps.

The fat junior ventured to peer out of the cart.

Mr. Redmay was disappearing in one direction with a vigorous stride, no doubt on his way to Courtfield. An ancient rural gentleman — evidently George—was toddling away in another direction towards a mass of buildings in the far distance, going to fetch a horse to take the cart away to Giles' Corner. The coast was clear!

Billy Bunter waited for both figures to disappear from sight, and then clambered out of the cart. It behoved him to be gone before George returned with the horse.

The fat Owl grinned as he blinked back towards the field he had crossed in his flight where the barn was.

He was quite as amused as the farmer and his man by Mr. Quelch's extraordinary predicament.

Nothing really could have happened more fortunately for Bunter.

Over the hedge he had a glimpse of the ancient barn and its thatched roof, and a figure clamped on the slope of that roof.

That was Mr. Quelch, watched by a terrifying-looking dog that would not have bitten him for love or money if he had tried to escape.

Billy Bunter chuckled

Bunter was not afraid of dogs that would not bite. A dog that was as gentle as a young lamb, and took children for rides on its back, had no terrors for Bunter. After what he had

heard, Bunter was not nervous about that dog.

Quelch evidently was. Blinking at the distant figure, squatting on the sloping thatch, Bunter could see that his Form-master was watching some object below the eaves. But he was making no movement.

"He, he, he!" chortled Bunter.

The farmer and George being gone, and Quelch crouching on the roof of the barn, the coast was clear for Bunter, and he started on his way.

But he stopped again.

He was clear of Quelch, so far as that went. Unfortunately, he had to see him again at Greyfriars. Quelch, obviously, would not remain a permanent fixture on the roof of that barn. Sooner or later he would blow in at the school, and it was fairly certain that his temper would not be improved by his experiences on Redmay Farm. It was a dismal prospect for Bunter.

But Billy Bunter's fat brain was working. It occurred to him that, if he rescued Quelch from that awful predicament, Quelch could hardly whop him afterwards, especially for something he hadn't done.

Rescuing Quelch from a dog that would not, according to his master, bite for love or money was not really a difficult or dangerous task.

Had it been either, Billy Bunter would have had no use for it. But it was neither. It was as easy as falling off a form.

Billy Bunter halted, turned, and rolled back the way he had come— towards the barn in the last field.

Standing in the gap in the hedge, he blinked at the barn, at Mr. Quelch cramped on the sloping thatch, and Toothy, squatted below the eaves, watching him.

Mr. Quelch's eyes, wandering round the landscape in a sort of hopeless hope of help, fell on Bunter, and he started. He had not expected to see the fat junior there again.

To his surprise, Bunter came rolling from the gap in the hedge towards the barn. Angry as he was with him, Mr. Quelch could not see him rolling into danger without warning him. He waved a hand at Bunter, and shouted:

"Bunter! Take care! There is a fierce dog here! You had better go away at once!"

Bunter rolled on, regardless. From information received, so to speak, he knew exactly how fierce that dog was.

"It's all right, sir!" he called out. "I've come back to help you!"

"Nonsense! Go away at once!"

"I can't leave you like this, sir," said the dutiful fat Owl. "I'll hold the dog while you get down, sir."

"I cannot allow you to take the risk. Go away at once, you foolish boy!" exclaimed Mr. Quelch.

"It's all right, sir. I've got a way with dogs," said Bunter cheerfully. "They—they like me, sir. I—I'll chance it!"

Gurrrrrggh!, came a deep growl from Toothy as he spotted the newcomer.

He turned his head towards Bunter, with a display of teeth that was positively terrifying. Bunter came to a sudden halt.

He liked Toothy's looks no more than Mr. Quelch did. A dreadful doubt came into his mind that perhaps the farmer over-rated the lamb-like docility of that mastiff. If Toothy's temper was anything like his looks, Bunter would have liked to be a hundred miles away from Toothy, and would have preferred a thousand.

The growl was followed by a hurri-

cane of barking. Toothy pranced at Bunter, and pranced round him, with bark after bark.

Almost did the fat Owl turn tail and bolt out of the field. Still, even Bunter could not fail to observe that, though the mastiff pranced round him, and barked like a machine-gun in action, he made no attempt to bite.

Taking his courage in both hands, as it were, Bunter advanced on the dog and stretched out a fat hand to him.

"G-g-g-good dog!" gasped Bunter. "G-g-g-good old d-d-doggie!"

Had Toothy snapped, Bunter would have bounded, and would probably not have stopped on the hither side of a couple of fields.

But Toothy did not snap. A fat hand fastened on his collar. Toothy took it like a lamb.

Bunter's courage revived.

He held on to that collar—an easy task, as Toothy made no objection whatever.

Mr. Quelch, from the roof of the barn, gazed in wonder.

"I've got him, sir!" called out Bunter victoriously.

"Bless my soul!" exclaimed Mr. Quelch. "Are—are—are you sure that you have that dog safely, Bunter?"

"Oh, yes, sir! Right as rain!" squeaked Bunter cheerily. "'Tain't easy to hold him, sir, but I've got him all right. I—I can hold him while you get out of the field, sir."

Mr. Quelch, though with considerable doubt, slipped off the roof of the barn. Toothy emitted a series of loud barks. But Billy Bunter's fat hand was firm on the collar.

"It's all right, sir!" called out Bunter. "If you get out of the field, sir——"

"I shall certainly not go and leave you with that dangerous dog, Bunter!" gasped Mr. Quelch.

"It—it's really all right, sir. Look how quiet he is now I've got him. I can hold him all right, really, sir."

"If you are sure, Bunter—really, the dreadful animal seems quite tame with you—if you are certain——"

"Oh, quite, sir!" chirruped Bunter. "He's all right with me. I—I know how to manage dogs, sir."

"Very well, Bunter! I will go. And I am very much obliged to you, my boy, and very pleased to see you display so much courage. The dog seems very quiet with you, but you have certainly run a very considerable risk. I shall excuse you for your disrespectful act, Bunter, for which I intended to punish you most severely——"

"But it wasn't me, sir! I never chucked anything at your hat!" gasped Bunter.

"Very well, Bunter. In the circumstances, I shall accept your assurance." said Mr. Quelch. "And if you are quite, quite sure that you are safe with that dog——"

"Oh, yes, sir! But—but he's getting a bit restive. If you wouldn't mind hurrying, sir——"

"I shall go at once."

Mr. Quelch started back towards the stile with long and rapid strides. A volley of barks followed him, and Mr. Quelch, though he disdained to run, certainly walked very quickly—very quickly indeed.

He disappeared across the meadow towards Redclyffe Wood.

Billy Bunter, his fat face wreathed in grins, released Toothy's collar at last. Toothy blinked at him and trotted away into the barn.

Bunter, with his fat grin extending almost from ear to ear, rolled on his way by the short cut across Redmay

THE MAGNET LIBRARY.—No. 1,566.

Farm, and rolled cheerily in at Greyfriars—the first man home from the paper-chase.

THE TWENTIETH CHAPTER.
All Right for Bunter !

"I SAY, you fellows !"

Most of the Remove were in the Rag after the run when Billy Bunter rolled in. For the last couple of hours Bunter had been adorning the study armchair with his fat person, resting his weary fat limbs. But it was tea-time now, and laziness had to take second place.

Many of the Removites were a little tired. It had been a hard run across country. Even Bob Cherry was glad to sit down. But the hares had got safely in, uncaptured, which was a satisfaction to them. Hardly more than seven or eight fellows had kept on the run to the finish, the weary ones tailing off at various points. Peter Todd was one of the few who had been in at the death, and he fixed a deadly glare on the fat Owl as he rolled into the Rag.

"You fat slacker !" hooted Peter. "You chucked it almost at the start ! Come over here and be booted !"

"Oh, really, Toddy—I had to stop, really !" explained Bunter. "You fellows remember passing Quelch and old Prout ! I say, which of you stopped behind and knocked Quelch's hat off with a turf ?"

"What ?" yelled Bob Cherry.

"Did anybody ?" exclaimed Harry Wharton.

"Gammon !" said Vernon-Smith.

"Well, somebody did !" declared Bunter. "I saw it knocked off ! I never saw who did it, but I saw the hat go. I say, Quelch thought it was me at first——"

"Wasn't it ?" asked Carter, with a laugh.

"No, it wasn't !" hooted Bunter.

"Is the surefulness terrific, my esteemed fat Bunter ?" chuckled Hurree Jamset Ram Singh.

"I tell you I didn't !" howled Bunter. "Quelch thought I did, because I was there, but I didn't. See ? I'd like to know which of you fellows stopped behind and pelted Quelch's hat !"

"Well, a lot of fellows tailed off," said Harry Wharton, "but—— Did any fellow here pelt Quelch ?"

There was no answer to that question.

"Where were you, Carter ?" asked Bob Cherry, with grim sarcasm.

"Find out !" retorted Carter.

"Well, I can't find out, but I can guess !" said Bob contemptuously.

"I say, you fellows, I shouldn't wonder if it was Carter; he's always playing some rotten trick to land me with Quelch ! But, as it happened, it turned out all right, Quelch took my word about it afterwards——"

"Quelch took your word !" yelled Skinner.

"Yes, he did——"

"Fan me, somebody !"

"Ha, ha, ha !"

"You see, it was after I'd rescued him from a savage bulldog," explained Bunter. "Quelch was cornered by a fearful, awful, howling bloodhound, and I rushed up and saved him."

"Suffering haddocks ! Go it !"

"I did, really ! You see, Quelch got on a barn, and there was the mastiff watching him, and I rushed up and seized him——"

"You seized Quelch ?"

"Ha, ha, ha !"

"Eh ? No, you ass ! I seized the bulldog—that is, the bloodhound—I mean, the mastiff—and——"

"And swung him round your head by his tail and hurled him across Redclyffe Wood ?" asked Skinner.

"Ha, ha, ha !" yelled the juniors.

"Oh, no ! I just seized him and—and held him by sheer strength and courage, you know, while Quelch escaped. That's why I never finished the run. And Quelch——"

"Shut up, you ass; here he comes !" whispered Bob Cherry, as the door of

the Rag opened and Mr. Quelch stepped in.

The Remove master glanced over the room.

"Bunter !" he said.

"Oh ! Yes, sir ?"

The Removites looked on curiously, Carter with a suppressed grin. The Remove schemer had no doubt that Mr. Quelch had looked in to call Bunter to account for knocking off his hat.

But there was a surprise in store for Carter—and for the rest of the Remove. Mr. Quelch bestowed quite an amiable smile on the fattest member of his Form. He had a parcel in his hand—apparently brought in with him after his walk. He held it out.

"This is for you, Bunter !" he said.

"Oh !" gasped Bunter.

"I am very much obliged to you, Bunter, for what you did at Redlmay Farm this afternoon," said the Remove master. "I have brought you a small reward—a box of chocolates, Bunter. I believe, my boy, that you had nothing to do with the disrespectful act in Redclyffe Wood, and I feel sure also that it was not you who destroyed the papers from my study yesterday. I have a very much better opinion of you than I had, Bunter."

"Oh, sir !" gasped the fat Owl.

Mr. Quelch left the Rag, leaving the Removites almost gasping.

Bob Cherry, glancing at Carter, chuckled at the expression on his face.

"I say, you fellows," gasped Bunter, "you heard that ? Perhaps you believe me now !"

He grabbed open the parcel. It contained a large and handsome box of chocolates. He grabbed off the lid. His remarks were resumed with his mouth full and came a little muffled.

"I say, this is all right ! I say, you fellows, have some of these chocs—there's lots ! Perhaps you believe now that I rescued Quelch from a savage bulldog—I mean, bloodhound—that is, Alsatian ! Mind, I never heard the farmer say that he was as tame as a lamb, and wouldn't bite for love or money. I never heard the farmer say anything at all—in fact, he wasn't there——"

"Ha, ha, ha !"

"Blessed if I see anything to cackle at ! It was just pluck—sheer grit !" said Bunter. "Pluck will tell, you know ! I say, you fellows, this looks good for my report this term, doesn't it ? You could see that Quelch was jolly pleased ! I say, these are ripping chocs ! Have some ?"

And the Removites, chuckling, had some.

THE END.

(Once again fortune has favoured the fat Owl! Next week Billy Bunter gets some of his own back on the scheming Carter! You'll learn all about it in: "A VENTRILOQUIST'S VENGEANCE!"—next Saturday's spanking fine story of Greyfriars.)

The Magnet

2D

Billy Bunter's Own Paper

THERE'S A MASTER WELL-KNONE TO THE SKOOL. WHO WOLLOPS THE CHAPS SOMETHING CROOL. HIS NAME'S KNONE TO YOU, IT BEGINS WITH A Q, AND WE AWL OF US THINK HIM A PHOOL!

AWKWARD FOR BUNTER!

Want the Latest News? Then Fall In and Follow—

The GREYFRIARS GUIDE

A TOUR OF THE SCHOOL. Inside the Tower.

(1)

A steep and spiral stair will take
You up to see the bell and clock,
So mind your step, for goodness' sake,
For visitors may get a shock
By treading on a stair
That isn't really there!

(2)

The rising-bell will meet your eye
Unless you keep a good look-out,
It's hung where passing heads go by
To give the visitor a clout,
And then its hollow tone
Is mingled with a groan!

(3)

The clock has frequently struck one,
For, as it swings from side to side,
The pendulum is sure to stun
The head with which it may collide,
While danger often lurks
Within the monster's works!

(4)

The bell-rope waits to trip your feet,
The beams will get you in the neck,
Go careful, for the sake of Pete,
Unless you want to be a wreck!
Ah, down the stairs at last,
The deadly peril's past!

A WEEKLY BUDGET OF FACT AND FUN

By
THE GREYFRIARS RHYMESTER

STRANGE STATISTICS

If all the words spoken by Coker in one year were collected in a book, there would be no sense in it whatever.

If all the money at Greyfriars were put into a heap, Fisher T. Fish would be on it like a bird.

If all the ink used in writing lines for Quelch were poured into a bucket and balanced on Loder's study door, it would serve a much more useful purpose.

If all the sausage rolls purchased from Mrs. Mimble by Greyfriars fellows last week were made of cast-iron, Bunter would weigh 48.625 tons more than he does now.

And if you want a PUZZLE this week, look at these 'ere proverbs——
(1) Where there's no sense there's no feeling.
(2) Bad news carries while good news tarries.
(3) A stitch in time saves nine.
(4) Live not to eat, but eat to live.
(5) There's bound to come a rainy day.
(6) Do unto others as you would have them do to you.
(7) Truth and oil come ever uppermost.
· (8) Riches take unto themselves wings and fly.
(9) Look before ye leap.
Buried in each proverb is a part of your body. Can you dig them out?
(*Solutions at foot of column.*)

If all the things Mr. Prout calls "unparalleled and unprecedented" were to happen at once, the result would be unparalleled and unprecedented.

If all the goals scored by the Upper Fourth against the Remove during the season were to be crammed into one match, the Remove would have to score a goal to win.

LOWER SCHOOL LAMENT

(To be sung with slow music.)

Weep for the brave! Oh, day of wrath!
My tears make heavy splashes!
Bring me a sack of blackest cloth
And on my head pour ashes!
Woe unto Greyfriars, fair and fine;
For thee I weep this bitter brine,
No words can cheer me up;
Oh, reader, join your tears with mine—
We've been and lost the Cup!

Forth, forth we went, so brave and young,
With Rookwood School to battle;
Supported there by many a tongue,
By many a rasping rattle!
And thus we played with "art" and "sole,"
And when we scored a splendid goal,
The Rookwood fellows gasped,
While tongues were heard from pole to pole
And rasping rattles rasped!

Oh, how our hearts within us burned,
We played with skill and science;
Undaunted, our opponents turned
And went for us like giants!
When Silver scored, and scored again,
We set our teeth and tried in vain
To beat the Rookwood skill,
While all the tongues were dumb with pain,
The rasping rattles still!

When Lovell popped in number three
We felt our fungus bristle!
And after that, the referee,
He went and blew his whistle!
We cannot always win, we know,
We're bound to lose at times, although
We're seldom sold a pup!
But now—— Oh, join my wail of woe,
We've been and lost the Cup!

THE GREYFRIARS ALPHABET

The Rev. HERBERT HENRY LOCKE, M.A., D.D.,

the Venerable Headmaster.

L is for LOCKE, the Reverend
Headmaster, who is clever and
A Doctor of Divinity
Of Cambridge (Lower Trinity);
He rules the school judiciously,
Not mildly or officiously,

But with a calm authority
That shows his seniority.
A constant careful tact is his
In all scholastic practices,
As daily he co-ordinates
The work of his subordinates,
Good judgment and ability
He uses with facility,
And muscles strong and sinister
A flogging can administer!

ANSWER TO PUZZLE

Nose, Leg, Chin, Toe, Ear, Tooth, Hand, Chest, and Eye.

A VENTRILOQUIST'S VENGEANCE!
By FRANK RICHARDS

Gurrrrrggh! The deep and savage growl of a particularly vicious dog seemed to come from under Carter's chair, and the new junior jumped up suddenly. His cup crashed in pieces and tea spread in a flood. "Carter!" rumbled Mr. Quelch. "How dare you?"

THE FIRST CHAPTER.

Shirty!

"OH!" gasped Mr. Quelch.

"Oh!" gasped all the Greyfriars Remove.

Only one fellow in that Form looked unconcerned.

That one was Billy Bunter.

And it was because Bunter, being short-sighted, could not see what every other fellow could see—the paper pinned on the blackboard.

Mr. Quelch had let his Form in for third school that morning. In break no fellow was supposed to enter the Form-room; but it was clear that someone had entered, for a paper was stuck on the blackboard with a couple of drawing-pins, which certainly had not been there in second lesson.

Mr. Quelch gave quite a convulsive start as he saw that paper. His eyes popped at it. So did the eyes of all the Remove—except Bunter's, which blinked unperturbed behind the fat Owl's big spectacles.

"Oh!" repeated Mr. Quelch.

"You fat chump, Bunter!" breathed Bob Cherry.

"Eh? What's up?" asked Bunter.

"You howling ass!" murmured Harry Wharton.

"Oh, really, Wharton——"

"Bunter's done it this time!" grinned Smithy.

"The donefulness is terrific!" murmured Hurree Jamset Ram Singh.

"You ass!" hissed Frank Nugent.

"I say, you fellows, what's up?" asked Bunter, in surprise. "What's Quelch staring at on the blackboard? Is there anything there?"

"You ought to know!" chuckled Carter, the new fellow in the Remove.

"Eh? How should I know?" asked Bunter.

Billy Bunter turned his big spectacles on the blackboard. He could make out a square of paper pinned there. He fancied that there was writing on it, but his limited vision could not make out the writing

"Upon my word!" said Mr. Quelch. "Upon my word!"

His eyes—and all other eyes but Bunter's—read the lines written on the paper on the board. They were written

A tip top, highly amusing school story of those world-wide favourites —Harry Whar on & Co, of Greyfriars.

in the well-known scrawl of Billy Bunter, and the spelling was Bunter's very own. It was a limerick that was written there, and a dozen fellows had seen Bunter showing that limerick about the Remove studies the evening before. But that even Bunter would be ass enough to pin it up on the blackboard in the Form-room for Quelch to see, no one had supposed for a moment. But there it was. It ran:

"There's a master well-knone in the skool,
Who wollops the chaps something crool.
    His name's knone to you,
    It begins with a Q,
And we awl of us think him a phool!"

Billy Bunter had made the Remove fellows laugh with that limerick. Bunter thought the limerick fearfully funny. The other fellows thought the spelling fearfully funny.

But Mr. Quelch, plainly, was amused neither by the limerick, nor by the way in which it was spelt For a long, long moment he stood staring at the paper on the blackboard, as if he could hardly believe his eyes—as, perhaps, he hardly could. Thunder gathered in his brow. Hs gimlet eyes glittered when at last he turned to his class.

"Bunter!"

"Yes, sir!" answered Bunter, quite cheerfully.

It was amazing to the Removites to see the fat Owl so cheery and unconcerned. Obviously he was booked for a record row, and if he had pinned that paper on the blackboard he could hardly fail to be aware of it. And as Bunter was known to be the author of the limerick, the fellows naturally supposed that he had put it there.

Mr. Quelch picked up his cane. He pointed with it at the paper on the blackboard.

"Look at that, Bunter! You placed it there!"

"Oh, no, sir!" answered Bunter, still cheerful. "Wharton did, sir."

Harry Wharton jumped.

"I!" he stuttered.

"Wharton!" exclaimed Mr. Quelch. "You, my head boy! Is it possible——"

"Certainly not!" gasped the captain of the Remove.

"Bunter, how dare you make such a statement!" exclaimed Mr. Quelch.

"But he did, sir!" gasped Bunter, THE MAGNET LIBRARY.—No. 1.567.

blinking at his Form-master. "Don't you remember, sir, in second lesson, you asked him to?"

"I—asked—him—to!" gurgled Mr. Quelch.

"Yes, sir. All the fellows heard you!" exclaimed Bunter. "You wanted the blackboard in the lesson, sir, and you asked Wharton to place it there. I never touched it, sir."

Mr. Quelch gazed at him.

"Is that intended for deliberate impertinence, Bunter?" he demanded. "You know perfectly well that I am not speaking of the blackboard."

"Ain't you, sir?" asked Bunter. "I thought you were, as you were pointing at it, sir."

There was a chortle in the Remove, instantly suppressed as Mr. Quelch's gimlet eye gleamed round.

"I am speaking of the paper pinned on the blackboard, Bunter!" thundered Mr. Quelch.

"Oh, are you, sir? I can't read it from here, sir," said the cheery Owl. "If it's for the lesson, sir, may I sit nearer? I'm a little short-sighted, sir, and I can't read it."

"You are well aware of what is written on the paper, Bunter, as you wrote it!" roared Mr. Quelch. "Stand out before the class, Bunter! You placed that paper there, and——"

"I didn't!" howled Bunter. His cheerfulness departed. He realised that there must be something on that paper that had made Quelch shirty. "I—I haven't been near the blackboard, sir!"

"That paper is written in your hand, Bunter, and in your disgraceful spelling!" said Mr. Quelch sternly. "Look at it, you disrespectful young rascal!"

Bunter, rolling out before the class, blinked at the paper on the blackboard. On a nearer view he was able to read it. He jumped almost clear of the Form-room floor as he did so. His little round eyes almost shot out of his big, round spectacles.

"Oh crikey!" gasped Bunter. "Oh lor'! Oh jiminy!"

"The blithering owl!" murmured Vernon-Smith. "Did he expect it to amuse Quelch, or what?"

"Bunter, I shall punish you with the greatest severity for having written such disrespectful nonsense, and, above all, for having pinned it up in the Form-room!" exclaimed Mr. Quelch.

"I didn't!" yelled Bunter. "I—I never! I never knew it was here, sir! I never put it on the blackboard! I—I never wrote it! I—I've never seen it before! It—it's quite strange to me, sir! I never wrote it, sir, and I never showed it to the fellows in the studies last night! You can ask them, sir—they all saw it!"

"Ha, ha, ha!"

"Silence! Bunter, bend over that desk! I shall cane you severely, Bunter, and I shall refer in your report this term to your disrespectful impudence. Not a word! Bend over that desk!"

"Oh lor'! But I never——"

"Bend over!" roared Mr. Quelch.

"Oh scissors!"

The fattest figure at Greyfriars School bent over the desk. Six times the cane rose, and six times it fell, and exactly half a dozen times an ear-splitting yell rang through the Remove Form-room. Six was the customary limit, but Mr. Quelch looked strongly inclined to keep on. However, he stopped at six, though reluctantly.

"Go back to your place, Bunter!"

"Yarooh!"

"You will take five hundred lines! I THE MAGNET LIBRARY.—No. 1,567.

shall give you a detention this afternoon. Now——"

"Yow-ow-ow-ow-ow!"

"If you utter another sound, Bunter, I shall cane you again!"

With a great effort, Billy Bunter suppressed the sounds of woe. He crawled back to his place.

Mr. Quelch unhooked the paper from the board, tore it across, and tossed it into the wastepaper-basket. And third lesson began in an atmosphere that was positively electric.

THE SECOND CHAPTER.
Bob With His Back Up!

"NO!" said Bob Cherry.

"Look here, Bob——"

"No!"

"My esteemed and idiotic Bob——"

"It's no good jawing!" said Bob Cherry. "I've said no, and I mean no! I'd rather chuck Soccer altogether than play in the same team with that cad Carter."

Bob Cherry's friends gazed at him in exasperation. It was utterly unlike the cheery, good-natured Bob, to take a line like this. He was good-tempered, good-natured, tolerant to a fault; he looked on the best side of everybody and everything; he often had a good word to say even for fellows like Skinner and Fisher T. Fish. So his attitude now was all the more disconcerting and exasperating.

All the Remove knew that he barred Carter, the new man in the Form. But carrying a private feud into football was beyond the limit, and quite unlike Bob. And as Tom Merry & Co. were coming over from St. Jim's that afternoon, Bob was wanted. To stand out of the team, simply because he disliked a fellow who was in it, was not a thing that any fellow could do. But Bob, apparently, was going to do it, all the same.

"You know you're wanted in the game!" said Harry Wharton tartly. "Smithy throws his weight about sometimes, because he can't be spared—are you taking a leaf out of Smithy's book, Bob?"

Bob crimsoned.

"Oh, don't be an ass!" he snapped. "I can't stand that man Carter, and I won't! He hacked me, in the Highcliffe match, and put me out of the game. He didn't care a bean if we were beaten, so long as he scored over me! That's not the man you ought to play for the Remove! I'd never play him, if I were skipper."

"That must have been an accident! Anyhow, you can chance it—are you afraid of a hack?" growled Johnny Bull.

"I tell you, I can't stand him, and won't! He would play the same trick over again, if he got a chance! But that's not all. The fellow's a reptile!" growled Bob. "He's been playing dirty, treacherous trickery ever since he came here. He's up against that fat ass, Bunter——"

"Oh, blow Bunter!" said Frank Nugent.

"For goodness' sake, let that drop!" exclaimed Harry Wharton. "Bunter and Carter, and their silly squabbles, have got nothing to do with footer."

"I tell you——"

"It's no good telling me what I know! Bunter's gabbled all over the Lower School that old Joseph Carter is turning down his nephew and taking up the fat chump—and I dare say it's all gas, and I don't care a boiled bean whether it is or not! Bother the pair of them,"

exclaimed the exasperated captain of the Remove. "What's all that got to do with Soccer?"

"Well, it's got something to do with it!" grunted Bob. "Carter hacked me in a match and stopped my game because I've stood up for Bunter, and for no other reason. And I tell you, I won't stand by and see that fat fool diddled and done by a cunning rascal."

"Do you feel fearfully concerned where old Joe Carter leaves his money if he's got any?" asked Johnny Bull sarcastically.

"Oh, don't talk rot! That's got nothing to do with me. But you all know that the old ass wrote to Quelch about Bunter's report this term—Quelch told Bunter so, and Bunter told everybody who would listen. Carter's out to get him a bad report, and dish him with the old bean. And he sticks at nothing at all to get by with it."

"And Bunter's so keen on a good report!" said Johnny Bull, still sarcastic. "He slacks in class, slacks at prep, slacks at games, snoops grub in the studies, and writes idiotic limericks about his beak—he doesn't need much help from Carter to get a rotten bad report."

"That's his look-out—so long as Carter leaves him alone! He's going to have fair play!" snorted Bob. "That limerick this morning was another sample—that was Carter's work, as I know jolly well."

"Why, you howling ass!" roared Johnny. "We all saw Bunter showing it off in the studies last night, like the blithering chump he is."

"I know that! But he never meant Quelch to see it—he's not such a fool as that! Who pinned it up in the Form-room?"

"Bunter, I suppose——"

"Well, you're an ass, then! It was Carter."

"You mean to say you saw him?" exclaimed Johnny.

"Of course I didn't!" howled Bob. "Does the rotter ever let anybody see him at his dirty tricks?"

"Then how do you know?"

"Well, I do know! I know Carter did it because it was done to land that fat frump in another row with Quelch, and nobody but Carter is worm enough to do it."

"Oh, my hat! Are you going to say next that Carter made Bunter write the limerick in the first place?"

"Bunter scribbled that rot because he's a fool! Carter put it up under Quelch's nose because he's a rogue."

"You'd make no end of a judge on the bench, old chap—finding people guilty without evidence because you've got a down on them."

"The downfulness on the absurd Carter is terrific!" remarked Hurree Jamset Ram Singh. "But——"

"But it's got nothing to do with Soccer!" said Harry Wharton. "I don't see putting everything on a fellow without any evidence; but even if you're right, Bob, it's got nothing to do with the St. Jim's match."

"Why do you want to play the fellow?" growled Bob. "He's new here—he only came this term. Plenty of good men in the Remove."

"That's rot!" said Wharton at once. "I don't like Carter much personally, and you may be right about him; but is that going to prevent me from seeing that he's one of the best wingers we've got? He's as good as Smithy—and doesn't put on such thumping airs about it, either."

"Well, he's good at Soccer!" admitted Bob. "Not what I should expect of such a cur; but he can play Soccer,

Still, you're not short of wingers! Franky here can play a good game."

"Thanks!" said Nugent, laughing. "I'd be glad, too! But that man Carter can play my head off, and you know it, Bob."

"Redwing's a good man—so is Russell —so is Ogilvy—old Oggy is the man you want. A good winger, and as straight as a string——"

Harry Wharton laughed.

"I'll take your advice about any man but Carter," he said. "We've got a prize-packet in that chap! The last few weeks he's come out wonderfully. You know it as well as I do, Bob! There's no reason why he shouldn't play, except that you've got a down on him——"

"Well, that's no reason!" said Bob. "You're skipper! If you're satisfied with him, play him, but leave me out!"

"That's not sense," said Harry, "and if you want it plain, it's not sporting either! You've no right to let the team down."

"I should have to let the team down, if that tricky cad got a chance of crocking me in the game, as he did before."

"Smithy's down on him, too, but he hasn't crocked Smithy."

"No—because Smithy told him that if he had any accidents with him, he'd smash him up afterwards. He won't have any accidents with the Bounder!" said Bob scornfully. "Smithy isn't the man to take it as I did."

"Well, it's no good talking!" said the captain of the Remove. "I can't leave out a good man simply because you bar him. Will you play or not?"

"No!"

"That does it, then!"

The Famous Five were discussing the matter in the Rag after dinner. The Remove football list was posted there.

Harry Wharton crossed over to it, taking a pencil from his pocket.

Bob's name was in the list, as right-half. Wharton had put it there, regardless of Bob's repeated declarations that he would not play in the same team with Arthur Carter. Now, however, he had to take it out.

He drew the pencil through "R. Cherry," and wrote underneath it "T. Redwing." His friends watched him in silence.

Bob Cherry opened his lips—but he closed them again.

It gave him a pang to see his name marked out—though he had asked for it, and indeed insisted on it. Neither was he quite satisfied with the line he was taking. Private rows had nothing to do with Soccer, and ought not to have been carried on to the football field. Still, if it takes two to make a quarrel, equally it takes two to keep the peace. Bob Cherry was willing, and eager, to dismiss personal animosities for ninety minutes, but he knew that Carter was not. The other fellows simply could not get it into their heads that any man could be base enough to crock a man on his own side, to pay out a private score, at the risk of throwing away the game. But Bob, who had been through it, knew.

Still, he was far from satisfied, and it was bitterly unpleasant to realise that he was falling in the estimation of his friends.

Harry Wharton, having finished making the alteration in the football list, looked round at him—a last mute appeal. He was more than willing to erase that alteration, if Bob made a sign.

Bob hesitated.

At that moment, Arthur Carter came into the Rag. At the sight of him, Bob's face hardened, and his eyes gleamed. The mere sight of the new

fellow seemed to have the effect on Bob of a red rag on a bull.

Carter glanced at the Famous Five, and then at the football list. He raised his eyebrows a little.

"Cherry out?" he asked. "What's up?" He looked round at Bob. "Not feeling fit, Cherry?"

Grunt!—from Bob. He did not choose to answer Carter. The new junior stared at him, and then smiled.

"Is it my fault?" he asked. "I've heard the fellows saying that Cherry won't play in the match if I do. Is that the truth, Cherry?"

"Yes!" growled Bob.

"Is that what you call sporting?"

Bob's eyes flashed.

"You know a lot about sporting!" he snorted. "Is it what you call sporting to stick Bunter's silly limerick up in the Form-room for Quelch to see?"

"Did I?" yawned Carter.

"I know you did!"

"You know more than I do, then!" said Carter, laughing. "I'd never even heard of the rot before I saw it where that fat ass stuck it up on the blackboard! As the fat ass is a relation of mine, I'd have stopped him if I could——"

"Oh, shut up!" snapped Bob, in disgust. "Bunter's always been a fool, but he was never incessantly landed for it before you came here!"

"Oh, give Bunter a rest!" exclaimed Harry Wharton. "I can tell you I'm fed-up with Bunter!"

"The fed-upfulness is terrific!"

"Let's get out!" growled Johnny Bull. "Bob can row with Carter without our help."

"But I'm not going to row," said Carter "I think it's rather hard lines that I'm to be held responsible for every silly trick played by the biggest fool at Greyfriars! If Cherry's so fearfully concerned about Bunter, he might have taken that silly limerick away from him and chucked it in the fire."

"So I would have if I'd known you had an eye on it and intended to pinch it to stick up in the Form-room!" grunted Bob. "You've not been so jolly successful as you fancy, though. You've landed that fat ass, but I'm going to Quelch about it. I'm going to square it for Bunter if I can."

Carter stared at him, and laughed.

"Best of luck!" he said. "Quelch may possibly want something in the nature of evidence if you mention my name."

"I'm not going to mention your name, as you jolly well know. But I'm going to tell Quelch that Bunter never stuck that cheeky rot on the blackboard as he believes. Quelch knows he wrote it, but it was sticking it up in the Form-room that got his goat; and I believe I can clear that up, anyhow."

And with that, Bob Cherry stalked out of the Rag, leaving Carter shrugging his shoulders. And the football list remained as it was

---

THE THIRD CHAPTER.

Not Pally!

"BE a pal, Toddy, old man!"

Peter Todd of the Remove grunted. Peter was feeling merry and bright that afternoon. It was a half-holiday, and he was in the team to play St. Jim's when they came. And he was sorry for Bunter—under detention, and with an imposition of five hundred lines hanging over his fat head. Still, he did not want to cash Billy Bunter's celebrated postal order, which was always expected, but never came. He groped in his pocket for a "bob"

"If a bob's any use——" he said.

"Oh, yes! Rather!" said Bunter. He held out a fat hand All was grist that came to Bunter's mill. "Thanks, old chap! I say, can you make it two?"

"No!" grunted Toddy

"I shouldn't like to be close with money, like you are, Toddy!" said Bunter, shaking his head. "Openhanded generosity—that's my way! Still, if a fellow's stingy, I suppose he can't help it!"

Having thus expressed his thanks to Toddy for the loan of a shilling, Bunter slipped the same into his pocket.

"I say, don't clear off Toddy!" he added. "I haven't said what I was going to say to you. Be a pal, old chap!"

Peter stared at him. He glared at him He had taken it for granted that Bunter was after a little loan. But it was, apparently, some other matter in which the fat Owl of the Remove wanted him to be a pal. That bob was a sheer waste, in the circumstances.

"It's about my detention," explained Bunter. "You know that awful beast Quelch has given me a detention this afternoon! I say, Toddy, don't walk out of the study when a fellow's talking to you! I say, old chap, I want you to be a pal. Quelch thinks I wrote that limerick——"

"He knows you did, you fat ass!"

"Well, he thinks I did because it was jolly clever, and he knows I'm a clever chap!" admitted Bunter. "But that ain't proof, you know."

"Oh crumbs!" said Toddy.

"I mean to say, putting down a clever thing to me because I'm clever ain't fair, any more than putting down silly things to you because you're a fool, old chap! You see that?" argued Bunter.

"Fan me!" murmured Toddy.

"Well, I want you to be a pal," said Bunter. "You go to Quelch, and tell him that I never wrote that limerick, and——"

"But you did!" yelled Peter.

"I wish you'd keep to the point, Toddy! What I want is to get off detention," explained Bunter. "You tell Quelch that I never wrote that limerick, to your certain knowledge—see? Ten to one he will believe you. If he doesn't there's no harm done. It's only just the trouble of walking to his study. I'd do more than that for a pal."

Peter Todd glanced round Study No. 7, as if in search of something.

Billy Bunter blinked at him impatiently through his big spectacles.

"You're not paying attention, Toddy!" he exclaimed. "What the thump are you looking for?"

"The cushion!"

"I'm sitting on it! You don't want the cushion now, Peter. What the dickens do you want the cushion for?" exclaimed Bunter irritably.

"All right! This book will do!" said Peter. "I only want to chuck it at you, old fat man! Here you are!"

Bang!

"Ow! Beast! Ow!" roared Bunter, as the volume banged on a fat chin. "Why, you rotter! Wharrer you chucking things at me for? Beast!"

Peter, chuckling, left the study without lingering to explain why he was chucking things at Bunter.

The fat junior was left rubbing his podgy chin and grunting with wrath.

There was a step in the passage, and Bob Cherry looked into Study No 7.

Bunter gave him a ferocious glare

"Get out, you beast!" he hooted.

"Hallo, hallo, hallo! What——"

"Oh! Is it you! I thought it was that other beast come back! I say,

Bob, Toddy's just gone down the passage! Go after him and kick him, will you?"

"Why?" asked Bob, laughing.

"Chucking a book at a chap, just because I asked him to go to Quelch's study!" said Bunter. "Lazy, you know! Rotten slacker! But I say, old chap, you can do it for me, if you like. Will you?"

"Yes, when I go down. What is it you want me to say to Quelch?"

"Tell him I never wrote that limerick, and——"

"But you did!" said Bob, staring.

"That's just what Toddy said when I asked him!" exclaimed Bunter, in great exasperation. "His very words! You seem to be just as fatheaded as Toddy! Can't you talk sense for once?"

"You fat, flabby, frabjous freak!" growled Bob. "I've a jolly good mind to boot you round your study! You ask me to go and tell Quelch lies again, and I'll do it, too!"

"Beast!"

Bob, who had stepped into the study, made a step back towards the door. He was strongly tempted to leave the fat Owl to his fate, but he stopped.

"Look here, Bunter, I came to speak to you," he said. "You've said that you did not stick up that limerick in the Form-room. Is that the truth?"

"If you're going to hint that I tell lies, Cherry——"

"You fat chump!" roared Bob. "Did you or not?"

"No, I didn't!" howled Bunter. "As if I'd get Quelch down on me like a ton of bricks! Some cad sneaked it from my study and stuck it up there!"

"Who do you think?"

"That cad Carter, I expect!" snorted Bunter "Isn't he always playing rotten tricks to land me with Quelch? He wants me to get a bad report this term. If I do, I lose my chance with old Joe Carter. That's what he wants. I believe he'd be glad if I got sacked—and me his relation, too! You'd expect a fellow to be proud to find a relation like me at his new school, wouldn't you? But is he? No fear!"

"Well, you're such a fearful fibber, no fellow can believe a word you say!" growled Bob. "But I believe you never put that cheeky rot up on the blackboard, and I'm going to Quelch to tell him so It may get you off."

Billy Bunter brightened.

"Good!" he exclaimed. "Now you're talking sense! Tell him at the same time that I never wrote it, won't you?"

"No!" roared Bob.

"I mean to say, you may as well do the job thoroughly!" urged Bunter. "What I want is to get off detention. That's important."

"I'm going to tell him the truth, you fat idiot—just that, and no more and no less!"

"You keep on wandering from the point, Cherry! Keep your mind on the main point—that's getting me off detention! And the lines, too, you know! If Quelch believes I never had anything to do with that limerick, he will let me off detention and lines! Dash it all, I think that's worth the trouble of going to his study and jawing for a few minutes!" said Bunter warmly. "Tell him that you know, for a fact, that I never had anything to do with it! Just go into his study and say—yarooooh! Leggo, you beast!"

Billy Bunter roared as his fat neck was grabbed and his fat head banged against the back of an armchair. He roared frantically

"There!" gasped Bob, and with a final bang, he released Bunter's fat

neck and walked out of Study No. 7.

"Beast!" roared Bunter. "Yah! Rotter! Beast! Wow! Beast!"

He rolled to the doorway, and shook a fat fist after Bob as he tramped away to the stairs.

Herbert Vernon-Smith came out of Study No. 4 and stared at him.

"What's that game?" he asked.

"I say, Smithy, hold on a minute, old chap!" said Bunter eagerly. "I say, think it would be any good if you went to Quelch and told him that I never wrote that limerick? I'd rather Cherry did, because Quelch knows you tell lies——"

"Eh?"

"Still, it's worth trying on," said Bunter. "Cherry makes out that he can't go and tell lies, but I know you don't mind, old chap—it's in your line, ain't it? A few more won't hurt you, Smithy! I'd ask Mauleverer, but, of course, he's not the sort of chap I could ask to do it—but you are, old fellow. Go to Quelch and say that I never—yoo—hooooop!"

Why Smithy cut along to his study door, and kicked him, Bunter did not know. But he knew that Smithy did—quite a hefty kick! The fat Owl bounded back into the study and slammed the door! It looked as if Bunter was booked for detention that afternoon, unless the truth could save him! And that was not a resource on which William George Bunter was accustomed to place much reliance!

THE FOURTH CHAPTER.

Alibi for Bunter!

BOB CHERRY stopped at the door of his Form-master's study, and hesitated. But he had made up his mind, and he tapped at the door.

"Come in!"

Bob entered.

Mr. Quelch was seated at his table, with a pile of Latin papers before him. He had about thirty papers to go through that afternoon before he was at leisure. It was a half-holiday for the Remove, but not for their Form-master. No doubt that was the reason why Quelch gave Bob a glance of impatient inquiry Interruptions were not welcome.

"What is it, Cherry?" he rapped.

Bob stood before the table, with the colour deep in his cheeks. He had determined to speak to Quelch—but it was not an easy task. Exasperating ass as Billy Bunter was, he was going to have fair play, if Bob could help. For the rivalry between the two relations of old Mr. Carter, Bob did not care a straw—it had not the slightest interest for him. But in that peculiar contest between a rogue and a fool, Bob was on the side of the fool!

"It's about Bunter, sir!" blurted out Bob "I think I ought to tell you, sir, that Bunter never put up that silly paper in the Form-room this morning."

"Nonsense!" snapped Mr. Quelch. "It was in Bunter's hand, and was certainly his work, Cherry! What do you mean? I have no doubt that many boys in the Form had seen it before. I judged so by their looks!"

"I know sir! Bunter did it, but he never put it up on the blackboard! He never meant you to see it."

"Oh!" said Mr. Quelch.

He laid down his pen and sat looking at Bob's flushed face, very attentively, across the table.

The limerick was, of course, extremely disrespectful, and ought never to have been composed by the fatuous fat Owl.

But Mr. Quelch was no fool—he was an experienced schoolmaster. He knew perfectly well that jokes and jests were constantly being made about the "beaks." They ought not to have been, doubtless; but they were! The fact that Bunter had written the limerick was a small matter, in comparison with his having posted it up in the Form-room. That was the head and front of his offending, so to speak. That was a direct insult and defiance, for which hardly any punishment could be too severe. If Bunter had not done that, the case was very much altered.

"Are you sure of this, Cherry?" asked Mr. Quelch, after a long pause.

"I'm quite sure of it, sir!" answered Bob. "I know Bunter never meant that silly thing to be seen outside the Form; and I know that he would never have had the nerve to put it where you saw it."

"Someone put it there!" said Mr. Quelch dryly.

"I know, sir—but not Bunter! Some other fellow picked it up in his study, and made that use of it."

Mr Quelch's look grew sharper.

"If that is the case, Cherry, such a boy must have known that the blame would be laid on Bunter!" he said.

Bob shifted uncomfortably. He could not mention Carter; that was sneaking, and sneaking was barred! Moreover, he had no atom of proof! He was certain; but his certainty was nothing to anyone but himself.

"I know it wasn't Bunter, sir!" he stammered. "I'm sure of that! I thought you ought to know."

"Certainly, I should be glad to know, if it is the case! But——"

"It was put up in break this morning, sir! Bunter was in sight of plenty of fellows most of the time. I saw him in the school-shop for quite ten minutes out of the fifteen."

"Can you state positively, Cherry, that Bunter had no opportunity, during break, of slipping away unobserved to the Form-room?"

"Well, I couldn't say so as a fact, sir, but I'm sure of it," said Bob. "I know he was under my eyes for two-thirds of the time, and he never went near the House at all. And I remember that when the bell went, he came cutting across the quad—he wasn't in the House."

Mr. Quelch drummed on the table for a moment or two, with his fingers. Bob could see that he was impressed.

"Unfortunately, Cherry, it is impossible to trust any statement made by Bunter," he said, at last. "And only Bunter can know for certain. However, there is certainly something in what you say. If Bunter was not guilty of that act of insolence in pinning the paper up in the Form-room, I shall certainly remit the remainder of his punishment."

He reflected for a moment.

"Break was at ten-forty-five this morning," he said. "You say that you saw Bunter for ten minutes——"

"Yes, sir—he cut across to the tuck-shop at once, and was there when I went in. It was only four or five minutes to eleven when he left. And third school was at eleven."

Mr. Quelch smiled faintly.

"I rely upon your word absolutely, Cherry! What you tell me of your own knowledge I take as a fact. If you can find some equally trustworthy boy who can account for Bunter's time until third school, you may ask him to come to my study and speak to me."

"Very well, sir!"

Bob left the study, and Quelch resumed Latin papers.

Bob's brow was thoughtful as he went.

" I say, can't you make it two, old chap ? " said Bunter, as Peter Todd placed a shilling in his fat palm. " No ! " grunted Toddy. " I shouldn't like to be close with money, like you are, Toddy," said Bunter. " Open generosity—that's my way. Still, some fellows can't help being stingy ! "

He walked across to the changing-room, where many of the Remove had already gathered.

"Oh, here you are, Cherry !" said Tom Redwing, with a cheery grin. "If you've changed your mind, I'm ready to stand down."

Bob shook his head.

"No—you go in and win, Reddy ! I say, did you happen to see Bunter in break this morning?"

"Yes, in the shop——"

"That's no good—I saw him there !" Bob looked round over a crowd of fellows. "Any of you see Bunter this morning after he got out of the grub-shop, and before the bell went?"

"What the dickens does it matter ?" demanded Johnny Bull.

"It matters a lot to Bunter !" answered Bob. "That putrid limerick was stuck on the blackboard in break. Bunter was in the shop till five minutes to eleven. If he did it, he did it in those minutes. I want to find some fellow who saw him at the time."

"Setting up as a detective ?" asked Carter, with a sneer.

Bob gave him a glare.

"I'm setting up to 'stop your rotten tricks !" he snorted. "When it's proved that Bunter never put that paper there, I'll leave it to all the fellows to guess who did !"

"Sing out, you men !" grinned Squiff. "Anybody see a fat pig rolling about just before third school ?"

"Ha, ha, ha !"

"Yes, I jolly well did !" said Ogilvy. "Bunter was trying to borrow a bob from me, just before the bell went."

"Bet you he never got it !" grinned Skinner.

"No he didn't ! But he jawed about his postal order," said Ogilvy. "He would have got one, if the bell hadn't rung."

Bob Cherry gave a chuckle

"That does it !" he said. "Was Bunter talking to you for five minutes, Oggy, old man ?"

"Quite ! It seemed more like fifty."

"Ha, ha, ha !"

"Come on, old man—Quelch wants to see a man who saw Bunter during that five minutes, and can say that he never went to the Form-room !" exclaimed Bob.

"He might have gone before I saw him——"

"No, he didn't; he was in the shop. I was there. This is a jolly old alibi for Bunter—clears him all along the line !" chuckled Bob. "Come on—you've got to tell Quelch that !"

"Oh, all right !" said the good-natured Scottish junior; and he left the changing-room with Bob.

Carter cast a dark and bitter look after Bob as he went. Bob Cherry was about the last fellow in the Remove who might have been expected to put in detective work like this ! Not for the first time Bob had put "paid " to the schemer of the Remove ! The thing had been landed on Bunter, without a spot of doubt in Quelch's mind—and Bob Cherry had knocked it completely on the head ! For it was clear that, with Bunter's time all through break accounted for, he could not have been the fellow who had slipped into the Form-room and pinned that disrespectful paper on the blackboard !

Harry Wharton gave Carter a sharp, searching look.

"So it seems that it was not Bunter, after all !" he said slowly. "Was it you, Carter?"

"Thanks for the question !" drawled Carter "Was it you ?"

"Wha-a-t ?"

"Well, you asked me ! Can't I ask you ?"

"Sauce for the goose is sauce for the gander !" grinned Skinner "Answer up, Wharton ! Was it you ?"

"Oh, shut up !" snapped Harry.

Ogilvy came back to the changing-room a few minutes later.

"Bunter's all right," he said.

"Quelch has sent for him to let him off detention ! Lucky old porpoise !" He glanced round. "But who the dickens found Bunter's silly paper and stuck it up in the Form-room? It was a dirty trick, whoever did it !"

Many eyes turned on Carter. He walked out of the changing-room with an air of indifference, but with bitter chagrin and rage in his heart.

———

THE FIFTH CHAPTER.
Bunter Knows How !

"I SAY, Bob——"

"Oh, don't bother !" grunted Bob.

Bob Cherry was not in the best of spirits.

His usually sunny face was clouded, and he was walking aimlessly under the elms, his hands driven deep in his pockets.

It was a fine, cold, clear afternoon, glorious for football. Bob fairly yearned to be in the Remove eleven. There were few things he would not have given to line up with his friends when Tom Merry & Co. arrived.

Instead of which he was strolling aimlessly about, keeping a distance from the cheery crowd in the changing-room. It was seldom that Bob felt "out of it " in matters of games; but he was utterly out of it now Three members of the Co. were in the team; Frank Nugent was with them, and Bob was left on his own

He was wondering, rather dismally, whether perhaps he had not made a mistake in standing out.

More than his own keen desire to play, there was the fact that he was wanted in the eleven And Carter, after all, was not likely to play the same treacherous trick twice—it would look a little too palpable. Bob realised that he had allowed his intense loathing for the cunning trickster to overcome his judgment. He was needed in the side, and he ought to have played, and that fact dawned on him as he thought it over—too late to be of any use. Wanted or not, he could not barge in now and claim the place that had been given to Redwing.

In that dismal frame of mind, he was far from pleased to see Bunter. He was feeling solitary; but there were worse things than solitude, and Bunter's company was one of them.

That, however, did not occur to Bunter. Bunter knew, if Bob did not, that his company was a boon and a blessing.

"Anything up, old chap?" asked Bunter affably.

"Oh, yes! No! Roll off!"

"I say, I've got off detention and the lines, too!" grinned Bunter. "You were rather a beast in the study, Cherry; but it was jolly decent of you to go and put it to Quelch. He's let me off with the licking I had in the Form-room. He said that that was sufficient punishment for having written disrespectful nonsense—and that he was satisfied that I never put it up in the Form-room! It's a bit odd that he took your word when he wouldn't take mine, ain't it?"

Bob laughed.

"I mean to say, a Form-master ought to take a fellow's word," said Bunter. "It would make things so much easier, you know. A chap could get by with anything. But the fact is, Quelch is no gentleman!"

"Ass!"

"Oh, really, Cherry! I say, ain't you playing football?"

"No!"

"Oh! Because Wharton's put that cad in the team! I know," said Bunter. "Quite right, old chap! I wouldn't play in the same team with him, either! No good Wharton asking me—I should refuse!"

"Fathead!"

"I say, I'm going to make that cad Carter sit up!" went on Bunter confidentially. "I've been thinking it out, and I know how, too! He keeps on landing me with Quelch, to get me a bad report. Well, sauce for the goose is sauce for the gander! I'm jolly well going to land him, see? I say, don't you mention to him about me being a ventriloquist."

"Bother you and your ventriloquism!"

"I mean, as he's new here, he doesn't know anything about it," explained Bunter. "I can pull his leg all right. You know what a wonderful ventriloquist I am, Cherry——"

"I know what a thumping ass you are!"

"Beast! I say, you seem in a jolly bad temper this afternoon," said the fat Owl, blinking at Bob's moody face. "You've done me a good turn, old chap! I'd like to cheer you up. I say, come over to Cliff House with me and see my sister Bessie!"

"Oh, my hat!" said Bob.

It did not seem to him that a view of Bunter's sister Bessie would have a fearfully cheering effect on his spirits.

"I'll take you, if you'll stand a taxi!" said Bunter. "I don't want to walk. Might see Marjorie Hazeldene. You can talk to Bessie, while I talk to Marjorie. She'd like that! What about it?"

"Chump!"

"Those St. Jim's chaps will be blowing in before long," remarked Bunter. "I want to see that fellow D'Arcy—

rather an old pal of mine. I'll tell you what, Cherry—you'd like to play——"

"Of course I should!" grunted Bob. "Don't be an ass!"

"Well, suppose Carter stood out——"

"He won't, ass!"

"Well, he might!" said Bunter. To Bob's surprise, the fat Owl gave him a sly, fat wink. "I might manage it!"

"You! You ass!"

"Oh, really, Cherry——"

"Give us a rest, for goodness' sake!" growled Bob, and he walked away, more than satisfied with what he had had of the pleasure of Billy Bunter's company.

"Beast!" squeaked Bunter.

The fat junior rolled away to the changing-room. There was a grin on his face and a sly twinkle in his little round eyes behind his spectacles. Bunter was on the warpath!

He had been thinking this over! In dealing with Carter, he was about as useful as a fat rabbit dealing with a fox. But there was one weapon in Bunter's fat hands of which Carter knew nothing.

The Remove fellows generally knew all about Bunter's ventriloquism. They were, in fact, fed up with it. They admitted that it was an extraordinary gift, and that Bunter did it well—but they had heard enough of it, in fact, a little too much, and did not want any more.

But Carter, the new junior, had no knowledge of it. Carter was the only man in the Remove on whom Bunter could hope to play ventriloquial tricks without getting spotted! But Carter was an easy victim! Now that this idea had occurred to Billy Bunter's fat brain, he saw ahead of him a chance of scoring over the fellow who was continually landing him in the soup.

He blinked in at the doorway of the changing-room.

"I say, you fellows, is Carter here?" he asked.

"He was—but he's gone!" answered Harry Wharton. "It's not time to change yet! Roll away!"

"But, I say, where is he?"

"I don't know—or care, either! Cut!"

"Beast!"

Billy Bunter rolled away in search of Carter. Quite a masterly scheme was outlined in Bunter's podgy brain—founded upon the circumstance that Arthur Carter did not know that he was a ventriloquist! That weird and wonderful gift was—Bunter hoped, at least—going to land Carter in the soup, in which he had so often landed Bunter that term.

He found Carter in his study—No. 1 in the Remove. The new junior was sitting by the window, looking over a newspaper, when Bunter opened the door and blinked in.

He put the paper hastily out of sight, as the door opened. It was a pink paper, devoted to "gee-gees" and the activities of bookmakers. That was a subject in which Arthur Carter was deeply interested. With all his cunning, and all his knavery, he was, in actual fact, one of the "mugs" on which that noble profession subsists! Since he had fallen from his old uncle's good graces, his pocket-money had been strictly limited; but, such as it was, most of it ran away on "dead certs" that came in tenth or eleventh!

But the fellow who had been sacked from St. Olaf's for "blagging" was very careful to keep up appearances, so far as he could, at Greyfriars. Only when he was alone did Carter's sporting papers or cigarettes come into view.

Now he was almost caught, as the study door opened suddenly, without a knock, and Billy Bunter's spectacles glimmered in.

But the pink paper vanished on the instant, and with the same movement Carter picked up a "Caesar."

Billy Bunter blinked across the study at him. He favoured him with a fat sneer, as he saw the school-book in his hand.

"Swotting?" jeered Bunter.

Carter suppressed a grin! That was exactly the impression he had wanted to give, if Bunter had only known it.

"Get out, you fat lout!" he said.

"Cheeky beast——"

Whiz!

Caesar's "Gallic War" flew across the study, and landed on Bunter's fat little nose! No schoolboy ever found the "Gallic War" grateful or comforting; but never had Billy Bunter found it so disagreeable as at that moment.

"Ow!" roared Bunter.

He tottered back into the passage.

"Shut that door!" snapped Carter. He was anxious to get back to the gee-gees and the odds.

The next moment, Carter gave a jump. From the passage, barking through the half-open doorway, came a familiar voice—the voice of Henry Samuel Quelch, master of the Remove—or else its twin!

"Carter! Are you in your study, Carter?"

"Oh! Yes, sir!" gasped Carter.

He jumped to his feet, deeply thankful that the pink paper was safely out of sight!

THE SIXTH CHAPTER.

Ventriloquial Vengeance!

"CARTER!"

"Yes, sir!"

"I have discovered who pinned that insolent paper in the Form-room this morning!"

"Oh!" gasped Carter.

He stood staring towards the doorway of the study. As Mr. Quelch was addressing him, he naturally expected his Form-master to step in.

But Mr. Quelch did not step in!

As Mr. Quelch, at that moment, was sitting in his own study, busy with Latin papers, he was not likely to step into a junior study!

Billy Bunter was alone, outside the door. That imperative bark, which any Remove man could have sworn was Mr. Quelch's voice, proceeded from the fat ventriloquist of the Remove!

Bunter was quite an adept in that kind of thing. Any voice that had any distinctive quality, Bunter could imitate like a parrot; and there was no doubt that Quelch's voice was distinctive.

"It was not I, sir!" gasped Carter, "I——"

"Silence, Carter!" came the bark, "I am perfectly well aware that you abstracted that paper, and pinned it up in the Form-room."

"I—I assure you, sir——"

"I repeat, silence! You will remain in detention this afternoon, Carter. Take your French books, and go to Class-room No. 10. You will report to Monsieur Charpentier that I have sent you."

"But, sir——" gasped Carter in dismay.

"Enough!"

"I'm in the football team, sir—the St. Jim's men will be here in half an hour, and——"

"Silence, Carter !"

The door slammed, pulled shut from outside.

Carter stood staring at it in blank surprise and rage.

How Mr. Quelch had spotted him, as the fellow who had pinned up the limerick. he could not begin to guess; but it seemed that Quelch had no doubt about it ! Anyhow, he was booked for the detention class, and there was no help for that !

In deep and concentrated fury, the schemer of the Remove sorted out his French class-books, to take down to Class-room No. 10.

Billy Bunter rolled down the passage to the stairs, grinning.

He had a pain in his fat little nose; but he hardly heeded it, in his satisfaction at having pulled Carter's leg so completely.

Carter had been completely taken in ! No doubt that he was surprised that his Form-master had barked at him, without looking into the study. But he could hardly doubt that Quelch was there, when he heard Quelch's voice. So far from suspecting Bunter of tricking him, he would hardly have believed that Bunter could have done it, had he been told. Without a doubt in his mind, Carter gathered his French books for the detention class.

Bunter was loafing at the foot of the staircase, when Carter came down. Carter gave him a scowl in passing. Bunter blinked at the books under his arm, and grinned from ear to ear.

He rolled after Carter, as the new fellow cut away hastily to the changing-room. He had to let his captain know that he would not be playing that afternoon.

Some of the footballers were changing now. Others were talking together

(*Continued on next page.*)

LEARN TO PLAY FOOTBALL!
OUR INTERNATIONAL COACH

NOW that we have dealt with all those players whose job it is to look after the defensive side of a football team, it is time we carried on to talk about the attackers. That is not to suggest that the attackers and defenders in a football side are separate, and have nothing to do with each other.

I have tried to make you realise, in these lessons, that the success of a football team depends upon the way all the players work together, and help one another. The attack and the defence are really closely linked. But for the sake of simplicity we usually divide footballers into two classes—attackers and defenders. I propose to tell you all I know about the work of the attackers.

Before we start. let me get something off my chest which I feel may be bothering you. I have an idea that some of you think a great deal of this fairly advanced stuff about football which I am passing on to you is not much good for the sort of football you are playing.

It is true that some of the things I tell you about football may not be necessary for you just yet But I imagine that every boy who plays football wants to keep on playing when he grows up, and yearns to be really good at the game. Hence I tell you of things which may seem a bit difficult, because I think that if you try to do things in the right way now, you will find it much easier to do them right when you get to the higher standard of football. You see the idea ? I am not content just with making you into good schoolboy footballers. I want to make you into Internationals. And I shan't do that if I leave out some of the most important lessons about the game just because they seem a bit unnecessary for the class of football in which you are playing now.

ALWAYS IN THE WARS

SO to progress with attacking ideas. We'll deal with the centre-forward first To be a centre-forward you have certainly to be a tough 'un—big, strong, and able to stand a lot of buffeting. You need only read the reports of first-class football matches to realise what some centre-forwards have to put up with.

To be a star centre-forward, chum, you've got to be a real tough 'un—able to take plenty of knocks and bruises. Our special reporter's had some and knows !

It is a fact that three of the best centre-forwards in the game to-day have been badly in the wars more or less all through this season. Ernest Glover, of Grimsby Town, hasn't played since the first day of the season. Ted Drake, one of the strongest fellows you could imagine. has been in and out of the Arsenal team with injury after injury, and Fred Steele, of Stoke, has been the same. Oh, yes, you must be tough to be a centre-forward.

You want to know why centre-forwards get hurt more than other players. I think I can explain fairly easily. The centre-forward is looked upon as the spear-head of the attack. He is the man who is expected to turn the good play of his colleagues into goals—the point of the attacking arrow. You know that if the point of an arrow gets blunted. the arrow doesn't do its job properly. Defenders of football teams know that, too. They realise that if they can shut the spear-head out of the game, the rest of the attack won't be nearly so effective, however well it plays.

I am not saying that it is the fault of the defenders that centre-forwards get hurt. Don't think for a moment that halves and full-backs set out to "blunt" the centre-forward by injuring him. What they do is to concentrate on seeing that the centre-forward doesn't get the ball, or be given much room to work in. Perhaps, in order to make sure he doesn't get a look in, two or three defenders go for him at the same time. Is it any wonder that groggy knees and strained muscles are the result?

It is because of this desire to blunt the spear-head of the attack that the stopper centre-half, whom I told you all about a week or two ago, has been invented. I mentioned that the instructions the centre-half gets when he goes out to play a game, are that he must stop the opposing centre-forward. So it comes about that the chief job of the centre-forward is to prevent himself being "blunted " by the stopper centre-half. And. believe me, that is no light job.

QUICK OFF THE MARK

PERHAPS the first essential for a centre-forward, after his strength and toughness, is that he should be quick. By that I don't mean that he must be able to run fast—do a hundred yards in ten seconds, or anything like that. He must be quick in his movements, and "quick off the mark." When footballers are running races they don't have them over long distances. They have races over twenty yards. You see, it's pace over the first few yards which matters in football. The man who starts quickest will get there first. So a centre-forward must be quick.

He must, of course, be a good dribbler —but that goes for all footballers, whatever position they play in. The ability to use both feet goes for all footballers, too; but the centre-forward must be specially good at it. He must be able to shoot accurately with either foot. If he has to change the ball over on to his best foot when he gets a chance to score, the odds are that the ball won't be there by the time he is ready. It is also important that a centre-forward should be specially good at heading, but we have agreed that there shall be none of that in our games for the time being, because somebody might get hurt.

Even with all these things in his favour, however, there can be no guarantee that the centre-forward will overcome the fellows who try to blunt him. To do this he will probably have to think out all sorts of dodges, and have secret plans with his colleagues, to change positions, and that sort of thing. But I will have some more to say next week about how the centre-forward can make himself a nuisance to the stopper centre-half, and how he can be helped to do this by his forward colleagues.

THE MAGNET LIBRARY.—No. 1,567

—and all of them looked round, at the sight of Carter's angry savage face.

"You've got to leave me out, Wharton," said Carter curtly.

"What the dickens do you mean?" asked the captain of the Remove, testily.

"I've got a detention."

Wharton stared at him.

"A detention! You were here a quarter of an hour ago—have you gone round collecting detentions since then?"

"That old fool Quelch came up to my study and told me!" snarled Carter. "He's got it into his head that I pinned up that paper in the Form-room this morning—you can thank Cherry for it; I've no doubt he worked it."

"Rubbish! I'm sure Bob never mentioned your name to Quelch."

"Looks as if he did!" sneered Carter, "I've got a detention, anyhow—and I've got to get to Mossoo's class-room! I thought I'd tell you."

"Well, my hat!"

Carter slouched savagely away. He was disappointed, as well as enraged. It was a redeeming point in his character that he was keen on Soccer, and played a good game. He was still keener, perhaps, on keeping Bob Cherry out of the game; and it was only his presence in the team that kept Bob out. He was in his blackest mood, as he tramped away to the detention-room.

Harry Wharton drew a deep breath.

"Well, this puts the lid on!" he said. "Another man gone from the team—thank goodness you're here, Oggy! You'll play?"

"Like a bird!" grinned Ogilvy.

"And Bob——" said Frank Nugent.

"Redwing's put in—we can't chop and change like that!" grunted the captain of the Remove. "All right, Reddy—you play."

"All wrong—I don't!" said Tom Redwing with a smile. "I'll go and find Cherry——"

"Look here——" began Vernon-Smith The Bounder was keen to see his chum in the St. Jim's match. "Look here. Reddy, don't be an ass——"

"Exactly!" agreed Tom. "I'm not ass enough to take Cherry's place, if he will play—and he will now! You want him, Wharton?"

"Well, yes, only it's not fair on you, said Harry, slowly.

"That's all right!"

Tom Redwing left the changing-room, to look for Bob. He found him "mooching" dismally in the quad, and dragged him along, explaining matters on the way.

Bob was looking rather bewildered, as he came into the changing-room, but his face was much brighter.

"Reddy says you want me——" he began.

"Yes; Reddy's standing out!" answered Harry. "So is Carter," he added, rather acidly, "so don't begin on that again."

Bob coloured.

"I'm ready and willing," he said. "I've been thinking it over, and I don't think I ought to have stood down."

"Glad you can see it!"

"But I can't understand Carter standing out," said Bob. "What the dickens is he chucking the match for? The only decent thing about him is that he's keen on footer."

"He's got a detention. Quelch thinks he played that silly trick with the limerick this morning. Carter thinks you put it into his head!"

"I never mentioned him to Quelch!" roared Bob.

"Well, Quelch seems to have jumped on him, anyhow—whether he's got it right or wrong."

"He's got it right!" growled Bob. "It was Carter! If Quelch has spotted him, serve him jolly well right! I'd like to see him spotted every time he plays a dirty trick."

"He, he, he!"

Billy Bunter, blinking into the changing-room through his big spectacles, chuckled gleefully Quelch, in his study, was blissfully unconscious of the fact that he was supposed to have sent Carter in to detention! Bunter found that reflection fearfully amusing.

Bob Cherry glanced round at him.

"Did you know that Carter was going to be detained, Bunter?" he asked.

"Eh? Oh, no! Not at all, old chap! How should I know?"

"You told me in the quad that he might stand out," said Bob. "Now he's got to stand out. Have you been to Quelch?"

"Oh, no! I had nothing to do with it!" said Bunter hastily "Besides, one good turn deserves another, you know."

"What?"

"I mean to say, you got me off with Quelch!" said Bunter. "Well, now you're going to play football. See?"

"What the dickens had you to do with it?" exclaimed Harry Wharton.

"Oh, nothing!"

"Then what do you mean, you fat ass?"

"Oh, nothing at all, old chap!" said Bunter: and he rolled away, leaving the footballers staring.

Certainly, no fellow in the changing-room had the faintest suspicion of Bunter's part in the affair.

There was general satisfaction in the team. Carter, good winger as he was, was little liked personally, and every fellow was glad to see Bob Cherry back in the eleven

That satisfaction was far from being shared by Arthur Carter. While the footballers were changing Carter was presenting himself at Class-room No. 10. where the French master had his detention class—a dozen hapless juniors who had extra French for their sins.

Monsieur Charpentier looked at him as he came in.

"Vat is it, Cartair?" he asked. "Vy you come here?"

"I'm in detention, sir!" grunted Carter sullenly.

"Mais, but Meester Quelch he have not given me your name!" said Mossoo.

"He's just told me to come here."

"Oh! Verree vell! You may take ze place, Cartair"

And Carter took his place in the detention class, and had the pleasure—or otherwise—of absorbing additional knowledge of the beautiful French language, while the Remove footballers were playing Tom Merry & Co., of St. Jim's.

<hr />

THE SEVENTH CHAPTER.

Pulling Smithy's Leg !

HERBERT VERNON-SMITH came up the Remove passage, with a black scowl on his face.

Billy Bunter, loafing in the doorway of Study No. 7, grinned at him.

Why Smithy was scowling so savagely Bunter did not know, but it rather amused him. When Smithy was in a

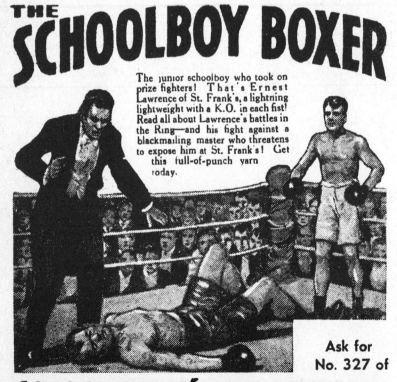

bad temper every fellow who had a view of him was made aware of the fact. Greyfriars fellows generally regarded a display of temper as one of the things that were "not done." but in such matters the Bounder was a law unto himself, which was one of the reasons why he had received his nickname.

Smithy had cause to be annoyed. Like other fellows in the Remove team, he had looked forward keenly to the St. Jim's match. Quite aware of his own quality, Smithy knew his value to the team, and he liked that value to be made quite clear in every match in which he played. On this occasion, the Bounder had not been at the top of his form, and the game had been anything but a triumph for him.

Not only had he failed to score, but he had lost his temper at a perfectly fair charge from Figgins of St. Jim's, which had washed out a promising chance, and he had dropped into some rough play, which had caused his captain to call him to order. So, when the game was over, Vernon-Smith got away from the changing-room as quickly as possible, instead of lingering with the cheery crowd there, and stalked away to his study with a black brow. And that black brow did not lighten, in the very least, at the sight of Billy Bunter's fat face grinning at him. In fact, it darkened still more.

"Bag any goals. Smithy?" squeaked Bunter.

He knew quite well, from the Bounder's look, that Smithy hadn't.

"Find out!" snarled the Bounder.

"He he, he!"

It was rather injudicious for Bunter to cackle, with the Bounder glaring at him, in the mood to punch the first head that came to hand!

Smithy passed his own study and came up the passage to Study No. 7. He grabbed the fat Owl's collar, slewed him round, and planted a boot on the tightest trousers at Greyfriars.

Bunter roared and sprawled

Feeling a little better—though leaving Bunter feeling a good deal worse—Smithy tramped back to Study No. 4, went in and slammed the door after him.

"Beast!" gasped Bunter

Bunter really had asked for it! But, like many people in this unreasonable universe, he did not like getting that for which he had asked.

He blinked out into the Remove passage, his eyes gleaming behind his spectacles.

The Bounder's slam had rung the length of the passage. So Bunter knew that he had closed his door

He crept on tiptoe to that door and stooped to the keyhole. Through the keyhole he emitted a howl.

"Yah! Cad! Swanking cad! You can't play footer for toffee! Marbles is your game! Yah!"

There was a sound of a chair scraping in the study as Smithy bounded up.

Bunter did not wait for him

He fairly shot into Study No. 3, which belonged to Ogilvy and Russell. They were down in the changing-room, and the study was empty. Bunter popped in. behind the door.

The next moment Smithy's door opened, and he tramped furiously out into the passage. Had Bunter been there something painful would undoubtedly have happened to Bunter. As Bunter was not there, Smithy supposed that he had cut back to his own study, and he tramped up to Study No. 7 after him.

Bunter, in a state of mingled glee and trepidation, grinned. Listening

intently with his fat ears, he heard the Bounder stamp into Study No. 7

He peered out into the passage. Smithy had gone into Study No. 7, and the coast, for the moment, was clear.

Bunter cut along to the next study, reached round the door, and extracted the key of Study No. 4 from the lock. Key in hand, he shot back into Ogilvy's study.

From Study No. 7 the Bounder's voice could be heard:

"You fat rotter, where are you? I'll burst you all over the Remove! Where are you, you fat pig?"

Bunter, safe in Ogilvy's study again, made no sound. He heard Smithy come back, a few moments later, and go into his own study. Another angry slam rang the length of the Remove passage.

Bunter did not need telling that Smithy had shut the door again.

He waited a couple of minutes, to give Vernon-Smith time to settle down. Then, on tiptoe, he crept along to Smithy's study and inserted the key into the outside of the lock.

Click !

The key turned.

Bunter suppressed a gleeful giggle. He heard an angry exclamation in the study as the Bounder heard the door locked on him.

Tramping feet came across the study to the door There was a wrench at the door-handle from within.

"By gad !" The Bounder's voice came in concentrated tones of rage. "Is that you, Bunter? Is that you, you fat fool? I'll smash you !"

Bunter made no answer to that.

Softly. on tiptoe, he crept away to Study No. 1, where he laid Smithy's key on the table There was a sound of sharp rapping on Smithy's door. The Bounder, a prisoner in his study, was raging. Whether it was Bunter or some other fellow who had played that trick on him, he did not know; but he wanted to get at the fellow, whoever he was.

Bunter grinned as he emerged from Study No. 1.

There was no one else up in the Remove at the time: the footballers had not come out of the changing-room, with the exception of Smithy. The Remove ventriloquist had a clear field. He walked along to Study No. 4, and at the sound of footsteps Vernon-Smith shouted from the interior of the study.

"Hold on, will you? I'm locked in !"

Smithy could not, of course, see who was in the passage, but he knew that it must be a Remove fellow

Bunter gave a little, fat cough, and answered, and his answer was in a voice quite unlike his own fat squeak. It was a rather high and sharp voice— the nearest imitation he could make of Carter's !

"Hallo! What's up?"

"Some fool's locked me in!" called back Smithy "Bunter, I think! Is that fat fool there?"

"I saw Bunter downstairs a minute or two ago," answered the sharp voice, which Smithy never dreamed of guessing came from Bunter.

"Somebody else, then! Is the key in the lock?"

"No."

"Is that Carter?" asked Vernon-Smith.

He thought that he recognised the sharp voice.

"You know it is!" answered the sharp voice.

"How should I know, you ass, when I can't see you?" snapped the Bounder. "Think I can see through an oak door?"

"You know my voice, I suppose,"

came the answering snap. "Why have you locked yourself in?"

"I haven't, you fool! Somebody bagged the key when I went out of the study and locked me in. Look here, see if you can find it."

"Likely !"

"Perhaps it was you locked me in !" snarled the Bounder.

"Perhaps it was."

"You cheeky fool——"

"Same to you, with knobs on !"

"By gum, if I could get at you, Carter, I'd wipe up the passage with you !" hissed Vernon-Smith. "Will you let me out or not?"

"No, I won't! Stick where you are !"

There was a savage wrench at the door-handle, and an enraged thump on the door.

"You cheeky rotter! I'll smash you for this !" yelled Vernon-Smith.

"You can't smash a fellow with your mouth, and you can't use anything else. I'd knock you spinning with one hand !"

"Open the door and try it on !" yelled the Bounder furiously.

"I expect you'd hide under the table if I did."

In Study No. 4, Herbert Vernon-Smith was almost foaming with rage. He had been in a bad temper to begin with. His temper was now the worst ever He had no doubt, by this time, that it was Carter who had locked him in, any more than he doubted that it was Carter talking to him from the other side of the door. He hammered furiously on the oak.

"Will you unlock this door, you cur?" he yelled. "I'll boot you up the passage and back again! You rotter! You're doing this because I paid you out for the dirty trick you played on me at the Three Fishers a week or two ago. By gum, I'll make you sorry for this !"

"Rats !"

"You funky worm, let me get at you !" roared the Bounder.

"You can come along to my study whenever you like. You'll find me at home if you want to go out at the end of a boot."

Bunter, grinning, walked away. Loud and furious hammering on the inside of Smithy's door followed him. Unheeding, the fat ventriloquist rolled away down the stairs.

Smithy was left a prisoner in his study, raging. How long it would be before he got out, Bunter did not know. Neither did he care. But he had no doubt that when Smithy did get out there would be a hectic time in store for Carter. He chuckled at the prospect.

The schemer of the Remove regarded Billy Bunter with too much contempt to dream of fearing any hitting back from the fat Owl. But, in view of his peculiar methods, there was no doubt that Bunter was quite a dangerous man when he was on the warpath.

THE EIGHTH CHAPTER.

A Row With the Bounder !

"CARTER !"

The new fellow in the Remove set his lips as he heard his Form-master's voice. But his manner was quite respectful as he turned round to Mr. Quelch. He disliked that gentleman extremely, but it was not his game to let Mr. Quelch become aware of that fact.

Carter was in a most unpleasant temper The detention class had been dismissed at half-past four, by which time Carter, as well as the rest of the class, had had more than enough of extra French.

The football match was over, and there was the usual noisy crowd in the changing-room. Carter heard that Grey-friars had won by three goals to two; but he was not much interested in a game in which he had not played, and he was not in a mood to join a cheery crowd.

He was disturbed deeply by the fact that Mr. Quelch had spotted him as the trickster in the Form-room that morning. How Quelch had spotted him he could not begin to guess, for he was certain that he had been unobserved when he crept into the Remove room in break to pin Bunter's absurd limerick up on the blackboard. But in the circumstances he could not doubt that Quelch had, and it was a blow to him.

His peculiar game at Greyfriars required caution and secrecy. It was as good as done for if Mr. Quelch came to know, or even suspect, that he was aiming to get Bunter a bad report for the term.

To his surprise, Mr. Quelch's expression was quite kindly. Carter was lounging moodily in the quad when Quelch called him. Certainly Mr. Quelch did not look as if he had been quite recently very displeased with the junior.

"Yes, sir!" muttered Carter.

"You are unoccupied at the present moment, I think, Carter. I should like you to go down to the post office."

"Oh, certainly, sir!" said Carter.

He had not the slightest desire to oblige Mr. Quelch, but his manner was quite meek and respectful.

"Thank you, my boy!" said Mr. Quelch, quite amiably "It was my intention to walk to the village, and I promised Mr. Hacker to bring back a postal order from Friardale. I am unable to go, however, and I should be obliged, Carter, if you would do so."

"I shall be glad, sir!" said Carter, not very truthfully. "I was thinking of a spin on my bike."

"Very good!" said Mr. Quelch. "Take this pound note, Carter, and bring a postal order for one pound, and take it to Mr. Hacker when you come back."

"Yes, sir."

Carter took the pound note and the odd coppers to pay for the postal order, and went away to get his bicycle.

His eyes gleamed under his knitted brows as he went.

It was a relief to see that Quelch appeared to be no longer incensed with him. Still, Quelch had, as he believed, given him a detention that afternoon, and now he had the cheek to use up what was left of his half-holiday. Carter had a malicious nature, and the thought occurred to his mind of letting that pound note blow away by accident—in which case, his Form-master would have had to indemnify Mr. Hacker for the loss.

But, malicious as he was, he did not allow malice to get the upper hand of caution. He wheeled his bike out, mounted it, and rode sullenly away to the village.

He was back in half an hour with the postal order in his pocket. Having put up his bike, he went into the House.

"Hallo, here he is!" called out Skinner, as he appeared.

Carter looked round. Half a dozen fellows were looking at him and grinning.

"Anything up?" asked Carter, puzzled.

THE MAGNET LIBRARY.—No. 1,567.

"You ought to know!" grinned Skinner.

"Smithy's as mad as a hatter!" said Hazeldene. "When are you going to let him out, you ass? Guard with your left when you do!"

"What the dickens do you mean?" exclaimed Carter impatiently. "Is anything up with Smithy? Not that I care."

"You don't know?" chuckled Skinner.

"How should I know? I've just been down to Friardale. Anything happened since the match?"

"Look here, wasn't it you?" asked Snoop. "Didn't you lock Smithy in his study?"

"Of course I didn't, fathead! Did anybody?"

"Somebody jolly well did, and Smithy thinks that it was you."

"What rot!"

Carter went on his way to the study of the master of the Shell to deliver the postal order, leaving Skinner & Co. chuckling.

He tapped at Mr. Hacker's door and opened it.

Mr Hacker and Mr. Capper were in the study, deep in talk.

Hacker glanced round impatiently at Carter.

"What is it?" he snapped. Hacker generally snapped.

"The postal order, sir. Mr. Quelch asked me to fetch it from Friardale for you as he was not going out."

"Oh, very well! Place it on the table, Carter; put a paper-weight on it," said Mr. Hacker, and he turned back to his conversation with the master of the Fourth.

Carter did as bidden and left the study.

He went up to the Remove passage, rather wondering what had happened there during his absence. There was a crowd of Remove fellows in the passage, mostly collected outside the door of Study No. 4.

Carter stared at them as he came up the passage from the stairs.

Thump, thump, thump! came from Study No. 4.

Following the thumps came the enraged voice of the Bounder.

"Will some of you get that key and let me out of this?"

"Nobody knows where the key is, Smithy!" called back Tom Redwing.

"That cad Carter's got it!" roared the Bounder. "Can't you find that rotter and get the key off him, you dummy?"

"I think he's gone out of gates. I've looked for him."

"Why on earth did the mad ass play this silly trick?" exclaimed Harry Wharton. "You'll have to wait till Carter comes in, Smithy."

"I'll smash him!" yelled the Bounder.

"I say, you fellows, here he comes!" squeaked Billy Bunter.

"Hallo, hallo, hallo! Here's Carter!"

"Carter, you ass, where's that key?" exclaimed Harry Wharton. "What the dickens do you mean by locking a fellow in his study and taking the key away?"

"Oh, don't be an ass!" snapped Carter. "I've done nothing of the sort! I haven't been up here at all since I came out of detention!"

"Is that Carter?" Vernon-Smith, in the study, heard the new junior's voice. "You rotten cur! Unlock that door! Do you hear me?"

"Is it locked?" asked Carter.

"Is it locked?" repeated Harry. "Yes, it's locked, and Smithy's been locked in for an hour or more. Didn't you——"

"No, I didn't!"

"Smithy seems to think you did!" said the captain of the Remove dryly. "If you've got the key, you'd better let Smithy out before he brings the prefects up here with that thundering row!"

"Where's the key, Carter?" asked Redwing

"How should I know where it is?" snapped Carter. "I know nothing at all about it."

"Will you make him hand over that key?" came the Bounder's fierce yell. "Take it away from him, Reddy! Are you afraid to handle that cur?"

"Oh, don't be a fathead, Smithy!" said Redwing. "Carter says he knows nothing about it."

"Fool! Idiot! He locked me in!"

"I did not!" snapped Carter. "What the thump's put that silly idea into your head, you ass?"

"I'll smash you! Give Redwing that key!"

"I haven't got any key, you dummy!" Thump, thump, thump!

"You'll have Quelch up here soon at this rate, Smithy!" said Peter Todd.

"I don't care! I'll have the whole school up if that cur doesn't unlock the door! Think I'm going to stay locked in this room?" yelled Vernon-Smith.

"He, he, he!"

"Make that cad hand the key over! I tell you he's got it! He slanged me from outside the study after he'd locked me in! He dared not do it with the door open! He locked me in, and told me to stick here! I tell you he told me so through the door! Now do you believe he's got the key?"

"I didn't!" yelled Carter.

"You did!" yelled back the Bounder.

"You're dreaming!"

"I'll smash you!"

"Look here, Carter, if you've got the key——" said Harry Wharton impatiently.

"I haven't, and I don't know anything about it! Don't be a fool!" snarled Carter.

And he went away to his own study, went in, and slammed the door.

The juniors in the passage looked at one another. They could not make this out.

From Study No. 4 came the sound of the Bounder's furious banging.

Thump, thump, thump! Bang! Thump!

THE NINTH CHAPTER.
Wingate Takes a Hand!

WINGATE of the Sixth came up the Remove staircase, with his ashplant under his arm and a grim frown on his face.

A "row" in the Remove was far from uncommon But the row that was going on now was rather outside the limit. The Bounder, in his rage, did not care who heard him banging on the locked door; he would not have cared if it had brought the headmaster on the scene. He banged and banged.

Bang, bang, bang! rang from Study No. 4 as Wingate came striding into the passage

The buzz of voices died away at the sight of the prefect.

"'Ware pre's!" murmured Nugent.

Bang, bang! on the door

"Stop it, Smithy! Wingate's coming!" called out Redwing anxiously.

"I don't care!"

Bang, bang, bang!

"Stop that row!" roared Wingate, as he strode up the passage. "You noisy young sweeps! Do you know you can be heard all over the House? Who's banging on that door?"

Click ! Billy Bunter heard an angry exclamation in the study, as Vernon-Smith heard his door locked on him. " By gad ! "
The Bounder's voice came in concentrated tones of rage. " Is that you, Bunter ? Is that you, you fat fool ? I'll smash
you ! " The fat Removite made no answer.

"Smithy !" said Wharton. "He's locked in."

Bang, bang !

"Stop that at once, Vernon-Smith !" And at the voice of the captain of the school even the reckless Bounder ceased to bang. "Now, what does this mean, Wharton? Is Vernon-Smith locked in his study?"

"Yes, Wingate."

"Some silly lark, I suppose. Who's got the key?"

"Nobody here," said Wharton. "We heard Smithy yelling and banging when we came up, that's all."

"Vernon-Smith ! Do you know who has the key?"

"Yes ! Carter !" howled the Bounder.

"Did Carter lock you in?"

"Yes."

"Where's Carter, Wharton?"

"In his study—my study," answered the captain of the Remove. "He says he doesn't know anything about it."

"Well, I'd better see him. If you make another sound from that study, Vernon-Smith, I'll give you six when the door's open !"

Wingate walked down the passage to Study No. 1, and the crowd of Removites followed him.

The Greyfriars captain threw open the door.

"You here, Carter?"

"I'm here."

"Vernon-Smith says you locked him in his study."

"Vernon-Smith's a fool !"

"An excitable ass, at any rate !" agreed Wingate. "Didn't you lock him in?"

"No !"

"Queer that he should think you did if you didn't !" said Wingate, with a sharp look at Carter. "You've not got the key?"

"No !"

"I say, you fellows, there's a key on the table !" squeaked Billy Bunter. "I say, is that Smithy's key?"

Wingate glanced at the study table. He had not noticed a key lying there, but he noticed it now. He picked it up.

"Is this yours, Carter?" he asked.

"No !"

"How did it come here, then?"

"I don't know ! I suppose it belongs to Wharton or Nugent; they share this study," answered Carter.

"Is this yours, Wharton?"

Wingate held up the key for inspection by the crowd of Remove fellows outside the doorway.

"No," answered Harry.

"Yours, Nugent?"

"Not mine."

Wingate's brow set grimly.

"So there's a key lying in your study, Carter, which appears to belong to nobody. We'll see whether it fits Vernon-Smith's door. It looks as if it might."

Carter stared at the key in Wingate's hand, breathing hard.

"I never put the key there," he said. "I never saw it in the study at all. I don't know anything about it."

"How did it get here, then?"

"I don't know, unless Wharton or Nugent left it there."

"We haven't been in the study," said Harry at once. "We heard Smithy kicking up a shindy when we came up, and went along there. Neither of us has been in the study at all."

"Well, I know nothing about the key," said Carter.

Wingate looked at him, and, without speaking again, walked out of the study, key in hand. He pushed it into the lock of Study No. 4 and turned it. Obviously, it was the right key. The door opened.

Vernon-Smith, red with rage, was revealed. He made a swift step to the open doorway, his hands clenched.

"Where's Carter?" he breathed.

"Hold on, Vernon-Smith !" said Wingate quietly. "Never mind where Carter is. I found this key in his study, but he says he never put it there. What made you think he had locked you in?"

Smithy made no reply to that. He wanted to get at Arthur Carter and hit out right and left, but he did not want to drag a Sixth Form prefect into the matter. But it was too late to think about that. Now that Wingate was on the scene, the matter was in official hands.

"I asked you a question, Vernon-Smith !" said the Greyfriars captain. "I'm waiting for an answer."

"I don't want a prefect to take it up !" muttered the Bounder.

"You should have thought of that before you kicked up such a hullaballoo ! I've taken it up now ! Answer my question at once !"

The Bounder stood silent. It was not the first time that he had had cause to regret the outbreak of his uncontrollable temper. He was now placed in the position of "telling" on Carter or refusing to answer a prefect—the first extremely disagreeable; the second hardly possible.

"Well?" rapped Wingate.

"I—I'd rather not——"

"You can cut that out ! You told me Carter had the key, and I found it in his study. How did you know it was Carter—if it was?"

"He slanged me through the door, after locking me in !" muttered the Bounder at last.

There was no help for it.

"That settles it, then !"

And Wingate walked back to Study No. 1, slipping his ashplant down from under his arm into his hand.

(*Continued on page* 16.)

THE HUNTING HEADMASTER!

New Serial—First Instalment

By DICKY NUGENT

GREYFRIAR

No. 281.

EDITED BY HARRY

" Where is he ? "

Jack Jolly, of the St. Sam's Fourth, asked that question in eggsasperated tones. His pals, Fearless and Merry and Bright, shook their heads.

" Give it up," said Bright.

" It's a mistery," said Merry. " It's not like the Head to disappear like this—especially at tea-time ! "

" Blow the blessed Head, anyway ! " said Frank Fearless, with tippical recklessness. " He said he wanted our impots by tea-time and we've done them. If we leave them in his study, we've done our bit—whether he's there or not ! "

Jolly and Merry and Bright looked dewbious. That mite have been all right with an ordinary headmaster. But Doctor Alfred Birchemall was no ordinary headmaster. Quite the reverse, in fakt !

When the Head had caught Jack Jolly & Co. bumping Snarler that morning he had ordered them all, Snarler included, to hand him fifty lines by tea-time. And when the Head said " hand," hand was what he meant !

But now that the heroes of the Fourth had done their lines they could not find the Head to hand him over the impots.

They had to look for him in all the likely places, including the tuck-shop, the Junior Common - room, and the Second Form-room— but without suxxess. Nobody had seen him in any of these places.

Where to look next was a bit of a puzzle ; and yet the Co. felt very dowbious about meerly dumping the impots on his study table.

" Your idea would be all right, Fearless, old chap," remarked Jolly, " if only the Head wasn't such a beestly tirant. The worst of it is, if we leave the impots in his study, as likely as not he'll say we weren't carrying out his instructions, and give us all a whopping with his birch."

" True enuff ! " nodded Fearless. " Hallo ! Here's Snarler ! Perhaps he knows. Seen the Head, Snarler ? "

" No ; I'm looking for him," growled Snarler. " I want to hand him this impot."

" Looks as if we're all in the same boat," grinned Jack Jolly. " I wonder where the thump——"

" Lissen ! " ejackulated Bright at that instant.

The Fourth Formers lissened.

To their grate releef, they then heard the Head's voice.

" That's the Head right enuff," said Fearless. " He's in the one place where we didn't look—the jim ! Come on, you fellows ! "

Grately serprized at the Head being in such a place at tea-time, the juniors moved off towards the jimmynasium. As they drew nearer, they distingwished his voice more clearly and their serprize increased when they found that he was shouting out cries usually heard on the hunting-field.

" Yoicks ! Gee-up ! Tally-ho ! " he was yelling.

" Grate pip ! What's the old buffer up to ? " asked Jack Jolly wonderingly. " Has he taken leave of his senses ? "

Frank Fearless grinned.

" If you ask my opinion, he said good-bye to them a long time ago ! "

" Ha, ha, ha ! "

" Tally-ho ! Tally-ho ! A-hunting we will go ! " came the Head's bellowing voice from the jim. " Yoicks ! Whoa, mare ! Gee-up ! "

" My hat ! "

The Fourth Formers broke into a run—and a cupple of seconds later broke into the jim.

An amazing site met th

There, as large as life as natcheral, was Doctor all. He was wearing a t place of his usual mor and he was sitting, of astride the vaulting-horse up and down in it just a a real horse, taking him good gallop !

More amazing still, he ing a hunting-horn whic round his sholder by a string ; and as the junic in, he raised this horn t and blew a loud, unmew on it.

Ta-ra ! Honk-honk !

" What the merry gasped Jack Jolly.

The next moment, Doc email reckernised that t introoders present and lo instrument again. His shifty eyes fixed sternl Fourth Formers.

" Well, boys ? " he wra

" Pretty well, thank gasped Jack Jolly. " W brought you the lines yo to do, sir."

" Good egg ! " said the his refined way. " Let's s

The Fourth Formers tr to the vaulting-horse an over their impots one Doctor Birchemall glance them breefly and nodded

" Very well, boys," " You may leave them on in my study till I retu scram—or, as the vulgar it, you may go ! "

The juniors turned to Jolly hezzitated.

" Ahem ! Are you sur all right, sir ? " he asked. like, sir, I'll call a doctor.

The Head looked serpri

" A doctor, Jolly ? Wl

" Why, to see if you potty, of corse ! "

" Ha, ha, ha ! "

Doctor Birchemall glan

" Potty ? How dare y such a thing, Jolly ? makes you think I've gon

" This funny game yo ing," answered the kapt Fourth, pointing to the horse. " You're sitting on horse and acting as if it's If that's not potty——"

But the Head didn't all finish that sentence.

" You silly yung hooted. " I'm not playir Jolly ! I'm practising ! hunting ! "

" Wha-a-at ? "

" Draw it mild, sir ! "

" It's true ! " roared " I've been invited to tur the County Hunt and getting in trim for it ! "

" Oh crums ! "

" Years ago," said Doc emall, calming himself mitey effort, " I was an o the saddle. But recently

---

TRAGEDY IN A FUN FAIR!

By S. Q. I. FIELD

What attracted Fishy about the new pin-table saloon in Courtfield High Street was the sign " ADMISSION FREE." Fishy never can resist anything free.

I was with Fishy, so, although fun fairs are all out of bounds, I went in with him.

The pin-tables, of course, were not free. They cost a penny a go. But there was one attraction from Fishy's point of view. Each pin-table contained an announcement that if you scored 5,000 you won a sixpenny box of chocolates.

Fishy gazed long and hard at that notice. Eventually he drew out his purse, took out a penny from it, and put it in the slot. It must have been an unusually thick one. It stuck.

Fishy tried to pull it back again. It wouldn't come. He tried to press it in. It wouldn't go. A look of alarm came into Fishy's hatchet face.

" I guess that penny looks like it's stuck," he said. " Where's the guy that looks after the joint ? "

Well, the guy that looked after the joint had gone out for a cup of tea. The only official left was an undersized kid who was new to the place and had no idea how the machines worked. What was still more alarming to Fish was that he had no pennies for refunds to dissatisfied customers, either.

Fishy went back to the pin-table. He thumped it, he rattled it, he rocked it, he kicked it, he climbed on top of it, he went down on his hands and knees underneath it. Nothing happened. The penny still obstinately refused to budge.

Fishy's alarm charged to complete panic.

" I guess we gotta do something ! " he yelled. " We've only got five minutes before we catch our train back. Maybe the guy won't be back from his tea."

" More than likely," I agreed. " What are you going to do about it ? "

Fishy answered by deeds —not words. With lips

tightly set and back hunched, he sprang at the pin-table. His thumb descended on the protruding portion of his penny and he made a desperate onslaught. Then he changed his tactics and started wrestling with the whole machine. Minute after minute the fearsome struggle went on, till at last,

with deep and tender sympathy. I told him the dreadful news that we could wait no longer or we would miss our train.

Never as long as I live, dear readers, shall I forget the heartrending groan that burst from Fishy's lips at that announcement.

I led him away. Blank

despair was in every line of his face. He was utterly bowed down with inexpressible grief.

" My penny ! " he kept on moaning.

Back at Greyfriars, he broke down completely. He was taken to the sanny and kept in bed in a darkened ward. Sorrow had shattered his health.

Since that black day he has slowly recovered, and now he is out and about again.

It would be nice to be able to say that everything turned out all right in the end—that he went back to the pin-table saloon and recovered his penny. Alas ! I can tell you nothing so pleasant as that.

When he did go back it was only to find that all the pin-tables had gone and the place was locked up. There was a sign up in one of the windows : " TO LET."

Fishy didn't collapse again. He was beyond it. He just uttered a bitter, hollow laugh and passed on. And though, to outward appearances, he is still the same, we who know him well know that the light has gone out of Fishy's life. He is a broken man because tragedy came to him in a fun fair.

Awful, isn't it ?

HARRY WHARTON CALLING!

We have become so used to regarding Bob Cherry as the champion boxer of the Remove that it seems quite strange to hear of anyone doubting his supremacy.

Yet some of our readers have taken it into their heads to ask whether there isn't a dark horse amongst us who might dispute Bob's claim to the title. Some of them have asked the pertinent question : "How long is it since he defended it, anyway ? "

The answer to that question is that the boxing championship of the Remove is not a cut-and-dried affair, ruled and judged by any kind of boxing board or athletic commission. It simply happens to be the opinion of most fellows that Bob Cherry is the best boxer in the Remove, and that's that !

But since some of you readers have raised the matter, it has occurred to me that it would be a bright idea if we got to work and held a series of contests to make sure that there is no mistake about it.

I have been turning it over in my mind for a week or two, and finally I have put it to an improvised committee of Remove sportsmen.

I feel you will all be pleased to know that the idea has met with an enthusiastic reception. The committee has decided definitely to hold a competition to find the champion boxer of the Remove, and the first round of the competition will be held next week.

How's that, chums ? Nice work, eh ? I knew you'd like it !

Let me add that the competition is going to be no hole - and - corner business, either. We have approached Mr. Lascelles and Wingate and obtained their sanction and support ; and the contests will all take place in the gym before qualified judges of the noble art. Seats will be provided round the ring for spectators, and all I wish is that our readers could be there to see the fun.

I am looking forward to the competition eagerly myself. and I may say that, in spite of our old friendship, I shall try my utmost to go one better than Bob.

I have arranged for Vernon-Smith to report on the fights, and you can rely on the Bounder giving you a crisp and racy account of all that happens. Look out for his first special article next week !

All the very best, chums !

HARRY WHARTON.

BUNTER IS SURE TO BE RATTLED !

The Head is thinking of forbidding the borrowing of other fellows' bikes.

If this compels Bunter to use his own old jigger again, it will be a "rattling" good idea.

PUNISHMENT TO FIT CRIME !

Coker, who is still at large with his motor-bike, wonders what he is likely to get for knocking down the kitchen garden fencing.

Our suggestion—a "gating."

---

lack of practice, my horsemanship has become a little rusty. I have come to the concloosion that I had better polish it up a bit before I go to the hounds. See ? "

"I bet it can do with it, sir ! " chuckled Jolly. "But what's the good of a wooden horse like this sir ? Take my tip and hire a horse from the stables at Muggleton, instead. We'll come with you to a quiet spot tomorrow and help you, if you like."

Doctor Birchemall's eyes gleemed.

"By Jove ! That's not at all a bad idea, Jolly. I will take advantage of your offer with plezzure. Meanwhile, I don't think I have wasted my time here to-day. To prove what I say, I will show you how I can do the galloping motion. Watch out ! "

With these words, the Head leaned forward in his imaginary saddle and started bobbing up and down so fewriously that the vaulting-horse farely rocked. The juniors jumped back hurriedly.

"Go it, sir ! " grinned Fearless.

Bump, bump, bump !

"Yoicks ! Tally-ho ! Gee-up, my bonny mare ! " cried Doctor Birchemall.

The wooden horse rocked wildly, but the Head was so eggsited that he failed to notiss any danger till it was too late.

The crash came at last. The horse rocked over on its side legs for an instant. Then it pitched to the floor with a bump that shook the jim, and the Head pitched over with it, yelling feendishly.

Bang ! Crash ! Wallop !

"Yarooooo ! Ow-wow ! "

Jack Jolly & Co. rushed to the reskew. But Snarler, who never wasted simperthy, did not join them. Instead, he opened his mouth and farely yelled with larfter.

"Ha, ha, ha ! Haw, haw, haw ! Ho, ho, ho ! " he roared. And he kept it up till Doctor Birchemall was on his feet again.

That was rather unforchunit for Snarler. The Head was just in the mood to look for a viktim, and Snarler fitted in with his requirements nicely.

"Snarler ! Ow ! How dare you larf at your headmaster's misfortunes ? Wow ! Follow me ! Wooooop ! " he gasped, as he limped away.

And Snarler stopped larfing and followed him. And pretty soon there was a sound like a carpet being beaten from the direction of the Head's study—accompanied by

shreeks and howls of aggerny from Snarler.

When Snarler staggered away from the Head's study at last, he was black and blue all over—and he was also seeing red !

"I'll get my own back for this ! " he vowed in vengeful axxents. "By the time I've finished with the Head, he'll wish he'd never had anything to do with horse riding ! "

(*What dark scheme is forming in Snarler's brain ? For the answer, read next week's hilarious installment !*)

THOUGHTLESS !

Skinner really should be more careful in class. What can you do with a chap who answers the geographical question : "Where do we get our tobacco ? " by saying : "At the back door of the cigar shop in Courtfield ! "

GREYFRIARS FROM FRESH ANGLES

1. Behind The Tuckshop Counter

By JESSIE MIMBLE

Dearie me ! A nice task you boys have set me, writing for the papers at my time of life ! Well, well, I can only tell folks in my own way how Greyfriars School appears to me from behind the tuckshop counter !

What it mostly seems like is just a collection of hungry boys, all clamouring to be served first ! Bless me ! The way they struggle and push, you would think they had had nothing to eat for a week ; and yet, as like as not, they have only just finished their dinner !

But that's not to say that all the customers in my shop are alike. Dearie me, no ! There are fat ones and thin ones and rich ones and poor ones—and, in fact, a more mixed collection of boys you could never wish to meet, I declare.

The boy who would like to be my best customer is really and truly the worst. His name is Billy Bunter, and a more greedy or silly boy I never wish to see. The things that boy has said to try to get me to allow him credit would fill a volume as big as my cookery-book !

Lord Mauleverer spends more than anybody else in my shop, and a very nice, agreeable young man his lordship is, too. But I don't want you to think I just like the boys for what they spend. Oh dear, no ! Some of the boys with very little to spend are great favourites of mine ; and, on the other hand, there are one or two of my most profitable customers of whom I have a very low opinion. Master Loder, for instance, comes in with all the airs and

graces imaginable and talks to me as if I were dirt beneath his feet. But I think maybe he will be more respectful after yesterday. He was even more rude than usual, and it provoked me so much that I took one of my jam tarts and squashed it on his face. It was a threepenny one, too ; but if it improves Master Loder's manners I shall consider it well worth the expense.

Yes, it's true that I have my trials and troubles in the tuckshop. But there's a lot that makes up for them. On a sunny summer's day I would not change my little shady nook under the elms for a mansion, I can assure you. It's nice to see the old school buildings across the quad and the green playing-fields in the distance. And even though the boys are bewildering with all their orders, their pranks and prattlings keep me young.

And now I can see a crowd of them walking over from football, with those nice boys, Master Wharton and Master Cherry, at the front. So I must stop writing and get back to my work !

(Spare our blushes !—Ed.)

A VENTRILOQUIST'S VENGEANCE!
By FRANK RICHARDS

(Continued from page 13.)

THE TENTH CHAPTER.
Quite a Mystery!

ARTHUR CARTER eyed the Greyfriars captain furtively and uneasily as he came back into Study No. 1.

Behind Wingate came a crowd of the Remove—the Bounder's red and angry face among the others.

Smithy's only desire just then was for Wingate to get off the scene so that he could begin on Carter! But even the reckless Bounder could hardly think of beginning the punching while the prefect was present.

Billy Bunter, wedged in the crowd in the passage, was grinning cheerily. All, from Bunter's point of view was going well.

Carter was going to get six! Serve him right! Smithy was going to thrash Carter when Wingate was gone! Serve him right again! Smithy would collect some damages in the process! Serve Smithy right! Altogether things looked good to the fat and fatuous Owl of the Remove. Both of them were beasts, and both of them were going to get toco—so that was all right!

Wingate swished his ash.

"It seems that you locked Vernon-Smith in his study, Carter! I dare say it was meant as a joke, but you can't play jokes that cause a row all over the House! Bend over that chair!"

Carter set his lips.

"I never did anything of the kind," he said. "If Vernon-Smith says I did he's either dreaming or lying."

"I found the key here——"

"I don't know who put it there—I hadn't been in the study!"

"Vernon-Smith says you slanged him through the door after locking him in."

"He must have dreamed it!"

Wingate looked quite perplexed. He was there to "whop" the cause of the uproar in the Remove; but he did not want to whop the wrong man. Carter's angry denials puzzled him.

"Well, one of you seems to be a regular young Ananias!" he said. "But I'm going to get at the truth! Step in here, Vernon-Smith!"

The Bounder pushed into the study, his eyes gleaming at Carter. It was only Wingate's presence that kept his knuckles away from Carter's features.

"You said that Carter slanged you through the door, Vernon-Smith?"

"Yes, he did!" grunted the Bounder.

"You say you did not, Carter?"

"I did not!"

"You lying cur!" hissed the Bounder. "I don't care whether Wingate believes you or not, but I'll make you sit up for it! I'll—— Wow!" The Bounder broke off, with a yelp, as Wingate gave him a flip with the ashplant.

"That's enough from you, Vernon-Smith!" said the Greyfriars captain. "Don't talk so much. One of you is lying—and that one is going to get the whopping of his life when I spot him. Did you see Carter when he locked you in?"

"No; he pinched the key while I was in another study."

"Then it was only his voice you heard?"

"Yes; but I know his voice! Besides, he said he was Carter!"

"Well, that sounds plain enough!" said Wingate. "Any of you know anything about it?" He glanced out at the crowd in the passage.

"No; most of us were in the changing-room after the football," answered Harry Wharton. "Nobody seems to have been up here. Smithy cleared off the minute he had changed, but the rest of us did not come up till some time later."

"I never came up at all!" snapped Carter. "I was in detention till half-past four, and after I came out of Mossoo's class Quelch asked me to go down to Friardale, and I went. I never came up here till after I got back."

"Liar!" said Vernon-Smith grimly. Whop!

"Ow!" gasped the Bounder. "Look here, Wingate, keep that ashplant to yourself!"

"I'll give you six with it if I have any more cheek from you, Vernon-Smith. What time was the football match over, Wharton?"

"Soon after four."

"How long before you came up to your study, Vernon-Smith?"

"About ten minutes," grunted the Bounder.

"How long after that before you were locked in?"

"A few minutes, I suppose."

"You were locked in before half-past four?"

"Yes, long before."

"Then, if Carter was in the detention-room till half-past, he cannot be the fellow who did it."

"He's lying!"

"We'll see about that! I suppose you know, Carter, that I shall ask Monsieur Charpentier what time he dismissed his class?"

"You can ask him as soon as you like, Wingate! If he doesn't tell you that I was in his class till half-past four you can give me six—or sixty, if you like!"

"By gum!" exclaimed Hazeldene, from the passage. "That's right, Wingate."

"How do you know, Hazeldene?"

Hazel grinned.

"Because I was in Froggy's detention class, too," he answered. "Mossoo turned us out when it struck half-past four."

"Carter was there?"

"Yes, he came in after the rest, but he left when we all did," answered Hazel. "There was another Remove chap in the class, too; he can tell you the same! You were there, Snoop."

"That's right," said Snoop. "Carter was with us there till half-past four, Wingate! If Smithy had told us the time he was locked in I could have told him that it wasn't Carter that did it."

Herbert Vernon-Smith's face was quite blank for a moment or two.

He had not doubted for a moment that it was the new junior who had locked him in and taunted him through the door. He had known nothing about the time at which Mossoo had dismissed the detention class. He would not have believed Carter's statement on that subject; but the evidence of Hazeldene and Snoop settled that.

The Bounder had to realise that it was a physical impossibility for Carter to have locked his study door before half-past four. And he knew that it was well before that time that it had been locked.

Wingate's face grew grimmer as he

fixed his eyes on the Bounder. He took a business-like grip on the ashplant.

"That clears Carter," he said. "Somebody else played that trick and landed the key in this study while Carter was in detention. Now, Vernon-Smith, I want to know why you named Carter."

There was a wriggle and a stirring in the crowd packed outside the study. Billy Bunter was trying to wriggle away.

Bunter had wanted, and had obtained, a front place to see the whoppings. Now he was very keen on getting out of that front place!

The turn the investigation was taking rather alarmed Bunter. It dawned upon his fat brain that it would be judicious to fade out of the picture.

But there was no escape for Bunter. Nearly all the Remove—a numerous Form—were packed round the doorway of Study No. 1! Nobody was going to shift to let the fat Owl wriggle away! Bunter had to stay where he was!

"Don't shove!" came several voices.

"I say, you fellows——"

"Shut up, Bunter! Stop shoving!"

"Now then, quiet there!" rapped Wingate. "I'm waiting for you to explain yourself, Vernon-Smith."

The Bounder stammered. He was quite at a loss.

"I—I—I thought it was Carter! The fellow owned up he was Carter—besides, it was Carter's voice——"

"That's rot!" said Carter. "I've heard no voice in the Form just like mine."

"Well, it sounded exactly like yours," snarled Vernon-Smith, "and I don't quite believe yet that it wasn't!"

"I say, you fellows, do let a fellow pass——"

"Shut up, Bunter!"

"I say, Bob, old chap, lemme get out——"

"Shut up, you ass!"

"You seem to have made a very extraordinary mistake, Vernon-Smith," said Wingate. "Some other fellow seems to have locked you in and led you to believe that it was Carter! I'm going to find that fellow out! Who was up here at the time?"

"Hardly anybody, I think," said Harry Wharton.

"Did you see anyone when you came up, Vernon-Smith?"

"Only Bunter."

"Bunter!" repeated Wingate. "Where's Bunter now? Oh, here you are, Bunter! Step in! Why, what's the matter with the young ass?"

Billy Bunter did not step into the study as bidden! Billy Bunter made a frantic effort to crash through the crowd behind him and escape!

There was a howl from Bob Cherry as a fat elbow crashed into his ribs—a yell from Peter Todd as his toes were ground under a heel. Billy Bunter barged like an insane hippopotamus in his desperate endeavour to escape! The crowd swayed round him.

"Bunter!" roared Wingate.

"Oh crikey!"

"Push that young ass in here!"

"Oh lor'! I—I say, you fellows—oh crikey! Ow!"

A dozen hands shoved Bunter, and he went headlong into the study.

"Ow!" spluttered Bunter. "Ooooh!"

And he sat down, with a heavy bump, at the feet of the Greyfriars captain.

THE ELEVENTH CHAPTER.
Alas for Bunter!

BILLY BUNTER sat and blinked up at Wingate of the Sixth, gasping.

Wingate stared down at Billy Bunter.

"You young ass!" hooted Wingate.

"I—I say——" Bunter scrambled up and backed as near the door as he could. "It—it wasn't me, Wingate!"

"What wasn't you?"

"Oh! Anything! I—I mean, nothing!" gasped Bunter. "I wasn't here, you know! I was downstairs when Smithy saw me up here——"

"Wha-a-t? Was it you played that trick on Vernon-Smith?" demanded Wingate.

That suspicion was in every mind now. It could hardly fail to be, after Bunter's frantic endeavour to get off the scene.

"Oh, no! You see, I—I wasn't here!" gasped Bunter. "Besides, the beast kicked me—you know you did, Smithy!"

"Ha, ha, ha!"

"That fat chump!" exclaimed the Bounder blankly. "I thought it was Bunter at first—and then I heard Carter's voice outside——"

"You didn't!" yapped Carter.

"I thought I did! It was that blithering Owl playing his rotten ventriloquial tricks—I see that now!"

"I wasn't!" yelled Bunter. "I never hid in Ogilvy's study while you went to mine, and I never got your key away. As for putting it in Carter's study, I never thought of such a thing! Why should I? I wasn't thinking of paying him out for getting me into such a row with Quelch this morning!"

"You fat chump!" gasped Bob Cherry.

"Ha, ha, ha!"

"Bunter all the time!" grinned Skinner. "Jolly old Bunter on the warpath! You might have guessed it, Smithy!"

"You shut up, Skinner! You'll make Wingate think it was me!" gasped Bunter. "I say, Wingate, I never had anything to do with it, you know. It was Carter that Smithy heard outside his study."

"You young ass," said Wingate. "We've already got it clear that Carter was in detention class till half-past four."

"Well, I never knew that, of course," said Bunter. "How was I to know what time Froggy sent them off?"

"Do you mean you'd have left it later if you'd known that?" asked Wingate, staring at him.

"Yes, of course!"

"Then it was you——"

"Oh, no! It wasn't!" gasped Bunter.

"It wasn't?" yelled Wingate.

"No, not at all! I wasn't here, you see! I couldn't have locked Smithy in when I wasn't here, could I? Besides, he heard Carter's voice—and my voice ain't anything like Carter's. I can't imitate voices, Wingate, or anything of that sort! You can ask any of these fellows! They've often heard me."

There was a howl of laughter in the passage. Even Vernon-Smith's angry face relaxed into a grin.

Carter was staring at the fat Owl blankly. It was quite a surprise to him to learn that Bunter was the man. But it was no surprise to the other fellows, well acquainted as they were with the fat Owl's ventriloquial trickery.

Wingate swished the ashplant. Evidently, he had got the right man at last! There was no further doubt on that point.

"You're up for six, you young ass!" he said. "Bend over that chair!"

"But it wasn't me, Wingate!" wailed Bunter. "I keep on telling you that I was somewhere else at the time! The fact is, I was out of gates. Besides, that beast Smithy kicked me. I only asked him whether he'd taken any goals, and he kicked me. You jolly well know you did, Smithy!"

"Oh, my hat!" said Wingate. "Where were you when Vernon-Smith was locked in his study, Bunter?"

"Out of gates!" answered Bunter promptly.

"And where did Vernon-Smith kick you?"

"On the trousers!"

"Ha, ha, ha!" came a shriek from the passage.

Wingate grinned—he could not help it.

"You benighted young ass, I mean, where were you when Vernon-Smith kicked you?" he gasped.

"Oh! I—I—I was—was—was—I mean, he never kicked me!" stuttered Bunter. "I wasn't here, you see, so—so he couldn't have! When—when I say he kicked me, I—I mean that he—he didn't!"

"Oh, gad!" said the Greyfriars captain. "Quelch must enjoy having you in his Form, Bunter! Sort of pupil to make a Form-master merry and bright! Now bend over that chair!"

"Wha-a-t for?" gasped Bunter. "I—I haven't done anything, Wingate! I—I hope you can take my word."

"Bend over that chair!"

"Oh lor'!"

Billy Bunter bent over the chair.

Wingate wielded the ashplant with a practised hand! Six times it swiped on Bunter's tight trousers, to an accompaniment of loud and lamentable howls from Bunter.

Then the prefect tucked the ash under his arm.

"That's that!" he said. "Any more tricks of this kind, Bunter, and you'll get it harder next time!"

"Yow-ow-ow-ow!"

"You'll take a hundred lines for kicking up that shindy in your study, Vernon-Smith! I'll mention it to your Form-master. Now, no more noise in this passage—if I have to come up again, I'll whop you all round."

And Wingate walked away to the stairs, his duty done.

Bunter was left wriggling.

Smithy gave him a look—and left the study! Six from a prefect's ash was enough for Bunter, even in Smithy's opinion, and he left it at that. But Carter's eyes were glinting at the wriggling fat Owl with a deadly glint.

"So it was you!" he said, between his teeth. "You made that fool Smithy believe it was I, to land me in a row?"

"Beast!"

Carter made a quick step towards the fat junior.

Bob Cherry made one just as quick, from the passage, and interposed.

"Hands off!" he said gruffly.

"Stand aside, Cherry!"

"Put me aside, if you want me aside!" retorted Bob. "I'll be glad to handle you, you cur!"

"You've heard that fat rotter admit playing a dirty trick—I might have got six from Quelch, as well as a row with Smith!" hissed Carter. "Are you standing up for foul play like that?"

"You know all about foul play!" answered Bob scornfully. "You've set that fat fool the example, and he's followed it! It was a dirty trick, if Bunter had sense enough to understand it—but it was no dirtier than sneaking his silly limerick and pinning it up for Quelch to see in the Form-room! You've got some of your own medicine, and if you don't like the taste of it, that's your look-out."

"I'll smash him!" roared Carter.

"Get on with it—you'll have to smash me first! Get out of the study, Bunter, you fat ass—I can't stay here for ever. That fellow makes me sick."

Billy Bunter rolled out of the study.

Carter made a movement to follow, but Bob, at the doorway, stood like a lion in the p——

Carter ended the matter by slamming the door.

A few minutes later Vernon-Smith and Redwing, in Study No. 4, looked round, as the door opened, and a fat face looked in.

Billy Bunter, still wriggling from the ashplant, blinked into the study.

"I say, Smithy——" he burbled.

The Bounder grasped a cushion! He had let Bunter off once, but if the fatuous Owl had come to ask for it, he was welcome to it.

"I say, old chap, ain't you going to lick Carter?" asked Bunter. "I say, I'd jolly well lick a chap for locking me in my study! I would, really! I say, Smithy, you ain't funking Carter, are you?"

Whiz!

Crash!

Bump!

The cushion landed almost like a cannon-ball on Bunter's well-filled waistcoat.

Bunter went backwards into the passage like a stone from a catapult, and landed there roaring.

"Come back when you want some more!" said Smithy, as he shut the door.

Bunter did not come back for more! He seemed satisfied with what he had had!

THE TWELFTH CHAPTER.

Bunter Begs for It!

"CARTER!"

Arthur Carter started as the sharp, acid voice of Mr. Hacker, master of the Shell, rapped out suddenly from an open study window.

It was in break, the following morning; and Carter was lounging in the quad on his own, with a far from pleasant expression on his face.

The trick Billy Bunter had played on him the previous day had surprised and startled him, and alarmed him a little also.

Hitherto, he had regarded the fat Owl of the Remove as an obtuse and unthinking ass, powerless against his scheming knavery—a sort of fat dartboard at which he could pitch darts without danger of any of them coming back at him.

It was quite a surprise to him, and not a pleasant one, to find that Bunter could hit back—though it was true that the hapless fat Owl had not had much luck in his hitting back. And there had been a spot of unscrupulousness in Bunter's fatuous scheme, not unlike Carter's own! It disconcerted Carter very much. A rogue does not like to be the victim of roguery—no burglar likes to be burgled! In truth, a rogue would have no chance in life at all, but for the fact that the average man plays the game.

Carter was thinking, not pleasantly, over this new and unexpected development, when Hacker's sharp voice rapped from the study window.

He suppressed a scowl, as he glanced round.

Hacker, as master of the Shell, had nothing to do with Remove fellows, and had no right to call them. Still, a beak was a beak!

"Yes, sir!" answered Carter, glancing up at the window.

"Kindly come to my study at once, Carter!" rapped the acid voice from within the study.

Carter breathed hard! Nobody but his own Form-master, or the Head, had a right to give him that order! However, he had to go. He supposed that Hacker must have something to say about the errand he had performed for him the day before

"Very well, sir!" he answered sulkily

And he went along to the door

He would hardly have done so, had he been aware that Mr. Hacker was in Common-room, and that a fat ventriloquist was grinning at him from behind the curtain of Hacker's window!

Billy Bunter was on the warpath again!

Having spotted Carter lounging on the path under the windows of Masters' Studies, this bright idea had occurred to the Remove ventriloquist.

As Carter started for the door of the House, Bunter started for the door of the study!

Carter, coming in, met him at the corner of the passage, and gave his fat, grinning face a scowl in passing.

"He, he, he!" followed him from Bunter, as he went up the passage.

In the sacred precincts of Masters' Studies a fellow could not kick a fellow; so Carter went on his way unheeding the fat Owl.

Bunter rolled cheerily out into the quad.

He rather hoped that Carter, finding nobody in the study, would wait there for Hacker, and get into a row! Hacker, who was called the "Acid Drop" in his Form, was not a nice-tempered man, and not likely to be pleased at finding a Remove fellow in his study—and he was certainly not likely to believe Carter's explanation that he had called him in, when he had done nothing of the kind!

Billy Bunter felt that he was getting on quite nicely—on the warpath! He rolled out into the quad, grinning.

Meanwhile, Carter arrived at Mr. Hacker's study, tapped, and entered He stared angrily round an empty study.

Why Hacker had called him from the window and gone away before he could arrive, was rather a mystery.

Undecided what to do, Carter stood waiting! If Hacker had called him, and stepped out for a moment to speak to some other beak, he would expect him to wait. He waited, with growing annoyance.

As he stood there, his eyes fell on the postal order he had placed on the study table the previous day. Hacker, evidently, had not posted it yet. It lay where Carter had left it, under the paper-weight.

He gave it only a careless glance. Then he glanced out of the doorway, to see whether Hacker was coming. Nobody was in sight.

Puzzled and angry, he waited. He had nothing special to do in break; but he did not want his time taken up like this, by the master of another Form. He stared impatiently from the window.

A fat and grinning face met his view! Billy Bunter, in the quad, was blinking at that window, through his big spectacles, and grinning from one fat ear to the other.

"Oh!" ejaculated Carter.

A sudden suspicion shot into his mind. He remembered the trick at Smithy's door the previous day. Bunter had got away with that, by some weird trick of imitating voices! He had met Bunter, as he came to Hacker's study—going away from some master's study evidently! All was suddenly clear to Carter! He had been tricked!

He drew a deep, deep breath!

Hacker had not called him at all—it was that fat idiot pulling his leg, with his weird ventriloquia trickery, as he had pulled Smithy's. And if Hacker came in and found him there——

A spasm of rage went through him. With all his cleverness, all his cunning, he had been taken in like a baby by a fellow he regarded as a fat fool, with hardly enough sense to go in when it rained!

He turned quickly towards the door. He did not want to be caught there by Hacker, to stammer out an explanation to a sharp-tempered and suspicious man.

But he paused as he passed the table. His eyes fixed on the postal order under the paper-weight!

He stood—with his face whitening. The thought that had come into his mind almost frightened him.

So far, in his peculiar campaign against Bunter he had taken advantage only of the fat Owl's own faults and foibles—of which the name is legion. But this——

Possibly, rascal as he was, he would never have done it, but for the spot of unscrupulousness Bunter had revealed. That seemed some sort of feeble justification to him—rogue against rogue!

For a long moment he stood undecided—then he peered, with a white face, from the door. Had anyone been in sight, he would have left the study without carrying out the dastardly scheme that had flashed into his mind. But there was no one in sight—the coast was clear.

He stepped back to the table, picked up the postal order, and slipped it into his pocket. Then he left the study swiftly.

A minute later he was in the quadrangle, strolling with his hands in his pockets, with a casual air.

He strolled away to the old Cloisters, and, having made sure that no eye was on him, folded the postal order and slipped it into a slit cut in the lining of his jacket with a penknife. It was safe there till wanted.

Relieved in his mind, though still undecided how the scheme was to be carried out, and indeed not quite certain that he would carry it out at all, he left the Cloisters.

A minute or two later the bell rang, and the Remove went in for third school.

Billy Bunter's fat voice was—as usual—audible as the juniors gathered at the Form-room door.

"I say, you fellows, my postal order never came——"

"It never does, does it?" asked Johnny Bull

"Well I was expecting a postal order from one of my titled relations, you know! These delays in the post office are a bit annoying!" said Bunter. "I say, Wharton, what about lending me the ten bob——"

"Nothing about lending you the ten bob, old fat man."

"I mean the five bob, old chap——" amended Bunter.

"Ha, ha ha!"

"It's practically certain to come to-morrow!" urged Bunter. "I've been expecting it for some time."

"Whole terms, in fact!" remarked Bob Cherry.

"Oh, really, Cherry! I say, old fellow, you might lend me the five bob! One good turn deserves another, you know!"

"You've done me a good turn?" asked Bob. "Is that how you describe bagging my toffee from my study?"

"I never bagged your toffee! I haven't been in your study! Besides, I suppose you're no going to make a fuss about a spot of toffee—there was only one chunk in the bag. I'm not talking about toffee. You were jolly glad to play in the football match yesterday, I know that."

"Jolly glad!" agreed Bob.

"Well, then, one good turn deserves another!" said Bunter

"Anybody know what the fat chump means, if he means anything?" asked Bob.

"Well, you wouldn't have played if Carter had played, you know that!" said Billy Bunter warmly. "And who got him into detention?"

"Eh! Quelch did!"

"He, he, he!"

"What are you going off like an alarm clock for, you fat ass?"

"He, he, he! That cad Carter thought it was Quelch!" chuckled Bunter. "But if he'd looked out of the study, he wouldn't have seen Quelch! He, he, he!"

Every fellow on the spot stared at Bunter. Carter, who had just arrived, stared with the rest. The short-sighted Owl of the Remove had not noticed him coming up the passage.

Harry Wharton, with a grim face, stepped to the fat Owl, and dropped a hand on a podgy shoulder.

"What do you mean by that, Bunter?" he asked, very quietly.

"Oh, nothing! I had nothing to do with it, of course! Still, one good turn deserves another, and Bob can't deny that he was jolly glad to play in the St. Jim's match after all. I think he might let me have the half-crown on my postal order, after all I've done for him."

"My only hat!" gasped Bob. "Is that what you meant when you were gabbling to me in the quad? Was Carter fool enough to let you pull his leg to that extent?"

"He, he, he!"

Carter, his face almost livid with rage, made a stride at the fat junior. He understood now. Bunter's words, added to his discovery of the fat Owl's ventriloquial trickery, made it all suddenly clear. That was why Mr. Quelch had not shown the expected signs of being "wrathy" with him. Quelch knew nothing of the matter. It was not Quelch who had ordered him into detention on Wednesday! It was the fat ventriloquist of the Remove, imitating Quelch's voice, outside his study!

"Why you—you—you rotter!" he gasped, almost choking. "You—you did that—you took me in—you got me a detention, and I thought——"

"Eh? I didn't see you, Carter! Oh, no! Nothing of the kind! I say, you fellows, keep him off!" yelled Bunter.

Bob Cherry interposed just in time, and spun Carter back with a heavy shove.

"'Ware beaks!" murmured Skinner, as Mr. Quelch appeared in the passage, coming up to the Form-room door.

Carter controlled his fury. He went into the Form-room with the rest of the Remove, his lips set hard.

He had sat through the previous afternoon, in the detention-class, at extra French, instead of playing football—and he owed it to Billy Bunter! The last spot of remorse was banished from his heart now—his mind was made up. The fat fool was not only asking for it; he was begging for it! and it was coming to him!

Billy Bunter had set his podgy feet on the warpath; but he little guessed where that path was to lead him!

" Someone seems to have locked you in your study, Vernon-Smith, and led you to believe that it was Carter," said Wingate.
" I'm going to find that fellow out. Who was up here at the time ? " There was a sudden commotion as Billy Bunter made a frantic effort to escape.

THE THIRTEENTH CHAPTER.

Stump for Bunter !

" LOOK here, Bob——"
"Oh rats !" said Bob gruffly.

Four exasperated glares were turned on Bob. His "feud" with the new fellow, Carter, had tried the patience of his chums many times that term ; but never so severely as now. Now it seemed tried to breaking-point.

The Famous Five were in the Rag, after class. Harry Wharton had a cricket stump in his hand.

That stump was intended for Billy Bunter ! Three members of the Co. were in full agreement ; so were all the Remove, except Bob Cherry. Bob, as usual, was standing up for Bunter.

He was the fat Owl's only defence. Behind Bob's sturdy figure Billy Bunter was blinking in alarm at the angry Removites. He had been walked into the Rag after class, to take his gruel ; and he would have been taking it, at the present moment, but for Bob ! Bob stood like a rock in the way.

"You're setting yourself up against the whole Form, Bob," said Frank Nugent.

"Cheek !" grunted Johnny Bull.

"The cheekfulness is a little terrific, my esteemed Bob !" said Hurree Jamset Ram Singh mildly.

"Chuck it, Bob !" said Mark Linley.

"Barge him out of the way !" exclaimed Bolsover major. "What are you wasting time talking to the cheeky ass for ?"

"I say, you fellows——" squeaked Bunter.

"Save your breath, old fat frump !" said Peter Todd. "You'll want it all for yelling, in a minute."

"Beast !" groaned Bunter. "Ain't you going to do anything for a pal, Toddy ?"

"Yes—I'm going to have a whack with that stump !"

"Beast !"

"Will you get out of the way, Bob, and stop playing the fool ?" asked Harry Wharton, very quietly.

"No !" answered Bob.

"Look here, Cherry !" exclaimed Squiff. "Don't be a goat ! You know what that fat porpoise has done. Nobody cares a straw for his rows with his relations ; but when it comes to keeping a man out of a football match——"

"We beat St. Jim's without Carter !" said Bob.

"That's not the point !"

"Oh, yes it is, to some extent," answered Bob coolly. "We mightn't have beaten them, with Carter in the team—crocking any man he happened to dislike."

"Oh, rot !"

"The rotfulness is terrific."

"What do you think, Smithy ?" asked Bob. "Carter had an accident with me in the Highcliffe match. What did you tell him ?"

The Bounder shrugged his shoulders.

"I told him that if he had an accident with me, I'd have one with him," he answered. "He hasn't yet !"

"That's rot, Smithy !" said Harry Wharton.

"Is it ?" sneered the Bounder. "Well, I can tell you this—if Carter ever hacks me like he did Cherry, accident or not, I'll give him the same back, and one over for interest ! He knows that, or he'd have done it already. He likes me no more than he does Cherry."

"Well, that's neither here nor there !" said Harry Wharton impatiently. "I happen to be football captain, and I put Carter into the eleven. Bunter took it on himself to shift him out. Is Bunter to decide who's going to play for the Remove ?"

"Hardly ! You're a fool to play Carter—but you're skipper !" said the Bounder. "I'd whop him black and blue for meddling, if I were skipper."

"A Daniel come to judgment !" said Peter Todd. "You hear that, Bob ?"

"You can leave Bunter alone !" said Bob. "That is, unless you give Carter the same ! Bunter kept a man out of the St. Jim's match with his silly tricks—well, Carter put a man out of the Highcliffe match with his foul play ! Bunter's a fool—but Carter's a rascal ! No sense in whopping the fool and letting off the rascal."

"Something in that !" agreed the Bounder. "Carter got away with it—why not Bunter ?"

"I say, you fellows, I never did it !" wailed Bunter. "I wasn't there at all, you know ! I was somewhere else when I did it ! Honour bright !"

"Shut up, you fat ass !" grunted Bob.

"Beast !"

"Look here, Bob——"

"Rats !"

"I say, you fellows, I never did it, and I won't do it again !" howled Bunter. "That cad Carter has been after me ever since he came. You jolly well know it. Well, if he's after me, why shouldn't I get after him ? Not that I did it—you know—I didn't !"

"You get after him all you like, you fat idiot, but not to the extent of meddling in the football !" said the captain of the Remove. "You've got to be made to understand that, you frabjous cuckoo !"

"I—I understand it all right, old chap !" gasped Bunter. "I—I understand perfectly, old fellow. I'll take your word for it ! I will, really."

"Ha, ha, ha !"

"You're going to have a dozen with this stump——"

"Beast !"

THE MAGNET LIBRARY.—No. 1,567.

"Will you get out of the way, Bob?"

"No!" answered Bob stubbornly

Harry Wharton breathed deep and hard. Next to Nugent, Bob was his best chum But he was captain of the Remove; and nobody but Bob was able to find any excuse for Bunter's trickery Football matches were important matters in the Remove—and for a selected player to be tricked into missing a match was altogether beyond pardon. The fact that Carter had not, after all, been specially wanted, made no difference to that Neither did Bob's contention that Carter was a foul player; for the general belief was that the unfortunate episode in the Highcliffe match had been an accident

The captain of the Remove would not have retreated had any other fellow stood in the way So he could hardly do so because it was one of his own friends who opposed the administration of justice!

"Last time of asking, Bob!" he said

"I'm sticking here!"

"We shall have to shift you!"

"Get on with it!"

Bob's jaw squared, and his blue eyes gleamed. He was not giving way an inch against all the Form.

Wharton compressed his lips

"Shift him!" he said curtly

The next few minutes were exciting Half a dozen fellows shifted Bob Cherry—but the shifting was no easy task!

He hit out on all sides. and he hit hard—and there was a wild and scrambling tussle Peter Todd and Johnny Bull mixed up on the floor—Ogilvy went across them—Russell spun one way, and Redwing another—Harry Wharton went over his back and Nugent stumbled over his legs, crashed into Hurree Singh, and brought the Nabob of Bhanipur to the floor

But more and more hands grasped at Bob, and he was dragged headlong away.

He went down at last, still resisting, and crashed and half a dozen fellows sat on him to keep him there

Harry Wharton staggered to his feet. He rubbed a painful nose.

"You silly fathead!" he gasped. "Now some of you put that fat chump across the table!"

"I say, you fellows, leggo! I say—yarooph!" roared Bunter

Bob, heavily sat on gasped and heaved. But half a dozen grinning fellows pinned him helplessly down Bunter was plumped on the long table, yelling with apprehension

Very soon he had something more serious to yell for The cricket stump rose and fell with rhythmic whacks

A dozen reports like pistol-shots rang through the Rag Then the captain of the Remove threw aside the stump

"You can cut you fat chump!" he snapped, rubbing his nose again

"Yarooph!"

"Boot him out!"

"Beast!"

Bunter flew Three or four boots helped him out of the Rag, and he disappeared, yelling.

Then Bob Cherry was allowed to rise to his feet

Red and rumpled, he glared at his friends. Then without a word he tramped out of the Rag

THE FOURTEENTH CHAPTER.

Tea in Study No. 13

AT tea-time Billy Bunter rolled into Study No 13, and blinked round that apartment through his big spectacles.

Mark Linley, kneeling at the study

fire, was making toast. Little Wun Lung, standing at the table, was buttering the same as fast as made. Bob Cherry was sitting on a corner of the table, with a rather moody expression on his face.

But if Bob had not forgotten the row in the Rag, Bunter had dismissed it from his fat mind. If he still felt a few twinges from the application of the stump, the prospect of tea comforted him. At the approach of a meal-time, all lesser matters naturally slipped from Bunter's thoughts.

"Early?" he asked breezily. "I thought I wouldn't keep you fellows waiting. Anything to cook? I'll lend a hand."

Bob Cherry gave him a rather grim look. He was championing Bunter, and he did not regret it; but Bunter was not exactly a credit to his champion He had told Bunter to come to his study for a talk with him—one of those heart-to-heart talks. But a heart-to-heart talk, though possibly instructive and beneficial, had no great attraction for William George Bunter; and he certainly would not have come for that alone. So Bob had asked him to tea.

"Oh, here you are!" he grunted.

"Yes, old chap," said Bunter cheerily "I say, did they damage you in the Rag? He, he, he! You looked awfully funny with all those fellows sitting on you. He, he, he!"

"Did I?" breathed Bob.

"Yes, fearfully; your arms and legs sticking out—just like a lobster, you know." said Bunter. "But, I say, what have you got for tea? Something beside toast, I hope? If my postal order had come——"

"I've got something to say to you, Bunter."

"All right. If you want me to cut down to the tuckshop, say the word, old chap, I'll go."

"About your row with Carter——"

"Oh. blow Carter!" said Bunter. "I've jolly well paid him out. I'll pay him out again, too—see if I don't! I say, have you got a cake?"

"Now, listen to me!" said Bob. Heart-to-heart talks were a little difficult with Bunter's eyes roving about the study in quest of foodstuffs. However, Bob got on with it. "That cad Carter is on your track, and he won't stop at any dirty trick to dish you. But dirty trickery isn't an example to be followed—see?"

"Isn't it?" asked Bunter.

"No!" roared Bob.

"All right, old chap. Can I get anything out of the cupboard?"

"Will you listen to me?"

"I'm listening, old fellow; but I may as well help get tea, while I'm listening. I don't mind if you go on talking, of course."

There was a chuckle from Mark Linley; and Wun Lung grinned. Bob Cherry restrained a natural impulse to boot Bunter out of the study.

"Look here," he said, "you can play all the tricks you like on Carter, as he plays them on you; but you ought to play the game, even if he doesn't—see?"

"Think so?" asked Bunter.

"Yes, you ass!"

"All right. If there's a cake, shall I get it out of the cupboard?" asked Bunter. "I don't mind telling you I'm rather hungry."

"That fellow's a sneaking, scheming cur!" said Bob "That's not the sort of fellow you'd like to be, Bunter."

"No fear! Upright and honourable—kindest friend and noblest foe, and

all that—that's my sort," said Bunter. "I say, shall I begin on the toast?"

"That trick you played at Smithy's study yesterday was mean," said Bob. "So it was tricking Carter out of the football match. You can't do dirty mean things because he does them, Bunter. Can't you see that?"

"Oh, yes! Any sardines?"

"What?"

"I like sardines with toast," explained Bunter.

"I've been standing up for you, because that rat is after you!" said Bob, heedless of the important question of sardines. "But I can't stand up for a fellow who plays dirty tricks the same as that cad himself. And, look here, Bunter, it pays better to keep straight."

"That doesn't appeal to me," said Bunter cheerily. "I dare say that's how you look at it, Cherry; but I don't care whether it pays or not. I just go straight, because it's my nature."

"Oh crumbs!" gasped Mark Linley.

"Fattee old Buntee velly funnee," chuckled Wun Lung. "Muchee good olde Bob Chelly talkee 'long Buntee."

"You fat idiot!" roared Bob.

"Oh, really, Cherry! If that's how you talk to a fellow after asking him to tea in your study——"

"Shut up, dummy, and listen to me! Try to get into your fat head that honesty is the best policy, even if there was no other reason for being decent. Look at that cad Carter, for instance! Where has all his trickery got him? Nowhere, so far. Can't you see that?"

"Well, I fancy I'm the fellow to put paid to a cad like that," said Bunter. "I've got brains."

"Oh crikey!"

"I'll handle him all right," said Bunter confidently. "I say, this is jolly good toast; but you might put the butter on a bit thicker, Wun. I like plenty of butter on my toast. I'll make that cad sit up, don't you worry You see, with my wonderful ventriloquism, I can pull his leg all right. I'm going to make Quelch think Carter's cheeking him in the Form-room. He, he, he!"

"You're not!" roared Bob.

"Eh? Why not?"

"Because it's a mean trick."

"Wouldn't Carter do it, if he could?" demanded Bunter, through a large mouthful of toast.

"Yes, he would; and that's a reason why you shouldn't, or any decent fellow. If I catch you playing dirty tricks, I'll jolly well boot you—see?"

"Well, I like that," said Bunter warmly. "I'm not the fellow for dirty tricks, I hope. I like that from you Who let his skipper down in a football match. just because he had a row on with one of the men?"

Bob gazed at him, speechless.

Bunter blinked round the study.

"I say, have you got any sardines, Linley?" he asked. "I don't seem to be able to get any sense out of Cherry. He can't talk about anything, except his silly rows with Carter."

"In the cupboard," said Mark, laughing.

"Oh, good!"

Bunter rolled across to the study cupboard, and got busy with sardines. Bob Cherry watched him in silence. He realised that he was not making much progress in that heart-to-heart talk with Bunter.

"Look here, Bunter!" he said, at last.

Any more sardines?" asked Bunter.

"No!" yelled Bob.

"Oh, all right! No need to howl at a fellow. I'm not deaf, like Dutton. One tin of sardines isn't much. Look here, if you fellows don't want any, I'll finish them. They go all right with toast. I suppose you're going to make some more toast, Linley. You don't seem to have much of a spread here; but a fellow can fill up on toast."

"Will you listen to me, Bunter?"

"Well, I'd rather you gave me a rest, old chap, if you don't mind. You're a bit like a sheep's head, you know—all jaw. Blessed if I ever saw such a fellow for chin-wag! If you'd let a fellow speak, I was going to tell you that there's a row on in the Shell."

"Never mind that!"

"Well, I don't mind it, of course," said Bunter. "Hacker can make out that the Shell fellows go pinching in his study, if he likes. I say, he's had a lot of them up, and asked them about a postal order he makes out he's missed. I dare say the old ass has got it in his pocket all the time—you know Hacker. Sure there ain't any more sardines? What about this jar of bloater paste? I suppose I can open it?"

"Oh, gum!" said Bob. "That's the fellow I've rowed with my pals about—that I punched Wharton's nose for——"

"Serve him right!" said Bunter. "It's time Wharton had his nose punched—altogether too stuck up, if you ask me. I wonder you've never punched it before, old chap, with the airs and graces he puts on! I used to be in his study when he first came, you know; but I had to get out—I couldn't stand it! Not that Toddy's much better—he's mean! I say, is there any more bloater paste? I suppose you've got something for tea, after asking a fellow here?"

There was a tramp of feet in the passage, and four fellows looked in. Mark Linley and Wun Lung grinned welcome. Bob Cherry stared. Harry Wharton, Frank Nugent, Johnny Bull, and Hurree Jamset Ram Singh walked in, and the captain of the Remove deposited a parcel on the table.

"Well, what do you fellows want?" asked Bob gruffly.

"Tea!" answered Harry cheerily. "We've brought our grub along!"

"I say, I'll unpack that for you!" exclaimed Billy Bunter eagerly.

And he proceeded to do so without delay.

"You've got Carter's company in your own study," said Bob, with sarcasm.

"We prefer yours, old bean!" said Frank Nugent affably.

"The preferfulness is terrific!" grinned Hurree Jamset Ram Singh.

"After sitting on my head in the Rag?" growled Bob.

"Nothing in it to damage, was there?" asked Johnny Bull.

Bob stared at him, and then grinned.

Billy Bunter, turning good things out of the parcel, beamed.

"I say, you fellows, this is a spread!" he exclaimed. "Cherry asked me to tea, but he doesn't seem to have anything but toast. I say, what a ripping cake! You fellows treated me rottenly after class, but I never was a chap to owe grudges! I say, there's two pots of jam. Shall I open them both?"

"Open anything you like except your mouth!" said Johnny Bull. "For goodness' sake keep that shut for a bit!"

"Beast!"

Bob Cherry looked rather uncertainly at his friends; but he was more than glad to meet them half-way and let the row in the Rag be abolished, as if it had never happened.

"Sit down, you chaps!" he said. "I was rather an ass to stick up for that fat frog. There's a cricket stump on the shelf, if you'd like to give him a few more whops."

"Why, you beast——" yelled Bunter, in alarm.

"Ha, ha, ha!"

"I say, you fellows——"

"Pack in the grub and shut up, Bunter!"

And Billy Bunter promptly obeyed the first half of that injunction, though not the second.

THE FIFTEENTH CHAPTER.
A Row in the Shell!

THAT there was a "row" on in the Shell, as Billy Bunter had mentioned in Study No. 13, most of the House knew before dorm that night.

Trouble in the Shell was not uncommon, for Mr. Hacker, the master of that Form, was a suspicious man, with a sour temper and an acid tongue. Shell fellows would gladly have "swopped" him for any other beak at Greyfriars. Hobson, the captain of the Shell, had been heard to breathe dire threats of coming back some day as an Old Boy, and whacking Hacker with his own cane.

But the present row was rather out of the common. In the Rag that evening several of the Shell fellows told fellows of other Forms about it, with deep and thrilling indignation.

(Continued on next page.)

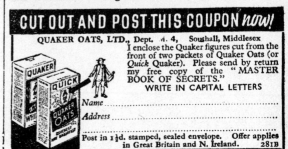

The Acid Drop it seemed, made out that there was a postal order missing from his study table! He had missed it when he had sat down to write a letter, in which he had intended to post it. That was just before tea Tea in the Shell studies had been disagreeably interrupted

Every Shell man who had been in Hacker's study since class, and a good many who hadn't, were called on the carpet.

"The old goat!" said Hobson, to a crowd of juniors in the Rag Thus disrespectfully did Hobby describe his Form-master "The bony old goat! Making out somebody's snooped a quid out of his study! Of course, nobody has! You all know Hacker!"

"Don't we!" said Bob Cherry sympathetically

"He says he got it yesterday—sent some Remove kid to fetch it I think," said Stewart of the Shell, "and left it on his table under a paper-weight till he wanted it. Well, if he did, it might have gone any time—and anybody might have had it. He never missed it till he came to write a silly letter to his silly nephew at some silly school"

"Silly old ass!" said the Bounder.

"Cheeky too!" said Hoskins of the Shell. "He rooted me out of the music-room to ask me about it, because I'd been in his study after class! I was practising Caskowiski's sonata in B major, you know and what do you think he said? Told me to stop that noise while he spoke to me!"

At which there was a chuckle in the Rag! Claude Hoskins was no end of a musician, with a taste for modern composers, and Hacker, with all his faults, was not the only man at Greyfriars who regarded Hobby's musical effects as a noise! Fellows had been heard to describe them as a horrid din!

Still, it was agreed that it was like Hacker's cheek to interrupt a fellow, inquiring about a postal order which, of course, he hadn't lost at all.

"In his trousers pocket, most likely!" said Hobson "That's the sort of old ass he is! He lost a letter once, and suspected every man in the Form in turn of snooping it out of his desk, and it turned out he'd shoved it into his trousers pocket, instead of the pocket he thought he had! That's the kind of footling ass Hacker is!"

"I suppose it's still in his study all the time!" said Harry Wharton

"Of course it is! He's laid a book on it, or something." said Stewart. "No good telling him so!"

"But he can't think it's pinched!" exclaimed Johnny Bull "That would be rather thick even for the Acid Drop."

"Well, he jolly well does think so!" said Hobson "He doesn't exactly say so—perhaps he's ashamed to but he's had man after man up, questioning him like a dashed detective! I jolly nearly told him to shut up! Only, of course, you can't to a beak that"

"Hardly!" grinned Bob Cherry

"You fellows grouse about Quelch, at times!" growled Hobson "Wouldn't I like to swop Hacker for him! Wouldn't I just! Quelch is a cough drop, but he's got sense! Hacker's a fool!"

"When did Hacker miss it?" asked Carter

"I've told you—just before tea!"

"But if he left it there since yesterday, it might have gone any time," said Carter

"Just what I was saying!" said THE MAGNET LIBRARY.—No. 1,567.

Stewart. "Of course it might—if it went at all! But, of course, it never did."

"Did you see anything of it, Bunter?" asked Carter.

Billy Bunter blinked round through his big spectacles

"Eh?" he ejaculated. "What?"

"Did you see anything of Hacker's postal order when you were in his study in break this morning?" asked Carter deliberately.

A sudden silence followed that question.

As nobody outside the Shell had any business in Hacker's study, it had not occurred to anyone, so far, to think of any fellow outside the Form in connection with the matter. Neither, apparently, had it occurred to Mr. Hacker! It was news to all the fellows that a Removite had been in Hacker's study that day.

Bob Cherry's eyes flashed.

In Study No. 13, after that heart-to-heart talk with Bunter, he had almost made up his mind to let the fat Owl, as it were, rip. But at that question from Carter, Bob saw the hand of the schemer at work again. He broke out angrily, before Bunter could answer.

"You rotter, are you trying to make out that Bunter was in Hacker's study? Are you trying to stick this on Bunter, you cur?"

Carter shrugged his shoulders.

"Before you sling out the compliments, why not ask Bunter whether he was there or not?" he suggested. "I've no doubt he will tell you."

"You weren't there, Bunter?" asked Bob, looking round at the fat Owl.

"Not if old Hacker's going to think that I snooped his postal order!" said Bunter "No fear!"

"Wha-a-at?" gasped Bob, while the other fellows yelled. "You howling ass, Carter says you were there. Were you, or not?"

"Well, you know what a fibber Carter is!" said Bunter "Don't you believe a word Carter says. He'd jolly well like to stick this on me! I don't believe that chap could tell the truth if he tried He's my relation, I know, but he's not truthful—not much of the Bunter side of the family in him! The Carters are a low lot!"

"Were you in Hacker's study this morning, you fat frump?"

Bunter appeared to be deep in reflection for a moment or two.

"Well, no," he answered. "On the whole I wasn't. I went nowhere near Hacker's study! Mind, I wouldn't mind telling you fellows, but if Hacker got to hear of it he might think I'd snaffled his putrid postal order. So the fact is, I wasn't there—nowhere near the place! Carter jolly well knows it, too, if he'd own up He passed me as I was coming away"

"Oh crumbs!"

"Did you see the postal order while you were there, you fat ass?" asked Harry Wharton

"No—I never looked round the room at all! Besides, I told you that I wasn't there!"

"Well, my hat!" said Hobson, staring at the fat Owl. "Hacker would want to know what a Remove man was up to in his study if he knew."

"Well, Carter was there, too," said Bunter. "He was going there when I came away! I—I mean, of course, when I never came away, as I wasn't there, you know."

"You benighted chump," said Bob Cherry. "Why on earth did you go to Hacker's study?"

"I didn't, old chap!"

"Was he there?" asked Peter Todd.

"Eh? No fear! I knew he was jawing in Common-room, or I shouldn't have picked his study to pull Carter's leg!" chuckled Bunter. "You see, I made that ass Carter think that Hacker was calling him, with my wonderful ventriloquism, you know! He cut off to Hacker's study at once! He, he, he!"

"Oh," said Bob, "that was why you went there, you fathead?"

"Oh, no, I never went there at all!" Bunter shook his head decidedly. "Don't you get making out that I went to Hacker's study while he was in Common-room, Cherry! He might hear of it, and you know what a suspicious beast he is."

Carter laughed.

"If that postal order doesn't turn up, I shall have my own opinion about what's become of it—but it's no bizney of mine. Hacker can sort it out for himself."

"You can keep your opinion to yourself, at any rate!" growled Bob. "It's the sort of rotten opinion a fellow like you would have."

"Thanks!" yawned Carter, and he walked out of the Rag, leaving the discussion still going on.

By bed-time, half the Lower School knew that Billy Bunter had been in the study from which the postal order had been missed. And a good many fellows wondered whether Bunter could have explained, had he liked, what had become of it!

THE SIXTEENTH CHAPTER.

Catching Carter!

GURRRRRRGGH!
Arthur Carter jumped.

The Remove were at breakfast, in the morning. Quelch, who always breakfasted with his Form, sat at the head of the table. Other beaks breakfasted in Common-room, or sometimes in their studies, and often the Remove wished that Quelch did the same: for there was no doubt that, early in the morning, Quelch was not at his bonniest.

Until he had disposed of eggs and bacon, Quelch was undoubtedly grim.

Like many middle-aged gentlemen, Quelch was a little nervy and testy before breakfast, but did not realise that an empty interior was the cause —he was more prone to think that the fault lay in others, who irritated him.

He improved considerably, and took a brighter view of life, after the very first mouthful and the first draught of tea! Before breakfast was over, he would often be quite genial.

Unluckily, Quelch had not yet started on the provender when Carter gave that sudden convulsive jump and dropped a cup.

It was hardly Carter's fault!

A deep and savage growl under his chair was enough to make any fellow jump. It sounded, to Carter, as if a particularly vicious dog was just at his legs, and he jumped. His cup crashed, in pieces, and tea spread in a flood.

A gimlet eye transfixed him from the head of the table.

"Carter!" came Quelch's deep rumble. "What on earth are you doing, Carter? How dare you! Sit down at once!"

"There's a dog under my chair, sir!" gasped Carter.

"What? Nonsense! Sit down immediately!"

Quelch's look, and tone, were awe-inspiring—almost terrifying! But Carter did not heed his master's voice.

"I say, you fellows—leggo! I say—yaroooooh!" roared Bunter. Whack, whack, whack! The stump rose and fell, and Bunter wriggled wildly. Bob Cherry gasped and heaved, but half-a-dozen grinning fellows pinned him helplessly down.

He was not going to sit down with his legs in reach of that vicious dog!

Standing up, he pushed his chair back and stared under it, and under the edge of the table. To his astonishment, no dog was to be seen.

"Carter!" almost roared Mr. Quelch.

"It—it was a dog, sir!" stammered Carter.

"Nonsense! I repeat, nonsense! There can be no dog in Hall! If there is a dog here, point it out to me."

"I—I can't see it, sir—but——"

"Take a hundred lines, Carter! If you do not sit down this instant, I shall send you out of Hall without your breakfast!"

Carter sat down.

He was angry and puzzled. The dog appeared to have growled savagely under his chair and then departed, which was perplexing. Other fellows, near Carter, had heard the growl, though Mr. Quelch, at the end of the long table, had been out of hearing, and they were puzzled, too.

Billy Bunter, blinking across the table at Carter grinned. And several fellows, spotting that grin on Bunter's fat face, caught on to the fact that the Remove ventriloquist was at work again.

Harry Wharton made a sign to the fat junior to "chuck" it. Bunter favoured him with a fat wink in response.

He was not disposed to chuck it! Ventriloquism was his only method of getting back at Carter, and Bunter was on the warpath!

Gurrrrrrh!

Carter jumped again at the growl under his chair, and dragged his legs up instinctively, with a gasp of alarm.

"Carter!" rapped Mr. Quelch. "Will you keep still? Cannot you sit still at table, Carter? What is the matter with you, Carter?"

"It's that dog again, sir!" gasped Carter. "I don't want to be bitten, sir!"

"Upon my word!" Mr. Quelch rose to his feet, with an expression on his face like that of Roderick Dhu, on the occasion when dark lightnings flashed from Roderick's eye! "I will ascertain for myself whether there is a dog present, Carter, and if there is not, as I am sure there is not, I shall cane you."

"I heard him growl under my chair, sir."

"You did nothing of the kind, Carter, as there is certainly no dog here. But we shall see!" said the Remove master grimly.

He came along the table, and the juniors rose from their places to give him a clear field for investigation.

No dog, certainly, was to be seen on the spot. Mr. Quelch stooped and glared under the table. He beheld a forest of legs and feet, but nothing else.

He rose again, with a grim brow.

"There is no dog here, Carter! I was perfectly assured that there was not, and I have now ascertained the fact! Explain yourself."

"I—I—I heard him, sir——" stammered Carter.

"If you heard a dog here, Carter, where is the dog? Point out the animal to me!" snorted Mr. Quelch.

Carter stood helplessly puzzled. He could not point out a non-existent dog! Mr. Quelch waited one moment—no more! The he pointed to the door.

"Go!" he said.

"I—I haven't finished my breakfast, sir——"

"Leave the Hall at once, Carter, and wait for me in my study!" said Mr. Quelch. "I shall cane you when I come there! Not a word more! Go!"

Carter, with set lips, went.

Mr. Quelch returned to his chair, and breakfast was resumed—Billy Bunter grinning with cheery satisfaction.

Some of the juniors, who had "tumbled" to the fat Owl's trick, gave him expressive looks. But expressive looks were wasted on Bunter! He had scored over Carter—and that was what Bunter wanted! Carter had a hundred lines, and was going to have a caning! The fat ventriloquist of the Remove had a happy and satisfied feeling that he was getting his own back.

"You fat chump!" whispered Bob Cherry. "Didn't I tell you yesterday not to play mean tricks——"

"Oh, really, Cherry——"

"You can't let Carter take that licking!"

"Can't I?" grinned Bunter.

"If you do," hissed Bob into a fat ear, "I'll jolly well boot you round the quad after brekker."

"Beast!"

"You pernicious porker——"

"Cherry!" came a deep rumble.

"Oh! Yes, sir!" gasped Bob, looking round.

"Are you quarrelling with another Remove boy at the breakfast-table, Cherry?"

"Oh, no, sir!"

"Indeed! I judged by your expression that you were doing so, Cherry. Kindly repeat to me what you were saying to Bunter."

"I—I—I——"

"I am waiting to hear you, Cherry."

"I—I—I——"

"Will you tell me, this instant, what you were saying to Bunter!" thundered Mr. Quelch.

"I—I—I was telling him he was a—a pernicious porker, sir!" gasped Bob.

"Ha, ha, ha!"

"Silence! Cherry, you will take a hundred lines for using such expressions. Now be silent."

And Bob said no more during brekker.

THE MAGNET LIBRARY.—No. 1.567.

THE SEVENTEENTH CHAPTER.

Carter's Chance !

ARTHUR CARTER went into his Form-master's study with an expression on his face like unto that of a demon in a pantomime.

He was still puzzled about that growl under his chair, and the remarkable disappearance of the dog after growling; but he knew that he had heard what he had heard, whether Quelch believed it or not. Now he had to wait a good twenty minutes in the Remove master's study, with a caning at the end of that long wait

He stared angrily round the study, wondering whether there was a chance of playing some trick there to worry Quelch—payment in advance, as it were, for the caning he was going to receive.

But he shook his head at that thought. Anything that happened in that study could hardly fail to be traced to the fellow who had waited there during breakfast in Hall

But that glance round brought to his attention a pile of letters that lay on the Form-master's table.

He knew that these would be the letters for Remove fellows. It was one of Mr. Quelch's many duties to look over correspondence addressed to members of his Form

Most of the letters, which naturally were from home, passed with a cursory glance, but occasionally there was one that the Form-master had to stop in transit, or order to be opened in his presence. But for the fact that all correspondence passed under a beak's eye, some Greyfriars fellows would certainly have received communications they were better without.

After Quelch had glanced over the letters it was Trotter's duty to put them up in the rack, to be taken by the boys in break. Quelch generally did the glancing after breakfast.

Seeing the pile of letters, Carter stepped to the table and looked at them. His reason was that there might be a letter for himself among them. At the moment he had no other thought in his mind.

But he forgot to look for a letter for himself as he spotted an envelope addressed to " W G. Bunter."

His eyes fixed on that letter.

In break that morning Billy Bunter was going to find a letter for himself, and no doubt would hope—until he opened it—that it might contain his long-expected postal order. After opening, that hope was likely to be dashed.

Carter stood looking fixedly at that letter.

A strange expression was coming over his face.

He stepped quickly to the door, which he had left open, and shut it quietly. Then he stepped back to the table.

His eyes fixed on Bunter's letter again. He picked it up with fingers that trembled a little.

His thoughts were racing.

Ever since he had purloined the postal order from Mr. Hacker's study the previous day he had been wondering and pondering how to " plant " it on the fat Owl in such a way as to make it impossible for suspicion to be directed towards himself

To barge into Bunter and thrust it into a pocket, or to drop it into his box in the dormitory, would have been easy, but futile. It would not be found without a search being made, and it was very unlikely that any search for Hacker's missing " quid " would be

made in Quelch's Form. But a still more deterring circumstance was the fact that Bob Cherry suspected him, and had a watchful eye on him. It was known that he, as well as Bunter, had gone to Hacker's study while the postal order was there He knew—at least, he did not doubt—that if that postal order turned up on Bunter, Bob Cherry would guess, and would announce at the top of his powerful voice that Carter had put it where it was found.

He had to think of something a little more subtle than that, and so far he had been unable to do so.

Bunter had to spend that postal order, or there was, he realised, nothing in the scheme at all.

He had thought of leaving it somewhere for Bunter to " find," for Bunter was exactly the ass to think that " findings were keepings." But even Bunter was hardly ass enough for that, since he had heard that the postal order had been missed by Hacker and inquired after.

The young rascal had been, therefore, at a loss—determined to carry on with the scheme somehow, but undecided how. Meanwhile, the postal order was hidden in the lining of his jacket, safe from discovery.

Now, with that letter for Bunter in his hand, he knew what he could do, and what he was going to do.

Bunter was expecting a postal order. Carter, of course, had heard all about that, like every other fellow in the Lower School at Greyfriars.

If he found a postal order in his letter, what could he think, except that it had been sent him from home?

The handwriting of Mr. Bunter on the envelope, and the Surrey postmark, showed that this letter came from Bunter's home. More likely than not it contained an answer to a request for cash, probably in the form of advice to Bunter to keep within his allowance. If there was a postal order in it, all the better Carter had only to change one for the other.

He breathed hard, his heart beating thickly

He wondered whether his evil counsellor, Gideon Gooch, would have approved of this scheme, or whether the cunning lawyer would have thought it too risky?

Yet where was the risk ?

He had at least ten minutes, more likely a quarter of an hour, before Mr. Quelch arrived in the study.

To open the letter with steam, slip in the purloined postal order, and close the flap again—what could be easier ?

He did not even need to leave the study.

In the fender stood a little copper electric kettle, which Mr. Quelch used when he needed hot water in the study for any purpose. Carter had only to switch it on and wait a minute or two for steam to issue from the spout.

He hesitated.

When Bunter found that postal order in his letter, what was he likely to do? Cut off to the tuckshop instantly—there was no doubt about that. He might ask Mrs. Mimble at the school shop to change it for him instead of waiting till he could go down to the post office. That mattered nothing, so long as he spent it.

The short-sighted Owl of the Remove was not likely to notice the stamp of the issuing office on the slip of paper which showed that it had been bought in Friardale Moreover, that stamping, like so much Post Office stamping, was indistinct. In detective stories letters are traced by postmarks, but in real life

a postmark is only too likely to be utterly undecipherable, if anyone wishes to make it out. It was the same with the stamping on postal orders sometimes, especially in little village post offices. Carter had to look closely to make out " Friardale " in the circular stamping. Bunter would have had to screw his eyes behind his spectacles to make it out, and he was not likely to look at it at all.

That was all right !

A greater difficulty was the fact that in sending his son a postal order Mr. Bunter would naturally fill in his name. This postal order was not filled in as payable to anybody.

If Carter thought of dipping Mr. Quelch's pen in the ink, and filling in Bunter's name as payee, he dismissed it at once. He dared not do such a thing.

Still, people sometimes omitted to fill in the payee's name before posting a postal order. If Bunter senior was anything like Bunter junior, he was very likely to be careless in such matters. Anyhow, Bunter, finding the postal order in his letter, could hardly fail to believe that his father had sent it to him, and the fact that his name was not on it would make no difference.

That, too, was all right

Three long minutes passed while Carter was thinking it out, with perspiration on his brow. Then he stooped and switched on the electric kettle and waited

He had plenty of time yet—more than ample time; but his heart beat in throbs as he waited for the kettle to boil.

But he had no doubts. This time he had the fat sweep on the hip. It was not merely a matter of getting him a bad report. This meant the sack from the school, and a crashing end to all Bunter's hopes and prospects with old Joseph Carter ! This scheme was perfect, without a flaw—unless, indeed, there was something in rascality itself that insured its own defeat. And Carter had not yet learned that honesty was the best policy.

Steam came bubbling from the spout of the copper kettle in the fender. Carter held the envelope over it, and in a few moments the flap loosened. He shut off the switch.

Carefully pulling open the flap of the envelope, he drew out the letter from within. He glanced at it. It was brief:

" Dear William,—I have received your letter—the seventh this term, all in the same strain. As I regret that I am unable to send you anything beyond your usual allowance, I recommend you not to spend so much money on postage stamps.—Your affectionate father,
                    " W. S. BUNTER."

Carter grinned for a moment over that letter from home. But his face became at once very serious. This was not the sort of letter that was likely to be accompanied by a postal order for a pound. Even Bunter, fathead as he was, would be surprised and puzzled to find a " quid " in the envelope with such a letter as that.

There was only one way of getting out of that difficulty. Carter dropped the letter into Mr. Quelch's study fire.

Bunter might be surprised at receiving a postal order without an accompanying line; but the postal order, after all, was what he wanted, and he would naturally suppose that Mr. Bunter had been in a hurry.

Taking the folded postal order from its hiding-place in the lining of his jacket, Carter slipped it into the empty envelope. He stuck down the flap again with a spot of Mr. Quelch's gum.

Then he replaced the letter where he had found it—in the pile on the study table.

Glancing at Mr. Quelch's clock, he was surprised to see that he had not yet been ten minutes in the study. It had seemed much longer than that.

He stepped to the window, which was open, to let in the morning air of early spring, and stood looking out into the quad while he waited for the Remove master to appear.

Ten minutes later there was a scurrying of feet and whooping of voices in the quad as the Greyfriars fellows came out.

Billy Bunter blinked at him standing at Mr. Quelch's window, with a fat grin. The next moment Bunter yelled as Bob Cherry's boot landed on his trousers.

Carter turned away from the window as Mr. Quelch entered the study.

After breakfast Quelch was in a bonnier mood. He picked up his cane, and told Carter to bend over; but it was merely a flick, and Carter hardly knew whether he was caned or not when Quelch told him to go.

He went.

Mr. Quelch sat down at the table to look over the letters, little dreaming what had happened there.

Carter went out into the quad, with a sour smile on his face. His thoughts were concentrated on what was going to happen in break when the letters were taken from the rack. First and second school seemed very long to Carter that morning.

THE EIGHTEENTH CHAPTER.

Like a Charm !

"I SAY, you fellows, is there one for me?"

Billy Bunter, in break, blinked anxiously up at the letter-rack.

Bunter was, as usual, expecting a postal order. He had been expecting it ever since the term started, and it had not yet arrived. But hope springs eternal in the human breast.

"Hallo, hallo, hallo! Here's one for you, Bunter!" said Bob Cherry; and he reached down a letter to the fat Owl.

"Oh, good!" said Bunter. "I say, you fellows, I wonder if this is my postal order?"

"The wonderfulness is terrific!" grinned Hurree Jamset Ram Singh.

"Well, it's really over-due, you know," said Bunter. "I've been expecting it for some time, really. But I'm afraid this letter is from home, by the fist."

"He's afraid it's a letter from home!" chuckled Smithy. "O dutiful and affectionate son and heir!"

"Ha, ha, ha!"

"Well, I mean to say, I was expecting a letter from one of my titled relations, with a postal order, you know; but this can't be it, as there's no crest on it," explained Bunter. "Besides, it's the pater's fist. But it may be all right. I've written to him half a dozen times at least——"

"Seven times!" said Peter Todd.

"Eh—how do you know it was seven, Toddy?"

"Because you borrowed a stamp from me every time. You'd have written oftener if I'd stood the stamps."

"Oh, really, Toddy, I'll pay for those stamps if my pater's sent me a tip in this letter!" said Bunter. "After all, he might. It doesn't feel as if there's much in it. Still, you never know, you know."

Bunter did not seem in an urgent hurry to open that letter. His pater's "fist" on the envelope seemed to have damped him down, as it were.

Possibly he knew how unlikely it was that Mr. William Samuel Bunter had weighed in with a remittance. That letter was more likely to contain sage advice on the subject of economy. Bunter had been there before, so to speak, and he knew. And he had little use for sage advice. It was not legal tender at the tuckshop!

However, he jabbed a fat thumb into the envelope at last, which was Bunter's elegant way of opening a letter, and groped within with his fat fingers.

One fellow, lounging at a little distance, was watching him covertly while affecting to read a letter.

That one was Carter.

Other fellows who happened to be there were concerned about their own correspondence. Some of them cast rather envious glances at Smithy, who carelessly drew a couple of pound notes from a letter. But no fellow in the Remove was likely to cast envious eyes at Bunter.

But a sudden chirrup of glee from the fat junior drew attention on him.

"Oh crumbs! Oh, good! Oh crikey! Ripping!" ejaculated Bunter.

Many eyes turned on him then.

"What on earth's that?" exclaimed Bob Cherry, staring at a printed slip of paper in Bunter's fat fingers. "Don't—oh, don't say it's your postal order! The shock would be too great, old chap!"

"Ha, ha, ha!"

"I say, you fellows," trilled Bunter, "it's come!"

"Fan me!" gasped Peter Todd.

"Oh day worthy to be marked with a white stone!" said Hurree Jamset Ram Singh solemnly.

"I say, you fellows, this is all right!" chortled Bunter. "I say, the pater's sent me a quid!"

"Glorious!" grinned Bob.

"Gratters, old fat man!" said Harry Wharton, laughing.

"You'll have to pay poundage on that postal order, Bunter!" declared Skinner.

"Eh—why?"

"It's been such a jolly long time coming, it must be out of date!" explained Skinner. "Any whiskers grown on it?"

"Ha, ha, ha!"

"Yah!" retorted Bunter. "You don't often get a quid, Skinner, and chance it! I say, you fellows, a whole quid! He, he, he!"

"Hold on, old fat bean!" said Toddy. "Make sure it's a tip! 'Member your last postal order; your pater sent it for something special. Better see what he says in his letter before you blow it on riotous living."

"There ain't any letter with it!" said Bunter, blinking into the envelope. "That's rather odd, too. Generally the pater sends a letter, but not a tip; this time he's sent a tip, but not a letter!"

"Well, that's a change for the better in his manners and customs!" remarked the Bounder. "I'd encourage him to keep that up!"

"Ha, ha, ha!"

"I say, you fellows, I'm going to stand a spread with this!" said Bunter. "I shall have to have a snack in break, of course. But a whole quid——"

"There won't be much left for a spread if you have a snack!" remarked Skinner. "Better stand the spread in break."

"I say, Wharton, change this for me, will you? I can't go down to the post office in break."

"Pleased!" said the captain of the Remove, laughing. "I've only got ninepence, but if you'll take that for it——"

"Oh, really, Wharton! Look here, Smithy, you've got lots! Cash this postal order for me, will you?"

"I will if it's a real one!" said the Bounder, with a chuckle.

"Well, look at it, you silly ass! It's not filled in, either, so you can fill your own name when you cash it—see? Give me a pound note for it, Smithy."

Vernon-Smith took the postal order and glanced at it. Obviously, it was a real and genuine postal order, and the Bounder slipped it carelessly into his notecase and handed the fat Owl one of his pound notes in exchange.

With that note clutched tight in a fat hand, Billy Bunter shot out of the House and headed for the tuckshop. After him walked Skinner and Snoop and Fisher T. Fish. With a whole quid in his possession, Billy Bunter was worth cultivating as an acquaintance—temporarily, at least!

Arthur Carter walked away, with a gleam of satisfaction in his eyes. It was through now!

Bunter had received that postal order —Hacker's postal order—without a glimmering of suspicion. He had changed it, and it was too late to recall that action. Whether he changed it at the tuckshop or the post office or with one of the Remove fellows mattered nothing. He had changed it, and the fact could, and would, be brought home to him.

When he was taxed with it, it would not be of much use for him to say that he had taken it out of that letter from home?

Who could—or would—believe such a statement? His father, if referred to, could only say that there had been no postal order in the letter at all.

That postal order could be proved to be Hacker's—the number on it would prove that; a reference to the village post office would establish the fact.

The scheme had worked like a charm —the fat Owl had taken the bait like a fat gudgeon. All that was needed now was for Hacker's attention to be drawn to the fact that Bunter had been seen changing a postal order for a pound—after having been seen in Hacker's study! To that, the hard-hearted young rascal now devoted his thoughts—while Billy Bunter, with the assistance of two or three temporary pals, disposed of his unexpected tip at the school shop—with very little left out of the pound, when the bell rang for third school.

THE NINETEENTH CHAPTER.
Spotted by Smithy!

HERBERT VERNON-SMITH breathed hard, and his eyes glittered.

He stood in his study—with a postal order for twenty shillings in his hand, staring at it, and his face hardened, and hardened, as he stared. His teeth came together.

"Spoofed!" he muttered aloud. "By gad! Spoofed! By gad! I'll——" He shut his teeth again.

He dropped the postal order into his pocket, and left the study. It was after dinner, and most of the fellows were out in the quad. The Bounder went out of the House, and looked about him.

"Cherry!" he called.

"Hallo, hallo, hallo!" Bob Cherry was punting a footer with some Remove fellows, but he glanced round as the Bounder called.

"I want you a minute."

"Oh, all right!"

Bob joined Vernon-Smith, rather wondering at the hard, grim look on the Bounder's face.

"Anything up?" he asked.

"Yes—lots! Come along with me—I don't want to shout it out all over the school—at present, at least!"

Bob, in wonder, walked with him under the elms, leaving the other fellows punting the ball.

"What on earth's up, Smithy?" he asked.

"I don't quite know! I'm going to know! I thought I'd speak to you first, as you seem to have set yourself up as that fat fool's chief champion! Where's Bunter?"

"In the tuckshop, I expect, if he's got any of his quid left."

"My quid!" said the Bounder grimly.

"What do you mean? You gave him a pound note for his postal order——"

"For old Hacker's postal order!" answered Smithy, in the same grim tone.

Bob Cherry stood quite still. That answer from the Bounder bereft him of speech for a moment or two.

"Are you mad, Smithy?" he asked, at last.

"No!"

"Has Carter been pulling your leg, you fool? I noticed in the Rag last night that he was trying to make capital out of old Hacker fancying that he had lost a postal order——"

"I noticed it, too!" said Vernon-Smith. "That's the chief reason why I'm speaking to you, instead of Quelch, and why Bunter isn't being taken to the Head to be sacked this minute."

"If you're not mad, what do you mean?" growled Bob. "Bunter seems to have gone to Hacker's study yesterday, but he never touched his postal order—he wouldn't, fool as he is. Carter put the idea into fellows' minds—that was his game, the cad! Are you idiot enough to think that Bunter's postal order to-day was the one Hacker missed?"

"Exactly—as it's the same one."

"Don't be an ass!"

"I've got it here," said Vernon-Smith quietly. "Look at it!"

"Looking at it won't make it Hacker's!" growled Bob. "Bunter got that postal order in a letter from his father this morning, as you jolly well know."

"I know he said so! Does Bunter's pater live in Friardale, a mile or so from Greyfriars?" asked the Bounder sarcastically.

"You know he doesn't."

"Think he'd drop in at Friardale post office to get a postal order then?"

"How could he, fathead, when he lives in another county?" snapped Bob. "What the dickens do you mean?"

"I mean that that postal order was bought in Friardale on Wednesday this week!" answered Smithy.

"It wasn't, and couldn't have been."

"Look at the post office stamp on it."

"Oh, rot!" growled Bob.

But he looked, and his face changed as he made out the blurred stamping— FRIARDALE, with the date. He gave the Bounder a startled, almost scared look.

"Smithy!" he gasped.

"If old Bunter sent young Bunter a postal order, it would be bought either in Surrey, where he lives, or in London, where he goes to business!" said Vernon-Smith. "It couldn't and wouldn't be bought in Kent, near this school."

"I know! But——"

"A postal order for a pound, bought at Friardale on Wednesday, has been taken from Hacker's study. This is a postal order for a pound, bought at Friardale on Wednesday. Don't be a fool, Cherry! You know this is Hacker's as well as I do."

"Good heavens!" breathed Bob.

He gazed at the Bounder in horror. It was Hacker's postal order in Smithy's hand; he knew that now The Bounder slipped it back into his pocket.

"What made you think——" gasped Bob.

"I'm no fool!" answered Smithy coolly. "I thought, this morning that

Printed in England and published every Saturday by the Proprietors, The Amalgamated Press Ltd. The Fleetway House, Farringdon Street, London, E.C.4. Advertisement offices The Fleetway House, Farringdon Street, London E.C.4. Registered for transmission by Canadian Magazine Post. Subscription rates Inland and Abroad. 11s. per annum, 5s. 6d for six months. Sole Agents for Australia and New Zealand Messrs. Gordon & Gotch. Ltd. and for South Africa : Central News Agency Ltd.—Saturday, February 26th, 1938.

Bunter had taken that postal order from his letter, as all the fellows thought. I was only surprised that he got it at all. But—it struck me as a bit of a coincidence, afterwards, Bunter getting a postal order for a pound, when a postal order for a pound had just been missed from a study he went into without having any business there. So I gave it the once-over before letting it go further! When I made out the post office stamp on it, of course, I knew it was Hacker's."

"But——" stammered Bob.

"But," said the Bounder, "I've been spoofed—but was it by Bunter, or somebody else?"

"Who else? What do you mean?"

"I've been thinking!" said the Bounder, with a sneer "I know what it looks like on the face of it. Bunter saw that postal order on the table when he sneaked into Hacker's study yesterday—he bagged it—and he pretended to receive it by post this morning, to account for having it. He thinks I shall cash it next time I pass the post office, and that that will be the end of it. Hacker's suspecting fellows up and down the Shell—never dreaming of a Remove man! Safe as houses! That's what it looks like."

"I can't make it out! I'd never have believed—I know he snoops tuck, and he's an unscrupulous little beast in a good many ways, but this——"

"I said that that's what it looks like!" said the Bounder deliberately. "But things are not always what they look like, old bean! Haven't you ever heard that appearances are deceptive?"

"How——"

"As soon as I saw what it was, I jumped to it at once that Bunter had bagged Hacker's postal order, and spoofed me into taking it off his hands. That will be the general opinion, if this gets out."

"It must get out!" said Bob. "If Bunter pinched it, the sooner he's sacked, the better I'd never stand by a thief, I know that."

"But did he?" said Vernon-Smith. "I'm not a fellow to act in a hurry—and I got some second thoughts on the subject. There's two or three queer little circumstances about this, Cherry. There's a fellow in the Form whom we know to be on that fat fool's track. Two or three weeks ago, he gave me away at the Three Fishers, thinking it was Bunter there—and nearly got me bunked. I paid him out for that, and let it drop! But I haven't forgotten! I've got a good memory! Well, Carter knew all about that postal order—he had gone to fetch it for Hacker, on Wednesday, when I was locked in my study—you remember? And Carter went to Hacker's study yesterday, as well as Bunter."

"He said he never went in——"

"That, for what he said!" The Bounder snapped his fingers. "Look here, Cherry, if Bunter pinched that postal order he's going to be sacked. But did he? Is it possible that that cad Carter wangled this somehow?"

"How could he?"

The Bounder shook his head.

"I don't know! If Bunter never pinched it, he found it in his letter from home, as he said; so Carter, if he wangled it, must have got it into that letter somehow."

"That's impossible, Smithy."

"Is it? Letters have been opened by steam before now! I know it sounds thick—but it's possible. Bunter said there was no letter with it—he needn't have said so—it was jolly odd. Suppose Carter found an old envelope of Bunter's, patched it up, and put it in

the rack. That would account for no letter being in it."

Bob started.

"You seem to think worse of Carter than I do!" he said, slowly. "Do you think any fellow could be such a reptile?"

"I think Carter could!"

"But—but——" muttered Bob. "It's possible, Smithy—but—but it's almost impossible! An old envelope, after Bunter had ripped it open and thrown it away—— And then, how would he get it in the rack with the others? He wasn't out of the Form-room before us."

"No—it doesn't sound very feasible!" admitted the Bounder. "But if that letter was delivered this morning, he couldn't have got at it—Quelch has them all in his study, till they're put out for the fellows." The Bounder broke off, with a sudden jump. "Why, you fool, Carter was in Quelch's study this morning—more than a quarter of an hour there by himself—don't you remember? Quelch sent him there, after Bunter played that fool trick of the growling dog under the table——!"

"Oh!" gasped Bob.

The two looked at one another! Bob's face was pale—the Bounder's bitter and cynically sardonic. Both knew, now.

"The reptile!" breathed Bob. "The worm! The snake in the grass! Smithy, is it really possible that—that——"

"Nobody would believe it, I suppose," said Smithy, with his sneering grin. "No proof—there never is any proof with Carter—I've found the cur out, and you've found him out; but your own pals are fed up with your down on him—they wouldn't believe this, ten to one! And yet I know that Carter had Hacker's postal order, all ready to plant on that fat fool, and that he got it into Bunter's letter, just as if I'd seen him doing it!"

"If we could prove it——"

"We can't—only to ourselves."

"I don't see even that——"

The Bounder laughed.

"If this is Carter's work, you've only got to wait for his next move! This won't serve his turn, unless he gets Hacker on Bunter's track. If he did this, and I know he did, that's his next step."

"The fellow's a crook!" muttered Bob, "just a crook!"

"All that!" agreed Smithy. "Bad to the bone! Well, I lose a quid over this—but I'd lose a dozen to dish that hound. Hacker's going to find his postal order in his study—and that will be that! I shall be late for class this afternoon."

"Eh, why?"

"Because I shall have to wait till Hacker's gone in with the Shell, before I can nip into his study! Hallo, here's dear old Bunter! He doesn't look as if he's under the chopper, does he?"

Billy Bunter rolled up, happy and shiny, and sticky. He gave the two juniors a cheeky blink through his big spectacles.

"I say, Smithy, I've been looking for you!" he said. "Look here, old chap, I was going to stand a spread, out of that quid pater sent me, but—it's gone! I hardly know how it all went—but it has! It's surprising how a few things at the tuck-shop mount up, ain't it?"

"Very!" agreed the Bounder.

"Well, look here, old chap," said Bunter. "I had a postal order this morning. You know that! Fellows make a lot of jokes about a chap expecting a postal order—but it came all right, didn't it?"

"It did!" assented Smithy, while Bob Cherry stood looking at Bunter's fat, sticky face in silence.

"Well, then, you jolly well know that it's all right, what?" said Bunter. "Now, I'm expecting another postal order—from one of my titled relations, you know. You can rely on it, Smithy—it will come, just like this one did, you know. I'd like to stand that spread, after saying I would! I'm going to ask you, Smithy! Will you lend me the quid?"

The Bounder laughed.

"No!" he answered.

"I mean to say, that postal order's certain to come to-morrow!" explained Bunter. "It won't hurt you to lend me a quid till to-morrow, Smithy! It will be in the rack to-morrow morning, just as this one was this morning! You can be absolutely sure of that."

"You're sure that one this morning came from your pater?" asked the Bounder, watching Bunter's fat face intently.

"Eh? Yes, of course!" Bunter blinked at him in astonishment. "It was in my letter from home."

"Sure it wasn't Hacker's?" asked Smithy.

"Hacker's!" Bunter jumped. "How could it be Hacker's, you ass? What are you getting at, Smithy?"

"Like me to ring up your pater, and ask him whether he sent you a pound postal order?" asked Vernon-Smith.

"Eh? You can if you like! Why should I care?" asked the amazed Owl. "No bizney of yours, but you can if you like, you silly fathead!"

"Well, I won't," said the Bounder, laughing, "and I won't lend you another quid, either! Roll away, old tub!"

"Beast!"

Billy Bunter rolled away.

Smithy and Bob Cherry exchanged a look. Both were quite certain now. It was clear enough to them, that Bunter believed that that postal order had come in the letter from Mr. Bunter.

"That settles it, I think?" drawled Smithy.

"It does! But—that reptile—that cur——" Bob almost choked. "That snake ought to be kicked out of Greyfriars—he ought to be sent to Borstal——"

"He may be, before he's much older! This kind of game doesn't pay, in the long run! I'd bet you ten to one that he will dish himself, instead of Bunter, by the time he's through! Anyhow, we're dishing him this time!"

Herbert Vernon-Smith was five minutes late for class in the Remove-room that afternoon. Mr. Quelch duly gave him fifty lines for the same—which did not disconcert the Bounder. He winked at Bob Cherry, as he went to his place.

THE TWENTIETH CHAPTER.

Not as Per Programme!

MR. HACKER breathed hard, and he breathed deep. He was intensely annoyed. Hacker was often annoyed—quite trivial things annoyed the Acid Drop. But this, really, was very annoying.

For a whole day he had been in a state of acid suspicion, on the subject of that missing postal order! Acid drop as he was, he shrank from the suspicion that it had been stolen from his study—neither was he anxious to make it appear that there was a pincher in his Form! But the thing was gone—and what had become of it?

And then, coming into his study after class, he found it!

He found it quite unexpectedly!

Glancing at his table, he saw a postal order lying there, with the ink-stand on the corner to keep it down.

It had not been there the last time he was in the study, he knew that. But it was there now. He picked it up and examined it. It was his twenty-shilling postal order—the one that Carter of the Remove had fetched for him on Wednesday. The Friardale Post Office stamp, and the date on it, demonstrated that. The only difference was that the counterfoil had been torn off. That mattered little, as it did not detract from the value of the postal order. But it showed that it had passed through some fellow's hands—whose?

Mr. Hacker would have given a good deal to know!

Most unpleasant of all was the knowledge that it could not have been a Shell fellow. He had been in his study till the bell rang for class. After that the Shell had been under his eye. The postal order had been put there, under the inkstand, while he was in the Shell Form Room. So the young rascal who had taken it and returned it must belong to some other Form—unless it was one of the servants. It was not a theft; it was an irritating and annoying trick. And he had ragged and worried and suspected the Shell all day—only to discover now that no Shell fellow could have been the culprit. It was really very annoying.

Mr. Hacker compressed his thin lips hard.

However, having found the missing postal order, after all, he sat down to address a letter to his nephew Eric, slipped the postal order into it, and sealed it. He slipped the letter into his pocket to post when he went out. It was safe now, at all events.

Then he concentrated his irritated mind on the problem who had played that trick on him. He was thinking that out, with a bitter brow, when a tap came at the door of his study.

"Come in!" snapped Mr. Hacker.

It was a Remove junior who entered. Hacker stared at Carter, not at all pleased to see one of Quelch's boys.

"What is it, Carter?" he asked sharply.

"Please excuse me, sir!" said Carter smoothly. "There is something I think I ought to mention to you. It's about your postal order, sir."

Mr. Hacker's eyes glinted. He was very anxious for information on that subject.

"Indeed!" he said. "Kindly explain, Carter!"

"I'm rather disturbed about it, sir, as Bunter is a relation—a distant relation —of mine," explained Carter. "But——"

"Bunter? What has Bunter to do with it?"

"He has a postal order for twenty shillings, sir," said Carter. "As he never has any money, and as a postal order for twenty shillings is missing

from your study, sir, I—I couldn't help being disturbed about it. I thought, sir, that perhaps you might ask Bunter to let you see it"

But for the fact that Mr. Hacker had already found the missing postal order, there was no doubt that he would have jumped at that.

Certainly he would have requested— or, rather, demanded—to see a postal order for twenty shillings in any junior's hands, and would not have been satisfied till he had seen it. That would have been quite natural and inevitable in the circumstances.

But as Mr. Hacker's postal order was now enclosed in a letter in Mr. Hacker's pocket, the case was altered. He sat gazing very hard at Carter.

"I think Bunter has changed it in the Form, sir," went on Carter. "But it is not yet changed outside the school. I hope you'll excuse me, sir; but if my relation has got himself into trouble, I'm very anxious——"

Mr. Hacker rose to his feet.

"That will do, Carter!" he said bitterly. "I have been the victim of a disrespectful trick! Some boy, whose identity I cannot guess, took the postal order away from my study yesterday and returned it here this afternoon——"

Carter jumped.

"Returned it!" he gasped.

He stared at the master of the Shell like a fellow in a dream.

"You did not expect to hear that, Carter?" said Mr. Hacker sardonically. "Had you been aware that the disrespectful practical joker had returned the postal order, you would not have come here with this cock-and-bull story."

Carter gazed at him—dumb.

That the purloined postal order was back in Mr. Hacker's possession seemed to him wildly impossible. Yet it was evidently the case, from Hacker's own words. With his brain in a whirl of

stupefied amazement, the wretched schemer stared at Hacker.

Mr. Hacker picked up a cane from the table.

"As a rule," he said, "I should not cane a boy outside my own Form. But as you have chosen to come to my study, Carter, to delude me with this tale, you will take the consequences! I shall be happy to explain to Mr. Quelch, if necessary! Bend over that table, Carter!"

"I—I——" stammered Carter. "I—I—I thought——"

"You thought it would be an excellent joke—a leg-pull, no doubt, you would call it—to cause me to intervene in Mr. Quelch's Form and follow a wild-goose chase!" said Mr. Hacker, still sardonic. "I quite understand! You and your friends would, no doubt, laugh heartily at wasting my time and causing me to ask disagreeable questions of a boy who knows nothing of the matter! Oh, quite! But I am not so easily deluded, Carter!"

"I—I——"

"If you do not bend over that table, Carter, I shall take you by the collar!" said Mr. Hacker grimly. "I am going to make you understand, beyond the possibility of doubt, that I am not a proper subject for your leg-pulling propensities! Will you bend over that table?"

Carter backed a step towards the door.

Mr. Hacker promptly grabbed him by the collar. With Carter's collar in his left, he wielded the cane with his right.

Whack, whack, whack, whack, whack, whack!

Hacker laid every whack on hard.

Carter squirmed and wriggled and yelled. But he had a full six, and every one of the six was a swipe!

Then Mr. Hacker opened the study door, bundled him into the passage, and shut the door on him. He was feeling more pleasant now. He had not discovered who had played tricks with his postal order, but he had, at least, soundly punished a cheeky young rascal who had intended to pull his leg on the subject—or so, at least, the Acid Drop believed.

Carter, squirming from the caning and red with rage, amazed and chagrined and disappointed, squirmed away down the passage. Two Remove fellows were waiting at the corner.

"Try again, you cur!" said Bob Cherry.

"Yes, try again—and book a room at Borstal; you'll want one!" said the Bounder.

Carter gave them a glare, and squirmed on. They knew—how, he could not guess, but they knew! Whether they knew or not, he was beaten; the outcome of his scheme had been a thrashing from Hacker—merely that, and nothing more! It was really enough to make the schemer of the Remove wonder whether honesty, after all, was not the best policy!

THE END.

(Having failed so many times to get Billy Bunter into trouble, will Carter give it up as a bad job? For the answer see next Saturday's MAGNET.)

The Magnet 2D

Billy Bunter's Own Paper

BUNTER GETS IT IN THE NECK!

Interesting Information About Greyfriars By the Man Who Knows—

The GREYFRIARS GUIDE

A TOUR OF THE SCHOOL.   Au Revoir.

(1)
You've seen all the sights,
    You've sighted the scene,
Up several flights
    Of stairs you have been,
All over the school you have travelled
In verses in this magazine.

(2)
Your feet must be tired,
    They're certain to be;
A rest is required,
    So leave it to me—
We'll sit for a while in the tuckshop,
And then you can pay for my tea!

(3)
You really can't wait?
    H'm! Just as I thought!
Well, here is the gate,
    A cab has been brought,
And Gosling's expecting a shilling,
And gets? No pounds, nothing, and
    naught!

(4)
Now jump in your car
    And give us your fin!
Good-bye, Oh revwah,
    Pip-pip and chin-chin!
In future, whenever you're passing
You mustn't forget to drop in!

(*Next week:* THE DAILY ROUND.)

FAR AWAY and LONG AGO

Now once there lived a man named Mr.
    Prout,
Whose head was absolutely full of
    hair.
His chief delight was to wander out,
    And with his rifle slay the grizzly
    bear!
But that was far away and long ago,
He's now as bald as any bag of lard,
And as for shooting—well, his eye's so
    slow
He couldn't hit a haystack at a yard!

Now once there lived a slim and slender
    youth
Whose name was Henri in his native
    France;
His ways were not regarded as uncouth,
He studied English when he had the
    chance.
But that was far away and long ago,
His figure now is fat enough for two.
He teaches French, is funnier than a
    show,
And now he's simply known as "Old
    Mossoo."

Now once there lived a lad of sterling
    blood
Who never drank or smoked or took a
    tip;
He sailed in Noah's Ark and braved the
    Flood—
Yes, William Gosling worked to save
    the ship!
But that was far away and long ago.
A pipe and glass he's since been known
    to fill.
To tips he's never eager to say "No,"
And work makes Gosling absolutely
    ill!

A silly old sportsman named Popper
Went shooting one day in a topper,
    Which made the birds think
    He'd been having a drink,
And they thought it extremely
    improper!

THE GREYFRIARS ALPHABET

GERALD LODER,
the unpopular prefect of the Sixth.

L is for LODER—the cad!
Who's almost impossibly bad;
There's hardly a vice, small or large,
Which cannot be laid to his charge;
His genius for being a beast
Is worth a tin medal, at least!
A bully, he makes the fags shriek;
A toady, he'll grease to a beak;

A gambler, he dabbles in bets;
A smoker, he likes cigarettes;
A rake, he plays billiards and nap;
A funk, he's not keen on a scrap;
A slacker, at games he can't shine;
A braggart, he thinks he is fine;
But greatest of all is the fact
That he's never been jolly well sacked!

ANSWER TO PUZZLE

He'll go by boat.

A WEEKLY BUDGET OF FACT AND FUN

By
THE GREYFRIARS RHYMESTER

GREYFRIARS GRINS

Quelch has just whopped me for being
slovenly and careless in the hundred
lines I sent in. I'll bind the next lot in
Morocco with gilt edges.

When we chargedh Wun Lung, the
Chinese chump, with putting smoke-
bombs on the Rag fire, he said: "No
savvy!" Had he been Japanese, he
would have apologised.

Fisher T. Fish has started a loan
club. At the moment, he's started
alone.

PUZZLE PAR

Mark Linley wants to go to
Lancashire without touching
Gloucestershire, Oxfordshire,
Northamptonshire, or Lincoln-
shire. How will he manage it?
Answer at foot of column 2.

Tubb of the Third claims to have
found a curious object he's never seen
before. Probably a piece of soap.

A dog bit Loder in Friardale last
Saturday. A statue of the animal will
probably be erected in the quad.

Carne confiscated Skinner's cigarettes
and took them away to burn them. No
doubt he will throw them into his mouth
and set fire to them.

Gosling says he likes to meet a man
with the right spirit. And two glasses,
of course.

Bolsover major won his recent fight
with Snoop, when Snoop's seconds threw
in the towel after the first blow.

Sir Hilton Popper has shot all the
rabbits and pheasants on his estate.
He's now starting on the tadpoles.

If Fisher T. Fish is ever a schoolmaster, he'll be too jolly mean to give
his scholars lines.

"I'VE GOTTA HOSS!" So says Billy Bunter, the prize porpoise of the Greyfriars Remove. But borrowing the necessary cash and "getting it on" is a problem—until Arthur Carter comes to the rescue. It's the chance Bunter's rascally cousin has long been waiting for!

BILLY BUNTER'S DEAD CERT!

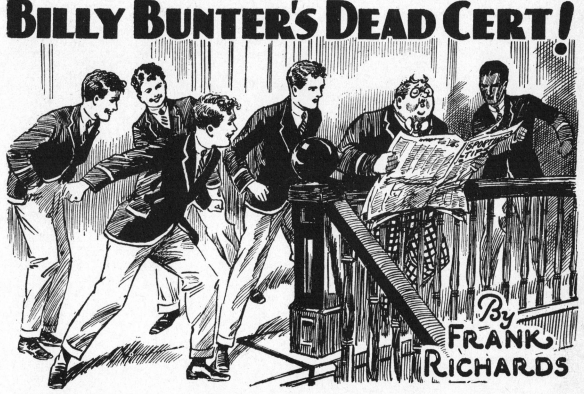

By FRANK RICHARDS

The Famous Five stood and gazed at Billy Bunter, as the fat junior held the sporting paper open in both hands, blinking at it with a fascinated blink!

THE FIRST CHAPTER.
A Special Snip!

"**B**Y gum!" said Billy Bunter.

Bunter's fat face was excited.

His eyes gleamed behind his spectacles.

The fat Owl of Greyfriars stood on the Remove landing, leaning on the banisters, with a newspaper open in his hands, and his eyes, and spectacles, glued on the same.

So deeply interested, or rather entranced, was Bunter, by what he was reading in that newspaper, that he was deaf and blind to his surroundings.

Even the fact that it was tea-time had slipped from his fat mind!

"By gum!" he repeated. "What a chance! Oh crikey! What a bit of luck finding this paper in Carne's study! Oh crumbs!"

Five juniors, coming up the Remove staircase, glanced at the fat Owl of the Remove. Harry Wharton & Co. glanced a second time—as they noticed that Bunter's paper was of a pink hue, and bore the title, in large letters, "Sporting Tips."

Racing papers were a variety of literature severely discouraged at Greyfriars. In fact, any junior found in possession of such a paper was liable to "six" from a prefect's ash! Any senior, in such circumstances, was due for an interview with his headmaster—likely to be a painful one!

And there was Bunter, with a sporting paper in his fat paws, prominent in the view of anyone that happened to pass!

Several fellows, passing, had glanced at it, and grinned. Beaks and prefects were not likely to come up to the Remove landing, unless for a special reason. But it was fearfully risky all the same.

Carter, the new fellow in the Remove, had passed and stared blankly at the fat Owl, and hurried down the stairs. Then the Famous Five came up, and, spotting Bunter and his sporting paper, stopped.

They stood and gazed at him. He did not heed them. He held the paper open in both fat hands, and blinked at it with a fascinated blink. He did not know that they were there, till Bob Cherry, stepping forward, took a kick at the pink paper which whipped it out

~~~~~~~~~~~~~~~~~~~~~~~~~~~~~~~~

UPROARIOUSLY FUNNY SCHOOL YARN OF HARRY WHARTON & CO., OF GREYFRIARS.

~~~~~~~~~~~~~~~~~~~~~~~~~~~~~~~~

of Bunter's hands and sent it fluttering on the landing. Then Bunter woke up, as it were.

"Oh! Beast! Who—what—" gasped Bunter. He plunged after the pink paper and grabbed it up. "I say, you fellows—"

"You howling ass!" exclaimed Harry Wharton. "What the dickens are you doing with that putrid rag?"

"Like Quelch to see you with it?" asked Frank Nugent.

"Eh? Old Quelch won't be coming up here," said Bunter. "Never mind Quelch! Blow Quelch! I say, you fellows, have you got a pound you don't want?"

"Likely, isn't it?" remarked Johnny Bull. Greyfriars juniors counted their cash in half-crowns rather than in pounds. And if a fellow had a pound, it was extremely unlikely that he would not want it!

"I mean to say, can you lend me a pound?" asked Bunter eagerly. "It's rather important! In fact, fearfully important."

"Must be frightfully important, for you to stuff at the tuckshop!" agreed Bob Cherry. "But have you really got room for a whole pound's worth of tuck? Not afraid of bursting in the quad?"

"'Tain't tuck!" snorted Bunter. "I'm not always thinking of tuck, like you fellows——"

"Oh, scissors!"

"Besides, I'll let you have a couple of pounds back for it, if you like, in a day or two!" explained Bunter. "If I have a pound to-day, I shall have six pounds on Thursday—see?"

"Not quite!" said Harry Wharton, staring at the fat Owl. "How are you going to turn one quid into six? Have you become a magician, as well as a fatheaded ventriloquist?"

"It's as easy as falling off a form!" grinned Bunter. "It's in this paper. You put a pound on Crackerjack——"

"Wha-a-t?"

"At five to one! Day after the race you collect six quids! Pretty easy money, what?"

"Great pip!"

"The easiness is terrific!" grinned Hurree Jamset Ram Singh "At least-fully, it is preposterously easy to put a

THE MAGNET LIBRARY.—No. 1,568.

pound on the esteemed Crackerjack. But it may not be so absurdly easy to collect the six pounds afterwards."

"Oh, that's all right!" said Bunter confidently. "You've only got to find a 'bookie' who pays—Smithy knows one! That's all right!"

"Well, my only hat!" said Bob Cherry blankly. "Are you taking up the Bounder's jolly old manners and customs, Bunter? Or are you taking Loder of the Sixth as a model? Specially looking for the sack?"

"Oh, don't be an ass!" said Bunter peevishly. "I can tell you, this is a tremendous chance—if only a fellow can get hold of a pound in time, you know. I happen to be short of money at the moment, owing to being disappointed about a postal order. Five pounds would come in jolly useful. Of course, it's not so much to me as it is to you fellows—still, I should be glad to have it. I can tell you, I could do with five quids!"

"And there's no doubt about the five quids?" asked Johnny Bull, with intense sarcasm.

"Oh, no! That's all right! You see, it's a special tip by a man who knows," explained Bunter. "Quick-Eye, of 'Sporting Tips,' gives it as his Special Snip! He knows, you know! He says here that he's been giving winners every day for weeks! Well, that shows, doesn't it?"

"The showfulness is not terrific, my esteemed Bunter!" chuckled Hurree Jamset Ram Singh. "The absurd Quick-Eye may be talking out of his absurd hat."

"Oh, don't be an ass! He knows," said Bunter. "I say, you fellows, Crackerjack is running on Wednesday, and you can get five to one against him to-day. Who's going to lend me a pound?"

"Boot him!" suggested Nugent.

"Better go along to Study No. 4 and boot Smithy!" growled Johnny Bull. "It's Smithy who's set that fat ass the example how to be a blackguard. I dare say that rotten paper is Smithy's."

"'Tain't!" hooted Bunter.

"Well, it's not yours!" snorted Johnny. "It cost twopence—and even you are not fool enough to give twopence for it."

"I found it in Carne's study! That beast Carne made me take his books to his study, when he came out of the Sixth after class. This paper happened to be there! I wasn't prying round his study, or anything like that, you know—it's not the sort of thing I should do. The paper wasn't hidden under the cushion in his armchair. I—I happened to see it, and looked at it, and when I saw this bit about Crackerjack, I thought I'd borrow the paper——"

"And Carne's a prefect!" snorted Johnny Bull.

"He wouldn't be a prefect long if the Head heard all this!" said Harry Wharton. "Hand over that rag, Bunter, and I'll shove it in the study fire."

"I'll watch it!" gasped Bunter. "There's lots of tips in this paper! If I get five quids in hand, after backing Crackerjack, I intend to go into it pretty deep—I may clear lots of money by the end of the week. I say, you fellows, who's going to lend me a quid?"

"Don't all speak at once!" grinned Bob Cherry.

"Ha, ha, ha!"

"Blessed if I can see anything to cackle at! I say, you fellows——"

"Look here, Bunter!" said the captain of the Remove. "Smithy plays

the goat in this style, but he has sense enough to look after himself! You haven't! Chuck it, see?"

"Beast!"

"As a warning not to go blagging like Smithy, we'll stuff that paper down the back of your silly neck!" continued Harry Wharton.

"Good egg!" said Bob. "Let's!"

"Look here, you beasts, you leave my paper alone!" roared Bunter, in great indignation. "Bob Cherry, you rotter, leggo that paper—Wharton, you beast, leggo my ears—if you don't leggo my hair, Nugent, I'll hack your shins. Ow! Beasts! Rotters! Yoooooogh!"

"Ha, ha, ha!"

Billy Bunter struggled and wriggled and squirmed frantically in the grasp of five pairs of hands. But he struggled and wriggled and squirmed in vain.

It was, perhaps, improbable that the fat Owl would ever raise the necessary pound, to begin a hectic career as an amateur blackguard. Still, the Famous Five considered it judicious to discourage him from following in the erring footsteps of the Bounder of Greyfriars. Stuffing that valuable publication "Sporting Tips" down the back of his fat neck seemed a good idea, to begin with—so they crumpled it and stuffed it down!

Then they walked on cheerily into the Remove passage, leaving Billy Bunter spluttering for breath, gurgling with indignation, and making frantic endeavours to extract "Sporting Tips" from the back of his neck!

THE SECOND CHAPTER.
Bunter in Luck!

"CARTER! What is it, Carter?" Mr. Quelch, master of the Remove, was in conversation with Hacker, master of the Shell, when the new member of his Form came downstairs.

Arthur Carter came over to the two masters, and Mr. Quelch inquired curtly what he wanted. When beaks were deep in chin-wag, they did not like the flow of verbosity to be interrupted.

"Please excuse me, sir!" said Carter, in his meekest manner. "But I think there is a chimney on fire in a Remove study—I thought that I had better let you know, sir."

"Oh!" said Mr. Quelch. "Quite! Thank you, Carter!"

He nodded to Hacker, and rustled away to the staircase at once. Mr. Hacker went his own way, while Mr. Quelch whisked up the stairs.

Carter stood looking after him, with a faint smile on his face; then, as he turned away, he came face to face with Herbert Vernon-Smith, of the Remove. He coloured a little under the Bounder's keen, scornful gaze.

"What rotten trick are you playing this time, Carter?" asked Smithy, in very distinct tones.

"Eh? I don't quite catch on!" drawled Carter.

"I heard what you said to Quelch."

"Are you picking up Bunter's way of listening to what doesn't concern you?" sneered Carter.

"You told Quelch that a chimney was on fire in the Remove!" said the Bounder, unheeding the sneer. "That was a lie, Carter!"

"I said I thought so!" corrected Carter. "There's a lot of smoke coming from somewhere—I saw it from my study window——"

"It was a lie!" said the Bounder grimly. "What did you want Quelch up in the Remove for? Is he going to

spot some fellow you dislike, up to something?"

"He won't spot you smoking in your study, or jotting down a letter to Bill Lodgey at the Three Fishers, anyhow, as you're down here!" answered Carter; and with that he turned away, and went out into the quad.

The Bounder cast a dark glance after him, and went up the stairs. He had just come into the House, and he knew that there was no chimney on fire, or he would have seen it from the quad. Plenty of fires were burning at Greyfriars, on a cold, clammy February day, and no doubt there was a good deal of smoke on the wind; and no doubt Mr. Quelch, when he found that nothing was the matter, would suppose that Carter had been mistaken. But Smithy had no doubt whatever that the schemer of the Remove had some personal motive for sending the Form-master up to the studies, and he wondered what it was, as he followed Mr. Quelch up. He was not far behind, when the Form-master stepped on the Remove landing.

On that landing, a fat figure was wriggling and squirming, gurgling and gasping, and making wild clutches at the back of its fat neck!

Mr. Quelch stopped, and stared at it.

A minute earlier, he would have caught Billy Bunter, with "Sporting Tips" wide-open in his fat hands, which would have meant something like a thunderclap for Bunter. Then Smithy would have known, at once, why Arthur Carter had pulled Quelch's leg, and sent him there!

But "Sporting Tips" was now out of sight, owing to the friendly ministrations of the Famous Five—stuffed down Billy Bunter's back, inside his collar. The fat junior's frantic endeavours had not yet extracted it.

"Beasts!" Bunter was howling, as his Form-master stepped on the landing. "Rotters! Cads! Swabs! Come and get this paper out of my neck, you rotters! Urrrggh! I'm all out of breath, you beastly cads! Yurrggh!"

"Bunter!" snapped Mr. Quelch.

"Oh!" Billy Bunter jumped, at his Form-master's voice, and ceased his antics all of a sudden. "Yes, sir! I didn't see you, sir! Oh crikey!"

"What is the matter with you, Bunter?"

"Oh! Nothing, sir!" gasped Bunter. Up to that moment, the fat Owl had been boiling with wrath and indignation. Now he was intensely glad that "Sporting Tips" was down his back, instead of in his fat hands!

Backing winners, at five to one, was fearfully attractive, but letting his Form-master catch him with a racing paper had no attraction at all for Bunter!

"Then what are you writhing in that ridiculous manner for, Bunter?" demanded Mr. Quelch.

"I—I wasn't, sir——"

"What?"

"I—I—I mean, I—I was doing some —some exercises, sir!" gasped Bunter. "Some—some physical jerks, sir! Exercising the—the muscles, sir——"

"If you tell me one more untruth, Bunter, I shall cane you! Has some-one pushed something inside your collar?"

"Oh! No, sir! There's nothing down my back—nothing at all. I wasn't trying to get it out, sir!" groaned Bunter. "Those beasts never shoved a news-paper down my neck, sir! Besides, it was only a—a—a lark."

"I do not approve of such absurd practical jokes!" said Mr. Quelch severely. "Had I witnessed this action, I should have punished such unthinking and boisterous horse-play! However, I am glad to see that you are not disposed to complain, Bunter."

"Oh! No, sir! Not at all, sir!" gasped Bunter.

"Vernon-Smith!" Mr. Quelch glanced round. "Kindly assist Bunter to extract a newspaper which some foolish boys have pushed down inside his collar."

"Oh, certainly, sir!" said Smithy.

Billy Bunter blinked almost in anguish at the Remove master, as Vernon-Smith stepped towards him to render first-aid! He was scared out of his fat wits at the bare idea of "Sporting Tips" coming to light under Quelch's gimlet eyes.

To his immense relief, Mr. Quelch turned, and walked up the Remove passage—in quest of that chimney which was on fire!

"Oh crikey!" gasped Bunter. "Oh crumbs! I say, hook it out, old chap, now—now he's gone! Oh lor'!"

The Bounder got hold of the crumpled newspaper, and hooked it out. He jumped as he saw what it was.

"You priceless idiot!" he gasped. "Jolly lucky for you Quelch never saw this! Who shoved it down your back?"

"Wharton and the other beasts——"

"Lucky for you they did! Get it out of sight, fathead, before Quelch comes back!" breathed the Bounder. "Take it to your study and shove it into the fire, you chump!"

Bunter crammed "Sporting Tips" under his tight jacket.

"That's all right," he said. "I say, Smithy, lend me a pound, will you?"

"No!"

"Beast!"

The Bounder laughed, and walked up the passage.

Billy Bunter promptly rolled into Study No. 7 to get "Sporting Tips" safely out of sight, till Mr. Quelch had gone down again.

Mr. Quelch, meanwhile, was looking into study after study, in the Remove passage, after that smoky chimney. He failed to find one. At Study No. 13, which was Bob Cherry's study, he found a numerous tea-party at tea—but no chimney on fire.

Having finished his investigation, Mr. Quelch was relieved to find that there was nothing the matter, though very annoyed with Carter for having made such an error, and given him all that trouble for nothing.

Vernon-Smith, in the passage, watched him depart, at last, with a sarcastic smile. Then the Bounder looked into Study No. 13, where Harry Wharton & Co. were at tea.

"Quelch been here after a smoky chimney?" he asked, with a grin.

"Yes; just gone!" answered Bob Cherry.

"What the dickens put the idea into his head?" asked Harry Wharton.

"Carter!" answered the Bounder.

"Carter pulling his leg?" asked the captain of the Remove. "What a rotten, silly trick!"

"Rotten enough!" agreed the Bounder. "But not so silly as it looks! Quelch very nearly caught Bunter with 'Sporting Tips'! I hear that you fellows shoved it down his back. If you hadn't, Quelch would have been on it."

"The fat ass!" said Harry. "He would have got six—as well as having Quelch's eye on him for the rest of the term."

"Exactly! That was Carter's game—and he nearly got by with it! Nice chap, ain't he?" grinned the Bounder, and he walked away to his own study —leaving the tea-party staring, and Bob Cherry frowning.

"That cur!" muttered Bob. "At it again——"

"Six on the bags would do Bunter good, if he's taking up blagging!" grunted Johnny Bull.

"That's not Carter's business!"

"Well, no!"

"I've a jolly good mind——" Bob half rose.

"Rot!" said Harry. "How the dickens do you know that Carter saw Bunter's idiotic paper at all, or that he sent Quelch up for that reason, if he did? You can't jump on a fellow for nothing. Sit down, fathead!"

Bob gave a grunt! But he sat down.

THE THIRD CHAPTER.

Nothing Doing!

"SEEN Hobson?" asked Hoskins, of the Shell.

"Blow Hobson!" answered Billy Bunter peevishly.

Claude Hoskins, at the end of the passage that led to the music-room, was looking about him with a rather irritated look.

Apparently he wanted Hobby, his studymate and pal in the Shell. Hobby was nowhere in the offing.

So, as Bunter was, he inquired of Bunter. Bunter was not in the least interested in either Hobson or Hoskins. Bunter was peeved.

He had reason to be peeved.

It was pretty rotten Bunter thought, for a fellow to be able to pick up five pounds on Wednesday as easily as picking up seashells on the seashore, and to be prevented by the lack of one single solitary pound in hand.

Chances like this did not often come a fellow's way. Horses, as Bunter knew from observation of some sporting fellows in the Lower School at Greyfriars, were fearfully uncertain animals. It was no end of a catch to get an absolutely sure snip—straight from the horse's own mouth, as it were.

Bunter had got it!

"Quick-Eye," of "Sporting Tips," gave Crackerjack as an absolutely certain winner—and "Quick-Eye" knew. At least, Bunter supposed that he did.

Knowing all this, "Quick-Eye" put his knowledge at the service of the public, through the medium of "Sporting Tips," instead of backing Crackerjack himself and making lots of money —which was very generous and self-denying of "Quick-Eye."

Bunter was in search of a quid to put on Crackerjack.

He had a penny!

Even that was a French penny, and had been refused again and again.

Bunter was prepared to plunge on Crackerjack—but plunging with a French penny was impracticable.

The Famous Five had refused to play up. Peter Todd had simply kicked him when he was told of the big idea. Skinner had laughed heartily, apparently greatly tickled by Billy Bunter as a bold, bad plunger on the races— but he had not produced any cash. Nobody to whom Bunter had applied had produced any cash. Often and often had Bunter suffered under a scarcity of that useful article cash—but never had there been such a scarcity as now.

With this deep problem on his fat mind, Billy Bunter was in no mood to be bothered by a fathead in the Shell. He could not borrow a quid of a Shell man. So he snorted a far from courteous reply to Hoskins' inquiry.

"Where the dickens is he?" went on Hoskins, heedless of Bunter's snort. "I told him I was playing my

'Fantasia in B minor' in the music-room after tea. I told him to wait for me here. He's not here."

At which Bunter's fat face relaxed into a grin.

Hobby was Claude's pal—but friendship had its limit. Hobby admired his musical friend immensely; he thought old Claude was fearfully clever to be able to produce all sorts of strange and startling noises on all sorts of instruments. But he did not want to listen to any of them.

If the amateur musician of the Shell was going to play one of his own compositions in the music-room it was a safe bet that James Hobson would get as far from the music-room as the extensive limits of Greyfriars School permitted.

Only Claude Hoskins did not know that—and Claude was surprised and irritated by Hobby's failure to appear.

"Well, I shan't wait for him!" went on Hoskins crossly. "That ass Gwynne of the Sixth wants the music-room in half an hour. I can't keep it when a Sixth Form man wants it. It's rotten, but there you are! I say, like to hear it, Bunter?" added Hoskins with a peculiar mixture of condescension and hopefulness.

Hoskins liked fellows to listen when he played his musical works.

It was not easy to get them to listen in. They would almost as soon have faced Hoskins with a machine-gun as with a musical instrument.

Billy Bunter blinked at Claude Hoskins through his big spectacles with a devastating blink. Life was a troublesome affair enough without Hoskins' music added as an extra and utterly unnecessary trouble to the rest. The fat Owl was about to make a reply as devastating as his blink, but he paused.

Bunter was not in need of music, but he was in sore need of a pound. He wondered whether it might be possible to "touch" that ass Hoskins for a quid if he put him into a good temper by listening to his tosh.

It was a chance, at least. Hoskins had plenty of pocket-money, most of which he spent on music paper to spoil in his study by writing down his compositions on it. He might have a quid. He might part with it if sufficiently buttered.

"It's rather good," went on Hoskins. "Here and there a bit like Smelowiski; but more modern, of course. I've got a succession of perfect fifths that I'm jolly sure Smelowiski never thought of. Come along, if you'd like to hear it."

"Jolly glad to, old chap!" said Bunter affably. "If there's anything I really like it's first-class music, Hoskins. And yours is really the thing!"

"Eh?" Hoskins gave him quite a pleasant smile. Hitherto he had thought of Bunter, whenever he thought of him at all, as a fat ass. He realised now that appearances were not everything. This remark of Bunter's showed a keen judgment, a fine taste, of which Hoskins had never suspected him before. "My dear chap, come on, then; I'll play the whole thing over to you with pleasure."

Bunter rolled down the passage after Hoskins.

He could not help feeling some inward misgivings. It would be pretty awful if he had to stand and listen for perhaps half an hour without extracting a quid from Hoskins of the Shell when the period of torment was over.

But he resolved to take the risk. After all, he could stick his fingers in his ears when Hoskins wasn't looking.

THE MAGNET LIBRARY.—No. 1,568.

Claude Hoskins sailed merrily into the music-room, pitched open the lid of the somewhat battered piano, and plumped on the music stool. He opened his music—which looked to Bunter as if flies, fresh from an inkpot, had been crawling over the paper. He dashed back a curl of hair from his eyes—not that it was anywhere near his eyes, but Hoskins cultivated that artistic curl with great care, and had a way of dashing it back. Then, as it seemed to Bunter, he hit the piano as if he hated it bitterly.

The crash of chords filled the music-room to overflowing. Claude thumped and crashed and banged. Bunter eyed him malevolently through his spectacles. He considered this too thick. He had come there to listen to Hoskins' fantasia—whatever a fantasia was—and he wanted Hoskins to get on with it and get it over. Having waited a few minutes for Hoskins to begin, Bunter ventured to tap him on the shoulder.

Hoskins gave him a far-away look.

"I say, never mind about practising now, old chap," suggested Bunter. "Get on with the fantasia—what?"

"You idiot!" said Hoskins.

"Eh?"

"I'm playing the fantasia!"

"Oh!" gasped Bunter.

"Shut up!" said Hoskins.

Bunter shut up.

He realised that Hoskins was not merely banging on the piano from sheer exuberance of spirits; he was playing his musical composition.

Bunter's mistake was, perhaps, a natural one. To any ear but the composer's it certainly sounded like random banging on the piano.

All that Bunter could do was to stand just behind Hoskins where the pianist could not see him, and press his fat paws tightly over his fat ears. This took off the edge of it, as it were.

Suddenly, with a terrific crash, Hoskins ceased. He spun round on the music stool, and Bunter whipped his hands away from his ears just in time.

"Splendid, old chap!" he gasped. "I say, that's ripping! I say, Hoskins, there's something I was going to ask you——"

"That's the first movement," said Hoskins.

"Eh?"

"Now I'll play you the second movement."

"Oh crikey!"

Bang! went Hoskins on the piano.

Smack! went Bunter's fat paws to his ears again.

Bang, bang, bang! went Hoskins merrily; and the much-thumped piano roared and thundered and groaned under his vigorous attack. Harder and harder Bunter pressed his fat hands to his ears, but he could not keep it out—and he could only wonder in dismay how long it was going to last.

It ceased, and Hoskins spun round again. This time Bunter did not succeed in getting his hands away from his ears quickly enough. Hoskins spotted them in transit.

"What the dickens are you up to?" demanded Hoskins.

"Oh, I—I was—was scratching my ear!" gasped Bunter. "I—I say, Hoskins, that—that's a splendid sonata——"

"Fantasia!" grunted Hoskins.

"I—I mean fantasia! I say, old chap, there was something I was going to ask you——"

"That's all right. If you'd like to hear the variation on the original theme, here you are."

Thump! Bang! Crash!

Hoskins was going strong again; and Bunter groaned miserably and clapped his hands to his ears once more. He could not help thinking that he would have earned that pound by the time he borrowed it—if he did borrow it!

But, to Bunter's enormous relief as well as surprise, Hoskins suddenly stopped, before he had tortured the atmosphere for more than five minutes. He grabbed a pencil from his pocket and started jabbing at the music paper.

Apparently he had thought of some improvement in his composition. It seemed, to Bunter in need of a few improvements. Anyhow, he was glad of the rest. Never had silence seemed so golden.

"I—I say, Hoskins——" bleated Bunter.

"Don't interrupt me!"

"But I wanted to ask you——"

"Yes, yes, I'll play it all over again from beginning to end if you like, but don't interrupt me for a minute."

Bunter shuddered at the prospect.

"I say, just listen a minute!" he gasped desperately. "I say, old chap, do you happen to have a pound?"

"Eh? No."

"I—I want you to lend me a pound and——"

"I've only got fourpence, and I want it. Shut up!"

"Oh crikey!"

"I shan't be a minute putting in a bit I've just thought of," said Hoskins. "Wait there. I'll play it over again and——"

"Beast!"

"Wha-a-t?"

"You—you—you—you silly idiot!" shrieked Bunter "You've driven me deaf with that awful row, and you've only got fourpence. Beast!"

Having thus expressed his gratitude for a musical treat, Billy Bunter rolled to the door.

Hoskins stared after him blankly.

With the door open, Bunter turned to give him a parting glare.

"Beast!" he roared. "Ass! Fathead! The Head ought to stop you kicking up that fearful row! Yah!"

Bunter rolled out. Hoskins shot from the piano stool, and his foot shot after Bunter as he rolled.

Crash!

There was a yell from Bunter, and, like Iser in the poem, he rolled rapidly. Hoskins slammed the door on him, and went back to the piano.

"Ow! Beast!" gasped Bunter, as he scrambled up. "Ow! Rotter! Oh crikey!"

He glared in wrath at the door of the music-room. But from the other side of that door came an outbreak of sound like an air-raid, mingled with a motor-bus accident! Bunter rolled away. He went minus the hoped-for pound—but it was something to get out of range of Hoskins' music!

THE FOURTH CHAPTER.

Corn in Egypt!

ARTHUR CARTER, by the next morning, was the only fellow in the Remove whom Billy Bunter had not asked to lend him a pound.

The Remove was a numerous Form, and among so many fellows a really determined borrowing campaign ought to have produced some result.

But the result was nil!

Fellows who had a pound, wanted, with a selfishness that disgusted Bunter,

to keep that pound! Once more it was borne in on Bunter's fat mind what a selfish world it was!

Instead of extracting what he wanted from the Remove fellows, Bunter obtained all sorts of things that he did not want.

The Famous Five had stuffed "Sporting Tips" down his back. Peter Todd had booted him. Lord Mauleverer told him that he was a dingy little beast. Mary Linley gave him five minutes of serious talk, for his own good—which Bunter would not have minded so much had Mark lent him the quid as well—which, however, Mark did not do! Skinner, and Snoop, and Stott laughed; Bolsover major roared; Hazeldene chortled. Squiff pulled his fat ear, Tom Brown shied a Latin grammar at him, Ogilvy sat him down in the Remove passage with a bump. Such were the responses of the Remove to Bunter's earnest and urgent request for a quid, that could easily be turned into six.

Turning one quid into six, by means of backing Crackerjack at five to one, seemed to appeal to nobody!

In sheer desperation, Bunter even tried Fisher T. Fish—and Fishy almost fell on his study floor at the bare idea of lending anybody anything! Needless to state, the quid was not forthcoming!

So, in break, on Tuesday morning, Bunter was still quidless, and that golden chance looked like passing him by. Unless he was "on" that day, the chance was gone, as the race was on the morrow.

The amount of tuck to be obtained for five pounds was dazzling to think of; and all that was needed was somebody's quid to begin with! And not a man in the Remove would play up!

Bunter even thought of asking Carter—but he shook his fat head at that hopeless thought.

Carter, of course, ought to have done it. He was Bunter's relation—a distant relation. He knew, of course, that Bunter was in fearful need of a quid. All the Remove knew that. Indeed, by this time, Bunter, as a bold, bad blackguard, was becoming a standing joke in the Form. But, relation as he was, Carter was unlikely to lend Bunter anything but a boot.

Catching sight of him in the quad, in break that morning, Billy Bunter gave him a devastating blink through his big spectacles. Carter was looking at him—and Bunter returned his look, with all the scorn and contempt he could express in his fat features.

"Beast!" murmured Bunter.

But for the fact that they were rivals for the riches of old Joseph Carter, Bunter's relation might have played up—perhaps!

But, as it was, there was no hope!

Old Joseph Carter had turned down his nephew for getting expelled from St. Olaf's, and the fact that he was considering whether to take up Billy Bunter in his place naturally did not produce harmony between them.

A great deal depended on Bunter's report that term—which Bunter was anxious should be a good one, and Carter equally anxious should be a bad one!

But old Joseph's wealth was far off, dim, and distant; and Bunter, at the moment, would have given his rather doubtful prospects of the same for a quid in hand, to put on Crackerjack! But for that rivalry, he might have extracted it from his relation in the Remove. As even Bunter, hopeful as he was, could not hope to pull that off, he indemnified himself by blinking

In angry amazement, Mr. Hacker rose to his feet and stared across the high back of the armchair. "BUNTER!" "Oh crikey!" gasped the fat Removite, spinning round in terror, the receiver dropping from his fat hand. "Oh jiminy!"

scorn and contempt at Carter, and as Carter came over to him the scorn and contempt intensified. His fat lip curled, and he turned up his little fat nose farther than Nature had intended, though Nature had started it well on the upward way

"Toothache?" asked Carter.

"Eh?" ejaculated Bunter in surprise. "No."

"What are you making those faces for, then?"

Bunter gazed at him in silent scorn. His lofty, supercilious look of contempt was described by Carter as "making faces."

"I wanted to speak to you," went on Carter.

"Well, don't!" retorted Bunter, disdainfully. "You're not the sort of fellow I want to speak to!"

"But——"

"Keep your distance! Think I don't know why you got Quelch up to the Remove studies yesterday?" sneered Bunter. "Think I don't know why you've played one rotten trick on me after another, since you've been here? Think I don't know that you want to get me a bad report from Quelch this term to dish me with old Joe Carter? Yah!"

"You fat ass——"

"Yah!"

"I've heard——"

"I don't care what you've heard—and I don't want to know! Just keep your distance!"

"I've heard that you've been trying to borrow a quid up and down the Form and——"

"No bizney of yours. I haven't asked you to lend me one, anyhow!" sneered Bunter. "Mind your own business—see?"

"If you really needed one——"

"Yah!"

"I could lend it to you——"

"Eh?"

"I shouldn't mind, if you're really hard pushed for a quid!" said Carter, while Bunter blinked at him in utter astonishment. "After all, we're relations, though we're not friends, and if you're in a hole I don't see why I shouldn't help you out!"

"Gammon!" said Bunter. "You can't pull my leg! Yah!"

"Look here, do you want a quid, or not?" asked Carter impatiently. "If you do, I'll lend you one, and here it is."

To Bunter's intensified amazement, Arthur Carter drew a pound note from his pocket.

The fat Owl gazed at it. He could not believe that Carter was in earnest. Why should a fellow who disliked him intensely, and who was his rival for the crumbs that fell from the rich man's table, lend him a pound, when no other fellow in the Form would do anything of the kind?

But when Carter shoved the pound note into his fat paw, even Bunter had to believe it!

"I—I—I say," he gasped. "D-d-do you mean it?"

"That looks as if I do, doesn't it?" asked Carter. "I don't know what you want it for, but if you're hard pushed, there it is!"

"Oh crikey!" gasped Bunter.

"Only one thing," added Carter, turning back as he was moving away. "I've heard some silly talk that you're backing a horse, or something. I suppose I can take it for granted that there's nothing in it."

"Oh, no—yes!" gasped Bunter.

"What I mean is, I couldn't lend you money for anything of that kind," said Carter. "If it's for anything else, you're more than welcome. See?"

"Oh! It's for anything else!" gasped Bunter. "I—I mean, it—it's for some-

thing else! I—I mean, what I really want this quid for is to make a—a—a contribution to—to—to the School Fund for—for—I—I forget what! See?"

"I see!" assented Carter. "That's all right, then! I thought I'd make it clear, that's all. You can settle it later in the term."

"Oh, I'll settle to-morrow, or Thursday, at the latest," said Bunter. "I shall have lots of money then."

"Right-ho!" said Carter. "Any time you like!"

And he walked away, leaving Billy Bunter's fat face irradiated by happy satisfaction.

Bunter blinked and blinked at that pound note before he tucked it away. Really, it seemed too good to be true! It had come like corn in Egypt in one of the lean years. It had dropped like manna on Bunter's fat head. It was a really amazing stroke of luck.

Up and down and round about the Remove had Bunter gone, seeking in vain to borrow that urgent quid. And the only fellow he had not asked—the fellow whom it seemed hopeless to ask —had lent it to him of his own accord! It was amazing, but immensely satisfactory.

Bunter had his quid now. All that was necessary was to get it "on" that wonderful horse, Crackerjack, while there was yet time. Bunter was going to manage that somehow, and he was going to roll in easy money for ever afterwards.

The thing was quite simple. He would win five pounds, and get his stake money back, too, making six pounds, out of which he would repay Carter his quid. That would leave him five pounds to work on as capital; and five pounds, at merely three to one on the next winner, would produce twenty pounds! Twenty pounds, laid out on

THE MAGNET LIBRARY.—No. 1,568.

another winner at, say, four to one, would produce one hundred pounds! It was dazzling to think of!

And Bunter realised that he was being quite moderate in his calculations. For there were six-to-one winners, seven-to-one winners; he had even heard of ten-to-one winners. Still, it was safer to be on the moderate side, he felt, in making his calculations. After all, one hundred pounds in, say, a fortnight would not be bad for a chap in the Lower Fourth.

Bunter quite forgot to consider whether there was anything dingy or disgraceful in such transactions. A fellow could not, after all, be expected to think of everything.

Easy money, in larger and larger sums, was enough for Bunter to think of, and he thought of it with ecstatic bliss.

His fat face was wreathed in smiles as he went in to third school with the Remove. He was almost walking on air. Indeed, he rather resembled the classical gentleman in Horace, who was like to strike the stars with his sublime head.

THE FIFTH CHAPTER.
Bunter Wants a "Bookie"!

"SMITHY!"

"No!" hooted the Bounder.

"But I say——"

"Clear off, you blithering ass!"

"For goodness' sake, chuck it, Bunter!" said Tom Redwing.

Vernon-Smith and his chum were walking in the quad after dinner when Billy Bunter joined them. Smithy naturally supposed that he was after that quid again; the fat Owl had already tried the Bounder twice, and this looked like a third attempt.

"If you ask me to lend you a quid again," said Vernon-Smith, "I'll boot you as far as the gym and back again! That's a tip!"

"Who's asking you to lend me a quid?" demanded Bunter, with all the dignity of a fellow who already had a quid in his possession. "I'm not!"

Vernon-Smith stared at him, and then grinned.

"Oh, if it's not that, cut on!" he said. "Mind, I mean what I said about booting you to the gym and back!"

"Oh, really, Smithy, I've got a quid!" explained Bunter

"Whose?" asked Smithy.

"Beast! I mean, a chap lent it to me, old chap! I say, Smithy—— You cut off, Redwing, will you, while I'm talking to Smithy?"

"No!" answered Tom Redwing.

"Oh, really, Redwing—I mean to say, this isn't the sort of thing you want to hear, you being a goody-goody nincompoop, if you don't mind my mentioning it!" explained Bunter.

Tom Redwing laughed.

"I don't mind what rot you talk, fat-head, only I'd rather you'd shut up! Why not shut up?"

"Beast! Well, look here, Smithy, I'm in a bit of a difficulty," said Bunter. "I've got the quid, and I've spotted a winner, but I've got to get on—see? Owing to the silly restrictions here, I can't walk out to the Cross Keys and ask them to put me in touch with a bookmaker. It might lead to a lot of trouble."

"It might," agreed the Bounder—"quite a lot, in fact."

"I don't want to be sacked. They're down on a fellow pretty heavy for that sort of thing," said Bunter, shaking his

head seriously. "But you know Bill Lodgey at the Three Fishers, Smithy. He takes bets for you, doesn't he?"

Vernon-Smith looked fixedly at Bunter. The statement was true; Smithy did know a dingy racing man at the Three Fishers, and that dingy racing man did take bets for the "bad hat" of the Remove

But it was not agreeable to the Bounder to find the Peeping Tom of the Lower School so conversant with his affairs. Neither did he like to hear them mentioned in open quad, where anyone might have passed and heard Bunter's squeak.

Redwing, rather uneasy at his chum's look, gave Bunter a push.

"Cut off!" he said curtly.

"Shan't! I'm talking to Smithy! Look here, Smithy, we can get out till school; and I want you to come along with me and give me an introduction to Lodgey—see? You know where to find him, don't you?"

"Oh gad!" said the Bounder.

Secretly and with great caution, the Bounder sometimes saw that racing man with whom he was acquainted. But the idea of walking off to the Three Fishers at a moment's notice with such a comrade in blackguardism as Billy Bunter was enough to make Smithy stare.

"Will you come now?" asked Bunter. "You see, I've got to get my bet on to-day, as the race is to-morrow. I can't get out in the morning to see Lodgey. It will have to be done to-day, or not at all. You can put a quid on at the same time, if you like; I don't mind letting you have my tip. Why shouldn't you win a fiver, too?" said Bunter generously. "Back Crackerjack, old chap! Put your shirt on him! He's the goods!"

"Listen to the man who knows!" chortled the Bounder

"Well, it's a sure thing!" said Bunter. "One of 'Quick-Eye's' special snips, you know. He gives lots of winners——"

"How do you know?"

"He says so in 'Sporting Tips,'" explained Bunter.

"Oh crikey!"

"This snip is practically from the horse's mouth! said Bunter. "You have a fiver on, Smithy, if you've got one! Fancy collecting thirty pounds on Thursday! Easy money—what?"

"Almost too easy!" grinned Smithy. "Want to get rich quick, Reddy? Take Bunter's tip, and put your socks on Crackerjack!"

"The fat ass!" said Redwing, who was staring at Bunter with a mingling of wonder and disgust. "I suppose Bunter's the kind of idiot those rogues like to get hold of."

"Just the kind!" chuckled Smithy. "Now, look here, Bunter, if you've really touched some silly ass for a quid, go and blow it in jam tarts, and make sure of it. You're going the right way to lose your quid, and get sacked over and above! That cad Carter would be glad to see you at this game; he would take jolly good care that Quelch heard of it somehow."

"Oh, that's rot!" said Bunter. "Carter isn't such a bad chap in his way. It was Carter lent me the quid."

"Wha-at?"

"Pretty decent of him—what?" said Bunter. "He's a cad and a worm and rotter, and all that, but that was pretty decent."

"You benighted idiot!" said Vernon-Smith. "Haven't you sense enough to see that he's done it just to help you land yourself in trouble?"

"Rot! He asked me specially if I was going to bet with it, and said he

wouldn't lend it to me if I was," said Bunter.

"And it doesn't occur to you that that was to cover up his tracks if it comes out, when you're sacked, that you got the money from him?" asked the Bounder sarcastically.

"Oh, really, Smithy, I wish you wouldn't keep on jawing about Carter when I want you to take me along to see Lodgey!" said Bunter peevishly. "Look here, will you come along to the Three Fishers?"

"No, fathead!"

"Beast! I suppose I had better ask Skinner; I believe Skinner knows him. I'm sure Angel of the Fourth does, I might ask Angel," said Bunter thoughtfully. "You can go and eat coke, Smithy! I suppose you're jealous because you can't spot winners and I can! Yah! Well, you won't get any more sure snips from me, I can tell you!"

"Hold on!" said the Bounder, as Bunter was about to roll off. "On second thoughts, old fat man, I'll take a walk with you before class."

Bunter turned back at once.

"Right-ho!" he said cheerily. "Be a sport, old fellow! Come on!"

"Look here, Smithy——" began Tom Redwing.

"You shut up, Redwing!" interrupted Bunter warmly. "You leave Smithy alone!"

Vernon-Smith closed one eye at Redwing, who stared, and then laughed, as the Bounder walked away with Bunter. Redwing guessed, though Bunter did not, that that walk before class would not terminate at the Three Fishers.

Arthur Carter was lounging near the gates, perhaps keeping an eye on Bunter to see whether he went out.

He glanced very curiously at Smithy and the fat Owl, as they went out together.

Probably, seeing Bunter setting forth in company with the bad hat of the Remove, Carter concluded that all was going well for his peculiar scheme.

It was worth a pound, the young rascal considered, to see the fatuous Owl dish himself completely.

It was for this kind of thing that Carter had been expelled from his last school, and had lost the favour of his rich uncle. Bunter was not likely to replace him in that favour if he was sacked from Greyfriars for the same kind of thing. If Carter had a conscience it was satisfied by the fact that Bunter, judged by his present actions, was no better than himself. Probably, however, his conscience did not trouble him very much.

Having seen Vernon-Smith and Bunter depart, and having noted the direction taken by them, Carter strolled back into the quad, with a sour smile on his face.

Smithy and Bunter walked up the road, Bunter happy and satisfied at the idea of getting his quid on Crackerjack before class, and nothing doubting that he was going to meet that estimable citizen, Bill Lodgey. The Bounder, who knew that Mr. Lodgey was absent at the races, and who had no intention of going anywhere near the Three Fishers, doubted it very much.

THE SIXTH CHAPTER.
Bamboozling Bunter!

HERBERT VERNON-SMITH halted.

"Here you are!" he said.

"Um!" said Bunter rather doubtfully.

They had stopped in Oak Lane, where

that winding lane was bordered by the high fence of the grounds of the Three Fishers.

A high fence did not appeal ery much to Bunter He was not fond of climbing as an exercise.

Moreover, there was a ditch along the bottom of the fence There was not much water in it, but there was a good deal of mud, and the mud was sticky, smelly, and unpleasant A fellow who slipped in climbing the fence was very likely to sit in that ditch—a most disagreeable possibility

"I say, why not go on to the gate?" asked Bunter. "We can see whether there's anybody about, you know, before we go in."

"Too jolly risky!" said the Bounder, shaking his head

"Well, look here, there's another gate on the towpath; let's go round that way."

"Too far; we should never get back in time. I'll give you a bunk up," said the Bounder. "I'll land you at the top of the fence all right."

"I'd rather go in by the gate."

"Go, then; I'm not stopping you!"

"Beast! I mean, give me a bunk up, old chap!"

"Buck up, then. We can't hang about here for ever!" said the Bounder impatiently.

Billy Bunter managed to get across the narrow ditch without tumbling in. From the ditch there was a narrow grassy slope up to the fence. Bunter got a rather precarious footing on it by holding on to the fence with his fat hands.

(*Continued on next page.*)

LEARN to PLAY FOOTBALL!
BY
OUR INTERNATIONAL COACH

CHANGING POSITIONS :

NOW, then, centre-forwards, we must set out to find ways and means of getting rid of that bogy of ours — the opposing centre-half. He has been put there to bottle us up. We mustn't allow him to do so—that's all there is to it.

We may try, as many centre-forwards have tried, to do the job by wandering. The centre-forward's real place is in the centre of the field But if he cannot get by the middle route to goal, he must find another road So he wanders about, out to the wings, back towards his own half of the field; anywhere, so long as he keeps the stopper centre-half on the move The idea is, you see, that the opposing centre-half, who has been given instructions to stick to his man like glue, will follow the centre-forward wherever he goes. If he does this, there will be a gap left down the middle of the field

That is where the inside-forwards come into this picture A football team without a centre-forward is not really a football team at all So when the centre goes wandering about, taking the centre-half with him, someone else must nip in to take the centre-forward's place. And that, of course, requires perfect understanding between the centre-forward and his colleagues.

I have never seen this interchanging of positions done so cleverly as it was done, and I believe is still being done, by Horatio Carter and Bob Gurney of Sunderland I don't think anyone will argue with me when I say that it was the clever combined play of these two which did more than anything else to win for Sunderland the Championship and the Cup in successive seasons.

Two seasons ago, when Sunderland won the Championship, they scored 109 goals in the season You might have expected that Bob Gurney, the centre-forward of the side, would have got most of those But he didn't. Carter, the inside-right, scored the same number of goals as Gurney in that season. The two of them "bagged" 31 each.

The reason was simple. Although he appeared on the programme as centre-forward, Gurney spent no more time in that position than did Carter. They kept changing places, so cleverly and

| The hardest worked players in a football team are undoubtedly the inside forwards. Our special sporting contributor explains their various duties in this interesting article. |

so quickly, that the opposing centre-half didn't know which one he was supposed to be marking. The result was that they helped one another to score no end of goals.

A BIT OF EVERYTHING !

IN present-day football there is definitely another job which falls to the lot of the inside-forward— to help the centre-forward carry out his task of beating the stopper centre-half. The addition of this extra duty has made the job of the inside man, without doubt, the hardest and most strenuous of all. He must be a bit of everything Defender, attacker, fine dribbler, able to give good passes, a marksman, and an all-round help to his colleagues.

I once heard Ray Westwood, Bolton Wanderers and England inside-left, and one of the best inside-forwards in the world at the present moment, sum up the inside-forward's job very well. He said that the inside-forward, if he is doing his job well, is a "fetcher, a schemer, and a finisher." Let's pull that to pieces, and see what the man who knows meant by it.

First of all, the inside man must be a fetcher. This means that, if the half-backs are a bit overrun, and can't give much time to feeding their forwards, as I told you they should, the inside-forwards must go back and fetch the ball for themselves, without waiting for it to be sent up to them. To do that they must be strong, as half-backs are, and good tacklers.

After they have gone back to fetch the ball, they must bring it up to their forwards. What do they need to enable them to do this? The ability to run with the ball, and keep it under complete control while they dribble up

field. So far, so good. They have gone back, and have brought the ball up to their other forwards. What now? They must either keep going on themselves, or pass to a colleague. But they can't do any passing until they have first of all drawn opponents out of position by beating one or two players and making other defenders leave their "posts" to come across to tackle them. That means tricks—the schemer part of Westwood's description coming in.

SURPRISING THE DEFENCE !

WE know, don't we, that you can't keep on doing the same thing in football? You must always be introducing something different. When the inside-forward has done his tricks, the defenders will soon get to know his ways if he always passes to a colleague. So sometimes he must go right through on his own, taking the defence by surprise, and doing his share in the goal-scoring line.

Ray Westwood himself is about the best of the lot at this surprise dash through. Watch him, if you get the chance. With the ball at his feet, and the defenders waiting for him to pass, he will suddenly get moving and go right through the whole defence like a streak of lightning. He has everything which enables him to do this Speed off the mark, a fine body swerve, ball control, and, once through the defence, he can finish with a shot which the goalkeeper sometimes never sees until he turns round to pick the ball out of the net. That's Westwood, that was! You know the sort of business.

Funnily enough, one of the greatest goal-scoring inside-forwards of all time was also a Bolton Wanderers inside-left. Way back in the season of 1920-21, Joe Smith scored 38 goals for the "Trotters," as Bolton Wanderers are called. Harry Clifton, the present Chesterfield inside-right, is going all out to beat that record this season. But I am pretty certain that, when the summer comes, Clifton, and many other inside-forwards, will feel like a good long rest. To be a fetcher, a schemer, and a finisher in football is no weak man's job.

THE MAGNET LIBRARY.—No. 1,568.

The more active Bounder joined him there, and proceeded to bunk him up Bunter was not easy to bunk.

He grabbed at the fence and dragged, and the Bounder heaved from below; but so much weight required a good deal of lifting. Progress was slow.

"Ow!" gasped Bunter. "Wow! You're pinching me, you beast! Ow!"

"Get on with it, fathead!" panted the Bounder. "Do you think I'm a steam crane? Get up!"

"Beast!" gurgled Bunter.

He clambered and the Bounder shoved, and he got his fat paws to the top of the fence. There he clung and hung, with his feet nearly a yard above the earth.

At that point in the proceedings Vernon-Smith ceased his efforts. Instead of bunking Bunter further, he jumped back across the ditch into the lane.

Bunter, hanging on, squeaked at him over a fat shoulder.

"I say, Smithy, you beast, bunk me up! I say——"

"Can't you pull yourself up now?" queried the Bounder.

"No!" howled Bunter.

"I rather fancied you couldn't," agreed Smithy.

"Will you help me up or not?" shrieked Bunter.

"Not," answered Vernon-Smith coolly.

"Why, you—you—you beast!" gasped Bunter. "You can't leave me hanging here like this, you awful rotter!"

"You won't hang long," said Smithy reassuringly. "Your weight's against it, old fat porpoise. You'll drop pretty soon."

"I shall fall into the ditch!" yelled Bunter.

"Exactly."

"Why, you—you—you awful beast!" gurgled the hapless fat sportsman. "Have you been pulling my leg all this time, you awful cad?"

"Have you guessed it? Gum! With a brain like that, Bunter, you oughtn't to be satisfied with spotting winners—you ought to be Prime Minister at least."

"Beast!" yelled Bunter.

"Go it!"

"Rotter!" shrieked Bunter. "Cad!"

"Hear, hear!"

"Give me a bunk up, you swab!"

"Bow-wow!"

"Help me get down, then!"

"You'll get down all right, soon. The law of gravitation will do that much for you!"

"Beast!"

Billy Bunter made a frantic effort to drag himself up the fence, but he made it in vain.

His fat hands clung to the top, but he had no chance whatever of pulling his weight up and getting an arm over.

All that Bunter could do was to hold on. And it was clear that he could not do that for very long.

It was only a matter of minutes before he would have to let go and drop, and there was no footing on the grassy slope under him; dropping meant going into the muddy ditch.

That was an awful prospect!

Bunter was not quick on the uptake, but he realised now that Smithy had had no intention of getting into touch with the desired bookie. Smithy had been simply pulling his fat leg. Really, Bunter might have guessed that one, for

the Bounder, when he went blagging, was not likely to take such a companion as the fat Owl on such an expedition. Bunter guessed it now, at all events. Smithy had bunked him up there with the intention of leaving him hanging till he dropped—as a warning to him not to play the goat. Certainly, after plumping in the ditch, Bunter was likely to be too busy scraping off mud to have any leisure for thinking about bookies.

He hung on, gasping and spluttering. Vernon-Smith watched him, with a cheerful grin, for a minute or two; then he walked away down the lane towards the school.

He was through with Bunter.

"Smithy!" yelled the fat Owl, as he heard the Bounder's receding footsteps. "I say, Smithy, don't go! You can't leave me here like this, you beast!"

"Good-bye, Bunter!" called back the Bounder.

"Come back, you cad!" roared Bunter. "Come and help me down! I say, old fellow—— Oh, you rotter! I say, dear old cad—I mean, dear old chap——"

"Ha, ha, ha!" floated back from the Bounder, and he turned a corner and disappeared.

"Beast!" shrieked Bunter.

Smithy was gone. He was walking back to Greyfriars, laughing—actually laughing—as he went, as if there was something funny in the predicament in which he had left that bold, bad blackguard Bunter!

"Oh crikey!" gasped Bunter.

He clutched desperately at the top of the fence. He made another frantic effort to drag himself up, but it was in vain.

One of his fat hands slipped from its hold. He clutched wildly to get hold again, but could not reach. He hung with one hand.

"Ow! Help!" yelled Bunter. "Oh crikey! Smithy, you beast! Ow! Help! I'm going! Yarooooh!"

The other hand slipped from the fence.

Bunter shot downward.

His feet hit the grassy slope below and slid, and there was a loud and heavy splash as Bunter sat in the ditch.

Splash!

"Gurrrggh!"

He sat and squashed in six inches of soft, slimy, odoriferous mud. The scents stirred up round him were most unpleasant. Slimy mud squashed and splashed over his trousers as he sat. His fat legs almost disappeared in it, and as he wriggled and squirmed the smell stirred up from the mud could almost have been cut with a knife.

"Ow! Ow! Groooogh! Ooooogh!" gurgled Bunter. "Urrrrggh! Wurrgh! Oh dear! Oh crikey! Ow! Oooooch!"

Crackerjack, and odds of five to one, quite disappeared from Billy Bunter's fat mind. He struggled and wriggled to get out of the ditch, wishing from the bottom of his fat heart that he had never set out as a wild and woolly backer of winners—at least, in company with Smithy!

THE SEVENTH CHAPTER.

Muddy!

"HALLO, hallo, hallo!"

"What the dickens——"

"Is that Bunter?"

"Taking a mud-bath, old fat man?"

"The mudfulness is terrific."

Five cyclists pulled up, and dismounted, in Oak Lane, at the sight of

a fat, muddy, gasping figure crawling out of a ditch.

Bob Cherry, leaning his bike against an oak, ran to render aid.

Bunter was in difficulties. He crawled and clambered; but the thick mud stuck to his fat legs, and it did not seem easy to extract them.

Bob Cherry grasped him, and the fat Owl was jerked out, almost like a cork from a bottle.

He sat in the road and spluttered.

"Urrgh! Beast! Trying to pull my arm off, or what?" he gasped. "I think you might help a fellow without pulling his arm off. Urrgh! Oh crikey, look at my bags!"

"How on earth did you get into that ditch?" asked Bob Cherry, quite puzzled. "Did you walk into it?"

"Oh, don't be a silly ass! Think I'd walk into a ditch?" snorted Bunter.

"Well, what were you in it for?" asked Harry Wharton. "Like mud?"

"Beast! It was that brute Smithy!" groaned Bunter. "He did it. Look at the state I'm in! Mud all over my bags! I'm soaked with mud!"

"Smithy shoved you in the ditch?" exclaimed Frank Nugent.

"Ow! Yes! The rotter! Groogh!"

Bunter staggered to his feet. He was splashed and spotted with mud from head to foot; but his trousers were in a really awful state. Thick, slimy mud caked them all over, and his boots were quite invisible in their coating of mud. Bunter was of the mud—muddy.

"I say, you fellows, I can't walk back to school like this!" he groaned. "I say, I shall have to scrape some of this mud off. All of you help, will you? Get handfuls of grass, and scrape—see?"

The Famous Five looked at him. They were out for a spin before afternoon class—not out on a mud-scraping expedition. On the other hand, Bunter was in an awful state, and evidently required a lot of scraping.

"Oh, we'll all help!" said Bob. "But, look here, Bunter, did Smithy shove you into that ditch? I can't make that out. Why did he?"

"Because he's a rotten cad!" hissed Bunter. "Pulling a fellow's leg. He bunked me up and left me there, the rotter!"

"Bunked you up?" repeated Bob blankly. "On that fence, do you mean? Why the thump did you want to be bunked up on that fence?"

"Oh, never mind that!" said Bunter hastily. "Look here! Get hold of some grass, and rub this mud off."

"All togetherfully!" said Hurree Jamset Ram Singh. "Many hands make light work go to the well, and save a stitch in time, as the English proverb remarks."

"Hold on!" said Bob quietly. "That's the fence of the Three Fishers. Is that where you were going, Bunter?"

"Find out!" snorted Bunter. "What's the good of standing there and jawing, when I've got to get all this mud off?"

"Smithy wouldn't help that fat idiot go out of bounds, Bob," said Johnny Bull. "He plays the giddy ox himself; but he wouldn't help that blithering chump do the same."

"Of course he wouldn't," said Harry Wharton. "He never did anything of the kind."

"Didn't he?" hooted Bunter. "He jolly well did, the cad! Bunked me up that fence, and left me sticking there, the beast, and walked off, laughing."

"Oh!" exclaimed Harry. He caught

on now. "Pulling your silly leg, I suppose. He knew you couldn't get over without a steam derrick to lift you."

"He left you to drop into the ditch?" ejaculated Nugent.

"Yes, the beast!" groaned Bunter. "Now look at me. I say, you fellows, do scrape off this mud, instead of jawing!"

"So you were going out of bounds?" asked Bob.

"Oh, no; not at all! I—I was—was just climbing that fence to—to look over!" explained Bunter. "Besides, I suppose I can do as I like. You ain't a Sixth Form prefect, Bob Cherry."

"No," said Bob. "I'm not a prefect, nor a mud-scraper, either!" He stepped back to his bicycle. "You fellows coming? I'm going on."

"I say, you fellows, don't go!" yelled Bunter. "I say, help me scrape this mud off! I wasn't going out of bounds. You needn't think I was going to see Bill Lodgey, and get my pound on Crackerjack—I wasn't! I don't know Lodgey. In fact, I've never heard the name."

"You fat, frowsy, foozling fathead!" said Johnny Bull. "Serve you jolly well right! I've a jolly good mind to stick you back in that ditch myself! Come on, you men!"

"Beasts!" roared Bunter, as the Famous Five remounted their machines, and rode onward. "I say, you fellows —— Oh crikey!"

The cyclists disappeared in a bunch down the lane. If Billy Bunter collected mud on an expedition to see a bookie, Bunter could clean that mud off himself—and he was left to do the same.

The fat junior shook a fat and muddy fist after the cyclists as they went, and set to work mud-scraping.

It was a weary task.

He grabbed handfuls of grass, and scraped at the mud. He scraped and scraped and scraped, and rubbed and rubbed.

Mud came off in lumps and chunks and showers. Billy Bunter gasped, and gurgled, and spluttered, breathless with his exertions.

But at long, long last he had cleaned off the worst of the mud, and ceased to scrape. He stood panting for breath.

There was a jingle of bicycle bells in the lane, and again cyclists came into view—three this time.

Bunter blinked round hopefully. He hoped to see Remove fellows of Greyfriars.

Instead of which, he beheld Ponsonby, Gadsby, and Monson of the Highcliffe Fourth.

They stared at him as they rode up; and Bunter gave them a muddy scowl. He had no help to expect from Highcliffians.

"Oh gad!" ejaculated Pon. "What's that?"

"Greyfriars cad!" grinned Monson. "I've heard that they never wash at Greyfriars; but that's the giddy limit!"

"What a specimen!" grinned Gadsby.

The three cyclists stopped and jumped down.

Billy Bunter, eyeing them uneasily, backed away

Ponsonby winked at his friends.

"Been in the ditch, Bunter?" he asked.

"Yes. I say, you fellows, you'd

better hurry. You'll be late for class at Highcliffe," said Bunter anxiously. "It's a long step from here."

"Oh, we've got a few minutes to spare, if you want any help!" said Ponsonby blandly. "I see you've been scraping off mud. Like any help?"

Bunter blinked at him suspiciously. He would have been glad of help to get off a little more of the mud before he rolled back to Greyfriars. But he did not trust the bland Pon. Like the wise old Trojan of ancient times, he feared the Greeks when they offered gifts.

"Oh, no; that's all right!" said the fat Owl hastily. "Don't you trouble. It's all right now."

"No trouble at all," said Ponsonby. "In fact, we're glad to have met you. Ain't we, you fellows?"

"Very!" grinned Gadsby.

"Fearfully!" agreed Monson.

"We're going, to help," said Ponsonby. "Can't miss a chance like this of doing a fellow a friendly turn. You seem to have scraped off a lot of mud, Bunter. We'll give you some more to scrape off—what?"

"Hear, hear!" chortled Monson.

"I—I say, keep off, you beasts!" yelled Bunter. "Oh, you rotters! Oh, you Highcliffe cads! Yaroooh!"

Pon & Co., with grinning faces, barged Bunter back into the ditch. He sat in mud once more, squelching.

"Ha, ha, ha!" yelled Pon & Co.

And they remounted their jiggers, and rode on, yelling.

"Oh crikey!" gasped Bunter.

Once more he struggled and crawled and clambered out of the ditch. Once more he stood in the road, streaming. After all his efforts and exertions, he was as muddy as ever, or a little muddier.

But he was tired of mud scraping. He set out for Greyfriars as he was, squelching mud at every step. It was a muddy, tired, dismal and dreary Owl that trailed in at last at the school gates.

THE EIGHTH CHAPTER.

Just Like Quelch!

ARTHUR CARTER eyed his relative, Bunter, very curiously, in class that afternoon. He was wondering whether the fat Owl had succeeded in getting "on."

He knew quite well why Bunter had left the school with Smithy—at least, he could guess accurately enough. But he did not know that Smithy had only been pulling the fat Owl's egregious leg.

He hoped that Bunter was on. Once the obtuse fat junior was involved in racing transactions with a disreputable racing man, the rest of the schemer's task would be easy enough.

Bunter was not the sort of fellow to be able to carry on such a game undetected. But if he had a chance of escaping detection, Carter was ready to put paid to that. He was going to make sure that Bunter was spotted—once he had put his podgy foot in it. But had he?

(Continued on next page.)

Bunter did not look like a fellow who had carried out a successful transaction. He looked morose and worried. Carter was left in doubt.

The Owl of the Remove was, in fact, deeply worried! Getting on that day meant laying the foundation of a fortune! And he was not on yet—owing to the iniquitous Bounder!

Mr. Quelch was giving his Form some valuable instruction in geography. But Bunter had no mind for geography that afternoon. His Form-master's voice was simply an irritating drone to Bunter's fat ears. His intellect, such as it was, was concentrated on the urgent business of getting on. It would be simply awful if "Quick-Eye's" special snip won that race on Wednesday with Bunter off instead of on!

Geography passed Billy Bunter by like the idle wind which he regarded not. If Mr. Quelch noticed his unusually thoughtful look, and fancied that he was giving unusual attention to the lesson, Mr. Quelch was in error. Bunter did not hear a word of Quelch's geographical instruction.

But all at once the cloud was chased from Bunter's fat brow, and he smiled. He had thought of a way.

Why not phone that man Lodgey?

Smithy, as many fellows knew, had sometimes bagged a master's phone to ring up a racing friend. It was the kind of reckless thing that the Bounder would do just to show fellows what a devil of a fellow he was!

Bunter would have liked to be a devil of a fellow like Smithy—but, on the other hand, he had no liking for risks. In fact, he disliked them extremely.

Calling up a racing man on the phone, at the risk of being caught in the act by a beak, did not appeal to Bunter. But suppose he could contrive it during class, when all the beaks were busy and the prefects in Form with the Head! That seemed a safe proposition.

All that was needed was an excuse for getting out of Form for ten minutes or so. Excuses came easily enough to a fellow who regarded the truth as a stranger with which he had no desire to make acquaintance.

Bunter thought this idea over, and thought that it looked good! It did not take him long to think of an excuse for getting away from the Form-room. Maps were required in that lesson. Bunter slipped his map under his desk out of sight and got going.

"Please, sir, may I fetch my map?"

Mr. Quelch had unrolled a big map of Europe over the blackboard, and was about to point out things which he, if not his Form, considered worthy of note, when Bunter squeaked.

He glanced round at the fat junior.

"Your map, Bunter!" he repeated.

"Yes, sir! I can't see that map from here, sir—I'm short-sighted! Can I fetch my map from my study, sir?"

"Instructions were given for maps to be brought in for this lesson, Bunter," said Mr. Quelch severely.

"I—I forgot, sir!"

"You should not have forgotten, Bunter! You will take a hundred lines for having forgotten your map, and you may look at Cherry's."

"Oh crikey!"

"What? What did you say, Bunter?"

"I—I—I said thank you, sir!" gasped Bunter.

Mr. Quelch gave him a grim look and resumed operations with the pointer. Bob shoved his map along so that Bunter could get a view of it. But Bunter did not favour it with a single blink. He was not interested in maps! This, he thought bitterly, was just THE MAGNET LIBRARY.—No. 1,568.

like Quelch! Instead of getting out of the Form-room he had got a hundred lines! For the next ten minutes Billy Bunter sat in bitter and morose reflection.

Then his fat squeak was heard again.

"Please, sir——"

"You are interrupting me, Bunter!"

"Yes, sir, but I left the tap turned on in the Remove passage, sir. May I go and turn it off?"

Mr. Quelch gave him a fixed look.

"You left a tap turned on in the Remove passage, Bunter?"

"Yes, sir!"

"And you have only just remembered it?"

"Ye-e-es, sir!"

"I shall cane you for having left a tap turned on, Bunter! Wharton, kindly go up to the Remove passage and turn off the tap there."

Mr. Quelch stepped towards Bunter, pointer in hand.

Harry Wharton rose to leave the Form-room.

Bunter could have groaned!

"You may hold out your hand, Bunter!" said Mr. Quelch.

"I—I—I—now I—I think of it, sir, I—I never left the tap turned on, sir!" gasped Bunter.

"You did not leave the tap turned on!" exclaimed Mr. Quelch.

"N-n-no, sir."

"Wharton, you may sit down! Bunter, stand up! Bend over that desk, Bunter! I shall cane you severely for this prevarication."

"Oh crikey!" gasped Bunter, in dismay.

Quelch had been going to give him one on the palm for having left the tap turned on! Now he was going to hand it out more severely! The hapless fat Owl had made matters worse instead of better!

"Do you hear me, Bunter?" rapped Mr. Quelch.

"Oh! Yes, sir! I—I mean, I did leave the tap turned on!" gasped Bunter.

"You did leave it turned on?" ejaculated Mr. Quelch.

"Yes, sir! Full on, running all over the shop, sir!" said Bunter eagerly.

"Shall—shall I hold out my hand, sir?"

Mr. Quelch gazed at him.

"Bunter, stand up! Bend over that desk immediately! I shall cane you with great severity, Bunter, for these repeated prevarications."

"Oh lor'!"

Whack, whack, whack!

"Oh! Ow! Wow!" roared Bunter.

Whack, whack, whack!

"Woo-hooop!"

Mr. Quelch returned to the blackboard.

Billy Bunter wriggled with anguish as he sat down again.

Geography resumed its weary way after that interruption. Billy Bunter gave it no more attention than before. But he did not interrupt again. He had quite given up the bright idea of phoning Billy Lodgey during class.

THE NINTH CHAPTER.

Quite a Surprise for Mr. Hacker!

"THAT old ass Hacker——" hissed Hoskins of the Shell.

"Yes, old chap——" murmured Hobson soothingly.

"That old swab——"

"Oh! Yes! But——"

"That—that—that skinny old gargoyle!" said Hoskins. "Does he think I'm going to stand it? Does he?"

"Um!" said Hobson.

Billy Bunter gave the two Shell fellows a blink of annoyance. He had worry enough on his fat mind without two silly asses in the Shell interrupting his reflections with their nonsense.

After class Bunter was in the quad—debating, in the depths of his podgy intellect, that troublesome problem how to get on. It was a settled thing that he had to get on—the only question was how?

That beast Smithy could get on when he liked, but the stars in their courses seemed to be fighting against Bunter, as they fought against Sisera of old.

Still off, Bunter was meditating that problem as he leaned on one of the old Greyfriars elms, when Hobson and Hoskins stopped quite near him.

Hobby was trying to soothe his chum. Hobby was a really devoted pal, and he would have done anything for Hoskins except listen to his music.

Apparently something of an untoward nature had happened in the Shell Form Room that afternoon. Claude Hoskins was deeply incensed against the Acid Drop, as Hacker was called in his Form.

"Taking it away, you know!" breathed Hoskins. "Actually taking it away—taking it away from a fellow."

"Well, if a chap starts writing music in class, old chap—after all, we were doing Latin prose with Hacker——"

"It came suddenly into my head. You know how things flash into a chap's mind!" said Hoskins. "I was never satisfied with that bit in my fantasia—I knew all the time there was something wanted—and then, this afternoon, it flashed into my mind—diminished sevenths, of course—the very thing."

"Oh! Yes! Quite!" Hobson made soothing gestures. Old Claude had the artistic temperament and often required soothing like a baby! "But Hacker, you know—he doesn't understand."

"The vandal!" said Hoskins.

"Yes; but——"

"The Goth!" hissed Hoskins.

"Oh, yes! But——"

"The Philistine!"

"You see, old chap, it was Latin prose, and Hacker doesn't know a thing about extinguished seventeenths——"

"Diminished sevenths, you ass!"

"I—I mean, diminished sevenths! Can't you write it out over again?" asked Hobson. "I—I'll help, if you like."

"Fathead!" said Claude ungratefully. But really, help from a fellow who called diminished sevenths "extinguished seventeenths" was not likely to be of much use to a musician. Hobby could kick a goal with any fellow in the Lower School at Greyfriars; but what he did not know about music would have filled large volumes. He admired his musical chum immensely; but it made his head ache to look at his musical works; while listening to them was beyond the powers of endurance.

"Think I can recall that phrase!" groaned Hoskins. "It flashed into my mind, and I jotted it down—a combination of diminished sevenths with perfect fifths that, I can tell you, would make them sit up and take notice at the Queen's Hall! I'd been at it a quarter of an hour before Hacker spotted me! Of course, I'd forgotten Hacker! I forgot I was in class, really! Then he takes it away! He's taken it to his study!"

"Couldn't you make up something else instead?" suggested Hobson helpfully. "I mean to say, it all sounds much the same when it's played, doesn't it?"

"Idiot!" said Hoskins.

"Ow !] Beasts ! " There was a loud howl from Billy Bunter, as the sash shut down across his podgy back, pinning him down. Outside the window, he twisted round his head and blinked furiously through his big spectacles. Inside, his fat legs thrashed wildly.

Hobson, discouraged, stood silent. So far as he could see, it did not matter much what old Claude jotted down on the music-paper. Whatever he jotted down, it made an unearthly row when it was played—and Hobby did not see much difference between one unearthly row and another. But he realised that these fine distinctions meant more to old Claude than to him.

"I'm going to have it back !" said Hoskins. "The finest composition of modern times isn't going to stick about Hacker's study, and so I can jolly well tell him !" There was no false modesty about the musical genius of the Greyfriars Shell.

"But, I say——" mumbled Hobson.

"The old Goth is gone out," said Hoskins. "I heard him tell Quelch ! He's gone to Courtfield. Ten to one he's left it on his study table."

"But he will miss it !" gasped Hobson. "He will be on your trail, old chap, if he misses it when he comes in."

"Let him !" said Hoskins recklessly. "So long as I get it back safe, never mind Hacker ! I'll give him time to get to Courtfield, and then I'm going to nip into his study and bag it !"

"But——" urged Hobby, in dismay.

"That's settled !" said Claude Hoskins. "Let's go down to the gates, and see whether the old Goth is out of sight yet."

Billy Bunter blinked after the two Shell fellows as they went. Bunter was not interested in the disaster to Hoskins' diminished sevenths. He did not know what a diminished seventh was, and did not want to know. But he was interested to learn that the master of the Shell had gone to Courtfield. There was a telephone in Hacker's study; and if Hacker was on his way to Courtfield, it was bound to be safe for a fellow to

borrow his phone. This looked as if the problem of getting on was solved !

Bunter rolled away to the House, while Hoskins and Hobby walked down to the gates to see the last of Hacker.

"Hallo, hallo, hallo ! Come and help us punt this ball, Bunter !" roared Bob Cherry, who was punting a footer, after class, with a dozen other Remove fellows.

Bunter snorted, and rolled on. He was not likely to waste time punting a footer, with a dazzling vision of vast wealth trembling in the balance !

He rolled into the House, and gave a cautious blink along Masters' Passage. No one was in sight there, and the doors were all closed.

On tiptoe, the fat junior crept past Mr. Quelch's door. Almost without a sound, he reached the Shell beak's study.

Swiftly he opened the door and stepped in, shutting the door after him. A Remove fellow had to be very careful about being seen entering the study of the master of another Form—where, of course, he had no business. Bunter got out of sight from the passage as quickly as possible.

Once safe inside Hacker's study, he breathed more freely. He was safe there for as long as he liked, if Hacker was on his way to Courtfield. It did not occur to Bunter, for the moment, that perhaps Hoskins' information was ill-founded.

Hoskins had heard Hacker tell Quelch that he was going to Courtfield after class. He supposed that he had gone ! But that, really, was no proof that Hacker really had gone ! Hoskins was liable to make mistakes ! In fact, he seldom made anything else !

Safe in the study with the door shut, Billy Bunter cut straight across to Mr. Hacker's telephone.

He did not even blink round the study first—but had he done so, he would only have observed the high back of the armchair in which Mr. Hacker—as an actual fact—was sitting at the moment !

Hacker, sitting there, and toasting his toes at the fire, was considering whether, after all, he would walk to Courtfield, as the weather seemed to threaten rain.

If he was going, it was more than time he started ! Hoskins, indeed, supposed he had started ! But he had not yet finally made up his mind that he was going to start at all. It was very cosy in his study. It was very clammy out of doors. In that undecided state, Mr. Hacker was rather startled and extremely surprised and annoyed, to hear his study door open without a knock—and then to hear a fellow cross the study to the telephone !

In angry amazement he rose to his feet and stared across the high back of the armchair.

He stood petrified as he gazed at Billy Bunter.

Bunter, at the phone, had his back partly turned towards Hacker, and, of course, did not see him.

Having no doubt that that study was unoccupied, after what he had heard from Hoskins, Bunter was thinking only of the urgent matter in hand—ringing up the Three Fishers, and getting in touch with Bill Lodgey there !

He lifted the receiver from the hooks. A voice came through from the exchange.

"Number, please !"

Billy Bunter never gave that number. There was a sudden roar of wrath in the study.

"Bunter !"

Bunter jumped.

"Oh crikey !" he gasped.

(*Continued on page* 16.)

HELPING THE HEAD!

Another Rollicking Instalment of
"THE HUNTING HEADMASTER!"

By DICKY NUGENT

GREYFRIAR

No. 282.   EDITED BY HA

On the morning after the commical insident in the jim, Jack Jolly & Co. duly kept their promise to give the Head a real lesson in riding on a real, live horse.

On the previous day, Doctor Birchemall had been all at sixes and sevens; but now he was dressed-up to the nines. He wore white riding-breeches, top-boots, and his usual scholistick gown. He had evidently decided to save up his topper for the day of the hunt, for he still wore his workaday mortar-board.

Altogether, he looked a bit of a freek. But, as Frank Fearless remarked, he had never looked anything else, so there was nothing serprizing about that!

The chums of the Fourth fansied they could detect a slite air of anxiety about him, as they walked down the lane with him to Muggleton, and when they reached Jobbs' Livery Stables, where they were hiring the horse, their suspishons became a certainty. The Head had one horse after another brought to him before he could find one that was docile enuff. A meer swish of the tail was suffishant to scare him.

"Take this feroshus beest away!" he cried, time after time. "I want a horse that is really quiet and inoffensive—not a fiery, untamed steed like this!"

Mr. Jobbs, the owner of the livery stables, began to turn quite sarkastick.

"If you want something really docile to ride on, sir," he said, "why not give up the idea of a horse and hire a sheep instead?"

"Bah!" retorted Doctor Birchemall; and Mr. Jobbs shrugged and walked off to fetch yet another of his mounts.

At last, however, the Head found one to his liking. It was an old cabhorse with nock neeze and bony ribs, and Jack Jolly & Co. sniffed ordibly when they saw it. But the Head gave a whinny of plezzure.

"Aha! This is the mare I've been waiting for!" he cried. "I can tell at a glance that she'll obey every order from the saddle—and at the same time there's a touch of class about her that makes a strong appeal to a shrewd judge of horseflesh like myself."

"True enuff, sir," grinned Mr. Jobbs. "That's eggsactly what the catsmeat man remarked about her this morning!"

"Ha, ha, ha!"

"Oh, ratts!" grunted the Head. And he stalked out of the stables in high dudgeon, the

grinning Fourth Formers following him, leading the cabhorse with them.

They adjerned to a field near the stables before Doctor Birchemall venchered to mount his hired steed.

As they did so, a St. Sam's junior, who had been waiting behind a tree at the side of the road, joined stelthily in the procession. If Jack Jolly & Co. had turned

round, they would have reckernised Snarler; but they failed to do so, and Snarler mannidged to draw near them without being notissed.

There was a gloating grin on the face of the cadd of the Fourth—and a misterious-looking tin in his hand.

"Ha, ha!" chuckled Snarler to himself. "Wouldn't the Head be wild if he knew that this tin of itching-powder was going to be emptied on his horse's back just underneeth the saddle? I only hoap nobody looks round before I do the desprit deed!"

The cadd of the Fourth was carrying out the thrett he had made to have his own back on the Head—and he was doing it in his own pekuliar way!

Not many fellows would have thought of the idea of putting itching powder on the back of the Head's horse; but when it came to weerd and wonderful ideas, you could always rely on Snarler to come up to scratch.

With an unplezzant leer on his lips, he crept nearer and nearer to the old cabhorse till he was near enuff to touch it. Then, while he lifted up the saddle slitely with one hand, with the other he emptied the contents of the tin of itching-powder underneeth it.

"Now to dodge back into a place of conseal-ment!" he mermered. "It will take a minnit or two for the powder to do its deadly work; but at the end of that time, the fun ought to be well worth watching!"

With these words, Snarler pockcted the empty tin and retrected silently to a hiding-place on the other side of the hedge.

"Now for it, boys!" he heard Doctor Birchemall say, as he reached the hedge. "Hold her tightly while I jump into the saddle!"

"I, I, sir!" grinned Jack Jolly & Co.

Grinning all over his face, Snarler peered out from the hedge.

Jack Jolly & Co. were holding the horse, ready for the Head to mount it. Jolly himself was holding its head and Fearless held its tail, while Merry and Bright each had one stirrup. As Snarler watched, he saw Doctor Birchemall put one foot into Merry's stirrup and swing himself up into the saddle. He mannidged it very well, too, eggsept that he swung his free leg rather wide and caught Bright a nasty biff on the chin with his foot.

Clonk!

"Yarooooo!" shreek-ed Bright, dropping his stirrup and dancing about like a cat on hot brix.

"Bright, you really should be more careful!" cried the Head. "Fansy dropping the stirrup just when I wanted it! Why, you mite have made me hurt myself!"

"You—you—"

"I sujjest that you stop your song and dance act at once," said the Head seveerly. "Then perhaps we can get on with the washing—or, as the vulgar mite put it, proseed with our equestrian rehearsal!"

"Shall I lead the mare, sir?" asked Jolly.

"Thanks, if you will, Jolly! I must say that this mare is just the animal to give konfidence to one who has been too long absent from the saddle. She is as steady as a rock and—— Ow! Wow! What the merry dickens!"

Doctor Birchemall broke off with a gasp of dismay. The mare, which had seemed as steady as a rock when he had started talking, had become as wobbly as a jelly by the time he finished! Its back started rippling like a corkscrew, its legs shook like aspirin leaves and its head began to go round in circles.

Snarler's itching-powder had begun to do its deadly work! But the Head and his helpers, of corse, knew nothing of this. The only thing they could think was

(continued in next column)

that to h "
mou safe
B easil Befo take the dene awa the star wou poss circu in mee Hea
F circl its gall with wild The stoo mad scra four
F rang as h this perf
Sav
B tall fron care free Joll that them
F blen solv itsel rear and roun Hea its was and the
B "
Jack pals resk
"
I've and box shot foot com mal
A to I out onc rem one fron

HARRY WHARTON CALLING!

The first bouts in the great Remove Boxing Championship have been fought, and in another column Vernon-Smith gives you a brief account of them and explains the present position. Next week, if things go according to programme, the air will be cleared considerably and we shall know who's who and what's what and be able perhaps to make a shrewd guess at the name of the probable champion.

Meanwhile, another topic is beginning to loom in sporting discussions at Greyfriars—the annual cross-country run. This hardy annual is run as an open handicap and as the handicapping is done by that keen judge of athletics, Mr. Lascelles, every entrant from the loftiest senior down to the

inkiest fag is assured of a sporting chance of winning. Half the school have entered already.

Not many fellows go into really serious training for it, most being content to rely on their normal quota of footer and gym work to keep them in trim. I have, however, seen one or two foot-slogging round the playing-fields during the past week and the Third and Second Forms have held a couple of paperchases by way of preparation.

Neither the handicap nor the course have yet been decided on, so we're all very much in the dark at present. Notwithstanding this, whispers as to the likely winner are already going the rounds. I have been told (1) that Blundell is unbeatable this year, (2) that nobody stands an

earthly against North and (3) that Coker is going all out for the event. About the first two I am unable to give an authoritative opinion, but Coker strikes me as a very probable winner if he can reproduce the form I saw him display near Friardale this week.

He happened to steer his motor-bike by accident through an open gateway into a farmyard crowded with chickens and the farmer came after him with a shotgun. Coker left his machine temporarily where it had crashed in the farmyard, and I don't think I am exaggerating when I tell you that he streaked out of that farmyard at a good thirty miles an hour!

But perhaps he will be unable to achieve that dizzy speed on the day of the race!

More Greyfriars titbits next week, chums!
—HARRY WHARTON.

GREYFRIARS FROM FRESH ANGLES

2. My Greyfriars Patients.

By DR. PILLBURY

The Greyfriars known to me is a particularly human school, made up of all sorts and conditions of boys.

There are some who want to go straight into the sanatorium for a finger-ache, and others who have to be carried in under violent protest even if they are dangerously ill!

Let me say this about them at once; a fitter crowd of youngsters I can never hope to find anywhere! The powers that be at Greyfriars believe in every boy getting his due share of fresh air and healthy exercise, and the result is a very high standard of general fitness.

Of course, there are exceptions. One young fellow named Bunter attains a very low standard of general fitness, but makes up for it by reaching a most exceptionally high standard of general FATNESS. Perhaps this is why I see more of him than of any other boy in the school. Bunter is apt to be taken ill at regular intervals. Incidentally, those intervals usually coincide with examinations!

On one occasion when I was called in to attend Bunter, I found him with a face that was deadly white and a tongue that was covered in spots. Only after a lengthy examination did I discover that the white on his face was French chalk, and that the spots on his tongue were splashes of paint!

But Bunter is a law unto himself, and there is nobody else like him in the school—luckily for Greyfriars!

Most of my calls at the school arise out of minor accidents on the playing fields or occurring in the course of some foolhardy prank or jape. How many times I have had to attend boys for broken bones or fractures following on a ride down the banisters or a climb up the School House wall to a dormitory I really cannot say. Hundreds at least, I imagine!

A high-spirited crowd, these Greyfriars boys, I assure you. And I would not have them otherwise!

---

e was going better dis- while you're Jack Jolly.

was more than done. Head could e foot out of the mad- had broken he chums of

Then it stunts that made it im- he cleverest to dismount et alone a like the

n round in g to catch . Then it and down k wobbling l directions. opped and ee legs and k efforts to ack with the

owls of fear n the Head, ried through d wonderful

Reskew! he shreeked. as rather a save a man nt that was und in this ion. Jack soon found was beyond

y, the pro- evenchally the horse suddenly its hind legs l spinning top, and the clinging to a few turns, at a tanjent n a heap on

w-ow-ow!" r?" asked s he and his l to the

s! Groooo! d my spine my brane- attered my ractured my Ow! Here beestly ani-

ead jumped nd scurried way of the mare with agility for s suffering e injuries.

The Head wore a very worried frown, as he watched the frantick anticks of the animal he had tried to ride.

"It's a beestly nuisance!" he groaned. "I simply must turn out with the County Hunt if it can possibly be mannidged. Yet how am I to do so if I can't ride?"

Jack Jolly gave a sudden wissle.

"I've got a branewave, sir! Suppose I turn up instead of you!"

"Wh-a-a-at?"

"I can easily do it, sir," said the kaptin of the Fourth eagerly. "I can put on a false beard and paint a lot of rinkles on my face and build up my nose with putty. It's the easiest thing in the world to imitate a funny face like yours, sir!"

"Ha, ha, ha!" roared Merry and Bright and Fearless.

Doctor Birchemall turned red.

"If you're trying to be funny, Jolly——"

"Not a bit of it, sir!" said Jolly cheerfully. "I can dress myself up

so that you and I will look as like as two peas. Mounted on horseback, nobody will twig that I'm not the right height. And after the hunt, of corse, I can slip away and you can join the party instead—just as though you've been with them all the time!"

The Head's eyes gleemed.

"By Jove! That's rather a ripping wheeze, Jolly, when you put it like that! Do you really think you can mannidge it?"

"Certain, sir!"

"Then it's a go!" grinned the Head. "Mum's the word, boys! Now we'll go back and tell Mr. Jobbs about the pekuliar behaviour of his horse."

Doctor Birchemall led the way back to the stables, grinning happily once more.

And as he and his helpers marched away, Snarler, who had heard every word, grinned even more happily in his hiding-place behind the hedge.

"Ha, ha, ha!" he

chortled. "Now that I know the old fogey's next move, I'm going to take a hand in it. This is going to be the joak of the term by the time I've finished! Ha, ha, ha!"

And Snarler returned to St. Sam's, farely hugging himself!

(*Look out for more fun and frolic in next week's sparkling instalment!*)

HE MUST HAVE LOST THE THREAD!

Before visiting the Sixth Form Debating Society recently, we were told that Gwynne had a remarkable gift for stringing words together.

So we were hardly surprised to find that he soon got himself tied up in knots.

GOSSIP FROM THE PREFECTS' ROOM

The prefects are to discuss a resolution "That the ashplant should be abolished."

The rumour that Loder will propose an addendum " . . . and replaced by the cat-o'-nine-tails" is stated to be premature.

COMPETITION BOUTS ALL THRILLS NO FRILLS!

Says H. VERNON-SMITH

If anyone tells you that I went to watch the preliminary bouts for the Remove boxing championship, wearing a hard, cynical grin, and came away dancing with enthusiasm and with my face illuminated with a new-born respect for young boxers, don't believe 'em—because I'm not that kind of a guy.

But if I did happen to be that kind of a guy, I assure you with my hand over my heart that nothing I have seen since I came to Greyfriars would have worked that change in me more effectively.

The fact is, my dear sportsmen, those preliminary bouts were an eye-opener to all those among the spectators who knew anything about the glove game. In brief, it was a case of all thrills and no frills!

Before the evening started with the first 3-round scrap between Bolsover major and Bulstrode, Larry Lascelles

warned the crowd that no applause was allowed except at the end of each round, and the warning proved very

necessary. If it had not been given, the crowd would have been on their feet and yelling in the first minute!

Mind you, there was about as much science in it as there would be in a boxing-match between a couple of wild elephants, but those who enjoy a good stand-up scrap with plenty of hard slogging and no quarter given, had a treat. Bulstrode, who displayed odd flashes of skill, beat his weightier opponent on points.

Squiff and Brown were next in the ring, and their display was just as refined as their predecessors' had been rough. Brown got the verdict, but it must have been by a very narrow margin of points.

Penfold and Delarey followed, and soon waded in on whirlwind lines. This was a rattling good fight, with science and hard-hitting both featured prominently, and both boxers out for blood. At the end of the second round, they floored each other simultaneously and honours were even. But Penfold took command in the third session and started punishing the Afrikander so severely that Larry stepped in and stopped the fight, awarding the palm to Penfold.

The first knock-out of the evening was delivered by

Russell, the victim being Peter Todd. I am told that Todd hit the boards so hard that the impact dislodged several bricks from one of the School House chimneys. This is what is commonly known as baloney, but it was certainly a genuine knock-out.

Redwing and Linley followed and gave a fine clean-cut display of the noble art. They were so close together on points at the finish that Larry took the unusual step of declaring them both winners, and passing them on to the next stage.

Cherry and Wharton received byes in the first stage, and the only fight left was that between Johnny Bull and your humble. Modesty forbids that I should describe in graphic detail what I did to Bull. I won by a knockout in the second round, and we'll leave it at that.

So now we are left with the following: Cherry, Wharton, Russell, Brown, Bulstrode, Redwing, Penfold, Linley, and myself.

Who will be the winner out of this little lot?

I'll give you one guess as to what I think myself!

BILLY BUNTER'S DEAD CERT!

By FRANK RICHARDS

(Continued from page 13.)

He spun round in terror, the receiver dropping from his fat hand. It hung at the end of the cord, while the hapless fat Owl blinked at Mr. Hacker, his eyes almost popping through his spectacles.

"Oh jiminy!" gurgled Bunter.

"How dare you?" roared Mr. Hacker. "Upon my word! The impertinence—the insolence—of Quelch's boys, passes all bounds! I shall take you to your Form-master, Bunter!"

"Oh lor'!"

"Number, please!" came impatiently from the exchange. "Will you please give the number?"

Mr. Hacker grabbed the receiver and jammed it back on the hooks. Then he grabbed Bunter. He marched Bunter by his collar out of the study, and down the passage, to Mr. Quelch's door.

"Oh crumbs!" came a startled gasp from the corner of the passage!

Claude Hoskins was just coming round that corner when he sighted Hacker and Bunter.

Having failed to spot Hacker from the gates, Claude had taken it for granted that he was well on his way to Courtfield, and was heading for his study, and a confiscated sheet of music there! But at the sight of Hacker, with a fat Removite wriggling in his grip, Claude Hoskins realised that Hacker, after all, hadn't gone—and Claude faded promptly out of the picture.

Billy Bunter would have been glad to do a fade-out, too! But Bunter had no chance of fading out!

Bunter was marched into his Form-master's study. He left it three minutes later—doubled up like a pocket-knife, and uttering sounds of woe! And for quite a long time after that, Billy Bunter forgot all about Crackerjack, and the urgent necessity for getting on

---

THE TENTH CHAPTER.

Loder Looks Into It!

LODER of the Sixth whistled. Walker shrugged his shoulders. Carne looked from one to the other, with a deep wrinkle of worry in his brow.

The three men of the Sixth had met in conclave in Carne's study, after class.

Carne of the Sixth was in difficult waters; and his pals were ready to help him, if they could—but they did not quite see how.

In Carne's armchair, the seat cushion was thrown back. It was a large and heavy flat cushion fitted to the chair; and Carne of the Sixth was in the habit of slipping under it any sort of paper he preferred to keep out of the general view. It was quite a safe hiding-place for such things—and never, till now, had it proved unsafe.

But now—the deep wrinkle of worry in the brow of Carne of the Sixth Form showed that something was amiss.

"That's where it was!" Carne pointed

to the chair. "Under that cushion! I always keep my racing papers there! But—it's gone!"

"Sure you didn't shift it yourself?" asked Walker.

"Of course I didn't!" snapped Carne irritably. "It was there yesterday. I went to the place for it to-day, and it was gone. I—I suppose the maids wouldn't think of spying under that cushion! Trotter wouldn't! But—who can have taken it?"

"Well, a beak wouldn't!" said Loder. "If a beak spotted 'Sporting Tips' in a Sixth Form man's study, that man would go up to the Head so quick it would make his head swim! Can't have been a beak, or you'd be telling Dr. Locke about it, not us, this minute."

"A prefect——" muttered Carne.

"We're prefects! No other pre could or would butt in, except head prefect, and that's Wingate. And Wingate would never dream of poking his nose under a cushion in a chair. Is he that sort?"

"Well, no," said Carne. "I don't like him—but I know that! Gwynne or Sykes or Bancroft——"

"They couldn't butt in! It wasn't a prefect, any more than it was a beak! Some junior——" said Loder.

"Some young scoundrel that you've whopped, perhaps!" suggested Walker. "By gum, if he shows that paper about, and tells where he found it——" Carne's face was quite pale.

"That's as good as the sack!" he said. "The Head might go easy with another man—never with a pre. He would call it betraying his confidence, and all that sort of bunk."

"We've got to get hold of that paper!" said Loder decisively. "If it comes out that it was found in your study, Carne, you're up for trouble—and you jolly well might never pull through. Look here, do you know of any junior who's been to the study since the last time you saw the paper?"

Carne reflected.

"Bunter!" he said. "I sent Bunter here with my books after class yesterday. I pulled the lazy little beast's ear, as he did not seem willing."

"Bunter! That's that fat little scoundrel in the Remove—always spying and prying!" said Loder. "Just the little swab to nose out a thing that a fellow wanted to keep out of sight."

"But—if he got it yesterday, it's blabbed all over his Form by now—twenty-four hours ago!" said Carne, in a scared voice.

Loder looked grim.

"If Bunter's got a racing paper, Bunter's breaking a very strict rule of this school!" he said. "He will take the consequences. I suppose there's nothing on the paper to show that it was yours?"

"Think I wrote my name, and the number of my study on it?" grunted Carne.

"That's all right, then!" Loder rose to his feet. "I've heard a rumour—I needn't mention that it was in this study—that Bunter of the Remove has a racing paper. I'm bound to look into it, as a prefect. If he spins any silly yarns about having found it in a Sixth Form study, the result will be pretty serious for him."

"Oh, my hat!" said Walker.

"I—I'd rather it was kept quiet!" gasped Carne. "I—I can't face the Head and tell lies, Loder. I haven't your nerve."

"Leave it to me," said Loder.

He put Carne's official ashplant under his arm and left the study.

Carne of the sixth was left in an

extremely uneasy mood. He was quite terrified by that mysterious disappearance of a racing paper from his study. Walker of the Sixth was feeling uneasy, too—wondering whether Carne, if he was up for the sack, might blurt out awkward things about other fellows.

But Gerald Loder was quite cool as he made his way to the Remove quarters. Loder had no doubt that he could handle this matter efficiently.

It was near tea-time, and Remove men were gathering in their passage. On the Remove landing Loder came on the new junior, Carter.

"Is Bunter in his study, Carter?" he asked.

"I think so, Loder," answered Carter—and his eyes gleamed as he watched the prefect walk up the passage.

"Hallo, hallo, hallo!" murmured Bob Cherry.

The Famous Five were in the passage near Study No. 13, and they all looked at Loder of the Sixth as he came up from the landing.

"What does that Sixth Form rotter want in our passage?" grunted Johnny Bull. "Oh, my hat! Is he after Bunter?"

Loder stopped at the door of Study No. 7.

"Looks as if he's heard something about Crackerjack," said Nugent. "Poor old Bunter!"

The Famous Five moved along towards Study No. 7. So did a dozen other Remove fellows. Loder had quite an audience as he threw open the door of Bunter's study and stepped in.

Three fellows were in that study—Bunter, Peter Todd, and Tom Dutton. All three looked startled at the sight of a Sixth Form prefect. Such a visit could only portend trouble for some member of the study.

"Bunter!" rapped Loder.

"Ye-e-es, Loder!" stammered the fat Owl, with his eyes and spectacles very uneasily on the bully of the Sixth. "It wasn't me, Loder!"

"What's this I hear about you having a racing paper, or something of the kind, Bunter?" demanded Loder.

"Oh crikey!" gasped Bunter.

Loder's idea was to startle Bunter into an admission if he had the missing paper. He succeeded perfectly!

Startled dismay and terror were only too clearly depicted on Billy Bunter's fat and fatuous countenance.

"Well?" rapped Loder.

"I—I—I haven't!" gasped Bunter. "Nothing of the kind, Loder! I—I've never seen 'Sporting Tips' in my life!"

"That will do!" said Loder. "Hand it over at once, you dingy young rascal! I don't know whether I ought to take you to your Form-master about this! Hand over that paper this instant!"

"I—I haven't got it!" gasped Bunter. "You can ask Toddy—he knows! He saw it——"

"Shut up, you fat ass!" hissed Peter.

"Oh, really, Toddy——"

"I'm waiting for that paper, Bunter!" said Loder. "If you keep me waiting, I shall call Mr. Quelch up!"

"But—but I haven't got it!" wailed Bunter. "I never had it, Loder, and it ain't hidden behind the books on the shelf——"

"He, he, he!" came from the passage.

Loder slipped the ash down into his hand. He was sure now, and fully entitled to exercise his authority as a prefect!

Whop!

"Wow!" roared Bunter.

"Will you hand over that paper?"

"Ow! No! Yes! All right! I say, Loder, I—I only found it! I—I did, really! I—I'll tell you where I found it——"

Whop!

"Yaroop!"

Bunter made a dive for the book-shelf and dragged "Sporting Tips" into view from its hiding-place behind the books there.

Loder took it from him, glanced at it, and slipped it into his pocket.

"Anything more of this kind here?" he demanded.

"Ow! No!" groaned Bunter.

"I shall keep an eye on this study!" said Loder. "This sort of thing in a junior Form—by gad! Bunter, bend over that chair!"

"Oh crikey!"

Six times Loder's ash rose and fell, amid loud howls from Bunter. Then Gerald Loder tucked the ash under his arm again and walked away.

Billy Bunter wriggled and groaned. Twice that day had Quelch whopped him for his sins—and now he had captured a third swiping from Loder of the Sixth!

Lightning, it is said, never strikes twice in the same place; but whoppings, unfortunately, did. And Billy Bunter was feeling very much hurt! He wriggled and writhed.

"Who wouldn't be a sportsman?" asked Skinner, in the passage.

"Ha, ha, ha!"

"Ow! Wow! I say, you fellows—wow! I say, what beast sneaked to a pre about that—wow—paper? Wow!"

"Perhaps Carne missed it!" grinned Johnny Bull. "Feeling bad, Bunter?"

"Ow! Yes!"

"Serve you jolly well right!"

"Beast!"

In Bunter's study there was tribulation and woe! But in Carne's, in the Sixth, there was satisfaction, at all events! That was no comfort to Bunter! Bunter wriggled, and could not be comforted—and almost wished that he had never started on the career of a bold, bad blagger at all!

THE ELEVENTH CHAPTER.
No Exit!

"THAT you have wronged me, doth appear in this!"

That surprising statement greeted Billy Bunter's fat ears as he toiled up the box-room staircase a couple of hours later.

It was the voice of William Wibley, of the Remove, that proceeded from the half-open door of the Remove box-room.

Billy Bunter breathed hard and deep.

Nobody, he had supposed, would be in the box-room. Instead of which several fellows were there, the light was on, and William Wibley's voice was rolling out Shakespearian lines.

Bunter reached the landing and blinked in, his eyes gleaming with wrath behind his spectacles.

It was past lock-up, after which no fellow could leave the House, except by special leave from a master.

Bunter had to leave the House if he was going to see Bill Lodgey; but he could not, of course, ask leave from a master to pay a visit to a disreputable bookmaker at a disreputable "pub."

Bunter was not bright; but he was bright enough to realise that.

He had to get out surreptitiously, if at all. The box-room window was the easiest way, well known in the Remove.

The fat sportsman had intended to cut out of gates after tea and get back before lock-up. But that licking from Loder had put paid to the idea. By the time Bunter had recovered from that severe whopping sufficiently to give his attention to the urgent business of getting on, it was too late, and he dared not risk being missed at call-over. After call-over came lock-up; and Bunter had either to break bounds in secret or else give up the whole idea of backing Crackerjack with Carter's quid, and thereby losing the chance of a life-time!

Bunter was not going to lose the chance of a life-time if he could help it. So here he was—with designs on the box-room window!

Unfortunately, there also was Wibley of the Remove, spouting Shakespeare. There also were five or six other Removites.

It was, apparently, a rehearsal. Wibley, the great chief of the Remove Dramatic Society, was getting ambitious —he was going to give "Julius Cæsar." Rehearsals were often difficult matters. In the Rag, fellows persisted in talking instead of sitting round like silent owls, as, of course, they ought to have done when Wib had a theatrical stunt on— in Wib's opinion, at least. There was not much room in a study; besides, fellows would barge into a study. How could fellows rehearse in Wib's study when Morgan might begin playing his flute, or Mick Desmond demand, in loud and vociferous tones:

"Have ye seen me Virgil? Where the jooce is that Virgil?"

Wibley had selected the box-room—convenient for a rehearsal, though inconvenient at the moment for Bunter.

"You have condemned and notes Lucius Pella for taking bribes here of the Sardians!" continued Wibley, who was, apparently, taking the part of Cassius in the play. "Where in my letters, praying on his side, because I knew the man, were slighted off?"

"You banged yourself to fight in such a corpse," answered Russell, who seemed to be Brutus, taking a squint at a rather tattered and indecipherable script.

Yell from Wibley!

"Get it right, fathead! What do you mean?"

Russell took another squint.

"You banged yourself to write in such a scrape," he amended.

"Idiot!" yelled Wibley.

"Here, I say," broke in Ogilvy, "that ain't in Shakespeare! You've got it wrong yourself, Wib!"

"Dummy!" roared Wibley.

"That ain't, either!" said Squiff. "Dash it all, Wibley, you might get your own lines right when you're taking the rehearsal and ragging fellows for forgetting their lines!"

"I've got my lines right!" roared Wibley.

"Well, there isn't either 'idiot' or 'dummy' in my copy," said Squiff. "What Cassius says next is: 'As such a time——'"

"I was talking to Russell, ass! You wronged yourself to write in such a cause, you ass!" roared Wibley.

"Eh—I haven't written anything!" said Russell. "What cause do you mean?"

"Fathead! Ass! That's Brutus' line!" raved Wibley.

"Oh! Is it?" said Russell, with another squint at his script. "Oh, all right! You wronged yourself to write in such a cause. You're sure it isn't scrape, Wibley?"

"Idiot!"

"I say, you fellows——"

"Get out, Bunter!" hooted Wibley. "You're not in this! Don't interrupt! Look here, get out! Shut that door!"

"Yes; get out, old fat man!" said Bob Cherry, who was sitting on Lord Mauleverer's big trunk, waiting till wanted. "Shut the door after you!"

"I say, you fellows, Quelch is coming up here!" said Bunter. "He's seen a light in the box-room, I think! You'd better clear!"

"Quelch can come up, if he likes, fat-head! No harm in rehearsing 'Julius Cæsar' in a box-room," answered Bob.

"I—I—I mean, he—he—he said there's a lot of row going on here," said Bunter. "He's bringing up his cane."

"If Quelch interrupts us, I'll jolly well shy 'Julius Cæsar' at him!" exclaimed the exasperated Wibley. "Shut up, Bunter! Now, then, Russell!"

"You wronged yourself to write in such a scrape—I mean, cause," said Brutus.

"At such a time as this, it is not meet——"

"I say, you fellows——"

"Shut up, Bunter!" shrieked Wibley.

"I say, I—I believe I can hear Quelch coming! He's in a fearful temper!" urged Bunter. "I—I came up specially to give you the tip."

"Shut up! At such a time as this, it is not meet——"

Wibley carried on with Cassius' speech regardless of Bunter. Bunter eyed him with an exasperated blink.

It was true that it was no business of the amateur theatrical performers if Bunter broke House bounds after lock-up. They had no right to stop him if he chose to crawl out of the box-room window and clamber down from the leads. But it was quite possible that they might, all the same—especially Bob Cherry, who was very likely to think it up to him to save the fat Owl from trouble. Bunter did not want to risk being stopped; this was almost his last chance of getting out. He could not get out in prep, and after prep came dorm.

"I say, Bob——" he recommenced.

"Shut up, old chap!"

"But, I say, Wharton asked me to tell you he wanted you in the study——"

"Tell him I'm busy!"

"I think it's rather important, old chap. I—I think he—he's fallen down and broken his leg——"

"Wha-at?"

"I'd go, old chap, if I were you!" said Bunter, eyeing Bob eagerly. "He —he was groaning in awful agony——"

Bob Cherry rose from Lord Mauleverer's trunk.

Bunter's fat face brightened. Once that beast was off the scene, he could risk it; Bob was the likeliest one to stop him in transit.

Bob came towards the box-room door. There, to Bunter's surprise and annoyance, he grasped the fat Owl by the neck.

"I don't know why you've come up here telling crammers, old fat porpoise!" said Bob. "But if you think it's funny, I don't! Take that!"

Tap!

"Yoooop!" roared Bunter, as his head tapped on the door.

"And that!"

Tap!

"Yow-wooop!"

"And now buzz off before I boot you down the stairs!" said Bob cheerfully.

He rolled Bunter out on the landing and slammed the box-room door on him.

The fat Owl, gurgling with wrath, stooped to the keyhole, and yelled through it:

"Beast!"

Then he rolled away.

Wibley & Co. carried on with "Julius Cæsar," evidently booked in that box-room till prep. There was no way out for Bunter

Already that day it had seemed as if the stars in their courses were fighting against Bunter getting that quid on Crackerjack. Now, clearly, they were up to the same game again. The fat sportsman began to wonder whether he ever would get that quid on Crackerjack

THE TWELFTH CHAPTER.

In or Out?

"I SAY, you fellows!"

Billy Bunter rolled into the Rag. After lock-up a good many of the Remove were there, among them the members of the famous Co. who were not attending the box-room rehearsal. Carter was there, and he was still in doubt as to whether his intended victim had got in touch with a bookie. He gave the fat junior a very penetrating look as he rolled in.

It was dark outside, and the light, of course, was on in the Rag.

Bunter rolled across to the windows.

The Rag had windows on the quadrangle. It was rather a long drop for a fellow like Bunter; still, it was practicable. Only it was rather awkward for a sportsman to break House bounds under the eyes of two or three dozen other fellows. Nobody was likely to call the attention of a master or a prefect; still, it was injudicious. But Bunter was—or thought he was—equal to that little difficulty. He pulled the curtain aside, opened the window, and blinked out into the dusky quad.

"Shut that window, fathead!" called out Bolsover major. "There's a beastly draught!"

Bunter did not heed. He blinked round at the Co.

"Help a chap out!" he said. "I've left my Latin grammar on the seat under the elms, where I was mugging it up after class. I shall want it in prep."

"Ass!" said Harry Wharton. "Ask Quelch for leave to go out and get it."

"I don't want to see Quelch. He whopped me this afternoon through Hacker making out that I went to his study. I can cut across and get it all right," said Bunter. "We've got Virgil in prep to-night, so I shall want my Æneid."

"Your Æneid!" said Harry, staring. "Have you left that out in the quad as well as your Latin grammar?"

"I—I mean, my Latin grammar!" amended Bunter hastily. "You might help a fellow down, Wharton. It's rather a drop."

"Fathead! Ask Quelch, and go out at the door."

"I'm not going to ask Quelch! He mightn't believe me," explained Bunter. "He's doubted my word before, as you know."

"What does that silly owl want to go out into the quad for?" asked Johnny Bull, staring at Bunter.

"Haven't I just told you?" demanded Bunter. "I've got to get my Algebra. I left it on the seat—I mean, my Virgil —that is, my Latin grammar. I want it in prep presently."

"Shall I cut out and get it for you?" asked Johnny sarcastically.

Had Bunter really left a book out of the House he would certainly have jumped at that offer. Now he did not jump.

"Oh, you'd never find it!" he said. "You're rather an ass, old chap—thanks all the same! Lend me a hand out of this window, Nugent."

"I'll lend you some school-books instead," suggested Nugent, with a grin.

"Oh, I'd rather have my own books, old chap! I don't believe in borrowing books—or borrowing at all, if you come to that. Neither a borrower nor a lender be, you know, as Spokeshave says—I mean Shakespeare. Inky, old chap, give me a hand out of this window, will you?"

"The answer is in the absurd negative, my idiotic Bunter!"

"Beast! I say, Smithy——"

"Go and eat coke!" said the Bounder, without looking round.

"Rotter! I say, Redwing——"

"Fathead!"

"Toddy, old man——"

"You're not going out, you howling ass!" said Peter Todd. "It's a whopping for breaking House bounds. Haven't you had enough whoppings for one day?"

"Well, you see, I've got to get my geometry book——"

"What a collection of books Bunter's left out in the quad!" remarked Skinner. "A whole school outfit!"

"Ha, ha, ha!"

"I mean my Algebra—that is, my Latin Virgil—grammar! Well, if you cads won't lend a fellow a hand, I can manage without. Keep that door shut."

"You fat chump!" exclaimed the captain of the Remove. "Stay where you are."

"Yah!" retorted Bunter. He put his head out of the window, and blinked into the February dusk. "I say, one of you might help a fellow!"

"Nobody's going to do anything of the kind, fathead!"

Carter came towards the window.

"I don't see why Bunter shouldn't fetch his book in, if he chooses," he said. "I'll help you out, if you like, Bunter."

"Oh, thanks!" said Bunter, in surprise.

This was the second time that day that Carter had unexpectedly come to the rescue. Bunter began to think that he had rather misjudged Arthur Carter. This, Bunter thought, was jolly good-natured of him!

Other fellows did not get that impression, however. Harry Wharton & Co. gave Carter rather grim looks. Wharton came over to the window.

"What do you mean by that, Carter?" he asked very quietly.

"I mean what I say," answered Carter. "If Bunter wants his book for prep, why shouldn't he fetch it in?"

"Yes, rather!" said Bunter. "Lend me a hand, old chap!"

"You know that Bunter is lying, the same as we do," said Harry Wharton unceremoniously. "I don't know why he wants to break bounds, but he's not left a book in the quad, and he's not going after it, and you know it."

"I don't know it. I don't see why you should set Bunter down as a liar every time he opens his mouth," said Carter coolly. "He says he has left a book out, and I suppose he knows what he's talking about. I'm going to help him out. Still, we may as well have it clear." He turned to Bunter. "You've really left a school-book out in the quad, Bunter?"

"Yes, rather! Certainly!" answered Bunter, promptly.

"Well, it's against the rules to go out in lock-ups, but Quelch wouldn't make much fuss about a fellow going out for a school-book. I shall certainly help you out if you want to go."

"Thanks, old chap!"

Vernon-Smith looked round.

"You fat frump!" he said. "Carter knows you're going out to hunt for trouble, and he's going to help you all he can."

"Yah!" retorted Bunter.

Harry Wharton set his lips. It was clear to every fellow in the Rag that Bunter was, as usual, prevaricating, and he could not believe that it was not as clear to Carter as to everyone else. Remembering Bunter's attempt to get in at the Three Fishers that day, Wharton could make a guess at his real intentions, and he strongly suspected that Carter could, also. At all events, he was not going to let the obtuse fat Owl get on with it.

Carter helped the fat junior into the window. As Bunter sprawled there, with his fat head outside, and his fat legs still inside, Harry Wharton grasped Carter by the shoulder and spun him away.

Then he grasped the window-sash and shut it down.

There was a loud howl from Bunter.

As he was half out of the window, the sash shut down across his podgy back and pinned him there.

Outside the window he twisted round his head, and blinked furiously through his big spectacles. Inside, his fat legs thrashed wildly.

There was a roar of laughter in the Rag.

Carter staggered three or four paces away. Then he recovered himself and came back towards the window with a red and angry face.

"You cheeky cad!" he panted.

"Stand back!" said the captain of the Remove quietly. "If you lay a finger on that sash, Carter, I'll knock you spinning!"

"Hear, hear!" grinned Johnny Bull.

Carter clenched his hands.

"What are you meddling for?" he exclaimed. "What business is it of yours if Bunter goes out to fetch a book?"

"Oh, shut up!" said Harry unceremoniously. "You're not landing that fat fool in trouble this time, Carter! Stand back, if you don't want a scrap on your hands!"

Carter, for a moment, looked like springing at the captain of the Remove; but he thought better of it, and stood back, with a shrug of the shoulders. He did not want a scrap with the captain of the Form; neither would it have been of any use to him, for the other members of the Co. were ready to see that he did not let Bunter out.

Meanwhile, Billy Bunter was struggling and kicking frantically. His infuriated voice was heard from without.

"Beast! Lemme go! I say, you fellows, make him open that sash!—I say, I've got to fetch my Crackerjack—I mean, my Latin Algebra—that is, my grammar! Will you let me out of this, you awful beast!"

"Will you come in if I lift the sash, fathead?" inquired Wharton.

"No!" yelled Bunter.

"Hand me that cushion, Mauly!"

"Yaas, old bean!" Lord Mauleverer handed over the cushion from his arm-chair.

Wharton swung it in the air.

"Coming in, Bunter?"

"Beast! No! Rotter! No!"

Whop!

" Hallo, what are you going to do with that rope ?" asked Peter Todd, genially, as he looked into the study. " How many necks have you got, Bunter ?" " Eh ? One, you ass ! Wharrer you mean ? " " I mean, you'd better not break it—you'll want it later ! " explained Peter.

The cushion descended, hard and heavy. The yell that emanated from William George Bunter rang across the quad.

"Yaroooh ! Ow ! Yow ! Stop it, Wharton, you beast ! I say, Carter, make him stop it ! Wow !"

"Coming in, old fat man ?"

"Yarooh ! No ! Beast ! Ow !"

Whop !

"Ha, ha, ha !"

"Like to come in ?"

"Ow ! Wow ! Yes, if you like !" howled Bunter. Two whops from the cushion seemed to be enough for Bunter. "Open that window, you beast ! I'll come in ! I—I want to come in."

Harry Wharton laughed.

"Well, if you want to come in I'll let you in !" he said.

"Ha, ha, ha !"

The captain of the Remove pushed up the sash.

Bunter, whose word was not often his bond, made a wild effort to wriggle out as soon as he was released from the pressure of the cushion.

But as Frank Nugent grasped one fat leg, and Johnny Bull the other, he had no chance of wriggling in. He landed on the floor of the Rag with a bump and a howl, and Harry Wharton closed the window.

Bunter sat on the floor and roared.

"Ow ! Beast ! I'll jolly well get that quid on Crackerjack, all the same, and blow the lot of you ! Beasts ! Ow !"

"What about booting him ?" asked Johnny Bull.

"Good egg ! Go it !"

Billy Bunter did not stay to be booted. He jumped away and scuttled out of the Rag, and the hour of prep found Bunter still within the walls of the House, and the quid as far as ever from getting on Crackerjack.

THE THIRTEENTH CHAPTER.

Roped In !

"PREP !" said Bunter bitterly.

He blinked morosely at the books on the table in Study No. 7, and at Peter Todd and Tom Dutton, who were sitting down to prep.

No fellow in the Remove, probably, really liked prep, but it was one of the things that had to be done. Toddy and Dutton were getting on with it. Bunter had no idea or intention of getting on with it. Much more important matters than prep occupied his fat mind.

Bunter was getting quite desperate. Somehow, anyhow, he had to get that quid on Crackerjack before it was too late.

He had no doubt that Bill Lodgey would take him on, once he got into touch with that frowsy gentleman. On that point, Bunter was right. He was, in fact, exactly the " mug" that Bill Lodgey liked to meet. Mr. Lodgey would have had no objection whatever to annexing Bunter's quid. But the difficulties in the way of getting in touch with Mr. Lodgey seemed insuperable. They were enough to discourage any fellow, except a fellow who saw before him a dazzling vision of wealth—easy money to be had for the trouble of picking it up. Bunter was not going to lose a fortune, simply because a lot of meddlesome fellows butted into his private affairs. Not Bunter.

Everybody seemed to be against Bunter—even the Bounder, who dabbled in bets and gee-gees himself. From only one fellow, in fact, had he received any help or sympathy —and that fellow was his rival, Carter. Which really might have enlightened Bunter, had he possessed the intellectual faculties of the average rabbit.

But the average rabbit was an intellectual prodigy, compared with the fat ornament of the Greyfriars Remove.

Bunter was as determined as ever. He did not touch his prep; he did not even think of it, except to dismiss the subject with a sniff of scorn.

Prep—at such a time as this ! Nero fiddling, while Rome burned, was nothing to it.

Peter and Dutton worked, while Bunter sat in the armchair, and glowered over his big spectacles.

He was anxious for prep to be over. Plans had formed in Bunter's fat brain; but to carry them out, he had to have the study to himself.

"You'll get into a row with Quelch,". Peter Todd warned him, when prep was half through.

"Blow Quelch !" snorted Bunter. "Who cares for Quelch ?"

"If he puts you on con——"

"Blow con !"

Bunter apparently was bent on understudying the schoolboy in the song, who "scamped his prep, and who skewed his con, whenever his Form beak put him on."

"Didn't you tell me you wanted to get a good report this term ?" asked Peter.

"Eh ? Yes."

"Is this how you're setting about getting it ?"

"Oh, rats !"

Peter gave a shrug and resumed work. Presently he stooped and glanced under the table. Several times his foot kicked against something there, and he wondered what it was.

He stared at a coil of rope.

"What the dickens——" he ejaculated.

Bunter sat up.

"Here, you leave that alone !" he exclaimed.

"You blithering Owl!" exclaimed. Peter. "What have you sneaked that rope into the study for?"

"Oh, nothing!" said Bunter hastily. "In—in fact, I—I didn't bring it here. I never got it out of the Fifth Form box-room, Peter I—I wonder how it got in the study really."

Peter Todd gave him a fixed look, and then resumed prep, without further remark, much to Bunter's relief.

Prep was over at last—to Bunter's further relief. And he was glad to see that Toddy prepared to leave the study at once. He had dreaded that the beast might hang about.

"Come on, Dutton!" said Peter. "Coming down to the Rag?"

The deaf junior glanced round the study.

"What bag?" he asked. "I can't see a bag. What do you want a bag for?"

"Rag!" roared Peter.

"Rag? A bag for rag? What do you mean, Toddy? You're not collecting rags. I suppose?" asked Dutton, in astonishment.

"Oh crumbs!"

"Plums! If you want a bag for plums, there's a paper bag in the cupboard, if that's what you mean. Where are the plums?"

Without answering that question, Peter took his deaf pal by the arm, and led him out of the study.

Bunter grinned with satisfaction when the door closed on them.

He got busy at once.

There was not much time, between prep and dorm, for an expedition out of bounds. But it was now or never. The fat junior dragged the coil of rope out from under the table. It was quite a long rope He had made a collection of box cords in the Fifth Form box-room. and joined them together with uncommon industry. He had doubled them and trebled them, to make sure that they would bear his weight

Now he fastened one end to a leg of the armchair, with a multiplicity of knots to make sure of it.

The other end he carried to the study window.

Descending from a study window, by means of a rope, was not an exploit that appealed to Bunter. But it was a case of any port in a storm. This was his last chance of getting on Crackerjack, unless he broke dormitory bounds after lights out—a very desperate resource. Bunter had thought it out, laid his plans, and made up his fat mind. Now he was going to do it—at least, he thought that he was.

Unfortunately, as he put a fat hand on the window to open it, the study door reopened. and Peter Todd looked in.

"Hallo! What are you going to do with that rope?" asked Peter genially.

Bunter blinked at him with a deadly blink.

"Beast, I thought you'd gone down to—"

"I sort of fancied you would," agreed Peter. "How many necks have you got, Bunter?"

"Eh? One, you ass! Wharrer you mean?"

"I mean, you'd better not break it. You'll want it later," explained Peter.

"Oh, don't be an ass! I say, is that Wharton calling you?"

"I don't seem to hear him."

"I think I'd go and see, Peter. I—I think he wants to speak to you about the football."

"What are you doing with that rope?"

"Oh, nothing!"

"Not thinking of sliding down it from the window?"

"Oh, no; nothing of the kind! I'm not going to get out of the window. Toddy."

"Right in one; you're not," assented Peter. "I'm going to see that you don't, old fat ass!"

Peter Todd grabbed the rope; then he grabbed Bunter.

"Hands off, you cheeky beast!" roared Bunter. "Look here— Ow! If you bump me over on the floor, you rotter, I'll— Yarooh!"

Bump!

Bunter landed on the study floor. Peter cheerfully looped the rope round him, and tied a knot. Bunter's fat arms were pinned down to his podgy sides. Then Peter wound the rest of the rope round the armchair, and knotted it again.

"That all right?" he asked.

"Beast!" roared Bunter.

"I'll give you a look in before dorm," said Peter. "Au revoir, you bold, bad blithering bloater!"

"Don't you leave me tied up like this, you beast!" yelled Bunter, wriggling wildly in the rope. "I say, Toddy— I say, you rotten brute— I say, old chap—dear old beast—I mean dear old chap— Oh crikey!"

Slam!

The study door closed after Peter Todd.

Bunter was left to wriggle.

THE FOURTEENTH CHAPTER.

In the Stilly Night!

WINGATE of the Sixth saw lights out for the Remove that night.

Probably he noticed a good many smiling faces in the dormitory. Among them, however, was one that was not smiling.

Billy Bunter's fat face was morose and grim.

By that time all the Remove knew that Bunter had, somehow or other, got hold of the necessary quid, and was frantically eager to get it on that wonderful horse, Crackerjack, who was going to win at five to one—perhaps! It was quite a joke in the Remove by this time.

The case of a fellow who was taking up blagging, and begging earnestly for the sack, had its serious aspects But it was rather difficult to take Bunter, the blackguard, seriously. His fatuous essay in blackguardism struck the Remove fellows chiefly as funny.

Now that it was bed-time, and the Lower Fourth shepherded off to their dormitory, most of the fellows considered that Bunter was safe.

Even if he thought of taking the desperate step of breaking bounds after lights out, he was not likely to get on with it. Once his fat head was on the pillow, Bunter was booked till morning. There were some things that Bunter could do really well. He could eat more than any other fellow at Greyfriars. He could talk the hind-leg off a mule. And he could sleep in a way that left Rip Van Winkle merely an also ran. In that line the Seven sleepers of Ephesus had nothing on Bunter. Whatever plans Bunter might make for that night, it was fairly certain that Morpheus would get the upper hand, and that the fat Owl would not stir again, when once slumber's chain had bound him.

That it was his intention to get up, after going to bed, the juniors soon had evidence, though fortunately for Bunter, Wingate did not suspect it.

"Bunter!" rapped out the prefect suddenly.

"Eh? Yes, Wingate." Bunter, about to clamber into bed, blinked round at the captain of Greyfriars.

"You frowsy little slacker, what the dickens do you mean by going to bed with your socks on?" demanded Wingate.

"Oh!" gasped Bunter.

And there was a general grin up and down the Remove dormitory.

Bunter, evidently, had left his socks on to save the trouble of putting them on when he turned out in the night. That was evident to the Remove, but to Wingate it appeared only a specimen of Bunter's lazy slackness.

"I—I— It—it's c-c-cold, Wingate!" stuttered Bunter. "I—I've kept them on to—to keep my feet warm, you know."

"Cold?" asked Wingate. He slipped his ashplant into his hand. "Like me to warm you?"

"Oh!" gasped Bunter. "N-n-no!"

He discarded the socks, and crawled into bed.

Wingate put out the lights, and the Remove were left to slumber.

Instead of slumbering, however, most of the juniors chuckled. Obviously, Bunter intended to break bounds that night. Equally obviously, he would be fast asleep when the time came! Wherefore did the juniors chuckle.

"Like me to call you, Bunter?" asked Skinner. "About midnight—what?"

"Ha, ha, ha!"

"Give Bill Lodgey my kind regards!" chortled the Bounder. "Put something on for me, won't you, Bunter?"

"I—I say, you fellows, I'm not going to break bounds to-night!" squeaked Bunter. "Don't any of you fellows stay awake."

"You're not, old fat man!" chuckled Peter Todd. "If I thought you were, old porpoise, I'd tie you up again."

"Beast!"

"This is Bunter's way of getting a good report from Quelch for the term," remarked Hazeldene. "Quelch is sure to give him a jolly good one if he catches him out of dorm to-night."

"Ha, ha, ha!"

"Oh, he won't be rough on a sleepwalker," said Smithy, "and Bunter won't go, unless he walks in his sleep!"

"I'm not going, you fellows—really, you know! I'm going to sleep! I don't suppose I shall open my eyes till rising-bell."

"Even Bunter tells the truth sometimes, by accident!" remarked Bob Cherry.

"Ha, ha, ha!"

Snore!

"Gone to sleep, Bunter?" called out Nugent.

"Yes, old chap—fast asleep!"

"Ha, ha, ha!"

"I say, you fellows, don't keep on cackling, when a fellow's asleep——"

"Ha, ha, ha!" yelled the Remove.

Snore!

Billy Bunter, with great astuteness, affected to go to sleep. He snored and snored! He could see that his intention was quite well known to all the Form, though he could not guess how they knew! But they did know, and it would be just like some of the beasts to stay awake and stop him when he started on the wild and woolly razzle! So he proceeded to convince them that he was fast asleep!

For about five minutes Bunter, wakeful, made sounds of snoring. Then the snore became genuine. Bunter had dropped off!

With his eyes shut and his mouth open, the fat Owl of the Remove slept and snored.

"Bunter!" called out Harry Wharton.

Snore!

"Like a doughnut?"

Snore!

Evidently, Bunter was really asleep this time!

Once asleep, he was safe till rising-bell. Other fellows went to sleep, and at ten o'clock only one member of the Form was awake.

That one was Arthur Carter!

Carter, of course, knew Bunter's plans for the night, as well as the rest. From that circumstance, he knew that Bunter had not yet made the plunge that he was so anxious for Bunter to make. He knew, too, that now Bunter was asleep nothing but the rising-bell was likely to awaken him—if even the rising-bell did. Billy Bunter often snored on while the rising-bell clanged, till roused out by a friendly boot or a wet sponge.

Carter lay awake, thinking it over. For another hour he waited. When half-past ten chimed, the chime was followed by Bunter's steady snore. Carter sat up in bed as eleven drew nigh.

In the glimmer of starlight from the high windows he could dimly make out the other beds—from one of which proceeded the unending melody of Billy Bunter's snore!

He reached out, and picked up a slipper. Taking careful aim, he whizzed it across to Bunter's bed.

It dropped fairly on a little fat nose! Smack!

Bunter's snore was suddenly changed into a startled squeak! Even Bunter awakened at a slipper smacking on his nose!

"Oooooh!" squeaked Bunter.

His eyes opened, and he blinked round him in the gloom. Carter's head was on his pillow again, and he made no sound.

"Oooogh!" repeated Bunter. "What—oogh!"

He sat up.

The slipper had slipped off, after smacking on his nose. Bunter did not know what had awakened him, but he had a pain in his nose, and he rubbed it. And he was awake!

With wakefulness came recollection. He realised that while fully intending to remain awake, he had dropped off to sleep! By sheer luck he had awakened. He crawled out of bed.

There was a gleam of light. Bunter had borrowed Toddy's electric flash-lamp from the study, all ready. By its beam he looked at his watch! The watch had stopped. Bunter breathed hard.

He knew that it must be late. He had intended to turn out at half-past ten, which was late enough to be safe, but not too late to catch Mr. Lodgey at the Three Fishers. He realised now that it was later than that. And as he stood shivering by his bed he heard eleven chimes, one after another, through the stilly night. It was eleven o'clock!

Evidently, he had no time to lose. With infinite caution Bunter dressed himself in the dark. There was no sound in the dormitory but that of steady breathing and a whisper of the wind in the old trees in the quad. The Remove were fast asleep—and Bunter was very careful not to awaken them.

Dressed at last, the fat Owl groped his way, slowly and cautiously, to the door, little dreaming that a wakeful ear was listening for the slightest sound.

That ear caught the sound of a door opening and closing.

Carter grinned in the darkness.

Bunter was gone!

Carter had succeeded perfectly. It had only been necessary to waken the fat Owl—and he had awakened him! The rest could safely be left to Bunter himself!

That unspeakable ass was going out of bounds, at eleven o'clock at night! Had Bunter desired to play Carter's game for him he could not have played it better!

One thing was needed now—the discovery, by Mr. Quelch, that Bunter's bed was empty in the Remove dormitory!

Carter smiled into the darkness.

Bunter, coming back from his night-prowl, would find his Form-master waiting for him! Whether he lied, or whether he owned up, there was no doubt that Quelch would learn where he had been, and why. It was, in all probability, the sack for Bunter—at the very least, it was a Head's flogging, and a report, that term, that would knock into small pieces any chance he had of getting into the good graces of old Joseph Carter! And the schemer of the Remove grinned into the darkness as he slipped out of bed, and crept to the door—after Bunter!

THE FIFTEENTH CHAPTER.
Three in the Dark!

"I—I wouldn't!" murmured Hobson of the Shell.

Claude Hoskins sniffed.

"Perhaps you wouldn't!" he said. "But I jolly well would—and I jolly well shall!"

"But suppose Hacker's up——"

"He goes to roost at half-past ten, like clockwork. That's why I've waited till eleven."

"Some of the other beaks may be up and——"

"I'm chancing that!"

"It means an awful row if you're copped, old man!" said Hobson, with almost tearful earnestness. He was sitting up in bed, in the Shell dormitory, peering at his chum, who was tucking pyjamas into trousers. "Hacker will miss that sheet of music from his study, in the morning, even if you get it——"

"Let him! It's mine, ain't it?"

"Yes, but——"

"I'd have had it this afternoon if the old goat had gone to Courtfield, as he told Quelch he would! Of course, he had to change his mind, and stick frowsting in his study! That's the sort of unreliable old fossil he is! But he's

not keeping my music, I know that! He's capable of pinching it, I believe, if he understood its value!"

Hoskins buckled his braces.

"Everybody's in bed now," he said. "It's safe as houses. Anyhow, I'm going. Catch me letting him keep my music!"

Claude Hoskins was grimly determined. He had spent quite a long time that afternoon—in class, before Mr. Hacker's eye fell on him—in scribbling down that remarkable combination of perfect fifths and diminished sevenths, which he had no doubt was one of the most remarkable things in modern music—as perhaps it was. To recall the exact phrasing of those marvellous bars was impossible; he had to get his copy back, or the masterpiece was in danger of being lost to Hoskins—and lost to the world!

It was worth a little risk—in fact, it was worth a lot: A lot or a little, Claude was going to risk it.

"But, I say——" murmured Hobby feebly. "Suppose Hacker——"

"I'm going."

And Hoskins went.

James Hobson was left in a state of dismay—the only fellow awake in the Shell, but too alarmed for his chum to think of going to sleep again.

Really it was a rather serious matter for any fellow to break dorm bounds at eleven at night and go down to root in a master's study for an article that had been confiscated by that master.

And really, Hobby could not help thinking old Hacker—Acid Drop, as he was—was not fearfully to blame for having taken away the music Claude had written down in class when he was supposed to be doing Latin prose.

(Continued on next page.)

Hacker was not an amiable Form-master, but even an amiable beak might have jibbed at that and come down rather heavy

It was certain that he would be awfully exasperated if he found that the confiscated paper had been taken from his study He would know at once, of course, that Hoskins had snooped it. In all Greyfriars, Hoskins was the only fellow who attached any value to that arrangement of perfect fifths and diminished sevenths.

On the other hand, it was quite pos-sible—indeed, probable—that Hacker had thrown it into his study fire or his wastepaper-basket. Hobby could not help hoping that he had done one or the other; for, in either case, he would not then miss it and get on old Claude's track in the morning

Hobby was anxious for his chum; but Hoskins was too keen on recovering his musical composition to be anxious for himself. Still, he was very quiet and very cautious as he stole away from the Shell dormitory

Late as it was, some of the masters might still be up, though there was no doubt that Hacker would have gone to bed. Some of the Sixth might still be up, in their studies, though that was unlikely.

Hoskins did not want to be "copped," as Hobby expressed it. He did not want whoppings, lines, or detention. All he wanted was that spot of mar-vellous music—merely that, and nothing more. "Copped" out of his dormi-tory, he was not likely to get hold of it, so he was cautious and doubly cautious.

Creeping across the big landing to-wards the stairs, Claude Hoskins stopped suddenly his heart beating.

The darkness was almost like pitch. He could see nothing; but he could hear—indeed, his ears were very much on the alert. And he heard a sound.

It seemed to him like the sound of a stealthy, shuffling footfall coming out of one of the many passages that opened from that extensive landing, all the dormitories being on the same floor.

He listened, with quickening heart-beats, for a repetition of the sound. If some beak were prowling about——

Again came the sound—soft, stealthy, and cautious; but to his intent ears unmistakably that of a cautious footfall.

He stared in the darkness in the direction of that sound.

A sudden gleam of light nearly blinded him He blinked. The next moment the light was gone again.

Hoskins knew what that meant. Someone coming along in the dark had turned on a flashlamp for a second to pick his way.

Who the dickens was it?

Some young rotter going out of bounds, perhaps. Vernon-Smith of the Remove, or Angel of the Fourth, or Price of the Fifth? Or was it a master, or a prefect, prowling? Beaks and prefects did prowl at times. Sometimes a master would come up to give a dor-mitory the once-over Hacker had been known to prowl when suspicious that some dormitory raid or pillow-fight was scheduled to take place after lights-out. Suppose it was Hacker? Or that gimlet-eyed blighter old Quelch?

Hoskins felt extremely uneasy.

But his cue was silence and cover; and he backed silently across the land-ing to the banisters and crouched there to give the unknown one plenty of space to pass on to the stairs.

Faint footfalls came in the silence;

then he heard a grunt. He started as he heard that.

It was wildly impossible that a pig could have got loose in the House and started wandering about in the middle of the night, but it sounded awfully like it.

But really it couldn't be that. Besides, a wandering pig could not have turned on a flashlamp.

Flash came again It was nowhere near Hoskins, but he crouched low against the banisters and watched. Whoever it was that was crossing the big landing to the stairs had turned on the beam of the flashlamp again to see his way.

There was an answering flash to the flash of the light: it came from a pair of big spectacles perched on a little fat nose.

The light was shut off again; but Hoskins knew who it was now—that fat ass Bunter of the Remove!

Why on earth Bunter of the Remove was wandering out of his dormitory at that hour was a mystery to Hoskins, but it did not interest him; he only hoped that the fat chump would not kick up a row and wake somebody while he—Hoskins—was on the track of the musical masterpiece.

Another glimmer came—this time from the staircase. Bunter was creep-ing down the stairs Hoskins watched over the banisters in the darkness.

A gleam again—from the lower land-ing. Apparently Bunter was heading for the Remove, for he did not approach the lower stairs. Anyhow, Hoskins was done with him. Bunter had gone up the Remove passage.

He crept away from the banisters and approached the staircase. Bunter was off the scent—if Bunter mattered. Hoskins reached the stairs—and there, with a sudden heart-beat as before, he halted again.

There was a stealthy step in the dark-ness behind him—at least, Claude Hos-kins was sure that there was.

He spun round and stared breath-lessly. Was some other fellow out of his dormitory as well as Bunter? Or was it a beak this time? Perhaps a beak after Bunter Hoskins panted a little as he tried to penetrate the gloom with his startled eyes. Possibly his panting reached ears as intent as his own. At all events, there was no further sound from the landing.

For a long minute Hoskins stood listening; but all was still, and he con-cluded at last that he must have been mistaken Mistaken or not, he was going down to Hacker's study after that musical masterpiece

And, stepping stealthily on the stairs, he went.

THE SIXTEENTH CHAPTER.

Tracked !

ARTHUR CARTER stood silent, listening, his ears intently on the strain.

He hardly breathed as he stood and strained his sharp ears.

He was not man minutes behind Bunter.

Silently and stealthily he had fol-lowed the fat junior from the Remove dormitory. He had to make sure that Bunter was actually out of the House before he caused Quelch to turn out and come on the scene

That Bunter had left the Remove dormitory with the intention of "break-ing out" and getting away to see the much-desired bookie, Carter had no doubt. All the Remove knew Bunter's

game, and Carter as well as anyone else. Still, he had to be sure.

Bunter was not, in ordinary circum-stances, given to breaking out. But he had been known more than once to pay a nocturnal visit to a study where some fellow had left a cake or a bag of doughnuts; it was even rumoured in the Remove that Bunter had burgled the larder in his time.

That, indeed, was much more like Bunter than breaking out at night to see a racing man.

Carter did not want to take the serious step of rousing Mr. Quelch and bringing him on the scene only to find that the fat Owl was guzzling a cake in Smithy's study or a bag of jam tarts in Bob Cherry's study.

It was easy enough to follow the fat Owl, watch him leave the House—if he did so—and then proceed to the awaken-ing of Quelch. Pitching a chair or something down the stairs would in-fallibly bring Quelch on the scene, whether he had gone to bed or not; and it would leave no clue to Carter's hand in the matter, as he would be back in the dormitory, in bed, before Quelch arrived on the spot. But first of all he had to make sure that Bunter was outside the House.

That there was another fellow from another Form abroad in the hours of darkness, naturally did not occur to Carter.

He was certainly not thinking of Hoskins of the Shell—whom he hardly knew, and of whose missing musical masterpiece he knew nothing whatever.

When he heard a soft and stealthy footfall on the landing he had not the slightest doubt that it was Bunter's.

Whose else could it be, creeping in the darkness?

Carter stopped. He heard a panting breath from the gloom and knew that an unseen fellow had turned at the top of the staircase and was listening.

He hardly ventured to breathe! He had no doubt—he never dreamed of doubting—that this was Bunter; and if Bunter took the alarm, the game was up—the fat junior would scuttle back to his dormitory like a fat rabbit to its burrow.

For a long minute Carter stood, anxious.

Then, to his relief, he heard faint sounds from the stairs, which showed that the fellow ahead of him was going down!

All was well!

With redoubled caution he followed. Feeling his way by the polished oak banisters, he trod on tiptoe, careful not to make the slightest sound.

But the fellow ahead of him was not quite so cautious. Relieved of his apprehensions, Claude Hoskins was pushing on his way; cautious, but not so cautious as the young rascal who was tracking him in the belief that he was Bunter.

On the lower landing Carter stopped again, listening intently! He rather expected Bunter to make for the Remove passage, and the box-room there, with its convenient window on the leads! As, in fact, Billy Bunter had actually done, hardly two minutes before!

But the fellow ahead of Carter did not do so! Hoskins had no business in the Remove passage!

Carter, to his surprise, picked up sounds which showed that the fellow ahead was descending the lower stair-case.

Although, at that hour, everybody, or nearly everybody, was in bed, this was more risky than breaking out by an upper window. Carter wondered,

" A boy of your Form, Quelch ! " said Mr. Hacker, in his most acid tones. " Perhaps you will ascertain why he is here—and has, apparently, been here all night ! " Mr. Quelch stared at Carter like a man in a dream. " Carter ! " he rapped. The junior slept on.

savagely, whether Bunter was, after all, heading for the pantry—in which case he had all his trouble for nothing ! He wanted his rival for riches snaffled, but for something rather more serious than bagging a pie from the pantry.

He followed on cautiously, as before.

Likely enough—he hoped, at least—the fat ass intended to climb out of a ground-floor window, or unfasten some back door—or perhaps sneak out by way of the Sixth Form lobby ! Anyhow, he was going to track him, wherever he went !

At the foot of the big staircase he paused to listen again. He could see nothing—not a glimpse of the fellow he was tracking; but again he heard faint and stealthy sounds ! To his amazement he realised that the breaker of bounds was heading for Masters' Passage.

It was true that there was a door on the quad, at the end of that passage. But it was fearfully risky to use it, if a beak happened to be up ! Still, Bunter might prefer that risk to that of clambering out of a window ! Bunter was no whale on climbing !

There was no gleam of light in Masters' Passage—not a single, solitary gleam from under any door. Neither was there a sound, nor a glimmer of light from the Common-room. Evidently all the masters had gone to bed.

Carter caught another stealthy footfall, and another ! Then they stopped—nowhere near the outer door at the passage's end. The unseen one had stopped at a master's study !

Carter heard a door handle turn.

In renewed amazement he realised that the breaker of bounds was entering a beak's study !

Evidently—to Carter—Bunter's game was to drop from a master's study window to the quad—quite an easy mode of egress, if a fellow had the

nerve to use a master's study as a way out !

A door opened quietly, and shut as quietly ! The breaker of bounds had gone into a study !

It was Mr. Hacker's study that he had entered.

Outside that door, Carter stood still —waiting !

Still in the firm and fixed belief that he had been tracking Bunter, he had no doubt that, in those moments, the fat Owl was clambering out of Hacker's window—and he gave him time to get on with it, and get through.

Listening intently, he could hear no sound of an opening window. Either Bunter was very stealthy and cautious, or he was already gone ! But Carter was in no haste. He gave his victim plenty of time. He allowed five long minutes to elapse.

Then, and not till then, he put his hand to the door-handle, turned it, and opened the door of Hacker's study.

THE SEVENTEENTH CHAPTER.

Hoskins Knows How !

CLAUDE HOSKINS shut off his electric-torch.

He shut it off promptly.

The sound of the door-handle stirring was enough for Hoskins !

Instantly the study was dark.

There had only been a tiny gleam of light from a tiny pocket-torch in Hoskins' hand—but sufficient for him to search among the books and papers on Mr. Hacker's table for that priceless sheet of music.

Quite reassured, and nothing doubting that he was the only fellow up, apart from the fat Removite who had gone up the Remove passage, Hoskins had

arrived in his beak's study, shut the door after him, and started looking for that sheet of music-paper, on which were written symbols that looked like mad ants and insane centipedes, but were really crotchets and quavers, semi-quavers and demi-semi-quavers, sharps and flats, perfect fifths and diminished sevenths, and other things of a like musical nature.

He had brought the tiny torch with him, and he flashed it over the table—hoping that it would reveal that musical masterpiece.

But it did not !

There were Latin papers, there were all sorts of exercises, there were books, there were some newspapers—but there was nothing that looked like a procession of mad ants and insane centipedes !

Hoskins' music was not there !

That Hacker would be Vandal enough, Goth enough, Philistine enough, to destroy that priceless work, hardly occurred to Hoskins. Confiscated articles were generally handed back at the end of the term, if of any value.

Unfortunately, Horace Hacker did not know that Hoskins' musical works were of any value. He never even suspected that !

Never for a moment had it occurred to him that he had in his Form a greater musician than Beethoven, Handel, or Mozart. Never had he dreamed that a fellow in the Shell out-Wagnered Wagner, and out Korsakoffed Korsakoff !

Sad to relate, Hacker regarded that amazing contraption of perfect fifths and diminished sevenths as rubbish, and, as rubbish, he had chucked it into his wastepaper-basket !

Hoskins could have found it in a minute, by looking into the place which THE MAGNET LIBRARY.—No. 1,568.

any other Greyfriars fellow could have told him was the proper place for it!

But Hoskins never thought of the wastepaper-basket.

He rooted anxiously over the table, silently and cautiously, but very thoroughly, and at the end of four or five minutes he had to realise that the masterpiece was not there!

Where had that unspeakable swab Hacker put it?

Locked it up in a drawer, perhaps! Desperate thoughts of smashing open a locked drawer flitted through Claude Hoskins' mind.

But they vanished suddenly at a sound from the door; Promptly he shut off the torch! He stood breathless.

The door was opening!

He was caught!

But was he?

Hoskins acted promptly.

Even as the door opened he ducked and dodged under the table.

Under the table he was out of sight, if the light came on—and he was, had he only known it, in close proximity to the missing masterpiece, for his elbow touched the wastepaper-basket as he crouched!

He tried to still his breathing!

If Hacker caught him there——

He had no doubt, of course, that it was Hacker! Who but Hacker would be coming to Hacker's study, between eleven o'clock and midnight? Why the master of the Shell had come down he could not guess; but he had not a vestige of doubt that it was Hacker!

He waited for the light to flash on!

But it did not come!

It was too dark in the study to see anything. For what mysterious reason Hacker entered without turning on the light had Hoskins guessing—but he was glad of it!

The draught along the floor told him that the door was still open. He heard a faint sound of soft footsteps crossing to the window. At the window was a pale gleam of starlight, between curtains partly drawn.

That glimmer was blocked by a form that stood and looked out of the window! Hoskins could discern that much.

He was lost in amazement!

Why Hacker came down at that hour, entered his study in the dark, and then stood staring out from the window into the quad was a mystery that no fellow could be expected to penetrate.

But there it was—amazing as it was, it was happening; and it gave Hoskins a chance to escape.

The figure at the window obviously did not know that he was in the study! If he stayed there without turning on the light for a few moments all was O.K. for Hoskins!

Silently Hoskins crept out from under the table and reached the open door. He was not thinking of further search for the missing music now, he was thinking only of getting away safe from Hacker.

In a matter of seconds he was in the doorway. The figure at the window had not stirred. He was quite unconscious of Claude Hoskins!

That was plain to Hoskins!

And—at the doorway—Claude stopped.

His eyes gleamed. That swab Hacker had confiscated his priceless music—and shoved it somewhere where he could not find it! That swab Hacker had come down in the middle of the night and stopped his search for the missing music! That swab Hacker was going to be about to sit up for the same—as easy as falling off a form! Hoskins knew how!

With great care and stealth Hoskins extracted the key from the inside of the door. He made no sound.

Equally soundlessly he inserted it in the outside of the lock!

Then suddenly he drew the door shut from the passage side and turned the key, with a sharp click!

He did not care if Hacker heard him now! Hacker could not see through a locked oak door!

From within the study came a startled exclamation!

Hoskins did not stay to listen to it! He cut away!

A fellow who had locked his beak in his study could not get off the scene too quickly! Hoskins got off it very quickly indeed! He almost raced!

In about a minute he was back in the Shell dormitory!

Hobby's voice came from the gloom.

"That you, Claude?"

"It's me!" breathed Hoskins. He was tearing off his trousers in great haste.

"Got it?"

"No! But I got Hacker!"

"Hacker?" gasped Hobson.

"The old goat came down, and never turned on the light—goodness knows why! He never saw me! I got out and locked him in!"

"Oh crikey!"

"He can rouse the House, or stay there till morning—blow him!"

"Oh crumbs!"

Claude Hoskins tumbled into bed.

"Oh jiminy!" said Hobson.

He was alarmed! Hoskins was amused! Neither of them dreamed that Mr. Hacker was fast asleep in bed, as he had been for the last hour—and that Arthur Carter of the Remove, locked in Hacker's study, was wondering dizzily who had locked him in, and why!

— — —

THE EIGHTEENTH CHAPTER.
Bolster for Bunter!

BILLY BUNTER breathed hard and deep.

He almost snorted with fury.

Bunter was at the door of the Remove box-room.

His plans were cut and dried. The rehearsal party had stopped him from using that mode of exit early in the evening. But the rehearsers were all fast asleep in the Remove dormitory now. There was nobody to stop Bunter!

All he had to do was to get into that box-room, clamber out of the window on to the leads, slide down the rain-pipe, and that would be that!

Why the box-room door did not open readily, as usual, to his fat hand Bunter did not realise at first. But he knew that it did not open! Then it dawned on him that the box-room was locked and the key gone.

He breathed fury.

That beast Bob Cherry had done this, of course! That beast had guessed why Bunter had interrupted the rehearsals of "Julius Cæsar" in the box-room. Bunter saw it all! The rehearsers were gone—but unfortunately one of them had locked the box-room door and taken away the key, lest the fat Owl should seek egress that way after the rehearsal.

"Beast!" hissed Bunter.

There was no way out by way of the Remove box-room for the sportive Owl of the Remove!

With deep feelings, the fat junior tramped down the box-room stair again into the Remove passage.

He had to find some other way out! He disliked the idea of going farther downstairs, but there was no choice in

the matter now! The door of the Sixth Form lobby was his next resource.

Breathing wrath, the fat Owl crept away down the Remove passage again to the landing at the end.

He had almost reached the lower staircase when a sudden alarming sound startled his fat ears—the sound of somebody running up the stairs in the dark!

Bunter jumped.

He almost squeaked aloud in his surprise and alarm!

In the darkness he could see nothing, but he could hear distinctly the hurried footfalls on the stairs.

Of the proceedings of Hoskins and Carter that eventful night Bunter, of course, knew nothing! He had not the remotest idea that any fellow but himself was up!

That Carter had tracked Hoskins to Hacker's study in mistake for Bunter, that Hoskins had locked him in in mistake for Hacker, and that Hoskins was cutting back to his dormitory with more speed than caution, after that exploit, the fat Owl naturally could not guess.

All Bunter knew was that somebody was running up the lower stairs in the dark directly towards him!

Visions of frowning beaks, of Sixth Form prefects on the prowl for breakers of bounds, danced before Bunter's terrified mind.

He turned and fled.

He cut across the landing to the upper stairs and bolted up those stairs like a frightened rabbit.

On the dormitory landing he paused a second to listen. The footfalls were following him, coming up the upper staircase.

He bolted on.

Breathless, scared out of his fat wits in terror of feeling an official hand grasping his fat shoulder, Bunter scudded into the passage leading to the Remove dormitory.

The footfalls behind him followed no farther. They died away in the direction of the Shell dormitory! Hoskins had got home!

By the time Hoskins reached the Shell dorm Bunter reached the Remove dorm. He grabbed open the door and scuttled in.

"Oh crikey!" gasped Bunter when he was safe inside, and he shut the door and cut across to his bed.

Bump!

Yell!

Bunter bumped into the bedstead in the dark. He stumbled and sat down. His startled howl echoed along the Remove dormitory.

Five or six fellows awoke! Three or four voices became audible.

"Who's that?"

"What's that row?"

"Is that Bunter?"

"That fat chump——"

Peter Todd sat up in bed, groped for a matchbox, and struck a match. The flicker revealed a fat, startled face and a pair of gleaming spectacles.

"Bunter!" howled Peter.

"Bunter, you blithering Owl!" hooted Bob Cherry.

"He woke up, after all!" chuckled the Bounder. "How the dooce did he wake up? Has there been a thunder-clap?"

"By gum, I'll boot him all round the dorm!" exclaimed Peter.

"I—I say, you fellows, quiet!" gasped Bunter. "For goodness' sake quiet! They're after me! Oh crumbs!"

"Who's after you, you Owl?"

"A prefect, I think—it might be Quelch! He nearly got me on the stairs! Oh crumbs! He may be here any minute!" gasped Bunter.

Bunter kicked off his shoes. Without

waiting to remove anything else he plunged headlong into bed and drew the bedclothes over him. He was in terror every moment of the dormitory door opening, to reveal the sternly inquiring countenance of Mr. Quelch.

"Have you been out?" demanded Peter.

"Nunno! I—I couldn't get the box-room door open!" gasped Bunter.

"Ha, ha, ha!"

"If it was you, Cherry, you beast——"

"Right on the nail, old fat man!" chuckled Bob.

"I say, Peter, put that light out, you idiot!" gasped Bunter, as Toddy ignited a candle-end. "I tell you they may be here any minute! I was chased up the stairs and across the landing!"

"Can't hear anybody coming!" said Smithy.

"He was after me! He must have spotted me somehow in the dark! I tell you he chased me up the stairs and across the landing! I—I think he missed me there and cut on towards the Shell dorm! But if he comes here——"

"If he comes here he will see me bolstering you for breaking bounds after lights out!" said Peter Todd, getting out of bed.

"Beast! Will you be quiet?" hissed Bunter. "I shall be taken up before the Head if I'm spotted!"

"Well, why shouldn't you be?"

"Beast!"

Peter Todd picked up the bolster from his bed. He stepped towards Bunter, with the bolster in both hands.

The fat junior blinked at him in mingled wrath and apprehension. He did not want the bolster—and still less did he want to be spotted, if the prowler of the night came to the Remove dormitory looking for the breaker of bounds!

But as there was no sound outside the dormitory, it was evident that nobody was coming to the other fellows, and Peter got on with the good work!

Swipe!

"Ow! Oh, you beast——"

Swipe!

"Yaroooh!"

Swipe, swipe, swipe!

Peter had a heavy hand with a bolster! He swiped hard, and he swiped fast.

Billy Bunter wriggled and howled under his blankets, as the swipes descended.

"Leave off! Gerraway! Oh, you rotter! I'll punch your head, Toddy! Wow! Oh crikey! Will you stoppit? Beast! Oh crumbs! Ow!"

"Give him a few more for me, Toddy!" called out Bob Cherry.

"I say, you fellows—wow! Ow! Wow!" roared Bunter.

Swipe, swipe, swipe, swipe!

"Oh! Ow! ow! Oooooh!" howled Bunter.

"There!" gasped Toddy. "Feel like breaking bounds again, old fat ass? Feel like going on the tiles now? What?"

"Wow! Beast! Oh scissors!"

Peter ceased swiping at last. He was rather breathless, and a little tired. Bunter was more than a little tired.

"Oh, my hat!" exclaimed the Bounder suddenly. "That fat ass wasn't the only man up! Look!"

"Carter!" exclaimed Harry Wharton.

"Great pip!"

"Carter's gone!"

The Bounder had been the first to notice Carter's empty bed, in the flicker of the candle-light! But a dozen pairs of eyes were turned on it now. The Remove fellows stared at the empty bed. Carter was not in the dormitory. The bedclothes lay turned back, as he

had left them when he jumped out, to follow Bunter.

The Bounder chuckled.

"If a beak comes up here after Bunter, Carter's game is up!" he said. "You'd better be fast asleep if a beak blows in, Bunter."

"Ow! Wow! Yow!"

Peter blew out the candle and got back into bed.

— —

THE NINETEENTH CHAPTER.

Schemer's Luck!

ARTHUR CARTER stood in Mr. Hacker's study in the dark in a state of mingled rage and terror and astonishment that was quite unenviable.

Never had a young rascal been taken so completely by surprise.

He had not doubted for a moment that Bunter had got out by way of Harker's study window. For what other reason could the breaker of bounds have come to Hacker's study at all?

Looking from the window into the starlit quad, he had had not the remotest suspicion that anyone was in the study with him.

Only the sudden shutting of the door and the clicking of the key in the outside of the lock apprised him of that fact—after the unseen one was gone!

He stood in dismay and rage.

Turning the door-handle only proved beyond doubt that the door was locked on the outside. He was a prisoner in Hacker's study.

Who had done this?

Bunter, of course! It could only have been Bunter—so far as Carter could see! The fat Owl had known that he was followed, and had deliberately trapped Carter in that study! It was the only explanation he could think of!

He stepped to the window again, and groped over the fastening. Then he was sure! The window was fastened on the inside! Nobody could have fastened the window on the inside after getting out. Bunter, therefore, had not, after all, got out of that window! He had been hiding in the study—to catch Carter! Carter had no doubt of it, after thinking it over for a few minutes. It seemed clear enough!

And where was Bunter now?

Gone out to see his bookie, or gone back to bed? He was hardly likely to go out, if he knew that Carter was up and after him. More likely gone back to bed!

A more pressing question was, what was Carter himself going to do?

He was a prisoner in the study! He would not be released until somebody opened the study door in the morning—unless he banged on the door, and woke up somebody to come and let him out sooner!

Had he been sure that Bunter was out of the House, Carter might have ventured on that desperate step. Whatever the outcome to himself, the breaker of bounds would have been spotted.

But he was not sure—in fact, he thought it very unlikely. Bunter must know that there was a risk, at least, of Carter making a row in Hacker's study, and waking up a beak! In such circumstances, even the fatuous Owl would never venture to carry on! No—he had gone back to bed! As, indeed, the fat Owl had done, though for different reasons from those imagined by Carter.

What was he going to do?

Bunter was safe—if he was back in the dormitory, there was no evidence that he had ever left it at all. Carter could not even say for certain that it was Bunter who had locked him in that study! He had seen no one!

For long minute after minute, the hapless schemer of the Remove thought it over and over.

The only conclusion to which he could come was that he could do nothing!

He was locked in that study; and he had to stay there. There was no way of egress but the window, which would only let him out of the House, and make matters worse.

He had to stay where he was! There was, perhaps, a remote chance of slipping out unseen, when someone unlocked the door in the morning! Remote as that chance was, it was all that was left to Carter.

In a state of bitter rage and fury, he had to make up his mind to it! He threw himself, at last, into Mr. Hacker's armchair—to sleep, if he could!

But it was not easy to sleep in the circumstances. What was he going to say when he was caught in the morning?

That he had spied on Bunter, and followed him, in the hope of betraying him? That was not exactly a story that any fellow could tell—especially as the fat Owl would promptly deny having left the dormitory at all!

Carter thought it over and over. The truth was useless to him, and he could not think of an untruth that would sound plausible.

He was still thinking it over, savagely and dismally, when midnight boomed out over Greyfriars. It was futile to keep on thinking over a problem that had no solution, and he shut his eyes and tried to sleep. But he was too alarmed and disturbed for slumber. After what seemed like a century to the wretched young rascal, he heard the stroke of one.

Then, at last, he nodded off.

Once asleep, he remained asleep. Hour after hour chimed from the clock-tower, unheard and unheeded.

The grey February dawn crept over the school at last; and another sound woke the echoes of Greyfriars; the clang of the rising-bell!

Carter did not hear it.

A fellow who had not gone to sleep till one o'clock in the morning was not easy to wake. He slept on.

The rising-bell ceased—unheard by Carter; and he did not hear the sounds of opening doors, and footsteps, and voices. Fast asleep in Mr. Hacker's armchair, he heard nothing. In the Remove dormitory, fellows turned out, and saw, with amazement, that Carter's bed was still empty—that Carter had been absent from the dormitory all night! Where he was, and what he was up to, they could not guess—and certainly did not dream of guessing that he was asleep in a Form-master's study.

Carter slept on—and did not wake at the sound of a surprised exclamation outside the door, and the click of a key in the lock.

Mr. Hacker had come down to his study, and was naturally surprised to find it locked on the outside.

Unlocking the door, and opening it, Mr. Hacker stepped in—and gave a jump, almost clear of the floor, in his astonishment at what he saw!

He stood almost petrified at the sight of a Remove junior in his armchair, half-dressed, and fast asleep!

"Upon my word!" gasped Mr. Hacker. Really, he could hardly believe his eyes!

He made a step towards Carter—then, pausing, he walked out of the study, returning a couple of minutes later with Mr. Quelch.

"A boy of your Form, Quelch!" said the Acid Drop, in his most acid tones.

THE MAGNET LIBRARY.—No. 1,568.

"Perhaps you will ascertain why he is here—he has, apparently, been here all night!"

Mr. Quelch stared at Carter like a man in a dream! Never had he been so astonished. And he was quite as angry as astonished.

"Carter!" he rapped.

Carter slept on.

The Remove master stepped to him, grasped him by the shoulder, and shook him vigorously.

Carter's eyes opened, and he stared round him.

"Oh!" he gasped.

He stood before the two masters, crimson.

"What does this mean, Carter?" demanded Mr. Quelch sternly. "Why are you out of your dormitory? Mr. Hacker informs me that he found his study door locked, and you here. Explain yourself at once!"

"I—I—I" gasped Carter.

"What have you done in my study?" asked Mr. Hacker bitterly. "What rascally prank have you played here, Carter?"

"Oh, nothing!" stammered Carter. "I—I—I was locked in, sir!"

"I am aware that you were locked in, as I found you so," answered Mr. Hacker. "I require to know why you were here at all."

"Explain yourself at once, Carter!" snapped Mr. Quelch.

"I—I—I woke up in the night, sir!" stammered Carter. "I—I heard a noise, and came down to see——"

"Nonsense!" said Mr. Hacker.

"If that is true, Carter, you should have done nothing of the kind," said Mr. Quelch sternly. "But someone else must have turned the key on you. Who was it?"

"I—I never saw anybody, sir. I—I heard a noise, and—and came down, and then suddenly the door was locked——"

"An utterly absurd story!" said Mr. Hacker. "Presumably you came here with others to play some reprehensible prank, and your associates played this trick on you. Is that the truth?"

"Oh, no, sir! I——"

"I leave you to deal with this boy, Mr. Quelch," said Mr. Hacker stiffly.

"I shall deal with this boy as he deserves, Mr. Hacker," answered the Remove master, with equal stiffness. "Follow me to my study, Carter!"

Carter almost limped after his Form-master to his study. In that apartment Mr. Quelch selected a cane.

"For what reason you left your dormitory during the night, Carter, I do not know," said Mr. Quelch grimly. "Your explanation is scarcely credible; but even if true, it does not alter the fact that you have broken dormitory bounds after lights-out, which is a very serious matter. I shall cane you very severely, Carter. Bend over that chair!"

The Remove did not see Carter again till prayers. Then they saw him wriggling like an eel.

THE TWENTIETH CHAPTER.

Sticking Like Glue!

BILLY BUNTER was in the worst temper ever that morning.

Carter gave him black and bitter looks, which the fat Owl did not even notice in his preoccupation. Morning classes were a dismal and dreary worry to Bunter.

Owing to the mishaps of the night, the fat sportsman had not, after all, got out, and morning found him as far as ever from being on that wonderful horse, Crackerjack.

There was trouble with Quelch, too. Bunter was put on con, which, he reflected bitterly, was just his luck. Having been too busy about sporting matters the previous evening to have any time for prep, Bunter's construe was even worse than usual. It was always the worst in the Remove, but on this occasion even Sammy Bunter of the Second Form might have blushed for it.

Quelch, fortunately, did not know that Bunter had neglected prep in favour of racing matters. But he knew that Bunter had done no prep, and he rewarded him for the same with two hundred lines.

All this was very discouraging to a sportsman. In break Bunter was strongly tempted to chuck up the whole thing, and expend Carter's quid on tuck.

The temptation was strong, and it was not the kind of temptation that Bunter was accustomed to resist. But, wonderful to relate, he resisted it. Only a few more hours, and—if he succeeded in getting on—that quid would be turned into six quids—the beginning of a stream of quids and quids and quids, and then more and more quids! Really it was worth waiting for.

Bunter resolved to wait. There was, after all, yet time. Crackerjack was going to run in the two-thirty. Any time up to half-past two a sportsman could get on. It was a half-holiday that afternoon. A fellow could get out on a bike immediately after dinner. It was the last, last chance, but the game was not up yet!

The fat Owl settled his plans during third school.

After dinner Billy Bunter strolled into the quad in a careless, casual sort of way—a way so very careless, and so very casual, that it would have excited suspicion, even if he had not been suspected already.

The Famous Five, with grinning faces, strolled in the quad also, and, intensely to Bunter's annoyance, wherever he strolled, they strolled.

He walked under the elms, and they walked under the elms. He went to the school library, and they went to the school library. He rolled into the gym, and they walked after him. He went down to the gates, and down to the gates they went in his wake. He repaired to Big Side, where Wingate and his merry men were at games practice. The Famous Five displayed an equal interest in Sixth Form Soccer. He joined a group in the quad who were listening to Coker of the Fifth saying uncomplimentary things about his Form-master, Prout. Harry Wharton & Co. lent an ear to Coker just as long as Bunter did. Finally, the enraged and exasperated Owl rolled down to the bike-shed, and the bike-shed proved equally attractive to the Famous Five.

Then Bunter resorted to strategy. He could see that they suspected him and were watching him. Even Bunter could see what was as plain as the sun at noonday. Still, he was the fellow for strategy!

"I say, you fellows, come over to Cliff House with me?" asked Bunter casually.

"Just the thing!" agreed Bob Cherry.

"We've got footer practice later, but lots of time for a spin first."

"I say, though, I'd stick to footer practice if I were you," said Bunter eagerly. "You want to be in form for the Rookwood match, you know. Why not go down to games practice now?"

"And miss the pleasure of a spin with you?" asked Johnny Bull. "No fear!"

Bunter breathed hard.

"My tyre's punctured," he remarked. "I shall have to go and ask some fellow to lend me a jigger. You fellows get your machines out while I'm gone."

"Oh, borrow Carter's!" said Bob. "I hear that he lent you a quid, and I'm sure he would be equally pleased to lend you a jigger for the same reason."

"I shall have to ask Carter. I—I shall have to go and look for him."

"All right, we'll help you look for him."

"Don't trouble——"

"No trouble at all, old chap!"

Billy Bunter rolled out of the bike-shed with feelings that could hardly have been expressed in words. His only hope now was to dodge those brutes after starting on the spin. Strategy might yet do it.

Carter was found in the quad.

"I say, Carter——"

"Get out, you fat rotter!" snarled Carter.

"Eh? What's up?" asked Bunter. "I say, will you lend me your bike?"

Carter's expression changed. He did not need telling why Bunter wanted a bike.

"Oh, all right," he answered; "you can have it if you like!"

Billy Bunter blinked round at the Famous Five. They were grouped at a little distance while he spoke to Carter. But they were not looking at him; they were looking towards the football ground. If this was a chance, Bunter was not going to lose it. He scuttled back to the bike-shed as fast as his fat little legs could go.

There he took Carter's machine from the stand and wheeled it out. He gave an eager blink round through his big spectacles. Had those beasts forgotten him? It looked like it, for they were not on hand. Swiftly Bunter ran the jigger out, mounted, and pedalled away up the Courtfield road.

This was an unexpected stroke of luck! Really, it seemed too good to be true!

Alas! It was!

Five minutes later there was a merry jingle of bikes behind Bunter.

The Famous Five came up with a rush. They smiled cheerily on Bunter.

"Nearly missed you, old man," said Bob. "Why did you start without us after asking us to ride over to Cliff House with you?"

Bunter did not answer that question. As he was riding with his back to the direction of Cliff House School, and as the Famous Five had come after him, it was evidently not in that direction that they had thought of seeking him. They knew his intended destination as well as Bunter did. Indeed, he doubted whether they had really lost sight of him at all, as he had so happily supposed.

"Going the long way round, Bunter?" asked Johnny Bull affably. "We shall have to go through Oak Lane and down the towpath to get to Cliff House this way."

Printed in England and published every Saturday by the Proprietors, The Amalgamated Press, Ltd., The Fleetway House, Farringdon Street, London, E.C.4. Advertisement offices: The Fleetway House, Farringdon Street, London, E.C.4. Registered for transmission by Canadian Magazine Post. Subscription rates: Inland and Abroad, 11s. per annum; 5s. 6d. for six months. Sole Agents for Australia and New Zealand: Messrs. Gordon & Gotch, Ltd., and for South Africa: Central News Agency, Ltd.—Saturday, March 5th, 1938.   LL

"**A** good spin while we're about it," said Frank Nugent. "We'll race you, if you like, Bunter, only we don't want a start."

Billy Bunter breathed fury as he turned into Oak Lane. On that lane were the gate and the fence of the Three Fishers. Bunter was heading for the gate; he had had enough of the fence already. But how he was to shake off those sticky beasts was a mystery.

"I—I say, you fellows, I'll race you, if you like," said Bunter suddenly, as the gate came into view. "I'll beat you to—to Cliff House! Put it on!"

"Right-ho!"

Five cheery cyclists shot on—and one fat rider slowed down. Once more Bunter could hardly believe in his good luck. They shot onward past the gate of the Three Fishers.

Bunter slowed, and jumped off at that gate.

Then, with lightning speed, five cyclists whirled round and came whizzing back. They circled round Bunter and dismounted.

"Stopping for a rest, old fat man?" asked Bob.

"I—I—I got a—a puncture!" gasped Bunter. "You fellows keep on; I—I'll overtake you when—when I've mended it."

"My dear old bean, I'll mend it for you!" said Bob Cherry. "I'm rather a dab at mending punctures. Where is it? The tyres seem quite hard."

"Oh, I—I thought it was a puncture, but—but it isn't!" gasped Bunter. "I—I'll get on again. You fellows start."

"Oh, we'll wait for you!" said Harry Wharton.

"The waitfulness will be an esteemed pleasure!" grinned Hurree Jamset Ram Singh. "Take your own time, my absurd and idiotic Bunter!"

And the Famous Five leaned on their jiggers and smiled at Bunter. He did not smile back. He glared.

"Look here, you beasts, you mind your own business!" yelled Bunter, giving up strategy at last as a bad job. "I don't want your company! Understand that? I'm fed-up with you! Get out, and leave a fellow alone!"

"You don't want our company?" asked Bob.

"No, I don't!"

"What a coincidence! We don't want yours, either!"

"Ha, ha, ha!"

"But we're sticking to you, all the same, old fat porpoise," grinned Bob—"sticking to you like glue till half-past two!"

"You'll be glad of it later!" said Harry Wharton, laughing. "It's really horrid to be sacked, Bunter."

"The gladfulness will be terrific."

"Beast!" roared Bunter. "Look here, I'm going in here, and you're jolly well not going to stop me—see?"

"Well, you may be right," remarked Bob, "but I've got quite a different opinion myself! My idea is that you're not. In fact, I think that if you don't get away from that gate, I'm going to boot you—like that!"

"Yaroooh!"

"I'll do the same," said Johnny Bull, "like that!"

"Yoo-hoop!"

"What about sitting him in the ditch again?" asked Nugent. "That did the trick all right when Smithy did it!"

"Good egg! Bag him!"

"Collar him!"

Billy Bunter rushed Carter's bike back into the middle of the lane, and remounted in hot haste. He did not want to sit in that ditch again. His experience in that ditch was one that no fellow could possibly want to repeat. He shot away on the bike.

COME INTO THE OFFICE, BOYS AND GIRLS!

Your Editor is always pleased to hear from his readers. Write to him: Editor of the "Magnet," The Amalgamated Press, Ltd., Fleetway House, Farringdon Street, London, E.C.4.

HALLO, everybody! Your Editor calling!

I feel that it is up to me this week, chums, to make some apology for having left out my little Chat this last week or two. Although I say it myself, I never realised this particular feature was so popular as it apparently is. As you know, I try to please everybody, and accordingly I have introduced new features, such as the "Greyfriars Guide," and the special Football Article, both of which seem to meet with everybody's approval. Well, as the saying is, one can't get a quart into a pint pot! Accordingly, something had to be "dropped" temporarily, to make room for the new features, and I decided that it would have to be my Chat. The result is, that I am in the black books of some of my readers. I therefore bow my head in humble apology, chums, for the omission. So much for that.

As well as receiving many letters, I very often get rung up on the phone. Only this morning a certain reader phoned me up to tell me that he disagreed with the answer to the puzzle that appeared in the "Greyfriars Guide"—issue of the MAGNET dated January 22nd, 1938—and which read as follows: "Two trains run from Courtfield to London and back each day. The first goes up at 60 m.p.h., and back at 30 m.p.h. The second does 45 m.p.h in each direction. Which gets back first?" The answer was: "The second train would arrive first. It's average speed is 45 m.p.h., while the other train's is 40 m.p.h." For my chum's benefit, I will prove the correctness of the answer. Suppose, for instance, that the distance from Courtfield to London is 60 miles, the first train would take one hour to do the outward journey, and two hours—travelling at 30 m.p.h.—to do the return journey, making three hours in all. 120 miles in three hours is therefore 40 m.p.h.—a slower speed than the second train, which travels at 45 m.p.h in both directions. Got it now, chum?

———

Did you notice the chap with football on page 21? It only took 61 Bournville Cocoa Coupons to secure it, and it is full size and just the very thing you are requiring for match practice. There are lots of other gifts obtainable, too, and you can learn all about them in the 44-page Book of Gifts offered in return for the coupon in the Bournville advertisement. If you read carefully you will find that there is also a Free coupon included with the book.

———

Now for next Saturday's super story of Greyfriars.

"CARTER TAKES THE COUNT!"
By Frank Richards.

With all his cunning, Arthur Carter has failed, so far, to black Billy Bunter's character and redeem his own. But he's not given up hope, by any means! Next week, he plays the most despicable trick imaginable. Fortunately, however, just when it looks like being all UP for Bunter—— No, to say more would give away the plot entirely, and this I don't want to do. Wait until next Saturday, chums, when you can read and enjoy this spanking fine story of Harry Wharton & Co.

YOUR EDITOR.

"After him!" roared Johnny Bull.

"Tally-ho!" yelled Bob.

There was a clatter of bikes behind Bunter. Puffing and blowing, the fat Owl put on desperate speed. He shot out of the lane into the Courtfield road again and whizzed on to the school. After him careered the Famous Five.

Arthur Carter, at the school gates, was looking up the road, wondering whether Bunter had at last got away with it and crossed the Rubicon, so to speak. He stared at the sight of the fat junior in frantic flight, with five laughing cyclists whizzing after him.

He gritted his teeth as he watched them coming. Only too clearly, Bunter had not got away with it. He was not yet on, and not likely to be on. The chums of the Remove had seen to that!

Many and various had been Billy Bunter's attempts to get going on the attractive career of an amateur blackguard. Every one of them had been nipped in the bud. Carter had given him all the help he wanted—in vain. There was going to be no blagging for Bunter.

It was a tired, breathless, and perspiring fat Owl that rolled into the bike-shed and let Carter's jigger run where it liked there. The look that Billy Bunter gave the Famous Five as they followed him in was really blood-curdling.

Quite uncurdled, they smiled at him.

"Ripping race!" said Bob Cherry heartily. "I never thought you could put it on like that, Bunter!"

"Beast!"

"Coming down for a spot of games practice now?" asked Nugent.

"Rotter!"

"Taking a rest?" asked Harry Wharton. "All right! We'll sit down, too!"

"Swab!"

"Anything the matter, Bunter?" asked Johnny Bull. "You seem shirty about something!"

"Yah!"

Half-past two chimed from the clock-tower. Billy Bunter groaned.

The game was up. Crackerjack was running now. It was too late for a sportsman to get on. After all his efforts, Billy Bunter was still off. Carter's quid was still in his pocket, but the dazzling vision of boundless wealth had vanished—gone like a mirage, as, in fact, it was.

Billy Bunter groaned dismally. And the chums of the Remove, heartlessly unsympathetic, went down to games practice and left him to groan.

THE TWENTY-FIRST CHAPTER.

The Founder of the Feast!

" A LSO ran?"

"Yes!"

"Not Crackerjack?"

"Yes!"

"Oh, my hat!"

Billy Bunter gave quite a jump.

Bunter, at the moment, was outside a study door in the Sixth Form passage. He was stooping outside that door; with his fat ear very near the keyhole.

Eavesdropping in the Sixth was rather a risky business. Even the Peeping Tom of Greyfriars would hardly have run the risk; but for a very important and urgent reason. Bunter was going into that study—but he wanted to make sure whether Carne of the Sixth was at home first! If Carne of the Sixth was at home, Bunter's visit had to be postponed.

Bitter as Bunter's disappointment was at not getting on, he had rallied. For a long, long time that afternoon, the fat Owl had mourned, like Rachel, and could find no comfort. But he had thought it over now! Obviously—to Bunter—having lost one chance, the best thing that he could do was to look for another. A squint at Carne's racing paper would do the trick!

That prophetic genius, "Quick-Eye," could scarcely have exhausted his prophetic gifts on one tip. Probably there were others, just as good, for races at a later date! A squint at "Sporting Tips" would ascertain that fact! If the paper was in the study, and Carno of the Sixth was out of it, Bunter was going to get that squint—and act accordingly. He had manfully resisted the lure of the tuck-shop, and the quid was still in his pocket.

So he stooped and pressed a fat ear to the keyhole, to find out whether anybody was in the study—and the sound of voices within apprised him that there was! And what they were saying glued that fat ear to the keyhole! They were talking about Bunter's own selected winner. Crackerjack!

"But look here, Loder," went on Carne's voice, "are you sure? That man 'Quick-Eye' in 'Sporting Tips' ain't bad! He gave Crackerjack as a Special Snip! Dash it all, I put ten bob on him both ways!"

"My dear chap, here it is in the evening paper!" drawled Loder. "I've never thought much of that tipster 'Quick-Eye'—too jolly cocksure for me! I got the paper at Courtfield, to see. Here you are—Bonny Boy, Trawler, Spoofer's Pride, the first three —six more ran—one of them Crackerjack——"

"Also ran! My hat!"

"Oh crumbs!" breathed Bunter.

He waited to hear no more!

The study was not empty; but if it had been, it would not have attracted Bunter now! He no longer desired a squint at Carne's sporting paper!

Bunter had had no doubt that Crackerjack was going to win! Had not "Quick-Eye," the expert tipster, said so? Instead of which, he had lost! He figured among the "also rans." "Quick-Eye," evidently, was not so quick-eyed as he supposed—he had got it wrong, as racing experts so often do!

Bunter rolled away down the passage. He had heard enough—more than enough! In his inside pocket was a quid, which he had not succeeded in getting on Crackerjack! Had he succeeded, that quid would not, as Bunter had fondly hoped, have produced quids and quids and quids and quids! It would have been gone from his gaze like a beautiful dream! Instead of laying the foundation of a fortune, the fat sportsman of the Remove would only have chucked away a pound, with the risk of getting sacked over and above!

Billy Bunter had had a lot of disappointments and discouragements, and he had rallied round from all of them! But he did not rally from this! Even on Bunter's remarkable intelligence, it dawned that a racing tipster was not a reliable guide to fortune!

If the stars in their courses had fought against Bunter getting that quid on Crackerjack, they had done him a good turn—for he still had the quid, which certainly he would not have had if he had got it on Crackerjack! That was a comfort!

There was, so to speak, balm in Gilead! Bunter was not going to make a fortune—and Carter was not going to see him sacked for blagging—but he still had a quid; and no longer had any reason for resisting the lure of the tuck-shop!

To that attractive establishment Bunter immediately bent his steps!

It was tea-time, and the Famous Five had come in, after games practice, for supplies for tea. They smiled as Bunter rolled in. They smiled still more when

the Owl produced a pound note, and proceeded to order foodstuffs in quite a reckless way. Bunter's pound notes were limited in number—limited, in fact, to the one he had borrowed from his kind relation, Carter! So this looked as if the fat sportsman had abandoned blagging in favour of guzzling!

Carter was in the tuckshop, and he, too, looked at Bunter—but without smiling! What he saw did not make him disposed to smile!

His pound note was going, but not, evidently, on the races! The net outcome of his scheming was, that he was standing the fat Owl a free feed—with his whopping from Quelch thrown in as a make-weight! Carter did not feel in the least like smiling!

"Hallo, hallo, hallo, old fat man!" chortled Bob Cherry. "Blowing it on tuck after all?"

Bunter blinked round at the Famous Five.

"I say, you fellows, have some of these tarts!" he said hospitably. "I've got lots! I've got a whole quid, you know! I say, that senior man Carne is a silly ass, to take any notice of what those rotten racing tipsters say in those rotten racing papers! I've just heard that his horse has lost! He, he, he! Some fellows are awful fools, ain't they?"

"They are!" grinned Bob. "They is! Especially when they're named Bunter!"

"Oh, really, Cherry! Catch me playing the fool like that!" said Bunter. "Too much sense, I hope! Besides, it's not the thing—it's not done, you know! My advice to you fellows is, to steer quite clear of that sort of thing! You'll only lose your money, you can take it from me."

"Oh, my hat!"

"But have some of these tarts!" said the fat Owl. "I've got lots! Do have some! They're good, I can tell you."

"Shove one over to Carter!" grinned Bob. "Let Carter have a whack! He's the founder of the feast, you know!"

"Ha, ha, ha!"

"I say, Carter, have a tart?"

But Arthur Carter did not answer, and he did not stay for a tart! He left the tuckshop, scowling—leaving the Famous Five chuckling, and Billy Bunter scoffing jam tarts.

THE END

(The next yarn in this grand series is better than ever. Note the title: "CARTER TAKES THE COUNT!" Order your copy of the MAGNET *to-day, chums!)*

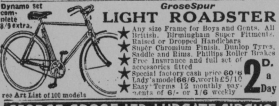